Wilbur Smith was born in Central Africa in 1933. He was educated at Michaelhouse and Rhodes University.

He became a full-time writer in 1964 after the successful publication of *When the Lion Feeds*, and has since written thirty novels, all meticulously researched on his numerous expeditions worldwide. His books are now translated into twenty-six different languages.

He owns a farm and game reserve and has an abiding concern for the peoples and wildlife of his native continent, an interest strongly reflected in his novels.

PRAISE FOR WILBUR SMITH

'Wilbur Smith rarely misses a trick'
Sunday Times

'The world's leading adventure writer'
Daily Express

'Action is the name of Wilbur Smith's game
and he is a master'
Washington Post

'The pace would do credit to a Porsche, and the invention
is as bright and explosive as a fireworks display'
Sunday Telegraph

'A violent saga . . . told with vigour and enthusiasm . . .
Wilbur Smith spins a fine tale'
Evening Standard

'A bonanza of excitement'
New York Times

'. . . a natural storyteller who moves confidently and
often splendidly in his period and sustains a flow of
convicing incident'
Scotsman

'Raw experience, grim realism, history and romance welded
with mystery and the bewilderment of life itself'
Library Journal

'A thundering good read'
Irish Times

WILBUR SMITH

EAGLE IN THE SKY
&
MEN OF MEN

PAN BOOKS

Eagle in the Sky first published 1974 by William Heinemann.
First published in paperback 1988 by Pan Books.
Men of Men first published 1981 by William Heinemann.
First published in paperback 1997 by Pan Books.

This omnibus first published in paperback 2006 by Pan Books
an imprint of Pan Macmillan Ltd
Pan Macmillan, 20 New Wharf Road, London N1 9RR
Basingstoke and Oxford
Associated companies throughout the world
www.panmacmillan.com

ISBN-13: 978-0-330-44680-8
ISBN-10: 0-330-44680-0

1 3 5 7 9 8 6 4 2

A CIP catalogue record for this book is available from
the British Library.

Typeset by SetSystems Ltd, Saffron Walden, Essex
Printed and bound in Great Britain by
Mackays of Chatham plc, Chatham, Kent

EAGLE IN THE SKY

Acknowledgements

While writing this story I had valuable help from a number of people. Major Dick Lord and Lieutenant Peter Cooke gave me advice on the technique and technicalities of modern fighter combat. Dr Robin Sandell and Dr David Davies provided me with the medical details. A brother angler, the Revd Bob Redrup, helped with the choice of the title. To them all I am sincerely grateful.

While in Israel many of the citizens of that state gave help and hospitality in generous measure. It grieves me that I may not mention their names.

As always my faithful research assistant gave comfort, encouragement and criticism when it was most needed. This book is dedicated to her son – my stepson – Dieter Schmidt.

'Three things are too wonderful for me,
four I do not understand,
The way of an eagle in the sky,
The way of a serpent on a rock,
The way of a ship on the high seas,
And the way of a man with a maiden.'

Proverbs 30: 18–20

There was snow on the mountains of the Hottentots' Holland and the wind came off it, whimpering like a lost animal. The instructor stood in the doorway of his tiny office and hunched down into his flight jacket, thrusting his fists deeply into the fleece-lined pockets.

He watched the black chauffeur-driven Cadillac coming down between the cavernous iron-clad hangars, and he frowned sourly. For the trappings of wealth Barney Venter had a deeply aching gut-envy.

The Cadillac swung in and parked in a visitors' slot against the hangar wall, and a boy sprang from the rear door with boyish enthusiasm, spoke briefly with the coloured chauffeur, then hurried towards Barney.

He moved with a lightness that was strange for an adolescent. There was no stumbling over feet too big for his body, and he carried himself tall. Barney's envy curdled as he watched the young princeling approach. He hated these pampered darlings, and it was his particular fate that he must spend so much of his working day in their company. Only the very rich could afford to instruct their children in the mysteries of flight.

He was reduced to this by the gradual running down of his body, the natural attrition of time. Two years previously, at the age of forty-five, he had failed the strict medical on which his position of senior airline captain depended, and now he was going down the other side of the hill, probably to end as a typical fly-bum, steering tired and beaten-up heaps on unscheduled and shady routes for unlicensed and unprincipled charter companies.

1

The knowledge made him growl at the child who stood before him. 'Master Morgan, I presume?'

'Yes, sir, but you may call me David.' The boy offered his hand and instinctively Barney took it – immediately wishing he had not. The hand was slim and dry, but with a hard grip of bone and sinew.

'Thank you, David.' Barney was heavy on irony. 'And you may continue to call me "sir".'

He knew the boy was fourteen years old, but he stood almost level with Barney's five-foot-seven. David smiled at him and Barney was struck almost as by a physical force by the boy's beauty. It seemed as though each detail of his features had been wrought with infinite care by a supreme artist. The total effect was almost unreal, theatrical. It seemed indecent that hair should curl and glow so darkly, that skin should be so satiny and delicately tinted, or that eyes possess such depth and fire.

Barney became aware that he was staring at the boy, that he was falling under the spell that the child seemed so readily to weave – and he turned away abruptly.

'Come on.' He led the way through his office with its fly-blown nude calendars and handwritten notices carrying terse admonitions against asking for credit, or making right-hand circuits.

'What do you know about flying?' he asked the boy as they passed through the cool gloom of the hangar where gaudily coloured aircraft stood in long rows, and out again through the wide doors into the bright mild winter sunshine.

'Nothing, sir.' The admission was refreshing, and Barney felt his mood sweeten slightly.

'But you want to learn?'

'Oh, yes sir!' The reply was emphatic and Barney glanced at him. The boy's eyes were so dark as to be almost black, only in the sunlight did they turn deep indigo blue.

'All right then – let's begin.' The aircraft was waiting on the concrete apron.

'This is a Cessna 150 high-wing monoplane.' Barney began the walk-around check with David following attentively, but when he started a brief explanation of the control surfaces and the principle of lift and wing-loading, he became aware that the boy knew more than he had owned up to. His replies to Barney's rhetorical questions were precise and accurate.

'You've been reading,' Barney accused.

'Yes, sir,' David admitted, grinning. His teeth were of peculiar whiteness and symmetry and the smile was irresistible. Despite himself, Barney realized he was beginning to like the boy.

'Right, jump in.'

Strapped into the cramped cockpit shoulder to shoulder, Barney explained the controls and instruments, then led into the starting procedure.

'Master switch on.' He flipped the red button. 'Right, turn that key – same as in a car.'

David leaned forward and obeyed. The prop spun and the engine fired and kicked, surged, then settled into a satisfying healthy growl. They taxied down the apron with David quickly developing his touch on the rudders, and paused for the final checks and radio procedure before swinging wide on to the runway.

'Right, pick an object at the end of the runway. Aim for it and open the throttle gently.'

Around them the machine became urgent, and it buzzed busily towards the far-off fence markers.

'Ease back on the wheel.'

And they were airborne, climbing swiftly away from the earth.

'Gently,' said Barney. 'Don't freeze on to the controls. Treat her like—' he broke off. He had been about to liken the aircraft to a woman, but realized the unsuitability of the simile. 'Treat her like a horse. Ride her light.'

Instantly he felt David's death-grip on the wheel relax, the touch repeated through his own controls.

'That's it, David.' He glanced sideways at the boy, and felt a flare of disappointment. He had felt deep down in his being that this one might be bird, one of the very rare ones like himself whose natural element was the blue. Yet here in the first few moments of flight the child was wearing an expression of frozen terror. His lips and nostrils were trimmed with marble white and there were shadows in the dark blue eyes like the shape of sharks moving beneath the surface of a summer sea.

'Left wing up,' he snapped, disappointed, trying to shock him out of it. The wing came up and held rock steady, with no trace of over-correction.

'Level her out.' His own hands were off the controls as the nose sank to find the horizon.

'Throttle back.' The boy's right hand went unerringly to the throttle. Once more Barney glanced at him. His expression had not altered, and then with a sudden revelation Barney recognized it not as fear, but as ecstasy.

'He is a bird.' The thought gave him a vast satisfaction, and while they flew on through the basic instruction in trim and attitude, Barney's mind went back thirty years to a battered old yellow Tiger Moth and another child in his first raptures of flight.

They skirted the harsh blue mountains, wearing their mantles of sun-blazing snow, and rode the tail of the wild winds that came down off them.

'Wind is like the sea, David. It breaks and swirls around high ground. Watch for it.' David nodded as he listened to his first fragments of flying lore, but his eyes were fixed ahead savouring each instant of the experience.

They turned north over the bleak bare land, the earth

naked pink and smoky brown, stripped by the harvest of its robes of golden wheat.

'Wheel and rudder together, David,' Barney told him. 'Let's try a steep turn now.' Down went the wing and boldly the nose swept around holding its attitude to the horizon.

Ahead of them the sea broke in long lines of cream on the white beaches. The Atlantic was cold green and ruffled by the wind, flecked with dancing white.

South again, following the coastline where small figures on the white sand paused to look up at them from under shading hands, south towards the great flat mountain that marked the limit of the land, its shape unfamiliar from this approach. The shipping lay thick in the bay and the winter sunlight flashed from the windows of the white buildings huddling below the steep wooded sides of the mountain.

Another turn, confident and sure, Barney sitting with his hands in his lap and his feet off the rudder bars, and they ran in over the Tygerberg towards the airfield.

'Okay,' said Barney. 'I've got her.' And he took them in for the touchdown and taxied back to the concrete apron beside the hangars. He pulled the mixture control fully lean and let the engine starve and die.

They sat silent for a moment, neither of them moving or speaking, both of them unwinding but still aware that something important and significant had happened and that they had shared it.

'Okay?' Barney asked at last.

'Yes, sir,' David nodded, and they unstrapped and climbed down on to the concrete stiffly. Without speaking they walked side by side through the hangar and office. At the door they paused.

'Next Wednesday?' Barney asked.

'Yes, sir.' David left him and started towards the waiting Cadillac, but after a dozen steps he stopped, hesitated, then turned back.

'That was the most beautiful thing that has ever happened to me,' he said shyly. 'Thank you, sir.' And he hurried away leaving Barney staring after him.

The Cadillac pulled off, gathering speed, and disappeared round a bend amongst the trees beyond the last buildings. Barney chuckled, shook his head ruefully and turned back into his office. He dropped into the ancient swivel chair and crossed his ankles on the desk. He fished a crumpled cigarette from the pack, straightened and lit it.

'Beautiful?' he grunted, grinning. 'Crap!' He flicked the match at the waste bin and missed it.

The telephone woke Mitzi Morgan and she crept out from under her pillows groping blindly for it.

'Lo.'

'Mitzi?'

'Hi, Dad, are you coming up?' She came half-awake at her father's voice, remembering that this was the day he would fly up to join the family at their holiday home.

'Sorry, baby. Something has broken here. I won't be up until next week.'

'Oh, Dad!' Mitzi expressed her disappointment.

'Where's Davey?' her father went on quickly to forestall any recriminations.

'You want him to call you back?'

'No, I'll hold on. Call him, please, baby.'

Mitzi stumbled out of bed to the mirror, and with her fingers tried to comb some order into her hair. It was off-blonde and wiry, and fuzzed up tight at the first touch of sun or salt or wind. The freckles were even more humiliating, she decided, looking at herself disapprovingly.

'You look like a Pekinese,' she spoke aloud, 'a fat little Pekinese – with freckles,' and gave up the effort of trying to change it. David had seen her like this a zillion times.

6

She pulled a silk gown over her nudity and went out into the passage, past the door to her parents' suite where her mother slept alone, and into the living area of the house.

The house was stacked in a series of open planes and galleries, glass and steel and white pine, climbing out of the dunes along the beach, part of sea and sky, only glass separating it from the elements, and now the dawn filled it with a strange glowing light and made a feature of the massive headland of the Robberg that thrust out into the sea across the bay.

The playroom was scattered with the litter of last night's party, twenty house guests and as many others from the big holiday homes along the dunes had left their mark – spilled beer, choked ashtrays and records thrown carelessly from their covers.

Mitzi picked her way through the debris and climbed the circular staircase to the guest rooms. She checked David's door, found it open, and went in. The bed was untouched, but his denims and sweat shirt were thrown across the chair and his shoes had been kicked off carelessly.

Mitzi grinned, and went through on to the balcony. It hung high above the beach, level with the gulls which were already dawn-winging for the scraps that the sea had thrown up during the night.

Quickly Mitzi hoisted the gown up around her waist, climbed up onto the rail of the balcony and stepped over the drop to the rail of the next balcony in line. She jumped down, drew the curtains aside and went into Marion's bedroom.

Marion was her best friend. Secretly she knew that this happy state of affairs existed chiefly because she, Mitzi, provided a foil for Marion's petite little body and wide-eyed doll-like beauty – and was a source of never-ending gifts and parties, free holidays and other good things.

She looked so pretty now in sleep, her hair golden and

soft as it fanned out across David's chest. Mitzi transferred all her attention to her cousin, and felt that sliding sensation in her breast and the funny warm liquid sensation at the base of her belly as she looked at him. He was seventeen years old now, but already he had the body of a grown man.

He was her most favourite person in all the world, she thought. He's so beautiful, so tall and straight, and his eyes can break your heart.

The couple on the bed had thrown aside their covering in the warmth of the night, and there was hair on David's chest now, thick and dark and curly, there was muscle in arm and leg, and breadth across the shoulders.

'David,' she called softly, and touched his shoulder. 'Wake up.'

His eyes opened, and he was awake instantly, his gaze focused and aware.

'Mitz? What is it?'

'Get your pants on, warrior. My papa's on the line.'

'God.' David sat up, dropping Marion's head on to the pillow. 'What time is it?'

'Late,' Mitzi told him. 'You should set the alarm when you go visiting.'

Marion mumbled a protest and groped for the sheets as David jumped from the bed.

'Where's the phone?'

'In my room – but you can take it on the extension in yours.'

She followed him across the balcony railing, and curled up on David's bed while he picked up the receiver and with the extension cord trailing behind him began pacing the thick carpet restlessly.

'Uncle Paul?' David spoke. 'How are you?'

Mitzi groped in the pocket of her gown and found a Gauloise. She lit it with her gold Dunhill, but at the third puff David turned aside from his pacing, grinned at her, took the cigarette from between her lips and drew deeply upon it.

Mitzi pulled a face at him to disguise the turmoil that his nakedness stirred within her, and selected another cigarette for herself.

'He'd die if he knew what I was thinking,' she told herself, and derived a little comfort from the thought.

David finished his conversation and cradled the receiver before turning to her.

'He's not coming.'

'I know.'

'But he is sending Barney up in the Lear to fetch me. Big pow-wow.'

'It figures,' Mitzi nodded, then began a convincing imitation of her father. 'We have to start thinking about your future now, my boy. We have to train you to meet the responsibilities with which destiny has entrusted you.'

David chuckled and rummaged for his running shorts in the drawer of his bureau.

'I suppose I'll have to tell him now.'

'Yes,' Mitzi agreed. 'You sure will have to do that.'

David pulled up his shorts and turned for the door.

'Pray for me, doll.'

'You'll need more than prayer, warrior,' said Mitzi comfortably.

The tide had swept the beach smooth and firm, and no other feet had marked it this early. David ran smoothly, long strides leaving damp footsteps in a chain behind him.

The sun came up casting a soft pink sheen on the sea, and touching the Outeniqua mountains with flame – but David ran unseeing. His thoughts were on the impending interview with his guardian.

It was a time of crisis in his life, high school completed and many roads open. He knew the one he had chosen would draw violent opposition, and he used these last few hours of solitude to gather and strengthen his resolve.

A conclave of gulls, gathered about the body of a stranded fish, rose in a cloud as he ran towards them, their wings catching the low sun as they hovered then dropped again when he passed.

He saw the Lear coming before he heard it. It was low against the dawn, rising and dropping over the towering bulk of the Robberg. Then swiftly, coming in on a muted shriek, it streaked low along the beach towards him.

David stopped, breathing lightly even after the long run, and raised both arms above his head in salute. He saw Barney's head through the Perspex canopy turned towards him, the flash of his teeth as he grinned and the hand raised, returning his salute as he went by.

The Lear turned out to sea, one wingtip almost touching the wave crests, and it came back at him. David stood on the exposed beach and steeled himself as the long sleek nose dropped lower and lower, aimed like a javelin at him.

Like some fearsome predatory bird it swooped at him and at the last possible instant David's nerve broke and he flung himself on to the wet sand. The jet blast lashed him as the Lear rose and turned inland for the airfield.

'Son of a bitch,' muttered David as he stood up brushing damp sand from his bare chest, and imagined Barney's amused chuckle.

'I taught him good,' thought Barney, sprawled in the co-pilot's seat of the Lear as he watched David ride the delicate line of altitude where skill gave way to chance.

Barney had put on weight since he had been eating Morgan bread, and his paunch peeked shyly over his belt. The beginning of jowls bracketed the wide downturned mouth that gave him the air of a disgruntled toad, and the cap of hair that covered his skull was sparser and speckled with salt.

Watching David fly, he felt the small warmth of his affection for him that his sour expression belied. Three years he had been chief pilot of the Morgan group and he knew well to whose intervention he owed the post. It was security he had now, and prestige. He flew great men in the most luxuriously fitted machines, and when the time came for him to go out to pasture he knew the grazing would be lush. The Morgan group looked after its own.

This knowledge sat comfortably on his stomach as he watched his protégé handle the jet.

Extended low flying like this required enormous concentration, and Barney watched in vain for any relaxation of it in his pupil.

The long golden beaches of Africa streamed steadily beneath them, punctuated by rock promontories and tiny resorts and fishing villages. Delicately the Lear followed the contours of the coastline, for they had spurned the direct route for the exhilaration of this flight.

Ahead of them stretched another strip of beach but as they howled low along it they saw that this one was occupied.

A pair of tiny feminine figures left the frothy surf and ran panic-stricken to where towels and discarded bikinis lay above the high-water mark. White buttocks contrasted sharply with a coffee-brown tan, and they laughed delightedly.

'Nice change for you to see them running away, David,' Barney grinned as they left the tiny figures far behind and bore onwards into the south.

From Cape Agulhas they turned inland, climbing steeply over the mountain ranges, then David eased back on the throttles and they sank down beyond the crests towards the city, nestling under its mountain.

As they walked side by side towards the hangar, Barney looked up at David who now topped him by six inches.

'Don't let him stampede you, boy,' he warned. 'You've made your decision. See you stick to it.'

David took his British racing green MG over De Waal Drive, and from the lower slopes of the mountain looked down to where the Morgan building stood four-square amongst the other tall monuments to power and wealth.

David enjoyed its appearance, clean and functional like an aircraft's wing – but he knew that the soaring freedom of its lines was deceptive. It was a prison and fortress.

He swung off the freeway at an interchange and rode down to the foreshore, glancing up at the towering bulk of the Morgan building again before entering the ramp that led to the underground garages beneath it.

When he entered the executive apartments on the top floor, he passed along the row of desks where the secretaries, hand-picked for their looks as well as their skill with a typewriter, sat in a long row. Their lovely faces opened into smiles like a garden of exotic blooms as David greeted each of them. Within the Morgan building he was treated with the respect due the heir apparent.

Martha Goodrich, in her own office that guarded the inner sanctum, looked up from her typewriter, severe and businesslike.

'Good morning, Mr David. Your uncle is waiting – and I do think you could have worn a suit.'

'You're looking good, Martha. You've lost weight and I like your hair like that.' It worked, as it always did. Her expression softened.

'Don't you try buttering me up,' she warned him primly. 'I'm not one of your floozies.'

Paul Morgan was at the picture window looking down over the city spread below him like a map, but he turned quickly to greet David.

'Hello, Uncle Paul. I'm sorry I didn't have time to change. I thought it best to come directly.'

'That's fine, David.' Paul Moran flicked his eyes over

David's floral shirt open to the navel, the wide tooled leather belt, white slacks and open sandals. On him they looked good, Paul admitted reluctantly. The boy wore even the most outlandish modern clothes with a furious grace.

'It's good to see you.' Paul smoothed the lapels of his own dark conservatively cut suit and looked up at his nephew. 'Come in. Sit down, there, the chair by the fireplace.' As always, he found that David standing emphasized his own lack of stature. Paul was short and heavily built in the shoulders, thick muscular neck and square thrusting head. Like his daughter, his hair was coarse and wiry and his features squashed and puglike.

All the Morgans were built that way. It was the proper course of things, and David's exotic appearance was outside the natural order. It was from his mother's side, of course. All that dark hair and flashing eyes, and the temperament that went with it.

'Well, David. First off, I want to congratulate you on your final results. I was most gratified,' Paul Morgan told him gravely, and he could have added ' – I was also mightily relieved.' David Morgan's scholastic career had been a tempestuous affair. Pinnacles of achievement followed immediately by depths of disgrace from which only the Morgan name and wealth had rescued him. There had been the business with the games master's young wife. Paul never did find out the truth of the matter, but had thought it sufficient to smooth it over by donating a new organ to the school chapel and arranging a teaching scholarship for the games master to a foreign university. Immediately thereafter David had won the coveted Wessels prize for mathematics, and all was forgiven – until he decided to test his housemaster's new sports car, without that gentleman's knowledge, and took it into a tight bend at ninety miles an hour. The car was unequal to the test, and David picked himself up out of the wreckage and limped away with a nasty scratch on his calf. It had taken all of Paul

13

Morgan's weight to have the housemaster agree not to cancel David's appointment as head of house. His prejudices had finally been overcome by the replacement of his wrecked car with a more expensive model, and the Morgan Group had made a grant to rebuild the ablution block of East House.

The boy was wild, Paul knew it well, but he knew also that he could tame him. Once he had done that he would have forged a razor-edged tool. He possessed all the attributes that Paul Morgan wanted in his successor. The verve and confidence, the bright quick mind and adventurous spirit – but above all he possessed the aggressive attitude, the urge to compete that Paul defined as the killer instinct.

'Thank you, Uncle Paul,' David accepted his uncle's congratulations warily. They were silent, each assessing the other. They had never been easy in the other's company, they were too different in many ways – and yet in others too much alike. Always it seemed that their interests were in conflict.

Paul Morgan moved across to the picture windows, so that the daylight back-lit him. It was an old trick of his to put the other person at a disadvantage.

'Not that we expected less of you, of course,' he laughed, and David smiled to acknowledge the fact that his uncle had come close to levity.

'And now we must consider your future.' David was silent.

'The choice open to you is wide,' said Paul Morgan, and then went on swiftly to narrow it. 'Though I do feel business science and law at an American university is what it should be. With this obvious goal in mind I have used my influence to have you enrolled in my old college—'

'Uncle Paul, I want to fly,' said David softly, and Paul Morgan paused. His expression changed fractionally.

'We are making a career decision, my boy, not expressing preferences for different types of recreation.'

'No, sir. I mean I want to fly – as a way of life.'

'Your life is here, within the Morgan Group. It is not something in which you have freedom of action.'

'I don't agree with you, sir.'

Paul Morgan left the window and crossed to the fireplace. He selected a cigar from the humidor on the mantel, and while he prepared it he spoke softly, without looking at David.

'Your father was a romantic, David. He got it out of his system by charging around the desert in a tank. It seems you have inherited this romanticism from him.' He made it sound like some disgusting disease. He came back to where David sat.

'Tell me what you propose.'

'I have enlisted in the air force, sir.'

'You've done it? You've signed?'

'Yes, sir.'

'How long?'

'Five years. Short service commission.'

'Five years—' Paul Morgan whispered, 'Well, David, I don't know what to say. You know that you are the last of the Morgans. I have no son. It will be sad to see this vast enterprise without one of us at the helm. I wonder what your father would have thought of this—'

'That's hitting low, Uncle Paul.'

'I don't think so, David. I think you are the one who is cheating. Your trust fund is a huge block of Morgan shares, and other assets given to you, on the unstated understanding that you assume your duties and responsibilities—'

'If only he would bawl me out,' thought David fiercely, knowing that he was being stampeded as Barney had warned him. 'If only he would order me to do it – so I could tell him to shove it.' But he knew he was being manipulated by a man skilled in the art, a man whose whole life was the manipulation of men and money, in whose hands a seventeen-year-old boy was as soft as dough.

'You see, David, you are born to it. Anything else is cowardice, self indulgence—' the Morgan Group reached out its tentacles, like some grotesque flesh-eating plant, to suck him in and digest him, ' – we can have your enlistment papers annulled. It will be the matter of a single phone call—'

'Uncle Paul,' David almost shouted, trying to shut out the all-pervasive flow of words. 'My father. He did it. He joined the army.'

'Yes, David. But it was different at that time. One of us had to go. He was the younger – and, of course, there were other personal considerations. Your mother—' he let the rest of it hang for a moment then went on, ' – and when it was over he came back and took his rightful place here. We miss him now, David. No one else has been able to fill the gap he left. I have always hoped that you might be the one.'

'But I don't want to.' David shook his head. 'I don't want to spend my life in here.' He gestured at the mammoth structure of glass and concrete that surrounded them. 'I don't want to spend each day poring over piles of paper—'

'It's not like that, David. It's exciting, challenging, endlessly variable—'

'Uncle Paul.' David raised his voice again. 'What do you call a man who fills his belly with rich food – and then goes on eating?'

'Come now, David.' The first edge of irritation showed in Paul Morgan's voice, and he brushed the question aside impatiently.

'What do you call him?' David insisted.

'I expect that you would call him a glutton,' Paul Morgan answered.

'And what do you call a man with many millions – who spends his life trying to make more?'

Paul Morgan froze into stillness. He stared at his ward for long seconds before he spoke.

'You become insolent,' he said at last.

'No, sir. I did not mean it so. You are not the glutton – but I would be.'

Paul Morgan turned away and went to his desk. He sat in the high-backed leather chair and lit the cigar at last. They were silent again for a long time until at last Paul Morgan sighed.

'You'll have to get it out of your system, the way your father did. But how I grudge you five wasted years.'

'Not wasted, Uncle Paul. I will come out with a Bachelor of Science degree in aeronautical engineering.'

'I suppose we'll just have to be thankful for little things like that.'

David went and stood beside his chair.

'Thank you. This is very important to me.'

'Five years, David. After that I want you.' Then he smiled slightly to signal a witticism. 'At least they will make you cut your hair.'

Four miles above the warm flesh-coloured earth, David Morgan rode the high heavens like a young god. The sun visor of his helmet was closed, masking with its dark cyclops eye the rapt, almost mystic expression with which he flew. Five years had not dulled the edge of his appetite for the sensation of power and isolation that flight in a Mirage interceptor awoke in him.

The unfiltered sunlight blazed ferociously upon the metal of his craft, clothing him in splendour – while far below the very clouds were insignificant against the earth, scattered and flying like a sheep flock before the wolf of the wind.

Today's flight was tempered by a melancholy, a sense of impending loss. The morrow was the last day of his enlistment. At noon his commission expired and if Paul Morgan prevailed he would become Mr David – new boy at Morgan Group.

He thrust the thought aside, and concentrated on the enjoyment of these last precious minutes; but too soon the spell was broken.

'Zulu Striker One, this is Range Control. Report your position.'

'Range Control, this is Zulu Striker One holding up range fifty miles.'

'Striker One, the range is clear. Your target-markers are figures eight and twelve. Commence your run.'

The horizon revolved abruptly across the nose of the Mirage, as the wings came over and he went down under power, falling from the heights, a controlled plunge, purposeful and precise as the stoop of a falcon.

David's right hand moved swiftly across the weapon selector panel, locking in the rocket circuit.

The earth flattened out ahead, immense and featureless, speckled with low bush that blurred past his wing-tips as he let the Mirage sink lower. At this height the awareness of speed was breathtaking, and as the first marker came up ahead it seemed at the same instant to flash away below the silvery nose.

Five, six, seven – the black numerals on their glaring white grounds flickered by.

A touch of left rudder and stick, both adjustments made without conscious effort – and ahead was the circular layout of the rocket range, the concentric rings shrinking in size around the central mound – the 'coke' of flight jargon, which was the bull's-eye of the target.

David brought the deadly machine in fast and low, his mach meter recording a speed that was barely subsonic. He was running off the direct line of track, judging his moment with frowning concentration. When it came he pulled the Mirage's nose in to the 'pitch up' and went over on to the target with his gloved right finger curled about the trigger lever.

The shrieking silver machine achieved her correct slightly nose-down attitude for rocket launch at the precise instant of time that the white blob of 'coke' was centred in the diamond patterns of the reflector sight.

It was an evolution executed with subtle mastery of many diverse skills, and David pressed against the spring-loaded resistance of the trigger. There was no change in the feel of the aircraft, and the hiss of the rocket launch was almost lost beneath the howl of the great jet, but from beneath his wings the brief smoke lines reached out ahead towards the target, and in certainty of a fair strike David pushed his throttle to the gate and waited for the rumbling ignition of his afterburners, giving him power for the climb out of range of enemy flak.

'What a way to go,' he grinned to himself as he lay on his back with the Mirage's nose pointed into the bright blue, and gravity pressing him into the padding of his seat.

'Hello, Striker One. This is Range Control. That was right on the nose. Give the man a coke. Nice shooting. Sorry to lose you, Davey.' The break in hallowed range discipline touched David. He was going to miss them – all of them. He pressed the transmit button on the moulded head of his joystick, and spoke into the microphone of his helmet. 'From Striker One, thanks and farewell,' David said. 'Over and out.'

His ground crew were waiting for him also. He shook hands with each of them, the awkward handshakes and rough jokes masking the genuine affection that the years had built between them. Then he left them and went down the vast metal-skinned cavern, redolent with the smell of grease and oil along which the gleaming rows of needle-nosed interceptors stood, even in repose their forward lines giving them speed and thrust.

David paused to pat the cold metal of one of them, and the orderly found him there peering up at the emblem of the Flying Cobra upon the towering tailplane.

'C.O.'s compliments, sir, and will you report to him right away.'

Colonel 'Rastus' Naude was a dried-out stick of a man, with a wizened monkey face, who wore his uniform and medal ribbons with a casually distracted air. He had flown Hurricanes in the Battle of Britain, Mustangs in Italy, Spitfires and Messerschmitt 109s in Palestine and Sabres in Korea – and he was too old for his present command – but nobody could muster the courage to tell him that, especially as he could out-fly and out-gun most of the young bucks on the squadron.

'So we are getting rid of you at last, Morgan,' he greeted David.

'Not until after the mess party, sir.'

'Ja,' Rastus nodded. 'You've given me enough hardship these last five years. You owe me a bucket of whisky.' He gestured to the hard-backed chair beside his desk. 'Sit down, David.'

It was the first time he had used David's given name, and David placed his flying helmet on the corner of the desk and lowered himself into the chair, clumsy in the constricting grip of his G-suit.

Rastus took his time filling his pipe with the evil black Magaliesberg shag and he studied the young man opposite him intently. He recognized the same qualities in him that Paul Morgan had prized, the aggressive and competitive drive that gave him a unique value as an interceptor pilot.

He lit the pipe at last, puffing thick rank clouds of blue smoke as he slid a sheath of documents across the desk to David.

'Read and sign,' he said. 'That's an order.' David glanced rapidly through the papers, then he looked up and grinned.

'You don't give in easily, sir,' he admitted.

One document was a renewal of his short service contract for an additional five years, the other was a warrant of promotion – from captain to major.

'We have spent a great deal of time and money in making you what you are. You have been given an exceptional talent, and we have developed it until now you are – I'll not mince words – one hell of a pilot.'

'I'm sorry, sir,' David told him sincerely.

'Damn it,' said Rastus angrily. 'Why the hell did you have to be born a Morgan. All that money – they'll clip your wings, and chain you to a desk.'

'It's not the money.' David denied it swiftly. He felt his own anger stir at the accusation.

Rastus nodded cynically. 'Ja!' he said. 'I hate the stuff also.' He picked up the documents David had rejected, and grunted. 'Not enough to tempt you, hey?'

'Colonel, it's hard to explain. I just feel that there is more to do, something important that I have to find out about – and it's not here. I have to go look for it.'

Rastus nodded heavily. 'All right then,' he said. 'I had a good try. Now you can take your long-suffering commanding officer down to the mess and spend some of the Morgan millions on filling him up with whisky.' He stood up and clapped his uniform cap at a rakish angle over his cropped grey head. 'You and I will get drunk together this night – for both of us are losing something, I perhaps more than you.'

It seemed that David had inherited his love of beautiful and powerful machines from his father. Clive Morgan had driven himself, his wife, and his brand new Ferrari sports car into the side of a moving goods train at an unlit level crossing. The traffic police estimated that the Ferrari was travelling at one hundred and fifty miles an hour at the moment of impact.

Clive Morgan's provision for his eleven-year-old son was detailed and elaborate. The child became a ward of his uncle Paul Morgan, and his inheritance was arranged in a series of trust funds.

On his majority he was given access to the first of the funds which provided an income equivalent to that of, say, a highly successful surgeon. On that day the old green MG had given way to a powder-blue Maserati, in true Morgan tradition.

On his twenty-third birthday, control of the sheep ranches in the Karroo, the cattle ranch in South-West Africa and Jabulani, the sprawling game ranch in the Sabi-Sand block, passed to him, their management handled smoothly by his trustees.

On his twenty-fifth birthday the number two fund interest would divert to him, in addition to a large block of negotiable paper and title in two massive urban holdings – office and supermarket complexes, and a high-rise housing project.

At age thirty the next fund opened for him, as large as the previous two combined, and transfer to him for the first of five blocks of Morgan stock would begin.

From then onwards, every five years until age fifty further funds opened, further blocks of Morgan stock would be transferred. It was a numbing procession of wealth that stretched ahead of him, daunting in its sheer magnitude; like a display of too much rich food, it seemed to depress appetite.

David drove fast southwards, with the Michelin metallics hissing savagely on the tarmac, and he thought about all that wealth, the great golden cage, the insatiable maw of Morgan Group yawning open to swallow him so that, like the cell of a jelly fish, he would become a part of the whole, a prisoner of his own abundance.

The prospect appalled him, adding a hollow sensation in his belly to the pulse of pain that beat steadily behind his eyes – testimony to the foolhardiness of trying to drink level with Colonel Rastus Naude.

He pushed the Maserati harder, seeking the twin opiates of power and speed, finding comfort and escape in the rhythms and precision of driving very fast, and the hours flew past as swiftly as the miles so it was still daylight when he let himself into Mitzi's apartment on the cliffs that overlooked Clifton beach and the clear green Atlantic.

Mitzi's apartment was chaos, that much had not changed. She kept open house for a string of transitory guests who drank her liquor, ate her food and vied with each other as to who could create the most spectacular shambles.

In the first bedroom that David tried there was a strange girl with dark hair curled on the bed in boys' pyjamas, sucking her thumb in sleep.

With the second room he was luckier, and he found it deserted, although the bed was unmade and someone had left breakfast dishes smeared with congealed egg upon the side table.

David slung his bag on the bed and fished out his bathing costume. He changed quickly and went out by the side stairs that spiralled down to the beach and began to run – a trot at first, and then suddenly he sprinted away, racing blindly as though from some terrible monster that pursued him. At the end of Fourth beach where the rocks began, he plunged into the icy surf and swam out to the edge of the kelp at Bakoven point, driving overarm through the water and the cold lanced him to the bone, so that when he came out he was blue and shuddering. But the hunted feeling was gone and he warmed a little as he jogged back to Mitzi's apartment.

He had to remove the forest of pantihose and feminine underwear that festooned the bathroom before he could draw himself a bath. He filled it to the overflow, and as he settled into it the front door burst open and Mitzi came in like the north wind.

'Where are you, warrior?' She was banging the doors. 'I saw your car in the garage – so I know you're here!'

'In here, doll,' he called, and she stood in the doorway and they grinned at each other. She had put on weight again, he saw, straining the seam of her skirt, and her bosom was bulky and amorphous under the scarlet sweater. She had finally given up her struggle with myopia and the metal-framed spectacles sat on the end of her little nose, while her hair fuzzed out at unexpected angles.

'You're beautiful,' she cried, coming to kiss him and getting soap down her sweater as she hugged him.

'Drink or coffee?' she asked, and David winced at the thought of alcohol.

'Coffee will be great, doll.'

She brought it to him in a mug, then perched on the toilet seat.

'Tell all!' she commanded and while they chatted the pretty dark-haired girl wandered in, still in her pyjamas and bug-eyed from sleep.

'This is my coz, David. Isn't he beautiful?' Mitzi introduced them. 'And this is Liz.'

The girl sat on the dirty linen basket in the corner and fixed David with such an awed and penetrating gaze that Mitzi warned her, 'Cool it, darling. Even from here I can hear your ovaries bouncing around like ping-pong balls.'

But she was such a silent, ethereal little thing that they soon forgot her and talked as if they were alone. It was Mitzi who said suddenly, without preliminaries, 'Papa is waiting for you, licking his lips like an ivy-league ogre. I ate with them Saturday night – he must have brought your name up one zillion times. It's going to be strange to have you sitting up there on Top Floor, in a charcoal suit, being bright at Monday morning conference—'

David stood up suddenly in the bath, cascading suds and steaming water, and began soaping his crotch vigorously. They watched him with interest, the dark-haired girl's eyes widening until they seemed to fill her face.

David sat down again, slopping water over the edge.

'I'm not going!' he said, and there was a long heavy silence.

'What you mean – you're not going?' Mitzi asked timorously.

'Just that,' said David. 'I'm not going to Morgan Group.'

'But you have to!'

'Why?' asked David.

'Well, I mean it's decided – you promised Daddy that when you finished with the air force.'

'No,' David said, 'I made no promise. He just took it. When you said a moment ago – being bright at Monday morning conference – I knew I couldn't do it. I guess I've known all along.'

'What are you going to do, then?' Mitzi had recovered from the first shock, and her plump cheeks were tinged pink with excitement.

'I don't know. I just know I am not going to be a caretaker for other men's achievements. Morgan Group isn't me. It's something that Gramps, and Dad and Uncle Paul made. It's too big and cold—'

Mitzi was flushed, bright-eyed, nodding her agreement, enchanted by this prospect of rebellion and open defiance.

David was warming to it also. 'I'll find my own road to go. There's more to it. There has to be something more than this.'

'Yes,' Mitzi nodded so that she almost shook her

25

spectacles from her nose. 'You're not like them. You would shrivel and die up there in the executive suite.'

'I've got to find it, Mitzi. It's got to be out there somewhere.'

David came out of the bath, his body glowing dull red-brown from the scalding water and steam rising from him in light tendrils. He pulled on a terry robe as he talked and the two girls followed him through to the bedroom and sat side by side on the edge of the bed, eagerly nodding their encouragement as David Morgan made his formal declaration of independence. Mitzi spoiled it, however.

'What are you going to tell Daddy?' she asked. The question halted David's flow of rhetoric, and he scratched the hair on his chest as he considered it. The girls waited attentively.

'He's not going to let you get away again,' Mitzi warned. 'Not without a stand-up, knock-down, drag-'em-out fight.'

In this moment of crisis David's courage deserted him. 'I've told him once, I don't have to tell him again.'

'You just going to cut and run?' Mitzi asked.

'I'm not running,' David replied with frosty dignity as he picked up the pigskin folder which held his thick sheaf of credit cards from the bedside table. 'I am merely reserving the right to determine my own future.' He crossed to the telephone and began dialling.

'Who are you calling?'

'The airline.'

'Where are you heading?'

'The same place as their first flight out.'

'I'll cover for you,' declared Mitzi loyally, 'you're doing the right thing, warrior.'

'You bet I am,' David agreed. 'My way – and screw the rest of them.'

'Do you have time for that?' Mitzi giggled, and the dark-haired girl spoke for the first time in a husky intense voice

26

without once taking her eyes off David. 'I don't know about the rest of them, but may I be first, please?'

With the telephone receiver to his ear David glanced at her, and realized with only mild surprise that she was in deadly earnest.

D avid came out into the impersonal concrete and glass arrivals hall of Schiphol Airport, and he paused to gloat on his escape and to revel at this sense of anonymity in the uncaring crowd. There was a touch at his elbow, and he turned to find a tall, smiling Dutchman quizzing him through rimless spectacles.

'Mr David Morgan, I think?' and David gaped at him.

'I am Frederick van Gent of Holland and Indonesian Stevedoring. We have the honour to act on behalf of Morgan Shipping Lines in Holland. It is a great pleasure to make your acquaintance.'

'God, no!' David whispered wearily.

'Please?'

'No. I'm sorry. It's nice to meet you.' David shook the hand with resignation.

'I have two urgent telex messages for you, Mr Morgan.' Van Gent produced them with a flourish. 'I have driven out from Amsterdam especially to deliver same.'

The first was from Mitzi who had sworn to cover for him.

'Abject apologies your whereabouts extracted with rack and thumbscrew stop Be brave as a lion stop Be ferocious as an eagle Love Mitzi.'

David said, 'Traitorous bitch!' and opened the second envelope.

'Your doubts understood, your action condoned stop Confident your good sense will lead you eventually on to

27

path of duty stop Your place here always open Affectionately Paul Morgan.'

David said, 'Crafty old bastard,' and stuffed both messages into his pocket.

'Is there a reply?' Van Gent asked.

'Thank you, no. It was good of you to take this trouble.'

'No trouble, Mr Morgan. Can I help you in any way? Is
there anything you require?'

'Nothing, but thanks again.' They shook hands and Van
Gent bowed and left him. David went to the Avis counter
and the girl smiled brightly at him.

'Good evening, sir.'

David slipped his Avis card across the desk. 'I want
something with a little jump to it, please.'

'Let me see, we have a Mustang Mach I?' She was pure
blonde with a cream and pink unlined face.

'That will do admirably,' David assured her, and as she
began filling the form in, she asked, 'Your first visit to
Amsterdam, sir?'

'They tell me it's the city with the most action in
Europe, is that right?'

'If you know where to go,' she murmured.

'You could show me?' David asked and she looked up at
him with calculating eyes behind a neutral expression,
made a decision and resumed her writings.

'Please sign here, sir. Your account will be charged,'
then she dropped her voice. 'If you have any queries on
this contract, you can contact me at this number – after
hours. My name is Gilda.'

Gilda shared a walk-up over the outer canal with three
other girls who showed no surprise, and made no objection
when David carried his single Samsonite case up the steep
staircase. However, the action that Gilda provided was in
a series of discotheques and coffee bars where lost little
people gathered to talk revolution and guru-babble. In two
days David discovered that pot tasted terrible and made

him nauseous, and that Gilda's mind was as bland and unmarked as her exterior. He felt the stirrings of uneasiness when he studied the others that had been drawn to this city by the news that it was wide open, with the most understanding police force in the world. In them he saw symptoms of his own restlessness, and he recognized them as fellow seekers. Then the damp chill of the lowlands seemed to rise up out of the canals like the spirits of the dead on doomsday, and when you have been born under the sun of Africa the wintry effusions of the north are a pale substitute.

Gilda showed no visible emotion when she said good-bye, and with the heaters blasting hot air into the cab of the Mustang, David sent it booming southwards. On the outskirts of Namur there was a girl standing beside the road. In the cold her legs were bare and brown, protruding sweetly from the short faded blue denim pants she wore. She tilted her golden head and cocked a thumb.

David hit the stick down, and braked with the rubber squealing protest. He reversed back to where she stood. She had flat-planed Slavic features and her hair was white-blonde and hung in a thick plait down her back. He guessed her age at nineteen.

'You speak English?' he asked through the window. The cold was making her nipples stand out like marbles through the thin fabric of her shirt.

'No,' she said. 'But I speak American – will that do?'

'Right on!' David opened the passenger door, and she threw her pack and rolled sleeping bag into the back seat.

'I'm Philly,' she said.

'David.'

'You in show biz?'

'God, no – what makes you ask?'

'The car – the face – the clothes.'

'The car is hired, the clothes are stolen and I'm wearing a mask.'

29

'Funny man,' she said and curled up on the seat like a kitten and went to sleep.

He stopped in a village where the forests of the Ardennes begin and bought a long roll of crisp bread, a slab of smoked wild boar meat and a bottle of Möet Chandon. When he got back to the car Philly was awake.

'You hungry?' he asked.

'Sure.' She stretched and yawned.

He found a loggers' track going off into the forest and they followed it to a clearing where a long golden shaft of sunlight penetrated the green cathedral gloom.

Philly climbed out and looked around her. 'Keen, Davey, keen!' she said.

David poured the champagne into paper cups and sliced the meat with a penknife while Philly broke the bread into hunks. They sat side by side on a fallen log and ate.

'It's so quiet and peaceful – not at all like a killing ground. This is where the Germans made their last big effort – did you know that?'

Philly's mouth was full of bread and meat which didn't stop her reply. 'I saw the movie, Henry Fonda, Robert Ryan – it was a complete crock.'

'All that death and ugliness, we should do something beautiful in this place,' David said dreamily, and she swallowed the bread, took a sip of the wine, before she stood up languidly and went to the Mustang. She fetched her sleeping bag and spread it on the soft bed of leaf mould.

'Some things are for talking about – others are for doing,' she told him.

For a while in Paris it looked as though it might be significant, as though they might have something for each other of importance. They found a room with a shower in a clean and pleasant little *pension* near the Gare St Lazare, and they walked through the streets all that day, from Concorde to Étoile, then across to the Eiffel Tower and back to Notre Dame. They ate supper at a sidewalk café on the 'Boul Mich', but halfway through the meal they reached an emotional dead end. Suddenly they ran out of conversation, they sensed it at the same time, each aware that they were strangers in all but the flesh and the knowledge chilled them both. Still they stayed together that night, even going through the mechanical and empty motions of love, but in the morning, when David came out of the shower, she sat up in the bed and said, 'You are splitting.'

It was a statement and not a question, and it needed no reply.

'Are you all right for bread?' he asked, and she shook her head. He peeled off a pair of thousand-franc notes and put them on the side table.

'I'll pay the bill downstairs.' He picked up his bag. 'Stay loose,' he said.

Paris was spoiled for him now, so he took the road south again towards the sun for the sky was filled with swollen black cloud and it rained before he passed the turn-off to Fontainebleau. It rained as he believed was only possible in the tropics, a solid deluge that flooded the concrete of the highway and blurred his windscreen so that the flogging of the wipers could not clear it swiftly enough for safe vision.

David was alone and discomforted by his inability to sustain communication with another human being. Although the other traffic had moderated its pace in the rain, he drove fast, feeling the drift and skate of his tyres on the slick surface. This time the calming effect of speed was ineffective and when he ran out of the rain south of Beaune it seemed that the wolf pack of loneliness ran close behind him.

However, the first outpouring of sunshine lightened his mood, and then far over the stone walls and rigid green lines of the vineyards he saw a wind-sock floating like a soft white sausage from its pole. He found the exit from the highway half a mile farther on, and the sign 'Club Aéro-nautique de Provence'. He followed it to a neat little airfield set among the vineyards, and one of the aircraft on the hard-stand was a Marchetti Aerobatic type F260. David climbed out of the Mustang and stared at it like a drunkard contemplating his first whisky of the day.

The Frenchman in the club office looked like an unsuccessful undertaker, and even when David showed him his logbook and sheafs of licences, he resisted the temptation of hiring him the Marchetti. David could take his pick from the others – but the Marchetti was not for hire. David added a five hundred franc note to the pile of documents, and it disappeared miraculously into the Frenchman's pocket. Still he would not let David take the Marchetti solo, and he insisted on joining him in the instructor's seat.

David executed a slow and stately four-point roll before they had crossed the boundary fence. It was an act of defiance, and he made the stops crisp and exaggerated. The Frenchman cried 'Sacré bleu!' with great feeling and froze in his seat, but he had the good sense not to interfere with the controls. David completed the manoeuvre and then immediately rolled in the opposite direction with the wing-tip a mere fifty feet above the tips of the vines. The Frenchman relaxed visibly, recognizing the masterly touch, and when David landed an hour later he grinned mourn-fully at him.

'Formidable!' he said, and shared his lunch with David – garlic polony, bread and a bottle of rank red wine. The good feeling of flight and the aroma of garlic lasted David all the way to Madrid.

In Madrid suddenly it began to happen, almost as though it had been arranged long before, as though his frantic flight across half of Europe was a pre-knowledge that something of importance awaited him in Madrid.

He reached the city in the evening, hurrying the last day's journey to be in time for the first running of the bulls that season. He had read Hemingway and Conrad and much of the other romantic literature of the bullring. He wondered if there might not be something for him in this way of life. It read so well in the books – the beauty, glamour and excitement – the courage and trial and the final moment of truth. He wanted to evaluate it, to see it here in the great Plaza Des Torros, and then, if it still intrigued him, go on to the festival at Pamplona later in the season.

David checked in at the Gran Via with its elegance faded to mere comfort, and the porter arranged tickets for the following day. He was tired from the long drive and he went to bed early, waking refreshed and eager for the day. He found his way out to the ring and parked the Mustang amongst the tourist buses that already crowded the parking lot so early in the season.

The exterior of the ring was a surprise, sinister as the temple of some pagan and barbaric religion, unrelieved by the fluted tiers of balconies and encrustations of ceramic tiles – but the interior was as he knew it would be from film and photograph. The sanded ring smooth and clean, the flags against the cloud-flecked sky, the orchestra pouring out its jerky, rousing refrain – and the excitement.

The excitement amongst the crowd was more intense than he had known at prize fights or football internationals, they hummed and swarmed, rank upon rank of white eager faces and the music goaded them on.

David was sitting amongst a group of young Australians who wore souvenir sombreros and passed goat-skins of bad wine about, the girls squealing and chittering like sparrows. One of them picked on David, leaning forward to tug his shoulder and offer him the wine-skin. She was pretty enough in a kittenish way and her eyes made it clear that the offer was for more than cheap wine, but he refused both invitations brusquely and went to fetch a can of beer from one of the vendors. His chilly experience with the girl in Paris was still too fresh. When he returned to his seat the Aussie girl eyed the beer he carried reproachfully and then turned brightly and smiling to her companions.

The late arrivals were finding their seats now and the excitement was escalating sharply. Two of them climbed the stairs of the aisle towards where David sat. A striking young couple in their early twenties, but what first drew David's attention was the good feeling of companionship and love that glowed around them, like an aura setting them apart.

They climbed arm in arm, passed where David sat, and took seats a row behind and across the aisle. The girl was tall with long legs clad in short black boots and dark pants over which she wore an apple-green suede jacket that was not expensive but of good cut and taste. In the sun her hair glittered like coal newly cut from the face and it hung to her shoulders in a sleek soft fall. Her face was broad and sun-browned, not beautiful for her mouth was too big and her eyes too widely spaced, but those eyes were the colour of wild honey, dark brown and flecked with gold. Like her, her companion was tall and straight, dark and strong-looking. He guided her to her seat with a brown, muscled arm and David felt a sharp stab of anger and envy for him.

'Big cocky son of a gun,' he thought. They leaned their heads together and spoke secretly, and David looked away, his own loneliness accentuated by their closeness.

The parade of the toreadors began, and they came out with the sunlight glittering on the sequins and embroidery of their suits, as though they were the scales of some flamboyant reptile. The orchestra blared, and the keys to the bull pens were thrown down on to the sand. The toreadors' capes were spread on the *barrera* below their favourites and they retired from the ring.

In the pause that followed David glanced at the couple again. He was startled to find that they were both watching him and the girl was discussing him. She was leaning on

34

her companion's shoulder, her lips almost touching his ear as she spoke and David felt his stomach clench under the impact of those honey-golden eyes. For an instant they stared at each other and then the girl jerked away guiltily and dropped her gaze – but her companion held David's eyes openly, smiling easily, and it was David who looked away.

Below them in the ring the bull came out at full charge, head high, and hooves skidding in the sand.

He was beautiful and black and glossy, muscle in the neck and shoulder bunching as he swung his head from side to side and the crowd roared as he spun and burst into a gallop, pursuing an elusive flutter of pink across the ring. They took him on a circuit, passing him smoothly from cape to cape, letting him show off his bulk and high-stepping style, and the perfect sickle of his horns with their creamy points, before they brought in the horse.

The trumpets ushered in the horse, and they were a mockery – a brave greeting from the wretched nag, with scrawny neck and starting coat, one rheumy old eye blinkered so he could not see the fearsome creature he was going to meet.

Clownish in his padding, seeming too frail to carry the big armoured man on his back, they led him out and placed him in the path of the bull – and here any semblance of beauty ended.

The bull went into him head down, sending the gawky animal reeling against the *barrera* and the man leaned over the broad black back and ripped and tore into the hump with the lance, worrying the flesh, working in the steel with all his weight until the blood poured out in a slick tide, black as crude oil, and dripped from the bull's legs into the sand.

Raging at the agony of the steel the bull hooked and butted at the protective pads that covered the horse's flanks. They came up as readily as a theatre curtain and the bull was into the scrawny roan body, hacking with the terrible horns, and the horse screamed as its belly split open and the purple and pink entrails spilled out and dangled into the sand.

David was dry-mouthed with horror as around him the crowd blood-roared, and the horse went down in a welter of equipment and its own guts.

They drew the bull away and flogged the fallen horse, twisting its tail and prodding its testicles, forcing it to rise at last and stand quivering and forlorn. Then beating it to make it move again they led it from the ring stumbling over its own entrails.

Then they went to work on the bull, slowly, torturously, reducing it from a magnificent beast to a blundering hunk of sweating and bleeding flesh, splattered with the creamy froth blown from its agonized lungs.

David wanted to scream at them to stop it, but sick to the stomach, frozen by guilt for his own part in this obscene ritual, he sat through it in silence until the bull stood in the centre of the ring, the sand about him ploughed and riven by his dreadful struggles. He stood with his head down, muzzle almost touching the sand and the blood and froth dripped from his nostrils and gaping mouth. The hoarse sawing of his breathing carried to David even above the crazed roaring of the crowd. The bull's legs shuddered and he passed a dribble of loose liquid yellow dung that fouled his back legs. It seemed to David that this was the final humiliation, and he found he was whispering aloud.

'No! No! Stop it! Please, stop it!'

Then the man in the glittering suit and ballet shoes came to end it, and the point of the sword struck bone and the blade arced then spun away in the sunlight, and the bull heaved and threw thick droplets of blood, before he stood again.

They picked up the sword from the sand and gave it to the man and he sighted over the quiescent, dying beast and again the thrust was deflected by bone and David found that at last he had power in his voice, and he screamed:

'Stop it! You filthy bastards.'

Twelve times the man in the centre tried with the sword, and each time the sword flicked out of his hand, and then at last the bull fell of its own accord, weak from the slow loss of much blood and with its heart broken by the torture and the striving. It tried to rise, lunging weakly, but the strength was not there and they killed it where it lay, with a dagger in the back of the neck, and they dragged it out with a team of mules – its legs waggling ridiculously in the air and its blood leaving a long brown smudge across the sand.

Stunned with the monstrous cruelty of it, David turned slowly to look at the girl. Her companion was leaning over her solicitously, whispering to her, trying to comfort her.

She was shaking her head slowly, in a gesture of incomprehension, and her honey-coloured eyes were blinded with weeping. Her lips were apart, quivering with grief, and her cheeks were awash, shiny with her tears.

Her companion helped her to her feet, and gently took her down the steps, leading her away blindly like a new widow from her husband's grave.

Around him the crowd was laughing and exhilarated, high on the blood and the pain – and David felt himself rejected, cut off from them. His heart went out to the weeping girl, she of all of them was the only one who seemed real to him. He had seen enough also, and he knew he would never get to Pamplona. He stood up and followed the girl out of the ring, he wanted to speak to her, to tell her that he shared her desolation, but when he reached the parking lot they were already climbing into a battered old Citroën CV100, and although he broke into a run, the car pulled away – blowing blue smoke and clattering like a lawn-mower – and turned into the traffic heading east.

David watched it go with a sense of loss that effectively washed away the good feeling of the last few days, but he saw the old Citroën again two days later, when he had abandoned all idea of the Pamplona Festival and headed south. The Citroën looked even sicker than before, under a layer of pale dust and with the canvas showing on a rear tyre. The suspension seemed to have sagged on the one side, giving it a rakishly drunken aspect.

It was parked at a filling station on the outskirts of Zaragoza on the road to Barcelona, and David pulled off the road and parked beyond the gasoline pumps. An attendant in greasy overalls was filling the tank of the Citroën under the supervision of the muscular young man from the bullring. David looked quickly for the girl – but she was not in the car. Then he saw her.

She was in a *cantina* across the street, haggling with the elderly woman behind the counter. Her back was turned towards him, but David recognized the mass of dark hair now piled on top of her head. He crossed the road quickly and went into the shop behind her. He was not certain what he was going to do, acting only on impulse.

The girl wore a short floral dress which left her back and shoulders bare, and her feet were thrust into open sandals. But in concession to the ice in the air she wore a shawl over her shoulders. Close to, her skin had a plastic smoothness and elasticity, as though it had been lightly oiled and polished, and down the back of her naked neck the hair was fine and soft, growing in a whorl in the nape.

David moved closer to her as she completed her purchase of dried figs and counted her change. He smelt her, a light summery perfume that seemed to come from her hair. He resisted the temptation to press his face into the dense pile of it.

She turned smiling and saw him standing close behind her. She recognized him instantly, his was not a face a girl would readily forget. She was startled. The smile flickered out on her face and she stood very still looking at him, her expression completely neutral, but her lips slightly parted and her eyes soft and glowing golden. This peculiar stillness of hers was a quality he would come to know so well in the time ahead.

'I saw you in Madrid,' he said, 'at the bulls.'

'Yes,' she nodded, her voice neither welcoming nor forbidding.

'You were crying.'

'So were you.' Her voice was low and clear, her enunciation flawless, too perfect not to be foreign.

'No,' David denied it.

'You were crying,' she insisted softly. 'You were crying inside.' And he inclined his head in agreement. Suddenly she proffered the paper bag of figs.

'Try one,' she said and smiled. It was a warm friendly smile. He took one of the fruits and bit into the sweet flesh as she moved towards the door, somehow conveying an invitation for him to join her. He walked with her and they looked across the street at the Citroën. The attendant had finished filling the tank, and the girl's companion was waiting for her, leaning against the bonnet of the weary old car. He was lighting a cigarette, but he looked up and saw them. He evidently recognized David also, and he straightened up quickly and flicked away the burning match.

There was a soft whooshing sound and the heavy thump of concussion in the air, as fire flashed low across the concrete from a puddle of spilled gasoline. In an instant the flames had closed over the rear of the Citroën, and were drumming hungrily at the coachwork.

David left the girl and sprinted across the road.

'Get it away from the pumps, you idiot,' he shouted, and the driver started out of frozen shock.

It was happy fifth of November, a spectacular pyrotechnic display – but David got the handbrake off and the gearbox into neutral, and he and the driver pushed it into an open parking area alongside the filling station while a crowd materialized, seeming to appear out of the very earth, to scream hysterical encouragement and suggestions while keeping at a discreet distance.

They even managed to rescue the baggage from the rear seat before the flames engulfed it entirely – and belatedly the petrol attendant arrived with an enormous scarlet fire extinguisher. To the delighted applause of the crowd, he drenched the pathetic little vehicle in a great cloud of foam, and the excitement was over. The crowd drifted away, still laughing and chattering and congratulating the amateur firefighter on his virtuoso performance with the extinguisher – while the three of them regarded the scorched and blackened shell of the Citroën ruefully.

'I suppose it was a kindness really – the poor old thing was very tired,' the girl said at last. 'It was like shooting a horse with a broken leg.'

'Are you insured?' David asked, and the girl's companion laughed.

'You're joking – who would insure that? I only paid a hundred US dollars for her.'

They assembled the small pile of rescued possessions, and the girl spoke quickly to her companion in foreign, slightly guttural language which touched a deep chord in David's memory. He understood what she was saying, so it was no surprise when she looked at him.

'We've got to meet somebody in Barcelona this evening. It's important.'

'Let's go,' said David.

They piled the luggage into the Mustang and the girl's companion folded up his long legs and piled into the back seat. His name was Joseph – but David was advised by the girl to call him Joe. She was Debra, and surnames didn't seem important at that stage. She sat in the seat beside David, with her knees pressed together primly and her

40

hands in her lap. With one sweeping glance, she assessed the Mustang and its contents. David watched her check the expensive luggage, the Nikon camera and Zeiss binoculars in the glove compartment and the cashmere jacket thrown over the seat. Then she glanced sideways at him, seeming to notice for the first time the raw silk shirt with the slim gold Piaget under the cuff.

'Blessed are the poor,' she murmured, 'but still it must be pleasant to be rich.'

David enjoyed that. He wanted her to be impressed, he wanted her to make a few comparisons between himself and the big muscular buck in the back seat.

'Let's go to Barcelona,' he laughed.

David drove quietly through the outskirts of the town, and Debra looked over her shoulder at Joe.

'Are you comfortable?' she asked in the guttural language she had used before.

'If he's not – he can run behind,' David told her in the same language, and she gawked at him a moment in surprise before she let out a small exclamation of pleasure.

'Hey! You speak Hebrew!'

'Not very well,' David admitted. 'I've forgotten most of it,' and he had a vivid picture of himself as a ten-year-old, wrestling unhappily with a strange and mysterious language with back-to-front writing, an alphabet that was squiggly tadpoles and in which most sounds were made in the back of the throat, like gargling.

'Are you Jewish?' she asked, turning in the seat to confront him. She was no longer smiling; the question was clearly of significance to her.

David shook his head. 'No,' he laughed at the notion. 'I'm a half-convinced non-practising monotheist, raised and reared in the Protestant Christian tradition.'

'Then why did you learn Hebrew?'

'My mother wanted it,' David explained, and felt again the stab of an old guilt. 'She was killed when I was still a kid. I just let it drop. It didn't seem important after she had gone.'

'Your mother—' Debra insisted, leaning towards him, ' – she was Jewish?'

'Yeah. Sure,' David agreed. 'But my father was a Protestant. There was all sorts of hell when Dad married her. Everyone was against it – but they went ahead and did it anyway.'

Debra turned in the seat to Joe. 'Did you hear that – he's one of us.'

'Oh, come on!' David protested, still laughing.

'*Mazaltov,*' said Joe. 'Come and see us in Jerusalem some time.'

'You're Israeli?' David asked, with new interest.

'Sabras, both of us,' said Debra, with a note of pride and deep satisfaction. 'We are only on holiday here.'

'It must be an interesting country,' David hazarded.

'Like Joe just said, why don't you come and find out some time?' she suggested offhandedly. 'You have the right of return.' Then she changed the subject. 'Is this the fastest this machine will go? We have to be in Barcelona by seven.'

There was a relaxed feeling between them now, as though some invisible barrier had been lowered, as though she had made some weighty judgement. They were out of the city and ahead the open road wound down into the valley of the Ebro towards the sea.

'Kindly extinguish cigarettes and fasten your seat belts,' David said, and let the Mustang go.

She sat very still beside him with her hands folded in her lap and she stared ahead when the bends leapt at them, and the straights streamed in a soft blue blur beneath the body of the Mustang. There was a small rapturous smile on her mouth and the golden lights danced in her eyes, and David was moved to know that speed affected her the way it did him.

He forgot everything else but the girl in the seat beside him and the need to keep the mighty roaring machine on the ribbon of tarmac.

Once when they went twisting down into a dry dusty valley in a series of tight curves and David snaked the Mustang down into it with his hands darting from wheel to gear leaver, and his feet dancing heel and toe on the foot pedals – she laughed aloud with the thrill of it.

They bought cheese and bread and a bottle of white wine at a village *cantina* and ate lunch sitting on the parapet of a stone bridge while the water swirled below them, milky with snow melt from the mountains.

David's thigh touched Debra's, as they sat side by side. He could feel the warmth and resilience of her flesh through the stuff of their clothing and she made no move to pull away. Her cheeks were flushed a little brighter than seemed natural, even in the chill little wind that nagged at them.

David was puzzled by Joe's attitude. He seemed to be completely oblivious of David's bird dogging his girl, and he was deriving a childlike pleasure out of tossing pebbles at the trout in the waters below them. Suddenly David wished he would put up a better resistance, it would make his conquest a lot more enjoyable – for conquest was what David had decided on.

He leaned across Debra for another chunk of the white, tangy cheese and he let his arm brush lightly against the tantalizing double bulge of her bosom. Joe seemed not to notice.

'Come on, you big ape,' David thought scornfully. 'Fight for it. Don't just sit there.'

He wanted to test himself against this buck. He was big, and strong, and David could tell from the way he moved and held himself that he was well co-ordinated and self-assured. His face was chunky and half ugly, but he knew that some women liked them that way, and he was not

43

fooled by Joe's slow and lazy grin – the eyes were quick and sharp.

'You want to drive, Joe?' he asked suddenly, and the slow grin spread like a puddle of spilled oil on Joe's face – but the eyes glittered with anticipation.

'Don't mind if I do,' said Joe, and David regretted the gesture as he found himself hunched in the narrow back seat. For the first five minutes Joe drove sedately, touching the brakes to test for grab and pull, flicking through the gears to feel the travel and bite of the stick, taking a burst of power through a bend to establish stability and detect any tendency for the tail to break out.

'Don't be scared of her,' David told him, and Joe grunted with a little frown of concentration creasing his broad forehead. Then he nodded to himself and his hands settled firmly, taking a fresh grip, and Debra whooped as he changed down to get the revs peaking. He slid the car through the first bend and David's right foot stabbed instinctively at a non-existent brake pedal and he felt his breathing jam in his throat.

When Joe parked them in the lot outside the airport at Barcelona and switched off the engine, all of them were silent for a few seconds and then David said softly, 'Son of a gun!'

Then they were all laughing. David felt a tinge of regret that he was going to have to take the girl away from him, for he was beginning to like him, despite himself, beginning to enjoy the slow deliberation of his speech and movements that was so clearly a put-on and finding pleasure in the big slow smile that took so long to reach its full bloom. David had to harden his resolve.

They were an hour early for the plane they were meeting and they found a table in the restaurant overlooking the runways. David ordered an earthenware jug of Sangria, and Debra sat next to Joe and put her hand on his arm while she chatted, a gesture that tempered David's new-found liking for him.

A private flight landed as the waiter brought the Sangria, and Joe looked up.

'One of the new executive Gulfstreams. They tell me she is a little beauty.' And he went on to list the aircraft's specifications in technical language that Debra seemed to follow intelligently.

'You know anything about aircraft?' David challenged him.

'Some,' admitted Joe, but Debra took the question.

'Joe is in the air force,' she said proudly, and David stared at them.

'So is Debs,' Joe laughed, and David switched his attention to her. 'She's a lieutenant in signals.'

'Only the reserve,' Debra demurred, 'but Joe is a flier. A fighter pilot.'

'A flier,' David repeated stupidly. He should have known from Joe's clear and steady gaze that was the peculiar mark of the fighter pilot. He should have known by the way he handled the Mustang. If he was an Israeli flier – then he would have flown a formidable number of operations. Hell, every time they took off, they were operational. He felt a vast tide of respect rising within him.

'What squadron are you on – Phantoms?'

'Phantoms!' Joe curled his lip. 'That isn't flying. That's operating a computer. No, we really fly. You ever heard of a Mirage?'

David blinked, and then nodded.

'Yeah,' said David, 'I've heard of them.'

'Well, I fly a Mirage.'

David began to laugh, shaking his head.

'What's wrong?' Joe demanded, his smile fading. 'What's funny about that?'

'I do too,' said David. 'I fly a Mirage.' It was no use

trying to get hot against this buck, he decided. 'I've got over a thousand hours on Mirages.' And it was Joe's turn to stare, then suddenly they were both talking at once – Debra's head turning quickly from one to the other.

David ordered another jug of Sangria, but Joe would not let him pay. He repeated for the fiftieth time, 'Well, that beats all,' and punched David's shoulder. 'How about that, Debs?'

Halfway through the second jug, David interrupted the talk which had been exclusively on aviation.

'Who are we meeting, anyway? We've driven across half of Spain and I don't even know who the guy is.'

'This guy is a girl,' Joe laughed, and Debra filled in.

'Hannah,' and she grinned at Joe, 'his fiancée. She is a nursing sister at Hadassah Hospital, and she could only get away for a week.'

'Your fiancée?' David whispered.

'They are getting married in June.' Debra turned to Joe. 'It's taken him two years to make up his mind.'

Joe chuckled with embarrassment, and Debra squeezed his arm.

'Your fiancée?' asked David again.

'Why do you keep saying that?' Debra demanded. David pointed at Joe, and then at Debra.

'What,' he started, 'I mean, who – what the hell?'

Debra realized suddenly and gasped. She covered her mouth with both hands, her eyes sparkling. 'You mean – you thought—? Oh, no,' she giggled. She pointed at Joe and then at herself. 'Is that what you thought?' David nodded.

'He is my brother,' Debra hooted. 'Joe is my brother, you idiot! Joseph Israel Mordecai and Debra Ruth Mordecai – brother and sister.'

Hannah was a rangy girl with bright copper hair and freckles like gold sovereigns. She was only an inch or two shorter than Joe but he lifted her as she came through the customs gate, swung her off her feet and then engulfed her in an enormous embrace.

It seemed completely natural that the four of them should stay together. By a miracle of packing they got all their luggage and themselves into the Mustang with Hannah perched on Joe's lap in the rear.

'We've got a week,' said Debra. 'A whole week! What are we going to do with it?'

They agreed that Torremolinos was out. It was far south, and since Michener had written *The Drifters*, it had become a hangout for all the bums and freaks.

'I was talking to someone on the plane. There is a place called Colera up the coast. Near the border.'

They reached it in the middle of the next morning and it was still so early in the season that they had no trouble finding pleasant rooms at a small hotel off the winding main street. The girls shared, but David insisted on a room of his own. He had certain plans for Debra that made privacy desirable.

Debra's bikini was blue and brief, hardly sufficient to restrain a bosom that was more exuberant than David had guessed. Her skin was satiny and tanned to a deep mahogany, although a strip of startling white peeped over the back of her costume when she stooped to pick up her towel. She was long in the waist, and leg, and a strong swimmer – pacing David steadily through the cool blue water when they set out for a rocky islet half a mile off shore.

They had the tiny island to themselves and they found a patch of flat smooth rock out of the wind and full in the sun. They lay side by side with their fingers entwined and the salt water had sleeked Debra's hair to her shoulders, like the coat of an otter.

They lay in the sun and they talked away the afternoon. There was so much they had to learn about each other.

Her father had been one of the youngest colonels in the American Air Force during World War II, but afterwards he had gone on to Israel. He had been there ever since, and was now a major-general. They lived in a house in an old part of Jerusalem which was five hundred years old, but was a lot of fun.

She was a senior lecturer in English at the Hebrew University in Jerusalem and, this shyly as though it was a rather special secret, she wanted to write. A small volume of her poetry had already been published. That impressed David, and he came up on one elbow and looked at her with new respect, and a twinge of envy, for someone who saw the way ahead clearly.

She lay with her eyes closed against the sun, and droplets of water sparkling like gems on her thick dark eyelashes. She wasn't beautiful, he decided carefully, but very handsome and very, very sexy. He was going to have her, of course. There was no doubt in David's mind about this, but there seemed little urgency in it now. He was enjoying listening to her talk, she had a quaint way of expressing herself, once she was in full flight, and her accent was strangely neutral – although there were faint echoes of her American background now he knew to look for them. She told him that the poetry was merely a beginning. She was going to write a novel about being young and living in Israel. She had the outline worked out, and it seemed like a pretty interesting story to David. Then she started to talk about her land and the people who lived in it. David felt something move within him as he listened – a nostalgia, a deep race memory. Again his envy stirred. She was so certain of where she was from and where she was going – she knew where she belonged, and what her destiny was, and this made her strong. Beside her he felt suddenly insignificant and without purpose.

She opened her eyes suddenly, squinting a little in the sunlight, and looked up at him.

'Oh dear,' she smiled. 'We are so sad, David. Do I talk too much?' He shook his head but did not answer her smile, and she became solemn also.

She studied his face carefully, with minute attention. The sun had dried his hair and fluffed it out, and it was soft and fine and very dark. The bone of his cheek and jaw was sculptured and finely balanced, the eyes very clear and slightly Asiatic in cast, the lips full and firm, and the nose delicately fluted with wide nostrils and a straight graceful line.

She reached up and touched his cheek.

'You are very beautiful, David. You are the most beautiful human being I have ever seen.'

He did not move, and she ran the finger down his neck on to his chest, twirling it slowly in the dark body hair.

Slowly he leaned forward and placed his mouth over hers. Her lips were warm and soft and tasted of sea salt. Her arms came up around the back of his head and folded around him. They kissed until he reached behind her and unfastened the clasp of her costume between the smooth brown shoulder blades. She stiffened immediately and tried to pull away from him.

David held her gently but firmly, murmuring little soothing noises as he kissed her again. Slowly she relaxed and he went on gentling her until her hands went to the back of his neck again, and she sighed and shuddered.

His hands were skilled and expert, masterful enough to prevent rebellion, not rough enough to panic her. He pushed up the thin material of her costume top and was surprised and enchanted with the firm rubbery weight of her breasts and the big dusky rose-brown nipples which were pebble-hard to his touch.

It was shocking, completely foreign to his experience, for David was not accustomed to check or denial, but Debra placed her hands on his shoulders and shoved him with such force that he lost his balance and slid down the rock, grazing his elbow and ending in a heap at the water's edge.

He scrambled angrily to his feet as Debra came up with a fluid explosive movement, fastening her costume as she did so. A single bound of her long brown legs carried her to the edge of the rocks and she dived outwards, hitting the water flat and surfacing to call back at him.

'I'll race you to the beach.'

David would not accept the challenge and followed her at his own dignified pace. When he emerged unsmilingly from the low surf, she studied his face a moment and then grinned.

'When you sulk you look about ten years old,' she told him, which was no great exercise of tact, and David stalked back to his room.

He was still being extremely dignified and aloof that evening when they discovered a discotheque named '2001 AD' run by a couple of English boys down on the seafront. They crowded round a table at which there were already two BEA hostesses and a couple of raggedy-looking beards. The music was loud enough and the rhythm hard enough to jar the spine and loosen the bowels, and when the two hostesses gazed at David with almost religious awe Debra forsook her attitude of cool amusement and suggested to David that they dance. Mollified by this little feminine by-play, David dropped his impersonation of the Ice King.

They moved well together, sharing the gut rhythms of the harsh music, executing the primeval movements that reeked of Africa with a grace that drew the attention of the other dancers.

When the music changed Debra came to him and laid her body against his. David felt some force flowing from her that seemed to charge every nerve of his body – and he knew that no relationship he had with this woman would

50

ever run calmly. It was too deeply felt for that, too volatile and triggered for momentary explosion.

When the record ended they left Joe and Hannah huddled over a carafe of red wine and they went out into the silent street and down to the beach.

There was a moon in the sky that lit the dark cliffs crowding in above the beach, and reflected off the sea in multiple yellow images. The low surf hissed and coughed on the pebble beach and they took off their shoes and walked along it, letting the water wash around their ankles.

In an angle of the cliff, they found a hidden place amongst the rocks and they stopped to kiss again, and David mistakenly took her new soft mood as an invitation to continue from where he had left off that afternoon.

Debra pulled away again, but this time with determination and said angrily, 'Damn you! Don't you ever learn? I don't want to do that. Do we have to go through this every time we are alone?'

'What's the matter?' David was immediately stung by her tone, and furious with this fresh check. 'This is the twentieth century, darling. The simpering virgin is out of style this season – hadn't you heard?'

'And spoilt little boys should grow up before they come out on their own,' she flashed back at him.

'Thanks!' he snarled. 'I don't have to stay around taking insults from any professional virgin.'

'Well, why don't you move out then?' she challenged him.

'Hey, that's a great idea!' He turned his back on her and walked away up the beach. She had not expected that, and she started to run after him – but her pride checked her. She stopped and leaned against the rock.

He shouldn't have rushed me, she thought miserably. I want him, I want him very much, but he will be the first since Dudu. If he will just give me time it will be all right, but he mustn't rush me. If he could only go at my speed, help me to do it right.

It is funny, she thought, how little I remember about Dudu now. It's only three years, but his memory is fading so swiftly, I wonder if I really did love him. Even his face is hazy in my mind, while I know every detail of David's – every plane and line of it.

Perhaps I should go after him and tell him about Dudu, and ask him to be patient and to help me a little. Perhaps I should do that, she thought, but she did not and slowly she walked up the beach, through the silent town to the hotel.

Hannah's bed across the room was empty. She would be with Joe, lying with him, loving with him. I should be with David also, she thought. Dudu was dead, and I'm alive, and I want David and I should be with him – but she undressed slowly and climbed into the bed and lay without sleeping.

David stood in the doorway of '2001 AD' and peered through the weirdly flashing lights and the smog, the warm palpable emanation from a hundred straining bodies. The BEA hostesses were still at the table, but Joe and Hannah had gone.

David made his way through the dancers. The one hostess was tall and blonde, with high English colour and china-doll eyes. She looked up and saw David, glanced around for Debra, made sure she was missing before she smiled.

They danced one cut of the record without touching each other and then David leaned close to her and placed both hands on her hips. She strained towards him with her lips parting.

'Have you got a room?' he asked, and she nodded, running the tip of her tongue lewdly around her lips.

'Let's go,' said David.

It was light when David got back to his own room. He shaved and packed his bag, surprised at the strength of his residual anger. He lugged his bag down to the proprietor's office and paid his bill with his Diners Club card.

Debra came out of the breakfast room with Joe and Hannah. They were all dressed for the beach with terry robes over their bathing gear, and they were happy and laughing – until they saw David.

'Hey!' Joe challenged him. 'Where are you going?'

'I've had enough of Spain,' David told them. 'I'm taking some good advice, and I'm moving out,' and he felt a flare of savage triumph as he saw the quick shadow of pain in Debra's eyes. Both Joe and Hannah glanced at her, and quickly she controlled the quiver of her lips. She smiled then, a little too brightly and stepped forward, holding out her hand.

'Thank you for all your help, David. I'm sorry you have to go. It was fun.' Then her voice dropped slightly and there was a tiny quiver in it. 'I hope you find what you are looking for. Good luck.'

She turned quickly and hurried away to her room. Hannah's expression was steely, and she gave David a curt nod before following Debra.

'So long, Joe.'

'I'll carry your bag.'

'Don't bother.' David tried to stop him.

'No trouble.' Joe took it out of his hand and carried it out to the Mustang. He dumped it on the rear seat.

'I'll ride up to the top of the hills with you and walk back.' He climbed into the passenger seat and settled comfortably. 'I need the exercise.'

David drove swiftly, and they were silent as Joe deliberately lit a cigarette and flicked the match out the window.

'I don't know what went wrong, Davey, but I can guess.'

David didn't reply, he concentrated on the road.

'She's had a bad time. These last few days she has been different. Happy, I guess, and I thought it was going to work out.'

Still David was silent, not giving him any help. Why didn't the big bonehead mind his own business?

'She's a pretty special sort of person, Davey, not because she's my sister. She really is, and I think you should know about her – just so you don't think too badly about her.'

They had reached the top of the hills above the town and the bay. David pulled on to the verge but kept the engine running. He looked down on the brilliant blue of the sea, where it met the cliffs and the pine-covered headlands.

'She was going to be married,' said Joe softly. 'He was a nice guy, older than she was, they worked together at the University. He was a tank driver in the reserve and he took a hit in the Sinai and burned with his tank.'

David turned and looked at him, his expression softening a little.

'She took it badly,' Joe went on doggedly. 'These last few days were the first time I've seen her truly happy and relaxed.' He shrugged and grinned like a big St Bernard dog. 'Sorry to give you the family history, Davey. Just thought it might help.' He held out a huge brown hand. 'Come and see us. It's your country also, you know. I'd like to show it to you.'

David took the hand. 'I might do that,' he said.

'*Shalom*.'

'*Shalom*, Joe. Good luck.' Joe climbed out of the car and when David pulled away he watched him standing on the side of the road with his hands on his hips. He waved and the first bend in the road hid him.

There was a school for aspiring Formula One racing drivers on a neglected concrete circuit near Ostia, on the road from Rome. The course lasted three weeks and cost $500 US.

David stayed at the Excelsior in the Via Veneto, and commuted each day to the track. He completed the full course, but after the first week knew it was not what he wanted. The physical limitation of the track was constricting after flying the high heavens, and even the crackling, snarling power of a Tyrell Ford could not match the thrust from the engine of a jet interceptor. Although he lacked the dedication and motivation of others in his class his natural talent for speed and his co-ordination brought him out high in the finishing order – and he had an offer to drive on the works team of a new and struggling company that was building and fielding a production team of Formula One racing machines. Of course, the salary was starvation, and it was a measure of his desperation that he came close to signing a contract for the season, but at the last moment he changed his mind and went on.

In Athens he spent a week hanging around the yacht basins of Piraeus and Glyfada. He was investigating the prospects of buying a motor yacht and running it out on charter to the islands. The prospect of sun and sea and pretty girls seemed appealing and the craft themselves were beautiful in their snowy paint and varnished teakwork. In one week he learned that charter work was merely running a sea-going boarding house for a bunch of bored, sunburned and seasick tourists.

On the seventh day the American Sixth Fleet dropped anchor in the bay of Athens. David sat at a table of one of the beach-front cafés and drank *ouzo* in the sun, while he studied the anchored aircraft carriers through his binoculars. On the great flat tops the rows of Crusaders and Phantoms were grouped with their wings folded. Watching them he felt a consuming hunger, a need that was almost spiritual. He had searched the earth, it seemed, and there was nothing for him upon its face. He laid the binoculars aside, and he looked up into the sky. The clouds were high, a brilliant silver against the blue.

He picked up the glass of milky *ouzo* that the sun had warmed and rolled its sweet liquorice taste about his tongue.

'East, west, home is best.'

He spoke aloud, and had a mental image of Paul Morgan sitting in his high office of glass and steel. Like a patient fisherman he tended his lines laid across the world. Right now the one to Athens was beginning to twitch. He could imagine the quiet satisfaction as he began to reel it in, drawing David struggling feebly back to the centre. What the hell, I could still fly Impalas as a reserve officer, he thought, and there was always the Lear – if he could get it away from Barney.

David drained the glass and stood up abruptly, feeling the fading glow of his defiance. He flagged a cab and was driven back to his room at the Grande Bretagne on Syndagma Square.

His defiance was dying so swiftly that one of his companions for dinner that night was John Dinopoulos, Morgan Group's agent for Greece, a slim elegant sophisticate with an unlined sun-tanned face, silver wings in his hair and an elegantly casual way of dressing.

John had selected for David's table companion the female star of a number of Italian spaghetti westerns. A young lady of ample bosom and dark flashing eye whose breathing and bosom had become so agitated when John introduced David as a diamond millionaire from Africa.

Diamonds were the most glamorous, although not the most significant, of Morgan Group's interests.

They sat upon the terrace of Dionysius, for the evening was mild. The restaurant was carved into the living rock of the hill-top of Lycabettus, under the church of St Paul.

56

Down the zig-zag path from the church, the Easter procession of worshippers unwound in a flickering stream of candle flames through the pine forest below them, and the singing carried sweetly on the still night air. On its far hill-top the stately columns of the Acropolis were flood-lit so that they glowed as creamily as ancient ivory, and beyond that again on the midnight waters of the bay the American fleet wore gay garlands of fairy lights.

'The glory that was Greece—' murmured the star of Italian westerns, as though she voiced the wisdom of the ages, and placed one heavily jewelled hand on David's thigh while with the other she raised a glass of red Samos wine to him and cast him a look under thick eyelashes that was fraught with significance.

Her restraint was impressive, and it was only after they had eaten the main course of savoury meats wrapped in vine leaves and swimming in creamy lemon sauce that she suggested that David might like to finance her next movie.

'Let's find some place where we can talk about it—' she murmured, and what better place than her suite?

John Dinopoulos waved them away with a grin and a knowing wink, a gesture that annoyed David for it made him see the whole episode for the emptiness that it was.

The star's suite was pretentious, with thick white carpets and bulky black leather furniture. David poured himself a drink while she went to change into clothing more suitable for a discussion of high finance. David tasted the drink, realized that he did not want it and left it on the bar counter.

The star came out of the bedroom in a bedrobe of white satin which was cut back from arm and bosom, and was so sheer that her flesh gleamed with a pearly pink sheen through the material. Her hair was loose, a great wild mane of swirling curls – and suddenly David was sick of the whole business.

'I'm sorry,' he said. 'John was joking – I'm not a millionaire, and I really prefer boys.'

He heard his untouched glass shatter against the door of the suite as he closed it behind him.

Back at his own hotel he ordered coffee from room service, and then on an impulse he picked up the telephone again and placed a Cape Town call. It came through with surprising speed, and the girl's voice on the other end was thickened with sleep.

'Mitzi,' he laughed. 'How's the girl?'

'Where are you, warrior? Are you home?'

'I'm in Athens, doll.'

'Athens – God! How's the action?'

'It's a drag.'

'Yeah! I bet,' she scoffed. 'The Greek girls are never going to be the same again.'

'How are you, Mitzi?'

'I'm in love, Davey. I mean really in love, it's far out. We are going to be married. Isn't that just something else?' David felt a spur of anger, jealous of the happiness in her voice.

'That's great, doll. Do I know him?'

'Cecil Lawley, you know him. He's one of Daddy's accountants.' David recalled a large, pale-faced, bespectacled man with a serious manner.

'Congratulations,' said David. He felt very much alone again. Far from home, and aware that life there flowed on without his presence.

'You want to talk to him?' Mitzi asked. 'I'll wake him up.' There was a murmur and mutter on the other end, then Cecil came on.

'Nice work,' David told him, and it really was. Mitzi's share of Morgan Group would be considerably larger than David's. Cecil had drilled himself an oil well in a most unconventional manner.

'Thanks, Davey.' Cecil's embarrassment at being caught

tending his oil well carried clearly over five thousand miles of telephone cable.

'Listen, lover. You do anything to hurt that girl, I'll personally tear out your liver and stuff it down your throat, okay?'

'Okay,' said Cecil, and his alarm was brittle in his tone. 'I'll put you back to Mitzi.'

She prattled on for another fifty dollars' worth before hanging up. David lay on the bed with his hands behind his head and thought about his dumpy soft-hearted cousin and her new happiness. Then quite suddenly he made the decision which had been lurking at the edge of his consciousness all these weeks since leaving Spain. He picked up the phone again and asked for the porter's desk.

'I'm sorry to trouble you at this time in the morning,' he said, 'but I should like to get on a flight to Israel as soon as possible, will you please arrange that.'

The sky was filled with a soft golden haze that came off the desert. The gigantic TWA 747 came down through it, and David had a glimpse of dark green citrus orchards before the solid jolt of the touch-down. Lod was like any other airport in the world but beyond its doors was a land like no other he had ever known. The crowd who fought him for a seat in one of the big black *sheruts*, communal taxis plastered with stickers and hung with gew-gaws, made even the Italians seem shining towers of restrained good manners.

Once aboard, however, it was as though they were on a family outing – and he a member of that family. On one side of him a paratrooper in beret and blouse with his winged insignia on the breast and an Uzi submachine-gun slung about his neck offered him a cigarette, on the other a big strapping lass also in khaki uniform and with the dark gazelle eyes of an Israeli, which became even darker and more soulful when she looked at David, which was often, shared a sandwich of unleaven bread and balls of fried chick-peas, the ubiquitous pitta and falafel, with him and practised her English upon him. All the occupants of the front seat turned around to join the conversation, and this included the driver who nevertheless did not allow his speed to diminish in the slightest and who punctuated his remarks with fierce blasts of his horn and cries of outrage at pedestrians and other drivers.

The perfume of orange blossom lay as heavily as sea mist upon the coastal lowlands, and always afterwards it would be for David the smell of Israel.

Then they climbed into the Judaean hills, and David felt a sense of nostalgia as they followed the winding highway through pine forests and across the pale shining slopes where the white stone gleamed like bone in the sunlight and the silver olive trees twisted their trunks in graceful agony upon the terraces which were the monuments to six thousand years of man's patient labour.

It was so familiar and yet subtly different from those fair and well-beloved hills of the southern cape he called home. There were flowers he did not recognize, crimson blooms like spilled blood, and bursts of sunshine-yellow blossoms upon the slopes – then suddenly a pang that was like a physical pain as he glimpsed the bright flight of chocolate and white wings amongst the trees, and he recognized the crested head of an African hoopoe – a bird which was a symbol of home.

He felt a sense of excitement building within him, unformed and undirected as yet but growing, as he drew closer to the woman he had come to see – and to something else of which he was as yet uncertain.

There was, at last, a sense of belonging. He felt in sympathy with the young persons who crowded close to him in the cab.

'See,' cried the girl, touching his arm and pointing to the wreckage of war still strewn along the roadside, the burned-out carapaces of trucks and armoured vehicles, preserved as a memorial to the men who died on the road to Jerusalem. 'There was fighting here.'

David turned in the seat to study her face, and he saw again the strength and certainty that he had so admired in Debra. These were a people who lived each day to its limit, and only at its close did they consider the next.

'Will there be more fighting?' he asked.

'Yes,' she answered him without hesitation.

'Why?'

'Because – if it is good – you must fight for it,' and she made a wide gesture that seemed to embrace the land and all its people, 'and this is ours, and it is good,' she said.

'Right on, doll,' David agreed with her, and they grinned at each other.

So they came to Jerusalem with its tall, severe apartment blocks of custard-yellow stone, standing like monuments upon the hills, grouped about the massive walled citadel that was its heart.

TWA had reserved a room at the Intercontinental Hotel for David while on board the inward flight. From his window he looked across the garden of Gethsemane at the old city, at its turrets and spires and the blazing golden Dome of the Rock – centre of Christianity and Judaism, holy place of the Moslems, battleground of two thousand years, ancient land reborn – and David felt a sense of awe. For the first time in his life, he recognized and examined that portion of himself that was Jewish, and he thought it was right that he should have come to this city.

'Perhaps,' he said aloud, 'it's just possible that this is where it's all at.'

It was early evening when David paid off the cab in the car park of the University and submitted to a perfunctory search by a guard at the main gate. Here body search was a routine that would soon become so familiar as to pass unnoticed. He was surprised to find the campus almost deserted, until he remembered it was Friday – and that the whole tempo was slowing for the Sabbath.

The red-bud trees were in full bloom around the main plaza and the ornamental pool, as David crossed to the admin block and asked for her at the inquiries desk where the porter was on the point of leaving his post.

'Miss Mordecai—' The porter checked his list. 'Yes. English Department. On the second floor of the Lauterman Building.' He pointed out through the glass doors. 'Third building on your right. Go right on in.'

Debra was in a students' tutorial, and while he waited for her, he found a seat on the terrace in the warmth of the sun. It was as well, for suddenly he felt a breath of uncertainty cooling his spine. For the first time since leaving Athens, he wondered if he had much cause to expect a hearty welcome from Debra Mordecai. Even at this remove in time, David had difficulty in judging his own behaviour towards her. Self-criticism was an art which David had never seriously practised; with a face and fortune such as his, it was seldom necessary. In this time of waiting he found it novel and uncomfortable to admit that it was just possible that his behaviour may have been, as Debra had told him, that of a spoiled child. He was still exploring this thought, when a burst of voices and the clatter of heels upon the flags distracted him and a group of students came out on to the terrace, hugging their books to their chests, and most of the girls glanced at him with quick speculative attention as they passed.

There was a pause then before Debra came. She carried books under her arm and a sling bag over one shoulder, and her hair was pulled back severely at the nape of her neck; she wore no make-up, but her skirt was brightly coloured in big summery whorls of orange. Her legs were bare and her feet were thrust into leather sandals. She was in deep conversation with the two students who flanked her, and she did not see David until he stood up from the parapet. Then she froze into that special stillness he had first noticed in the *cantina* at Zaragoza.

David was surprised to find how awkward he felt, as though his feet and hands had grown a dozen sizes. He grinned and made a shrugging, self-deprecatory gesture.

'Hello, Debs.' His voice sounded gruff in his own ears, and Debra stirred and made a panicky attempt to brush back the wisps of hair at her temples, but the books hampered her.

'David—' She started towards him, a pace before she hesitated and stopped, glancing at her students. They sensed her confusion and melted, and she swung back at him.

'David—' she repeated, and then her expression crumbled into utter desolation. 'Oh God, and I haven't even a shred of lipstick on.'

David laughed with relief and went towards her, spreading his arms, and she flew at him and it was all confusion with books and sling bag muddled, and Debra making breathless exclamations of frustration before she could divest herself of them. Then at last they embraced.

'David,' she murmured with both arms wound tightly around his neck. 'You beast – what on earth took you so long? I had almost given you up.'

Debra had a motor scooter which she drove with such murderous abandon that she frightened even the Jerusalem taxi-drivers who crossed her path – men with a reputation for steel nerves and disregard for danger.

Perched on the pillion David clung to her waist and

remonstrated with her gently as she overtook a solid line of traffic and then cut smartly across a stream coming in the opposite direction with her exhaust popping merrily.

'I'm happy,' she explained over her shoulder.

'Fine! Then let's live to enjoy it.'

'Joe will be surprised to see you.'

'If we ever get there.'

'What's happened to your nerve?'

'I've just this minute lost it.'

She went down the twisting road into the valley of Ein Karem as though she was driving a Mirage, and called a travelogue back to him as she went.

'That's the Monastery of Mary's Well where she met the mother of John the Baptist – according to the Christian tradition in which you are a professed expert.'

'Hold the history,' pleaded David. 'There's a bus around that bend.'

The village was timeless amongst the olive trees, dug into the slope with its churches and monasteries and high-walled gardens, an oasis of the picturesque, while the skyline above it was cluttered with the high-rise apartments of modern Jerusalem.

From the main street Debra scooted into the mouth of a narrow lane, where high walls of time-worn stone rose on each hand, and braked to a halt outside a forbidding iron gate.

'Home,' she said, and wheeled the scooter into the gatehouse and locked it away before letting them in through a side gate hidden in a corner of the wall.

They came out into a large garden court enclosed by the high rough plastered walls which were lime-washed to glaring white. There were olive trees growing in the court with thick twisted trunks. Vines climbed the walls and spread their boughs overhead; already there were bunches of green grapes forming upon them.

'The Brig is a crazy keen amateur archaeologist.' Debra

indicated the Roman and Greek statues that stood amongst the olive trees, the exhibits of pottery amphorae arranged around the walls, and the ancient mosaic tiles which paved the pathway to the house. 'It's strictly against the law, of course, but he spends all his spare time digging around in the old sites.'

The kitchen was cavernous with an enormous open fireplace in which a modern electric stove looked out of place, but the copper pots were burnished until they glowed and the tiled floor was polished and sweet-smelling.

Debra's mother was a tall slim woman with a quiet manner, who looked like Debra's older sister. The family resemblance was striking and, as she greeted them, David thought with pleasure that this was how Debra would look at the same age. Debra introduced them and announced that David was a guest for dinner, a fact of which he had been unaware until that moment.

'Please,' he protested quickly, 'I don't want to intrude.' He knew that Friday was a special night in the Jewish home.

'You don't intrude. We will be honoured,' she brushed aside his protest. 'This house is home for most of the boys in Joe's squadron, we enjoy it.'

Debra fetched David a Goldstar beer and they were sitting on the terrace together when her father arrived. He came in through the wicket gate, stooping his tall frame under the stone lintel and taking off his uniform cap as he entered the garden.

He wore uniform casually cut, and open at the throat with cloth insignia or rank and wings at the breast pocket. He was slightly round-shouldered, probably from cramming his lanky body into the cramped cockpits of fighter aircraft, and his head was brown and bald with a monk's fringe of hair and a fierce spiky moustache through which a gold tooth gleamed richly. His nose was big and hooked, the nose of a biblical warrior, and his eyes were dark and

65

snapping with the same golden lights as Debra's. He was a man of such presence that he commanded David's instant respect. He stood to shake the General's hand and called him 'sir' completely naturally.

The Brig subjected David to a rapid, raking scrutiny and reserved his judgement, showing neither pleasure nor disdain.

Later David would learn that the nickname 'The Brig' was a shortened version of 'The Brigand', a name the British had given him before 1948 when he was smuggling warplanes and arms into Palestine for the *Haganah*. Everyone, even his children, called him that and only his wife used his given name, Joshua.

'David is sharing the Sabbath meal with us tonight,' Debra explained to him.

'You are welcome,' said the Brig, and turned to embrace his women with love and laughter, for he had seen neither of them since the previous Sabbath, his duties keeping him at air bases and control rooms scattered widely across the land.

When Joe arrived, he was also in uniform, the casual open-necked khaki of summer, and when he saw David he dropped his slow manner and hurried to him, laughing, and enfolded him in a bear hug, speaking over his shoulder to Debra.

'Was I right?'

'Joe said you would come,' Debra explained.

'It looks like I was the only one who didn't know,' David protested.

There were fifteen at dinner, and the candlelight gleamed on the polished wood of the huge refectory table and the silver Sabbath goblets. The Brig said a short prayer, the satin and gold embroidered yarmulke looking slightly out of place on his wicked bald head, then he filled the wine goblets with his own hand murmuring a greeting to each of his guests. Hannah was with Joe, her copper hair glowing handsomely in the candlelight, and she greeted David with reserve. There were two of the Brig's brothers with their wives and children and grandchildren, and the talk was loud and confusing as the children vied with their elders for a hearing and the language changed at random from Hebrew to English. The food was exotic and spicy, although the wine was too sweet for David's taste. He was content to sit quietly beside Debra and enjoy the sense of belonging to this happy group. He was startled then when one of Debra's cousins leaned across her to speak to him.

'This must be very confusing for you – your first day in such an unusual country as Israel, and not understanding Hebrew, you not being Jewish—'

The words were not meant unkindly, but all conversation stopped abruptly and the Brig looked up, frowning swiftly, quick to sense an unkindness to guest at his board.

David was aware of Debra staring at him intently, as if to will words from him, and suddenly he thought how three denials finalized any issue – in the New Testament, in Mohammedan law, and perhaps in that of Moses as well. He did not want to be excluded from this household, from these people. He didn't want to be alone again. It was good here.

He smiled at the cousin and shook his head. 'It's strange, yes – but not as bad as you would think. I understand Hebrew, though I don't speak it very well. You see, I am Jewish, also.'

Beside him Debra gave a soft gasp of pleasure and exchanged quick glances with Joe.

'Jewish?' the Brig demanded. 'You don't look it,' and David explained, and when he was through the Brig nodded. It seemed that his manner had thawed a little.

'Not only that, but he is a flier also,' Debra boasted, and the Brig's moustache twitched like a living thing so that he had to soothe it with his napkin while he reappraised David carefully.

'What experience?' he demanded brusquely.

'Twelve hundred hours, sir, almost a thousand on jets.'

'Jets?'

'Mirages.'

'Mirages!' The Brig's gold tooth gleamed secretly.

'What squadron?'

'Cobra Squadron.'

'Rastus Naude's bunch?' The Brig stared at David as he asked.

'Do you know Rastus?' David was startled.

'We flew in the first Spitfires from Czechoslovakia together – back in '48. We used to call him Butch Ben Yok – Son of a Gentile – in those days. How is he, he must be getting on now? He was no spring chicken even then.'

'He's as spry as ever, sir,' David answered tactfully.

'Well, if Rastus taught you to fly – you might be half good,' the Brig conceded.

As a general rule the Israeli Air Force would not use foreign pilots, but here was a Jew with all the marks of a first-class fighter pilot. The Brig had noticed the marvellous élan and thrust which that other consummate judge of young men, Paul Morgan, had recognized also and valued so highly. Unless he had read the signs wrongly, something he seldom did, then here was a rare one. Once more he appraised the young man in the candlelight and noticed that clear and steady gaze that seemed to seek a distant horizon. It was the eye of the gunfighter, and all his pilots were gunfighters.

To train an interceptor pilot took many years and nearly a million dollars. Time and money were matters of survival in his country's time of trial – and rules could be bent.

He picked up the wine bottle and carefully refilled David's goblet. 'I will place a telephone call to Rastus Naude,' he decided silently, 'and find out a bit more about this youngster.'

Debra watched her father as he began to question David searchingly on his reasons, or lack of them, for coming to Israel – and on his future plans.

She knew precisely how the Brig's mind was working, for she had anticipated it. Her reasons for inviting David to dinner and for exposing him to the Brig were devious and calculated.

She switched her attention back to David, feeling the tense warm sensation in the pit of her stomach and the electric prickle of the skin upon her forearms as she looked at him.

'Yes, you big cocky stallion,' she thought comfortably, 'you aren't going to find it so easy to escape again. This time I'm playing for keeps, and I've got the Brig on to you also.'

She lifted her goblet to him, smiling sweetly at him over the rim.

'You're going to get exactly what you are after, but in trumps and with bells on,' she threatened silently, and aloud she said, '*Lechaim!* To life!' and David echoed the toast.

'This time I'm not going to be put off so easily,' he promised himself firmly as he watched the candlelight explode in tiny golden sparks in her eyes. 'I'm going to have you, my raven-haired beauty, no matter how long it takes or what it costs.'

T he telephone beside his bed woke David in the dawn, and the Brig's voice was crisp and alert, as though he had already completed a day's work.

'If you have no urgent plans for today, I'm taking you to see something,' he said.

'Of course, sir.' David was taken off balance.

'I will fetch you from your hotel in forty-five minutes, that will give you time for breakfast. Please wait for me in the lobby.'

The Brig drove a small nondescript compact with civilian plates, and he drove it fast and efficiently. David was impressed with his reaction time and co-ordination – after all the Brig must be well into his fifties, and David allowed himself to contemplate such immense age with awe.

They took the main highway west towards Tel Aviv, and the Brig broke a long silence.

'I spoke with your old CO last night. He was surprised to hear where you were. He tells me that you were offered promotion to staff rank before you left—'

'It was a bribe,' said David, and the Brig nodded and began to talk. David listened to him quietly while he watched with pleasure the quickly changing landscape as they came down out of the hills and turned southwards through the low rolling plains towards Beersheba and the desert.

'I am taking you to an air force base, and I might add that I am flouting all sorts of security regulations to do so. Rastus assured me that you can fly, and I want to see if he was telling me the truth.'

David looked at him quickly.

'We are going to fly?' and he felt a deep and pleasurable excitement when the Brig nodded.

'We are at war here, so you will be flying a combat sortie, and breaking just about every regulation in the book. But you'll find we don't go by the book very much.'

He went on quietly, explaining his own particular view of Israel, its struggle and its chances of success, and David remembered odd phrases he used.

' – We are building a nation, and the blood we have been forced to mix into the foundations has strengthened them—'

' – We don't want to make this merely a sanctuary for all the beaten-up Jews of the world. We want the strong bright Jews also—'

' – There are three million of us, and one hundred and fifty million enemies, sworn to our total annihilation—'

' – If they lose a battle, they lose a few miles of desert, if we lose one we cease to exist—'

' – We'll have to give them one more beating. They won't accept the others. They believe their ammunition was faulty in 1948, after Suez the lines were restored so they lost nothing, and in '67 they think they were cheated. We'll have to beat them one more time before they'll leave us alone—'

He talked as to a friend or an ally and David was warmed by his trust, and enlivened by the prospect of flying again.

A plantation of eucalyptus trees grew as a heavy screen alongside the road, and the Brig slowed to a gate in the barbed wire fence and a sign that proclaimed in both languages: 'Chaim Weissmann Agricultural Experimental Centre.'

They turned on to the side road through the plantation, and there was a secondary fence and a guard post amongst the trees.

A guard at the gate checked the Brig's papers briefly, they clearly knew him well. Then they drove on, emerging from the plantation into neatly laid-out blocks of different cereal crops. David recognized oats, barley, wheat and maize – all of it flourishing in the warm spring sunshine. The roads between each field were surveyed long and straight and paved with concrete that had been tinted to the colour of the surrounding earth. There was something unnatural in these smooth two-mile long fairways bisecting each other at right angles, and to David they were familiar. The Brig saw his interest and nodded. 'Yes,' he said, 'runways. We are digging in – not to be taken by the same tactics we used in '67.'

David pondered it while they drove rapidly towards a giant concrete grain silo that stood tall in the distance. In the fields scarlet tractors were at work, and overhead irrigation equipment threw graceful glittering ostrich feathers of spray into the air.

They reached the concrete silo and the Brig drove the compact through the wide doors of the barn-like building that abutted it. David was startled to see the lines of buses and automobiles parked in neat lines along the length of the barn. There was transport here for many hundreds of men – and yet he had noticed less than a score of tractor-drivers.

There were guards here again, in paratrooper uniform, and when the Brig led David to the rounded bulk of the silo, he realized suddenly that it was a dummy. A massive bomb-proof structure of solid concrete, housing all the sophisticated communications and radar equipment of a modern fighter base. It was combined control tower and plot for four full squadrons of Mirage fighters, the Brig explained briefly as they entered an elevator and sank below the earth.

They emerged into a reception area where again the Brig's papers were examined, and a paratrooper major was called to pass David through, a duty he performed reluctantly and at the Brig's insistence. Then the Brig led David along a carpeted and air-conditioned underground tunnel to the pilots' dressing-room. It was tiled and spotless, with showers and toilets and lockers like a country club changing-room.

The Brig had ordered clothing for David, guessing his size and doing so accurately. The orderly corporal had no trouble fitting him out in overalls, boots, G-suit, gloves and helmet.

The Brig dressed from his own locker and both of them went through into the ready room, moving stiffly in the constricting grip of the G-suits and carrying their helmets under their arms.

The duty pilots looked up from chess games and magazines as they entered, recognized the general and stood to greet him, but the atmosphere was easy and informal. The Brig made a small witticism and they all laughed and relaxed, while he led David through into the briefing-room.

Swiftly, but without overlooking a detail, he outlined the patrol that they would fly, and checked David out on radio procedure, aircraft identification, and other parochial details.

'All clear?' he asked at last, and when David nodded, he went on, 'Remember what I told you, we are at war. Anything we find that doesn't belong to us we hit it, hard! All right?'

'Yes, sir.'

'It's been nice and quiet the last few weeks, but yesterday we had a little trouble down near Ein Yahav, a bit of nastiness with one of our border patrols. So things are a little sensitive at the moment.' He picked up his helmet and map case then turned to face David, leaning close to him and fixing him with those fierce brown and golden eyes.

'It will be clear up there today, and when we get to forty thousand, you will be able to see it all, every inch of it from Rosh Hanikra to Suez, from Mount Hermon to Eilat, and you will see how small it is and how vulnerable to the enemies that surround us. You said you were looking for something worthwhile – I want you to decide whether guarding the fate of three million people might not be a worthwhile job for a man.'

They rode on a small electric personnel carrier down one of the long underground passages, and they entered the concrete bunker dispersed at one point of a great star whose centre was the concrete silo, and they climbed down from the cart.

The Mirages stood in a row, six of them, sleek and needle-nosed, crouching like leashed and impatient animals, so well remembered in outline, but vaguely unfamiliar in their desert brown and drab green camouflage with the blue Star of David insignia on the fuselage.

The Brig signed for two machines, grinning as he wrote 'Butch Ben Yok' under David's numeral.

'As good a name as any to fly under,' he grunted. 'This is the land of the pseudonym and alias.'

David settled into the tiny cockpit with a sense of homecoming. In here it was all completely familiar and his hands moved over the massed array of switches, instruments and controls like those of a lover as he began his pre-flight check.

In the confined space of the bunkers the jet thunder assaulted the eardrums, their din only made bearable by the perforated steel baffles set into the rear of the structure.

The Brig looked across at David, his head enclosed in the garishly painted helmet, and gave him the high sign. David returned it and reached up to pull the Perspex canopy closed. Ahead of them, the steel blast doors rolled swiftly upwards, and the ready lamps above them switched from red to green.

There was no taxiing to take-off areas; no needless ground exposure. Wing-tip to wing-tip they came up the ramp out of the bunker into the sunlight. Ahead of them stretched one of the long brown runways, and David pushed open his throttle to the gate, and then ignited his afterburners, feeling the thrust of the mighty jet through the cushioning of his seat. Down between the fields of green corn they tore, and then up, with the swooping sensation in the guts and the rapier nose of the Mirage pointed at the sapphire of the sky that arched unbroken and unsullied above them, and once again David experienced the euphoria of jet-powered flight.

They levelled out at a little under forty thousand feet

avoiding even altitudes or orderly flight patterns, and David placed his machine under the Brig's tail and eased back on the throttles to cruising power, his hands delighting in the familiar rituals of flight while his helmeted head revolved restlessly in the search routine, sweeping every quarter of the sky about him, weaving the Mirage to clear the blind spot behind his own tail.

The air had an unreal quality of purity, a crystalline clarity that made even the most distant mountain ranges stand out in crisp silhouette, hardly shaded with the blue of distance. In the north the Mediterranean blazed like a pool of molten silver in the sunlight, while the sea of Galilee was soft cool green, and farther south the Dead Sea was darker, forbidding in its sunken bed of tortured desert.

They flew north over the ridge of Carmel and the flecked white buildings of Haifa with its orange-gold beaches on which the sea broke in soft ripples of creamy lacework. Then they turned together easing back on the power and sinking slowly to patrol altitude at twenty thousand feet as they passed the peak of Mount Hermon where the last snows still lingered in the gullies and upon the high places, streaking the great rounded mountain like an old man's pate.

The softly dreaming greens and pastels delighted David who was accustomed to the sepia monochromes of Africa. The villages clung to the hill-tops, their white walls shining like diadems above the terraced slopes and the darker areas of cultivated land.

They turned south again, booming down the valley of the Jordan, over the Sea of Galilee with its tranquil green waters enclosed by the thickets of date palm and the neatly tended fields of the Kibbutzim, losing altitude as the land forsook its gentle aspect and the hills were riven and tortured, rent by the wadis as though by the claws of a dreadful predator.

On the left hand rose the mountains of Edom, hostile

and implacable, and beneath them Jericho was a green oasis in the wilderness. Ahead lay the shimmering surface of the Dead Sea. The Brig dropped down, and they thundered so low across the salt-thickened water that the jet blast ruffled the surface behind them.

The Brig's voice chuckled in David's earphones. 'That's the lowest you are ever going to fly – twelve hundred feet below sea level.'

They were climbing again as they crossed the mineral works at the southern end of the sea, and faced the blasted and mountainous deserts of the south.

'Hello, Cactus One, this is Desert Flower.' Again the radio silence was broken, but this time David recognized the call sign of command net. They were being called directly from the Operations Centre of Air Force Command, situated in some secret underground bunker at a location that David would never learn. On the command plot their position was being accurately relayed by the radar repeaters.

'Hello, Desert Flower,' the Brig acked, and immediately the exchange became as informal as two old friends chatting, which was precisely what it was.

'Brig, this is Motti. We've just had a ground support request in your area,' he gave the co-ordinates quickly, 'a motorized patrol of border police is under sneak lowlevel attack by an unidentified aircraft. See to it, will you?'

'*Beseder*, Motti, okay.' The Brig switched to flight frequency. 'Cactus Two, I'm going to interception power, conform to me,' he told David, and they turned together on to the new heading.

'No point in trying a radar scan,' the Brig grumbled aloud. 'He'll be down in the ground clutter. We'll not pick the swine off amongst those mountains. Just keep your eyes open.'

'*Beseder*.' David had already picked up the word. The favourite Hebrew word in a land where very little was really 'okay'.

David spotted it first, a slim black column of smoke beginning to rise like a pencil line drawn slowly against the windless and dazzling cobalt blue of the horizon.

'Ground smoke,' he said into his helmet microphone. 'Eleven o'clock low.'

The Brig squinted ahead silently, searching for it and then saw it on the extreme limit of his vision range. He grunted; Rastus had been right in one thing at least. The youngster had eyes like a hawk.

'Going to attack speed now,' he said, and David acked and lit his afterburners. The upholstery of his seat smacked into his back under the mighty increase in thrust and David felt the drastic alteration in trim as the Mirage went shooting through the sonic barrier.

Near the base of the smoke column, something flashed briefly against the drab brown earth, and David narrowed his eyes and made out the tiny shape, flitting swiftly as a sunbird, its camouflage blending naturally into the back-drop of desert, so it was as ethereal as a shadow.

'Bandit turning to port of the smoke,' he called the sighting.

'I have him,' said the Brig, and switched to command net.

'Hello, Desert Flower, I'm on an intruder. Call strike, please.' The decision to engage must be made at command level, and the answering voice was laconic, and flat.

'Brig, this is Motti. Hit him!'

While they spoke they were rushing down so swiftly that the details of the little drama being played out below sprang into comprehension.

Along a dusty border track three patrol vehicles of the border police were halted. They were camouflaged half-tracks, tiny as children's toys in the vastness of the desert.

One of the half-tracks was burning. The smoke was greasy black and rose straight into the air, the beacon that had drawn them. Lying spread-eagled in the road was a

77

human body, flung down carelessly in death, and the sight of it stirred in David a deeply bitter feeling of resentment such as he had last felt in the bullring at Madrid.

The other vehicles were pulled off the track at abandoned angles, and David could see their crews crouching amongst the scrub and rock. Some of them were firing with small arms at their attacker who was circling for his next run down upon them.

David had never seen the type before, but knew it instantly from the recognition charts that he had studied so often. It was a Russian MiG 17 of the Syrian Air Force. The high tailplane was unmistakable. The dappled brown desert camouflage was brightened by the red, white and black roundels with their starred green centres on the fuselage and the stubby swept wings.

The MiG completed its turn, settling swiftly down and levelling off for its next strafing run upon the parked vehicles. The pilot's attention was concentrated on the helpless men cowering amongst the rocks and he was unaware of the terrible vengeance bearing down upon him on high.

The Brig lined up for his pass, turning slightly to bring himself down on the Syrian's tail, attacking in classic style from behind and above, while David dropped back to weave across his rear, covering him and backing up to press in a supporting attack if the first failed.

The Syrian opened fire again and the cannon bursts twinkled like fairy lights amongst the men and trucks. Another truck exploded in a dragon's breath of smoke and flame.

'You bastard,' David whispered as he levelled out behind the Brig, and saw the havoc that was being wrought amongst his people. It was the first time he had thought of them as that, his people, and he felt the cold anger of the shepherd whose flock is under attack.

A line of poetry popped up in his mind, 'The Assyrian came down like a wolf on the fold', and his hands went purposefully to the chore of locking in his cannons-selectors and flicking the trigger forward out of its recess in the moulded grip of the joystick. The soft green glow lit his gunsight as it came alive and he squinted through it.

The Brig was pressing his attack in to close range, rapidly overhauling the slower clumsy-looking MiG, and at that moment he knew he would open fire David saw the Syrian's wing-shape alter. At the fatal instant he had become aware of his predicament, and he had done what was best in the circumstances. He had pulled on full flap and while his speed fell sharply he dropped one wing in a slide towards the earth a hundred feet below.

The Brig was committed and he loosed his salvo of cannon fire at the instant that the Syrian dropped, ducking under it like a boxer avoiding a heavy punch. David saw the blaze of shot pass high, rending the air above the sand-coloured aircraft. Then the Brig was through, missing with every shell, spiralling up and around in a great flashing circle, raging internally at his failure.

At the instant that David recognized the MiG's manoeuvre he reacted with a rapidity that was purely reflexive. He closed down his power, and hit his air brakes to punch a little speed off the Mirage.

The MiG turned steeply away to port, standing on one wing-tip that seemed to be pegged into the bleak desert earth. David released his air brakes, to give his wings lift for the next evolution, and then he dropped his own wing-tip and went sweeping round to follow the Syrian's desperate twists with the Mirage hovering on the edge of the stall.

The Syrian was turning inside him, slower and more manoeuverable; David could not bring his sights to bear, his right forefinger was curled around the trigger but always the dark shape of the MiG was out of centre in the illuminated circle of the sight as the aiming pipper dipped and rose to the pull of gravity.

Ahead of the two circling aircraft rose a steep and forbidding line of cliffs, rent by deep defiles and gullies.

The MiG made no attempt to climb above them, but selected a narrow pass through the hills and went into it like a ferret into its run, a desperate attempt to shake off the pursuit.

The Mirage was not designed for this type of flying, and David felt the urge to hit his afterburners and ride up over the jagged fangs of rock – but to do so was to let the MiG escape, and his anger was still strong upon him.

He followed the Syrian into the rock pass, and the walls of stone on either hand seemed to brush his wing-tips, the gully turned sharply to starboard and David dropped his wing and followed its course. Back upon itself the rock turned, and David swung the needle nose from maximum rate turn starboard to port, and the stall warning device winked amber and red at him as he abused the Mirage's delicate flying capabilities.

Ahead of him the MiG clawed its way through the tunnel of rock. The pilot looked back over his shoulder and he saw the Mirage following him, creeping slowly up on him, and he turned back to his controls and forced his machine lower still, hugging the rugged walls of stone.

The air in the hills was hot and turbulent, and the Mirage bucked and fought against restraint wanting to be free and high, while ahead of it the Syrian drifted tantalizingly off-centre in David's gunsight.

Now the valley turned again and narrowed, before climbing and ending abruptly against a solid dark purple wall of smooth rock.

The Syrian was trapped, he levelled out and climbed steeply upwards, his flight path dictated by the rocks on each side and ahead.

David pushed his throttle to the gate and lit his afterburners, and the mighty engine rumbled, thrusting him powerfully forward, up under the Syrian's stern.

The eternal micro-seconds of mortal combat dragged by, as the Syrian floated lazily into the circle of the gunsight, expanding to fill it as the Mirage's nose seemed to touch the other's tailplane and David felt the buffeting of the Syrian's slipstream.

He pressed the cannon trigger and the Mirage lurched as she hurled her deadly load into the other machine in a clattering double stream of cannon fire and an eruption of incendiary shells.

The Syrian disintegrated, evaporating in a gush of silvery smoke, rent through with bright white lightning, and the ejecting pilot's body was blown clear of the fuselage. For an instant it was outlined ahead of David's screen, cruciform in shape with arms and legs thrown wide, the helmet still on the head, and the clothing ballooning in the rush of air. Then it flickered past the Mirage's canopy as David climbed swiftly up out of the valley and into the open sky.

The soldiers were moving about amongst their vehicles, tending their wounded and covering their dead, but they all looked up as David flew back low along the road. He passed so close that he could see their faces clearly. They were sunbrowned, some with beards or moustaches, strong young faces, their mouths open as they cheered him, waving their thanks.

My people, he thought. He was still high on the adrenalin that had poured into his blood, and he felt a fierce elation. He grinned wolfishly at the men below him and lifted one gloved hand in salute before climbing up to where the Brig was circling, waiting for him.

The artificial lights of the bunker were dim after the brilliance of the sun. An engineer helped David from the cockpit as his mates swarmed over the Mirage to refuel and rearm it. This was one of the vital skills of this tiny air force, the ability to ready a warplane for combat in a fraction of the time usually required for the task. Thus in emergency the machine could return to the battle long before its adversary.

Moving stiffly from the confines of the cockpit, David crossed to where the Brig was already in conversation with the flight controller.

He stood with the gaudy helmet tucked under one arm as he stripped off his gloves, but as David came up he turned to him and his wintry smile exposed the gold tooth in its nest of fur.

Lightly he punched David's arm. '*Ken!* Yes!' said Major-General Joshua Mordecai. 'You'll do.'

D avid was late to fetch Debra for dinner that evening, but she had already learned the reason from her father.

They went to the Select behind David's Tower, inside the Jaffa Gate of the old city. Its unpretentious interior, decorated with patterns of rope upon the walls, did not fully prepare David for the excellent meal that the Arab proprietor served with the minimum of delay – mousakha chicken, with nuts and spices on a bed of kous-kous.

They ate almost in silence, Debra quickly recognizing and respecting David's mood. He was in the grip of post-combat *tristesse*, the adrenalin hangover of stress and excitement, but slowly the good food in his belly and the heavy Carmel wine relaxed him, until over the thimble-sized cups of Turkish coffee, black and powerfully reeking of cardamon seed, Debra could ask, 'What happened today, David?'

He sipped the coffee before replying.

'I killed a man.' She set down her cup and studied his

face solemnly, and he began to speak, telling her the detail of it, the chase and the kill, until he ended lamely, 'I felt only satisfaction at the time. A sense of achievement. I knew I had done what was right.'

'And now?' she prompted him.

'Now I am sad,' he shrugged. 'I am saddened that I had to do it.'

'My father, who has always been a soldier, says that only those who do the actual fighting can truly know what it is to hate war.'

David nodded. 'Yes, I understand that now. I love to fly, but I hate to destroy.'

They were silent again, both of them considering their own personal vision of war, both of them trying to find words to express it.

'And yet it is necessary,' Debra broke the silence. 'We must fight – there is no other way.'

'There is no other way – with the sea at our backs and the Arabs at our throats.'

'You speak like an Israeli,' Debra challenged him softly.

'I made a decision today – or rather I was press-ganged by your father. He has given me three weeks to brush up my Hebrew, and complete the immigration formalities.'

'And then?' Debra leaned towards him.

'A commission in the air force. That was the only point I scored on, I had just enough strength to hold out for the equivalent rank I would have had back home. He haggled like a secondhand clothes dealer, but I had him, and he knew it. So he gave in at last. Acting major, with confirmation of rank at the end of twelve months.'

'That's wonderful, Davey, you'll be one of the youngest majors in the service.'

'Yeah,' David agreed, 'and after I've paid my taxes I'll have a salary a little less than a bus-driver back home.'

'Never mind,' Debra smiled for the first time. 'I'll help you with your Hebrew.'

'I was going to talk to you about that,' he answered her smile. 'Come on, let's get out of here. I'm restless tonight – and I want to walk.'

They strolled through the Christian quarter. The open stalls on each side were loaded with garish and exotic clothes, and leather work and jewellery, and the smells of spices and food and drains and stale humanity was almost solid in the narrow lanes where the arches met overhead.

Debra drew him into one of the antique stores in the Via Dolorosa, and the proprietor came to them, almost wriggling with pleasure.

'Ah, Miss Mordecai – and how is your dearly esteemed father?' Then he rushed into the back room to brew more coffee for them.

'He's one of the half-honest ones, and he lives in mortal fear of the Brig.'

Debra selected an antique solid gold Star of David on a slim golden neck chain, and though he had never before worn personal jewellery, David bowed his head and let her place it about his neck. The golden star lay against the coarse dark curls of his chest.

'That's the only decoration you'll ever get – we don't usually give medals,' she told him laughingly. 'But welcome to Israel anyway.'

'It's beautiful,' David was touched and embarrassed by the gift, 'thank you.' And he buttoned his shirt over it and then reached awkwardly to kiss her – but she drew away and warned him.

'Not in here. He's a Moslem, and he'd be very offended.'

'All right,' said David. 'Let's go and find some place where we won't hurt anybody's sensibilities.'

They went out through the Lion Gate in the great wall and found a stone bench in a quiet place amongst the olive trees of the Moslem cemetery. There was a half moon in the sky, silver and mysterious, and the night was warm and waiting, seemingly as expectant as a new bride.

'You can't stay on at the Intercontinental,' Debra told him, and they both looked up at its arched and lighted silhouette across the valley.

'Why not?'

'Well, first of all it's too expensive. On your salary you just can't afford it.'

'You don't really expect me to live on my salary?' David protested, but Debra ignored him and went on.

'And what is more important, you aren't a tourist any more. So you can't live like one.'

'What do you suggest?'

'We could find you an apartment.'

'Who would do the housework, and the laundry, and the cooking?' he protested vehemently. 'I haven't had much practice at that sort of thing.'

'I would,' said Debra, and he froze for an instant and then turned slowly on the seat to look at her.

'What did you say?'

'I said, I would,' she repeated firmly, and then her voice quavered. 'That's if you want me to.' He was silent for a long moment.

'See here, Debs. Are you talking about living together? I mean, playing house-house on a full-time basis – the whole bit?'

'That's precisely what I am talking about.'

'But—' He could think of nothing further to say. The idea was novel, breathtaking, and alive with enchanting possibilities. All David's previous experiences with the opposite sex had been profuse rather than deep, and he found himself on the frontiers of unexplored territory.

'Well?' Debra asked at last.

'Do you want to get married?' His voice cracked on the word, and he cleared his throat.

'I'm not sure that you are the finest marriage material in the market, my darling David. You are as beautiful as the dawn, and fun to be with – but you are also selfish, immature and spoiled stupid.'

'Thank you kindly.'

'Well, there is no point in me mincing words now, David, not when I am about to throw all caution aside and become your mistress.'

'Wow!' he exclaimed, with all the frost thawing from his voice. 'When you say it straight out like that – it almost blows my mind.'

'Me too,' Debra confessed. 'But one condition is that we wait until we have our own special place, you may recall that I'm not so high on public beaches or rocky islands.'

'I'll never forget,' David agreed. 'Does this mean that you *don't* want to marry me?' He found his mortal terror of matrimony fading under this slur on his potential marriage worth.

'I didn't say that either,' Debra demurred. 'But let's make that decision when both of us are ready for it.'

'Right on, doll,' said David, with an almost idiot grin of happiness spreading over his face.

'And now, Major Morgan, you may kiss me,' she said. 'But do try and help me remember the conditions.'

A long while later, they drew a little apart to breathe and a sudden thought made David frown with worry.

'My God,' he exclaimed, 'what will the Brig say!'

'He won't be joining us,' she told him, and they both laughed together, excited by their own wickedness.

'Seriously, what will you tell your parents?'

'I'll lie to them graciously, and they'll pretend to believe me. Let me worry about that.'

'*Beseder*,' he agreed readily.

'You are learning,' she applauded. 'Let's just try that kiss again – but this in time in Hebrew, please.'

'I love you,' he said in that language.

'Good boy,' she murmured. 'You are going to make a prize pupil.'

There was one more doubt to be set at rest, and Debra voiced it at the iron gate to the garden, when at last he took her home.

'Do you know what the *Bris*, the Covenant, is?'

'Sure,' he grinned, and made scissors out of his first and second finger. It seemed in the uncertain light that she blushed, and her voice was only just audible.

'Well, what about you?'

'That,' David told her severely, 'is a highly personal question, the answer to which little girls should find out for themselves,' and his expression became lascivious, 'the hard way.'

'All knowledge is precious as gold,' she said in a small voice, 'and be sure that I will seek the answer diligently.'

D avid discovered that the acquisition of an apartment in Jerusalem was a task much like the quest for the Holy Grail. Although the high-rise blocks were being thrown up with almost reckless energy, the demand for accommodation far outweighed the supply.

The father of one of Debra's students was an estate agent and the poor man took their problem to his heart; the waiting-list for the new blocks was endless, but an occasional apartment in one of the older buildings fell vacant, and he used all his influence for them.

At unexpected moments of the day, Debra would send out an urgent signal, and David would fetch her in a taxi at the University and they would get the hell across town, urging on the driver, to inspect the latest offering.

The last of these reminded David of a movie set from *Lawrence of Arabia* complete with a dispirited palm tree out front, a spectacular display of bright laundry hanging from every balcony and window, and all the sounds and smells of an Arab camel market and a nursery-school playground at recess rising from the courtyard.

There were two rooms and an alleged bathroom. The roses and wreathes of the wallpaper had faded, except in patches where hangings had protected their original pristine virulent colouring.

David pushed open the door of the bathroom and, without entering, inspected the raggedy linoleum floor-covering and the stained and chipped bath tub; then pushing the door further he discovered the toilet bowl festering quietly in the gloom with its seat set at a rakish angle like the halo of a drunken angel.

'You and Joe could work on it,' Debra suggested uncertainly. 'It's not really *that* bad.'

David shuddered, and closed the door as though it were the lid of a coffin.

'You're joking – of course,' he said, and Debra's determinedly bright smile cracked and her lip quivered.

'Oh, David, we are never going to find a place!'

'And I can't wait much longer.'

'Nor can I,' admitted Debra.

'Right.' David rubbed his hands together briskly. 'It's time to send in the first team.'

He was not sure what form the presence of Morgan Group would take in Jerusalem, but he found it listed in the business directory under 'Morgan Industrial Finance' and the Managing Director was a large mournful-looking gentleman named Aaron Cohen who had a suite of offices in the Leumi Bank building opposite the main post office. He was overcome with emotion to discover that one of the Morgan family had been ten days in Jerusalem without his knowledge.

David told him what he wanted, and in twenty hours he had it signed and paid for. Paul Morgan picked his executives with care, and Cohen was an example of this attention. The price David must pay for this service was that Paul Morgan would have a full report of David's transaction, present whereabouts and future plans on his desk the next morning – but it was worth it.

Above the Hinnom canyon, facing Mount Zion with its impressive array of spires, the Montefiore quarter was being rebuilt as an integrated whole by some entrepreneur. All of it was clad in the lovely golden Jerusalem stone, and the designs of the houses were traditional and ageless. However, the interiors were lavishly modernized with tall cool rooms, mosaic-tiled bathrooms, and ceilings arched like those of a crusader church. Most of them had their own walled and private terraces. The one that Aaron Cohen procured for David was the pick of those that fronted Malik Street. The price was astronomical. That was the first question that Debra asked, once she had recovered her voice. She stood stunned upon the terrace beneath the single olive tree. The stone of the terrace had been cut and polished until it resembled old ivory, and she ran her fingers lightly over the carved front door. Her voice was hushed and her expression bemused.

'David! David! How much is this going to cost?'

'That's not important. What is important is whether you like it.'

'It's too beautiful. It's too much, David. We can't afford this.'

'It's paid for already.'

'Paid for?' She stared at him. 'How much, David?'

'If I said half a million Israeli pounds or a million, what difference would it make? It's only money.'

She clapped her hands over her ears. 'No!' she cried. 'Don't tell me! I'd feel so guilty I wouldn't be able to live in it.'

'Oh, so you are actually consenting to live in it.'

'Try me,' she said with emphasis. 'You just try me, lover!'

They stood in the central room that opened on to the

terrace, and although it was light and airy enough for the savage heat of summer that was coming, it smelled now of new paint and varnished woodwork.

'What are we going to do about furniture?' David asked.

'Furniture?' Debra repeated. 'I hadn't thought that far ahead.'

'For what I have in mind, we'll need at least one king-size bed.'

'Sex-maniac,' she said, and kissed him.

No modern furniture looked at home under the domed roof, or upon the stone-flagged floors. So they began to furnish from the bazaars and antique shops.

Debra solved the main problem with the discovery in a junk yard of an enormous brass bedstead from which they scraped the accumulated dirt; they polished it until it glowed, fitted it with a new inner-spring mattress, and covered it with a cream-coloured lace bedspread from Debra's bottom drawer.

They purchased *kelim* and woven woollen rugs by the bale from the Arab dealers in the old city, and scattered them thickly upon the stone floors, with leather cushions to sit upon and a low olive-wood table, inlaid with ebony and mother-of-pearl, to eat off. The rest of the furniture would come when they could find it for sale, or, failing that, have it custom-made by an Arab cabinet-maker that Debra knew of. Both the bed and the table were enormously heavy, and they needed muscle to move them, so they called for Joe. He and Hannah arrived in his tiny Japanese compact, and after they had recovered from the impact of the Morgan palace they fell to work enthusiastically with David supervising. Joe grunted and heaved, while Hannah disappeared with Debra into the modern American kitchen to exclaim with envy and admiration over the washing-machine, dryer, dish-washer and all the other appliances that went with the house. She helped to cook the first meal.

David had laid in a case of Goldstar beer, and after their labours they all gathered about the olive-wood table to warm the house and wet the roof.

David had expected Joe to be a little reserved, after all it was his baby sister who was being set up in a fancy house; but Joe was as natural as ever and enjoyed the beer and the company so well that Hannah had to intervene at last.

'It's late,' she said firmly.

'Late?' asked Joe. 'It's only nine o'clock.'

'On a night like tonight, that's late.'

'What do you mean?' Joe looked puzzled.

'Joseph Mordecai, diplomat extraordinary,' Hannah said with heavy sarcasm, and suddenly Joe's expression changed as he glanced from Debra to David guiltily, swallowed his beer in a single gulp, and hoisted Hannah to her feet by one arm.

'Come on,' he said. 'What are we sitting here for?'

David left the terrace lights burning, and they shone through the slats of the shuttered windows, so the room was softly lit, and the sounds from the outside world were so muted by distance and stone walls as to be a mere murmur that drifted from afar, and seemed rather to accentuate their aloneness than to spoil it.

The brass of the bedstead gleamed softly in the gloom, and the ivory lacework of the bedspread smelled of lavender and moth balls.

He lay upon the bed and watched her undress slowly, conscious of his eyes upon her and shy now as she had never been before.

Her body was slim and with a flowing line of waist and leg, young and tender-looking, with a child's awkward grace, and yet with a womanly thrust of hip and bosom.

She came to sit upon the edge of the bed, and he marvelled once again at the lustre and plasticity of her skin, at the subtlety of colouring where the sun had darkened it from soft cream to burned honey, and at the contrast of her dusky rose-tipped breasts and the dark thick bush of curls at the base of her softly curving stomach.

She leaned over him, still shyly, and touched his cheek with one finger, running down his throat on to his chest where the gold star lay upon the hard muscle.

'You are beautiful,' she whispered, and she saw it was true. For he was tall and straight with muscled shoulders and lean flanks and belly. The planes of his face were pure and perfect, perhaps its only fault lying in its very perfection. It was almost unreal, as though she were lying with some angel or god from out of mythology.

She twisted her legs up on to the bed, stretching out beside him upon the lace cover, and they lay on their sides facing each other, not touching but so close that she could feel the warmth of his belly upon her own like a soft desert wind, and his breath stirred the dark soft hair upon her cheek.

She sighed then, with happiness and contentment, like a traveller reaching the end of a long lonely journey.

'I love you,' she said for the first time, and reaching out she took his head, her fingers twining in the thick springing hair at the nape of his neck, and drew it tenderly to her breast.

Long afterwards the chill of night oozed into the room, and they came half-awake and crept together beneath the covers.

As they began drifting back into sleep she murmured sleepily, 'I'm so glad that surgery won't be necessary, after all,' and he chuckled softly.

'Wasn't it better finding out for yourself?'

'Much better, lover. Much, much better,' she admitted.

Debra spent one entire evening explaining to David that a high-performance sports car was not a necessity for travel between his base and the house on Malik Street, for she knew her man's tastes by then. She pointed out that this was a country of young pioneers, and that extravagance and ostentation were out of place. David agreed vehemently, secure in the knowledge that Aaron Cohen and his minions were scouring the country for him.

Debra suggested a Japanese compact similar to Joe's, and David told her that he would certainly give that his serious consideration.

Aaron Cohen's henchman tracked down a Mercedes Benz 350 SL belonging to the German Chargé d'Affaires in Tel Aviv. This gentleman was returning to Berlin and wished to dispose of his auto, for a suitable consideration in negotiable cash. A single phone call was sufficient to arrange payment through the Crédit Suisse in Zurich.

It was golden bronze in colour, with a little under twenty thousand kilometres on the clock, and it had clearly been maintained with the loving care of an enthusiast.

Debra, returning on her motor scooter from the University, found this glorious machine parked at the top end of Malik Street, where a heavy chain denied access by all motor-driven vehicles to the village.

She took one look at it, and knew beyond all reasonable doubt who it belonged to. She was really quite angry when she stormed on to the terrace, but she pretended to be angrier than that.

'David Morgan, you really are absolutely impossible.'

'You catch on fast,' David agreed amiably; he was sunbathing on the terrace.

'How much did you pay for it?'

'Ask me another question, doll. That one is becoming monotonous.'

'You are really—' Debra paused and searched frantically

for a word of sufficient force. She found it and delivered it with relish, 'decadent!'

'You don't know the meaning of the word,' David told her gently as he rose from the cushions in the sun and drifted lazily in her direction. Though she had been his lover for only a mere three days she recognized the look in his eye and she began backing away.

'I will teach you the meaning,' he said. 'I am about to give you a practical demonstration of decadence in such a sensitive spot that you are likely to remember it for a long time.'

She ducked behind the olive tree as he lunged, and her books spilled across the terrace.

'Leave me! Hands off, you beast.'

He feinted right, and caught her as she fell for it. He picked her up easily across his chest.

'David Morgan, I warn you, I shall scream if you don't put me down this instant.'

'Let's hear it. Go ahead!' and she did, but in a ladylike fashion so as not to alarm the neighbours.

Joe, on the other hand, was delighted with the 350. The four of them took it on a trial run down the twisting road through the Wilderness of Judaea to the shores of the Dead Sea. The road challenged the car's suspension and David's driving skill, and they whooped with excitement through the bends. Even Debra was able to overcome her initial disapproval, and finally admitted it was beautiful – but still decadent.

They swam in the cool green waters of the oasis of Ein Gedi where they formed a deep rock pool before overflowing and running down into the thick saline water of the sea itself.

Hannah had brought her camera and she photographed Debra and David sitting together on the rocks beside the pool.

They were in their bathing costumes, Debra's brief

bikini showing off her fine young body as she half-turned to laugh into David's face. He smiled back at her, his face in profile and the dark sweep of his hair falling on to his forehead. The desert light picked out the pure features and the boldly stated facets of his beauty.

Hannah had a print of the photograph made for each of them, and later those squares of glossy photographic paper were all they had left of it, all that remained of the joy and the laughter of those days, like a lovely flower taken from the growing tree of life and pressed and dried, flattened and desiccated, deprived of its colour and perfume.

But the future threw no shadow over their happiness on that bright day, and with Joe driving this time they ran back for Jerusalem. Debra insisted that they stop for a group of tank corp boys hitch-hiking home on leave, and although David protested it was impossible, they squeezed three of them into the small cab. It was Debra's sop to her feelings of guilt, and she sat in the back seat with her arms around David's neck and they all sang the song that was that year a favourite with the young people of Israel, 'Let There be Peace'.

In the last few days while David waited to enter the air force, he loafed shamelessly, frittering the time away in small chores like having his uniforms tailored. He resisted Debra's suggestion that if regulation issue were good enough for her father, a general officer, then they might be good enough for David. Aaron Cohen supplied him with an introduction to his own tailor. Aaron was beginning to develop a fine respect for David's style.

Debra had arranged membership for David at the University Athletic Club, and he worked out in the first-class modern gym every day, and finished with twenty lengths of the Olympic-size swimming pool to keep himself in shape.

However, at other times, David merely lay sunbathing on the terrace, or fiddled with electrical plugs or other small tasks Debra had asked him to see to about the house.

As he moved through the cool and pleasant rooms, he would find an item belonging to Debra, a book or a brooch perhaps, and he would pick it up and fondle it briefly. Once a robe of hers thrown carelessly across the foot of the bed and redolent of her particular perfume gave him a physical pang as it reminded him sharply of her, and he held the silkiness to his face and breathed the scent of her, and grudged the hours until her return.

However, it was amongst her books that he discovered more about her than years of study would have revealed. She had crates of these piled in the unfurnished second bedroom which they were using as a temporary storeroom until they could find shelves and cupboards. One afternoon David began digging around in the crates. It was a literary mixed grill – Gibbon and Vidal, Shakespeare and Mailer, Solzhenitsyn and Mary Stewart, amongst other strange bedfellows. There was fiction and biography, history and poetry, Hebrew and English, softbacks and leather-bound editions – and a thin green-jacketed volume which he almost discarded before the author's name caught his attention. It was by D. Mordecai and with a feeling of discovery he turned to the flyleaf. *This Year, in Jerusalem*, a collection of poems, by Debra Mordecai.

He carried the book through to the bedroom, remembering to kick off his shoes before lying on the lace cover – she was very strict about that – and he turned to the first page.

There were five poems. The first was the title piece, the two-thousand-year promise of Jewry. 'Next year in Jerusalem' had become reality. It was a patriotic tribute to her land and even David, whose taste in writing ran to Maclean and Robbins, recognized that it had a superior quality. There were lines of startling beauty, evocative phrasing and penetrative glimpses. It was good, really good, and

David felt a strange proprietary pride – and a sense of awe. He had not guessed at these depths within her, these hidden areas of the mind.

When he came to the last poem, he found it was the shortest of the five, and it was a love poem – or rather it was a poem to someone dearly loved who was gone – and suddenly David was aware of the difference between that which was good and that which was magic.

He found himself shivering to the music of her words, felt the hair on his forearms standing erect with the haunting beauty of it, and then at last he felt himself choking on the sadness of it, the devastation of total loss, and the words swam as his eyes flooded, and he had to blink rapidly as the last terrible cry of the poem pierced him to the heart.

He lowered the book on to his chest, remembering what Joe had told him about the soldier who had died in the desert. A movement attracted his attention and he made a guilty effort to hide the book as he sat up. It was such a private thing, this poetry, that he felt like a thief.

Debra stood in the doorway of the bedroom watching him, leaning against the jamb with her hands clasped in front of her, studying him quietly.

He sat up on the bed and weighed the book in his hands. 'It's lovely,' he said at last, his voice was gruff with the emotions that her words had evoked.

'I'm glad you like it,' she said, and he realized that she was shy.

'Why did you not show it to me before?'

'I was afraid you might not like it.'

'You must have loved him very much?' he asked softly.

'Yes, I did,' she said, 'but now I love you.'

Then, finally, his posting came through and the Brig's hand was evident in it all, though Joe admitted that he had used his own family connections to influence the orders.

He was ordered to report to Mirage squadron 'Lance' which was a crack interceptor outfit based at the same hidden airfield from which he had first flown. Joe Mordecai was on the same squadron, and when he called at Malik Street to tell David the news, he showed no resentment that David would out-rank him, but instead he was confident that they would be able to fly together as a regular team. He spent the evening briefing David on squadron personnel, from 'Le Dauphin' the commanding officer, a French immigrant, down to the lowest mechanic. In the weeks ahead David would find Joe's advice and help invaluable, as he settled into his niche amongst this tightly-knit team of fliers.

The following day the tailor delivered his uniforms, and he wore one to surprise Debra when she backed in through the kitchen door, laden with books and groceries, using her bottom as a door buffer, her hair down behind and her dark glasses pushed up on top of her head.

She dropped her load by the sink, and circled him with her hands on her hips, her head cocked at a critical angle.

'I should like you to wear that, and come to pick me up at the University tomorrow afternoon, please,' she said at last.

'Why?'

'Because there are a few little bitches that lurk around the Lauterman Building. Some of them my students and some my colleagues. I want them to get a good look at you – and eat their tiny hearts out.'

He laughed. 'So you aren't ashamed of me?'

'Morgan, you are too beautiful for one person, you should have been born twins.'

It was their last day together, so he indulged her whimsy and wore his uniform to fetch her at the English Literature Department, and he was surprised to find how the dress affected the strangers he passed on the street – the girls smiled at him, the old ladies called *shalom*, even the guard at the University gates waved him through with a grin and a joke. To them all he was a guardian angel, one of those that had swept death from the very sky above them.

Debra hurried to meet and kiss him, and then walked beside him, her hand tucked proudly and possessively into the crook of his elbow. She took him to eat an early dinner at the staff dining-room in the rounded glass Belgium Building.

While they ate, a casual question of his revealed the subterfuge she had used to protect her reputation.

'I'll probably not get off the base for the first few weeks, but I'll write to you at Malik Street—'

'No,' she said quickly, 'I won't be staying there. It would be too lonely without you in that huge bed.'

'Where then? At your parents' home?'

'That would be a dead give-away. Every time you arrive back in town, I leave home! No, they think I am staying at the hostel here at the University. I told them I wanted to be closer to the department—'

'You've got a room here?' He stared at her.

'Of course, Davey. I have to be a little discreet. I couldn't tell my relatives, friends and employers to contact me care of Major David Morgan. This may be the twentieth century, and modern Israel, but I am still a Jewess, with a tradition of chastity and modesty behind me.'

For the first time David began to appreciate the magnitude of Debra's decision to come to him. He had taken it lightly compared to her.

'I'm going to miss you,' he said.

'And I you,' she replied.

'Let's go home.'

'Yes,' she agreed, laying aside her knife and fork. 'I can eat any old time.'

However, as they left Belgium House she exclaimed with exasperation: 'Damn, I have to have these books back by today. Can we go by the library? I'm sorry, Davey, it won't take a minute.'

So they climbed again to the main terrace and passed the brightly-lit plate-glass windows of the Students' Union Restaurant, and went on towards the solid square tower of the library whose windows were lighted already against the swiftly falling darkness. They had climbed the library steps and reached the glass doors when a party of students came pouring out, and they were forced to stand aside.

They were facing back the way they had come, across the plaza with its terraces and red-bud trees, towards the restaurant.

Suddenly the dusk of evening was lit by the searing white furnace glare of an explosion, and the glass windows of the restaurant were blown out in a glittering cloud of flying glass. It was as though a storm surf had burst upon a rock cliff, flinging out its shining droplets of spray, but this was a lethal spray that scythed down two girl students who were passing the windows at that moment.

Immediately after the flash of the explosion the blast swept across the terrace, a draught of violence that shook the red-bud trees and sent David and Debra reeling against the pillars of the library veranda. The air was driven in upon them so that their eardrums ached with the blow, and the breath was sucked from their lungs.

David caught her to him and held her for the moments of dreadful silence that followed the blast. As they stared so, a soft white fog of phosphorus smoke billowed from the gutted windows of the restaurant and began to roll and drift across the terrace.

Then the sounds reached them through their ringing

eardrums, the small tinkle and crunch of glass, the patter and crack of falling plaster and shattered furniture. A woman began to scream, and it broke the spell of horror.

There were shouts and running feet. One of the students near them began in a high hysterical voice, 'A bomb. They've bombed the café.'

One of the girls who had fallen under the storm of glass fragments staggered up and began running in small aimless circles, screaming in a thin passionless tone. She was white with plaster dust through which the blood poured in dark rivulets, drenching her skirt.

In David's arms Debra began to tremble. 'The swine,' she whispered, 'oh, the filthy murdering swine.'

From the smoking destruction of the shattered building another figure shambled with slow deliberation. The blast had torn his clothing from his body, and it hung from him in tatters, making him a strange scarecrow figure. He reached the terrace and sat down slowly, removed from his face the spectacles that were miraculously still in place and began fumbling to clean them on the rags of his shirt. Blood dripped from his chin.

'Come on,' grated David, 'we must help.' And they ran down the steps together.

The explosion had brought down part of the roof, trapping and crushing twenty-three of the students who had come here to eat and talk over the evening meal.

Others had been hurled about the large low hall, like the toys of a child in tantrum, and their blood turned the interior into a reeking charnel house. Some of them were crawling, creeping, or moving spasmodically amongst the tumbled furniture, broken crockery and spilled food. Some lay contorted as though in silent laughter at death's crude joke.

Afterwards they would learn that two young female members of El Fatah had enrolled in the university under false papers, and they had daily smuggled small quantities of explosive on to the campus until they had accumulated sufficient for this outrage. A suitcase with a timing device had been left under a table and the two terrorists had walked out and got clean away. A week later they were on Damascus television, gloating over their success.

Now, however, there was no reason or explanation for this sudden burst of violence. It was as undirected, and yet as dreadfully effective as some natural cataclysm. Chilling in its insensate enormity, so that they, the living, worked in a kind of terrified frenzy, to save the injured and to carry from the shambles the broken bodies of the dead.

They laid them upon the lawns beneath the red-bud trees and covered them with sheets brought hurriedly from the nearest hostel. The long white bundles in a neat row upon the green grass was a memory David knew he would have for ever.

The ambulances came, with their sirens pulsing and rooflights flashing, to carry away death's harvest and the police cordoned off the site of the blast before David and Debra left and walked slowly down to where the Mercedes was parked in the lot. Both of them were filthy with dust and blood, and wearied with the sights and sounds of pain and mutilation. They drove in silence to Malik Street and showered off the smell and the dirt. Debra soaked David's uniform in cold water to remove the blood. Then she made coffee for them and they drank it, sitting side by side in the brass bed.

'So much that was good and strong died there tonight,' Debra said.

'Death is not the worst of it. Death is natural, it's the logical conclusion to all things. It was the torn and broken flesh that still lived which appalled me. Death has a sort of dignity, but the maimed are obscene.'

She looked at him with almost fear in her eyes. 'That's cruel, David.'

'In Africa there is a beautiful and fierce animal called

102

the sable antelope. They run together in herds of up to a hundred, but when one of them is hurt – wounded by a hunter or mauled by a lion – the lead bulls turn upon him and drive him from the herd. I remember my father telling me about that, he would say that if you want to be a winner then you must avoid the company of the losers for their despair is contagious.'

'God, David, that's a terribly hard way to look at life.'

'Perhaps,' David agreed, 'but then, you see, life is hard.'

When they made love, there was for the first time a quality of desperation in it, for it was the eve of parting and they had been reminded of their mortality.

In the morning David went to join his squadron and Debra locked the house on Malik Street.

E ach day for seventeen days David flew two, and sometimes three, sorties. In the evenings, if they were not flying night interceptions, there were lectures and training films, and after that not much desire for anything but a quick meal and then sleep.

The Colonel, Le Dauphin, had flown one sortie with David. He was a small man with a relaxed manner and quick, shrewd eyes. He had made his judgement quickly.

After that first day, David and Joe flew together, and David moved his gear into the locker across from Joe in the underground quarters that the crews on standby used.

In those seventeen days the last links in an iron friendship were forged. David's flair and dash balanced perfectly with Joe's rock-solid dependability.

David would always be the star while Joe seemed destined to be the accompanist, the straight guy who was a perfect foil, the wingman without personal ambition for glory whose talent was to put his number one into the position for the strike.

Quickly they developed into a truly formidable team, so perfectly in accord that communication in the air was almost extra-sensory, similar to the instantaneous reaction of the bird flock or the shoal of fish.

Joe sitting out there behind him was for David like a million dollars in insurance. His tail was secure and he could concentrate on the special task that his superior eyesight and lightning reactions were so suited to. David was the gunfighter, in a service where the gunfighter was supreme.

The IAF had been the first to appreciate the shortcomings of the-air-to-air missile, and relied heavily on the classic type of air combat. A missile could be induced to 'run stupid'. It was possible to make its computer think in a set pattern and then sucker it with a break in the pattern. For every three hundred missile launches in air-to-air combat, a single strike could be expected.

However, if you had a gunfighter coming up into your six o'clock position with his finger on the trigger of twin 30-mm cannons, capable of pouring twelve thousand shells a minute into you, then your chances were considerably lighter than three hundred to one.

Joe also had his own special talent. The forward scanning radar of the Mirage was a complicated and sophisticated body of electronics, that required firstly a high degree of manual dexterity. The mechanism was operated entirely by the left hand, and the fingers of that hand had to move like those of a concert pianist. However, more important was the 'feel' for the instrument, a lover's touch to draw the optimum results from it. Joe had the 'feel', David did not.

They flew training interceptions, day and night, against high-flying and low-altitude practice targets. They flew low-level training strikes, and at other times they went out high over the Mediterranean and engaged each other in plane-to-plane dogfights.

However, Desert Flower steered them tactfully away from any actual or potential combat situation. They were watching David.

At the end of the period, David's service dossier passed over Major-General Mordecai's desk. Personnel was the Brig's special responsibility and although each officer's dossier was reviewed by him regularly, he had asked particularly to see David's.

The dossier was still slim, compared to the bulky tomes of some of the old salts, and the Brig flicked quickly over his own initial recommendation and the documents of David's acting commission. Then he stopped to read the later reports and results. He grinned wolfishly as he saw the gunnery report. He could pick them out of a crowd, he thought with satisfaction.

At last he came to Le Dauphin's personal appraisal:

'Morgan is a pilot of exceptional ability. Recommended that acting rank be confirmed and that he be placed on fully operational basis forthwith.'

The Brig picked up the red pen that was his own special prerogative and scrawled 'I agree' at the foot of the report.

That took care of Morgan, the pilot. He could now consider Morgan, the man. His expression became bleak and severe. Debra's sudden desire to leave home almost immediately David arrived in Jerusalem had been too much of a coincidence for a man who was trained to search for underlying motives and meanings.

It had taken him two days and a few phone calls to learn that Debra was merely using the hostel room at the University as an accommodation address, and that her real domestic arrangements were more comfortable.

The Brig did not approve, very definitely not. Yet he knew that it was beyond his jurisdiction. He had learned that his daughter had inherited his own iron will. Confrontations between them were cataclysmic events that shook the family to its foundations and seldom ended in satisfactory results.

Although he spent much of his time with young people, still he found the new values hard to live with – let alone accept. He remembered the physical agony of his long and chaste engagement to Ruth with pride, like a veteran reviewing an old campaign.

'Well, at the least she has the sense not to flaunt it, not to bring shame on us all. She has spared her mother that.' The Brig closed the dossier firmly.

Le Dauphin called David into his office and told him of his change in status. He would go on regular 'green' standby, which meant four nights a week on base.

David would have to undergo his paratrooper training in unarmed combat and weapons. A downed pilot in Arab territory had a much better chance of survival if he was proficient in this type of fighting.

David went straight from Le Dauphin's office to the telephone in the crew-room. He caught Debra before she left the Lauterman Building for lunch.

'Warm the bed, wench,' he told her, 'I'll be home tomorrow night.'

He and Joe drove up to Jerusalem in the Mercedes, and he wasn't listening to Joe's low rumbling voice until a thumb like an oar prodded his ribs.

'Sorry, Joe, I was thinking.'

'Well, stop it. Your thoughts are misting up the windows.'

'What did you say?'

'I was talking about the wedding – Hannah and me.'

David realized it was only a month away now, and he expected the excitement amongst the women was heavy as static on a summer's day before the rain. Debra's letters had been filled with news of the arrangements.

'I would be happy if you will stand up with me, and be

my witness. You fly as wingman for a change, and I'll take on the target.'

David realized that he was being honoured by the request and he accepted with proper solemnity. Secretly he was amused. Like most young Israelis David had spoken to, both Debra and Joe claimed not to be religious. He had learned that this was a pose. All of them were very conscious of their religious heritage, and well versed in the history and practice of Judaism. They followed all the laws of living that were not oppressive, and which accorded with a modern and busy existence.

To them 'religious' meant dressing in the black robes and wide-brimmed hats of the ultra-orthodox Mea Shearim, or in following a routine for daily living that was crippling in its restrictions.

The wedding would be a traditional affair, complete with all the ceremony and the rich symbolism, complicated only by the security precautions which would have to be most rigorously enforced.

The ceremony was to take place in the Brig's garden, for Hannah was an orphan. Also the secluded garden and fortress-like walls about it were easier to protect.

Amongst the guests would be many prominent figures in the government and the military.

'At the last count we have five generals and eighteen colonels on the list,' Joe told him, 'to which add most of the cabinet, even Golda has promised to try and be there. So you see, it's going to make a nice juicy target for our friends in Black September.' Joe scowled and lit two cigarettes, passing one to David. 'If it wasn't for Hannah, you know how women feel about weddings, I would just as soon go down to a registry office.'

'You are fooling nobody,' David grinned. 'You are looking forward to it.'

'Sure.' Joe's scowl cleared. 'It's going to be good to have

our own place, like you and Debs. I wish Hannah had been sensible. A year of pretending.' He shook his head. 'Thank God it's nearly over.'

He dropped Joe in the lane outside the Brig's house in Ein Karem.

'I won't bother to invite you in,' Joe said. 'I guess you've got plans.'

'Good guess,' David smiled. 'Will we see you and Hannah? Come to dinner tomorrow night.'

Joe shook his head again. 'I'm taking Hannah down to Ashkelon to visit her parents' graves. It's traditional before a wedding. Perhaps we'll see you Saturday.'

'Right then, I'll try and make it. Debra will want to see you. *Shalom*, Joe.'

'*Shalom, shalom*,' said Joe and David pulled away, flicking the gears in a racing change as he put the Mercedes at the hill. Suddenly he was in a hurry.

The terrace door stood open in welcome, and she was waiting for him. Debra was vibrant and tense with expectation, sitting in one of the new leather chairs with her legs curled under her. Her hair was freshly washed and shimmering like a starling's wing. She was dressed in a billowing kaftan of light silk and subtle honey colours that picked out the gold in her eyes.

She came out of the chair in a swirl of silk, and ran barefooted across the rugs to meet him.

'David! David!' she cried and he caught her up and spun on his heels, laughing with her.

Afterwards she led him proudly about the rooms and showed him the changes and additions that had turned it into a real home during his absence. David had convinced her that cost was not fundamental and they had chosen the designs for the furniture together. These had been made and delivered by Debra's tame Arab and she had arranged them as they had planned it. It was all in soft leather and dark wood, lustrous copper and brass, set off by the bright rugs. However, there was one article he had never seen before – a large oil painting on canvas, and Debra had hung it unframed on the freshly painted white wall facing the terrace. It was the only decoration upon the wall, and any other would have been insignificant beside it. It was a harsh dominant landscape, a desert scene which captured the soul of the wilderness; the colours were hot and fierce and seemed to pour through the room like the rays of the desert sun itself.

Debra held his hand and watched David's face anxiously for a reaction as he studied it.

'Wow!' he said at last.

'You like it?' She was relieved.

'It's terrific. Where did you get it?'

'A gift from the artist. She's an old friend.'

'She?'

'That's right. We are driving up to Tiberias tomorrow to have lunch with her. I've told her all about you, and she wants to meet you.'

'What's she like?'

'She's one of our leading artists, and her name is Ella Kadesh, but apart from that I can't begin to describe her. All I can do is promise you an entertaining day.'

Debra had prepared a special dish of lamb and olives and they ate it on the terrace under the olive tree. Again the talk turned to Joe's wedding, and in the midst of it David asked abruptly, 'What made you decide to come with me – without marrying?'

She replied after a moment. 'I discovered that I loved you, and I knew that you were too impatient to play the waiting game. I knew that if I didn't, I might lose you again.'

'Until recently, I didn't realize what a big decision it was,' he mused, and she sipped her wine without replying.

'Let's get married, Debs,' he broke the silence.

'Yes,' she nodded. 'That's a splendid idea.'

'Soon,' he said. 'Soon as possible.'

'Not before Hannah. I don't want to steal her day from her.'

'Right,' David agreed, 'but immediately afterwards.'

'Morgan, you have got yourself a date,' she told him.

It was a three-hour drive to Tiberias so they rose as soon as the sun came through the shutters and tiger-striped the wall above the brass bed. To save time, they shared one bath, sitting facing each other, waist-deep in suds.

'Ella is the rudest person you'll ever meet,' Debra warned him. She looked like a little girl this morning with her hair piled on top of her head and secured with a pink ribbon. 'The greater the impression you make on her, the ruder she will be, and you are expected to retaliate in kind. So please, David, don't lose your temper.'

David scooped up a dab of suds with a finger and smeared it on the tip of her nose.

'I promise,' he said.

They drove down to Jericho, and then turned north along the valley of the Jordan, following the high barbed-wire fence of the border with its warning notice boards for the minefields, and the regular motorized patrols grinding deliberately along the winding road.

It was hot in the valley and they drove with the windows open and Debra pulled her skirt high around her waist to cool her long brown legs.

'Better not do that if you want to be in time for lunch,' David warned her, and she smoothed them down hurriedly.

'Nothing is safe with you around,' she protested.

They came at last out of the barren land into the fertile basin of the Kibbutzim below Galilee, and again the smell of orange blossom was so strong on the warm air that it was difficult to breathe.

At last they saw the waters of the lake flashing amongst the date palms and Debra touched his arm.

'Slow down, Davey. Ella's place is a few miles this side of Tiberias. That's the turn-off, up ahead.'

It was a track that led down to the lake shore and it ended against a wall of ancient stone blocks. Five other cars were parked there already.

'Ella's having one of her lunch parties,' Debra remarked and led him to a gate in the wall. Beyond was a small ruined castle. The tumbled walls formed weird shapes and the stone was black with age; over them grew flamboyant creepers of bougainvillaea and the tall palms clattered their fronds in the light breeze that came off the lake. Other exotic flowering shrubs grew upon the green lawns.

Part of the ruins had been restored and renovated into a picturesque and unusual lakeside home, with a wide patio and a stone jetty against which a motor-boat was moored. Across the green waters of the lake rose the dark smooth whale-back of the Golan Heights.

'It was a crusader fortress,' Debra explained. 'One of the guard posts for traffic across the lake and part of the series leading up to the great castle on the Horns of Hittem that the Moslems destroyed when they drove the crusaders out of the Holy Land. Ella's grandfather purchased it during the Allenby administration, but it was a ruin until she did it up after the War of Independence.'

The care with which the alterations had been made so as not to spoil the romantic beauty of the site was a tribute to Ella Kadesh's artistic vision, which was completely at odds with the woman herself.

She was enormous; not simply fat or tall, but big. Her hands and her feet were huge, her fingers clustered with rings and semi-precious stones and her toenails through the open sandals were painted a glaring crimson, as if to flaunt their size. She stood as tall as David, but the tent-like dress that billowed about her was covered with great explosive designs that enhanced her bulk until she seemed to make up two of him. She wore a wig of tiered curls, flaming red in colour and dangling gold earrings. It seemed she must have applied her eye make-up with a spade, and her rouge with a spray gun. She removed the thin black cheroot from her mouth and kissed Debra before she turned to study David. Her voice was gravelly, hoarse with cheroot smoke and brandy.

'I had not expected you to be so beautiful,' she said, and Debra quailed at the expression in David's eyes. 'I do not like beauty. It is so often deceptive, or inconsequential. It usually hides something deadly – like the glittering beauty of the cobra – or like the pretty wrapper of a candy bar, it contains cloying sweetness and a soft centre.' She shook the stiffly lacquered curls of her wig, and fixed David with her shrewd little eyes. 'No, I prefer ugliness to beauty.'

David smiled at her with all his charms upon display. 'Yes,' he agreed, 'having met you, and seen some of your work, I can understand that.'

She let out a cackle of raucous laughter, and clapped the cheroot back in her mouth. 'Well now, at the very least we are not dealing with a chocolate soldier.' She placed a huge masculine arm about David's shoulders and led him to meet the company.

They were a mixed dozen, all intellectuals – artists, writers, teachers, journalists – and David was content to sit beside Debra in the mild sunshine and enjoy the beer and the amusing conversation. However, Ella would not let him relax for long and when they sat down to the gargantuan *alfresco* meal of cold fish and poultry, she attacked him again.

'Your martial airs and affectations, your pomp and finery. A plague on it I say, a pox on your patriotism, and courage – on your fearlessness and your orders of chivalry. It is all sham and pretence, an excuse for you to stink up the earth with piles of carrion.'

'I wonder if you will feel the same when a platoon of

Syrian infantry break in here to rape you,' David challenged her.

'My boy, I find it so difficult to get laid these days that I should pray for such a heaven-sent opportunity.' She let out a mighty hoot of laughter and her wig slipped forward at an abandoned angle. Nothing was safe from her, and she pushed the wig back into place and streamed straight into the attack again.

'Your male bombast, your selfish arrogance. To you this woman—' and she indicated Debra with a turkey leg, ' – to you she is merely a receptacle for your seething careless sperm. It matters not to you that she is a promise for the future, that within her are the seeds of a great writing talent. No, to you she is a rubbing block, a convenient means to a—'

Debra interrupted her. 'That definitely is enough, I will not allow a public debate on my bedroom,' and Ella turned towards her with the battle lust lighting her eyes.

'Your gift is not yours to use as you wish. You hold it in trust for all mankind, and you have a duty to them. That duty is to exercise your gift, to allow it to grow and blossom and give forth fruit.' She used the turkey leg like a judge's gavel, banging the edge of her plate with it, to silence Debra's protests.

'Have you written a word since you took young Mars to your heart? What of the novel we discussed on this very terrace a year ago? Have your animal passions swamped all else? Has the screeching of your ovaries—'

'Stop it, Ella!' Debra was angry now, her cheeks flushed and her brown eyes snapping.

'Yes! Yes!' Ella tossed the bone aside and sucked her fingers noisily. 'Ashamed you should be, angry with your-self—'

'Damn you,' Debra flared at her.

'Damn me if you will – but you are damned yourself if you do not write! Write, woman, write!' She sat back and the wicker chair protested at the movement of her vast body. 'All right, now we will all go for a swim. David has not seen me in a bikini yet – much he will care for that skinny little wench when he does!'

They drove back to Jerusalem in the night, flushed with the sun, and although the Mercedes seats had not been designed for lovers, Debra managed to sit close up against him.

'She's right, you know,' David broke a long contented silence. 'You must write, Debs.'

'Oh, I will,' she answered lightly.

'When?' he persisted, and to distract him she snuggled a little closer.

'One of these days,' she whispered as she made her dark head comfortable on his shoulder.

'One of these days,' he mimicked her.

'Don't bug me, Morgan.' She was already half-asleep.

'Stop being evasive.' He stroked her hair with his free hand. 'And don't go to sleep while I'm talking to you.'

'David, my darling, we have a lifetime – and more,' she murmured. 'You have made me immortal. You and I shall live for a thousand years, and there will be time for everything.'

Perhaps the dark gods heard her boast, and they chuckled sardonically and nudged each other.

On Saturday Joe and Hannah came to the house on Malik Street, and after lunch they decided on a tourist excursion for David and the four of them climbed Mount Zion across the valley. They entered the labyrinth of corridors that led to David's tomb, covered with splendid embroidered cloth and silver crowns and Torah covers. From there it was a few steps to the room of Christ's last supper in the same building, so closely interwoven were the traditions of Judaism and Christianity in this citadel.

Afterwards they entered the old city through the Zion gate and followed the wall around to the centre of Judaism, the tall cliff of massive stone blocks, bevelled in the fashion of Herodian times, which was all that remained of the fabulous second temple of Herod, destroyed two thousand years before by the Romans.

They were searched at the gate and then joined the stream of worshippers flocking down towards the wall. At the barrier they stood for a long time in silence. David felt again the stirring of a deep race memory, a hollow feeling of the soul which longed to be filled.

The men prayed facing the wall, many of them in the long black coats of the Orthodox Jew with the ringlets dangling against their cheeks as they rocked and swayed in religious ecstasy. Within the enclosure of the right-hand side, the women seemed more reserved in their devotions.

Joe spoke at last, a little embarrassed and in a gruff tone. 'I think I'll just go say a *sh'ma*.'

'Yes,' Hannah agreed. 'Are you coming with me, Debra?'

'A moment.' Debra turned to David, and took something from her handbag. 'I made it for you for the wedding,' she said. 'But wear it now.'

It was a yarmulke, an embroidered prayer cap of black satin.

'Go with Joe,' she said. 'He will show you what to do.'

The girls moved off to the women's enclosure and David placed the cap upon his head and followed Joe down to the wall.

A *shamash* came to them, an old man with a long silver beard, and he helped David bind upon his right arm a tiny leather box containing a portion of the Torah.

'So you shall lay these words upon your heart and your soul, and you shall bind them upon your right arm—'

Then he spread a *tallit* across David's shoulders, a tasselled shawl of woven wool, and he led him to the wall, and he began to repeat after the *shamash*:

'Hear, O Israel, the Lord our God, the Lord is one—'

His voice grew surer as he remembered the words from

long ago, and he looked up at the wall of massive stone blocks that towered high above him. Thousands of previous worshippers had written down their prayers on scraps of paper and wedged them into the joints between the blocks, and around him rose the plaintive voices of spoken prayer. It seemed to David that in his imagination a golden beam of prayer rose from this holy place towards the heavens.

Afterwards they left the enclosure and climbed the stairs into the Jewish quarter, and the good feeling remained with David, glowing warmly in his belly.

That evening they sat together on the terrace drinking Goldstar beer and splitting sunflower seeds for the nutty kernels, and naturally the talk turned to God and religion.

Joe said, 'I'm an Israeli and then a Jew. First my country, and a long way behind that comes my religion.'

But David remembered the expression on his face as he prayed against the wailing wall.

The talk lasted until late, and David glimpsed the vast body of his religious heritage.

'I would like to learn a little more about it all,' he admitted, and Debra said nothing but when she packed for him to go on base that night she placed a copy of Herman Wouk's *This is My God* on top of his clean uniforms.

He read it and when next he returned to Malik Street, he asked for more. She picked them for him, English works at first but then Hebrew, as his grip upon the language became stronger. They were not religious works only, but histories and historical novels that excited his interest in this ancient centre of civilization which for three thousand years had been a crossroads and a battleground.

He read anything and everything that she put into his case, from Josephus Flavius to Leon Uris.

This led to a desire to see and inspect the ground. It became so that much of the time that they were free together was spent in these explorations. They began with the hill-top fortress of Herod at Masada where the zealots had killed each other rather than submit to Rome, and from there they moved off the tourist beat to the lesser-known historical sites.

In those long sunlit days they might eat their basket lunch sitting on the ruins of a Roman aqueduct and watching a falcon working the thermals that rose off the floor of the desert, after they had searched the bed of a dry wadi for coins and arrowheads brought down by the last rains.

Around them rose the tall cliffs of orange and golden stone, and the light was so clean and stark that it seemed they could see for ever, and the silence so vast that they were the only living things in the world.

They were the happiest days that David had ever known, and they gave point and meaning to the weary hours of squadron standby, and when the day had ended there was always the house on Malik Street with its warmth and laughter and love.

J oe and David arranged leave of absence from the base for the wedding. It was a time of quiet, and Le Dauphin let them go without protest, for he would be a guest.

They drove up to Jerusalem the day before and were immediately conscripted to assist with the arrangements. David laboured mightily as a taxi-driver and trucker. The Mercedes transported everything from flowers to musical instruments and distant relatives.

The Brig's garden was decorated with palm leaves and coloured bunting. In the centre stood the *huppah*, a canopy worked with religious symbols in blue and gold, the Star of David and the grapes and ears of wheat, the pomegranates and all the other symbols of fertility. Beneath it, the marriage ceremony would take place. Trestle tables covered with bright cloths and set with bowls of flowers and dishes of fruit were arranged beneath the olive trees. There were places for three hundred guests, an open space for the dancing, a raised timber stand hung with flags for the band.

The catering was contracted out to a professional firm and the menu had been carefully decided upon by the chef and the women. It would have two high points – an enormous stuffed tuna, again a symbol of fertility, and a lamb dish in the bedouin style served upon enormous copper salvers.

On the Sunday of the wedding, David drove Debra to the home of the chief surgeon of Hadassah Hospital. Hannah was one of his theatre sisters and he had insisted that she use his home to prepare for the wedding. Debra was to assist her, and David left them and drove on to Ein Karem. The lane leading to the house was cordoned off and thick with Secret Service men and paratroopers.

While he watched Joe dressing, losing and finding the ring, and sweating with nerves, David lay on Joe's bed and gave him bad advice. They could hear the guests gathering in the garden below, and David stood up and went to the window. He watched an air force colonel being carefully scrutinized and searched at the gates, but taking it all in good part.

'They are being pretty thorough,' David remarked.

'Hannah has asked to have as few as possible of the guards in the garden. So they are being damned careful about who they let in.' Joe had at last completed dressing and already he was beginning to sweat through the armpits of his uniform.

'How do I look?' he asked anxiously.

'God, you handsome beast,' David told him.

'Piss off, Morgan,' Joe grinned at him, crammed his cap on to his head and glanced at his watch. 'Let's go,' he said.

The Chief Rabbi of the army was waiting with the Brig and the others in the Brig's study. The Rabbi was the mild-mannered man who had personally liberated the Tomb of the Patriarchs in the war of '67. During the advance on Hebron, he had driven a jeep through the disintegrating Arab lines, shot open the door to the tomb with a submachine-gun and chased the Arab guards screaming over the rear wall.

Joe sat at the Brig's desk and signed the *ketubbah*, the marriage contract, then the Rabbi handed him a silken cloth which Joe lifted in a formal act of acquisition to a chorus of congratulatory 'Mazal tovs' from the witnesses.

The bridegroom's party trooped out into the crowded garden now to await the arrival of the bride, and she came accompanied by the chief surgeon standing in for her dead father, and a party of festively dressed women, including Debra and her mother. They all carried lighted candles.

To David, Hannah had never been particularly attractive, she was too tall and severe in body and expression; however, in her white bridal dress and veil she was transformed.

She seemed to float cloudlike upon the billowing white skirts, and her face was softened by the veil and by the inner happiness that seemed to glow through her green eyes. Red-gold hair framed her cheeks, and the freckles were disguised under make-up applied by Debra's cunning hand. She had used it to mute the rather harsh lines of Hannah's bony nose, and the result was that Hannah was as near to beautiful as she would ever come.

Joe, looking big and handsome in his air force tans, went forward eagerly to meet her at the gate to the garden and to lower the veil over her face in the ceremony of *bedeken dikalle*.

Joe moved to the *chuppah* canopy where the Rabbi waited with a *tallit* over his shoulders. After Joe the women led Hannah, each of them still carrying a burning candle, and the Rabbi chanted a blessing as the women and the bride circled Joe seven times in a magical circle which in olden times would serve to ward off evil spirits. At last bride and groom stood side by side, facing towards the site of the Temple with the guests and witnesses pressed closely about them and the ceremony proper began.

The Rabbi spoke the benediction over a goblet of wine from which bride and groom both drank. Then Joe turned to Hannah, her face still veiled, and he placed the plain gold ring upon her right forefinger.

'Behold you are consecrated unto me by this ring, according to the law of Moses and Israel.'

Then Joe broke the glass under his heel and the sharp crunch was a signal for an outburst of music and song and gaiety. David left Joe's side and worked his way through the joyous crowd of guests to where Debra waited for him.

She wore a gown of yellow and she had fresh flowers in the dark sheen of her hair. David smelled their perfume as he hugged her surreptitiously about the waist and whispered in her ear, 'You next, my beauty!' and she whispered back, 'Yes, please!'

Joe took Hannah on his arm, and then went to the improvised dance floor. The band began with a light bouncy tune and all the younger ones flocked to join them – while the elders spread out at the tables beneath the palm-decked trellis.

Yet amongst all the laughter and the gaiety, the uniforms added a sombre touch; almost every second man was adorned with the trappings of war, and at the garden gate and the entrance to the kitchens were uniformed paratrooper guards each with an Uzi submachine-gun slung at his shoulder. It was easy to pick out the Secret Service men. They were the ones in civilian clothes who moved without smiling, alert and vigilant, amongst the guests.

David and Debra danced together, and she was so light and warm and strong in his arms that when the band paused for breath he resented it. He led her to a quiet corner, and they stood together, discussing the other guests in the most disrespectful terms until Debra giggled at some particularly outrageous remark and struck his arm lightly.

'You are terrible.' She leaned against him. 'I'm dying of thirst, won't you get me something to drink?'

'A glass of cold white wine?' he suggested.

'Lovely,' she said, smiling up into his face. For a moment they studied each other, and suddenly David felt something dark welling up from within him, a terrible despair, a premonition of impending loss. It was a physical thing and he could feel the chill of it enclose his chest and squeeze out all the happiness and the joy.

'What is it, David?' Her own expression altered in sympathy with his, and she tightened her grip on his arm.

'Nothing.' Abruptly he pulled away from her, trying to fight off the feeling. 'It's nothing,' he repeated, but it was still strong in his belly and he felt a wave of nausea from it. 'I'll get you the wine,' he said and turned away.

He made his way towards the bar, pushing gently through the throng. The Brig caught his eye and smiled bleakly across the garden at him. Joe was with his father and he called to David, laughing, with one arm around his bride. Hannah had her veil pushed up and her freckles were beginning to emerge from under the make-up, glowing vividly against the snow-white lace. David waved at them but went on towards the open-air bar at the end of the garden, the mood of sadness was still on him and he didn't want to talk to Joe now.

So he was cut off from Debra at the moment when, with a flourish, a procession of white-jacketed waiters came in through the iron gate of the garden. Each of them carried a huge copper salver from which, even in the warm sun, rose tendrils of steam, and the odour of meat and fish and spices filled the garden. There were gasps and cries of appreciation from the guests.

A way opened for them towards the high table on the

raised terrace which led to the kitchen doors and the house.

The procession of waiters passed close to David, and suddenly his attention was drawn from the display of fine food to the face of the second waiter in line. He was a man of medium height and dark complexion, a mahogany face with a thickly drooping moustache.

He was sweating. That was what had drawn David's attention, his face was shiny with sweat. Droplets clung in his moustache and slid down his cheeks. The white jacket was sodden at the armpits as he lifted the gigantic platter on high.

At the moment that he drew level with David their eyes met for an instant. David realized that the man was in the grip of some deep emotion – fear, perhaps, or exhilaration. Then the waiter seemed to become aware of David's scrutiny and his eyes slid nervously away.

David felt suspicion begin to chill his arms as the three figures climbed the stone stairs, and filed behind the table.

The waiter glanced again at David, saw that his gaze was still locked upon his face, and then he said something out of the corner of his mouth to one of his companions. He also glanced at David, and caught his stare, and his expression was sufficient to send alarm flaring urgently through David's chest and brain. Something was happening, something dangerous and ugly, he was certain of it.

Wildly he looked about for the guards. There were two of them on the terrace behind the line of waiters, and one near David beside the gate.

David shoved his way desperately towards him, mindless of the outraged comments of those in his way. He was watching the three waiters and so he saw it begin to happen.

It had obviously been carefully rehearsed, for as the three waiters placed the salvers upon the table to the laughter and applause of the guests crowded in the garden below them, so they drew back the sheets of plastic on which a thin display of food had been arranged to cover the deadly load that each copper salver carried.

The brown-faced waiter lifted a machine-pistol from under the plastic sheet, and turned swiftly to fire a traversing burst into the two paratroopers behind him at point-blank range. The clattering thunder of automatic fire was deafening in the walled garden, and the stream of bullets slashed through the bellies of the two guards like a monstrous cleaver, almost cutting them in half.

The waiter on David's left was a wizened monkey-faced man, with bright black berries for eyes. He, too, lifted a machine pistol from his salver, and he crouched over it and fired a burst at the paratrooper by the gate.

They were going for the guards, taking them out first. The pistol shook and roared in his fists, and the bullets socked into human flesh with a rubbery thumping sound.

The guard had cleared his Uzi, and was trying to aim as a bullet hit him in the mouth and snapped his head back, his paratrooper beret spinning high into the air. The machine-gun flew from his arms as he fell, and it slid across the tiles towards David. David dropped flat below the stone steps of the terrace as the Arab gunners turned their pistols on the wedding crowd, hosing the courtyard with a triple stream of bullets, and unleashing a hurricane of screams and shouts and desperate cries to join the roar of the guns.

Across the yard, a security agent had the pistol out of his shoulder holster and he dropped into the marksman crouch, holding the pistol with both arms extended as he aimed. He fired twice and hit the monkey-faced gunman, sending him reeling back against the wall, but he stayed on his feet and returned the agent's fire with the machine-pistol, knocking him down and rolling him across the paving stones.

The yard was filled with a panic-stricken mob, a struggling mass of humanity, that screamed and fell and crawled and died beneath the flail of the guns.

Two bullets caught Hannah in the chest, smashing her backwards over a table of glasses and bottles that shattered about her. The bright blood spurted from the wounds, drenching the front of her white wedding gown.

The centre gunman dropped his pistol as it emptied, and he stooped quickly over the copper salver and came up with a grenade in each hand. He hurled them into the struggling, screaming throng and the double blast was devastating, twin bursts of brightest white flame and the terrible sweep of shrapnel. The screams of the women rose louder, seeming as deafening as the gunfire – and the gunman stooped once more and his hands held another load of grenades.

All this had taken only seconds, but a fleeting moment of time to turn festivity into shocking carnage and torn flesh.

David left the shelter of the stone steps. He rolled swiftly across the flags towards the abandoned Uzi, and he came up on his knees, holding it at the hip. His paratrooper training made his actions automatic.

The wounded gunman saw him, and turned towards him, staggering slightly, pushing himself weakly away from the wall. His one arm was shattered and hung loosely in the tattered, blood-soaked sleeve of his jacket, but he lifted the machine-pistol and aimed at David.

David fired first, the bullets struck bursts of plaster from the wall behind the Arab and David corrected his aim. The bullets drove the gunman backwards, pinning him to the wall, while his body jumped and shook and twitched. He slumped down leaving a glistening wet smear of blood down the white plaster.

David swivelled the gun on to the Arab beside the kitchen door. He was poised to throw his next grenade, right arm extended behind him, both fists filled with the deadly steel balls. He was shouting something, a challenge or a war cry, a harsh triumphant screech that carried clearly above the screams of his victims.

Before he could release the grenade, David hit him with a full burst, a dozen bullets that smashed into his chest and belly, and the Arab dropped both grenades at his feet and doubled over clutching at his broken body, trying to stem the flood of his life blood with his bare hands.

The grenades were short fused and they exploded almost immediately, engulfing the dying man in a net of fire and shredding his body from the waist down. The same explosion knocked down the third assassin at the end of the terrace, and David came to his feet and charged up the steps.

The third and last Arab was mortally wounded, his head and chest torn by grenade fragments, but he was still alive, thrashing about weakly as he groped for the machine-pistol that lay beside him in a puddle of his own blood.

David was consumed by a terrible rage. He found that he was screaming and raging like a maniac, and he crouched at the head of the stairs and aimed at the dying Arab.

The Arab had the machine-pistol and was lifting it with the grim concentration of a drunken man. David fired, a single shot that slapped into the Arab's body without apparent effect, and then suddenly the Uzi in David's hands was empty, the pin falling with a hollow click on an empty chamber.

Across the terrace, beyond range of a quick rush, the Arab's face was streaked with sweat and blood as he frowned heavily, trying to aim the machine-pistol as it wavered. He was dying swiftly, the flame fluttering towards extinction, but he was using the last of his strength.

David stood frozen with the empty weapon in his hand, and the blank eye of the pistol sought him out, and fastened upon him. He watched the Arab's eyes narrow, and his sudden murderous grin of achievement as he saw David in his sights, and his finger tightening on the trigger.

At that range the bullets would hit like the solid stream of a fire hose. He began to move, to throw himself down the stairs, but he knew it was too late. The Arab was at the instant of firing, and at the same instant a revolver shot crashed out at David's side.

Half the Arab's head was cut away by the heavy lead slug, and he was flung backwards with the yellow custard contents of his skull splattering the white-washed wall behind him, and his death grip on the trigger emptied the machine-pistol with a shattering roar harmlessly into the grape vines above him.

Dazedly David turned to find the Brig beside him, the dead security guard's pistol in his fist. For a moment they stared at each other, and then the Brig stepped past him and walked to the fallen bodies of the other two Arabs. Standing over each in turn he fired a single pistol shot into their heads.

David turned away and let the Uzi drop from his hands. He went down the stairs into the garden.

The dead and the wounded lay singly and in piles, pitiful fragments of humanity. The soft cries and the groans of the wounded, the bitter weeping of a child, the voice of a mother, were sounds more chilling than the screaming and the shouting.

The garden was drenched and painted with blood. There were splashes and gouts of it upon the white walls, there were puddles and snakes of it spreading and crawling across the paving, dark slicks of it sinking into the dust, ropes of it dribbling and pattering like rain from the body of a musician as he hung over the rail of the bandstand. The sickly sweetish reek of it mingled with the smell of spiced food and spilled wine, with the floury taste of plaster dust and the bitter stench of burned explosive.

The veils of smoke and dust that still drifted across the garden could not hide the terrible carnage. The bark of the olive trees was torn in slabs from the trunks by flying steel, exposing the white wet wood. The wounded and dazed survivors crawled over a field of broken glass and shattered crockery. They swore and prayed, and whispered and groaned and called for succour.

David went down the steps, his feet moving without his bidding; his muscles were numb, his body senseless and only his finger-tips tingled with life.

Joe was standing below one of the torn olive trees. He stood like a colossus, with his thick powerful legs astride, his head thrown back and his face turned to the sky, but his eyes were tight-closed and his mouth formed a silent cry of agony – for he held Hannah's body in his arms.

Her bridal veil had fallen from her head, and the bright copper mane of her hair hung back – almost to the ground. Her legs and one arm hung loosely also, slack and lifeless. The golden freckles stood out clearly on the milky-white skin of her face – and the bloody wounds bloomed like the petals of the poinsettia tree upon the bosom of her wedding-gown.

David averted his eyes. He could not watch Joe in his anguish, and he walked on slowly across the garden, in terrible dread of what he would find.

'Debra!' he tried to raise his voice, but it was a hoarse raven's croak. His feet slipped in a puddle of thick dark blood, and he stepped over the unconscious body of a woman who lay, face down, in a floral dress, with her arms thrown wide. He did not recognize her as Debra's mother.

'Debra!' He tried to hurry, but his legs would not respond. He saw her then, at the corner of the wall where he had left her.

'Debra!' He felt his heart soar. She seemed unhurt, kneeling below one of the marble Grecian statues, with the

127

flowers in her hair and the yellow silk of her dress bright and festive.

She knelt, facing the wall, and her head was bowed as though in prayer. The dark wing of her hair hung forward screening her and she held her cupped hands to her face.

'Debra.' He dropped to his knees beside her, and timidly he touched her shoulder.

'Are you all right, my darling?' And she lowered her hands slowly, but still holding them cupped together. A great coldness closed around David's chest as he saw that her cupped hands were filled with blood. Rich red blood, bright as wine in a crystal glass.

'David,' she whispered, turning her face towards him. 'Is that you, darling?'

David gave a small breathless moan of agony as he saw the blood-glutted eye sockets, the dark gelatinous mess that congealed in the thick dark eyelashes and turned the lovely face into a gory mask.

'Is that you, David?' she asked again, her head cocked at a blind listening angle.

'Oh God, Debra.' He stared into her face.

'I can't see, David.' She groped for him. 'Oh David – I can't see.'

And he took her sticky wet hands in his, and he thought that his heart would break.

The stark modern silhouette of Hadassah Hospital stood upon the skyline above the village of Ein Karem. The speed with which the ambulances arrived saved many of the victims whose lives were critically balanced, and the hospital was geared to sudden influxes of war casualties.

The three men – the Brig, Joe and David – kept their

vigil together all that night upon the hard wooden benches of the hospital waiting-room. When more was learned of the planning behind the attack, a security agent would come to whisper a report to the Brig.

One of the assassins was a long-term and trusted employee of the catering firm, and the other two were his 'cousins' who had been employed as temporary staff on his recommendation. It was certain that their papers were forged.

The Prime Minister and her cabinet had been delayed by an emergency session, but had been on their way to the wedding when the attack was made. A fortunate chance had saved them, and she sent her personal condolences to the relatives of the victims.

At ten o'clock, Damascus radio gave a report in which El Fatah claimed responsibility for the attack by members of a suicide squad.

A little before midnight, the chief surgeon came from the main theatre, still in his theatre greens and boots, with his mask pulled down to his throat. Ruth Mordecai was out of danger, he told the Brig. They had removed a bullet that had passed through her lung and lodged under her shoulder blade. They had saved the lung.

'Thank God,' murmured the Brig and closed his eyes for a moment, imagining life without his woman of twenty-five years. Then he looked up. 'My daughter?'

The surgeon shook his head. 'They are still working on her in the small casualty theatre.' He hesitated. 'Colonel Halman died in theatre a few minutes ago.'

The toll of the dead was eleven so far, with four others on the critical list.

In the early morning the undertakers arrived for the bodies with their long wicker baskets and black limousines. David gave Joe the keys of the Mercedes, that he might follow by the hearse bearing Hannah's body and arrange the details of the funeral.

David and the Brig sat side by side, haggard and with sleepless bruised eyes, drinking coffee from paper cups.

In the late morning the eye surgeon came out to them. He was a smooth-faced, young-looking man in his forties, the greying of his hair seeming incongruous against the unlined skin and clear blue eyes.

'General Mordecai?'

The Brig rose stiffly. He seemed to have aged ten years during the night.

'I am Doctor Edelman. Will you come with me, please?'

David rose to follow them, but the doctor paused and looked to the Brig.

'I am her fiancé,' said David.

'It might be best if we spoke alone first, General.' Edelman was clearly trying to pass a warning with his eyes, and the Brig nodded.

'Please, David.'

'But—' David began, and the Brig squeezed his shoulder briefly, the first gesture of affection that had ever passed between them.

'Please, my boy,' and David turned back to the hard bench.

In the tiny cubicle of his office Edelman hitched himself on to the corner of the desk and lit a cigarette. His hands were long and slim as a girl's, and he used the lighter with a surgeon's neat economical movements.

'You don't want it with a sugar coating, I imagine?' He had appraised the Brig carefully, and went on without waiting for a reply. 'Neither of your daughter's eyes are damaged,' but he held up a hand to forestall the rising expression of relief on the Brig's lips, and turned to the scanner on which hung a set of X-ray plates. He switched on the back light.

'The eyes were untouched, there is almost no damage to her facial features – however, the damage is here—' He touched a hard frosty outline in the smoky grey swirls and patterns of the X-ray plate. ' – That is a steel fragment, a tiny steel fragment, almost certainly from a grenade. It is no larger than the tip of a lead pencil. It entered the skull through the outer edge of the right temple, severing the large vein which accounted for the profuse haemorrhage, and it travelled obliquely behind the eyeballs without touching them or any other vital tissue. Then, however, it pierced the bony surrounds of the optic chiasma,' he traced the path of the fragment through Debra's head, 'and it seems to have cut through the canal and severed the chiasma, before lodging in the bone sponge beyond.' Edelman drew heavily on the cigarette while he looked for a reaction from the Brig. There was none.

'Do you understand the implications of this, General?' he asked, and the Brig shook his head wearily. The surgeon switched off the light of the X-ray scanner, and returned to the desk. He pulled a scrap pad towards the Brig and took a propelling pencil from his top pocket. Boldly he sketched an optical chart, eyeballs, brain, and optical nerves, as seen from above.

'The optical nerves, one from each eye, run back into this narrow tunnel of bone where they fuse, and then branch again to opposite lobes of the brain.'

The Brig nodded, and Edelman slashed the point of his pencil through the point where the nerves fused. Understanding began to show on the Brig's strained and tired features.

'Blind?' he asked, and Edelman nodded.

'Both eyes?'

'I'm afraid so.'

The Brig bowed his head and gently massaged his own eyes with thumb and forefinger. He spoke again without looking at Edelman.

'Permanently?' he asked.

'She has no recognition of shape, or colour, of light or darkness. The track of the fragment is through the optic

131

chiasma. All indications are that the nerve is severed. There is no technique known to medical science which will restore that.' Edelman paused to draw breath, before going on. 'In a word then, your daughter is permanently and totally blinded in both eyes.'

The Brig sighed, and looked up slowly. 'Have you told her?' and Edelman could not hold his gaze.

'I was rather hoping that you would do that.'

'Yes,' the Brig nodded, 'it would be best that way. Can I see her now? Is she awake?'

'She is under light sedation. No pain, only a small amount of discomfort, the external wound is insignificant – and we shall not attempt to remove the metal fragment. That would entail major neurosurgery.' He stood up and indicated the door. 'Yes, you may see her now. I will take you to her.'

The corridor outside the row of emergency theatres was lined along each wall with stretchers, and the Brig recognized many of his guests laid out upon them. He stopped briefly to speak with one or two of them, before following Edelman to the recovery room at the end of the corridor.

Debra lay on the tall bed below the window. She was very pale, dry blood was still clotted in her hair and a thick cotton wool and bandage dressing covered both her eyes.

'Your father is here, Miss Mordecai,' Edelman told her, and she rolled her head swiftly towards them.

'Daddy?'

'I am here, my child.'

The Brig took the hand she held out, and stooped to kiss her. Her lips were cold, and she smelled strongly of disinfectant and anaesthetic.

'Mama?' she asked anxiously.

'She is out of danger,' the Brig assured her, 'but Hannah—'

'Yes. They told me,' Debra stopped him, her voice choking. 'Is Joe all right?'

'He is strong,' the Brig said. 'He will be all right.'

'David?' she asked.

'He is here.'

Eagerly she struggled up on to one elbow, her face lighting with expectation, the heavily bound eyes turned blindly seeking.

'David,' she called, 'where are you? Damn this bandage. 'Don't worry, David, it's just to rest my eyes.'

'No,' the Brig restrained her with a hand on her arm. 'He is outside, waiting,' and she slumped with disappointment.

'Ask him to come to me, please,' she whispered.

'Yes,' said the Brig, 'in a while, but first there is something we must talk about – something I have to tell you.'

She must have guessed what it was, she must have been warned by the tone of his voice for she went very still. That peculiar stillness of hers, like a frightened animal of the veld.

He was a soldier, with a soldier's blunt ways, and although he tried to soften it, yet even his tone was roughened with his own sorrow, so that it came out brutally. Her hand in his was the only indication that she had heard him, it spasmed convulsively like a wounded thing and then lay still, a small tense hand in the circle of his big bony fist.

She asked no questions and when he had done they sat quietly together for a long time. He spoke first.

'I will send David to you now,' he said, and her response was swift and vehement.

'No.' She gripped his hand hard. 'No, I can't meet him now. I have to think about this first.'

The Brig went back to the waiting-room and David stood up expectantly, the pure lines of his face seemingly carved from pale polished marble, and the dark blue of his eyes in deep contrast.

The Brig forestalled him harshly. 'No visitors.' He took David's arm. 'You will not be allowed to see her until tomorrow.'

'Is something wrong? What is it?' David tried to pull away, but the Brig held him and steered him towards the door.

'Nothing is wrong. She will be all right – but she must have no excitement now. You'll be able to see her tomorrow.'

They buried Hannah that evening in the family plot on the Mountain of Olives. It was a small funeral party attended by the three men and a mere handful of relatives, many of whom had others to mourn from the previous day's slaughter.

There was an official car waiting to take the Brig to a meeting of the High Command, where retaliatory measures would certainly be discussed, another revolution in the relentless wheel of violence that rolled across the troubled land.

Joe and David climbed into the Mercedes and sat silently, David making no effort to start the engine. Joe lit cigarettes for them, and they both felt drained of purpose and direction.

'What are you going to do now?' David asked him.

'We had two weeks,' Joe answered him. 'We were going down to Ashkelon—' His voice trailed off. 'I don't know. There isn't anything to do now, is there?'

'Shall we go and have a drink somewhere?'

Joe shook his head. 'I don't feel like drinking,' he said. 'I think I'll go back to base. They are flying night interceptions tonight.'

'Yes,' David agreed quickly, 'I'll come with you.' He could not see Debra until tomorrow, and the house on

134

Malik Street would be lonely and cold. Suddenly he longed for the peace of the night heavens.

The moon was a brightly curved Saracen blade against the soft darkness of the sky, and the stars were fat and silver and gemlike in their clarity.

They flew high above the earth, remote from its grief and sorrow, wrapped in the isolation of flight and lost in the ritual and concentration of night interception.

The target was a Mirage of their own squadron, and they picked it up on the scanner far out over the Negev. Joe locked on to it and called the track and range while David searched for and at last spotted the moving star of the target's jet blast, burning redly against the velvety blackness of the night.

He took them in on a clean interception creeping up under the target's belly and then pulling steeply up past its wing-tip, the way a barracuda goes for the lure from below and explodes out through the surface of the sea. They shot past so close that the target Mirage broke wildly away to port, unaware of their presence until that moment.

Joe slept that night, exhausted with grief, but David lay in the bunk beneath him and listened to him. In the dawn he rose and showered and left Joe still asleep. He drove into Jerusalem and reached the hospital just as the sun came up and lit the hills with its rays of soft gold and pearly pink.

The night sister at the desk was brusque and preoccupied. 'You shouldn't be here until visiting hours this afternoon,' but David smiled at her with all the charm he could muster.

'I just wanted to know if she is doing well. I have to rejoin my squadron this morning.'

The sister was not immune either to his smile or the air force uniform, and she went to consult her lists.

'You must be mistaken,' she said at last. 'The only Mordecai we have is Mrs Ruth Mordecai.'

'That's her mother,' David told her, and the sister flipped the sheet on her clipboard.

'No wonder I couldn't find it,' she muttered irritably. 'She was discharged last night.'

'Discharged?' David stared at her uncomprehendingly.

'Yes, she went home last night. I remember her now. Her father came to fetch her just as I came on duty. Pretty girl with eye bandages—'

'Yes,' David nodded. 'Thank you. Thank you very much,' and he ran down the steps to the Mercedes, his feet light with relief, freed at last from the gnawing doubt and dread.

Debra had gone home. Debra was safe and well.

The Brig opened the door to him, and let him into the silent house. He was still in his uniform, and it was wilted and rumpled. The Brig's face was fine-drawn, the lines crudely chiselled around his mouth, and his eyes were swollen and bloodshot from worry and sorrow and lack of sleep.

'Where is Debra?' David demanded eagerly, and the Brig sighed and stood aside for him to enter.

'Where is she?' David repeated, and the Brig led him to his study and waved him to a chair.

'Why don't you answer me?' David was becoming angry, and the Brig slumped into a chair across the large bare room, with its severe monastic furnishings of books and archaeological relics.

'I couldn't tell you yesterday, David, she asked me not to. I'm sorry.'

'What is it?' David was fully alarmed now.

'She had to have time to think – to make up her mind.' The Brig stood up again and began to pace, his footsteps echoing hollowly on the bare wooden floor, pausing every now and then to touch one of the pieces of ancient statuary, caressing it absently as he talked, as though to draw comfort from it.

David listened quietly, occasionally shaking his head as though to deny that what he was hearing was the truth.

'So you see it is permanent, final, without hope. She is blind, David, totally blind. She has gone into a dark world of her own where nobody else can follow her.'

'Where is she? I want to go to her,' David whispered, but the Brig ignored the request and went on steadily.

'She wanted time to make her decision – and I gave it to her. Last night, after the funeral, I went back to her and she was ready. She had faced it, come to terms with it, and she had decided how it must be.'

'I want to see her,' David repeated. 'I want to talk to her.'

Now the Brig looked at him and the bleakness in his eyes faded, his voice dropped, becoming gruff with compassion.

'No, David. That was her decision. You will not see her again. For you she is dead. Those were her words. "Tell him I am dead, but he must only remember me when I was alive—"'

David interrupted him, jumping to his feet. 'Where is she, damn you?' His voice was shaking. 'I want to see her now.' He crossed swiftly to the door and jerked it open, but the Brig went on.

'She is not here.'

'Where is she?' David turned back.

'I cannot tell you. I swore a solemn oath to her.'

'I'll find her—'

'You might, if you search carefully – but you will forfeit any respect or love she may have for you,' the Brig went on remorselessly. 'Again I will give you her exact words. "Tell him that I charge him on our love, on all we have ever been to each other, that he will let me be, that he will not come looking for me."'

'Why, but why?' David demanded desperately. 'Why does she reject me?'

'She knows that she is altered beyond all hope or promise. She knows that what was before can never be again. She knows that she can never be to you again what you have a right to expect—' He stopped David's protest with an angry chopping gesture of his hand. 'Listen to me, she knows that it cannot endure. She can never be your wife now. You are too young, too vital, too arrogant—' David stared at him. ' – She knows that it will begin to spoil. In a week, a month, a year perhaps, it will have died. You will be trapped, tied to a blind woman. She doesn't want that. She wants it to die now, swiftly – mercifully, not to drag on—'

'Stop it,' David shouted. 'Stop it, damn you. That's enough.' He stumbled to the chair and fell into it. They were silent for a while, David crouched in the chair with his face buried in his hands. The Brig standing before the narrow window casement, the early morning light catching the fierce old warrior's face.

'She asked me to make you promise—' He hesitated, and David looked up at him. ' – To promise that you would not try to find her.'

'No.' David shook his head stubbornly.

The Brig sighed. 'If you refused, I was to tell you this – she said you would understand, although I don't – she said that in Africa there is a fierce and beautiful animal called the sable antelope, and sometimes one of them is wounded by a hunter or mauled by a lion.'

The words were as painful as the cut of a whiplash, and David remembered himself saying them to her once when they were both young and strong and invulnerable.

'Very well,' he murmured at last, 'if that's what she wants – then I promise not to try and find her, though I don't promise not to try and convince her she is wrong.'

'Perhaps it would be best if you left Israel,' the Brig told him. 'Perhaps you should go back to where you came from and forget all of this ever happened.'

David paused, considering this a moment, before he answered, 'No, all I have is here. I will stay here.'

'Good.' The Brig accepted the decision. 'You are always welcome in this house.'

'Thank you, sir,' said David and went out to where the Mercedes was parked. He let himself into the house on Malik Street, and saw instantly that someone had been there before him.

He walked slowly into the living-room; the books were gone from the olive-wood table, the Kadesh painting no longer hung above the leather couch. In the bathroom he opened the wall cabinet and all her toilet articles had been removed, the rows of exotic bottles, the tubes and pots, even the slot for her toothbrush beside his was empty.

Her cupboard was bare, the dresses gone, the shelves blank, every trace of her swept away, except for the lingering scent of her perfume on the air, and the ivory lace cover upon the bed.

He went to the bed and sat upon it, stroking the fine lace-work, remembering how it had been.

There was the hard outline of something thin and square upon the pillow, beneath the cover. He turned back the lace and picked up the thin green book.

This Year, in Jerusalem. It had been left there as a parting gift.

The title swam and went misty before his eyes. It was all he had left of her.

It seemed as though the slaughter at Ein Karem was the signal for a fresh upsurge of hostility and violence throughout the Middle East. A planned escalation of international tensions, as the Arab nations rattled their impressive, oil-purchased array of weaponry and swore once more to leave not a single Jew in the land they still called Palestine.

There were savage and merciless attacks on soft targets, ill-protected embassies and consulates around the world, letter bombs, and night ambushes on school buses in isolated areas.

Then the provocations grew bolder, more directly aimed at the heart of Israel. Border infringements, commando-style raids, violations of air space, shellings, and a threatening gathering and massing of armed might along the long vulnerable frontiers of the wedge-shaped territories of the tiny land.

The Israelis waited, praying for peace – but gird for war.

Day after day, month after month, David and Joe flew to maintain that degree of expertise, where instinct and instantaneous reaction superseded conscious thought and reasoned action.

At those searing speeds beyond sound, it was only this training that swung the advantage from one combat team to another. Even the superior reaction times of these carefully hand-picked young men were unequal to the tasks of bringing their mighty machines into effective action, where latitudes of error were measured in hundredths of a second, until they had attained this extra-sensory perfection.

To seek out, to recognize, to close, to destroy, and to disengage – it was a total preoccupation that blessedly left little time for brooding and sorrow.

Yet the sorrow and anger, that David and Joe shared, seemed doubly to arm them. Their vengeance was all-consuming.

Soon they joined that select half-dozen strike teams that Desert Flower called to undertake the most delicate of sorties. Again and again they were ordered into combat, and each time the confidence that Command had in them was strengthened.

As David sat in his cockpit, dressed from head to foot in the stiff constricting embrace of a full-pressure suit, breathing oxygen from his closed face mask, although the Mirage still crouched upon the ground, there were four black, red and white miniature roundels painted on the fuselage below his cockpit. The scalps of the enemy.

It was a mark of Desert Flower's trust that Bright Lance flight had been selected for high altitude 'Red' standby. With the starter lines plugged ready to blow compressed air into the compressors and whirl the great engines into life, and the ground crew lounging beside the motor, the Mirages were ready to be hurled aloft in a matter of seconds. Both David and Joe were suited to survive the almost pressureless altitudes above sixty thousand feet where an unprotected man's blood would fizzle like champagne.

David had lost count of the weary uncomfortable days and hours he had sat cramped in his cockpit on 'Red' standby with only the regular fifteen-minute checks to break the monotony.

'Checking 11.15 hours – fifteen minutes to stand-down.' David said into the microphone, and heard Joe's breathing in his ears before the reply.

'Two standing by. *Beseder.*'

Immediately after stand-down, when another crew would assume the arduous waiting of standby, David would change into a track suit and run for five or six miles to get the stiffness out of his body and to have his sweat wash away the staleness. He was looking forward to that, afterwards he would—

There was a sharp crackle in his earphones and a new voice.

'Red standby – Go! Go!'

The command was repeated over loudspeakers in the underground bunker, and the ground crew boiled into action. With all his pre-flight checks and routine long ago completed, David merely pushed his throttle to starting position, and the whine of the starters showed immediate results. The engine caught and he ran up his power to one hundred per cent.

Ahead of him the blast doors were lifting.

'Bright Lance Two, this is Leader going to take off power.'

'Two conforming,' said Joe and they went screaming up the ramp and hurled themselves at the sky.

'Hallo, Desert Flower, this is Bright Lance airborne and climbing.'

'Bright Lance, this is the Brig,' David was not surprised to find that he was in charge of command plot. Distinctive voices and the use of personal names would prevent any chance of the enemy confusing the net with false messages. 'David, we have an intruder approach at high level that should enter our airspace in four minutes, if it continues on its present course. We are tracking him at seventy-five thousand feet which means it is either an American U2, which is highly unlikely, or that it is a Russian spy plane coming over to have a look at our latest dispersals.'

'*Beseder*, sir,' David acked.

'We are going to try for a storm-climb to intercept as soon as the target becomes hostile in our air space.'

'*Beseder*, sir.'

'Level at twenty thousand feet, turn to 186 and go to maximum speed for storm-climb.'

At twenty thousand, David went to straight and level flight and glanced into his mirror to see Joe's Mirage hanging out on his tail.

'Bright Lance Two, this is Leader. Commencing run now.'

'Two conforming.'

David lit his tail and pushed the throttle open to maximum afterburner position. The Mirage jumped away, and David let the nose drop slightly to allow the speed to build up quickly. They went blazing through the sound barrier without a check, and David retrimmed for supersonic flight, thumbing the little top-hat on the end of his stick.

Their speed rocketed swiftly through Mach 1.2, Mach 1.5.

The Mirages were stripped of all but their essentials, there were no missiles dangling beneath them, no auxiliary fuel tanks to create drag, the only weapons they carried were their two 30-mm cannons.

Flying lightly, they drove on up the Mach scale, streaking from Beersheba to Eilat in the time it would take a man to walk a city block. Their speed stabilized at Mach 1.9 just short of the heat barrier.

'David, this is the Brig. We are tracking you. You are on correct course and speed for interception. Prepare to commence climb in sixteen seconds.'

'*Beseder*, sir.'

'Counting now. Eight, seven, six . . . two, one. Go! Go!'

David tensed his body and as he pulled up the nose of the Mirage, he opened his mouth and screamed to fight off the effects of gravity. But despite these precautions and the constricting grip of his pressure suit, the abrupt change of direction crammed him down into his seat and the blood drained out of his head so that his vision went grey and then black.

The Mirage was standing on her tail still flying at very nearly twice the speed of sound and, as his vision returned, David glanced at the G-meter and saw that he had subjected his body to nearly nine times the force of gravity to achieve this attitude of climb without loss of speed.

Now he lay on his back and stared up at the empty sky while the needle of his altimeter raced upwards, and his speed gradually eroded away.

A quick sweep showed Joe's Mirage rock steady in position below him, climbing in concert with him, and his voice came through calm and reassuring.

'Leader, this is Two. I have contact with target.'

Even under the stress of storm-climb, Joe was busy manipulating his beloved radar, and he had picked up the spy plane high above them.

In this manoeuvre they were trading speed for height, and as one increased so the other drained away.

They were like a pair of arrows aimed directly upwards. The bowstring could throw them just so far and then they would hang there in space for a few moments, until they were drawn irresistibly back to earth. In those few moments they must find and kill the enemy.

David lay back in his seat and watched with fresh wonder as the sky turned darker blue and then slowly became the midnight black of space, shot through with the fiery prickings of the stars.

They were at the top edge of the stratosphere, high above the highest clouds or signs of weather as known to earth. Outside the cockpit the air was thin and weak, insufficient for life, hardly sufficient to keep the jets of the Mirage's engines burning – and the cold was a fearsome sixty degrees of frost.

The two aircraft slowly ran out of energy, and they came out together at the top of a mighty parabola. The sensation of flight was gone, they swam through the dark forbidding oceans of space and far below them the earth glowed strangely, with a weird unnatural light.

There was no time to admire the view, the Mirage was wallowing in the thin and treacherous air, her control surfaces skidding and sliding without bite.

Joe was on the target, tracking quietly and steadily and they came round carefully on to the heading, with the aircraft staggering mushily and beginning to fall away from these inhospitable heights.

David stared ahead, holding the Mirage's nose up for sustained altitude but already the stall warning device was flicking amber and red at him. He was running out of time and height.

Then suddenly he saw it, seeming startlingly close in the rare air, ghosting along on its immense wings, like a black manta-ray through the sable and silent sea of space – ahead and slightly below them – calmly and silently, it drifted along, its height giving it a false sense of invulnerability.

'Desert Flower, this is Bright Lance visual on the intruder and requesting permission for strike.' David's cool tone hid the sudden gust of his anger and hatred that the sighting had released.

'Report your target.' The Brig was hedging, it was a dangerous decision to call the strike on an unknown target.

'Desert Flower, it's an Ilyushin Mark 17–11. No apparent markings.'

It needed no marking, it could only belong to one nation. David was closing fast, he could fly no slower than this, and he was rapidly overhauling the other machine. Those huge wings were designed to float upon the feeble air of the stratosphere.

'Closing fast,' he warned Desert Flower. 'Opportunity for strike will pass in approximately ten seconds.'

The silence in his headphones hummed quickly, and he readied his cannons and watched the spy plane blowing up rapidly in size as he dropped down upon it.

Suddenly the Brig made the decision, perhaps committing his country to heavy retaliation, but knowing that the spy plane's cameras were steadily recording vital details of their ability to resist aggression, information that would be passed quickly to their enemies.

'David,' his voice was curt and harsh, 'this is the Brig. Hit him!'

'*Beseder.*' David let the Mirage's nose drop a fraction, and she responded gratefully.

'Two, this is Leader attacking.'

'Two conforming.'

He went down on the Ilyushin so fast, that as she came into his sights he knew he had time for only a few seconds of fire.

He pressed the trigger with the aiming pipper on the spy plane's wing roots, and he saw her rear up like a great fish struck by the steel of the harpoon.

For three seconds he poured his cannon shells into her, and watched them flash and twinkle against the massive black silhouette. Then he was through, falling away below the giant's belly, with his power spent, dropping away like the burned-out shell of a rocket.

Joe came down astern of him, backing up the attack, and in his sights the spy plane hung helplessly on its wide wings, its long rounded nose pointing to the black sky with its cold uncaring stars.

He pressed the trigger and the plane broke up amidst the bright flashes of exploding cannon shells. One wing snapped off at its roots and the carcass began its long slow tumble down the heavens.

'Hello, Desert Flower, this is Bright Lance Leader. Target destroyed.' David tried to keep his voice level, but he found his hands were trembling and his guts were aching cold from the spill-over of his hatred that not even the enemy's death could expunge.

Again he pressed the button to open the flight net. 'Joe, that's one more for Hannah,' he said, but for once there was no reply, and after he had listened in vain to the throb of the carrier beam for a few seconds he closed it, and activated his doppler gear for a homing signal, and silently Joe followed him back to base.

D ebra had been a steadying and maturing influence, but now David reacted so wildly to her going that Joe had to continue his role of wingman, even when they were off base.

They spent much of their leisure time together, for although they seldom mentioned their loss, yet the sharing of it drew them closer.

Often Joe slept over at Malik Street, for his own home was a sad and depressing place now. The Brig was seldom there in these troubled times, Debra gone and his mother was so altered by her terrible experience that she was grey and broken, aged beyond her years. The bullet wound in her body had closed, but there was other damage that would never heal.

David's wildness was a craving for the forgetfulness of constant action. He was only truly at peace when he was in the air, and on the ground he was restless and mercurial. Joe moved, big and calm beside him, steering him tactfully out of trouble with a slow grin and an easy word.

As a consequence of the downed spy plane, the Syrians began a policy of provocative patrols, calculated infringement of Israeli airspace, which was discontinued as soon as retaliation was drawn. As the interceptors raced to engage they would swing away, declining combat, and move back within their own borders.

Twice David saw the greenish luminous blur of these hostile patrols on the screen of his scanning radar, and each time he had surprised himself with the icy feeling of anger and hatred that had lain heavy as a rock upon his heart and lungs as he led Joe in on the interception. Each time, however, the Syrians had been warned by their own radar and they had turned away, increasing speed, and withdrawn discreetly and mockingly.

'Bright Lance, this is Desert Flower. Target is no longer hostile. Discontinue attack pattern.' The Syrian MiG 21s had crossed their own frontier, and each time David had answered quietly, 'Two, this is Leader. Discontinuing attack pattern and resuming scan.'

The tactics were designed to wear on the nerves of the defenders, and in all the interceptor squadrons the tension was becoming explosive. The provocation was pushing them to the edge of restraint. Incidents were only narrowly being averted, as the hot-bloods crowded their interceptions to the very frontiers of war. Finally, however, there had to come intervention from above as Desert Flower tried to hold them on a tighter leash. They sent the Brig to talk to his crews and as he stood on the dais and looked about the crowded briefing room, he realized that it was unfair to train the hawk and then keep the hood over his eyes and the thong upon his leg, to hold him upon the wrist, when the wild duck were flighting overhead.

He started at a philosophical level, taking advantage of the regard that he knew his young pilots had for him.

' – the object of war is peace, the ultimate strategy of any commander is peace—' There was no response from his audience. The Brig caught the level scrutiny of his own son. How could he talk of placation to a trained warrior who had just buried the multilated body of his bride? The Brig ploughed on manfully.

'Only a fool allows himself to be drawn on to a field of the enemy's choosing,' he was reaching them now, 'I won't have one of you young pups pushing us into something we are not ready for. I don't want to give them an excuse. That is what they want—' They were thawing now, he saw a head nod thoughtfully and heard a murmur of agreement.

'Any of you looking for big trouble, you don't have to go to Damascus, you know my address.' He tried for his first laugh, and got it. They were chuckling now. 'All right, then. We don't want trouble. We are going to lean right over backwards to prevent it – but we are not going to fall on our arses. When the time comes, I'll give you the word and it won't be the soft word, or the other cheek—' they growled then, a fierce little sound, and he ended it, ' – but you wait for that word.'

Le Dauphin stood up and took over from the Brig.

'All right, while I've got you all together, I've a little news for you that may help to cool the hot-heads who want to follow the MiGs over the border.' He motioned to the projection box at the end of the briefing-room, the lights went down and there was a shuffling of feet, and an outburst of coughing. A voice protested resignedly.

'Not *another* film show!'

'Yes,' the colonel took it up. '*Another* film show.' Then as the images began to flash upon the screen he went on, 'This is a military intelligence film, and the subject is a new ground-to-air missile system that has been delivered by the Soviet Army to the armies of the Arab Union. The code name for the system is "Serpent" and it updates the existing "Sam III" system. As far as we know, the system has been installed and is operative in the Syrian defensive perimeter, and will shortly be installed by the Egyptians. It is manned at present by Russian instructors.' As the colonel went on talking, the Brig sat back in his chair and watched their faces in the silver reflection from the screen. They were intent and serious, men looking for the first time on the terrible machines that might be the instrument of their own deaths.

'The missile is fired from a tracked vehicle. Here you see aerial reconnaissance shots of a mobile column. Notice that each vehicle carries a pair of missiles, and you will realize that they constitute an enormous threat—'

The Brig picked out the marvellously pure profile of David Morgan as he leaned forward to study the screen, and he felt a pang of sympathy and sorrow for him – and yet this was underlined by a new respect, a realignment of judgement. The boy had proved himself to be constant, capable of embracing an ideal and remaining loyal to it.

'The improvements in design of the "Serpent" are not

certain, but it is believed that the missile is capable of greater speeds, probably in the order of Mach 2.5, and that the guidance system is a combination of both infra-red heat seeker and computerized radar control.'

Watching the handsome young face, he wondered if Debra had not misjudged his reserves. It was possible that he would have been capable of – no, the Brig shook his head and groped for a cigarette. He was too young, too greedy for life, spoiled by good looks and riches. He would not be capable of it. Debra was right, as so often was the case. She had chosen the correct course. She could never hold him, she must set him free.

'It is expected that the "Serpent" is capable of engaging targets at altitudes between 1,500 feet and 75,000 feet.'

There was a stir amongst the listeners, as they assessed the threat of this new weapon.

'The warhead delivers a quarter of a ton of explosive and it is armed with a proximity fuse which is set to fire if the target is passed at range less than 150 feet. Within these limits the "Serpent" is lethal.'

The Brig was still watching David. Ruth and he had not seen the boy at their home for many months. He had come with Joe to spend the Sabbath evening with them twice after the outrage. However, the atmosphere had been stiff and artificial, everybody carefully avoiding mention of Debra's name. He had not come again after the second time, nearly six months ago.

'Evasive tactics at this stage will be the same as for "Sam III".'

'Prayer and good luck!' someone interjected and that raised a laugh.

' – maximum-rate turn towards the missile, to screen the radiation from your jet blasts, and attempt to force the "Serpent" to overshoot. In the event that the missile continues to track, you should climb into the sun and then make another maximum-rate turn. The missile may then accept the sun's infra-red radiation as a more tempting target—'

'And if that doesn't work?' a voice called, and another answered flippantly, 'Repeat the following: "Hear O Israel, the Lord our God, the Lord is one."' But this time nobody laughed at the old blasphemy.

The Brig timed his departure from the briefing-room to fall in beside David.

'When are we going to see you, David? It's been a long time.'

'I'm sorry, sir. I hope Joe made my apologies.'

'Yes, of course. But why don't you come with Joe this evening? God knows, there will be enough food.'

'I'll be very busy tonight, sir,' David declined lamely.

'I understand.' And as they reached the door of the OC's office the Brig paused, 'Remember you are always welcome,' and he turned away.

'Sir!' The Brig stopped and looked back at him. David spoke rapidly – almost guiltily.

'How is she, sir?' and then again, 'how is Debra? Have you seen her – I mean, recently?'

'She is well,' the Brig answered heavily. 'As well as she can be.'

'Will you tell her I asked?'

'No,' answered the Brig, ignoring the pleading in the dark blue eyes. 'No. You know I can't do that.'

David nodded and turned away. For a moment the Brig looked after him and then with a frown he went on into the colonel's office.

David dropped Joe in Ein Karem, at the entrance to the lane, and then he drove on into the main shopping area of East Jerusalem and parked outside the big new supermarket in Melech George V to do his shopping for the weekend ahead.

He was hanging over the freezer tray pondering the delicate choice between lamb cutlets and steak, when he became aware that he was being watched.

David looked up quickly and saw that she was a statuesque woman with a thick mane of blond curls. She stood beside the shelves farther down the aisle. Her hair was dyed, he could see the dark shadow of the roots, and she was older than he was, with a womanly heaviness in her hips and bosom and tiny lines at the corners of her eyes. She was eyeing him, a steady appraisal so unashamedly sensual that he felt the check in his breathing and the quick stirring of his lions. He looked back at the meat in the freezer, guilty and angry with the treachery of his body. It had been so long, so very long since he had experienced sexual awareness. He had believed that he never would again. He wanted to throw the pack of steak back into the freezer and leave, but he stood rooted with the breathless feeling squeezing his lungs, and he was aware of the woman's presence at his side. He could feel the warmth of her on his arm, and smell her – the flowery perfume mingled with the natural musky odour of the sexually aroused female.

'The steak is very good,' she said. She had a light sweet voice and he recognized the same breathless quality as his own. He looked at her. Her eyes were green, and her teeth were a little crooked but white. She was even older than he had thought, almost forty. She wore her dress low in front, he could see the crêpe effect of the skin between her breasts. The breasts were big and motherly, and suddenly David wanted to lay his head against them. They looked so soft and warm and safe.

'You should cook it rare, with mushrooms and garlic and red wine,' she said. 'It's very good that way.'

'Is it?' he asked hoarsely.

'Yes,' she nodded, smiling. 'Who will cook it for you? Your wife? Your mother?'

'No,' said David. 'I will cook it myself. I live alone,' and she leaned a little closer to him, her breast touching his arm.

David was dizzy and hot with the brandy. He had bought a bottle of it at the supermarket, and he had drunk it mixed with ginger ale to mask the spiritous taste. He had drunk it fast, and now he leaned over the basin in the bathroom and felt the house rock and sway about him. He steadied himself, gripping the edge of the basin.

He splashed cold water on to his face and shook off the drops, then he grinned stupidly at himself in the mirror above the basin. His hair was damp and hung on to his forehead; he closed one eye and the wavering image in the mirror hardened and squinted back at him.

'Hi there, boy,' he muttered and reached for the towel. He had dripped water down his tunic and this annoyed him. He threw the towel over the toilet seat and went back into the living-room.

The woman was gone. The leather couch still carried the indentation of her backside, and the dirty plates were on the olive-wood table. The air was thick with cigarette smoke and her perfume.

'Where are you?' he called thickly, swaying slightly in the doorway.

'Here, big boy.' He went to the bedroom. She lay on the bed, naked, plump and white with huge soft breasts and swelling belly. He stared at her.

'Come on, Davey.' Her clothing was thrown across the dressing-table, and he saw that her corsets were grey and unwashed. Her hair was yellow against the soft ivory lacework.

'Come to Mama,' she whispered hoarsely, opening her limbs languidly in invitation. She was spread upon the brass bed, upon the lace cover which had been Debra's – and David felt his anger surge within him.

'Get up,' he said, slurring his words.

153

'Come on, baby.'

'Get off that bed,' his voice tightened and she heard the tone and sat up with mild alarm.

'What is it, Davey?'

'Get out of here,' his voice was rising sharply. 'Get out, you bitch. Get out of here!' He was shaking now, his face pale and his eyes savage blue.

Quivering with panic, she climbed hurriedly from the bed, the great white breasts and buttocks wobbling with ridiculous haste as she stuffed them into the grey corset.

When she had gone, David went through into the bathroom and vomited into the toilet bowl. Then he cleaned the house, scouring pans and plates, polishing the glasses until they shone, emptying the ashtrays, opening the shutters to blow out the stench of cigarette and perfume – and finally, going through into the bedroom, he stripped and remade the bed with fresh sheets and smoothed the lace cover carefully until not a crease or wrinkle showed.

He put on a clean tunic and his uniform cap, and drove to the Jaffa gate. He parked the car in the lot outside the gate and walked through the old city to the reconstructed Sephardic synagogue in the Jewish quarter.

It was very quiet and peaceful in the high-domed hall and he sat a long time on the hard wooden bench.

Joe sat opposite David with a worried expression creasing his deep forehead as he studied the board. Three or four of the other pilots had hiked their chairs up and were concentrating on the game also. These chessboard conflicts between David and Joe were usually epics and attracted a partisan audience.

David had been stalking Joe's rook for half a dozen moves and now he had it trapped. Two more moves would shatter the king-sized defence, and the third must force a resignation. David grinned smugly as Joe reached a decision and moved a knight out.

'That's not going to save you, dear boy.' David hardly glanced at the knight, and he hit the rook with a white bishop. 'Mate in five,' he predicted, as he dropped the castle into the box, and then – too late – he realized that Joe's theatrical expression of anguish had slowly faded into a beatific grin. Joseph Mordecai used any deception to bait his traps, and David looked with alarm at the innocuous-seeming knight, suddenly seeing the devious plotting in which the castle was merely bait.

'Oh, you bastard,' David moaned. 'You sneaky bastard.'

'Check!' Joe gloated as he put the knight into a forked attack, and David had to leave his queen exposed to the horseman.

'Check,' said Joe again with an ecstatic little sigh as he lifted the white queen off the board, and again the harassed king took the only escape route open to him.

'And mate,' sighed Joe again as his own queen left the back file to join the attack. 'Not in five, as you predicted, but in three.' There was a loud outburst of congratulation and applause from the onlookers and Joe cocked an eye at David.

'Again?' he asked, and David shook his head.

'Take on one of these other patsies,' he said. 'I'm going to sulk for an hour.' He vacated his seat and it was filled by another eager victim as Joe reset the board. David crossed to the coffee machine, moving awkwardly in the grip of his G-suit, and drew a mug of the thick black liquid, stirred in four spoons of sugar and found another seat in a quieter corner of the crew-room beside a slim curly-headed young kibbutznik, with whom David had become friendly. He was reading a thick novel.

'*Shalom*, Robert. How you been?'

Robert grunted without looking up from his book, and David sipped the sweet hot coffee. Beside him, Robert moved restlessly in his seat and coughed softly. David was lost in his own thoughts, for the first time in months thinking of home, wondering about Mitzi and Barney Venter, wondering if the yellowtail were running hot in False Bay this season, and remembering how the proteas looked upon the mountains of the Helderberg.

Again Robert stirred in his chair and cleared his throat. David glanced at him, realized that he was in the grip of a deep emotion as he read, his lips quivering, and his eyes too bright.

'What are you reading?' David was amused, and he leaned forward to read the title. The picture on the dust jacket of the book was instantly familiar. It was a deeply felt desert landscape of fierce colours and great space. Two distant figures, man and woman, walked hand in hand through the desert and the effect was mystic and haunting. David realized that only one person could have painted that – Ella Kadesh.

Robert lowered the book. 'This is uncanny,' his voice was muffled with emotion. 'I tell you, Davey, it's beautiful. It must be one of the most beautiful books ever written.'

With a strange feeling of pre-knowledge, with a sense of complete certainty, of what it would be, David took the book out of his hands and turned it to read the title, *A Place of Our Own*.

Robert was still talking. 'My sister made me read it. She works for the publisher. She cried all night when she read it. It is very new, only published last week, but it's got to be the biggest book ever written about this country.'

David hardly heard him, he was staring at the writer's name in small print below the title.

'Debra Mordecai.'

He ran his fingers lightly over the glossy paper of the jacket, stroking the name.

'I want to read it,' he said softly.

'I'll let you have it when I'm finished,' Robert promised.

'I want to read it now!'

'No way!' Robert exclaimed with evident alarm, and almost snatched the book out of David's hands.

'You wait your turn, comrade!'

David looked up. Joe was watching him from across the room, and David glared at him accusingly. Joe dropped his eyes quickly to the chessboard again, and David realized that he had known of the publication. He started to go up to him, to challenge him, but at the moment the tannoy echoed through the bunker.

'All flights Lance Squadron to Red standby,' and on the readiness board the red lamps lit beside the flight designations.

'Bright Lance.

'Red Lance.

'Fire Lance.'

David snatched up his flying helmet and joined the lumbering rush of G-suited bodies for the electric personnel carrier in the concrete tunnel outside the crew-room door. He forced a place for himself beside Joe.

'Why didn't you tell me?' he demanded.

'I was going to, Davey, I really was.'

'Yeah, I bet,' David snapped sarcastically. 'Have you read it?'

Joe nodded, and David went on, 'What's it about?'

'I couldn't begin to tell you. You'd have to read it yourself.'

'Don't worry about that,' David muttered grimly, 'I will,' and he jumped down as they reached their hangar and strode across to his Mirage.

Twenty minutes later they were airborne and Desert Flower sent them hastening out over the Mediterranean at interception speed to answer a Mayday call from an El Al Caravelle who reported that she was being buzzed by an Egyptian MiG 21 J.

The Egyptian sheered off and raced for the coast and

the protection of his own missile batteries as the Mirages approached. They let him go and picked up the airliner. They escorted her into the circuit over Lod before returning to base.

Still in his G-suit and overalls, David stopped off at Le Dauphin's office and got himself a twenty-four-hour pass.

Ten minutes before closing time he ran into one of the bookstores in the Jaffa Road.

There was a pyramid display of A *Place of Our Own* on the table in the centre of the store.

'It's a beautiful book,' said the salesgirl as she wrapped it.

He opened a Goldstar, and kicked off his shoes before stretching out on the lace cover of the bed.

He began to read, and paused only once to switch on the overhead lights and fetch another beer. It was a thick book, and he read slowly – savouring every word, sometimes going back to re-read a paragraph.

It was their story, his and Debra's, woven into the plot she had described to him that day on the island off the Costa Brava, and it was rich with the feeling of the land and its people. He recognized many of the secondary characters, and he laughed aloud with the pleasure and the joy of it. Then at the end, he choked on the sadness as the girl of the story lies dying in Hadassah Hospital, with half her face torn away by a terrorist's bomb, and she will not let the boy come to her. Wanting to spare him that, wanting him to remember her as she was.

It was dawn then, and David had not noticed the passage of the night. He rose from the bed, light-headed from lack of sleep, and filled with a sense of wonder that Debra had captured so clearly the way it had been – that she had seen so deeply into his soul, had described emotions for which he had believed there were no words.

He bathed and shaved and dressed in casual clothes and went back to where the book lay upon the bed. He studied the jacket again, and then turned to the flyleaf for confirmation. It was there. 'Jacket design by Ella Kadesh.'

So early in the morning he had the road almost to himself and he drove fast, into the rising morning sun. At Jericho he turned north along the frontier road, and he remembered her sitting in the seat beside him with her skirts drawn high around her long brown legs and her thick dark hair shaking in the wind.

The whisper of the wind against the body of the Mercedes seemed to urge him, 'Hurry, hurry.' And the urgent drumming of the tyres carried him up towards the lake.

He parked the Mercedes beside the ancient crusader wall and went through into the garden on the lake shore.

Ella sat upon the wide patio before her easel. She wore a huge straw hat the size of a wagon wheel adorned with plastic cherries and ostrich feathers, her vast overalls covered her like a circus tent and they were stiff with dried paint in all her typically vivid colours.

Calmly she looked up from her painting with her brush poised.

'Hail, young Mars!' she greeted him. 'Well met indeed, and why do you bring such honour on my humble little home?'

'Piss on it, Ella, you know damn well why I'm here.'

'So sweetly phrased.' She was shifty, he could see it in her bright little eyes. 'Shame on it that such vulgar words pass such fair lips. Would you like a beer, Davey?'

'No, I don't want a beer. I want to know where she is.'

'Just who are we discussing?'

'Come on, I read the book. I saw the cover. You know, damn you, you know.'

159

She was silent then, staring at him. Then slowly the ornate head-dress dipped in acquiescence.

'Yes,' she agreed. 'I know.'

'Tell me where she is.'

'I can't do that, Davey. You and I both made a promise. Yes, I know of yours, you see.'

She watched the bluster go out of him. The fine young body with the arrogant set of shoulders seemed to sag, and he stood uncertainly in the sunlight.

'How about that beer now, Davey?' She heaved herself up from her stool and crossed the terrace with her stately tread. She came back and gave him a tall glass with a head of froth and they took a seat together at the end of the terrace out of the wind, in the mild winter sunlight.

'I've been expecting you for a week now,' she told him. 'Ever since the book was published. I knew it would set you on fire. It's just too damned explosive – even I wept like a leaky faucet for a couple of days,' she giggled shyly. 'You'd hardly believe it possible, would you?'

'That book was us – Debra and me,' David told her. 'She was writing about us.'

'Yes,' Ella agreed, 'but it does not alter the decision she had made. A decision which I think is correct, by the way.'

'She described exactly how I felt, Ella. All the things I felt and still feel – but which I could never have put into words.'

'It's beautiful and it's true, but don't you see that it confirms her position?'

'But I love her, Ella – and she loves me,' he cried out violently.

'She wants it to stay that way. She doesn't want it to die, she doesn't want it to sicken.' He began to protest, but she gripped his arm in a surprisingly powerful grip to silence him. 'She knows that she can never keep pace with you now. Look at you, David, you are beautiful and vital and swift – she must drag you back, and in time you must as certainly resent it.'

Again he tried to interrupt, but she shook his arm in her huge fist. 'You would be shackled, you could never leave her, she is helpless, she would be your charge for all your life – think on it, David.'

'I want her,' he muttered stubbornly. 'I had nothing before I met her, and I have nothing now.'

'That will change. Perhaps she has taught you something and young emotions heal as swiftly as young flesh. She wants happiness for you, David. She loves you so much that her gift to you is freedom. She loves you so much that for your sake she will deny that love.'

'Oh, God,' he groaned. 'If only I could see her, if I could touch her and talk to her for a few minutes.'

She shook her massive head, and her jowls wobbled dolefully.

'She would not agree to that.'

'Why, Ella, tell me why?' His voice was rising again, desperate with his anguish.

'She is not strong enough, she knows that if you came near her, she would waver and bring even greater disaster upon you both.'

They sat silently together then and looked out across the lake. High mountains of cloud rose up beyond the heights of Golan, brilliant white in the winter sunlight, shaded with blue and bruised grey, and range upon range they bore down upon the lake. David shivered as an icy little wind came ferreting across the terrace and sought them out.

He drank the rest of his beer, and then revolved the glass slowly through his fingers.

'Will you give her a message from me, then?' he asked.

'I don't think—'

'Please, Ella. Just this one message.'

She nodded.

'Tell her that what she wrote in the book is exactly how much I love her. Tell her that it is big enough to rise above this thing. Tell her that I want the chance to try.'

She listened quietly, and David made a groping gesture with his hands as though to pluck words from the air that might convince her.

'Tell her—' He paused, then shook his head. 'No, that's all. Just tell her I love her, and I want to be with her.'

'All right, David. I'll tell her.'

'And you will give me her answer?'

'Where can I reach you?'

He gave her the number of the telephone in the crew ready room at the base.

'You'll ring me soon, Ella? Don't keep me waiting.'

'Tomorrow,' she promised. 'In the morning.'

'Before ten o'clock. It must be before ten.'

He stood up, and then suddenly he leaned forward and kissed her sagging and raddled cheek.

'Thank you,' he said. 'You are not a bad old bag.'

'Away with you, you and your blarney. You'd have the sirens of the *Odyssey* themselves come a-running to your bidding.' She sniffed moistly. 'Get away with you now, I think I'm going to cry, and I want to be alone to enjoy it.'

She watched him go up across the lawns under the date palms and at the gate in the wall he paused and looked back. For a second they stared at each other and then he stepped through the gate.

She heard the engine of the Mercedes whirr and pull away slowly up the track, then the note of it rose as it hit the highway and went racing away southwards. Ella rose heavily and crossed the terrace, went down the steps towards the jetty and its stone boathouses screened from the house by part of the ancient wall.

Her speedboat rode at its mooring, restless in the wind and the chop of the lake. She went on down to the farthest and largest of the boathouses and stood in the open doorway.

The interior had been stripped and repainted with clean white. The furniture was simple and functional. The rugs on the stone floor were for warmth, plain woven wool, thick and rough. The large bed was built into a curtained alcove in the wall beside the fireplace.

On the opposite wall was a gas stove with a double cooking ring above which a number of copper cooking pots hung. A door beyond led through to a bathroom and toilet which Ella had added very recently.

The only decoration was the Ella Kadesh painting from the house on Malik Street, which hung on the bare white wall, facing the door. It seemed to lighten and warm the whole room; below it the girl sat at a working table. She was listening intently to her own voice speaking in Hebrew from the tape recorder. Her expression was rapt and intent, and she stared at the blank wall before her.

Then she nodded her head, smiling at what she had just heard. She switched off the recorder and turned in the swivel chair to the second recorder and punched the record button. She held the microphone close to her lips as she began to translate the Hebrew into English.

Ella stood in the doorway and watched her work. An American publisher had purchased the English-language rights of A Place of Our Own. They had paid Debra an advance of thirty thousand American dollars for the book, and an additional five thousand for her services as translator. She had almost completed the task now.

From where she stood, Ella could see the scar on Debra's temple. It was a glazed pinkish white against the deeply tanned skin of her face, a dimple like a child's drawing of a seagull in flight; V-shaped and no bigger than a snowflake, it seemed to enhance her fine looks, almost like a beauty spot, a tiny blemish that gave a focus point for her strong regular features.

She had made no attempt to conceal it for her dark hair was drawn back to the nape of her neck and secured there with a leather thong. She wore no make-up, and her skin looked clean and glowing, tanned and smooth.

Despite the bulky fisherman's jersey and woollen slacks her body appeared firm and slim for she swam each day, even when the snow winds came down from the north.

Ella left the doorway and moved silently closer to the desk, studying Debra's eyes as she so often did. One day she would paint that expression. There was no hint of the damage that lay behind, no hint that the eyes could not see. Rather their calm level gaze seemed to penetrate deeper, to see all. They had a serenity that was almost mystic, a depth and understanding that Ella found strangely disquieting.

Debra pressed the switch of the microphone, ending the recording, and then she spoke again without turning her head.

'Is that you, Ella?'

'How do you do it?' Ella demanded with astonishment.

'I felt the air move when you walked in, and then I smelt you.'

'I'm big enough to blow up a storm, but do I smell so bad?' Ella protested, chuckling.

'You smell of turpentine, and garlic and beer,' Debra sniffed, and laughed with her.

'I've been painting, and I was chopping garlic for the roast, and I was drinking beer with a friend.' Ella dropped into one of the chairs. 'How does it go with the book?'

'Nearly finished. It can go to the typist tomorrow. Do you want some coffee?' Debra stood up and crossed to the gas stove. Ella knew better than to offer her help, even though she gritted her teeth every time she watched Debra working with fire and boiling water. The girl was fiercely independent, utterly determined to live her life without other people's pity or assistance.

The room was laid out precisely, each item in its place where Debra could put her hand to it without hesitation. She could move confidently through her little world, doing her own housework, preparing her own food and drink, working steadily, and paying her own way.

Once a week, a driver came up from her publisher's office in Jerusalem to collect her tapes and her writing was typed out along with her other correspondence.

Weekly also she would go with Ella in the speedboat up the lake to Tiberias to do their shopping together, and each day she swam for an hour from the stone jetty. Often an old fisherman with whom she had become friendly would row down the lake to fetch her and she would go out with him, baiting her own lines and taking her turn at the oars.

Across the lawns from the jetty, in the crusader castle, there was always Ella's companionship and intelligent conversation – and here in her little cottage there was quietness and safety and work to fill the long hours. And in the night there was the chill of terrible aloneness and silent bitter tears into her solitary pillow, tears which only she knew about.

Debra placed a mug of coffee beside Ella's chair and carried her own back to her work bench.

'Now,' she said, 'you can tell me what is keeping you fidgeting around in your seat, and drumming your fingers on the arm of the chair.' She smiled towards Ella, sensing the surprise. 'You have got something to tell me, and it's killing you.'

'Yes,' Ella spoke after a moment. 'Yes, you are right, my dear.' She took a deep breath and then went on. 'He came, Debra. He came to see me, as we knew he must.'

Debra set the mug down on the table, her hand was steady and her face expressionless.

'I didn't tell him where you were.'

'How is he, Ella? How does he look?'

'He is thinner, a little thinner, I think, and paler than when I last saw him, but it suits him. He is still the most beautiful man I have ever seen.'

'His hair,' Debra asked, 'has he let it grow a little?'

'Yes, I think so. It's soft and dark and thick around his ears and curly down the back.'

Debra nodded, smiling. 'I'm glad he didn't cut it.' They were silent again, and then almost timidly Debra asked, 'What did he say? What did he want?'

'He had a message for you.'

'What was it?'

And Ella repeated it faithfully in his exact words. When she had finished, Debra turned away to face the wall above her desk.

'Please go away now, Ella. I want to be alone.'

'He asked me to give him your reply. I promised to speak to him tomorrow morning.'

'I will come to you later – but please leave me now.' And Ella saw the drop of bright liquid that slid down the smooth brown curve of her cheek.

Mountainously Ella came to her feet and moved towards the door. Behind her she heard the girl sob, but she did not turn back. She went across the stone jetty and up to the terrace. She sat before her canvas and picked up her brush and began to paint. Her strokes were broad and crude and angry.

D avid was sweating in the stiff shiny skin of his full pressure suit and he waited anxiously beside the telephone, glancing every few minutes at the crew-room clock.

He and Joe would go on high-altitude 'Red' standby at ten o'clock, in seven minutes' time, and Ella had not called him.

David's depression was thunderous and there was black anger and despair in his heart. She had promised to call before ten o'clock.

'Come on, Davey,' Joe called from the doorway and he stood up heavily and followed Joe to the electric carrier. As he took his seat beside Joe he heard it ring in the crew-room.

'Hold it,' he told the driver, and he saw Robert answer the telephone and wave through the glass panel at him.

'It's for you, Davey,' and he ran back into the crew-room.

'I'm sorry, David,' Ella's voice was scratchy and far away. 'I tried earlier but the exchange here—'

'Sure, sure,' David cut her short, his anger was still strong. 'Did you speak to her?'

'Yes, Davey. Yes, I did. I gave her your message.'

'What was her reply?' he demanded.

'There was no reply.'

'What the hell, Ella. She must have said something.'

'She said—' Ella hesitated, ' – and these are her exact words – " the dead cannot speak with the living. For David, I died a year ago."'

He held the receiver with both hands but still it shook. After a while she spoke again.

'Are you still there?'

'Yes,' he whispered, 'I'm still here.'

They were silent again, but David broke it at last.

'That's it, then,' he said.

'Yes. I'm afraid that's it, Davey.'

Joe stuck his head around the door.

'Hey, Davey. Cut it short, will you. Time to go.'

'I have to go now, Ella. Thanks for everything.'

'Goodbye, David,' she said, and even over the scratchy connection he could hear the compassion in her tone. It heightened the black anger that gripped him as he rode beside Joe to the Mirage bunker.

For the first time ever, David felt uncomfortable in the cockpit of a Mirage. He felt trapped and restless, sweating and angry, and it seemed hours between each of the fifteen-minute readiness checks.

His ground crew were playing back-gammon on the concrete floor below him, and he could see them laughing and joshing each other. It made him angrier than ever to see others happy.

'Tubby!' he barked into his microphone, and his voice was repeated by the overhead loudspeakers. The plump, serious young man, who was chief engineer for Lance squadron, climbed quickly up beside his cockpit and peered anxiously through the canopy at him.

'There is dirt on my screen,' David snapped at him. 'How the hell do you expect me to pick up a MiG when I'm looking through a screen you ate your bloody breakfast off?'

The cause of David's distress was a speck of carbon that marred the glistening perfection of his canopy. Tubby himself had supervised the polishing and buffing of it, and the carbon speck was wind-carried since then. Carefully he removed the offending spot, and lovingly he polished the place where it had been with a chamois leather.

The reprimand had been public and unfair, very unlike their top boy Davey. However, they all made allowances for 'Red' standby nerves – and spots on a canopy played hell with a pilot's nerves. Every time it caught his eye it looked exactly like a pouncing MiG.

'That's better,' David gruffed at him, fully aware that he had been grossly unfair. Tubby grinned and gave him a high sign as he climbed down.

At that moment there was a click and throb in his earphones and the distinctive voice of the Brig.

'Red standby – Go! Go!'

Under full reheat and with the driving thrust of the

afterburners hurling him aloft David called, 'Hello, Desert Flower, Bright Lance airborne and climbing.'

'Hello, David, this is the Brig. We have a contact shaping up for intrusion on our airspace. It looks like another teaser from the Syrians. They are closing our border at twenty-six thousand and should be hostile in approximately three minutes. We are going to initiate attack plan Gideon. Your new heading is 42° and I want you right down on the deck.'

David acked and immediately rotated the Mirage's nose downwards. Plan Gideon called for a low-level stalk so that the ground clutter would obscure the enemy radar and conceal their approach until such time as they were in position to storm-climb up into an attack vector above and behind the target.

They dropped to within feet of the ground, lifting and falling over the undulating hills, so low that the herds of black Persian sheep scattered beneath them as they shrieked eastwards towards the Jordan.

'Hello, Bright Lance, this is Desert Flower – we are not tracking you.' Good, thought David, then neither is the enemy. 'Target is now hostile in sector' – the Brig gave the co-ordinates – 'scan for your own contact.'

Almost immediately Joe's voice came in. 'Leader, this is Two. I have a contact.'

David dropped his eyes to his own radar screen and manipulated his scan as Joe called range and bearing. It was a dangerous distraction when flying in the sticky phase of high subsonic drag at zero feet, and his own screen was clear of contact.

They raced onwards for many more seconds before David picked up the faint luminous fuzz at the extreme range of his set.

'Contact firming. Range figures nine six nautical miles. Parallel heading and track. Altitude 25,500 feet.'

David felt the first familiar tingle and slither of his anger and hatred, like the cold of a great snake uncoiling in his belly.

'*Beseder*, Two. Lock to target and go to interception speed.'

They went supersonic and David looked up ahead at the crests of the thunderheads that reared up from the solid banks of cumulo nimbus lower down. These mountainous upthrusts of silver and pale blue were sculptured into wonderful shapes that teased the imagination – towers and turrets embattled and emblazoned, heroic human shapes standing proud or hunched in the attitude of mourning, the rearing horsemen of the chessboard, a great fleecy pack of wolves, and other animal shapes of fantasy – with the deep crevasses between them bridged in splendour by the rainbows. There were hundreds of these, great blazes of colour, that turned and followed their progress across the sky, keeping majestic station upon them. Above them, the sky was a dark unnatural blue, dappled like a Windsor grey by the thin striation of the cirrocumulus, and the sunlight poured down to shimmer upon the two speeding warplanes. As yet there was no sight of the target. It was up there somewhere amongst the cloud mountains. He looked back at his radar screen. He had taken his radar out of scan and locked it into the target, and now as they closed rapidly he could appraise their relative positions.

The target was flying parallel to them, twenty miles out on their starboard side, and it was high above them and moving at a little more than half their speed. The sun was beyond the target, just short of its zenith, and David calculated his approach path to bring him into an attack vector from above and into the target's starboard quarter.

'Turning to starboard now,' he warned Joe, and they came around together, crossing the target's rear to put themselves in the sun. Joe was calling the range and bearing, it showed a leisurely patrol pattern. There was no indication as yet that the target was aware of the hunters behind and far below.

'Two, this is Leader. Arm your circuits.'

Without taking his eyes from the radar screen, David pressed the master switch on his weapon console. He activated the two air-to-air Sidewinder missiles that hung under each wing-tip, and immediately heard the soft electronic tone cycling in his earphones. That tone indicated that the missiles were dormant, they had not yet detected an infra-red source to excite them. When they did they would increase the volume and rate of cycle, growling with anticipation, clamouring like hunting dogs on the leash. He turned them down so he could no longer hear them.

Now he selected his cannon switch, readying the twin 30-mm weapons in their pods just below his seat. The trigger flicked forward out of its recess in the head of the joystick and he curled his forefinger about it to familiarize himself with the feel of it.

'Two, this is Leader. I am commencing visual.' It was a warning to Joe to concentrate all his attention on the screen and feed David with directional data.

'Target is now ten o'clock high, range figures two seven nautical miles.'

David searched carefully, raking the billowing walls of blinding white, breaking off the search to look away at a ground point or a pinnacle of cloud to prevent his eyes focusing short, and to sweep the blind spot behind them, lest the hunters become the hunted.

Then he saw them. There were five of them, and they appeared suddenly out of cloud high above and were immediately outlined against it like tiny black fleas on a newly ironed bedsheet. Just then Joe called the range again.

'Figures one three nautical miles,' but the targets were outlined so crisply against their background that David could make out the delta-winged dart shape, and the high tailplane that identified them beyond all doubt as MiG 21 J.

'I have target visual,' he told Joe. 'Five MiG 21 Js.' His tone was flat and neutral, but it was a lie, for now at last his anger had something on which to fasten, and it changed its shape and colour, it was no longer black and aching but cold and bright and keen as a rapier's blade.

'Target is still hostile,' Joe confirmed that they were within Israeli territory, but his tone was not as well guarded as David's. David could detect the huskiness in it, and knew that Joe was feeling that anger also.

It would be another fifteen seconds before they had completed their turn across the enemy's stern, and David assessed the relative positions and saw that so far it had been a perfect approach. The formation sailed on serenely, unaware of the enemy beneath their tail, creeping up in the blind spot where the forward scanning radar could not discover them and rapidly moving into a position up toward the sun. Once there, David would go to attack speed and climb steeply up into a position of superior height and tactical advantage over the enemy formation. Looking ahead now, he realized that chance had given him an added bonus; one of the huge tower blocks of cloud was perfectly placed to screen his climb into the sun. He would use it to cover his stalk, the way the Boer huntsman of Africa stalked wild buffalo from behind a herd of domestic oxen.

'Target is altering course to starboard,' Joe warned him, the MiGs were turning away, edging back towards the Syrian border. They had completed their taunting gesture, they had flaunted the colours of Islam in the face of the infidel, and were making for safety.

David felt the blade of anger in his guts burn colder, sting sharper, and with an effort of restraint he waited out the last few seconds before making his climb. The moment came and his voice was still flat and without passion as he called to Joe, 'Two, this is Leader, commencing storm-climb.'

'Two conforming.'

David eased back on the controls and they went up in a climb so vicious that it seemed to tear their bowels from their bellies.

Almost immediately, Desert Flower picked up the radar images as they emerged from the ground clutter.

'Hullo both units Bright Lance. We are now tracking you. Show friend or foe.'

Both David and Joe were lying on their backs in the thrust of storm-climb, but at the order they punched in their IFF systems. Identification Friend or Foe would show a distinctive pattern, a bright halo, around their radar images on command plot identifying them positively even while they were locked with the enemy in the close proximity of the dogfight.

'*Beseder* – we are tracking you in IFF,' said the Brig, and they went plunging into the pillar of cloud and raked upwards through it. David's eyes darted between the boulé that contained his blind-flying instruments and the radar screen on which the enemy images shone bright and with hard outline, so close now that the individual aircraft in the enemy formation stood out clearly.

'Target is increasing speed and tightening starboard turn,' Joe intoned and David compensated for the enemy's manoeuvre.

David was certain that they had not detected his approach, the turn away was coincidental. Another glance at the screen showed that he had achieved his height advantage. He was now two miles off their quarter above them, with the sun at his back. It was the ideal approach.

'Turning now into final leg of attack pattern.' He alerted Joe to his intention and they began to pitch in. The last-second strike which would send their speed rocketing as they closed.

The target centred dead ahead, and the gunsight lit up, glowing softly on the screen ahead of him. The Sidewinder missiles caught the first emanations of infra-red rays from their victims, and they began to growl softly in David's earphones.

Still blinded by thick grey cloud they raced in, and suddenly they burst out into the clear. Ahead and below them opened a deep trough of space, a valley between cloud ranges and close below them the five MiGs sparkled silvery in the sunlight, pretty and toylike, their red, white and green markings festive and gay, the clean geometrical sweeps of wing and tail nicely balanced and the shark-like mouths of the jet intakes gaping, as they sucked in air.

They were in loose V-formation, two stacked back on each flank of the leader and in the fleeting seconds that David had to study them, he had assessed them. The four wingmen were Syrians, there was an indefinable sloppiness in their flying, a looseness of control. They flew with that lack of polish and confidence of the pupil. They were soft targets, easy pickings.

However, it did not need the three red rings about the leader's fuselage to identify him as a Russian instructor. Some leery old veteran with hawk's blood in his veins, tough and canny, and dangerous as an angry black mamba.

'Engage two port targets,' David ordered Joe, reserving the MiG leader and the starboard echelon for his attack. In David's headphones the missiles were growling their anxiety, they had sniffed out the massed jet blasts below them and already they were tracking, howling their eagerness to kill.

David switched to command net. 'Hello, Desert Flower, this is Bright Lance on target and requesting strike.'

Almost instantly the voice came back, 'David, this is the Brig—' he was speaking, rapidly, urgently, ' – discontinue attack pattern. I repeat, disengage target. They are no longer hostile. Break off attack.'

Shocked by the command, David glanced down the deep valley of cloud and saw the long brown valley of the Jordan falling away behind them. They had crossed over a line on the earth and immediately their roles had changed from defender to aggressor. But they were closing the target rapidly. It was a fair bounce, they were still unaware.

'We are going to hit them,' David made the decision through the cold bright thing that burned within him and he closed command net and spoke to Joe.

'Two, this is Leader attacking.'

'Negative! I say again negative!' Joe called urgently. 'Target is no longer hostile!'

'Remember, Hannah!' David shouted into his mask. 'Conform to me!' and he curled his finger about the trigger and touched left rudder, yawing fractionally to bring the nearest MiG into the field of his sights. It seemed to balloon in size as he shrieked towards it.

There was a heart-beat of silence from Joe, and then his voice strangled and rough.

'Two conforming.'

'Kill them, Joe,' David yelled and pressed against the spring-loaded tension of the trigger. There was a soft double hiss, hardly discernible above the jet din, and from under each wing-tip the missiles unleashed, they skidded and twisted as they aligned themselves on the targets, leaving darkly etched trails of vapour across David's front, and at that moment the MiGs became aware.

At a shouted warning from their leader, the entire formation burst into its five separate parts, splintering silvery swift like a shoal of sardines before the driving charge of the barracuda.

The rearmost Syrian was slow, he had only just begun to turn away when one of the Sidewinders flicked its tail, followed his turn and united with him in an embrace of death.

The shock wave of the explosion jarred David's

machine, but the sound of it was muted as the MiG was enveloped in the greenish-tinted cloud of the strike and it shattered into fragments. A wing snapped off and went whirling high and the brief blooming flower of smoke blew swiftly past David's head.

The second missile had chosen the machine with the red ring, the formation leader, but the Russian reacted so swiftly and pulled his turn so tight that the missile slid past him in an overshoot, and it lost the scent, unable to follow the MiG around. As David hauled the Mirage round after the Russian, he saw the missile destroy itself in a burst of greenish smoke, far out across the valley of clouds.

The Russian was in a hard right-hand turn, and David followed him. Staring across the imaginary circle that separated them, he could see every detail of the enemy machine; the scarlet helmet of the pilot, the gaudy colours of its roundels, the squiggle of Arabic script that was its identification markings – even the individual rivets that stitched the polished metal skin of the MiG.

David pulled back with all his strength against his joystick, for gravity was tightening the loading of his controls, opposing his efforts to place additional stress on the Mirage lest he tear its wings off the fuselage.

Gravity had hold of David also, its insidious force sucked the blood away from his brain so that his vision dimmed, the colour of the enemy pilot's helmet faded to dull brown, and David felt himself crushed down into his seat.

About his waist and legs his G-suit tightened its coils, squeezing brutally like a hungry python, attempting to prevent the drainage of blood from his upper torso.

David tensed every muscle in his body, straining to resist the loss of blood, and he took the Mirage up in a sliding, soaring yo-yo, up the side of an imaginary barrel. Like a motor-cyclist on a wall of death he whirled aloft, trying once more for the advantage of height.

His vision narrowed, greyed out, until his field was

176

reduced to the limits of his cockpit, and he was pinned heavily to his seat, his mouth sagging open, his eyelids dragging downwards; the effort of holding his right hand on the control column was Herculean.

In the corner of his vision the stall indicator blinked its little eye at him, changing from amber to red, warning him that he was on the verge of catastrophe, courting the disaster of supersonic stall.

David filled his lungs and screamed with all his strength, his own voice echoing through the grey mist. The effort forced a little blood back to his brain and his vision cleared briefly, enough to let him see that the MiG had anticipated his yo-yo and had come up under him, sliding up the wall of death towards his unprotected flank and belly.

David had no alternative but to break out of the turn before the MiG's cannons could bear. He rolled the Mirage out, and went instantly into a tight climbing left-hander, his afterburners still thundering at full power, consuming fuel at a prodigious rate, and placing a limit upon these desperate manoeuvres.

Neatly and gracefully as a ballet dancer, the Russian followed him out of the turn and locked into his next manoeuvre. David saw him coming up into an attack position in his rear-view mirror and he rolled out again and went up and right, blacking out with the rate of turn.

Roll and turn, turn for life, David had judged the Russian fairly. He was a deadly opponent, quick and hard, anticipating each of David's turns and twists, riding always within an ace of strike. Turn, and turn again, in great winging parabolas, climbing always, turning always, vapour trails spinning out from their wing-tips in silky arabesque patterns against the hard blue of the sky.

David's arms and shoulders ached as he fought the control dampers and the weight of gravity, sickened by the drainage of blood and the adrenalin in his system. His cold battle rage turned gradually to icy despair as each of his efforts to dislodge the Russian were met and countered, and always the gaping shark's maw of the MiG hung and twisted a point off his shoulder or belly. All David's expertise, all the brilliance of his natural flying gifts were slowly being discounted by the store of combat experience upon which his enemy could draw.

At one stage, when for an instant they flew wing-tip to wing-tip, David glanced across the gap and saw the man's face. Just the eyes and forehead above the oxygen mask; the skin was pale as bone and the eyes were deeply socketed like those of a skull – and then David was turning again, turning and screaming and straining against gravity, screaming also against the first enfolding coils of fear.

He rolled half out of the turn and then, without conscious thought, reversed the roll. The Mirage shuddered with protest and his speed bled off. The Russian saw it and came down on him from high on his starboard quarter. As David pushed the stick fully forward and left he kicked on full left rudder, ducking under the blast of cannon fire, and the Mirage went down in a spiralling dive. The blood which gravity had sucked from his head was now flung upwards through his body, filling his head and his vision with bright redness, the red-out of inverted gravitational force. A vein in his nose popped under the pressure and suddenly his oxygen mask was filled with a flood of warm choking blood.

The Russian was after him, following him into the dive, lining him up for his second burst.

David screamed with the metallic salty taste of blood in his mouth and hauled back on the stick with all his strength, the nose came up and over, climbing out of the dive, and again the blood drained from his head – going from red-out to black-out in the fraction of a second and he saw the Russian following him up, drawn up by the ploy. At the top David kicked it out in a breakaway roll. It caught the Russian, he was one-hundredth of a second slow in countering and he swung giddily through David's gunsight, an almost impossible deflection shot that sluiced cannon fire wildly across the sky, spraying it like water from a garden hose. The MiG was in David's sight for perhaps one-tenth of a second, but in that time David saw a flash of light, a bright wink of it below the pilot's canopy, and then David rolled and turned out, coming around hard and finding the Russian still hanging in the circuit, but losing air space, swaying out with a feather of white vapour streaming back from below his cockpit canopy.

I've hit him, David exulted, and his fear was gone, become anger again, a fierce triumphant anger. He took the Mirage up in another soaring yo-yo and this time the MiG could not hold station on him and David flickrolled off the top and came out with the Russian centred in his gunsight.

He fired a one-second burst and saw the incendiary shells lace in and burst in quick little stabbing stars in the silver fuselage of the MiG.

The Russian came out of his turn, in a gentle dive, flying straight, no longer taking evasive action, probably dead at his controls, and David sat on his tail, and settled the pipper of his gunsight.

He fired another one-second burst and the MiG began to break up. Small unidentifiable pieces of wreckage flew back at David, but the Russian stayed with his machine.

Again David hit him with a two-second burst, and now the MiG's nose sank until she was in a vertical dive still under full power and she went down like a silver javelin. David could not follow her without tearing off his own wings. He pulled out and watched the Russian fly into the earth at a speed that must have exceeded Mach 2. He burst like a bomb in a tall tower of dust and smoke that stood for long seconds on the brown plains of Syria.

David shut down his afterburners and looked to his fuel gauges. They were all showing only a narrow strip above the empty notch, and David realized that the last screaming dive after the MiG had taken him down to an altitude of five thousand, he was over enemy territory and too low – much too low.

Expending precious fuel he came around on a westerly heading and went to interception speed, climbing swiftly out of range of flak and searching the heavens about him for sign of either Joe or the other MiGs – although he guessed that the Syrians were either with Allah in the garden of the Houris, or back home with mother by this time.

'Bright Lance Two, this is Leader. Do you read me?'

'Leader, this is Two,' Joe's voice answered him immediately. 'I have you visual. In the name of God, get out of there!'

'What is my position?'

'We are fifty miles within Syrian territory, our course for base is 250°.'

'How did you go?'

'I took out one of mine. The other one ran for it, after that I was too busy keeping an eye on you—'

David blinked his eyes and was surprised to find that sweat was pouring down his forehead from under his helmet and his mask was slick and sticky with blood from his nosebleed. His arms and shoulders still ached, and he felt drunken and light-headed from the effects of gravity and combat and his hands on the control column were shaky and weak.

'I got two,' he said, 'two of the swines – one for Debra, and one for Hannah.'

'Shut up, Davey.' Joe's voice was stiff with tension. 'Concentrate on getting out of here. You are within range of both flak and ground missiles. Light your tail – and let's go.'

'Negative,' David answered him. 'I'm low on fuel. Where are you?'

'Six o'clock high at 25,000.' As he answered, Joe sat up in his seat, leaning forward against his shoulder straps to watch the tiny wedge shape of David's machine far below. It was climbing slowly up to meet him, slowly – too slowly, and low – too low. David was vulnerable and Joe was afraid for him, frowning heavily into his face mask and searching restlessly, sweeping heaven and earth for the first hint of danger. Two minutes would see them clear, but they would be two long, slow minutes.

He almost missed the first missile. The ground crew must have allowed David to overfly their launch pad before they put it up in pursuit – for Joe picked up its vapour trail as it streaked in from behind David, closing rapidly with him.

'Missile, break left,' Joe yelled into his mask. 'Go! Go! Go!' and he saw David begin his turn instantly, steeply, side-stepping the sizzling attack of the missile.

'It's lost you!' Joe called, as the missile continued its crazy career through space, beginning to yaw from side to side as it hunted for a target and at last bursting in self-destruction.

'Keep going, Davey,' Joe encouraged him, 'but keep awake, there will be more.'

They both saw the next one leave the ground from its camouflaged vehicle. There was a nest of them on a rocky ridge above a sun-blasted plain. The Serpent slid off the rock and lifted into the sky, climbing rapidly towards David's little machine.

'Light your tail,' Joe told him, 'and wait for it!' He watched the missile boring in, converging with dazzling speed on David's Mirage.

'Break right! Go! Go! Go!' Joe yelled and David twisted violently aside. Again the Serpent slid past him, over-shooting, but this time not losing contact and coming around to attack again, its seekers locked to David's machine.

'He's still on you,' Joe was screaming now. 'Go for the sun, Davey. Try for the sun,' and the Mirage pointed its nose at the great blazing orb that burned above the mountain ranges of dark cloud. The Serpent followed him upwards, hunting him with the dreadful single-mindedness of the automaton.

'He's on to you, Davey. Flip out now! Go! Go! Go!'

David flicked the Mirage out of her vertical climb, and fell like a stone – while the Serpent fastened its attention upon the vast infra-red output from the sun and streaked on towards it, losing the Mirage.

'You've lost it. Get out, Davey, get out!' Joe pleaded with him, but for the moment the Mirage was helpless. In her desperate climb for the sun she had lost manoeuvring speed and was wallowing clumsily now. It would be many seconds before she became agile and lithe once more – and by then it would be too late – for Joe saw the third missile become airborne and dart upwards on its feather of flame and smoke aiming at David's Mirage.

Joe did not consciously realize what he was going to do until he had winged over and commenced his dive under full power. He came down with his Mach meter indicating twice the speed of sound, and he levelled across David's tail, cutting obliquely across his track under the nose of the oncoming Serpent.

The Serpent saw him with its little cyclops radar eye, and it sensed the heat of his exhausts – fresher, more tantalizing than David's, and it accepted him as an alternative target and swung away after him, leaving David to fly on unscathed.

David saw Joe's aircraft flash past his wing-tip at searing speed, and but an instant behind him followed the Serpent. It took him only a second to realize that Joe had deliberately pulled the missile off him, had accepted the attack that must surely have destroyed David.

He watched with fascinated horror as Joe pulled out of

his dive, and used his speed to climb into the sun. The missile followed him smoothly, angling upwards, overhauling Joe's Mirage with effortless ease. Joe was watching the missile in his mirror, and at the last instant he flipped out of the climb – but this time the Serpent was not deceived; as Joe dropped so it swivelled also, and as earlier David had wallowed helplessly now Joe was in the same predicament. He had taken his chance and it had not worked for him. The missile found him, and in a brusque burst of flame, Joe and his Mirage died together.

David flew on alone, his Mirage once more at manoeuvring speed and his throat dry with horror and fear and grief. He found himself talking aloud.

'Joe, no, Joe. Oh God no! You shouldn't have done it.'

Ahead of him through the gaps in the massive cloud bases he saw the Jordan.

'It should be you that's going home, Joe,' he said. 'It should be you, Joe,' and felt the hard ball of sorrow in his throat.

But the instinct of survival was still strong and David yawned and glanced back to clear his blind spot – and he saw the last missile coming in on him. It was just a small black speck far behind, with a little frill of dark smoke around it, but it was watching him hungrily with its wicked little eye.

As he saw it, he knew beyond doubt that this one was his, the one that the fates had reserved for him. The attacks he had evaded so far had worn his nerves and strained his judgement, he felt a sense of fatalistic dismay as he watched the attacking missile gaining on him; nevertheless he gathered his scattered reserves for one more supreme effort.

His eyes narrowed to slits, the sweat sliding down his face and drenching his mask, his left hand holding the throttle fully open and his right gripping the control column with the strength of despair, he judged his moment.

The missile was almost upon him and he screamed with

all his might and hurled the Mirage into the turn, but he had misjudged it by the smallest part of a second. As he turned away the missile slid past him and it was close enough to pick up the shadow of the Mirage in the photo-electric eye of its fusing device. The eye winked at him and the missile exploded.

The Mirage was in the critical attitude of its turn, and the cockpit canopy was exposed entirely to the centre of the blast. It hit the plane with a blow that sent it tumbling; like a running man tripping it went over, and it lost life and flying capability.

The canopy was penetrated by flying steel. A piece struck David's armoured seat with a clang and then it glanced off and struck his arm above the elbow, snapping the bone cleanly so that the arm dropped uselessly and hung into his lap.

An icy wind raged through the torn canopy as the Mirage hurled itself through space with suicidal force, whipping its nose through the vicious motions and flat plane of high-speed spin. David was thrown against his straps, his ribs bruised and his skin smeared from his shoulders, and the broken arm flailing agonizingly.

He tried to hold himself upright in his seat as he reached up over his head, caught hold of the handle of the ejector mechanism and hauled the blind down over his face. He expected to have the charge explode beneath his seat and hurl him free of the doomed Mirage – but nothing happened.

Desperately he released the handle and strained forward to reach the secondary firing mechanism under his seat between his feet. He wrenched it and felt despair as there was no response. The seat was not working, the blast had damaged some vital part of it. He had to fly the Mirage out of it, with one arm and very little altitude left to him. He fastened his right fist on to the moulded grip of the stick, and in the crazy fall and flutter and whirl, David began to fight for control, flying now by instinct alone, for he was badly hurt, and sky and horizon, earth and cloud spun giddily across his vision.

He was aware that he was losing height rapidly, for every time the earth swayed through his line of vision it was closer and more menacing, but doggedly he continued his attempts to roll against the direction of spin.

The earth was very close before he felt the first hint of response, and the ferocity of her gyrations abated slightly. Stick and rudder together, he tried again and the Mirage showed herself willing at last. Gently, with the touch of a lover, he wooed her and suddenly she came out and he was flying straight and level, but she was hard hit. The blast of the missile had done mortal damage, and she was heavy and sick in his hands. He could feel the rough vibration of the engine shaking her, and he guessed that the compressor had thrown a blade and was now out of balance. Within minutes or seconds she would begin to tear herself to pieces. He could not try for climbing power on her.

David looked quickly about him and realized with a shock how far he had fallen in that terrible tumble down the sky. He was only two or three hundred feet above the earth. He was not sure of his direction, but when he glanced at his doppler compass, he found with mild surprise that he was still heading in the general direction of home.

The engine vibration increased, and he could hear the shrill screech of rending metal. He wasn't going to make it home – that was certain – and there was insufficient height to jettison the canopy, release his straps and attempt to scramble out of the cockpit. There was only one course still remaining, he must fly the Mirage in.

Even as he made the decision his one good hand was busy implementing it. Holding the stick between his knees, he let down his landing gear; the nose wheel might hold him up long enough to take some of the speed off her and prevent her cartwheeling.

He looked ahead, and saw a low ridge of rocky ground and sparse green vegetation. Disaster lurked for him there – but beyond it were open fields, ploughed land, orderly blocks of orchards, neatly laid-out buildings. That in itself was cheering. Such order and industry could only mean that he had returned across the border to Israel.

David skimmed over the ridge of broken rocks, sucking in his own belly as though to lift the Mirage bodily over the hungry teeth of granite, and ahead of him lay the fields. He could see women working in one of the orchards, stopping and turning to look at him. So close that he could clearly see the expressions of surprise and apprehension on their faces.

There was a man on a blue tractor and he jumped from his seat and fell to the earth as David passed only feet above his head.

All fuel cocks closed, all switches off, master switch off – David went into the final ritual for crash-landing.

Ahead of him lay the smooth brown field, open and clear. He might just be lucky enough, it might just come off.

The Mirage was losing flying speed, her nose coming up, the airspeed needle sinking back, 200 miles per hour, 190, 180, dropping back to her stalling speed of 150.

Then suddenly David realized that the field ahead of him was latticed with deep concrete irrigation channels. They were twenty feet wide, and ten deep, a deadly hazard – enough to destroy a Centurion tank.

There was nothing David could do now to avoid their gaping jaws. He flew the Mirage in, touching down smoothly.

'Smooth as a tomcat pissing on a sheet of velvet,' he thought bitterly, aware that all his skill was unavailing now. 'Even Barney would have been proud of me.' The field was rough, but the Mirage settled to it, pitching and lurking, shaking David ruthlessly about the cockpit, but she was up on all three wheels, losing speed handily, her undercart taking the strain. However, she was still travelling at ninety miles an hour when she went into the irrigation ditch.

It snapped her undercart off like pretzel sticks and she nosed in, struck the far bank of concrete that sheered through metal like a scythe, and sent the fuselage cartwheeling across the field with David still strapped within it. The wings broke away and the body slid on across the soft earth to come to rest at last, right way up like a stranded whale.

The whole of David's left side was numb, no feeling in his arm or leg, the straps had mauled him with their rude grasp, and he was stunned and bewildered in the sudden engrossing silence.

For many seconds he sat still, unable to move or think. Then he smelled, it, the pervasive reek of Avtur jet fuel from the ruptured tanks and lines. The smell of it galvanized him with the pilot's deadly fear of fire.

With his right hand he grabbed the canopy release lever and heaved at it. He wasted ten precious seconds with it, for it was jammed solid. Then he turned his attention to the steel canopy breaker in its niche below the lever. This was a tool specially designed for this type of emergency. He lifted it, lay back in his seat and attacked the Perspex dome above his head. The stink of jet fuel was overpowering, filling the cockpit, and he could hear the little pinging and tinkling sound made by white-hot metal.

His left arm hampered him, he had no feeling or use in it. The straps bound him tightly to his seat and he had to pause in his assault upon the canopy to loosen them.

Then he began again. He tore an opening in the Perspex, the size of a hand, and as he worked to enlarge it, a ruptured fuel-pressure line somewhere in the shattered fuselage sprayed a jet of Avtur high in the air. It fell in a heavy drizzle upon the canopy like a garden sprinkler, poured down the curved sides and dribbled through the hole David was cutting. It fell into his face, icy cold on his cheeks and stinging his eyes, it drenched his shoulders and the front of his pressure suit, and David began to pray. For the first time ever in his life the words took on meaning and he felt his terror receding.

'Hear O Israel, the Lord our God, the Lord is one.'

He prayed aloud, striking up at the softly yielding Perspex and feeling the soft rain of death in his face. He tore at the opening with his hands, bringing away slabs of transparent material, but ripping his gloves and leaving his blood smearing the jagged edges of the opening.

'Blessed be His name, whose glorious kingdom is for ever—'

The opening was large enough. He hauled himself up in the seat, and found himself caught by the oxygen and radio lines attached to his helmet. He could not reach them with his crippled left arm. He stared down at the offending limb, and saw the blood welling out of the torn sleeve of the suit. There was no pain but it was twisted at a comical angle from the elbow.

'You shall love the Lord your God with all your heart—' he whispered, and with his right hand he tore loose the chin strap and let his helmet drop to the floor-boards. The Avtur soaked into the soft dark mop of his hair and ran down his neck behind his ears, and he thought about the flames of hell.

Painfully he dragged himself out through the opening in the canopy, and now not even prayer could hold off the dark hordes of terror that assaulted his soul.

'For the anger of God will kindle against you—'

Laboriously he crawled across the slippery sleek metal of the wing root and fell to the ground. He fell face down and lay for a moment, exhausted by fear and effort.

' – remember all the commands of God—'

He heard voices then as he lay with his face against the

dusty earth, and he lifted his head and saw the women from the orchard running towards him across the open field. The voices were shrill but faint and the words were in Hebrew. He knew that he was home.

Steadying himself against the shattered body of the Mirage, he came to his feet with the broken arm dangling at his side, and he tried to shout to them.

'Go back! Beware!' but his voice was a throaty croak, and they ran on towards him. Their dresses and aprons were gay spots of colour against the dry brown earth.

He pushed himself away from the aircraft and staggered to meet the running women.

'Go back!' he croaked in his own terrible distress, with the grip of his G-suit strangling his movements and the evaporating fuel cold as ice in his air and down his face.

Within the battered hull of the Mirage a puddle of Avtur had been heated by the white-hot shell of the jet compressor. Its low volatility at last was raised to flash point and a dying spark from the electronic equipment was enough to ignite it.

With a dull but awful roar, the Mirage bloomed with dark crimson flame and sooty black smoke, the wind ripped the flames outwards in great streamers and pennants that engulfed all around them, and David staggered onwards in the midsts of the roaring furnace that seemed to consume the very air.

He held his breath – if he had not, the flame would have scorched his lungs. He closed his eyes tightly against the agony and ran on blindly. His body and his limbs were protected by the fireproof pressure suit and boots and gloves – but his head was bare and soaked with jet fuel.

As he ran his head burned like a torch. His hair frizzled off in a stinking puff of flame and the skin of his scalp and neck and face were exposed. The flames burnt his ears off and most of his nose, they flayed off his skin in a blistering sheet and then they ate into the raw flesh, they burnt away his lips and exposed his teeth and part of the bone of his jaw. They ate through his eyelids and stripped the living meat from his cheeks.

David ran on through the burning air and smoke, and he did not believe that such pain was possible. It exceeded all his imaginings and swamped all the senses of his body and mind – but he knew he must not scream. The pain was a blackness and the vivid colours of flame in his tightly closed eyes, it was a roaring in his ears like all the winds of the world, and in his flesh it was the goads and whips and burning hooks of hell itself. But he knew he could not let this terrible fire enter his body and he ran on without screaming.

The women from the orchard were brought up short by the sudden forest of flame and black smoke that rose up in front of them, engulfing the squashed-insect body of the aircraft, and closing around the running figure of the pilot.

It was a solid impenetrable wall of heat and smoke that blotted out all ahead of them, and forced them to draw back, awed and horrified, before its raging hot breath. They stood in a small group, panting and wild-eyed.

Then abruptly a freak gust of wind opened the heavy oily curtains of smoke, and out of them stumbled a dreadful thing with a scorched and smoking body and a head of flame.

Blindly it came out of the smoke, one arm hanging and its feet dragging and staggering in the soft earth. They stared at this thing in horror, frozen in silence, and it came towards them.

Then a strapping girl, with a strong brown body and a man of dark hair, uttered a cry of compassion – and raced to meet him.

As she ran, she stripped off her heavy voluminous skirt of thick wool, leaving her strong brown legs bare. She reached David and she swirled the skirt over his head, smothering the flames that still ate into his flesh. The other women followed her, using their clothing to wrap him as he fell and rolled on the earth.

Only then did David begin to scream, from that lipless mouth with the exposed teeth. It was a sound that none of them would ever forget. As he screamed the eyes were open, with the lashes and brow and most of the lids burned away. The eyes were dark indigo blue in the glistening mask of wet scorched meat, and the little blood vessels, sealed by the heat, popped open and dribbled and spurted. As he screamed, the blood and lymph bubbled from the nostril holes where his nose had been, and his body writhed and heaved and convulsed as spasm after spasm of unbearable agony hit him.

The women had to hold him down to control his struggles, and to prevent him tearing with clawed fingers at the ruins of his face.

He was still screaming when the doctor from the kibbutz slashed open the sleeve of his pressure suit with a scalpel and pressed the morphine needle into the twitching, jumping muscles of his arm.

The Brig saw the last bright radar image fade from the plot and heard the young radar officer report formally, 'No further contact.' And a great silence fell on the command bunker.

They were all watching him. He stood hunched over the plot and his big bony fists were clasped at his sides. His face was stiff and expressionless, but his eyes were terrible.

It seemed that the frantic voices of his two pilots still echoed from the speakers above his head, as they called to each other in the extremes of mortal conflict.

They had all heard David's voice, hoarse with sorrow and fear.

'Joe! No, Joe! Oh God, no!' and they knew what that

meant. They had lost them both, and the Brig was still stunned by the sudden incalculable turn that the sortie had taken.

At the moment he had lost control of his fighters he had known that disaster was unavoidable – and now his son was dead. He wanted to cry out aloud, to protest against the futility of it. He closed his eyes tightly for a few seconds, and when he opened them, he was in control again.

'General alert,' he snapped. 'All squadrons to "Red" standby—' he knew they faced an international crisis. 'I want air cover over the area they went down. They may have ejected. Put up two Phantom flights and keep an umbrella over them. I want helicopters sent in immediately, with paratrooper guards and medical teams—'

Command bunker moved swiftly into general alert procedure.

'Get me the Prime Minister,' he said. He was going to have to do a lot of explaining, and he spared a few vital seconds to damn David Morgan roundly and bitterly.

T he air force doctor took one look at David's charred and scorched head and he swore softly.

'We'll be lucky to save this one.'

Loosely he swathed the head in Vaseline bandages and they hurried with David's blanket-wrapped body on the stretcher to the Bell 205 helicopter waiting in the orchard.

The Bell touched down on the helipad at Hadassah Hospital and a medical team was ready for him. One hour and fifty-three minutes after the Mirage hit the irrigation canal David had passed through the sterile lock into the special burns unit on the third floor of the hospital – into a quiet and secluded little world where everybody wore masks and long green sterile robes and the only contact with the outside world was through the double-glazed windows and even the air he breathed was scrubbed and cleaned and filtered.

However, David was enfolded in the soft dark clouds of morphine and he did not hear the quiet voices of the masked figures as they worked over him.

'It's third degree over the entire area—'

'No attempt to clean it or touch it, Sister, not until it stabilizes. I am going to spray with Epigard, and we'll go to intra-muscular Tetracycline four-hourly against infection—

'It will be two weeks before we dare touch it.'

'Very well, Doctor.'

'Oh, and Sister, fifteen milligrams of morphine six-hourly. We are going to have a lot of pain with this one.'

Pain was infinity, an endless ocean across which the wave-patterns marched relentlessly to burst up the beaches of his soul. There were times when the surf of pain ran high and each burst of it threatened to shatter his reason. Again there were times when it was low, almost gentle in its throbbing rhythm and he drifted far out upon the ocean of pain to where the morphine mists enfolded him. Then the mists parted and a brazen sun beat down upon his head, and he squirmed and writhed and cried out. His skull seemed to bloat and swell until it must burst, and the open nerve-ends screamed for surcease.

Then suddenly there was the sharply beloved sting of the needle in his flesh, and the mists closed about him once more.

'I don't like the look of this at all. Have we taken a culture, Sister?'

'Yes, Doctor.'

'What are we growing?'

'I'm afraid it's strep.'

'Yes. I thought so. I think we'll change to Cloxacillin – see if we get a better response with that.'

With the pain, David became aware of a smell. It was the smell of carrion and things long dead, the smell of vermin in dirty blankets, of vomit and excreta, and the odour of wet garbage festering in dark alleys – and at last he came to know that the smell was the rotting of his own flesh as the bacteria of Streptococcus infection attacked the exposed tissue.

They fought it with the drugs, but now the pain was underlined with the fevers of infection and the terrible burning thirsts which no amount of liquids could slake.

With the fever came the nightmares and the fantasies to plague and goad him even further beyond the limits of his endurance.

'Joe—' he cried out in his agony, 'try for the sun, Joe. Break left now – Go! Go!' And then he was sobbing from the ruined and broken mouth. 'Oh, Joe! Oh God, no! Joe.'

Until the night-sister could no longer bear it and she came hurrying with the syringe, and his screams turned into babbling and then into the low whimper and moan of the drug sleep.

'We'll start with the acriflavin dressings now, Sister.'

When they changed the dressings every forty-eight hours it was under general anaesthetic for the entire head was of raw flesh, a bland expressionless head, a head like a child's drawing, crude lines and harsh colours, hairless, earless, streaked and mottled with yellow runs and patches of soft pus and corruption.

'We are getting a response from the Cloxacillin, it's looking a lot healthier, Sister.'

The naked flesh of his eyelids had contracted, pulling back like the glistening petals of a pink rose, exposing the eyeballs to the air without respite. They had filled the eyes' sockets with a yellow ointment to soothe and moisten them, to keep out the loathsome infection that covered his head. The ointment prevented vision.

'I think we'll go for an abdominal pedicel now. Will you prep for afternoon theatre, please, Sister?'

Now it was time for the knife, and David was to learn that the pain and the knife lived together in terrible sin. They lifted a long flap of skin and flesh from his belly, leaving it still attached at one end, and they rolled it into a fat sausage, then they strapped his good arm, the one without the plaster cast, to his side and they stitched the free end of the sausage to his forearm, training it to draw its blood supply from there. Then they brought him back from theatre and left him trussed and helpless and blind with the pedicel fastened to his arm, like a remora to the belly of a shark.

'Well, we have saved both eyes.' The voice was proud, fond almost, and David looked up and saw them for the first time. They were gathered around his cot, a circle of craning heads, mouths and noses covered by surgical masks, but his vision was still smeary with ointment and distorted by the drip irrigation that had replaced it.

'Now we will go for the eyelids.'

It was the knife again, the contracted and bunched-up eyelids split and re-shaped and stitched, the knife and pain and the familiar sickly taste and stink of anaesthetic that saturated his body and seemed to exude from the very pores of his skin.

'Beautiful, really lovely – we have cleaned up the infection nicely. Now we can begin.'

The head was cleansed of its running rivers of pus, and now it was glistening and wet, bald and bright red, the colour of a cocktail cherry as granulation tissue formed. There were two gnarled and twisted flaps for ears, the double row of teeth startlingly white and perfect where the lips had been eaten away, a long white blade of exposed bone outlined the point of the jaw, the nose was a stump with the nostrils like the double muzzles of a shotgun, and only the eyes were still beautiful – dark indigo and flawlessly white between lids of shocking crimson and neatly laid back stitches.

'We'll begin at the back of the neck. Will you prep for this afternoon's theatre, please, Sister?'

It was a variation on the theme of the knife. They planed sheets of live skin from his thighs and meshed them to allow a wider spread, then they laid them over the exposed flesh, covering a little at each session, and evaluating each attempt while David lay in his cot and rode the long swells of pain.

'That one is no good. I'm afraid we will have to scrap it and try again.'

While his thighs grew a new crop of skin, they planed fresh sheets from his calves, so that each donor-site became a new source of pain.

'Lovely! An edge-to-edge take with that graft.'

Slowly the cap of skin extended up across the nape of his neck and over his scalp. The meshing of the skin grafts gave them a patterned effect, regular as the scales of a fish, and the new grafts were hard-looking and raised.

'We can move the pedicel up now.'

'This afternoon's theatre, Doctor?'

'Yes, please, Sister.'

David came to know that they operated every Thursday in the burns unit. He came to dread the Thursday morning rounds when the consultant and his staff crowded around his cot and touched and prodded and discussed the restructuring of his flesh with an impersonal candour that chilled him.

They freed the fat sausage of flesh from his belly and it dangled from his arm like some grotesque white leech, seeming to have a life of its own, drawing blood and sustenance from its grip upon his forearm.

They lifted his arm and strapped it across his chest, and

the raw end of the pedicel they split and stitched to his jaw and to the stump of his nose.

'It's taken very nicely. We will begin shaping it this afternoon. We'll have him at the head of the theatre list. Will you see to that please, Sister?'

With the living flesh that they had stolen from his belly they fashioned a crude lump of a nose, taut, narrow lips and a new covering for his jawbone.

'The oedema has settled. This afternoon I will go for the bone-graft on the jaw.'

They opened his chest and split his fourth rib laterally, robbing it of a long sliver of bone, and they grafted this to the damaged jaw-bone, then they spread the flesh of the pedicel over it and stitched it all into place.

On Thursdays it was the knife and the stink of anaesthetic, and for the days in between it was the ache and pain of abused and healing flesh.

They fined down the new nose, piercing it with nostrils, they finished the reconstruction of his eyelids. They laid the last grafts behind his ears, they cut a double zig-zag incision around the base of his jaw where the contracting scar tissue was trying to draw his chin down on to his chest. The new lips took firm hold on the existing muscles and David gained control of them so he could form his words again and speak clearly.

The last area of raw flesh was closed beneath the patchwork of skin grafts, flesh grafts and stitches. David was no longer a high-infection risk and he was moved from a sterile environment. Once again he saw human faces, not merely eyes peering over white surgical masks. The faces were friendly, cheerful faces. Men and women proud of their achievement in saving him from death and refleshing his ravaged head.

'You'll be allowed visitors now, and I expect you'll welcome that,' said the consultant. He was a distinguished-looking young surgeon who had left a highly paid post at a Swiss clinic to head this burns and plastic surgery unit.

'I don't think I will be having any visitors,' David had lost contact with the reality of the outside world during the nine months in the burns unit.

'Oh, yes, you will,' the surgeon told him. 'We've had regular enquiries on your progress from a number of people. Isn't that correct, Sister?'

'That's right, Doctor.'

'You can let them know that he is allowed visitors now.'

The consultant and his group began to move on.

'Doctor,' David called him back. 'I want a look at a mirror,' and they were all silent, immediately embarrassed. This request of his had been denied many times over the last months.

'Damn it,' David became angry. 'You can't protect me from it for ever.'

The consultant gestured for the others to leave and they filed out of the ward, while he came back to David's bed.

'All right, David,' he agreed gently. 'We'll find you a mirror – though we don't have much use for them around here.' For the first time in the many months he had known him, David glimpsed the depths of his compassion, and he wondered at it. That a man who lived constantly amongst great pain and terrible disfigurement could still be moved by it.

'You must understand that how you are now is not how you will always be. All I have been able to do, so far, is heal your exposed flesh and make you functional again. You are once more a viable human being. You have not experienced the loss of any of your faculties – but I will not pretend that you are beautiful. However, there remains much that I can still do to change that. Your ears, for example, can be reconstructed with the material I have reserved for that purpose—' He indicated the stump of the pedicel that still hung from David's forearm. ' – There is much fine work still to be done about the nose and mouth and eyes.' He paced slowly the length of the ward and looked out into the sunlight for a moment before turning back again and coming forward to face David.

'But let me be truthful with you. There are limitations to what I can do. The muscles of expression, those delicate little muscles around the eyes and mouth, have been destroyed. I cannot replace those. The hair follicles of your lashes and brows and scalp have been burned away. You will be able to wear a wig, but—'

David turned to his bedside locker and took from the drawer his wallet. He opened it and drew out a photograph. It was the one which Hannah had taken so long ago of Debra and David sitting at the rock-pool in the oasis of Ein Gedi and smiling at each other. He handed it to the surgeon.

'Is that what you looked like, David? I never knew.' The regret showed like a quick shadow in his eyes.

'Can you make me look like that again?'

The surgeon studied the photograph a moment longer, the young god's face with the dark mop of hair and the clean pure lines of the profile.

'No,' he said. 'I could not even come close.'

'That's all I wanted to know.' David took the photograph back from him. 'You say I'm functional now. Let's leave it at that, shall we?'

'You don't want further cosmetic surgery? We can still do a lot—'

'Doctor, I've lived under the knife for nine months. I've had the taste of antibiotics and anaesthetic in my mouth, and the stink of it in my nostrils for all that time. Now all I want is a little escape from pain – a little peace and the taste of clean air.'

'Very well,' the surgeon agreed readily. 'It is not important that we do it now. You could come back at any time in the future.' He walked to the door of the ward. 'Come on. Let's go find a mirror.'

There was one in the nurses' room beyond the double doors at the end of the passage. The room itself was empty and the mirror was set into the wall above the wash basin.

The surgeon stood in the doorway and leaned against the jamb. He lit a cigarette and watched as David crossed towards the mirror and then halted abruptly as he saw his own image.

He wore the blue hospital dressing-gown over his pyjamas. He was tall and finely proportioned. His shoulders were wide, his hips narrow, and he had the same lithe and beautiful man's body.

However, the head that topped it was something from a nightmare. Involuntarily he gasped out aloud and the gash of a mouth parted in sympathy. It was a tight lipless mouth, like that of a cobra, white-rimmed and harsh.

Drawn by the awful fascination of the horror, David drew closer to the mirror. The thick mane of his dark hair had concealed the peculiar elongation of his skull. He had never realized that it jutted out behind like that, for now the hair was gone and the bald curve was covered with meshed skin, thickened and raised.

The skin and flesh of his face was a patchwork, joined by seams of scar tissue drawn tightly over his cheekbones, giving him a vaguely Asiatic appearance, but the eyes were round and startled, with clumsy lids and puffed dead-looking flesh beneath.

His nose was a shapeless blob, out of balance with his other coarsened features, and his ears were gnarled excrescences, seemingly fastened haphazardly to the sides of his head. The whole of it was bland and bald and boiled-looking.

The gash of a mouth twisted briefly in a horrid rictus, and then regained its frozen shape.

'I can't smile,' said David.

'No,' agreed the surgeon. 'You will have no control of your expressions.'

That was the truly horrifying aspect of it. It was not the twisted and tortured flesh, with the scarring and stitch marks still so evident – it was the expressionlessness of this mask. The frozen features seemed long dead, incapable of human warmth or feeling.

'Yeah! But you should have seen the other guy!' David said softly, and the surgeon chuckled without mirth.

'We'll have those last few stitches behind your ears out tomorrow – I shall remove what remains of the pedicel from your arm – and then you can be discharged. Come back to us when you are ready.'

David ran his hand gingerly over the bald patterned skull.

'I'm going to save a fortune in haircuts and razor blades,' he said, and the surgeon turned quickly away and walked down the passage, leaving David to get to know his new head.

The clothes that they had found for him were cheap and ill-fitting – slacks and open-neck shirt, a light jacket and sandals – and he asked for some head covering, anything to conceal the weird new shape of his scalp. One of the nurses found him a cloth cap, and then told him that a visitor was waiting for him in the hospital superintendent's department.

He was a major from the military provost marshal's office, a lean grey-haired man with cold grey eyes and a tight hard mouth. He introduced himself without offering to shake hands and then opened the file on the desk in front of him.

'I have been instructed by my office to ask for the formal resignation of your commission in the Israeli Air Force,' he started, and David stared at him. In the long pain-filled, fever-hot nights, the thought of flying once more had seemed like a prospect of paradise.

'I don't understand,' he mumbled, and reached for a cigarette, breaking the first match and then puffing quickly as the second flared. 'You want my resignation – and if I refuse?'

'Then we shall have no alternative other than to convene a court martial and to try you for dereliction of duty, and refusing in the face of the enemy to obey the lawful orders of your superior officer.'

'I see,' David nodded heavily, and drew on the cigarette. The smoke stung his eyes.

'It doesn't seem I have any choice.'

'I have prepared the necessary documents. Please sign here, and here, and I shall sign as witness.'

David bowed over the papers and signed. The pen scratched loudly in the silent room.

'Thank you.' The major gathered his papers, and placed them in his briefcase. He nodded at David and started for the door.

'So now I am an outcast,' said David softly, and the man stopped. They stared at each other for a moment, and then the major's expression altered slightly, and the cold grey eyes became ferocious.

'You are responsible for the destruction of two warplanes that are irreplaceable and whose loss has caused us incalculable harm. You are responsible for the death of a brother officer, and for bringing your country to the very brink of open war which would have cost many thousands more of our young people's lives – and possibly our very existence. You have embarrassed our international friends – and given strength to our enemies.' He paused and drew a deep breath. 'The recommendation of my office was that you be brought to trial and that the prosecution be instructed to ask for the death penalty. It was only the personal intervention of the Prime Minister and of Major-General Mordecai that saved you from that. In my view, instead of bemoaning your fate, you should consider yourself highly fortunate.'

He turned away and his footsteps cracked on the stone floor as he strode from the room.

In the bleak impersonal lobby of the hospital, David was suddenly struck by a reluctance to walk on out into the spring sunshine through the glass swing doors. He had heard that long-term prisoners felt this way when the time came for their release.

Before he reached the doors he turned aside and went down to the hospital synagogue. In a corner of the quiet square hall he sat for a long time. The stained-glass windows, set high in the nave, filled the air with shafts of coloured lights when the sun came through, and a little of the peace and beauty of that place stayed with him and gave him courage when at last he walked out into the square and boarded a bus for Jerusalem.

He found a seat at the rear, and beside a window. The bus pulled away and ground slowly up the hill towards the city.

He became aware that he was being watched, and he lifted his head to find that a woman with two young children had taken the seat in front of him. She was a poorly dressed, harassed-looking woman, prematurely aged and she held the grubby young infant on her lap and fed it from the plastic bottle. However, the second child was an angelic little girl of four or five years. She had huge dark eyes and a head of thick curls. She stood on the seat facing backwards, with one thumb thrust deeply into her mouth. She was watching David steadily over the back of the seat, studying his face with that total absorption and candour of the child. David felt a sudden warmth of emotion for the child, a longing for the comfort of human contact, of which he had been deprived all these months.

He leaned forward in his seat, trying to smile, reaching out a gentle hand to touch the child's arm.

She removed her thumb from her mouth and shrank away from him, turning to her mother and clinging to her arm, hiding her face in the woman's blouse.

At the next stop David stepped down from the bus and left the road to climb the stony hillside.

The day was warm and drowsy, with the bee murmur and the smell of the blossoms from the peach orchards. He climbed the terraces and rested at the crest, for he found he was breathless and shaky. Months in hospital had left him unaccustomed to walking far, but it was not that alone. The episode with the child had distressed him terribly.

He looked longingly towards the sky. It was clear and brilliant blue, with high silver cloud in the north. He wished he could ascend beyond those clouds. He knew he would find peace up there.

A taxi dropped him off at the top of Malik Street. The front door was unlocked, swinging open before he could fit his key in the lock.

Puzzled and alarmed he stepped into the living-room. It was as he had left it so many months before, but somebody had cleaned and swept, and there were fresh flowers in a vase upon the olive-wood table – a huge bouquet of gaily coloured dahlias, yellow and scarlet.

David smelled food, hot and spicy and tantalizing after the bland hospital fare.

'Hello,' he called. 'Who is there?'

'Welcome home!' There was a familiar bellow from behind the closed bathroom door. 'I didn't expect you so soon – and you've caught me with my skirts up and pants down.'

There was a scuffling sound and then the toilet flushed thunderously and the door was flung open. Ella Kadesh appeared majestically through it. She wore one of her huge kaftans, it was a blaze of primary colours. Her hat was apple-green in colour, the brim pinned up at the side like an Australian bush hat by an enormous jade brooch and a bunch of ostrich feathers.

Her heavy arms were flung wide in a gesture of welcome, and the face was split in a huge grin of anticipation. She came towards him, and the grin persisted long after the horror had dawned in her bright little eyes. Her steps slowed.

'David?' Her voice was uncertain. 'It is you, David?'

'Hello, Ella.'

'Oh God. Oh, sweet holy name of God. What have they done to you, my beautiful young Mars—'

'Listen, you old bag,' he said sharply, 'if you start blubbering I'm going to throw you down the steps.'

She made a huge effort to control it, fighting back the tears that flooded into her eyes, but her jowls wobbled and her voice was thick and nasal as she enfolded him in her huge arms and hugged him to her bosom.

'I've got a case of cold beers in the refrigerator – and I made a pot of curry for us. You'll love my curry, it's the thing I do best—'

David ate with enormous appetite, washing down the fiery food with cold beer, and he listened to Ella talk. She spouted words like a fountain, using their flow to cover her pity and embarrassment.

'They would not let me visit you, but I telephoned every week and kept in touch that way. The sister and I got very friendly, she let me know you were coming today. So I drove up to make sure you had a welcome—'

She tried to avoid looking directly at his face, but when she did the shadows appeared in her eyes, even though she made a convincing effort at gaiety. When he finished eating at last, she asked, 'What will you do now, David?'

'I would have liked to go back and fly. It's the thing I like to do best – but they have forced me to resign my commission. I disobeyed orders, Joe and I followed them across the border, and they don't want me any more.'

'There was nearly open war, David. It was a crazy thing that you and Joe did.'

David nodded. 'I was mad. I wasn't thinking straight – after Debra—'

Ellen interrupted quickly. 'Yes, I know. Share another beer?'

David nodded distractedly. 'How is she, Ella?' It was the question he had wanted to ask all along.

'She is just fine, Davey. She has begun the new book, and if anything it's better than the first. I think she will become a very important writer—'

'Her eyes? Is there any improvement?'

Ella shook her head. 'She had come to terms with that now. It doesn't seem to bother her any longer, just as you will come to accept what has happened—'

David was not listening. 'Ella, in all that time, when I was in hospital, every day I hoped – I knew it was useless, but I hoped to hear from her. A card, a word—'

'She didn't know, Davey.'

'Didn't know?' David demanded and leaned across the table to grip Ella's wrist. 'What do you mean?'

'After Joe – was killed, Debra's father was very angry. He believed that you were responsible.'

David nodded, the blank mask of his face concealing his guilt.

'Well, he told Debra that you had left Israel, and gone back to your home. We were all sworn to silence – and that's what Debra believes now.'

David released Ella's wrist, picked up his beer glass and sipped at the head of froth.

'You still haven't answered my question, David. What are you going to do now?'

'I don't know, Ella. I guess I'll have to think about that.'

A harsh warm wind came off the hills and ruffled the surface of the lake, darkening it to black and flecking it with white crests. The fishing boats along the curve of the shore tugged restlessly at their mooring ropes, and the fishing nets upon their drying racks billowed like bridal veils.

The wind caught Debra's hair and shook it out in a loose cloud. It pressed the silk dress she wore against her body, emphasizing the heavy roundness of her breasts and the length of her legs.

She stood on the battlements of the crusader castle, leaning both hands lightly on the head of her cane, and she stared out across the water, almost as though she could see beyond it.

Ella sat near her, on a fallen block of masonry out of the wind, but she pinned her hat down with one hand as she spoke, watching Debra's face intently to judge her reactions.

'At the time it seemed the kindest thing to do. I agreed to keep the truth from you, because I did not want you to torture yourself—'

Debra spoke sharply. 'Don't ever do that again.'

Ella made a moue of resignation and went on. 'I had no way of knowing how bad he was, they would not let me see him, and so I suppose I was a coward and let it drift.'

Debra shook her head angrily, but she remained silent. Ella wondered again that sightless eyes could contain so much expression, for Debra's emotions blazed clearly in the honey-coloured sparks as she turned her head towards Ella.

'It was not the time to distract you. Don't you see, my dear? You were adjusting so nicely – working so well on your book. I did not see that we could gain anything by telling you. I decided to co-operate with your father – and see how things turned out later.'

'Then why are you telling me all this now?' Debra

demanded. 'What has happened to change your mind – what has happened to David?'

'Yesterday at noon David was discharged from Hadassah Hospital.'

'Hospital?' Debra was puzzled. 'You don't mean he has been in hospital all this time, Ella? Nine months – it's impossible!'

'It's the truth.'

'He must have been terribly hurt,' Debra's anger had changed to concern. 'How is he, Ella? What happened? Is he healed now?'

Ella was silent a moment, and Debra took a pace towards her. 'Well?' she asked.

'David's plane flamed out and he was very badly burned about the head. He has recovered completely now. His burns have healed – but—'

Ella hesitated again, and Debra groped for her hand and found it. 'Go on, Ella! But—'

'David is no longer the most beautiful man I have ever seen.'

'I don't understand?'

'He is no longer swift and vital and – any woman who sees him now will find it difficult to be near him, let alone love him.'

Debra was listening intently, her expression rapt and her eyes soft-focused.

'He is very conscious of the way he looks now. He is searching for some place to hide, I think. He talks of wanting to fly as though it is some form of escape. He knows he is alone now, cut off from the world by the mask he wears—'

Debra's eyes had misted, and Ella made her gravelly voice gentler and she went on.

'But there is someone who will never see that mask.' Ella drew the girl closer to her. 'Somebody who remembers only the way he was before.' Debra's grip tightened on

Ella's hand, and she began to smile – it was an expression that seemed to radiate from deep within her.

'He needs you now, Debra,' Ella said softly. 'That is all there is left for him. Will you change your decision now?'

'Fetch him to me, Ella,' Debra's voice shook. 'Fetch him to me as soon as you can.'

D avid climbed the long line of stairs towards Ella's studio. It was a day of bright sunlight and he wore open sandals and light silk slacks of a bronze colour and a short-sleeved shirt with a wide V-neck. His arms were pale from lack of sun, the dark hair of his chest contrasting strongly against the soft cream – and upon his head he wore a wide-brimmed white straw hat to guard the cicatrice from the sun and to soften his face with shadow.

He paused, and he could feel the break of sweat under the shirt and the pumping of his lungs. He despised the weakness of his body and the quivering of his legs as he came out on the terrace. It was deserted, and he crossed to the shuttered doors and went into the gloom.

Ella Kadesh sitting on a Samarkand carpet in the centre of the paved floor was an astonishing sight. For she was dressed in a brief bikini costume adorned with pink roses that almost disappeared under the rolls of ponderous flesh that hung over it from belly and breast. She was in the yoga position of Padmasana, the sitting lotus, and her massive legs were twisted and entwined like mating pythons. Her hands were held before her palm to palm and her eyes were closed in meditation; upon her head her ginger wig was set four square like that of a judge.

David leaned in the doorway and before he could recover his breath he began to laugh. It began as a wheezy little chuckle, and then suddenly he was really laughing, from deep down – great gusts of it that shook his helpless body, and flogged his lungs. It was not mirth but a catharsis of the last dregs of suffering, it was the moment of accepting life again, a taking up once more of the challenge of living.

Ella must have recognized it as such, for she did not move, squatting like some cheerful Buddha on the brilliant carpet, and she opened one little eye. The effect was even more startlingly comic, and David reeled away from the door, and fell into one of the chairs.

'Your soul is a desert, David Morgan,' said Ella. 'You have no recognition of beauty, all loveliness would wither on the dung heap which—' But the rest of it was lost as she also began to giggle and the yoga pose broke down, melting like a jelly on a hot day, and she traded him hoot for hoot and bellow for bellow of laughter.

'I'm stuck,' she gasped at last. 'Help me, Davey, you oaf—' And he staggered to her, knelt and struggled to help her unlock her interwoven legs. They came apart with little creaking and popping sounds and Ella collapsed face down on the carpet groaning and giggling at the same time.

'Get out of here,' she moaned. 'Leave me to die in peace. Go and find your woman, she is down on the jetty.'

She watched him go quickly, and then she dragged herself up and went to the door. The laughter dried up and she whispered aloud, 'My two poor little crippled kittens – I wonder if I have done the right thing.' The shadows of doubt crossed her face, and then faded. 'Well, it's too damn late for worry now, Kadesh, you interfering old bag, you should have thought about that before.'

A gaudily coloured towel and beach jacket were spread upon the jetty and a transistor radio, with its volume turned high, blared out a heavy rock tune. Far out in the bay Debra was swimming alone, a steady powerful overarm crawl. Her brown arms flashed wetly in the sun at each stroke and the water churned to froth at the beat of her legs.

She stopped to tread water. Her bathing cap was plain white, and he could see that she was listening for the sound of the radio for she began to swim again, heading directly in towards the jetty.

She came out of the water, pulling off the cap and shaking out her hair. Her body was dark, sun-browned and bejewelled with drops, the muscles looked firm and hard and her tread was confident and sure as she came up the stone steps and picked up her towel.

As she dried herself David stood near and watched her avidly, seeming to devour her with his eyes, trying to make up in that first minute for all those many months. He had pictured her so clearly, and yet there was much he had forgotten. Her hair was softer, cloudier than he remembered. He had forgotten the plasticity and lustre of her skin, it was darker also than it had been before – almost the colour of her eyes – she must have spent many hours each day in the sun. Suddenly and unaffectedly she threw her towel down and adjusted the top of her brief costume, pulling open the thin fabric and cupping one fat breast in her hand to settle it more comfortably, David felt his need for her so strongly that it seemed he could not contain it all within the physical bounds of his chest. He moved slightly and the gravel crunched softly under his shoes.

Instantly the lovely head turned towards him and froze in the attitude of listening. The eyes were wide open, intelligent and expressive, they seemed to look slightly to one side of him – and David had a powerful impulse to turn and glance behind him, following their steady gaze.

211

'David?' she asked softly. 'Is that you, David?'

He tried to answer her, but his voice failed him and his reply was a small choking sound. She ran to him, swiftly and long-legged as a roused foal, with her arms reaching out and her face lighting with joy.

He caught her up, and she clung to him fiercely, almost angrily – as though she had been too long denied.

'I've missed you, David.' Her voice was fierce also. 'Oh, God, you'll never know how I have missed you,' and she pressed her mouth to the stark gash in his mask of flesh.

This was the first human being who had treated him without reserve – without pity or revulsion – in all those months, and David felt his heart swell harder and his embrace was as fierce as hers.

She broke at last, leaning back to press her hips unashamedly against his, exulting in the hard thrustingness of his arousal, proud to have evoked it – and quickly, questioningly she ran her hands over his face, feeling the new contours and the unexpected planes and angles.

She felt him begin to pull away, but she stopped him and continued her examination.

'My fingers tell me that you are still beautiful—'

'You have lying fingers,' he whispered, but she ignored his words, and pushed forward teasingly with her hips.

'And I'm getting another very powerful message from further south.' She gave a breathless little laugh. 'Come with me, please, sir.'

Holding his hand, she ran lightly up the steps, dragging him after her. He was amazed at the agility and confidence with which she negotiated the climb. She drew him into the cottage and as he looked about him, quickly taking it all in, she closed and bolted the door. Immediately the room was cool and dim and intimate.

On the bed her body was still damp and cold from the lake, but her lips were hot as she strained against him urgently. The two beautiful young bodies meshed hungrily,

212

almost as if they were attempting to find sanctuary within each other, desperately flesh sought haven within flesh, within each other's encircling arms and legs they searched for and found surcease from the loneliness and the darkness.

The physical act of love, no matter how often repeated, was insufficient for their needs; even in the intervals between they clung desperately to each other; sleeping pressed together, they groped drowsily but anxiously for each other if the movements of sleep separated them for even an instant. They talked holding hands, she reaching up to touch his face at intervals, he staring into her golden eyes. Even when she prepared their simple meals, he stood close beside or behind her so that she could sway against him and feel him there. It was as though they lived in momentary dread of being once more separated.

It was two days before they left the sanctuary of the cottage and walked together along the lake shore or swam from the jetty and lay in the warm sun. But even when Ella looked down at them from the terrace and waved, David asked, 'Shall we go up to her?'

'No,' Debra answered quickly. 'Not yet. I'm not ready to share you with anybody else yet. Just a little while more, please, David.'

And it was another three days before they climbed the path to the studio. Ella had laid on one of her gargantuan lunches, but she had invited no other guests and they were grateful to her for that.

'I thought I'd have to send down a party of stretcher-bearers to carry you up, Davey,' Ella greeted him, with a lecherous chuckle.

'Don't be crude, Ella,' Debra told her primly, flushing to a dark rose brown, and Ella let fly with one of her explosive bursts of mirth that was so contagious they must follow it.

They sat beneath the palm trees and drank wine from the earthenware jugs, and ate hugely, laughing and talking without restraint, David and Debra so involved with each other that they were not aware of Ella's shrewdly veiled appraisal.

The change in Debra was dramatic, all the coolness and reserve were gone now, the armour in which she had clad her emotions was stripped away. She was vital and eager and blooming with love.

She sat close beside David, laughing with delight at his sallies, and leaning to touch and caress him, as though to reassure herself of his presence.

Ella glanced again at David, trying to smile naturally at him, but guiltily aware of the sneaking sensation of repulsion she still felt – repulsion and aching pity – when she looked at that monstrous head. She knew that if she saw it every day for twenty years, it would still disturb her.

Debra laughed again at something David had said and turned her face to him, offering her mouth with a touching innocence.

'What a terrible thing to say,' she laughed. 'I think a gesture of contrition is called for,' and responded eagerly as the great ravaged head bent to her and the thin slit of a mouth touched hers.

It was disquieting to see the lovely dark face against that mask of ruined flesh, and yet it was also strangely moving.

'It was the right thing. For once I did the right thing,' Ella decided, watching them, and feeling a vague envy. These two were bound together completely, made strong by their separate afflictions. Before it had been a mutual itching of the flesh, a chance spark struck from two minds meeting, but now it was something that transcended that.

Ella recalled regretfully a long line of lovers stretching back to the shadowy edges of her memory, receding images which seemed unreal now. If only there had been something to bind her to one of those, if only she had been left with something more valuable than half-remembered words and faded memories of brief mountings and furtive couplings. She sighed, and they looked at her questioningly.

'A sad sound, Ella, darling,' Debra said. 'We are selfish, please forgive us.'

'Not sad, my children,' Ella denied hotly, scattering the old phantoms of her memory. 'I am happy for you. You have something very wonderful – strong and bright and wonderful. Protect it as you would your life.'

She took up her wine glass. 'I give you a toast. I give you David and Debra – and a love made invincible by suffering.' And they were serious for a moment while they drank the toast together in golden yellow wine, sitting in golden yellow sunlight, then the mood resumed and they were gay once more.

Once the first desperate demands of their bodies had been met, once they had drawn as close together as physical limits would allow, then they began a coupling of the spirit. They had never really spoken before, even when they had shared the house on Malik Street they had used only the superficial word symbols.

Now they began learning really to talk. Some nights they did not sleep but spent the fleeting hours of darkness in exploring each other's minds and bodies, and they delighted to realize that this exploration would never be completed – for the areas of their minds were boundless.

During the day the blind girl taught David to see. He found that he had never truly used his eyes before, and now that he must see for both of them he had to learn to make the fullest use of his sight. He must learn to describe colour and shape and movement accurately and incisively, for Debra's demands were insatiable.

In turn, David, whose own confidence had been shattered by his disfigurement, taught confidence to the girl. She learned to trust him implicitly as he grew to anticipate her needs. She learned to step out boldly beside him, knowing that he would guide or caution her with a light touch or a word. Her world had shrunk to the small area about the cottage and the jetty within which she could find her way surely. Now with David beside her, her frontiers fell back and she was free to move wherever she chose.

Yet they ventured out together only cautiously at first, wandering along the lakeside together or climbing the hills towards Nazareth, and each day they swam in the green lake waters and each night they made love in the curtained alcove.

David grew hard and lean and sun-tanned again, and it seemed they were complete for when Ella asked, 'Debra, when are you going to make a start on the new book?' she laughed and answered lightly:

'Sometime within the next hundred years.'

A week later she asked of David this time.

'Have you decided what you are going to do yet, Davey?'

'Just what I'm doing now,' he said, and Debra backed him up quickly. 'For ever!' she said. 'Just like this for ever.'

Then without thinking about it, without really steeling themselves to it, they went to where they would meet other people in the mass.

David borrowed the speedboat, picked up a shopping list from Ella, and they planed down along the lake shore to Tiberias, with the white wake churning out behind them and the wind and drops of spray in their faces.

They moored in the tiny harbour of the marina at Lido Beach and walked up into the town. David was so engrossed with Debra that the crowds around him were unreal, and although he noticed a few curious glances they meant very little to him.

Although it was early in the season, the town was filled with visitors, and the buses were parked in the square at the foot of the hill and along the lake front, for this was full on the tourist route.

David carried a plastic bag that grew steadily heavier until it was ready to overflow.

'Bread, and that's the lot,' Debra mentally ticked off the list.

They went down the hill under the eucalyptus trees and found a table on the harbour wall, beneath the gaily coloured umbrella.

They sat touching each other and drank cold beer and ate pistachio nuts, oblivious of everything and everybody about them even though the other tables were crowded with tourists. The lake sparkled and the softly rounded hills seemed very close in the bright light. Once a flight of Phantoms went booming down the valley, flying low on some mysterious errand, and David watched them dwindle southward without regrets.

When the sun was low they went to where the speedboat was moored, and David handed Debra down into it. On the wall above them sat a party of tourists, probably on some package pilgrimage, and they were talking animatedly – their accents were Limehouse, Golders Green and Merseyside, although the subtleties of pronunciation were lost on David.

He started the motor and pushed off from the wall, steering for the harbour mouth with Debra sitting close beside him and the motor burbling softly.

A big red-faced tourist looked down from the wall and, supposing that the motor covered his voice, nudged his wife.

'Get a look at those two, Mavis. Beauty and the beast, isn't it?'

'Cork it, Bert. They might understand.'

'Go on, luv! They only talk Yiddish or whatever.'

Debra felt David's arm go rigid under her hand, felt him begin to pull away, sensing his outrage and anger – but she gripped his forearm tightly and restrained him.

'Let's go, Davey, darling. Leave them, please.'

Even when they were alone in the safety of the cottage, David was silent and she could feel the tension in his body and the air was charged with it.

They ate the evening meal of bread and cheese and fish and figs in the same strained silence. Debra could think of nothing to say to distract him for the careless words had wounded her as deeply. Afterwards she lay unsleeping beside him. He lay on his back, not touching her, with his arms at his sides and his fists clenched. When at last she could bear it no longer, she turned to him and stroked his face, still not knowing what to say. It was David who broke the silence at last.

'I want to go away from people. We don't need people – do we?'

'No,' she whispered. 'We don't need them.'

'There is a place called Jabulani. It is deep in the African bushveld, far from the nearest town. My father bought it as a hunting lodge thirty years ago – and now it belongs to me.'

'Tell me about it.' Debra laid her head on his chest, and he began stroking her hair, relaxing as he talked.

'There is a wide plain on which grow open forests of mopani and mohobahoba, with some fat old baobabs and a few ivory palms. In the open glades the grass is yellow gold and the fronds of the ilala palms look like beggars' fingers. At the end of the plain is a line of hills, they turn blue at a distance and the peaks are shaped like the turrets of a fairy castle with tumbled blocks of granite. Between the hills rises a spring of water, a strong spring that has never dried and the water is very clear and sweet—'

'What does Jabulani mean?' Debra asked when he had described it to her.

'It means the "place of rejoicing",' David told her.

'I want to go there with you,' she said.

'What about Israel?' he asked. 'Will you not miss it?'

'No,' she shook her head. 'You see, I will take it with me – in my heart.'

Ella went up to Jerusalem with them, filling the back seat of the Mercedes. She would help Debra select the furniture they would take with them from the house and have it crated and shipped. The rest of it she would sell for them. Aaron Cohen would negotiate the sale of the house, and both David and Debra felt a chill of sadness at the thought of other people living in their home.

David left the women to it and he drove out to Ein Karem and parked the Mercedes beside the iron gate in the garden wall.

The Brig was waiting for him in that bleak and forbidding room above the courtyard. When David greeted him from the doorway he looked up coldly, and there was no relaxation of the iron features, no warmth or pity in the fierce warrior eyes.

'You come to me with the blood of my son on your hands,' he said, and David froze at the words and held his gaze. After a few moments the Brig indicated the tall-backed chair against the far wall, and David crossed stiffly to it and sat down.

'If you had suffered less, I would have made you answer for more,' said the Brig. 'But vengeance and hatred are barren things – as you have discovered.'

David dropped his eyes to the floor.

'I will not pursue them further, despite the dictates of my heart, for that is what I am condemning in you. You are a violent young man, and violence is the pleasure of fools and only the last resort of wise men. The only excuse for it is to protect what is rightfully yours – any other display of violence is abuse. You abused the power I gave you – and in doing it you killed my son, and brought my country to the verge of war.'

The Brig stood up from his desk, and he crossed to the window and looked down into the garden. They were both silent while he stroked his moustache and remembered his son.

At last the Brig sighed heavily and turned back into the room.

'Why do you come to me?' he asked.

'I wish to marry your daughter, sir.'

'You are asking me – or telling me?' the Brig demanded, and then without waiting for an answer returned to his desk and sat down. 'If you abuse this also – if you bring her pain or unhappiness, I will seek you out. Depend upon it.'

David stood up and settled the cloth cap over his gross head, pulling the brim well down.

'We would like you to be at the wedding. Debra asked that particularly – for you and her mother.'

The Brig nodded. 'You may tell her that we will be there.'

The synagogue at Jerusalem University is a gleaming white structure, shaped like the tent of a desert wanderer, with the same billowing lines.

The red-bud trees were in full bloom and the wedding party was larger than they had planned, for apart from the immediate family there were Debra's colleagues from the university, Robert and some of the other boys from the squadron, Ella Kadesh, Doctor Edelman the baby-faced eye surgeon who had worked on Debra, Aaron Cohen and a dozen others.

After the simple ceremony, they walked through the university grounds to one of the reception rooms that David had hired. It was a quiet gathering with little laughter or joking. The young pilots from David's old squadron had to leave early to return to base, and with them went any pretence of jollity.

Debra's mother was still not yet fully recovered, and the

prospect of Debra's departure reduced her to quiet grey weeping. Debra tried without success to comfort her.

Before he left, Dr Edelman drew David aside.

'Watch for any sign of atrophy in her eyes, any cloudiness, excessive redness – any complaints of pain, headaches—'

'I will watch for it.'

'Any indications, no matter how trivial – if you have any doubts, you must write to me.'

'Thank you, Doctor.'

They shook hands. 'Good luck in your new life,' said Edelman.

Through it all Debra showed iron control, but even she at last succumbed and she, her mother, and Ella Kadesh all broke down simultaneously at the departure barrier of Lod airport and hung around each other's necks, weeping bitterly.

The Brig and David stood by, stiff and awkward, trying to look as though they were not associated with the weeping trio, until the first warning broadcast gave them an excuse for a brief handshake and David took Debra's arm and drew her gently away.

They climbed the boarding ladder into the waiting Boeing without looking back. The giant aircraft took off and turned away southwards, and as always the sensation of flight soothed David; all the cares and tensions of these last few days left on the earth behind and below, he felt a new lightness of the spirit – excitement for what lay ahead.

He reached across and squeezed Debra's arm.

'Hello there, Morgan,' he said, and she turned towards him and smiled happily – blindly.

It was necessary to spend some time in Cape Town before they could escape to the sanctuary of Jabulani in the north.

David took a suite at the Mount Nelson Hotel, and from there he was able to settle the numerous issues that had piled up in his absence.

The accountants who managed his trust funds demanded ten days of his time and they spent it in the sitting-room of the suite, poring over trust documents and accounts.

In two years his income had grossly exceeded his spending, and the unused portion of his income had to be re-invested. In addition the third trust fund would soon pass to him and there were formalities to be completed.

Debra was hugely impressed by the extent of David's wealth.

'You must be almost a millionaire,' she said in a truly awed voice, for that was as rich as Debra could imagine.

'I'm not just a pretty face,' David agreed, and she was relieved that he could talk so lightly about his appearance.

Mitzi and her new husband came to visit them in their suite. However, the evening was not a success. Although Mitzi tried to act as though nothing had changed, and though she still called him 'warrior', yet it was apparent that she and her feelings had altered.

She was heavily pregnant and more shapeless than David would have thought possible. It was halfway through the evening before David realized the true reason for all the reserve. At first he thought that his disfigurement was worrying them, but after Mitzi had given a half-hour eulogy of the strides that Cecil was making at Morgan Group and the immense trust that Paul Morgan had placed in him, Cecil had asked innocently, 'Are you thinking of joining us at the Group? I'm sure we could find something useful for you to do – ha, ha!'

David could assure them quietly.

'No, thank you. You won't have to worry about me,

Cecil, old boy. You take over from Uncle Paul with my blessing.'

'Good Lord, I didn't mean that.' Cecil was shocked, but Mitzi was less devious.

'He really will be very good, warrior, and you never were interested, were you?'

After that evening they did not see the couple again, and Paul Morgan was in Europe, so David fulfilled his family obligations without much pain or suffering and he could concentrate on the preparations for the move to Jabulani.

Barney Venter spent a week with them in choosing a suitable aircraft to handle the bush airstrip and yet give David the type of performance he enjoyed. At last they decided on a twin-engined Piper Navajo, a six-seater with two big 300-hp Lycoming engines and a tricycle under-cart, and Barney walked around it with his hands on his hips.

'Well, she's no Mirage.' He kicked the landing-wheel and then checked himself and glanced quickly at David's face.

'I've had enough of Mirages,' David told him. 'They bite!'

On the last day David drove out with Debra to a farm near Paarl. The owner's wife was a dog breeder and when they went down to the kennels one of her Labrador pups walked directly to Debra and placed a cold nose on her leg as he inhaled her scent. Debra squatted and groped for his head and after fondling for a few moments she in her turn leaned forward and sniffed the pup's fur.

'He smells like old leather,' she said. 'What colour is he?'

'Black,' said David. 'Black as a Zulu.'

'That's what we'll call him,' said Debra. 'Zulu.'

'You want to choose this one?' David asked.

'No,' Debra laughed. 'He chose us.'

When they flew northwards the next morning the pup was indignant at being placed in the back seat and with a flying scrambling leap he came over Debra's shoulder and took up position in her lap, which seemed to suit them both very well.

'It looks like I have competition,' David muttered ruefully.

From the brown plateau of the high veld, the land dropped away steeply down the escarpment to the bush veld of southern Africa.

David picked up his landmark on the little village of Bush Buck Ridge and the long slim snake of the Sabi River as it twisted through the open forests of the plain. He altered course slightly northwards and within ten minutes he saw the low line of blue hills which rose abruptly out of the flat land.

'There it is, ahead of us,' David told Debra and his tone was infectious. She hugged the dog closer to her and leaned towards David.

'What does it look like?'

The hills were forested with big timber, and turreted with grey rock. At their base the bush was thick and dark. The pools glinted softly through the dark foliage. He described them to her.

'My father named them "The String of Pearls", and that's what they look like. They rise out of the run-off of rain water from the sloping ground beyond the hills. They disappear just as suddenly again into the sandy earth of the plain,' David explained as he circled the hills, slowly losing height. 'They are what give Jabulani its special character, for they provide water for all the wild life of the plain. Birds and animals are drawn from hundreds of miles to the Pearls.' He levelled out and throttled back, letting the aircraft sink lower. 'There is the homestead, white walls and thatch to keep it cool in the hot weather, deep shaded verandas and high rooms – you will love it.'

The airstrip seemed clear and safe, although the windsock hung in dirty tatters from its pole. David circled it carefully before lining up for the landing, and they taxied towards the small brick hangar set amongst the trees. David kicked on the wheel brakes and cut the engines.

'This is it,' he said.

J abulani was one of a block of estates that bounded the Kruger National Park – the most spectacular nature reserve on earth. These estates were not productive, in that they were unsuitable for the growth of crops and few of them were used for grazing of domestic animals; their immense value lay in the unspoiled bush veld and the wild life – in the peace and space upon which wealthy men placed such a premium that they would pay large fortunes for a piece of this *Lebensraum*.

When David's grandfather had purchased Jabulani he had paid a few shillings an acre, for in those days the wilderness was still intact.

It had been used as a family hunting estate down the years, and as Paul Morgan had never shown interest in the veld, it had passed to David's father and so to David.

Now the eighteen thousand acres of African bush and plain, held as freehold land, was a possession beyond price.

Yet the Morgan family had made little use of it these last fifteen years. David's father had been an enthusiastic huntsman, and with him most of David's school holidays had been spent here. However, after his father's death, the visits to Jabulani had become shorter and further apart.

It was seven years since the last visit, when he had brought up a party of brother officers from Cobra Squadron.

Then it had been immaculately run by Sam, the black overseer, butler and game ranger.

Under Sam's management there had always been fresh

crisp linen on the beds, highly polished floors, the exterior walls of the buildings had been snowy white and the thatch neat and well-tended. The deep-freeze had been well stocked with steak and the liquor cupboard filled – with every bottle accounted for.

Sam ran a tight camp, with half a dozen willing and cheerful helpers.

'Where is Sam?' was the first question David asked of the two servants who hurried down from the homestead to meet the aircraft.

'Sam gone.'

'Where to?' And the answer was the eloquent shrug of Africa. Their uniforms were dirty and needed mending, and their manners disinterested.

'Where is the Land-Rover?'

'She is dead.'

They walked up to the homestead and there David had another series of unpleasant surprises.

The buildings were dilapidated, looking forlorn and neglected under their rotting black thatch. The walls were dingy, grey-brown with the plaster falling away in patches.

The interiors were filthy with dust, and sprinkled with the droppings of the birds and reptiles that had made their homes in the thatch.

The mosquito gauze, that was intended to keep the wide verandas insect-free, was rusted through and breaking away in tatters.

The vegetable gardens were overgrown, the fences about them falling to pieces. The grounds of the homestead itself were thick with rank weed, and not only the Land-Rover had died. No single piece of machinery on the estate – water pump, toilet cistern, electricity generator, motor vehicle – was in working order.

'It's a mess, a frightful mess,' David told Debra as they sat on the front step and drank mugs of sweet tea.

Fortunately David had thought to bring emergency supplies with them.

'Oh, Davey. I am so sorry, because I like it here. It's peaceful, so quiet. I can just feel my nerves untying themselves.'

'Don't be sorry. I'm not. These old huts were built by Gramps back in the twenties – and they weren't very well built even then.' David's voice was full of a new purpose, a determination that she had not heard for so long. 'It's a fine excuse to tear the whole lot down, and build again.'

'A place of our own?' she asked.

'Yes,' said David delightedly. 'That's it. That's just it!'

They flew into Nelspruit, the nearest large town, the following day. In the week of bustle and planning that followed they forgot their greater problems. With an architect they planned the new homestead with care, taking into consideration all their special requirements – a large airy study for Debra, workshop and office for David, a kitchen laid out to make it safe and easy for a blind cook, rooms without dangerous split levels and with regular easily learned shapes, and finally a nursery section. When David described this addition Debra asked cautiously, 'You making some plans that I should know about?'

'You'll know about it, all right,' he assured her.

The guest house was to be separate and self-contained and well away from the main homestead, and the small hutment for the servants was a quarter of a mile beyond that, screened by trees and the shoulder of the rocky kopje that rose behind the homestead.

David bribed a building contractor from Nelspruit to postpone all his other work, load his workmen on four heavy trucks and bring them out to Jabulani.

They began on the main house, and while they worked, David was busy resurfacing the airstrip, repairing the water pumps and such other machinery as still had life left in it.

However, the Land-Rover and the electricity generator had to be replaced.

Within two months the new homestead was habitable, and they could move. Debra set up her tape recorders beneath the big windows overlooking the shaded front garden, where the afternoon breeze could cool the room and waft in the perfume of the frangipani and poinsettia blooms.

While David was completely absorbed in making Jabulani into a comfortable home, Debra made her own arrangements.

Swiftly she explored and mapped in her mind all her immediate surroundings. Within weeks she could move about the new house with all the confidence of a person with normal sight and she had trained the servants to replace each item of furniture in its exact position. Always Zulu, the Labrador pup, moved like a glossy black shadow beside her. Early on he had decided that Debra needed his constant care, and had made her his life's work.

Quickly he learned that it was useless staring at her or wagging his tail, to attract her attention he must whine or pant. In other respects she was also slightly feeble-minded, the only way to prevent her doing stupid things like falling down the front steps or tripping over a bucket left in the passage by a careless servant was to bump her with his shoulder, or with his nose.

She had fallen readily into a pattern of work that kept her in her workroom until noon each day, with Zulu curled at her feet.

David set up a large bird bath under the trees outside her window, so the tapes she made had as a background the chatter and warble of half a dozen varieties of wild birds. She had discovered a typist in Nelspruit who could speak Hebrew, and David took the tapes in to her whenever he flew to town for supplies and to collect the mail, and he brought each batch of typing back with him for checking.

They worked together on this task, David reading each batch of writing or correspondence aloud to her and making the alterations she asked for. He made it a habit of reading almost everything, from newspapers to novels, aloud.

'Who needs braille with you around,' Debra remarked, but it was more than just the written word she needed to hear from him. It was each facet and dimension of her new surroundings. She had never seen any of the myriad of birds that flocked to drink and bathe below her window, though she soon recognized each individual call and would pick out a stranger immediately.

'David, there's a new one, what it is? What does he look like?'

And he must describe not only its plumage, but its mannerisms and its habits. At other times he must describe to her exactly how the new buildings fitted into their surroundings, the antics of Zulu the Labrador, and supply accurate descriptions of the servants, the view from the window of her workroom – and a hundred other aspects of her new life.

In time the building was completed and the strangers left Jabulani, but it was not until the crates from Israel containing their furniture and other possessions from Malik Street arrived that Jabulani started truly to become their home.

The olive-wood table was placed under the window in the workroom.

'I haven't been able to work properly, there was something missing—' and Debra ran her fingers caressingly across the inlaid ivory and ebony top ' – until now.'

Her books were in shelves on the wall beside the table, and the leather suite in the new lounge looked very well with the animal-skin rugs and woven wool carpets.

David hung the Ella Kadesh painting above the fireplace, Debra determining the precise position for him by sense of touch.

'Are you sure it shouldn't be a sixteenth of an inch higher?' David asked seriously.

'Let's have no more lip from you, Morgan, I have to know exactly where it is.'

Then the great brass bedstead was set up in the bedroom, and covered with the ivory-coloured bedspread. Debra bounced up and down on it happily.

'Now, there is only one thing more that is missing,' she declared.

'What's that?' he asked with mock anxiety. 'Is it something important?'

'Come here.' She crooked a finger in his general direction. 'And I'll show you just how important it is.'

During the months of preparation they had not left the immediate neighbourhood of the homestead, but now quite suddenly the rush and bustle was over.

'We have eighteen thousand acres and plenty of four-footed neighbours – let's go check it all out,' David suggested.

They packed a cold lunch and the three of them climbed into the new Land-Rover with Zulu relegated to the back seat. The road led naturally down to the String of Pearls for this was the focal point of all life upon the estate.

They left the Land-Rover amongst the fever trees and went down to the ruins of the thatched summer house on the bank of the main pool.

The water aroused all Zulu's instincts and he plunged into it, paddling out into the centre with obvious enjoyment. The water was clear as air, but shaded to black in the depths.

David scratched in the muddy bank and turned out a thick pink earthworm. He threw it into the shallows and a dark shape half as long as his arm rushed silently out of the depths and swirled the surface.

'Wow!' David laughed. 'There are still a few fat ones around. We will have to bring down the rods. I used to spend days down here when I was a kid.'

The forest was filled with memories and as they wandered along the edge of the reed banks he reminisced about his childhood, until gradually he fell into silence, and she asked:

'Is something wrong, David?' She had grown that sensitive to his moods.

'There are no animals.' His tone was puzzled. 'Birds, yes. But we haven't seen a single animal, not even a duiker, since we left the homestead.' He stopped at a place that was clear of reeds, where the bank shelved gently. 'This used to be a favourite drinking place. It was busy day and night – the herds virtually lining up for a chance to drink.' He left Debra and went down to the edge, stooping to examine the ground carefully. 'No spoor even, just a few kudu and a small troop of baboon. There has not been a herd here for months, or possibly years.'

When he came back to her she asked gently, 'You are upset?'

'Jabulani without its animals is nothing,' he muttered. 'Come on, let's go and see the rest of it. There is something very odd here.'

The leisurely outing became a desperate hunt, as David scoured the thickets and the open glades, followed the dried water courses and stopped the Land-Rover to examine the sand beds for signs of life.

'Not even an impala.' He was worried and anxious. 'There used to be thousands of them. I remember herds of them, silky brown and graceful as ballet dancers, under nearly every tree.'

He turned the Land-Rover northwards, following an overgrown track through the trees.

'There is grazing here that hasn't been touched. It's lush as a cultivated garden.'

A little before noon they reached the dusty, corrugated public road that ran along the north boundary of Jabulani. The fence that followed the edge of the road was ruinous, with sagging and broken wire and many of the uprights snapped off at ground level.

'Hell, it's a mess,' David told her, as he turned through a gap in the wire on to the road, and followed the boundary for two miles until they reached the turn-off to the Jabulani homestead.

Even the signboard hanging above the stone pillars of the gateway, which David's father had fashioned in bronze and of which he had been so proud, was now dilapidated and hung askew.

'Well, there's plenty of work to keep us going,' said David with a certain relish.

Half a mile beyond the gates the road turned sharply, hedged on each side by tall grass, and standing full in the sandy track was a magnificent kudu bull, ghostly grey and striped with pale chalky lines across the deep powerful body. His head was held high, armed with the long corkscrew black horns, and his huge ears were spread in an intent listening attitude.

For only part of a second he posed like that, then, although the Land-Rover was still two hundred yards off, he exploded into a smoky blur of frantic flight. His great horns laid along his back as he fled through the open bush in a series of long, lithe bounds, disappearing so swiftly it seemed he had been only a fantasy, and David described it to Debra.

'He took off the very instant he spotted us. I remember when they were so tame around here that we had to chase them out of the vegetable garden with sticks.'

Again he swung off the main track and on to another overgrown path, on which the new growth of saplings was already thick and tall. He drove straight over them in the tough little vehicle.

'What on earth are you doing?' Debra shouted above the crash and swish of branches.

'In this country, when you run out of road, you just make your own.'

Four miles farther on, they emerged abruptly on to the fire-break track that marked the eastern boundary of Jabulani, the dividing line between them and the National Park which was larger than the entire land area of the state of Israel, five million acres of virgin wilderness, three hundred and eighty-five kilometres long and eighty wide, home of more than a million wild animals, the most important reservoir of wildlife left in Africa.

David stopped the Land-Rover, cut the engine and jumped down. After a moment of shocked and angry silence he began to swear.

'What's made you so happy?' Debra demanded.

'Look at that – just look at that!' David ranted.

'I wish I could.'

'Sorry, Debs. It's a fence. A game fence!'

It stood eight feet high and the uprights were hardwood poles thick as a man's thigh, while the mesh of the fence was heavy gauge wire. 'They have fenced us off. The National Park's people have cut us off. No wonder there are no animals.'

As they drove back to the homestead David explained to her how there had always been an open boundary with the Kruger National Park. It had suited everybody well enough, for Jabulani's sweet grazing and the perennial water of the pools helped to carry the herds through times of drought and scarcity.

'It's becoming very important to you, this business of the wild animals.' Debra had listened silently, fondling the Labrador's head, as David spoke.

'Yes, suddenly it's important. When they were here, I

guess I just took them for granted – but now they are gone it's suddenly important.'

They drove on for a mile or two without speaking and then David said with determination, 'I'm going to tell them to pull that fence down. They can't cut us off like that. I'm going to get hold of the head warden, now, right away.'

David remembered Conrad Berg from his childhood when he had been the warden in charge of the southern portion of the park, but not yet the chief. There was a body of legend about the man that had been built up over the years, and two of these stories showed clearly the type of man he was.

Caught out in a lonely area of the reserve after dark with a broken-down truck, he was walking home when he was attacked by a full-grown male lion. In the struggle he had been terribly mauled, half the flesh torn from his back and the bone of his shoulder and arm bitten through. Yet he had managed to kill the animal with a small sheath knife, stabbing it repeatedly in the throat until he hit the jugular. He had then stood up and walked five miles through the night with the hyena pack following him expectantly, waiting for him to drop.

On another occasion one of the estate owners bounding the park had poached one of Berg's lions, shooting it down half a mile inside the boundary. The poacher was a man high in government, wielding massive influence, and he had laughed at Conrad Berg.

'What are you going to do about it, my friend? Don't you like your job?'

Doggedly, ignoring the pressure from above, Berg had collected his evidence and issued a summons. The pressure had become less subtle as the court date approached, but he had never wavered. The important personage finally stood in the dock, and was convicted. He was sentenced to a thousand pounds fine or six months at hard labour.

Afterwards he had shaken Berg's hand and said to him,

'Thank you for a lesson in courage,' and perhaps this was one of the reasons Berg was now chief warden.

He stood beside his game fence where he had arranged over the telephone to meet David. He was a big man, broad and tall and beefy, with thick heavily muscled arms still scarred from the lion attack, and a red sunburned face.

He wore the suntans and slouch hat of the Park's service, with the green cloth badges on his epaulettes.

Behind him was parked his brown Chevy truck with the Park Board's emblem on the door, and two of his black game rangers seated in the back. One of them was holding a heavy rifle.

Berg stood with his clenched fists on his hips, his hat pushed back and a forbidding expression on his face. He so epitomized the truculent male animal guarding his territory that David muttered to Debra, 'Here comes trouble.'

He parked close beside the fence and he and Debra climbed down and went to the wire.

'Mr Berg. I am David Morgan. I remember you from when my father owned Jabulani. I'd like you to meet my wife.'

Berg's expression wavered. Naturally he had heard all the rumours about the new owner of Jabulani; it was a lonely isolated area and it was his job to know about these things. Yet he was unprepared for this dreadfully mutilated young man, and his blind but beautiful wife.

With an awkward gallantry Berg doffed his hat, then realized she would not see the gesture. He murmured a greeting and when David thrust his hand through the fence he shook it cautiously.

Debra and David were working as a team and they turned their combined charm upon Berg, who was a simple and direct man. Slowly his defences softened as they chatted. He admired Zulu, he also kept Labradors and it served as a talking-point while Debra unpacked a Thermos of coffee and David filled mugs for all of them.

'Isn't that Sam?' David pointed to the game ranger in the truck who held Berg's rifle.

'*Ja.*' Berg was guarded.

'He used to work on Jabulani.'

'He came to me of his own accord,' Berg explained, turning aside any implied rebuke.

'He wouldn't remember me, of course, not the way I look now. But he was a fine ranger, and the place certainly went to the bad without him to look after it,' David admitted before he went into a frontal assault. 'The other thing which has ruined us is this fence of yours.' David kicked one of the uprights.

'You don't say?' Berg swished the grounds of his coffee around the mug and flicked it out.

'Why did you do it?'

'For good reason.'

'My father had a gentleman's agreement with the Board, the boundary was open at all times. We have got water and grazing that you need.'

'With all respects to the late Mr Morgan,' Conrad Berg spoke heavily, 'I was never in favour of the open boundary.'

'Why not?'

'Your daddy was a *sportsman*.' He spat the word out, as though it were a mouthful of rotten meat. 'When my lions got to know him and learned to stay this side of the line – then he used to bring down a couple of donkeys and parade them along the boundary – to tempt them out.'

David opened his mouth to protest, and then closed it slowly. He felt the seamed scars of his face mottling and staining with a flush of shame. It was true, he remembered the donkeys and the soft wet lion skins being pegged out to dry behind the homestead.

'He never poached,' David defended him. 'He had an owner's licence and they were all shot on our land.'

'No, he never poached,' Berg admitted. 'He was too damned clever for that. He knew I would have put a rocket

236

up him that would have made him the first man on the moon.'

'So that's why you put up the fence.'

'No.'

'Why then?'

'Because for fourteen years Jabulani has been under the care of an absentee landlord who didn't give a good damn what happened to it. Old Sam here—' he motioned at the game ranger in the truck ' – did his best, but still it became a poachers' paradise. As fast as the grazing and water you boast of pulled my game out of the Park, so they were cut down by every sportsman with an itchy trigger finger. When Sam tried to do something about it, he got badly beaten up, and when that didn't stop him somebody put fire into his hut at night. They burned two of his kids to death—'

David felt his very soul quail at the thought of the flames on flesh, his cheeks itched at the memory.

'I didn't know,' he said gruffly.

'No, you were too busy making money or whatever is your particular form of pleasure.' Berg was angry. 'So at last Sam came to me and I gave him a job. Then I strung this fence.'

'There is nothing left on Jabulani – a few kudu, and a duiker or two – but otherwise it's all gone.'

'You are so right. It didn't take them long to clean it out.'

'I want it back.'

'Why?' Berg scoffed. 'So you can be a sportsman like your daddy? So you can fly your pals down from Jo'burg for the weekend to shoot the shit out of my lions?' Berg glanced at Debra, and immediately his red face flushed a deep port-wine colour. 'I'm sorry, Mrs Morgan, I did not mean to say that.'

'That's perfectly all right, Mr Berg. I think it was very expressive.'

'Thank you, ma'am.' Then he turned furiously back to David. 'Morgan's Private Safari Service, is that what you are after?'

'I would not allow a shot fired on Jabulani,' said David.

'I bet – except for the pot. That's the usual story. Except for the pot, and you've got the Battle of Waterloo being fought all over again.'

'No,' said David. 'Not even for the pot.'

'You'd eat butcher's beef?' Berg asked incredulously.

'Look here, Mr Berg. If you pull your fence out, I'll have Jabulani declared a private nature reserve—'

Berg had been about to say something, but David's declaration dried the words, and his mouth remained hanging open. He closed it slowly.

'You know what that means?' he asked at last. 'You place yourself under our jurisdiction, completely. We'd tie you up properly with a lawyer's paper and all that stuff: no owner's licence, no shooting lions because they are in a cattle area.'

'Yes. I know. I've studied the act. But there is something more. I'd undertake to fence the other three boundaries to your satisfaction, and maintain a force of private game rangers that you considered adequate – all at my own expense.'

Conrad Berg lifted his hat and scratched pensively at the long sparse grey hairs that covered his pate.

'Man,' he said mournfully, 'how can I say no to that?' Then he began to smile, the first smile of the meeting. 'It looks like you are really serious about this then.'

'My wife and I are going to be living here permanently. We don't want to live in a desert.'

'Ja,' he nodded, understanding completely that a man should feel that way. The strong revulsion that he had originally felt for the fantastic face before him was fading.

'I think the first thing we should work on is these

poachers you tell me about. Let's snatch a couple of those and make a few examples,' David went on.

Berg's big red face split into a happy grin.

'I think I'm going to enjoy having you as a neighbour,' he said, and again he thrust his hand through the fence. David winced as he felt his knuckles cracking in the huge fist.

'Won't you come to dinner with us tomorrow night? You and your wife?' Debra asked with relief.

'It will be a mighty great pleasure, ma'am.'

'I'll get out the whisky bottle,' said David.

'That's kind of you—' said Conrad Berg seriously, 'but the missus and I only drink Old Buck dry gin, with a little water.'

'I'll see to it,' said David just as seriously.

Jane Berg was slim woman of about Conrad's age. She had a dried-out face, lined and browned by the sun. Her hair was sunbleached and streaked with grey, and, as Debra remarked, she was probably the only thing in the world that Conrad was afraid of.

'I'm talking, Connie,' was enough to halt any flow of eloquence from her huge spouse, or a significant glance at her empty glass sent him with elephantine haste for a refill. Conrad had a great deal of trouble finishing any story or statement, for Jane had to correct the details during the telling, while he waited patiently for an opportunity to resume.

Debra chose the main course with care so as not to give offence, beefsteaks from the deep freeze, and Conrad ate four of them with unreserved pleasure although he spurned the wine that David served.

'That stuff is poison. Killed one of my uncles,' and stayed with Old Buck gin, even through the dessert.

Afterwards they sat about the cavernous fireplace with its logs blazing cheerfully and Conrad explained, with Jane's assistance, the problems that David would face on Jabulani.

'You get a few of the blacks from the tribal areas coming in from the north—'

'Or across the river,' Jane added.

'Or across the river, but they are no big sweat. They set wire snares mostly, and they don't kill that much—'

'But it's a terribly cruel way, the poor animals linger on for days with the wire cutting down to the bone,' Jane elaborated.

'As I was saying, once we have a few rangers busy that will stop almost immediately. It's the white poachers with modern rifles and hunting lamps—'

'Killing lamps,' Jane corrected.

' – killing lamps, that do the real damage. They finished off all your game on Jabulani in a couple of seasons.'

'Where do they come from?' David asked. His anger was rising again, the same protective anger of the shepherd that he had felt as he flew the skies of Israel.

'There is a big copper mine fifty miles north of here at Phalabora, hundreds of bored miners with a taste for venison. They would come down here and blaze away at every living thing – but now it's not worth the trip for them. Anyway they were just the amateurs, the weekend poachers.'

'Who are the professionals?'

'Where the dirt road from Jabulani meets the big national highway, about thirty miles from here—'

'At a place called Bandolier Hill,' Jane supplied the name.

' – there is a general dealer's store. It's just one of those trading posts that gets a little of the passing trade from the main road, but relies on the natives from the tribal areas. The person who owns and runs it has been there eight years now, and I have been after him all that time, but he's the craftiest bastard – I'm sorry, Mrs Morgan – I have ever run into.'

'He's the one?' David asked.

'He's the one,' Conrad nodded. 'Catch him, and half your worries are over.'

'What's his name?'

'Akkers. Johan Akkers,' Jane gave her assistance; the Old Buck was making her slightly owl-eyed, and she was having a little difficulty with her enunciation.

'How are we going to get him?' David mused. 'There isn't anything left on Jabulani to tempt him – the few kudu we have got are so wild, it wouldn't be worth the effort.'

'No, you haven't got anything to tempt him right now, but about the middle of September—'

'More like the first week in September,' Jane said firmly with strings of hair starting to hang down her temples.

' – the first week in September the marula trees down by your pools will come into fruit, and my elephants are going to visit you. The one thing they just can't resist is marula berries, and they are going to flatten my fence to get at them. Before I can repair it a lot of other game are going to follow the jumbo over to your side. You can lay any type of odds you like that our friend Akkers is oiling his guns and drooling at the mouth right this minute. He will know within an hour when the fence goes.'

'This time he may get a surprise.'

'Let's hope so.'

'I think—' David said softly ' – that we might run down to Bandolier Hill tomorrow to have a look at this gentleman.'

'One thing is for sure—' said Jane Berg indistinctly, ' – a gentleman, he is not.'

The road down to Bandolier Hill was heavily corrugated and thick with white dust that rose in a banner behind the Land-Rover and hung in the air long after they had passed. The hill was rounded and thickly timbered and stood over the main metalled highway.

The trading post was four or five hundred yards from the road junction, set back amidst a grove of mango trees with their deep green and glistening foliage. It was a type found all over Africa – an unlovely building of mud brick with a naked corrugated-iron roof, the walls plastered thickly with posters advertising goods from tea to flashlight batteries.

David parked the Land-Rover in the dusty yard beneath the raised stoep. There was a faded sign above the front steps:

'Bandolier Hill General Dealers'.

At the side of the building was parked an old green Ford one-ton truck with local licence plates. In the shade of the stoep squatted a dozen or so potential customers, African women from the tribal area, dressed in long cotton print dresses, timeless in their patience and their expressions showing no curiosity about the occupants of the Land-Rover. One of the women was suckling her infant with an enormously elongated breast that allowed the child to stand beside her and watch the newcomers without removing the puckered black nipple from his mouth.

Set in the centre of the yard was a thick straight pole, fifteen feet tall, and on top of the pole was a wooden structure like a dog kennel. David exclaimed as from the kennel emerged a big brown furry animal. It descended the pole in one swift falling action, seemingly as lightly as a bird, and the chain that was fastened to the pole at one end was, at the other, buckled about the animal's waist by a thick leather strap.

'It's one of the biggest old bull baboons I've ever seen.' Quickly he described it to Debra, as the baboon moved out to the chain's limit, and knuckled the ground as he made a leisurely circle about his pole, the chain clinking as it swung behind him. It was an arrogant display, and he ruffled out the thick mane of hair upon his shoulders. When he had completed the circle, he sat down facing the Land-Rover, in a repellently humanoid attitude, and thrust out his lower jaw as he regarded them through the small brown, close-set eyes.

'A nasty beast,' David told Debra. He would weigh ninety pounds, with a long dog-like muzzle and a jaw full of yellow fangs. After the hyena, he was the most hated animal of the veld – cunning, cruel and avaricious, all the vices of man and none of his graces. His stare was unblinking and, every few seconds, he ducked his head in a quick aggressive gesture.

While all David's attention was on the baboon, a man had come out of the store and now leaned on one of the pillars of the veranda.

'What can I do for you, Mr Morgan?' he asked in a thick accent. He was tall and spare, dressed in slightly rumpled and not entirely clean khaki slacks and open-neck shirt, with heavy boots on his feet and braces hooked into his pants, crossing his shoulders.

'How did you know my name?' David looked up at him, and saw he was of middle age with close-cropped greying hair over a domed skull. His teeth were badly fitting with bright pink plastic gums and his skin was drawn over the bones of the cheeks, and his deep-set eyes gave him a skull-like look. He grinned at David's question.

'Could only be you, scarred face and blind wife – you the new owner of Jabulani. Heard you built a new house and all set to live there now.'

The man's hands were huge, out of proportion to the rest of his rangy body, they were clearly very powerful and the lean muscles of his forearms were as tough as rope.

He slouched easily against the pillar and took from his

pocket a clasp knife and a stick of black wind-dried meat –
the jerky of North America, boucan of the Caribbean, or
the biltong of Africa – and he cut a slice as though it were
a plug of tobacco, popping it into his mouth.

'Like I asked – what can we do for you?' He chewed
noisily, his teeth squelching at each bite.

'I need nails and paint.' David climbed out of the Land-
Rover.

'Heard you did all your buying in Nelspruit.' Akkers
looked him over with a calculated insolence, studying
David's ruined face with attention. David saw that his
deep-set eyes were a muddy green in colour.

'I thought there was a law against caging or chaining
wild animals.' Akkers had roused David's resentment
almost immediately, and the needle showed in his tone.
Akkers began to grin again easily, still chewing.

'You a lawyer – are you?'

'Just asking.'

'I got a permit – you want to see it?'

David shook his head, and turned to speak to Debra in
Hebrew. Quickly he described the man.

'I think he can guess why we are here, and he's looking
for trouble.'

'I'll stay by the car,' said Debra.

'Good.' David climbed the steps to the veranda.

'What about the nails and paint?' he asked Akkers.

'Go on in,' he was still grinning. 'I got a nigger helper
behind the counter. He will look after you.'

David hesitated and then walked on into the building.
It smelled of carbolic soap and kerosene and maize meal.
The shelves were loaded with cheap groceries, patent
medicines, blankets and bolts of printed cotton cloth. From
the roof hung bunches of army surplus boots and greatcoats,
axe-heads and storm lanterns. The floor was stacked with
tin trunks, pick handles, bins of flour and maize meal and
the hundreds of other items that traditionally make up the

stock of the country dealer. David found the African assistant and began his purchase.

Outside in the sunlight Debra climbed from the Land-Rover and leaned lightly against the door. The Labrador scrambled down after her and began sniffing the concrete pillars of the veranda with interest where other dogs before him had spurted jets of yellow urine against the white-washed plaster.

'Nice dog,' said Akkers.

'Thank you.' Debra nodded politely.

Akkers glanced quickly across at his pet baboon, and his expression was suddenly cunning. A flash of understanding passed between man and animal. The baboon ducked its head again in that nervous gesture, then it rose from its haunches and drifted back to the pole. With a leap and bound it shot up the pole and disappeared into the opening of its kennel.

Akkers grinned and carefully cut another slice of the black biltong.

'You like it out at Jabulani?' he asked Debra, and at the same time he offered the scrap of dried meat to the dog.

'We are very happy there,' Debra replied stiffly, not wanting to be drawn. Zulu sniffed the proffered titbit, and his tail beat like a metronome. No dog can resist the concentrated meat smell and taste of biltong. He gulped it eagerly. Twice more Akkers fed him the scraps, and Zulu's eyes glistened and his soft silky muzzle was damp with saliva.

The waiting women in the shade of the veranda were watching with lively interest now. They had seen this happen before with a dog, and they waited expectantly. David was in the building, out of sight. Debra stood blind and unsuspecting.

Akkers cut a larger piece of the dried meat and offered it to Zulu, but when he reached for it he pulled his hand away, teasing the dog. With his taste for biltong now firmly established, Zulu tried again for the meat as it was offered. Again it was pulled away at the last moment. Zulu's black wet nose quivered with anxiety, and the soft ears were cocked.

Akkers walked down the steps with Zulu following him eagerly, and at the bottom he showed the dog the biltong once more, letting him sniff it. Then he spoke softly but urgently, 'Get it, boy,' and threw the scrap of biltong at the base of the baboon's pole. Zulu bounded forward, still slightly clumsy on his big puppy paws, into the circle of the chain where the baboon's paws had beaten the earth hard. He ran on under the pole and grubbed hungrily for the biltong in the dust.

The bull baboon came out of his kennel like a tawny grey blur and dropped the fifteen feet through the air; his limbs were spread and his jaws were open in a snarl like a great red trap, and the fangs were vicious, long and yellow and spiked. He hit the ground silently, and his muscles bunched as they absorbed the shock and hurled the long lithe body feet first at the unsuspecting pup. The baboon crashed into him, taking him on the shoulder with all the weight of his ninety pounds.

Zulu went down and over, rolling on his back with a startled yelp, but before he could find his feet or his wits, the baboon was after him.

Debra heard the pup cry, and started forward, surprised but not yet alarmed.

As he lay on his back, Zulu's belly was unprotected, sparsely covered with the silken black hair, the immature penis protruding pathetically, and the baboon went onto him in a crouching leap, pinning him with powerful furry legs as he bowed his head and buried the long yellow fangs deep into the pup's belly.

Zulu screamed in dreadful agony, and Debra screamed in sympathy and ran forward.

Akkers shot out a foot as she passed him and tripped her, sending her sprawling on her hands and knees.

'Leave it, lady,' he warned her, still grinning. 'You'll get hurt if you interfere.'

The baboon locked its long curved eye teeth into the tender belly, and then hurled the pup away from it with all the fierce strength of its four limbs. The thin wall of the stomach was ripped through, and the purple ropes of the entrails came out, hanging festooned in the baboon's jaws.

Again the disembowelled pup screamed, and Debra rolled blindly to her feet.

'David!' she cried wildly. 'David – help me!'

David came out of the building running; pausing in the doorway he took in the scene at a glance and snatched up a pick handle from the pile by the door. He jumped off the veranda, and in three quick strides he had reached the pup.

The baboon saw him coming and released Zulu. With uncanny speed, he whirled and leapt for the pole, racing upwards to perch on the roof of the kennel, his jowls red with blood, as he shrieked and jabbered, bouncing up and down with excitement and triumph.

David dropped the pick and gently lifted the crawling crippled black body. He carried Zulu to the Land-Rover and ripped his bush jacket into strips as he tried to bind up the torn belly, pushing the hanging entrails back into the hole with his fist.

'David, what is it?' Debra pleaded with him, and as he worked he explained it in a few terse Hebrew sentences.

'Get in,' he told her and she clambered into the passenger seat of the Land-Rover. He laid the injured Labrador in her lap, and ran around to the driver's seat.

Akkers was back at the doorway of his shop, standing with his thumbs hooked into his braces, and he was laughing. The false teeth clucked in the open mouth as he laughed, rocking back and forth on his heels.

On its kennel the baboons shrieked and cavorted, sharing its master's mirth.

'Hey, Mr Morgan,' Akkers giggled, 'don't forget your nails!'

David swung round to face him, his face felt tight and hot, the cicatrice that covered his cheeks and forehead were inflamed and the dark blue eyes blazed with a terrible anger. He started up the steps. His mouth was a pale hard slit, and his fists were clenched at his sides.

Akkers stepped backwards swiftly and reached behind the shop counter. He lifted out an old double-barrelled shotgun, and cocked both hammers with a sweep of his thick bony thumb.

'Self defence, Mr Morgan, with witnesses,' he giggled with sadistic relish. 'Come one step closer and we will get a look at your guts also.'

David paused at the top of the steps, and the gun – held in one huge fist – pointed at his belly.

'David, hurry – oh, please hurry,' Debra called anxiously from the Land-Rover, with the weak squirming body of the pup in her lap.

'We'll meet again.' David's anger had thickened his tongue.

'That will be fun,' said Akkers, and David turned away and ran down the steps.

Akkers watched the Land-Rover pull away and swing into the road in a cloud of dust, before he set the shotgun aside. He went out into the sunlight, and the baboon scrambled down from its pole and rushed to meet him. It jumped up on to his hip and clung to him like a child.

Akkers took a boiled sweet from his pocket and placed it tenderly between the terrible yellow fangs.

'You lovely old thing,' he chuckled, scratching the high cranium with its thick cap of grey fur and the baboon squinted up at his face with narrow brown eyes, chattering softly.

D espite the rough surface, David covered the thirty miles back to Jabulani in twenty-five minutes. He skidded the vehicle to a halt beside the hangar, and ran with the pup in his arms to the aircraft.

During the flight Debra nursed him gently in her lap, and her skirts were sodden with his dark blood. The pup had quieted, and except for an occasional whimper now lay still. Over the W/T David arranged for a car to meet them at Nelspruit airfield and forty-five minutes after take-off they had Zulu on the theatre table in the veterinary surgeon's clinic.

The veterinary surgeon worked with complete concentration for over two hours at repairing the torn entrails and suturing the layers of abdominal muscle.

The pup was so critically injured, and infection was such a real danger, that they dared not return to Jabulani until it had passed. Five days later, when they flew home with Zulu still weak and heavily strapped but out of danger, David altered his flight path to bring them in over the trading store at Bandolier Hill.

The iron roof shone like a mirror in the sun, and David felt his anger very cold and hard and determined.

'The man is a threat to us,' he said aloud. 'A real threat to each of us, and to what we are trying to build at Jabulani.'

Debra nodded her agreement, stroking the pup's head and not trusting herself to speak. Her own anger was as fierce as David's.'

'I'm going to get him,' he said softly, and he heard the Brig's voice in his memory.

'The only excuse for violence is to protect what is rightfully yours.'

He banked steeply away and lined up for his approach to the landing-strip at Jabulani.

Conrad Berg called again to sample the Old Buck gin, and to tell David that his application to have Jabulani declared a private nature reserve had been approved by the Board and that the necessary documentation would soon be ready for signature.

'Do you want me to pull the fence out now?'

'No,' David answered grimly. 'Let it stand. I don't want Akkers frightened off.'

'Ja,' Conrad agreed heavily. 'We have got to get him.' He called Zulu to him and examined the scar that was ridged and shaped like forked lightning across the pup's belly. 'The bastard,' he muttered, and then glanced guiltily at Debra. 'Sorry, Mrs Morgan.'

'I couldn't agree more, Mr Berg,' she said softly, and Zulu watched her lips attentively when she spoke – his head cocked to one side.

Like all young things, he had healed cleanly and quickly.

The marula grove that ran thickly along the base of the hills about the String of Pearls came into flower.

The boles were straight and sturdy, each crowned with a fully rounded, many-branched head of dense foliage, and the red flowers made a royal show.

Almost daily David and Debra would wander together through the groves, down the rude track to the pools, and Zulu regained his strength on these leisurely strolls which always culminated in a swim and a lusty shaking off of water droplets, usually on to the nearest bystander.

Then the green plum-shaped fruits that covered the female marulas thickly began to turn yellow as they ripened, and their yeasty smell was heavy on the warm evening breeze.

The herd came up from the Sabi, forsaking the lush reed beds for the promise of the marula harvest. They were led by two old bulls, who for forty years had made the annual pilgrimage to the String of Pearls, and there were fifteen breeding cows with calves running at heel and as many adolescents.

They moved up slowly from the south, feeding spread out, sailing like ghostly grey galleons through the open bush, overloaded bellies rumbling. Occasionally a tall tree would catch the attention of one of the bulls and he would place his forehead upon the thick trunk and, swaying rhythmically as he built up momentum, he would strain suddenly and bring it crackling and crashing down. A few mouthfuls of the tender tip leaves would satisfy him, or he might strip the bark and stuff it untidily into his mouth before moving on northwards.

When they reached Conrad Berg's fence the two bulls moved forward and examined it, standing shoulder to shoulder as though in consultation, fanning their great grey ears, and every few minutes picking up a large pinch of sand in their trunks to throw over their own backs against the worrisome attention of the stinging flies.

In forty years they had travelled, and knew exactly all the boundaries of their reserve. As they stood there contemplating the game fence, it was as though they were fully aware that its destruction would be a criminal act, and injurious to their reputations and good standing.

Conrad Berg was deadly serious when he discussed 'his' elephants' sense of right and wrong with David. He spoke of them like schoolboys who had to be placed on good behaviour, and disciplined when they transgressed. Discipline might take the form of driving, darting with drugs, or formal execution with a heavy rifle. This ultimate punishment was reserved for the incorrigibles who raided cultivated crops, chased motor-cars or otherwise endangered human life.

Sorely tempted, the two old bulls left the fence and ambled back to the breeding herd that waited patiently for their decision amongst the thorn trees. For three days the herd drifted back and forth along the fence, feeding and resting and waiting – then suddenly the wind turned westerly and it came to them laden with the thick, cloyingly sweet smell of the marula berries.

David parked the Land-Rover on the fire-break road and laughed with delight.

'So much for Connie's fence!'

For reasons of pachyderm prestige, or perhaps merely for the mischievous delight of destruction, no adult elephant would accept the breach made by another.

Each of them had selected his own fence pole, hard wood uprights embedded in concrete, and had effortlessly snapped it off level with the ground. Over a length of a mile the fence was flattened, and the wire mesh lay across the firebreak.

Each elephant had used his broken pole like a tightrope, to avoid treading on the sharp points of the barbed wire. Then once across the fence they had streamed in a tight bunch down to the pools to spend a night in feasting, an elephantine gorge on the yellow berries, which ended at dawn when they had bunched up into close order and dashed back across the ruined fence into the safety of the Park – perhaps pursued by guilt and remorse and hoping that Conrad Berg would lay the blame on some other herd.

However, the downed fence provided ready access for many others who had long hankered after the sweet untouched grazing and deep water holes.

Ugly little blue wildebeest with monstrous heads, absurdly warlike manes and curved horns in imitation of the mighty buffalo. Clowns of the bush, they capered with glee and chased each other in circles. Their companions the zebra were more dignified, ignoring their antics, and trotted in businesslike fashion down to the pools. Their rumps were striped and glossy and plump, their heads up and ears pricked.

Conrad Berg met David at the remains of his fence,

climbing out of his own truck and picking his way carefully over the wire. Sam, the African ranger, followed him.

Conrad shook his head as he surveyed the destruction, chuckling ruefully.

'It's old Mahommed and his pal One-Eye, I'd know that spoor anywhere. They just couldn't help themselves – the bastards—' He glanced quickly at Debra in the Land-Rover.

'That's perfectly all right, Mr Berg,' she forestalled his apology.

Sam had been casting back and forth along the soft break road and now he came to where they stood.

'Hello, Sam,' David greeted him. It had taken a lot of persuasion to get Sam to accept that this terribly disfigured face belonged to the young *nkosi* David who he had taught to track, and shoot and rob a wild beehive without destroying the bees.

Sam saluted David with a flourish. He took his uniform very seriously and conducted himself like a guardsman now. It was difficult to tell his age, for he had the broad smooth moonface of the Nguni – the aristocratic warrior tribes of Africa – but there was a frosting of purest white on the close-curled hair of his temples under the slouch hat, and David knew he had worked at Jabulani for forty years before leaving. The man must be approaching sixty years of age.

Quickly he made his report to Conrad, describing the animals and the numbers which had crossed into Jabulani.

'There is also a herd of buffalo, forty-three of them.' Sam spoke in simple Zulu that David could still follow. 'They are the ones who drank before Ripape Dam near Hlangulene.'

'That will bring Akkers running – the sirloin of a young buffalo makes the finest biltong there is,' Conrad observed dryly.

'How long will it be before he knows the fence is down?'

David asked, and Conrad fell into a long rapid-fire discussion with Sam that lost David after the first few sentences. However, Conrad translated at the end.

'Sam says he knows already, all your servants and their wives buy at his store and he pays them for that sort of information. It turns out that there is bad blood between Sam and Akkers. Sam suspects him of arranging to have him beaten, on a lonely road on a dark night. Sam was in hospital three months – he also accused Akkers of having his hut fired to drive him off Jabulani.'

'It adds up, doesn't it?' David agreed.

'Old Sam is dead keen to help us grab Akkers – and he has a plan of action all worked out.'

'Let's hear it.'

'Well, as long as you are in residence at Jabulani Akkers is going to restrict his activities to night poaching with a killing lamp. He knows every trick there is and we will never get him.'

'So?'

'You must tell your servants that you are leaving for two weeks, going to Cape Town on business. Akkers will know as soon as you leave and he will believe he has the whole of Jabulani to himself—' For an hour more they discussed the details of the plan, then they shook hands and parted.

As they drove back to the homestead they emerged from the open forest into one of the glades of tall grass, and David saw the brilliant white egrets floating like snowflakes over the swaying tops of golden grass.

'Something in there,' he said and cut the engine. They waited quietly until David saw the movement in the grass, the opening and closing at the passage of heavy bodies. Then three egrets, sitting in row, moved slowly towards him, borne on the back of a concealed beast as it grazed steadily forward.

'Ah, the buffalo!' David exclaimed as the first of them appeared, a great black bovine shape. It stopped as it saw the Land-Rover on the edge of the trees and it regarded them intently from beneath the wide spread of its horns, with its muzzle lifted high. It showed no alarm for these were Park animals, almost as tame as domestic cattle.

Gradually the rest of the herd emerged from the tall grass. Each in turn scrutinized the vehicle and then resumed feeding once more. There were forty-three of them, as Sam had predicted, and amongst them were some fine old bulls standing five and a half feet tall at the shoulder and weighing little less than 2,000 lb. Their horns were massively bossed, meeting in the centre of the head and curving downwards and up to blunt points, with a rugged surface that became polished black at the tips.

Crawling over their heavy trunks and thick short legs were numbers of ox-peckers, dull-plumaged birds with scarlet beaks and bright beady eyes. Sometimes head down they scavenged for the ticks and other blood-sucking body vermin in the folds of skin between the limbs. Occasionally one of the huge beasts would snort and leap, shaking and swishing its tail, as a sharp beak pried into a delicate portion of its anatomy, under the tail or around the heavy dangling black scrotum. The birds fluttered up with hissing cries, waited for the buffalo to calm down and then settled again to their scurrying and searching.

David photographed the herd until the light failed, and they drove home in the dark.

Before dinner David opened a bottle of wine and they drank it together on the stoep, sitting close and listening to the night sounds of the bush – the cries of the night birds, the tap of flying insects against the wire screen and the other secret scurrying and rustling of small animals.

'Do you remember once I told you that you were spoiled, and not very good marriage material?' Debra asked softly, nestling her dark head against his shoulder.

'I'll never forget it.'

'I'd like to withdraw that remark formally,' she went on,

and he moved her gently away so that he could study her face. Sensing his eyes upon her she smiled, that shy little smile of hers. 'I fell in love with a little boy, a spoiled little boy, who thought only of fast cars and the nearest skirt—' she said, ' – but now I have a man, a grown man,' she smiled again, 'and I like it better this way.'

He drew her back to him and kissed her, their lips melded in a lingering embrace before she sighed happily and laid her head back upon his shoulder. They were silent for a while before Debra spoke again.

'These wild animals – that mean so much to you—'

'Yes?' he encouraged her.

'I am beginning to understand. Although I have never seen them, they are becoming important to me also.'

'I'm glad.'

'David, this place of ours – it's so peaceful, so perfect. It's a little Eden before the fall.'

'We will make it so,' he promised, but in the night the gunfire woke him. He rose quickly, leaving her lying warm and quietly sleeping, and he went out on the stoop.

It came again, faintly on the still night, distance muting it to a small unwarlike popping. He felt his anger stirring again, as he imagined the long white shaft of the killing lamp, questing relentlessly through the forest until it settled suddenly upon the puzzled animal, holding it mesmerized in the beam, the blinded eyes glowing like jewels, making a perfect aiming point in the field of the telescopic rifle sight.

Then suddenly the rifle blast, shocking in the silence, and the long licking flame of the muzzle flash. The beautiful head snapping back at the punch of the bullet and the soft thump of the falling body on the hard earth, the last spasmodic kicking of hooves and again the silence.

He knew it was useless to attempt pursuit now, the gunman would have an accomplice in the hills above them ready to flash a warning if any of the homestead lights came on, or if an auto engine whirred into life. Then the killing lamp would be doused and the poacher would creep away. David would search the midnight expanse of Jabulani in vain. His quarry was cunning and experienced in his craft of killing, and would only be taken by greater cunning.

David could not sleep again. He lay awake beside Debra, and listened to her soft breathing – and at intervals to the distant rifle fire. The game was tame and easily approached, innocent after the safety of the Park. It would run only a short distance after each shot, and then it would stand again staring without comprehension at the mysterious and dazzling light that floated towards it out of the darkness.

David's anger burned on through the night, and in the dawn the vultures were up. Black specks against the pink dawn sky, they appeared in ever-increasing numbers, sailing high on wide pinions, tracing wide swinging circles before beginning to drop towards the earth.

David telephoned Conrad Berg at Skukuza Camp, then he and Debra and the dog climbed into the Land-Rover, warmly dressed against the dawn chill. They followed the descent of the birds to where the poacher had come on the buffalo herd.

As they approached the first carcass, the animal scavengers scattered – slope-backed hyena cantering away into the trees, hideous and cowardly, looking back over their misshapen shoulders, grinning apologetically – little red jackal with silvery backs and alert ears, trotting to a respectful distance before standing and staring back anxiously.

The vultures were less timid, seething like fat brown maggots over the carcass as they squawled and squabbled, fouling everything with their stinking droppings and loose feathers, leaving the kill only when the Land-Rover was very close and then flapping heavily up into the trees to crouch there grotesquely with their bald scaly heads outthrust.

There were sixteen dead buffalo, lying strung out along the line of the herd's flight. On each carcass the belly had been split open to let the vultures in, and the sirloin and fillet had been expertly removed.

'He killed them just for a few pounds of meat?' Debra asked incredulously.

'That's all,' David confirmed grimly. 'But that's not bad – sometimes they'll kill a wildebeest simply to make a fly whisk of its tail, or they'll shoot a giraffe for the marrow in its bones.'

'I don't understand,' Debra's voice was hopeless. 'What makes a man do it? He can't need the meat that badly.'

'No,' David agreed. 'It's deeper than that. This type of killing is a gut thing. This man kills for the thrill of it, he kills to see an animal fall, to hear the death cry, to smell the reek of fresh blood—' his voice choked off, 'this is one time you can be thankful you cannot see,' he said softly.

Conrad Berg found them waiting beside the corpses, and he set his rangers to work butchering the carcasses.

'No point in wasting all that meat. Food there for a lot of people.'

Then he put Sam to the spoor. There had been four men in the poaching party, one wearing light rubber-soled shoes and the others bare-footed.

'One white man, big man, long legs. Three black men, carry meat, blood drip here and here.'

They followed Sam slowly through the open forest as he patted the grass with his long thin tracking staff, and moved towards the unsurfaced public road.

'Here they walk backwards,' Sam observed, and Conrad explained grimly.

'Old poacher's trick. They walk backwards when they cross a boundary. If you cut the spoor while patrolling the fence you think they have gone the other way – leaving instead of entering – and you don't bother following them.'

The spoor went through a gap in the fence, crossed the

road and entered the tribal land beyond. It ended where a motor vehicle had been parked amongst a screening thicket of wild ebony. The tracks bumped away across the sandy earth and rejoined the public road.

'Plaster casts of the tyre tracks?' David asked.

'Waste of time.' Conrad shook his head. 'You can be sure they are changed before each expedition, he keeps this set especially and hides it when it's not in use.'

'What about spent cartridge shells?' David persisted.

Conrad laughed briefly. 'They are in his pocket, this is a fly bird. He's not going to scatter evidence all over the country. He picks up as he goes along. No – we'll have to sucker him into it.' And his manner became businesslike. 'Right, have you selected a place to stake old Sam out?'

'I thought we would put him up on one of the kopjes, near the String of Pearls. He'll be able to cover the whole estate from there, spot any dust on the road, and the height will give the two-way radio sufficient range.'

After lunch David loaded their bags into the luggage compartment of the Navajo. He paid the servants two weeks' wages in advance.

'Take good care,' he told them. 'I shall return before the end of the month.'

He parked the Land-Rover in the open hangar with the key in the ignition facing the open doorway, ready for a quick start. He took off and kept on a westerly heading, passing directly over Bandolier Hill and the buildings amongst the mango trees. They saw no sign of life, but David held his course until the hill sank from view below the horizon, then he came around on a wide circle to the south and lined up for Skukuza, the main camp of the Kruger National Park.

Conrad Berg was at the airstrip in his truck to meet the Cessna, and Jane had placed fresh flowers in the guest room. Jabulani lay fifty miles away to the north-west.

It was like squadron 'Red' standby again, with the Navajo parked under one of the big shade trees at the end of the Skukuza airstrip, and the radio set switched on, crackling faintly on the frequency tuned to that of Sam's transmitter, as he waited patiently on the hill-top above the pools.

The day was oppressively hot, with the threat of a rainstorm looming up out of the east, great cumulus thunderheads striding like giants across the bushveld.

Debra and David and Conrad Berg sat in the shade of the aircraft's wing, for it was too hot in the cockpit. They chatted in desultory fashion, but always listening to the radio crackle, and they were tense and distracted.

'He is not going to come,' said Debra a little before noon.

'He'll come,' Conrad contradicted her. 'Those buffalo are too much temptation. Perhaps not today – but tomorrow or the next day he'll come.'

David stood up and climbed in through the open door of the cabin. He went forward to the cockpit.

'Sam,' he spoke into the microphone. 'Can you hear me?'

There was a long pause, presumably while Sam struggled with radio procedure, then his voice, faint but clear: 'I hear you, *Nkosi*.'

'Have you seen anything?'

'There is nothing.'

'Keep good watch.'

'*Yebho, Nkosi*.'

Jane brought a cold picnic lunch down to the airstrip. They ate heartily despite the tension, and they were about to start on the milk tart, when suddenly the radio set throbbed and hummed. Sam's voice carried clearly to where they sat.

'He has come!'

'Red standby – Go! Go!' shouted David, and they rushed

for the cabin door, Debra treading squarely in the centre of Jane's milk tart before David grabbed her arm and guided her to her seat.

'Bright Lance, airborne and climbing.' David laughed with excitement and then memory stabbed him with a sharp blade. He remembered Joe hanging out there at six o'clock but he shut his mind to it and he banked steeply on to his heading, not wasting time in grabbing for altitude but staying right down at tree-top level.

Conrad Berg was hunched in the seat behind them, and his face was redder than usual – seeming about to burst like an over-ripe tomato.

'Where is the Land-Rover key?' he demanded anxiously.

'It's in the ignition – and the tank is full.'

'Can't you go faster?' Conrad growled.

'Have you got your walkie-talkie?' David checked him.

'Here!' It was gripped in one of his huge paws, and his double-barrelled .450 magnum was in the other.

David was hopping the taller trees, and sliding over the crests of higher ground with feet to spare. They flashed over the boundary fence and ahead of them lay the hills of Jabulani.

'Get ready,' he told Conrad, and flew the Navajo into the airstrip, taxiing up to the hangar where the Land-Rover waited.

Conrad jumped down at the instant that David braked to a halt, then he slammed the cabin door behind him and raced to the Land-Rover. Immediately David opened the throttle and swung the aircraft around, lining up for his take-off before the Navajo had gathered full momentum.

As he climbed, he saw the Land-Rover racing across the airstrip, dragging a cloak of dust behind it.

'Do you read me, Conrad?'

'Loud and clear,' Conrad's voice boomed out of the speaker, and David turned for the grey ribbon of the public road that showed through the trees, beyond the hills.

He followed it, flying five hundred feet above it, and he searched the open parkland.

The green Ford truck had been concealed from observation at ground level, again in a thicket of wild ebony, but it was open from the sky. For Akkers had never thought of discovery coming from there.

'Connie, I've got the truck. He's stashed it in a clump of ebony about half a mile down the bank of the Luzane stream. Your best route is to follow the road to the bridge, then go down into the dry river bed and try and cut him off before he gets to the truck.'

'Okay, David.'

'Move it, man.'

'I'm moving.' David saw the Land-Rover's dust above the trees, Conrad must have his foot down hard.

'I'm going to try and spot the man himself – chase him into your arms.'

'You do that!'

David started a long climbing turn towards the hills, sweeping and searching, up and around. Below him the pools glinted and he opened the throttles slightly, seeking altitude to clear the crests.

From the highest peak, a tiny figure waved frantically.

'Sam,' he grunted. 'Doing a war dance.' He altered course slightly to pass him closely, and Sam stopped his imitation of a windmill and stabbed with an extended arm towards the west. David acknowledged with a wave, and turned again, dropping down the western slopes.

Ahead of him the plain spread, dappled like a leopard's back with dark bush and golden glades of grass. He flew for a minute before he saw a black mass, moving slowly ahead of him, dark and amorphous against the pale grass. The remains of the buffalo herd had bunched up and were running without direction, desperate from the harrying they had received.

'Buffalo,' he told Debra. 'On the run. Something has alarmed them.' She sat still and intent beside him, hands in her lap, staring unseeingly ahead.

'Ah!' David shouted. 'Got him – with blood on his hands!'

In the centre of one of the larger clearings lay the black beetle-like body of a dead buffalo, its belly swollen and its legs sticking out stiffly as it lay on its side.

Four men stood around it in a circle, obviously just about to begin butchering the carcass. Three of them were Africans, one with a knife in his hand.

The fourth man was Johan Akkers. There was no mistaking the tall gaunt frame. He wore an old black fedora hat on his head, strangely formal attire for the work in which he was engaged, and his braces criss-crossed his tan-coloured shirt. He carried a rifle at the trail in his right hand, and at the sound of the aircraft engines he swung round and stared into the sky, frozen with the shock of discovery.

'You swine. Oh, you bloody swine,' whispered David, and his anger was strong and bright against the despoilers.

'Hold on!' he warned Debra, and flew straight at the man, dropping steeply on to him.

The group around the dead buffalo scattered, as the aircraft bore down on them, each man picking his own course and racing away on it, but David selected the lanky galloping frame with the black hat jammed down over the ears and sank down behind him. The tips of the propellers clipped the dry grass, as he swiftly overtook the running Akkers.

He was set to fly into him, driven by the unreasoning anger of the male animal protecting his own, and he lined up to cut him down with the spinning propeller blades.

As David braced himself for the impact Akkers glanced back over his shoulder, and his face was muddy grey with fright, the skull eyes dark and deeply set. He saw the murderous blades merely feet from him, and he threw himself flat into the grass.

The Navajo roared inches over his prone body, and David pulled it round in a steep turn, with the wing-tip brushing the grass. As he came round he saw that Akkers was up and running, and that he was only fifty paces from the edge of the trees.

David levelled out, aimed for the fugitive again but realized that he could not reach him before he was into the trees. Swiftly he sped across the clearing, but the lumbering figure drew slowly closer to the timber line and as he reached the sanctuary of a big leadwood trunk, Akkers whirled and raised the rifle to his shoulder. He aimed at the approaching aircraft; although the rifle was unsteady in his hands the range was short.

'Down,' shouted David, pushing Debra's head below the level of the windshield, and he pulled open the throttles and climbed steeply away.

Even above the bellow of the engines David heard the heavy bullet clang into the fuselage of the aircraft.

'What's happening, David?' Debra pleaded.

'He fired at us, but we've got him on the run. He'll head back for his truck now, and Conrad should be there waiting for him.'

Akkers kept under cover of the trees, and circling above him David caught glimpses of the tall figure trotting purposefully along his escape route.

'David, can you hear me?' Conrad's voice boomed suddenly in the tense cockpit.

'What is it, Connie?'

'We've got trouble. I've hit a rock in your Land-Rover and knocked out the sump. She's had it, pouring oil all over the place.'

'How the hell did you do that?' David demanded.

'I was trying a short cut.' Conrad's chagrin carried clearly over the ether.

'How far are you from the Luzane stream?'

'About three miles.'

'God, he'll beat you to it,' David swore. 'He's two miles from the truck and going like he's got a tax collector after him.'

'You have not seen old Connie move yet. I'll be there waiting for him,' Berg promised.

'Good luck,' David called, and the transmission went dead.

Below them Akkers was skirting the base of the hills, his black hat bobbing along steadily amongst the trees. David kept his starboard wing pointed at him and the Navajo turned steadily, holding station above him.

Other movement caught David's eye on the open slope of the hill above Akkers. For a moment he thought it was an animal, then with an intake of breath he realized that he was mistaken.

'What is it?' Debra demanded, sensing his concern.

'It's Sam, the damned fool. Connie told him not to leave his post – he's unarmed – but he's haring down the slope to try and cut Akkers off.'

'Can't you stop him?' Debra asked anxiously, and David didn't bother to answer.

He called Conrad four times before there was a reply. Conrad's voice was thick and wheezing with the effort of running.

'Sam is on to Akkers. I think he's going to confront him.'

'Oh God damn him,' groaned Conrad. 'I'll kick his black ass for him.'

'Hold on,' David told him, 'I'm going around for a closer look.'

David saw it all quite plainly, he was only three hundred

feet above them when Akkers became aware of the running figure on the slope above him. He stopped dead, and half-lifted the rifle; perhaps he shouted a warning but Sam kept on down, bounding over the rocky ground towards the man who had burned his children to death.

Akkers lifted the rifle to his shoulder and aimed deliberately, the rifle jumped sharply, the barrel kicking upwards at the recoil and Sam's legs kept on running while his upper torso was flung violently backwards by the strike of the heavy soft-nosed bullet.

The tiny brown-clad body bounced and rolled down the slope, before coming to a sprawling halt in a clump of scrub.

David watched Akkers reload the rifle, stooping to pick up the empty cartridge shell. Then he looked up at the circling aircraft above him, David may have been mistaken but it seemed the man was laughing – that obscene tooth-clucking giggle of his – then he started off again at a trot towards the truck.

'Connie,' David spoke hoarsely into his handset, 'he just killed Sam.'

Conrad Berg ran heavily over the broken sandy ground. He had lost his hat and sweat poured down his big red face, stinging his eyes and plastering the lank grey hair down his forehead. The walkie-talkie set bounced on his back, and the butt of the rifle thumped rhythmically against his hip.

He ran with grim concentration, trying to ignore the swollen pounding of his heart and the torture of breath that scalded his lungs. A thorn branch clawed at his upper arms, raking thin bloody lines through his skin, but he did not break the pattern of his run.

He turned his red and streaming face to the sky and saw

David's aircraft, circling ahead of him and slightly to his left. That marked for him Akkers' position – and it was clear that Conrad was losing ground in his desperate race to head off the escape.

The radio set on his back buzzed, but he ignored the call, he could not halt now. To break his run would mean he would only slump down exhausted. He was a big, heavy man, the air was hot and enervating, and he had run three miles through loose and difficult going – he was almost finished. He was burning the last of his reserves now.

Suddenly the earth seemed to fall away under him, and he pitched forward and half-slid – half-rolled – down the steep bank of the Luzane stream, to finish lying on his back in the white river sand, clean and grainy as sugar. The radio was digging painfully into his flesh and he dragged it out from under him.

Still lying in the sand he panted like a dog, blinded by sweat, and he fumbled the transmit button of the set.

'David—' he croaked thickly, 'I am in the bed of the stream – can you see me?'

The aircraft was arcing directly overhead now, and David's answer came back immediately.

'I see you, Connie, you are a hundred yards downstream from the truck. Akkers is there, Connie, he has just reached the truck, he'll be coming back down the river bed at any moment.'

Painfully, gasping, choking for breath, Conrad Berg dragged himself to his knees – and at that moment he heard the whirr and catch and purr of an engine. He unstrapped the heavy radio and laid it aside, then he unslung his rifle, snapped open the breech to check the load, and pulled himself to his feet.

Surprised at the weakness of his own massive body, he staggered into the centre of the river bed.

The dry river bed was eight feet deep with banks cut sheer by flood water, and it was fifteen feet wide at this point, and the floor was of smooth white sand, scattered with small water-rounded stones no bigger than a baseball. It made a good illegal access road into Jabulani, and the tracks of Akkers' truck were clearly etched in the soft sand.

Around a bed in the stream Conrad heard the truck revving and roaring as it came down a low place in the bank into the smooth bed.

Conrad stood squarely in the middle of the river bed with the rifle held across his hip, and he fought to control his breathing. The approaching roar of the truck reached a crescendo as it came skidding wildly around the bend in the stream, and raced down towards him. Showers of loose sand were thrown out from under the spinning rear wheels.

Johan Akkers crouched over the steering wheel, with the black hat pulled down to his eyebrows, and his face was grey and glistening with sweat, and he saw Conrad blocking the river bed.

'Stop!' Conrad shouted, hefting the rifle. 'Stop or I shoot!'

The truck was swaying and sliding, the engine screamed in tortured protest. Akkers began to laugh, Conrad could see the open mouth and the shaking shoulders. There was no slackening in the truck's roaring, rocking charge.

Conrad lifted the rifle and sighted down the stubby double barrels. At that range he could have put a bullet through each of Johan Akkers' deep-set eyes, and the man made no effort to duck or otherwise avoid the menace of the levelled rifle. He was still laughing, and Conrad could clearly see the teeth lying loosely on his gums. He steeled himself with the truck fifty feet away, and racing down upon him.

It takes a peculiar state of mind before one man deliberately and cold-bloodedly shoots down another. It must either be the conditioned reflex of the soldier or law-enforcement officer, or it must be the terror of the hunted, or again it must be the unbalanced frenzy of the criminal lunatic.

None of these was Conrad Berg. Like most big, strong men, he was essentially a gentle person. His whole thinking was centred on protecting and cherishing life – he could not pull the trigger.

With the truck fifteen feet away, he threw himself aside, and Johan Akkers swung the wheel wildly, deliberately driving for him.

He caught Berg a glancing blow with the side of the truck, hurling him into the earthen bank of the stream. The truck went past him, slewing out of control. It hit the bank farther down the stream in a burst of earth and loose pebbles, swaying wildly as Akkers fought the bucking wheel. He got it under control again, jammed his foot down on the accelerator and went roaring on down the river bed, leaving Conrad lying in the soft sand below the bank.

As the truck hit him, Conrad felt the bone in his hip shatter like glass, and the breath driven from his lungs by the heavy blow of metal against his rib cage.

He lay in the sand on his side and felt the blood well slowly into his mouth. It had a bitter salt taste, and he knew that one of the broken ribs had pierced his lung like a lance and that the blood sprang from deep within his body.

He turned his head and saw the radio set lying ten paces away across the river bed. He began to drag himself towards it and his shattered leg slithered after him, twisted at a grotesque angle.

'David,' he whispered into the microphone. 'I couldn't stop him. He got away,' and he spat a mouthful of blood into the white sand.

David picked the truck up as it came charging up the river bank below the concrete bridge of the Luzane, bounced and bumped over the drainage ditch and swung on to the road. It gathered speed swiftly and raced westwards towards Bandolier Hill and the highway. Dust boiled out from behind the green chassis, marking its position clearly for David as he turned two miles ahead of it.

After crossing the Luzane the road turned sharply to avoid a rocky outcrop, and then ran arrow-straight for two miles, hedged in with thick timber and undulating like a switchback, striking across the water shed and the grain of the land.

As David completed his turn he lowered his landing gear, and throttled back. The Navajo sank down, lined up on the dusty road as though it was a landing-strip.

Directly ahead was the dust column of the speeding truck. They were on a head-on course, but David concentrated coldly on bringing the Navajo down into the narrow lane between the high walls of timber. He was speaking quietly to Debra, reassuring her and explaining what he was going to attempt.

He touched down lightly on the narrow road, letting her float in easily, and when she was down he opened the throttles again, taking her along the centre of the road under power but holding her down. He had speed enough to lift the Navajo off, if Akkers chose a collision rather than surrender.

Ahead of them was another hump in the road, and as they rolled swiftly towards it the green truck suddenly burst over the crest, not more than a hundred yards ahead.

Both vehicles were moving fast, coming together at a combined speed of almost two hundred miles an hour, and the shock of it was too much for Johan Akkers.

The appearance of the aircraft dead in the centre of the road, bearing down on him with the terrible spinning discs of the propellers was too much for nerves already run raw and ragged.

He wrenched the wheel hard over, and the truck went

into a broadside dry skid. It missed the port wing-tip of the Navajo as it went rocketing off the narrow road.

The front wheels caught the drainage ditch and the truck went over, cartwheeling twice in vicious slamming revolutions that smashed the glass from her windows and burst the doors open. The truck ended on its side against one of the trees.

David shut the throttles and thrust his feet hard down on the wheel brakes, bringing the Navajo up short.

'Wait here,' he shouted at Debra, and jumped down into the road. His face was a frozen mask of scar tissue, but his eyes were ablaze as he sprinted back along the road towards the wreckage of the green truck.

Akkers saw him coming, and he dragged himself shakily to his feet. He had been thrown clear and now he staggered to the truck. He could see his rifle lying in the cab, and he tried to scramble up on to the body to reach down through the open door. Blood from a deep scratch in his forehead was running into his eyes blinding him, he wiped it away with the back of his hand and glanced around.

David was close, hurdling the irrigation ditch and running towards him. Akkers scrambled down from the battered green body, and groped for the hunting knife on his belt. It was eight inches of Sheffield steel with a bone handle, and it had been honed to a razor edge.

He hefted it under-handed, in the classic grip of the knife-fighter, and wiped the blood from his face with the palm of his free hand.

He was crouching slightly, facing David, and the haft of the knife was completely covered by the huge bony fist.

David stopped short of him, his eyes fastened on the knife, and Akkers began to laugh again. It was a cracked falsetto giggle, the hysterical laughter of a man driven to the very frontiers of sanity.

The point of the knife weaved in the slow mesmeric movement of an erect cobra, and it caught the sunlight in

271

bright points of light. David watched it, circling and crouching, steeling himself, summoning all the training of paratrooper school, screwing up his nerve to go in against the naked steel.

Akkers feinted swiftly, leaping in, and when David broke away, he let out a fresh burst of high laughter.

Again they circled, Akkers mouthing his teeth loosely, sucking at them, giggling, watching with those muddy green eyes from their deep, close-set sockets. David moved back slowly ahead of him, and Akkers drove him back against the body of the truck, cornering him there.

He came then, flashing like the charge of a wounded leopard. His speed and strength were shocking, and the knife hissed upwards for David's belly.

David caught the knife hand at the wrist, blocking the thrust and trapping the knife low down. They were chest to chest now, face to face, like lovers, and Akkers' breath stank of unwashed teeth.

They strained silently, shifting like dancers to balance each other's heaves and thrusts.

David felt the knife hand twisting in his grip. The man had hands and arms like steel, he could not hold him much longer. In seconds it would be free, and the steel would be probing into his belly.

David braced his legs and twisted sideways. The move caught Akkers off-balance and he could not resist it. David was able to get his other hand on to the knife arm, but even with both hands he was hard put to hold on.

They swayed and shuffled together, panting, grunting, straining, until they fell, still locked together, against the bonnet of the truck. The metal was hot and smelled of oil.

David was concentrating all his strength on the knife, but he felt Akkers' free hand groping for his throat. He ducked his head down on his shoulders, pressing his chin against his chest, but the fingers were steel hard and powerful as machinery. They probed mercilessly into his flesh, forcing his chin up, and settling on his throat, beginning to squeeze the life out of him.

Desperately David hauled at the knife arm, and found it more manageable now that Akkers was concentrating his strength on strangling him.

The open windscreen of the truck was beside David's shoulder, the glass had been smashed out of it, but jagged shards of it still stood in the metal rim, forming a crude but ferocious line of saw-teeth.

David felt the fingers digging deep into his throat, crushing the gristle of his larynx and blocking off the arteries that fed his brain. His vision starred and then began to fade darkly, as though he were pulling eight Gs in a dogfight.

With one last explosive effort David pulled the knife arm around on to the line of broken glass, and he dragged it down, sawing it desperately across the edge.

Akkers screamed and his strangling grip relaxed. Back and forth David sawed the arm, slashing and ripping through skin and fat and flesh, opening a wound like a ragged-petalled rose, hacking down into the nerves and arteries and sinews so that the knife dropped from the lifeless fingers and Akkers screamed like a woman.

David broke from him and shoved him away. Akkers fell to his knees still screaming and David clutched at his own throat massaging the bruised flesh, gasping for breath and feeling the flow of fresh blood to his brain.

'God Jesus, I'm dying. I'm bleeding to death. Oh sweet Jesus, help me!' screamed Akkers, holding the mutilated arm to his belly. 'Help me, oh God, don't let me die. Save me, Jesus, save me!'

Blood was streaming and spurting from the arm, flooding the front of his trousers. As he screamed his teeth fell from his mouth, leaving it a dark and empty cave in the palely glistening face.

'You've killed me. I'll bleed to death!' he screamed at

David, thrusting his face towards David. 'You've got to save me – don't let me die.'

David pushed himself away from the truck and took two running steps towards the kneeling man, then he swung his right leg and his whole body into a flying kick that took Akkers cleanly under the chin and snapped his head back.

He went over backwards and lay still and quiet, and David stood over him, sobbing and gasping for breath.

For purposes of sentence Mr Justice Barnard of the Transvaal division of the Supreme Court took into consideration four previous convictions – two under the Wildlife Conservation Act, one for aggravated assault, and the fourth for assault with intent to do grievous bodily harm.

He found Johan Akkers guilty of twelve counts under the Wildlife Conservation Act, but considered these as one when sentencing him to three years at hard labour without option of a fine, and confiscation of firearms and motor vehicles used in commission of these offences.

He found him guilty of one count of aggravated assault, and sentenced him to three years at hard labour without option.

The prosecutor altered one charge from attempted murder to assault with intent to do grievous bodily harm. He was found guilty as charged on this count, and the sentence was five years' imprisonment without option.

On the final charge of murder he was found guilty and Justice Barnard said in open court:

'In considering sentence of death on this charge, I was obliged to take into account the fact that the accused was acting like an animal in a trap, and I am satisfied that there was no element of premeditation—'

The sentence was eighteen years' imprisonment, and all

sentences were to run consecutively. They were all confirmed on appeal.

As Conrad Berg said from his hospital bed with one
heavily plastered leg in traction, and a glass of Old Buck
gin in his hand, 'Well, for the next twenty-eight years we
don't have to worry about that bastard – I beg your pardon,
Mrs Morgan.'

'Twenty-nine years, dear,' Jane Berg corrected him
firmly.

In July the American edition of *A Place of Our Own*
was published, and it dropped immediately into that
hungry and bottomless pool of indifference wherein so
many good books drown. It left not a sign, not a ripple of
its passing.

Bobby Dugan, Debra's new literary agent in America,
wrote to say how sorry he was – and how disappointed. He
had expected at least some sort of critical notice to be
taken of the publication.

David took it as a personal and direct insult. He ranted
and stormed about the estate for a week, and it seemed
that at one stage he might actually journey to America to
commit a physical violence upon that country – a sort of
one-man Vietnam in reverse.

'They must be stupid,' he protested. 'It's the finest book
ever written.'

'Oh, David!' Debra protested modestly.

'It is! And I'd love to go over there and rub their noses
in it,' and Debra imagined the doors of editorial offices all
over New York being kicked open, and literary reviewers
fleeing panic-stricken, jumping out of skyscraper windows
or locking themselves in the women's toilets to evade
David's wrath.

'David, my darling, you are wonderful for me,' she

giggled with delight, but it had hurt. It had hurt very badly. She felt the flame of her urge to write wane and flutter in the chill winds of rejection.

Now when she sat at her desk with the microphone at her lips, the words no longer tumbled and fought to escape, and the ideas no longer jostled each other. Where before she had seen things happening as though she were watching a play, seen her characters laugh and cry and sing, now there was only the dark cloud banks rolling across her eyes – unrelieved by colour or form.

For hours at a time she might sit at her desk and listen to the birds in the garden below the window.

David sensed her despair, and he tried to help her through it. When the hours at the desk proved fruitless he would insist she leave it and come with him along the new fence lines, or to fish for the big blue Mozambique bream in the deep water of the pools.

Now that she had completely learned the layout of the house and its immediate environs, David began to teach her to find her way at large. Each day they would walk down to the pools and Debra learned her landmarks along the track; she would grope for them with the carved walking-stick David had given her. Zulu soon realized his role in these expeditions, and it was David's idea to clip a tiny silver bell on to his collar so that Debra could follow him more readily. Soon she could venture out without David, merely calling her destination to Zulu and checking him against her own landmarks.

David was busy at this time with the removal of Conrad's game fence, as he was still laid up with the leg, and with building his own fences to enclose the three vulnerable boundaries of Jabulani. In addition there was a force of African rangers to recruit and train in their duties. David designed uniforms for them, and built outposts for them at all the main access points to the estate. He flew into Nelspruit at regular intervals to consult Conrad Berg on these arrangements, and it was at his suggestion that David began a water survey of the estate. He wanted surface water on the areas of Jabulani that were remote from the pools, and he began studying the feasibility of building catchment dams or sinking bore-holes. His days were full and active, and he became hard and lean and sunbrowned. Yet always there were many hours spent in Debra's company.

The 35-mm colour slides that David had taken of the buffalo herd before Johan Akkers had decimated it, were returned by the processing laboratory and they were hopelessly inadequate. The huge animals seemed to be standing on the horizon, and the ox-peckers on their bodies were tiny grey specks. This failure spurred David, and he returned from one trip to Nelspruit with a 600-mm telescopic lens.

While Debra was meant to be working, David set up his camera beside her and photographed the birds through her open window. The first results were mixed. Out of thirty-six exposures, thirty-five could be thrown away, but one was beautiful, a grey-headed bush shrike at the moment of flight, poised on spread wings with the sunlight catching his vivid plumage and his sparkling eye.

David was hooked by the photography bug, and there were more lenses and cameras and tripods, until Debra protested that it was a hobby which was completely visual, and from which she was excluded.

David had one of his inspirations of genius. He sent away for pressings of June Stannard's bird song recordings – and Debra was enchanted. She listened to them intently, her whole face lighting with pleasure when she recognized a familiar call.

From there it was a natural step for her to attempt to make her own bird recordings, which included the tinkle of Zulu's silver bell, the buzz of David's Land-Rover, the voices of the servants arguing in the kitchen yard – and faintly, very faintly, the chatter of a glossy starling.

'It's no damned good,' Debra complained bitterly. 'I wonder how she got hers so clear and close.'

David did some reading, and built a parabolic reflector for her. It did not look particularly lovely, but it worked. Aimed at a sound source it gathered and directed the sound waves into the microphone.

From the window of Debra's study they became more adventurous and moved out. He built permanent and comfortable hides beside the drinking places at the pools, and when his rangers reported a nesting site of an interesting bird species, they would build temporary blinds of thatch and canvas – sometimes on tall stilts – where David and Debra spent many silent and enjoyable hours together, shooting film and catching sound. Even Zulu learned to lie still and silent with his bell removed on these occasions.

Slowly they had begun to build up a library of photographs and recordings of a professional standard – until at last David plucked up sufficient courage to send to *African Wild Life Magazine* a selection of a dozen of his best slides. Two weeks later, he received a letter of acceptance, with a cheque for a hundred dollars. This payment represented a return of approximately one-twentieth of one per cent of his capital outlay on equipment. David was ecstatic, and Debra's pleasure almost as great as his. They drank two bottles of Veuve Clicquot for dinner, and under the spell of excitement and champagne their love-making that night was particularly inventive.

When David's photographs were published in *Wild Life* accompanied with Debra's text they reaped an unexpected harvest of letters from persons of similar interest all over the world, and a request from the editors for a full-length, illustrated article on Jabulani, and the Morgans' plans for turning it into a game sanctuary.

Debra made a lovely model for David's photographs that he compiled for the article, and she also worked with care on the text – while David fed her ideas and criticism.

Debra's new book lay abandoned, but her disappointment was forgotten in the pleasure of working together.

Their correspondence with other conservationists provided them with sufficient intellectual stimulus, and the occasional company of Conrad Berg and Jane satisfied their need for human contact. They were still both sensitive about being with other people, and this way they could avoid it.

The *Wild Life* article was almost complete and ready for posting, when a letter arrived from Bobby Dugan in New York. The editor of *Cosmopolitan* magazine had chanced upon one of the few copies of *A Place of Our Own* in circulation. She had liked it, and the magazine was considering serialization of the book – possibly linked with a feature article on Debra. Bobby wanted Debra to let him have a selection of photographs of herself, and four thousand words of autobiographical notes.

The photographs were there, ready to go to *Cosmopolitan*, and Debra ran through the four thousand words in three hours with David making suggestions, some helpful and some bawdy.

They sent off the tape and pictures in the same post as the article to *Wild Life*. For nearly a month they heard nothing more about it and then something happened to drive it from their minds.

They were in the small thatch and daub hide beside the main pool, sitting quietly and companionably during a lull in the evening activity. David had his camera tripod set up in one of the viewing windows and Debra's reflector was raised above the roof of the hide, daubed with camouflage paint and operated by a handle above her head.

The water was still and black, except where a surface-feeding bream was rising near the far reed banks. A flock of laughing doves was lining up with a chittering troop of spotted guinea fowl at the water's edge, sipping water and then pointing their beaks to the sky as they let it run down their throats.

Suddenly David took her wrist as a cautionary signal, and by the intensity of his grip she knew that he had seen something unusual and she leaned close against him so that she could hear his whispered descriptions, and with her right hand she switched on the recorder and then reached up to aim the reflector.

A herd of the rare and shy nyala antelope were approaching the drinking place timidly, clinging until the last possible moment to the security of the forest. Their ears were spread, and their nostrils quivered and sucked at the air, huge dark eyes glowing like lamps in the gloom.

There were nine hornless females, delicate chestnut in colour, striped with white, dainty-stepping and suspicious, as they followed the two herd bulls. These were so dissimilar from their females as though to belong to a different species. Purplish black, and shaggy with a rough mane extending from between the ears to the crupper, their horns were thick and corkscrewed, tipped with cream, and between their eyes was a vivid white chevron marking.

Advancing only a step at a time, and then pausing to stare with the limitless patience of the wild, searching for a hint of danger, they came slowly down the bank.

They passed the hide so closely that David was afraid to press the trigger of his camera lest the click of the shutter frighten them away.

He and Debra sat frozen as they reached the water; Debra smiled happily as she picked up the soft snort with which the lead bull blew the surface before drinking, and the liquid slurping with which he drew his first mouthful.

Once they were all drinking, David aimed and focused with care, but at the click of the shutter the bull nearest him leapt about and uttered a hoarse, throbbing alarm bark. Instantly the entire herd whirled and raced away like pale ghosts through the dark trees.

'I got it! I got it!' exulted Debra. 'Wow! He was so close, he nearly burst my eardrums.'

The excitement on Jabulani was feverish. Nyala antelope had never been seen on the estate before, not even in David's father's time, and all steps were taken to encourage them to remain. The pools were immediately placed out of bounds to all the rangers and servants, lest the human presence frighten the herd off before they had a chance to settle down and stabilize their territory.

Conrad Berg arrived, still using a stick and limping heavily as he would for the rest of his life. From the hide he watched the herd with David and Debra, and then back at the homestead he sat before the log fire, eating prime beef steak and drinking Old Buck while he gave his opinion.

'They aren't from the Park, I shouldn't think. I would have recognized a big old bull like that if I'd ever seen him before – they have probably sneaked in from one of the other estates – you haven't got the south fence up yet, have you?'

'Not yet.'

'Well, that's where they have moved from – probably sick of being stared at by all the tourists. Come up here for a bit of peace.' He took a swallow of his gin. 'You're getting a nice bit of stuff together here, Davey – another few years and it will be real show-place. Have you got any plans for visitors – you could make a good thing out of this place, like they have at Mala-Mala. Five-star safaris at economy prices—'

'Connie, I'm just too damn selfish to want to share this with anybody else.'

The distractions and the time had given Debra an opportunity to recover from the American failure of *A Place of Our Own*, and one morning she sat down at her desk and began working again on her second novel. That evening she told David:

'One of the blocks I have had is that I hadn't a name for it. It's like a baby – you have to give it a name or it's not really a person.'

'You have got a name for it?' he asked.

'Yes.'

'Would you like to tell me?'

She hesitated, shy at saying it to some other person for the first time. 'I thought I'd call it – *A Bright and Holy Thing*,' she said, and he thought about it for a few moments, repeating it softly.

'You like it?' she asked anxiously.

'It's great,' he said. 'I like it. I really do.'

With Debra once more busy on her novel it seemed each day was too short for the love and laughter and industry which filled it.

T he call came through while David and Debra were sitting around the barbecue in the front garden. David ran up to the house when the telephone bell insisted.

'Miss Mordecai?' David was puzzled, the name was vaguely familiar.

'Yes. I have a person-to-person call from New York, for Miss Debra Mordecai,' the operator repeated impatiently, and David realized who she was talking about.

'She'll take it,' he said, and yelled for Debra. It was Bobby Dugan, and the first time she had heard his voice.

'Wonder girl,' he shouted over the line. 'Sit down, so you don't fall down. Big Daddy has got news for you that will blow your mind! *Cosmopolitan* ran the article on you two weeks ago. They did you real proud, darling, full-page photograph – God, you looked good enough to eat—'

Debra laughed nervously and signalled David to put his ear against hers to listen.

' – the mag hit the stands Saturday, and Monday morning was a riot at the book stores. They were beating the doors down. You've caught the imagination of everybody here, darling. They sold seventeen thousand hardback in five days, you jumped straight into the number five slot on the *New York Times* bestseller list – it's a freak, a phenomenon, a mad crazy runner – darling, we are going to sell half a million copies of this book standing on our heads. All the big papers and mags are screaming for review copies – they've lost the ones we sent them three months ago. Doubleday are reprinting fifty thousand – and I told them they were crazy – it should have been a hundred thousand – it's only just starting – next week will see the West Coast catch fire and they'll be screaming for copies across the whole country—' There was much more, Bobby Dugan riding high, shouting his plans and his hopes, while Debra laughed weakly and kept saying, 'No! I can't believe it!' and 'It's not true!'

They drank three bottles of Veuve Clicquot that night, and a little before midnight Debra fell pregnant to David Morgan.

'Miss Mordecai combines superb use of language and a sure literary touch with the readability of a popular bestseller,' said the *New York Times*.

'Who says good literature has to be dull?' asked *Time*. 'Debra Mordecai's talent burns like a clean white flame.'

'Miss Mordecai takes you by the throat, slams you against the wall, throws you on the floor and kicks you in the guts. She leaves you as shaken and weak as if you had been in a car smash,' added the *Free Press*.

Proudly David presented Conrad Berg with a signed

copy of *A Place of Our Own*. Conrad had finally been prevailed upon to drop the 'Mrs Morgan' and call Debra by her given name. He was so impressed with the book that he had an immediate relapse.

'How do you think of those things, Mrs Morgan?' he asked with awe.

'Debra,' Debra prompted him.

'She doesn't think of them,' Jane Berg explained helpfully. 'It just comes to her – it's called *inspiration*.'

Bobby Dugan was correct, they had to reprint another fifty thousand copies.

It seemed as though the fates, ashamed of the cruel pranks they had played upon them, were determined to shower Debra and David with gifts.

As Debra sat at her olive-wood table, growing daily bigger with her child, once again the words flowed as strongly and as clearly as the spring waters of the String of Pearls. However, there was still time to help David with the illustrated publication he was compiling on the birds of prey of the bushveld, and to accompany him on the daily expeditions to different areas of Jabulani, and to plan the furnishings and the layout of the empty nursery.

Conrad Berg came to her secretly to enlist her aid in his plan to have David nominated to the Board of the National Parks Committee. They discussed it in length and great detail. A seat on the Board carried prestige and was usually reserved for men of greater age and influence than David. However, Conrad was confident that the dignity of the Morgan name combined with David's wealth, ownership of Jabulani, demonstrated interest in conservation and his ability to devote much time to the affairs of the Board would prevail.

'Yes,' Debra decided. 'It will be good for him to meet

people and get out a little more. We are in danger of becoming recluses here.'

'Will he do it?'

'Don't worry,' Debra assured him. 'I'll see to it.'

Debra was right. After the initial uneasiness of the first meeting of the Board, and once the other members became accustomed to that dreadful face and realized that behind it was a warm and forceful person, David gathered increasing confidence with each subsequent journey to Pretoria where the Board met. Debra would fly up with him and while they were at their deliberations she and Jane Berg shopped for the baby and the other items of luxury and necessity that were not readily come by in Nelspruit.

However, by November Debra was carrying low and she felt too big and uncomfortable to make the long flight in the cockpit of the Navajo, especially as the rains were about to break and the air was turbulent with storm cloud and static and heavy thermals. It would be a bumpy trip, and she was deeply involved in the last chapters of the new book.

'I'll be perfectly all right here,' she insisted. 'I've got a telephone and I have also got six game rangers, four servants and a fierce hound to guard me.'

David argued and protested for five days before the meeting and agreed only after he had worked out a timetable.

'If I leave here before dawn I'll be at the meeting by nine, we'll be finished by three and I can be back here by six-thirty at the latest,' he muttered. 'If it wasn't the budget and financial affairs vote, I would cut it – tell them I was sick.'

'It's important, darling. You go.'

'You sure now?'

'I won't even notice you're not here.'

'Don't get too carried away by it,' he told her ruefully. 'I might stay just to punish you.'

In the dawn the thunderheads were the colour of wine and flame and ripe fruit, fuming and magnificent, towering high above the tiny aircraft, high above the utmost ceiling of which it was capable.

David flew the corridors of open sky alone and at peace, wrapped in the euphoria of flight which never failed for him. He altered course at intervals to avoid the mountainous upsurges of cloud; within them lurked death and disaster, great winds that would tear the wings from his machine and send the pieces whirling on high, up into the heights where a man would perish from lack of oxygen.

He landed at Grand Central where a hire car was waiting for him, and spent the journey into Pretoria reading through the morning papers. It was only when he saw the meteorological prediction of a storm front moving in steadily from the Mozambique channel that he felt a little uneasy.

Before he entered the conference-room he asked the receptionist to place a telephone call to Jabulani.

'Two-hour delay, Mr Morgan.'

'Okay, call me when it comes through.'

When they broke for lunch he asked her again.

'What happened to my call?'

'I'm sorry, Mr Morgan. I was going tell you. The lines are down. They are having very heavy rainfull in the low veld.'

His vague uneasiness became mild alarm.

'Would you call the meteorological office for me, please?'

The weather was down solid. From Barberton to Mpunda Milia and from Lourenço Marques to Machadodorp, the rain was heavy and unrelenting. The cloud ceiling was above twenty thousand feet and it was right down on the ground. The Navajo had no oxygen or electronic navigational equipment.

'How long?' David demanded of the meteorological officer. 'How long until it clears?'

'Hard to tell, sir. Two or three days.'

'Damn! Damn!' said David bitterly, and went down to the canteen on the ground floor of the government building. Conrad Berg was at a corner table with two other members of the Board, but when he saw David he jumped up and limped heavily but urgently across the room.

'David,' he took his arm, and his round face was deadly serious. 'I've just heard – Johann Akkers broke jail last night. He killed a guard and got clean away. He's been loose for seventeen hours.'

David stared at him, unable to speak with the shock of it.

'Is Debra alone?'

David nodded, his face stiff with scar tissue, but his eyes dark and afraid.

'You'd better fly down right away to be with her.'

'The weather – they've grounded all aircraft in the area.'

'Use my truck!' said Conrad urgently.

'I need something faster than that.'

'Do you want me to come with you?'

'No,' said David. 'If you aren't there this afternoon, they won't approve the new fencing allocations. I'll go on my own.'

D ebra was working at her desk when she heard the wind coming. She switched off her tape recorder and went out on to the veranda with the dog following her closely.

She stood listening, not sure of what she was hearing. It was a soughing and sighing, a far-off rushing like that of a wave upon a pebble beach.

The dog pressed against her leg and she squatted beside him, placing one arm around his neck, listening to the gathering rush of the wind, hearing the roar of it building up swiftly, the branches of the marula forest beginning to thrash and rattle.

Zulu whimpered, and she hugged him a little closer.

'There, boy. Gently. Gently,' she whispered and the wind struck in a mighty squalling blast, crashing through the tree-tops, tearing and cracking the upper branches.

It banged into the insect screen of the veranda with a snap like a mainsail filling, and unsecured windows and doors slammed like cannon shots.

Debra sprang up and ran back into her workroom, the window was swinging and slamming, dust and debris boiling in through it. She put her shoulder to it, closing it and securing the latch, then she ran to do the same to the other windows and bumped into one of the house servants.

Between them they battened down all the doors and windows.

'Madam, the rain will come now. Very much rain.'

'Go to your families now,' Debra told them.

'The dinner, madam?'

'Don't worry, I'll make that,' and thankfully they streamed away through the swirling dust to their hutments beyond the kopje.

The wind blew for fifteen minutes, and Debra stood by the wire screen and felt it tugging and whipping her body. Its wildness was infectious, and she laughed aloud, elated and excited.

Then suddenly the wind was passed, as swiftly as it had come, and she heard it tearing and clawing its way over the hills above the pools.

In the utter silence that followed the whole world waited, tensed for the next onslaught of the elements. Debra felt the cold, the sudden fall in temperature as though the door to a great ice-box had opened, and she hugged her arms and shivered; she could not see the dark cloud banks that rolled across Jabulani, but somehow she sensed their menace and their majesty in the coldness that swamped her.

The first lightning bolt struck with a crackling electric explosion that seemed to singe the air about her, and Debra was taken so unawares that she cried out aloud. The thunder broke, and seemed to shake the sky and rock the earth's very foundations.

Debra turned and groped her way back into the house, locking herself into her room, but walls could not diminish the fury of the rain when it came. It drummed and roared and deafened, battering the window panes, and striking the walls and doors, pouring through the screen to flood the veranda.

As overpowering as was the rainstorm, yet it was the lightning and the thunder that racked Debra's nerves. She could not steel herself for each mighty crack and roar. Each one caught her off-balance, and it seemed that they were aimed directly at her.

She crouched on her day bed, clinging to the soft warm body of the dog for a little comfort. She wished she had not allowed the servants to leave, and she thought that her nerve might crack altogether under the bombardment.

Finally she could stand it no longer. She groped her way into the living-room. In her distress she had almost lost her way about her own home, but she found the telephone and lifted it to her ear.

Immediately she knew that it was dead, there was no tone to it, but she cranked the handle wildly, calling desperately into the mouthpiece, until finally she let it fall and dangle on its cord.

She began to sob as she stumbled back to her workroom, hugging the child in her big belly, and she fell upon the day bed and covered her ears with both hands.

'Stop it,' she screamed. 'Stop it, oh please God, make it stop.'

The new national highway as far as the coal-mining town of Witbank was broad and smooth, six lanes of traffic, and David eased the hired Pontiac into the fast lane and went flat, keeping his foot pressed down hard. She peaked out at a hundred and thirty miles an hour, and she sat so solid upon the road that he hardly needed to drive her. His mind was free to play with horror stories, and to remember Johan Akkers' face as he stood in the dock glaring across the Court Room at them. The deep-set muddy eyes, and the mouth working as though he were about to spit. As the warders had led him to the stairs down to the cells he had pulled free and shouted back.

'I'm going to get you, Scarface,' he giggled. 'If I have to wait twenty-nine years – I'm going to get you,' and they took him away.

After Witbank the road narrowed. There was heavy traffic and the bends had dangerous camber and deceptive gradients. David was able to concentrate on keeping the big car on the road, and to drive the phantoms from his mind.

He took the Lyndenburg turn off, cutting the corner of the triangle, and the traffic thinned out to an occasional truck. He was able to go flat out again, and race along the edge of the high escarpment. Then suddenly the road turned and began its plunge down into the low veld.

When he emerged from the Erasmus tunnel David ran into the rain. It was a solid grey bank of water that filled the air and buffeted the body of the Pontiac. It flooded the road, so David had difficulty following its verge beneath the standing sheets of water, and it swamped the windshield, so that the efforts of the wipers to clear it were defeated.

David switched on his headlights and drove as fast as he dared, craning forward in his seat to peer into the impenetrable blue-grey curtains of rain.

Darkness came early in the rain, beneath the lowering

black clouds, and the wet road dazzled him with the reflections of his own headlights, while the fat falling drops seemed as big as hailstones. He was forced to moderate his speed a little more, creeping down the highway towards Bandolier Hill.

In the darkness he almost missed the turning, and he reversed back to it, swinging on to the unmade surface.

It was slushy with mud, puddled and swampy, slippery as grease. Again he was forced to lower his speed. Once he lost it, and slid broadside into the drainage ditch. By packing loose stones under the wheels and racing the engine he pulled the Pontiac out and drove on.

By the time he reached the bridge over the Luzane stream, he had been six hours at the wheel of the Pontiac, and it was a few minutes after eight o'clock in the evening.

As he reached the bridge the rain stopped abruptly, a freak hole in the weather. Directly overhead the stars showed mistily, while around them the cloud banks swirled, turning slowly, as though upon the axis of a great wheel.

David's headlights cut through the darkness, out across the mad brown waters to the far bank a hundred yards away. The bridge was submerged under fifteen feet of flood water, and the water was moving so swiftly that its waves and whirlpools seemed sculpted in polished brown marble, and the trunks of uprooted trees dashed downstream upon the flood.

It seemed impossible that the bed of this raging torrent had been the narrow sandy bed in which Johan Akkers had run down Conrad with the green Ford truck.

David climbed out of the Pontiac and walked down to the edge of the water. As he stood there he saw the level creeping up perceptibly towards his feet. It was still rising.

He looked up at the sky, and judged that the respite in the weather would not last much longer.

He reached his decision and ran back to the Pontiac. He reversed well back onto the highest ground and parked it off the verge with the headlights still directed at the river edge. Then, standing beside the door, he stripped down to his shirt and underpants. He pulled his belt from the loops of his trousers and buckled it about his waist, then he tied his shoes to the belt by their laces.

Barefooted he ran to the edge of the water, and began to feel his way slowly down the bank. It shelved quickly and within a few paces he was knee-deep and the current plucked at him, viciously trying to drag him off-balance.

He posed like that, braced against the current, and waited, staring upstream. He saw the tree trunk coming down fast on the flood, with its roots sticking up like beseeching arms. It was swinging across the current and would pass him closely.

He judged his moment and lunged for it. Half a dozen strong strokes carried him to it and he grasped one of the roots. Instantly he was whisked out of the beams of the headlight into the roaring fury of the river. The tree rolled and bucked, carrying him under and bringing him up coughing and gasping.

Something struck him a glancing blow and he felt his shirt tear and the skin beneath it rip. Then he was under water again, swirling end over end and clinging desperately to his log.

All about him the darkness was filled with the rush and threat of crazy water, and he was buffeted and flogged by its raw strength, grazed and bruised by rocks and driftwood.

Suddenly he felt the log check and bump against an obstruction, turning and swinging out into the current again.

David was blinded with muddy water and he knew there was a limit to how much more of this treatment he could survive. Already he was weakening quickly. He could feel his mind and his movements slowing, like a battered prize fighter in the tenth round.

He gambled it all on the obstruction which the log had

encountered being the far bank, and he released his death-grip on the root and stuck out sideways across the current with desperate strength.

His overarm stroke ended in the trailing branches of a thorn tree hanging over the storm waters. Thorns tore the flesh of his palm as his grip closed over them, and he cried out at the pain but held on.

Slowly he dragged himself out of the flood and crawled up the bank, hacking and coughing at the water in his lungs. Clear of the river, he fell on his face in the mud and vomited a gush of swallowed water that shot out of his nose and mouth.

He lay exhausted for a long while, until his coughing slowed and he could breathe again. His shoes had been torn from his belt by the current. He dragged himself to his feet and staggered forward into the darkness. As he ran, he held his hand to his face, pulling the broken thorns from the flesh of his palm with his teeth.

Stars were still showing overhead and by their feeble light he made out the road, and he began to run along it, gathering strength with each pace. It was very still now, with only the dripping of the trees and the occasional far-off murmur of thunder to break the silence.

Two miles from the homestead, David made out the dark bulk of something on the side of the road, and it was only when he was a few paces from it that he realized it was an automobile – a late model Chevy. It had been abandoned, bogged down in one of the greasy mudholes that the rains had opened.

The doors were unlocked and David switched on the interior and parking lights. There was dried blood on the seat, a dark smear of it, and on the back seat was a bundle of clothing. David untied it quickly and recognized immediately the coarse canvas suiting as regulation prison garb. He stared at it stupidly for a moment, until the impact of it struck him.

The car was stolen, the blood probably belonging to the unfortunate owner. The prison garb had been exchanged for other clothing, probably taken from the body of the owner of the Chevy.

David knew then beyond all possible doubt that Johan Akkers was at Jabulani, and that he had arrived before the bridge over the Luzane stream had become impassable – probably three or four hours previously.

David threw the prison suiting back into the car, and he began to run.

Johan Akkers drove the Chevy across the Luzane bridge with the rising waters swirling over the guard rail, and with the rain teeming down in blinding white sheets.

The muddy water shoved at the body of the car, making steering difficult, and it seeped in under the doors, flooding the floorboards and swirling about Akkers' feet; but he reached the safety of the far bank and raced the engine as he shot up it. The wheels spun on the soft mud, and the Chevy skidded and swayed drunkenly in the loose footing.

The closer he drew to Jabulani the more reckless he became in his haste.

Before his conviction and imprisonment, Akkers had been a twisted and blighted creature, a man of deep moods and passionate temper. Feeling himself rejected and spurned by his fellow men he had lived in a world of swift defensive violence, but always he had kept within the bounds of reason.

However, during the two years that he had laboured and languished within prison walls, his anger and his lust for vengeance had driven him over that narrow boundary.

Vengeance had become the sole reason for his existence,

and he had rehearsed it a hundred times each day. He had planned his prison break to give himself three days of freedom — after that it did not matter. Three days would be enough.

He had infected his own jaw, running a needle poisoned with his excreta deeply into the gum. They had taken him to the dental clinic as he had planned. The guard had been easily handled, and the dentist had co-operated with a scalpel held to his throat.

Once clear of the prison, Akkers had used the scalpel, vaguely surprised by the volume of blood that could issue from a human throat. He had left the dentist slumped over his steering wheel on a plot of waste ground and, with his white laboratory gown over his prison suit, he had waited at a set of traffic lights.

The shiny new Chevy had pulled up for a red light and Akkers had opened the passenger door and slid in beside the driver.

He had been a smaller man than Akkers, plump and prosperous-looking, with a smooth pale face and soft little hairless hands on the steering wheel. He had obeyed meekly Akkers' instruction to drive on.

Akkers had rolled his soft white body, clad only in vest and shorts, into a clump of thick grass beside a disused secondary road and pulled the grass closed over him, then he had beaten the first road block out of the city area by forty minutes.

He stayed on the side roads, picking his way slowly eastwards. The infection in his jaw had ached intolerably despite the shot of antibiotics the dentist had given him, and his crippled claw of a hand had been awkward and clumsy on the gear lever — for the severed nerves and sinews had never knitted again. The hand was a dead and insensate thing.

Using the caution of a natural predator and helped by

the newsflashes on the radio, he had groped his way carefully through the net that was spread for him, and now he was on Jabulani and he could restrain himself no longer.

He hit the mud hole at forty and the Chevy whipped and spun, slewing her back end deep into the mud and high-centring her belly on the soft ooze.

He left her there and went on swiftly through the rain, loping on long legs. Once he giggled and sucked at his teeth, but then he was silent again.

It was dark by the time be climbed the kopje behind Jabulani homestead. He lay there for two hours peering down into the driving rain, waiting for the darkness.

Once night fell, he could see no lights, and he began to worry; there should have been lights burning.

He left the kopje and moved cautiously through the darkness down the hill. He avoided the servants' quarters, and went through the trees to the landing-strip.

He ran into the side of the hanger in the dark and followed the wall to the side doorway.

Frantically he spread his arms and felt for the aircraft that should be here – and when he realized that it was not he let out a groan of frustration.

They were gone. He had planned and schemed in vain, all his desperate striving was in vain.

Growling like an animal, he smashed the fist of his good hand against the wall, enjoying the pain of it in his frustration, and his anger and his hatred was so strong that it shook his body like a fever, and he cried out aloud, a formless animal cry without coherence or sense.

Suddenly the rain stopped. The heavy drum of it upon the iron roof of the hangar ceased so abruptly that Akkers was distracted. He went to the opening and looked out.

The stars were swimming mistily above him, and the only sound was the gurgle and chuckle of running water and the dripping of the trees.

There was the glimmering of light now, and he saw the

white walls of the homestead shine amongst the trees. He could do damage there, Akkers realized. He could find there some outlet for his terrible frustration. There was furniture to smash, and the thatch would burn – if lit from inside, the thatch would burn even in this weather.

He stared towards the homestead through the dark sodden trees.

D ebra woke in the silence. She had fallen asleep in the midst of the storm, perhaps as a form of escape.

Now she groped for the warm comforting body of the dog but he was gone. There was a patch of warmth on the bed beside her where he had lain.

She listened intently and there was nothing but the soft sounds of water in the guttering and far-off the growl of thunder. She remembered her earlier panic and she was ashamed.

She stood up from the bed and she was shivering with the cold in her loose, free-flowing dark blue maternity blouse, and the elastic-fronted slacks that were adjustable to her expanding waistline. She felt with her toes and found the light ballet pumps on the stone floor and pushed her feet into them.

She started towards her dressing-room for a sweater, then she would make herself a cup of hot soup, she decided.

Zulu started barking. He was outside in the front garden. Clearly he had left the house through the small hinged doorway that David had built especially for him in the veranda wall.

The dog had many barks, each with a different meaning which Debra understood.

A self-effacing woof, that was the equivalent of the watch-man's 'Ten o'clock on a June night – and all's well.'

297

Or a longer-drawn-out yowl, that meant, 'There is a full moon out tonight, and the wolf's blood in my veins will not allow me to sleep.'

A sharper, meaningful bark, 'Something is moving down near the pumphouse. It may be a lion.'

And then there was an urgent clamouring chorus, 'There is dire danger threatening. Beware! Beware!'

It was the danger bark now, and then growling through closed jaws as though he were worrying something.

Debra went out on to the veranda and she felt the puddled rainwater soaking through her light shoes. Zulu was harrying something in the front garden, she could hear the growling and scuffling, the movement of bodies locked in a struggle. She stood silently, uncertain of what to do, knowing only that she could not go out to Zulu. She was blind and helpless against the unknown adversary. As she hesitated she heard clearly the sound of a heavy blow. It cracked on bone, and she heard the thump of a body falling. Zulu's growls were cut off abruptly, and there was silence. Something had happened to the dog. Now she was completely alone in the silence.

No, not silence. There was the sound of breathing – a heavy panting breath.

Debra shrank back against the veranda wall, listening and waiting.

She heard footsteps, human footsteps coming through the garden towards the front door. The footsteps squelched and splashed in the rain puddles.

She wanted to call out a challenge, but her voice was locked in her constricted throat. She wanted to run, but her legs were paralysed by the sound of the intruder climbing the front steps.

A hand brushed against the wire screening, and then settled on the handle, rattling it softly.

At last Debra found her voice. 'Who is that?' she called, a high panicky cry that ran out into the night silence.

Instantly the soft sounds ceased. The intruder was frozen by her challenge. She could imagine whoever it was standing on the top step, peering through the screening into the darkness of the veranda, trying to make her out in the gloom. Suddenly she was thankful for the dark blouse and black slacks.

She waited motionlessly, listening, and she heard a little wind shake the tree-tops, bringing down a sudden quick patter of droplets. A hunting owl called down near the dam. She heard the thunder murmur bad-temperedly along the hills, and a nightjar screeched harshly from amongst the poinsettia bushes.

The silence went on for a long time, and she knew she could not stand it much longer. She could feel her lips beginning to quiver and the cold and fear and the weight of the child were heavy upon her bladder, she wanted to run – but there was nowhere to run to.

Then suddenly the silence was broken. In the darkness there was the sound of a man giggling. It was shockingly close and clear, and it was a crazy sound. The shock of it seemed to clutch at her heart and crush the air from her lungs. Her legs went weak under her, beginning to shake, and the pressure on her bladder was intolerable – for she recognized the sound of that laughter, the sick insane sound of it was graven upon her mind.

A hand shook the door handle, jerking and straining at it. Then a shoulder crashed into the narrow frame. It was a screen door – not built to withstand rough treatment. Debra knew it would yield quickly.

She screamed then, a high ringing scream of terror, and it seemed to break the spell which held her. Her legs would move again, and her brain would work.

She whirled and ran back into her workroom, slamming the door and locking it swiftly.

She crouched beside the door, thinking desperately. She knew that as soon as he broke into the house Akkers need only switch on a light. The electricity generator would automatically kick in on demand, and in the light he would have her at his mercy. Her only protection was darkness. In the darkness she would have the advantage, for she was accustomed to it.

She had heard the nightjar and the owl calling so she knew that night had fallen, and it was probable that the raincloud still blanketed moon and stars. Darkness was out there in the forest. She must get out of the house, and try to reach the servants' quarters.

She hurried through the rooms towards the rear of the house, and as she went she thought of a weapon. The firearms were locked in the steel cabinet in David's office – and the key was with him. She ran through to the kitchen and her heavy walking-stick was in its place by the door. She grasped it thankfully and slipped open the door catch.

At that moment she heard the front door crash open, with the lock kicked in, and she heard Akkers charge heavily into the living-room. She closed the kitchen door behind her and started across the yard. She tried not to run, she counted her steps. She must not lose her way. She must find the track around the kopje to the servants' hutments.

Her first landmark was the gate in the fence that ringed the homestead. Before she reached it she heard the electricity generator throb to life in the power house beyond the garages. Akkers had found a light switch.

She was slightly off in her direction and she ran into the barbed-wire fence. Frantically she began to feel her way along it, trying for the gate. Above her head she heard the buzz and crackle of the element in one of the arc lamps that lined the fence and could flood the gardens with light.

Akkers must have found the switch beside the kitchen door, and Debra realized that she must be bathed in the light of the arcs.

She heard him shout behind her, and knew that he had seen her. At that moment she found the gate, and with a sob of relief she tore it open and began to run.

She must get out of the light of the arcs, she must find the darkness. Light was mortal danger, darkness was sanctuary.

The track forked, left to the pools, right to the hutments. She took the right-hand path and ran along it. Behind her she heard the gate clank shut. He was after her.

She counted as she ran, five hundred paces to the rock on the left side of the path that marked the next fork. She tripped over it, falling heavily and barking her shins.

She rolled to her knees, and she had lost the walking-stick. She could not waste precious seconds in searching for it. She groped for the path and ran on.

Fifty paces and she knew she was on the wrong fork. This path lead down to the pumphouse – and she was not familiar with it. It was not one of her regular routes.

She missed a turn and ran into broken ground. She stumbled on until rank grass wrapped about her ankles and brought her down again, falling heavily on her side so that she was winded.

She was completely lost, but she knew she was out of the arc lights now. With luck she was shielded by complete darkness – but her heart was racing and she felt nauseous with terror.

She tried to control her gulping, sobbing breath, and to listen.

She heard him coming then, pounding footsteps that rang clearly, even on the rain-soaked earth. He seemed to be coming directly to where she lay, and she shrank down against the wet earth and she pressed her face into her arms to hide her face and muffle her breathing.

At the last moment his blundering footsteps passed her closely, and ran on. She felt sick with relief, but it was premature for abruptly the footsteps ceased and he was so close she could hear him panting.

He was listening for her, standing close beside where she lay in the grass. They stayed like that during the long slow passage of minutes. For Debra it seemed an eternity of waiting – broken at last by his voice.

'Ah! There you are,' he giggled, 'there you are. I can see you.'

Her heart jumped with shock, he was closer than she had thought. Almost she jumped up and began to run again – but some deeper sense restrained her.

'I can see you hiding there,' he repeated, giggling and snickering. 'I've got a big knife here, I'm going to hold you down and cut—'

She quailed in the grass, listening to the awful obscenities that poured from his mouth. Then suddenly she realized that she was safe here. She was covered by the night and the thick grass, and he had lost her. He was trying to panic her, make her run again and betray her position. She concentrated all her attention on remaining absolutely still and silent.

Akkers' threats and sadistic droolings ended in silence again. He listened for her with the patience of the hunter, and the long minutes dragged by.

The ache in her bladder was like a red-hot iron, and she wanted to sob out loud. Something loathsome crawled out of the wet grass over her arm. Her skin prickled with fresh horror at the feel of multiple insect feet on her skin, but she steeled herself not to move.

The thing, scorpion or spider, crawled across her neck and she knew her nerves would crack within seconds.

Suddenly Akkers spoke again. 'All right!' he said, 'I'm going back to fetch a flashlight. We'll see how far you get then. I'll be back soon – don't think you'll beat old Akkers. He's forgotten more tricks than you'll ever learn.'

He moved away heavily, noisily, and she wanted to strike the insect from her cheek and run again, but some instinct warned her. She waited five minutes, and then ten. The insect moved up into her hair.

Akkers spoke again out of the darkness near her. 'All right, you clever bitch. We'll get you yet,' and she heard him move away. This time she knew he had gone.

She brushed the insect from her hair, shuddering with horror. Then she stood up and moved quietly into the forest. Her fingers were stiff and cold on the fastenings of her slacks, but she loosened them and squatted to relieve the burning ache in her lower belly.

She stood up again and felt the child move within her body. The feel of it evoked all her maternal instincts of protection. She must find a safe place for her child. She thought of the hide by the pools.

How to reach them? For she was now completely lost.

Then she remembered David telling her about the wind, the rain wind out of the west, now reduced to an occasional light air, and she waited for the next breath of it on her cheek. It gave her direction. She turned her back to the next gust and set off steadily through the forest with hands held out ahead to prevent herself running into one of the trunks. If only she could reach the pools, she could follow the bank to the hide.

As the cyclonic winds at the centre of the storm turned upon their axis, so they swung, changing direction constantly and Debra followed them faithfully, beginning a wide aimless circle through the forest.

Akkers raged through the brightly lit homestead of Jabulani, jerking open drawers and kicking in locked cupboard doors.

He found the gun cabinet in David's office, and ransacked the desk drawers for keys. He found none, and giggled and swore with frustration.

He crossed the room to the built-in cupboard unit. There was a sealed-cell electric lantern on the shelf with a dozen packets of shotgun shells. He took down the lantern eagerly and thumbed the switch. The beam was bright white, even in the overhead lights – and he sucked his teeth and chuckled happily.

Once more he ran into the kitchen, pausing to select a long stainless-steel carving knife from the cutlery drawer before hurrying across the yard to the gate and along the path.

In the lantern beam, Debra's footprints showed clearly in the soft earth with his own overlaying them. He followed them to where she had blundered off the path, and found the mark of her body where she had lain.

'Clever bitch,' he chuckled again and followed her tracks through the forest. She had laid an easy trail to follow, dragging a passage through the rain-heavy grass and wiping the droplets from the stems. To the hunter's eye it was a clearly blazed trail.

Every few minutes he paused to throw the beam of the lantern ahead of him amongst the trees. He was thrilling now to the hunter's lust, the primeval force which was the mainspring of his existence. His earlier set-back made the chase sweeter for him.

He went on carefully, following the wandering trail, the aimless footprints turning haphazardly in a wide circle.

He stopped again and panned the lantern beam across the rain-laden grass tops, and he saw something move at the extreme range of the lamp, something pale and round.

He held it in the lantern beam, and saw the woman's pale strained face as she moved forward slowly and hesitantly. She went like a sleep-walker, with arms extended ahead of her, and with shuffling uncertain gait.

She was coming directly towards him, oblivious of the light which held her captive in its beam. Once she paused to hug her swollen belly and sob with weariness and fear.

The legs of her trousers were sodden with rain water and her flimsy shoes were already torn, and as she hobbled closer he saw that her arms and her lips were blue and shivering with the cold.

Akkers stood quietly watching her coming towards him, like a chicken drawn to the swaying cobra.

Her long dark hair hung in damp ropes down her shoulders, and dangled in her face. Her thin blouse was wet also with drops fallen from the trees, and it was plastered over the thrusting mound of her belly.

He let her come closer, enjoying the fierce thrill of having her in his power. Drawing out the final consummation of his vengeance – hoarding each moment of it like a miser.

When she was five paces from him he played the beam full in her face, and he giggled.

She screamed, her whole face convulsing, and she whirled like a wild animal and ran blindly. Twenty flying paces before she ran headlong into the stem of a marula tree.

She fell back, collapsing to her knees and sobbed aloud, clutching at her bruised cheek.

Then she scrambled to her feet and stood shivering, turning her head and cocking it for the next sound.

Silently he moved around her, drawing close and he giggled again, close behind her.

She screamed again and ran blindly, panic-stricken, witless with terror until an ant-bear hole caught her foot and flung her down heavily to the ground, and she lay there sobbing.

Akkers moved leisurely and silently after her, he was enjoying himself for the first time in two years. Like a cat he did not want to end it, he wanted it to last a long time.

He stooped over her and whispered a filthy word, and instantly she rolled to her feet and was up and running again – wildly, sightlessly, through the trees. He followed her, and in his crazed mind she became a symbol of all the thousand animals he had hunted and killed.

D avid ran barefooted in the soft earth of the road. He ran without feeling his bruised and torn skin, without feeling the pounding of his heart nor the protest of his lungs.

As the road rounded the shoulder of the hill and dipped towards the homestead he stopped abruptly, and stared panting at the lurid glow of the arc lights that floodlit the grounds and garden of Jabulani. It made no sense that the floodlights should be burning, and David felt a fresh flood of alarm. He sprinted on down the hill.

He ran through the empty, ransacked rooms shouting her name – but the echoes mocked him.

When he reached the front veranda he saw something moving in the darkness, beyond the broken screen door.

'Zulu!' He ran forward. 'Here, boy! Here, boy! Where is she?'

The dog staggered up the steps towards him, his tail wagged a perfunctory greeting, but he was obviously hurt. A heavy blow along the side of his head had broken the jaw, or dislocated it, so that it hung lopsided and grotesque. He was still stunned, and David knelt beside him.

'Where is she, Zulu? Where is she?' The dog seemed to make an effort to gather his scattered wits. 'Where is she, boy? She's not in the house. Where is she? Find her, boy, find her.'

He led the Labrador out into the yard, and he followed gamely as David circled the house. At the back door Zulu picked up the scent on the fresh damp earth. He started resolutely towards the gate, and David saw the footprints in the floodlights, Debra's and the big masculine prints which ran after them.

As Zulu crossed the yard, David turned back into his office. The lantern was missing from its shelf, but there was a five-cell flashlight near the back. He shoved it into his pocket and grabbed a handful of shotgun shells. Then he went quickly to the gun cabinet and unlocked it. He snatched the Purdey shotgun from the rack and loaded it as he ran.

Zulu was staggering along the path beyond the gates, and David hurried after him.

Johann Akkers was no longer a human being, he had become an animal. The spectacle of the running quarry had roused the predator's single-minded passion to chase and drag down and kill – yet it was seasoned with a feline delight in torment. He was playing with his wounded dragging prey, running it when he could have ended it, drawing it out, postponing the climax, the final consuming thrill of the kill.

The moment came at last, some deep atavistic sense of the ritual of the hunt – for all sport killing has its correct ceremony – and Akkers knew it must end now.

He came up behind the running figure and reached out to take a twist of the thick dark hair in the crippled claw of his hand, wrapping it with a quick movement about his wrist and jerking back her head, laying open the long pale throat for the knife.

She turned upon him with a strength and ferocity he had not anticipated. Her body was hard and strong and supple, and now that she could place him she drove at him with the wild terror of a hunted thing.

He was unprepared, her attack took him off-balance, and he went over backwards with her on top of him, and he dropped the knife and the lantern into the grass to protect his eyes, for she was tearing at them with long sharp nails. He felt them rip into his nose and cheek, and she screeched like a cat – for she was also an animal in this moment.

He freed the stiff claw from the tangle of her hair, and he drew it back, holding her off with his right hand – and he struck her. It was like a wooden club, stiff and hard and without feeling. A single blow with it had stunned the Labrador and broken his jaw. It hit her across the temple, a sound like an axe swung at a tree trunk. It knocked all the fight out of her, and he came up on his knees, holding her with his good hand and with the other he clubbed her mercilessly, beat her head back and across with a steady rhythm. In the light of the fallen lantern, the black blood spurted from her nose, and the blows cracked against her skull, steady and unrelenting. Long after she was still and senseless he continued to beat her. Then at last he let her drop, and he stood up. He went to the lantern and played the beam in the grass. The knife glinted up at him.

There is an ancient ceremony with which a hunt should end. The culminating ceremony of the gralloch, when the triumphant huntsman slits open the paunch of his game, and thrusts his hand into the opening to draw out the still-warm viscera.

Johan Akkers picked the knife out of the grass and set down the lantern so the beam fell upon Debra's supine figure.

He went to her and, with his foot, rolled her onto her back. The dark black mane of sodden hair smothered her face.

He knelt beside her and hooked one iron-hard finger into the front of her blouse. With a single jerk he ripped it cleanly open, and her big round belly bulged into the lantern light. It was white and full and ripe with the dark pit of the navel in its centre.

Akkers giggled and wiped the rain and sweat from his

face with his arm. Then he changed his grip on the knife, reversing it so the blade would go shallow, opening the paunch neatly from crotch to rib cage without cutting into the intestines, a stroke as skilful as a surgeon's that he had performed ten thousand times before.

Movement in the shadows at the edge of the light caused him to glance up. He saw the black dog rush silently at him, saw its eyes glow in the lantern light.

He threw up his arm to guard his throat and the furry body crashed into him. They rolled together, with Zulu mouthing him, unable to take a grip with his injured jaws.

Akkers changed his grip on the hilt of the carving knife and stabbed up into the dog's rib cage, finding the faithful heart with his first thrust. Zulu yelped once, and collapsed. Akkers pushed his glossy black body aside, pulling out the knife and he crawled back to where Debra lay.

The distraction that Zulu had provided gave David a chance to come up.

David ran to Akkers, and the man looked up with the muddy green eyes glaring in the lantern light. He growled at David with the long blade in his hand dulled by the dog's blood. He started to come to his feet, ducking his head in exactly the same aggressive gesture as the bull baboon.

David thrust the barrels of the shotgun into his face and he pulled both triggers. The shot hit solidly, without spreading, tearing into him in the bright yellow flash and thunder of the muzzle blast, and it took away the whole of Akkers' head above the mouth, blowing it to nothingness. He dropped into the grass with his legs kicking convulsively, and David hurled the shotgun aside and ran to Debra.

He knelt over her and he whispered, 'My darling, oh my darling. Forgive me, please forgive me. I should never have left you.' Gently he picked her up and holding her to his chest, he carried her up to the homestead.

Debra's child was born in the dawn. It was a girl, tiny and wizened and too early for her term. If there had been skilled medical attention available she might have lived, for she fought valiantly. But David was clumsy and ignorant of the succour she needed. He was cut off by the raging river and the telephone was still dead, and Debra was still unconscious.

When it was over he wrapped the tiny little blue body in a clean sheet and laid it tenderly in the cradle that had been prepared for her. He felt overwhelmed by a sense of guilt at having failed the two persons who needed him.

At three o'clock that afternoon, Conrad Berg forced a passage of the Luzane stream with the water boiling above the level of the big wheels of his truck, and three hours later they had Debra in a private ward of the Nelspruit hospital. Two days later she became conscious once more, but her face was grotesquely swollen and purple with bruises.

Near the crest of the kopje that stood above the homestead of Jabulani there was a natural terrace, a platform which overlooked the whole estate. It was a remote and peaceful place and they buried the child there. Out of the rock of the kopje David built a tomb for her with his own hands.

It was best that Debra had never felt the child in her arms, or at her breast. That she had never heard her cry or smelled the puppy smell of her.

Her mourning was therefore not crippling and corrosive, and she and David visited the grave regularly. One Sunday morning as they sat upon the stone bench beside it, Debra talked for the first time about another baby.

'You took so long with the first one, Morgan,' she complained. 'I hope you've mastered the techinque.'

They walked down the hill again, put the rods and a picnic basket into the Land-Rover and drove down to the pools.

The Mozambique bream came on the bite for an hour just before noon and they fought over the fat yellow wood grubs that David was baiting. Debra hung five, all around three pounds in weight, and David had a dozen of the big blue fish before it went quiet and they propped the rods and opened the cold box.

They lay together on the rug beneath the outspread branches of the fever trees, and drank white wine cold from the icebox.

The African spring was giving way to full summer, filling the bush with bustle and secret activity. The weaver birds were busy upon their basket nests, tying them to the bending tips of the reeds, fluttering brilliant yellow wings as they worked with black heads bobbing. On the far bank of the pool a tiny bejewelled kingfisher sat his perch on a dead branch above the still water, plunging suddenly, a speck of flashing blue to shatter the surface and emerge with a silver sliver wriggling in his outsize beak. Hosts of yellow and bronze and white butterflies lined the water's edge below where they lay, and the bees flew like golden motes of light to their hive in the cliff, high above the quiet pools.

The water drew all life to it, and a little after noonday David touched Debra's arm.

'The nyala are here—' he whispered.

They came through the grove on the far side of the pool. Timid and easily spooked, they approached a few cautious steps at a time before pausing to stare about them with huge dark eyes, questing muzzles and wide-spread ears; striped and dainty and beautiful they blended with the shadows of the grove.

'The does are all belly now,' David told her. 'They'll be dropping their lambs within the next few weeks. Everything

311

is fruitful.' He half-turned towards her and she sensed it and moved to meet him. When the nyala had drunk and gone, and a white-headed fish eagle circled high above them on dark chestnut wings, chanting its weird and haunting cry, they made love in the shade beside the quiet water.

David studied her face as he loved her. She lay beneath him with her eyes closed, and her dark hair spread in a shiny black sheet upon the rug. The bruise on her temple had faded to soft yellow and palest blue, for it was two months since she had left hospital. The white fleck of the grenade scar stood out clearly against the pale bruising. The colour rose in Debra's cheeks, and the light dew of perspiration bloomed across her forehead and upper lip and she made little cooing sounds, and then whimpered softly like a suckling puppy.

David watched her, his whole being engorged and heavy with the weight of his love. From above them an errant beam of sunlight broke through the canopy of leaves and fell full upon her upturned face, lighting it with a warm golden radiance so that it seemed to be the face of a madonna from some medieval church window. It was too much for David and his love broke like a wave, and she felt it and cried out. Her eyes flew wide, and he looked down into their gold-flecked depths. The pupils were huge black pools but as the sunlight struck full into them they shrank rapidly to black pinpoints.

Even in the extremity of his love, David was startled by the phenomenon, and long afterwards when they lay quietly together she asked, 'What is it, David? Is something wrong?'

'No, my darling. What could possibly be wrong?'

'I feel it, Davey. You send out the strongest signals – I am sure I could pick them up from halfway around the world.'

He laughed, and drew away from her almost guiltily. He

had imagined it perhaps, a trick of the light, and he tried to dismiss it from his mind.

In the cool of the evening he packed up the rods and the rug and they strolled back to where he had parked and they took the fire-break road home, for David wanted to check the southern fence line. They had driven for twenty minutes in silence before Debra touched his arm.

'When you are ready to tell me about whatever is bugging you – I'm ready to listen,' and he began talking again to distract both her and himself, but a little too glibly.

In the night he rose and went to the bathroom. When he returned he stood for many seconds beside their bed looking down at her dark sleeping shape. He would have left it then, but at that moment a lion began roaring down near the pools. The sound carried clearly through the still night across the two miles that separated them.

It was the excuse that David needed. He took the five-cell flashlight from his bedside table and shone it into Debra's face. It was serene and lovely, and he felt the urge to stoop and kiss her, but instead he called.

'Debra! Wake up, darling!' and she stirred and opened her eyes. He shone the beam of the flashlight full into them and again, unmistakably, the wide black circles of the pupils contracted.

'What is it, David?' she murmured sleepily, and his voice was husky as he replied.

'There is a lion holding a concert down near the pools. Thought you might want to listen.' She moved her head, averting her face slightly, almost as though the powerful beam of the flashlight was causing discomfort, but her voice was pleased.

'Oh yes. I love that big growly sound. Where do you suppose this one is from?'

David switched out the flashlight and slipped back into bed beside her.

'Probably coming up from the south. I bet he has dug a hole under the fence you could drive a truck through.' He tried to speak naturally as they reached for each other beneath the bedclothes and lay close and warm, listening to the far-away roaring until it faded with distance as the lion moved back towards the reserve. They made love then, but afterwards David could not sleep and he lay with Debra in his arms until the dawn.

Still it was a week before David could bring himself to write the letter:

Dear Dr Edelman,

We agreed that I should write to you if any change occurred in the condition of Debra's eyes, or her health.

Recently Debra was involved in unfortunate circumstances, in which she was struck repeated heavy blows about the head and was rendered unconscious for a period of two and half days.

She was hospitalized for suspected fracture of the skull, and concussion, but was discharged after ten days.

This occurred about two months ago. However, I have since noticed that her eyes have become sensitive to light. As you are well aware, this was not previously the case, and she has showed no reaction whatsoever until this time. She has also complained of severe headaches.

I have repeatedly tested my observations with sunlight and artificial light, and there can be no doubt that under the stimulus of a strong light source, the pupils of her eyes contract instantly and to the same degree as one would expect in a normal eye.

It now seems possible that your original diagnosis might have to be revised, but – and I would emphasize this most strongly – I feel that we should approach this very carefully. I do not wish to awaken any false or ill-founded hope.

314

For your advice in this matter I would be most grateful, and I wait to hear from you.

Cordially yours,

David Morgan.

David sealed and addressed the letter, but when he returned from the shopping flight to Nelspruit the following week, the envelope was still buttoned in the top pocket of his leather jacket.

The days settled into their calmly contented routine. Debra completed the first draft of her new novel, and received a request from Bobby Dugan to carry out a lecture tour of five major cities in the United States. A *Place of Our Own* had just completed its thirty-second week on the *New York Times* bestseller list – and her agent informed her that she was 'hotter than a pistol'.

David said that as far as he was concerned she was probably a lot hotter than that. Debra told him he was a lecher, and she was not certain what a nice girl like herself was doing shacked up with him. Then she wrote to her agent, and refused the lecture tour.

'Who needs people?' David agreed with her, knowing that she had made the decision for him. He knew also that Debra as a lovely, blind, bestselling authoress would have been a sensation, and a tour would have launched her into the superstar category.

This made his own procrastination even more corrosive. He tried to re-think and rationalize his delay in posting the letter to Dr Edelman. He told himself that the light-sensitivity did not mean that Debra could ever regain her vision; that she was happy now, had adjusted and found her place and that it would be cruel to disrupt all this and offer her false hope and probably brutal surgery.

In all his theorizing he tried to make Debra's need take priority, but it was deception and he knew it. It was special pleading, by David Morgan, for David Morgan – for if

Debra ever regained her sight, the delicately balanced structure of his own happiness would collapse in ruin.

One morning he drove the Land-Rover alone to the farthest limits of Jabulani and parked in a hidden place amongst camel thorn trees. He switched off the engine and, still sitting in the driving-seat, he adjusted the driving-mirror and stared at his own face. For nearly an hour he studied that ravage expanse of inhuman flesh, trying to find some redeeming feature in it – apart from the eyes – and at the end he knew that no sighted woman would ever be able to live close to that, would ever be able to smile at it, kiss and touch it, to reach up and caress it in the critical moments of love.

He drove home slowly, and Debra was waiting for him on the shady cool stoep and she laughed and ran down the steps into the sunlight when she heard the Land-Rover. She wore faded denims and a bright pink blouse, and when he came to her she lifted her face and groped blindly but joyously with her lips for his.

Debra had arranged a barbecue for that evening, and although they sat close about the open fire under the trees and listened to the night sounds, the night was cool. Debra wore a cashmere sweater over her shoulders, and David had thrown on his flying jacket.

The letter lay against his heart, and it seemed to burn into his flesh. He unbuttoned the leather flap and took it out. While Debra chatted happily beside him, spreading her hands to the crackling leaping flames, David examined the envelope turning it slowly over and over in his hands.

Then suddenly, as though it were a live scorpion, he threw it from him and watched it blacken and curl and crumple to ash in the flames of the fire.

It was not so easily done, however, and that night as he lay awake, the words of the letter marched in solemn procession through his brain, meticulously preserved and perfectly remembered. They gave him no respite, and though his eyes were gravelly and his head ached with fatigue, he could not sleep.

During the days that followed he was silent and edgy. Debra sensed it, despite all his efforts to conceal it – and she was seriously alarmed, believing that he was angry with her. She was anxiously loving, distracted from all else but the need to find and cure the cause of David's ills.

Her concern only served to make David's guilt deeper.

Almost in an act of desperation they drove one evening down to the String of Pearls, and leaving the Land-Rover they walked hand in hand to the water's edge. They found a fallen log screened by reeds and sat quietly together. For once neither of them had anything to say to each other.

As the big red sun sank to the tree-tops and the gloom thickened amongst the trees of the grove, the nyala herd came stepping lightly and fearfully through the shadows.

David nudged Debra, and she turned her head into a listening attitude and moved a little closer to him as he whispered.

'They are really spooky this evening, they look as though they are standing on springs and I can see their muscles trembling from here. The old bulls seem to be on the verge of a nervous breakdown, they are listening so hard their ears have stretched to twice their usual length, I swear. There must be a leopard lurking along the edge of the reed bed—' He broke off, and exclaimed softly, 'Oh, so that's it!'

'What is it, David?' Debra tugged at his arm insistently, her curiosity spurring her.

'A new fawn!' David's delight was in his voice. 'One of the does has lambed. Oh God, Debra! His legs are still wobbly and he is the palest creamy beige—' He described the fawn to her as it followed the mother unsteadily into the open. Debra was listening with such intensity, that it was clear the act of birth and the state of maternity had touched some deep chord within her. Perhaps she was remembering her own dead infant. Her grip on his arm tightened, and her blind eyes seemed to glow in the gathering dusk – and suddenly she spoke, her voice low, but achingly clear, filled with all the longing and sadness which she had suppressed.

'I wish I could see it,' she said. 'Oh God! God Let me see. Please, let me see!' and suddenly she was weeping, great racking sobs that shook her whole body.

Across the pool the nyala herd took fright, and dashed away among the trees. David took Debra and held her fiercely to his chest, cradling her head, so her tears were wet and cold through the fabric of his shirt – and he felt the icy winds of despair blow across his soul.

He re-wrote the letter that night by the light of a gas lamp while Debra sat across the room knitting a jersey she had promised him for the winter and believing that he was busy with the estate accounts. David found that he could repeat the words of the original letter perfectly and it took him only a few minutes to complete and seal it.

'Are you working on the book tomorrow morning?' he asked casually, and when she told him she was, he went on, 'I have to nip into Nelspruit for an hour or two.'

David flew high as though to divorce himself from the earth. He could not really believe he was going to do it. He could not believe that he was capable of such sacrifice. He wondered whether it was really possible to love somebody so deeply that he would chance destroying that love for the good of the other – and he knew that it was, and as he flew on southwards he found that he could face it at last.

Of all persons, Debra needed her vision, for without it the great wings of her talent were clipped. Unless she could see it, she could not describe it. She had been granted the gift of the writer, and then half of it had been taken from her. He understood her cry, 'Oh God! God! Let me see. Please, let me see,' and he found himself wishing it for her also. Beside her need his seemed trivial and petty, and silently he prayed.

'Please God, let her see again.'

He landed the Navajo at the airstrip and called the taxi and had it drive him directly to the Post Office, and wait while he posted the letter and collected the incoming mail from the box.

'Where now?' the driver asked as he came out of the building, and he was about to tell him to drive back to the airfield when he had inspiration.

'Take me down to the bottle store, please,' he told the driver and he bought a case of Veuve Clicquot champagne.

He flew homewards with a soaring lightness of the spirit. The wheel was spinning and the ball clicking, nothing he could do now would dictate its fall. He was free of doubt, free of guilt – whatever the outcome, he knew he could meet it.

Debra sensed it almost immediately, and she laughed aloud with relief, and hugged him about the neck.

'But what *happened*?' she kept demanding. 'For weeks you were miserable. I was worrying myself sick – and then you go off for an hour or two and you come back humming like a dynamo. What on earth is going on, Morgan?'

'I have just found out how much I love you,' he told her, returning her hug.

'Plenty?' she demanded.

'Plenty!' he agreed.

'That's my baby!' she applauded him.

The Veuve Clicquot came in useful. In the batch of mail that David brought back with him from Nelspruit was a letter from Bobby Dugan. He was very high on the first chapters of the new novel that Debra had airmailed to him, and so were the publishers; he had managed to hit them for an advance of $100,000.

'You're rich!' David laughed, looking up from the letter.

'The only reason you married me,' agreed Debra. 'Fortune hunter!' but she was laughing with excitement, and David was proud and happy for her.

'They like it, David.' Debra was serious then. 'They *really* like it. I was so worried.' The money was meaningless, except as a measure of the book's value. Big money is the sincerest type of praise.

'They would have to be feeble-minded not to like it,' David told her, and then went on. 'It just so happens that I have a case of French champagne with me, shall I put a bottle or ten on the ice?'

'Morgan, man of vision,' Debra said. 'At times like this, I know why I love you.'

The weeks that followed were as good then as they had ever been. David's appreciation was sharper, edged by the storm shadows on the horizon, the time of plenty made more poignant by the possibility of the drought years coming. He tried to draw it out beyond its natural time. It was five weeks more before he flew to Nelspruit again, and then only because Debra was anxious to learn of any further news from her publishers and agent, and to pick up her typing.

'I would like to have my hair set, and although I know we don't really need them, David, my darling, we should keep in touch with people – like once a month – don't you think?'

'Has it been that long?' David asked innocently, although each day had been carefully weighed and tallied, the actuality savoured and the memory stored for the lean times ahead.

David left Debra at the beauty salon, and as he went out he could hear her pleading with the girl not to 'put it up into those tight little curls and plaster it with lacquer' and even in the anxiety of the moment, David grinned for he had always thought of the hairstyle she was describing as 'Modern Cape Dutch' or 'Randburg Renaissance'.

The postbox was crammed full and David sorted quickly through the junk mail and picked out three letters from Debra's American agent, and two envelopes with Israeli stamps. Of these one was addressed in a doctor's prescription scrawl, and David was surprised that it had found its destination. The writing on the second envelope was unmistakable, it marched in martial ranks, each letter in step with the next, and the high strokes were like the weapons of a company of pike men, spiky and abrupt.

David found a bench in the park under the purple jacaranda trees, and he opened Edelman's letter first. It was in Hebrew, which made deciphering even more difficult.

Dear David,

Your letter came as a surprise, and I have since studied the X-ray plates once more. They seem unequivocal, and upon an interpretation of them I would not hesitate to confirm my original prognosis—

Despite himself, David felt the small stirrings of relief.

– However, if I have learned anything in twenty-five years of practice, it is humility. I can only accept that your observations of light-sensitivity are correct. Having done so, then I must also accept that there is at least partial function of the optic nerves. This presupposes that the nerve was not completely divided, and it seems reasonable to believe now that it was only partially severed, and that now – possibly due to the head blows that Debra received – it has regained some function.

The crucial question is just how great that recovery is, and again I must warn you that it may be as minimal as it is at the present time, when it amounts to nothing more than light sensitivity without any increase to the amount of vision. It may, however, be greater, and it is

321

within the realms of possibility that with treatment some portion of sight may be regained. I do not expect, however, that this will ever amount to more than a vague definition of light or shape, and a decision would have to be made as to whether any possible benefit might not be outweighed by the undesirability of surgery within such a vulnerable area.

I would, of course, be all too willing to examine Debra myself. However, it will probably be inconvenient for you to journey to Jerusalem, and I have therefore taken the liberty of writing to a colleague of mine in Cape Town who is one of the leading world authorities on optical trauma. He is Dr Ruben Friedman and I enclose a copy of my letter to him. You will see that I have also dispatched to him Debra's orginal X-ray plates and a clinical history of her case.

I would recommend most strongly that you take the first opportunity of presenting Debra to Dr Friedman, and that you place in him your complete confidence. I might add that the optical unit of Groote Schuur Hospital is rightly world-renowned and fully equipped to provide any treatment necessary – they do not restrict their activities to heart transplants!

I have taken the liberty of showing your letter to General Mordecai, and of discussing the case with him—

David folded the letter the carefully. 'Why the hell did he have to bring the Brig into it, talk about a war horse in a rose garden—' and he opened the Brig's letter.

Dear David,

Dr Edelman has spoken with me. I have telephoned Friedman in Cape Town, and he has agreed to see Debra.

For some years I have been postponing a lecture tour

to South Africa which the S.A. Zionist Council has been urging upon me. I have today written to them and asked them to make the arrangements.

This will give us the excuse to bring Debra to Cape Town. Tell her I have insufficient time to visit you on your farm but insist upon seeing her.

I will give you my dates later, and expect to see you then—

It was in typical style, brusque and commanding, presupposing acquiescence. It was out of David's hands now. There was no turning back, but there was still the chance that it would not work. He found himself hoping for that – and his own selfishness sickened him a little. He turned over the letter and on the reverse he drafted a dummy letter from the Brig setting out his plans for the forthcoming tour. This was for Debra, and he found faint amusement in aping the Brig's style, so that he might read it aloud to Debra convincingly.

Debra was ecstatic when he read it to her and he experienced a twinge of conscience at his deceit.

'It will be wonderful seeing him again, I wonder if Mother will be coming out with him—?'

'He didn't say, but I doubt it.' David sorted the American mail into chronological order from the post marks, and read them to her. The first two were editorial comment on *Burning Bright* and were set aside for detailed reply – but the third letter was another with hard news.

United Artists wanted to film *A Place of Our Own* and were talking impressively heavy figures for the twelve-month option against an outright purchase of the property and a small percentage of the profits. However, if Debra would go to California and write the screenplay, Bobby Dugan felt sure he could roll it all into a quarter-million-dollar package. He wanted her to weigh the fact that even established novelists were seldom asked to write their own screenplays – this was an offer not to be lightly spurned, and he urged Debra to accept.

'Who needs people?' Debra laughed it away quickly, too quickly – and David caught the wistful expression before she turned her head away and asked brightly, 'Have you got any of that champagne left, Morgan? I think we can celebrate – don't you?'

'The way you're going, Morgan, I'd best lay in a store of the stuff,' he replied, and went to the gas refrigerator. It foamed to the rim of the glass as he poured the wine, and before it subsided and he had carried the glass to her, he had made his decision.

'Let's take his advice seriously, and think about you going to Hollywood,' he said, and put the glass in her hand.

'What's to think about?' she asked. 'This is where we belong.'

'No, let's wait a while before replying—'

'What do you mean?' She lowered the glass without tasting the wine.

'We will wait until – let's say, until after we have seen the Brig in Cape Town.'

'Why?' She looked puzzled. 'Why should it be different then?'

'No reason. It's just that it is an important decision – the choice of time is arbitrary, however.'

'*Beseder!*' she agreed readily, and raised the glass to toast him. 'I love you.'

'I love you,' he said, and as he drank he was glad that she had so many roads to choose from.

The Brig's arrangements allowed them three more weeks before the rendezvous in Cape Town, and David drew upon each hour to the full, anticipating his chances of expulsion from their private Eden.

They were happy days and it seemed that nature had conspired to give them of her best. The good rains fell steadily, always beginning in the afternoon after a morning of tall clouds and heavy air filled with static and the feel of thunder. In the sunset the lightning played and flickered across the gilt cloud banks, turned by the angry sun to the colour of burnished bronze and virgins' blushes. Then in the darkness as they lay entwined, the thunder struck like a hammer blow and the lightning etched the window beyond the bed to a square of blinding white light, and the rain came teeming down with the sound of wild fire and running hooves. With David beside her, Debra was unafraid.

In the morning it was bright and cool, the trees washed sparkling clean so that the leaves glinted in the early sun and the earth was dark with water and spangled with standing pools.

The rains brought life and excitement to the wild things, and each day held its small discoveries – unexpected visitations, and strange occurrences.

The fish eagles moved their two chicks from the great shaggy nest in the mhobahoba at the head of the pools and taught them to perch out on the bare limb that supported it. They sat there day after day, seeming to gather their courage. The parent birds were frenetic in their ministrations, grooming their offspring for the great moment of flight.

Then one morning, as he and Debra ate breakfast on the stoop, David heard the swollen chorus of their chanting cries, harsh with triumph, and he took Debra's hand and they went down the steps into the open. David looked up and saw the four dark shapes spread on wide wings against the clear blue of the sky – and his spirit soared with them in their moment of achievement. They flew upwards in great sweeping circles, until they dwindled to specks and vanished, gone to their autumn grounds upon the Zambezi River, two thousand miles to the north.

There was, however, one incident during those last days that saddened and subdued them both. One morning, they walked four miles northwards beyond the line of hills to a narrow wedge-shaped plain on which stood a group of towering leadwood trees.

A pair of martial eagles had chosen the tallest leadwood as their mating ground. The female was a beautiful young bird but the male was past his prime. They had begun constructing their nest on a high fork, but the work was interrupted by the intrusion of a lone male eagle, a big young bird, fierce and proud and acquisitive. David had noticed him lurking about the borders of the territory, carefully avoiding overflying the airspace claimed by the breeding pair, choosing a perch on the hills overlooking the plain and gathering his confidence for the confrontation he was so clearly planning. The impending conflict had its particular fascination for David and his sympathy was with the older bird as he made his warlike show, screeching defiance from his perch upon the high branches of the leadwood or weaving his patrols along his borders, turning on his great wings always within the limits of that which he claimed as his own.

David had decided to walk up to the plain that day, in order to choose a site for the photographic blind he planned to erect overlooking the nest site, and also in curiosity as to the outcome of this primeval clash between the two males.

It seemed more than chance that he had chosen the day when the crisis was reached.

David and Debra came up through the gap in the hills and paused to sit on an outcrop of rock overlooking the plain while they regained their breath. The battlefield was spread below them.

The old bird was at the nest, a dark hunched shape with white breast and head set low on the powerful shoulders. David looked for the invader, sweeping the crests of the hills with his binoculars, but there was no sign of him. He dropped the binoculars to his chest and he and Debra talked quietly for a while.

Then suddenly David's attention was attracted by the behaviour of the old eagle. He launched suddenly into flight, striking upwards on his great black pinions, and there was an urgency in the way he bored for height.

His climb brought him close over their heads, so that David could clearly see the cruel curve of the beak and the ermine black splashes that decorated the imperial snow of his breast.

He opened the yellow beak and shrieked a harsh challenge, and David turned quickly in the old fighter pilot's sweep of sky and cloud. He saw the cunning of it immediately. The younger bird had chosen his moment and his attack vector with skill beyond his years. He was towering in the sun, high and clear, a flagrant trespasser, daring the old eagle to come up at him, and David felt his skin crawl in sympathy as he watched the defender climb slowly on flogging wings.

Quickly, and a little breathlessly, he described it to Debra and she reached for his hand, her sympathy with the old bird also.

'Tell me!' she commanded.

The young bird sailed calmly in waiting circles, cocking his head to watch his adversary's approach.

'There he goes!' David's voice was taut, as the attacker went wing over and began his stoop.

'I can hear him,' Debra whispered, and the sound of his wings carried clearly to them, rustling like a bush fire in dry grass as he dived on the old bird.

'Break left! Go! Go! Go!' David found he was calling to the old eagle as though he were flying wingman for him, and he gripped Debra's hand until she winced. The old eagle seemed almost to hear him, for he closed his wings and flicked out of the path of the strike, tumbling for a single turn so that the attacker hissed by him with talons reaching uselessly through air, his speed plummeting him down into the basin of the plain.

The old bird caught and broke out of his roll with wings half-cocked, and streaked down after the other. In one veteran stroke of skill he had wrested the advantage.

'Get him!' screamed David. 'Get him when he turns! Now!'

The young bird was streaking towards the tree-tops and swift death, he flared his wings to break his fall, turning desperately to avoid the lethal stoop of his enemy. In that moment he was vulnerable and the old eagle reached forward with his terrible spiked talons and without slackening the searing speed of his dive he hit the other bird in the critical moment of his turn.

The thud of the impact carried clearly to the watchers on the hill and there was a puff of feathers like the burst of explosives, black from the wings and white from the breast.

Locked together by the old bird's honed killing claws, they tumbled, wing over tangled wing, feathers streaming from their straining bodies and then drifting away like thistledown on the light breeze.

Still joined in mortal combat, they struck the top branches of one of the leadwood trees, and fell through them to come to rest at last in a high fork as an untidy bundle of ruffled feathers and trailing wings.

Leading Debra over the rough ground David hurried down the hill and through the coarse stands of arrow grass to the tree.

'Can you see them?' Debra asked anxiously, as David focused his binoculars on the struggling pair.

'They are trapped,' David told her. 'The old fellow has his claws buried to the hilt in the other's back. He will never be able to free them and they have fallen across the fork, one on either side of the tree.'

The screams of rage and agony rang from the hills about

them, and the female eagle sailed anxiously above the leadwood. She added her querulous screeching to the sound of conflict.

'The young bird is dying.' David studied him through the lens, watching the carmine drops ooze from the gaping yellow beak to fall and glisten upon the snowy breast, like a dying king's rubies.

'And the old bird—' Debra listened to the clamour with face upturned, her eyes dark with concern.

'He will never get those claws loose, they lock automatically as soon as pressure is applied and he will not be able to lift himself. He will die also.'

'Can't you do something?' Debra was tugging at his arm. 'Can't you help him?'

Gently he tried to explain to her that the birds were locked together seventy feet above the earth. The bole of the leadwood was smooth and without branches for the first fifty feet of its height. It would take days of effort to reach the birds, and by then it would be too late.

'Even if one could reach them, darling, they are two wild creatures, fierce and dangerous, those beaks and talons could tear the eyes out of your head or rip you to the bone – nature does not like interference in her designs.'

'Isn't there anything we can do?' she pleaded.

'Yes,' he answered quietly. 'We can come back in the morning to see if he has been able to free himself. But we will bring a gun with us, in case he has not.'

In the dawn they came together to the leadwood tree. The young bird was dead, hanging limp and graceless, but the old bird was still alive, linked by his claws to the carcass of the other, weak and dying but with the furious yellow flames still burning in his eyes. He heard their voices and twisted the shaggy old head and opened his beak in a last defiant cry.

David loaded the shotgun, snapping the barrels closed and staring up at the old eagle. 'Not you alone, old friend,' he thought, and he lifted the gun to his shoulder and hit him with two charges of buckshot. They left him hanging in tatters with trailing wings and the quick patter of blood slowing to a dark steady drip. David felt as though he had destroyed a part of himself in that blast of gunfire, and the shadow of it was cast over the bright days that followed.

These few days sped past too swiftly for David, and when they were almost gone he and Debra spent the last of them wandering together across Jabulani, visiting each of their special places and seeking out the various herds or individual animals almost as if they were taking farewell of old friends. In the evening they came to the place amongst the fever trees beside the pools, and they sat there until the sun had fallen below the earth in a splendour of purples and muted pinks. Then the mosquitoes began whining about their heads, and they strolled back hand in hand and came to the homestead in the dark.

They packed their bags that night and left them on the stoep, ready for an early start. Then they drank champagne beside the barbecue fire. The wine lifted their mood and they laughed together in their little island of firelight in the vast ocean of the African night – but for David there were echoes from the laughter, and he was aware of a sense of finality, of an ending of something and a new beginning.

When they took off from the landing-strip in the early morning, David circled twice over the estate, climbing slowly, and the pools glinted like gunmetal amongst the hills as the low sun touched them. The land was lush with the severe unpromising shade of green, so different from that of the lands of the northern hemisphere, and the servants stood in the yard of the homestead, shading their eyes and waving up at them, their shadows lying long and narrow against the ruddy earth.

David came around and steadied on course.

'Cape Town, here we come,' he said, and Debra smiled

and reached across to lay her hand upon his leg in warm and companionable silence.

They had the suite at the Mount Nelson Hotel, preferring its ancient elegance and spacious palmy gardens to the modern slabs of glass and concrete upon the foreshore and the rocks of Sea Point. They stayed in the suite for the two days, awaiting the Brig's arrival, for David had grown unaccustomed to humanity in its massed and unlovely multitudes, and found the quick inquisitive glances and murmurs of pity that followed him hard to stomach.

On the second day the Brig arrived. He knocked on the door of the suite and then entered with his aggressive and determined stride. He was lean and hard and brown, as David remembered, and when he and Debra had embraced, he turned to David and his hand was dry and leathery – but it seemed that he looked at David with a new calculation in the fierce warrior eyes.

While Debra bathed and dressed for the evening, he took David to his own suite and poured whisky for him without asking his preference. He gave David the glass and began immediately to discuss the arrangements he had made.

'Friedman will be at the reception. I will introduce him to Debra and let them talk for a while, then he will be seated next to her at the dinner-table. This will give us the opportunity to persuade Debra to undergo an examination later—'

'Before we go any further, sir,' David interrupted, 'I want your assurance that at no time will it ever be suggested to her that there is a possibility of Debra regaining her sight.'

'Very well.'

'I mean, at no time whatsoever. Even if Friedman determines that surgery is necessary, it must be for some other reason than to restore sight—'

'I don't think that is possible,' the Brig snapped angrily.

'If matters go that far, then Debra must be told. It would not be fair—'

It was David's turn for anger, although the frozen mask of his features remained immobile, the lipless slit of mouth turned pale and the blue eyes glared.

'Let me determine what is fair. I know her as you never can, I know what she feels and what she is thinking. If you offer her a chance of sight, you will create for her the same dilemma in which I have been trapped since the possibility first arose. I would spare her that.'

'I do not understand you,' the Brig said stiffly. The hostility between them was a tangible essence that seemed to fill the room with the feel of thunder on a summer's day.

'Then let me explain,' David held his eyes, refusing to be brow-beaten by this fierce and thrusting old warrior. 'Your daughter and I have achieved an extraordinary state of happiness.'

The Brig inclined his head, acknowledging. 'Yes, I will accept your word for that – but it is an artificial state. It's a hot-house thing, reared in isolation – it has no relation to the real world. It's a dream state.'

David felt his anger begin to shake the foundations of his reason. He found it offensive that anybody should speak of Debra and his life in those terms – but at the same time he could see the justification.

'You may say so, sir. But for Debra and me, it is very real. It is something of tremendous value.'

The Brig was silent now.

'I will tell you truly that I thought long and hard before I admitted that there was a chance for Debra, and even then I would have hidden it for my own selfish happiness—'

'You still do not make sense. How can Debra regaining her sight affect you?'

'Look at me,' said David softly, and the Brig glared at

him ferociously, expecting more, but when nothing further came his expression eased and he did look at David – for the first time truly seeing the terribly ravaged head, the obscene travesty of human shape – and suddenly he thought on it from David's side, whereas before he had considered it only as a father.

His eyes dropped and he turned to replenish his whisky glass.

'If I can give her sight, I will do it. Even though it will be an expensive gift for me, she must take it.' David felt his voice trembling. 'But I believe that she loves me enough to spurn it, if she were ever given the choice. I do not want her ever to be tortured by that choice.'

The Brig lifted his glass and took a deep swallow, half the contents at a gulp.

'As you wish,' he acquiesced, and it may have been the whisky, but his voice sounded husky with an emotion David had never suspected before.

'Thank you, sir.' David set down his own glass, still untasted. 'If you'll excuse me, I think I should go and change now.' He moved to the door.

'David!' the Brig called to him and he turned back. The gold tooth gleamed in the dark bristly patch of moustache, as the Brig smiled a strangely embarrassed but gentle smile.

'You'll do,' he said.

The reception was in the banquet-room at the Heerengracht Hotel, and as David and Debra rode up together in the elevator, she seemed to sense his dread, for she squeezed his arm.

'Stay close to me tonight,' she murmured. 'I'll need you,' and he knew it was said to distract him and he was grateful to her. They would be a freak show, and even though he was sure most of the guests had been prepared, yet he knew it would be an ordeal. He leaned to brush her cheek with his.

Her hair was loose and soft, very dark and glossy – and the sun had gilded her face to gold. She wore a plain green sheath that fell in simple lines to the floor, but left her arms and shoulders bare. They were strong and smooth, with the special lustre of the skin highlighting the smooth flow of her flesh.

She wore little make-up, a light touch on the lips only, and the serene expression of her eyes enhanced the simple grace of her carriage as she moved on his arm, giving David just that courage he needed to face the crowded room.

It was an elegant gathering, women in rich silks and jewellery, the men dark-suited, with the heaviness of body and poise which advertises power and wealth – but the Brig stood out amongst them, even in a civilian suit, lean and hard where they were plump and complacent – like a falcon amongst a flock of pheasants.

He brought Reuben Friedman to them and introduced them casually. He was a short, heavily built man, with a big alert head seeming out of proportion to his body. His hair was cropped short and grizzled to the round skull, but David found himself liking the bright bird eyes and the readiness of his smile. His hand was warm, but dry and firm. Debra was drawn to him also, and smiled when she picked up the timbre of his voice and the essential warmth of his personality.

As they went into dinner, she asked David what he looked like, and laughed with delight when he replied.

'Like a koala bear,' and they were talking easily together before the fish course was served. Friedman's wife, a slim girl with horn-rimmed spectacles, neither beautiful nor plain, but with her husband's forthright friendly manner, leaned across him to join the conversation and David heard her say, 'Won't you come to lunch tomorrow? If you can stand a brood of squalling kids.'

'We don't usually—' Debra replied, but David could hear her wavering, and she turned to him. 'May we—?' and he agreed and then they were laughing like old friends, but David was silent and withdrawn, knowing it was all subterfuge and suddenly oppressed by the surging chorus of human voices and the clatter of cutlery. He found himself longing for the night silence of the bushveld, and the solitude which was not solitude with Debra to share it.

When the master of ceremonies rose to introduce the speaker, David found it an intense relief to know the ordeal was drawing to a close and he could soon hurry away with Debra to hide from the prying, knowing eyes.

The introductory speech was smooth and professional, the jokes raised a chuckle – but it lacked substance, five minutes after you would not remember what had been said.

Then the Brig rose and looked about him with a kind of Olympian scorn, the warrior's contempt for the soft men, and though these rich and powerful men seemed to quail beneath the stare, yet David sensed that they enjoyed it. They derived some strange vicarious pleasure from this man. He was a figurehead – he gave to them a deep confidence, a point on which their spirits could rally. He was one of them, and yet apart. It seemed that he was a storehouse of the race's pride and strength.

Even David was surprised by the power that flowed from the lean old warrior, the compelling presence with which he filled the huge room and dominated his audience. He seemed immortal and invincible, and David's own emotions stirred, his own pulse quickened and he found himself carried along on the flood.

' – but for all of this there is a price to pay. Part of this price is constant vigil, constant readiness. Each of us is ready at any moment to answer the call to the defence of what is ours – and each of us must be ready to make without question whatever sacrifice is demanded. This can be life itself, or something every bit as dear—'

Suddenly David realized that the Brig had singled him out, and that they were staring at each other across the room. The Brig was sending him a message of strength, of courage – but it was misinterpreted by others in the gathering.

They saw the silent exchange between the two men, and many of them knew that David's terrible disfigurement and Debra's blindness were wounds of war. They misunderstood the Brig's reference to sacrifice, and one of them began to applaud.

Immediately it was taken up, a smattering here and there amongst the tables, but quickly the sound rose – became thunder. People were staring at David and Debra as they clapped, other heads turned towards them. Chairs began to scrape as they were pushed back and men and women came to their feet, their faces smiling and their applause pounding, until it filled the hall with sound and they were all standing.

Debra was not sure what it was all about, until she felt David's desperate hand in hers and heard his voice.

'Let's get out of here – quickly. They are all staring. They are staring at us—'

She could feel his hand shaking and the strength of his distress at being the subject of their ghoulish curiosity.

'Come, let's get away.' And she rose at his urging with her heart crying out in pain for him, and followed him while the thunder of applause burst upon his defenceless head like the blows of an enemy and their eyes wantonly raked his ravaged flesh.

Even when they reached the sanctuary of their own suite, he was still shaking like a man in fever.

'The bastard,' he whispered, as he poured whisky in a

glass and the neck of the bottle clattered against the crystal rim. 'The cruel bastard – why did he do that to us?'

'David.' She came to him groping for his hand. 'He didn't mean it to hurt. I know he meant it well, I think he was trying to say he was proud of you.'

David felt the urge to flee, to find relief from it all within the sanctuary of Jabulani. The temptation to say to her 'Come' and lead her there, knowing that she would do so instantly, was so strong that he had to wrestle with it, as though it were a physical adversary.

The whisky tasted rank and smoky. It offered no avenue of escape and he left the glass standing upon the counter of the private bar and turned instead to Debra.

'Yes,' she whispered into his mouth. 'Yes, my darling,' and there was a woman's pride, a woman's joy in being the vessel of his ease. As always she was able to fly with him above the storm, using the wild winds of love to drive them both aloft, until they broke through together into the brightness and peace and safety.

David woke in the night while she lay sleeping. There was a silver moon reflecting from the french windows and he could study her sleeping face, but after a while it was not sufficient for his need and he reached across gently and switched on the bedside lamp.

She stirred in her sleep, coming softly awake with small sighs and tumbling black hair brushed from her eyes with a sleep-clumsy hand, and David felt the first chill of impending loss. He knew he had not moved the bed when he lit the lamp, what had disturbed her he knew beyond doubt was the light itself – and this time not even their loving could distract him.

Reuben Friedman's dwelling proclaimed his station in the world. It was built above the sea with lawns that ran down to the beach and big dark green melkhout trees surrounding the swimming-pool, with an elaborate cabana and barbecue area. Marion Friedman's horde of kids were especially thinned out for the occasion, probably farmed out with friends, but she retained her two youngest. These came to peer in awe at David for a few minutes, but at a sharp word from their mother they went off to the pool and became immersed in water and their own games.

The Brig had another speaking engagement, so the four adults were left alone, and after a while they relaxed. Somehow the fact that Reuben was a doctor seemed to set both David and Debra at their ease. Debra remarked on it, when the conversation turned to their injuries and Reuben asked solicitously, 'You don't mind talking about it?'

'No, not with you. Somehow it's all right to bare yourself in front of a doctor.'

'Don't do it, my dear,' Marion cautioned her. 'Not in front of Ruby anyway – look at me, six kids, already!' And they laughed.

Ruby had been out early that morning and taken half a dozen big crayfish out of the crystal water, from a kelp-filled pool in the rocks which he boasted was his private fishing-ground.

He wrapped them in fresh kelp leaves and steamed them over the coals until they turned bright scarlet and the flesh was milk white and succulent as he broke open the carapaces.

'Now, if that isn't the finest spring chicken you have ever seen—' he crowed as he held up the dismembered shellfish, ' – you all bear witness that it's got two legs and feathers.'

David admitted that he had never tasted poultry like it

and as he washed it down with a dry Cape Riesling he found it was no terrible hardship to reach for another. Both he and Debra were enjoying themselves, so that it came as a jolt when Reuben at last began on the real purpose of their meeting.

He was leaning across Debra to refill her wine glass, when he paused and asked her.

'How long is it since your eyes were last checked out, my dear?' and gently he placed his hand under her chin and tilted her face to look into her eyes. David's nerves snapped taut, and he moved quickly in his chair, watching intently.

'Not since I left Israel – though they took some X-rays when I was in hospital.'

'Any headaches?' Ruby asked, and she nodded. Ruby grunted and released her chin.

'I suppose they could strike me off, drumming up business, but I do think that you should have periodic checks. Two years is a long time, and you have foreign matter lodged inside your skull.'

'I hadn't even thought about it.' Debra frowned slightly and reached up to touch the scar on her temple. David felt his conscience twinge as he joined actively in the conspiracy.

'It can't do any harm, darling. Why not let Ruby give you a going over while we are here? Heaven knows when we will have another opportunity.'

'Oh, David—' Debra disparaged the idea. 'I know you are itching to head for home – and so am I.'

'Another day or two won't matter, and now that we have thought about it, it's going to worry us.'

Debra turned her head in Ruby's direction. 'How long will it take?'

'A day. I'll give you an examination in the morning, and then we'll shoot some X-ray plates in the afternoon.'

'How soon could you see her?' David asked, his voice

unnatural for he knew that the appointment had been arranged five weeks previously.

'Oh, I'm sure we could fit her in right away – tomorrow – even if we have to do a little juggling. Yours is rather a special case.'

David reached across and took Debra's hand. 'Okay, darling?' he asked.

'Okay, David,' she agreed readily.

R uby's consulting-rooms were in the Medical Centre that towered above the harbour and looked out across Table Bay to where the black south-easter was hacking the tops from the waves in bursts of white, and shrouding the far shores of the bay in banks of cloud as grey as wood smoke.

The rooms were decorated with care and taste: two original landscapes by Pierneef and some good carpets, Samarkand and a gold-washed Abedah – even Ruby's receptionist looked like a hostess from a Playboy Club, without the bunny ears and tail. It was clear that Dr Friedman enjoyed the good things of life.

The receptionist was expecting them, but still could not control the widening of her eyes and the shocked flight of colour from her cheeks as she looked at David's face.

'Dr Friedman is waiting for you, Mr and Mrs Morgan. He wants you both to go through, please.'

Ruby looked different without his prosperous paunch bulging over the waistband of a bathing costume, but his greeting was warm as he took Debra's arm.

'Shall we let David stay with us?' he asked Debra in mock conspiracy.

'Let's,' she answered.

After the usual clinical history, which Ruby pursued relentlessly, he seemed satisfied and they went through into his examination-room. The chair looked to David to be identical to a dentist's, and Ruby adjusted it for Debra to lie back comfortably while he made a physical examination, directing light through her pupils deep into the body of each eye.

'Nice healthy eyes,' he gave his opinion at last, 'and very pretty also, what do you say, David?'

'Smashing,' David agreed, and Ruby sat Debra upright while he attached electrodes to her arm and swung forward a complicated-looking piece of electronic equipment.

'ECG,' David guessed, and Ruby chuckled and shook his head.

'No – it's a little invention of my own. I'm quite proud of it, but in reality it's only a variation on the old-fashioned lie-detector.'

'Question time again?' Debra asked.

'No. We are going to flash lights at you, and see just what sort of subconscious reaction you have to them.'

'We know that already,' Debra told him, and they both heard the edge in her voice now.

'Perhaps. It's just an established routine we work to.' Ruby soothed her, and then to David. 'Stand back here, please. The lights are pretty fierce, and you don't want to be looking into them.'

David moved back and Ruby adjusted the machine. A roll of graph paper began running slowly under a moving stylus which settled almost immediately into a steady rhythmic pattern. On a separate glass screen a moving green dot of light began to repeat the same rhythm, leaving a fading trail across the screen like the tail of a comet. It reminded David of the interceptor radar screen on the instrument panel of a Mirage jet. Ruby switched out the top lights, plunging the room into utter darkness, except for the pulsing green dot on the screen.

'Are we ready now, Debra? Look straight ahead, please. Eyes open.'

Soundlessly a brilliant burst of blue light filled the room, and distinctly David saw the green dot on the screen jump out of its established pattern, and for a beat or two it went haywire, then settled again into the old rhythm. Debra had seen the light flash, even though she was unaware of it; the pulse of light had registered on her brain and the machine had recorded her instinctive reaction.

The play with light went on for another twenty minutes while Ruby adjusted the intensity of the light source and varied the transmissions. At last he was satisfied, and turned the top lights up.

'Well?' Debra demanded brightly. 'Do I pass?'

'There's nothing more I want from you,' Ruby told her. 'You did just great, and everything is the way we want it.'

'Can I go now?'

'David can take you to lunch, but this afternoon I want you at the radiologist's. My receptionist arranged it for 2.30, I believe, but you had best check with her.' Neatly Ruby countered any attempt of David's to get him alone.

'I shall let you know as soon as I have the X-ray results. Here, I'll write down the radiologist's address.' Ruby scribbled on his prescription pad and handed it to David.

See me alone *tomorrow 10 a.m.*

David nodded and took Debra's arm. He stared at Ruby a moment trying to draw some reaction from him, but he merely shrugged his shoulders and rolled his eyes in a music-hall comedian's gesture of uncertainty.

The Brig joined them for lunch in their suite at the Mount Nelson, for David still could not endure the discomfort of the public rooms. The Brig drew upon some hidden spring of charm, as though sensing that his help was needed, and he had both of them laughing naturally with stories of Debra's childhood and the family's early days after leaving America. David was grateful to him, for the time passed so quickly that he had to hurry Debra to her appointment.

'I am going to use two different techniques on you, my dear—' David wondered what it was about her that made all males over forty refer to Debra as though she were twelve years old. 'First of all we will do five of what we call police mug shots, front, back, sides and top—' The radiologist was a red-faced, grey-haired man with big hands and heavy shoulders like a professional wrestler. 'We aren't even going to make you take your clothes off—' He chuckled, but David thought he detected a faint note of regret. 'Then after that, we are going to be terribly clever and take a continuous moving shot of the inside of your head. It's called tomography. We are going to clamp your head to keep it still and the camera is going to describe a circle around you, focused on the spot where all the trouble is. We are going to find out everything that's going on in that pretty head of yours—'

'I hope it doesn't shock you too much, Doctor,' Debra told him, and he looked stunned for a moment, then let out a delighted guffaw, and later David heard him repeating it to the sister with gusto.

It was a long tedious business, and afterwards when they drove back to the hotel, Debra leaned close to him and said, 'Let's go home, David. Soon as we can?'

'Soon as we can,' he agreed.

David did not want it that way, but the Brig insisted on accompanying David on his visit to Ruby Friedman the following morning. For one of the very few times in his life David had lied to Debra, telling her he was meeting with the Morgan Trust accountants, and he had left her in a lime-green bikini lying beside the hotel swimming pool, brown and slim and lovely in the sunlight.

Ruby Friedman was brusque and businesslike. He seated them opposite his desk and came swiftly to the core of the business.

'Gentlemen,' he said. 'We have a problem, a hell of a problem. I am going to show you the X-ray plates first to illustrate what I have to tell you—' Ruby swivelled his chair to the scanner and switched on the book-light to bring the prints into high relief. 'On the side are the plates that Edelman sent me from Jerusalem. You can see the grenade fragment.' It was stark and hard edged, a small triangular shard of steel lying in the cloudy bone structure. 'And here you can see the track through the optic chiasma, the disruption and shattering of the bone is quite evident. Edelman's original diagnosis – based on these plates, and on the complete inability to define light or shape – seems to be confirmed. The optic nerve is severed, and that's the end of it.' Quickly he unclipped the plates, and fitted others to the scanner. 'All right. Now here are the second set of plates, taken yesterday. Immediately notice how the grenade fragment has been consolidated and encysted.' The stark outline was softened by the new growth of bone around it. 'That is good, and expected. But here in the channel of the chiasma we find the growth of some sort that leaves itself open to a number of interpretations. It could be scarring, the growth of bone chips, or some other type of growth either benign or malignant.' Ruby arranged another set of plates upon the scanner. 'Finally, this is the plate exposed by the technique of tomography, to establish the contours of this excrescence. It seems to conform to the shape of the bony channel of the chiasma, except here—' Ruby touched a small half-round notch which was cut into the upper edge of the growth, ' – this little spot runs through the main axis of the skull, but is bent upwards in the shape of an inverted U. It is just possible that this may be the most significant discovery of our whole examination.' Ruby switched off the light of the scanner.

'I don't understand any of this.' The Brig's voice was sharp. He did not like being bludgeoned by another man's special knowledge.

'No, of course.' Ruby was smooth. 'I am merely setting

the background for the explanations that will follow.' He turned back to the desk, and his manner changed. He was no longer lecturing, but leading with authority.

'Now as to my own conclusions. There can be absolutely no doubt that certain function of the optic nerve remains. It is still conveying impulses to the brain. At least a part of it is still intact. The question arises as to just how much that is, and to what extent that function can be improved. It is possible that the grenade fragment cut through part of the nerve – severing five strands of a six-strand rope, or four or three. We do not know the extent, but what we do know is that damage of that nature is irreversible. What Debra may be left with is what she has now – almost nothing.'

Ruby paused and was silent. The two men opposite him watched his face intently, leaning forward in their seats.

'That is the dark side – if it is true, then Debra is for all practical purposes blind and will remain that way. However, there is another side to the question. It is possible that the optic nerve has suffered little damage, or none at all, please God—'

'Then why is she blind?' David asked angrily. He felt baited, driven by words, goaded like the bull from so long ago. 'You can't have it both ways.'

Ruby looked at him, and for the first time saw beyond that blank mask of scarred flesh and realized the pain he was inflicting, saw the hurt in the dark eyes, blue as rifle steel.

'Forgive me, David. I have been carried away by the intriguing facts of this case, seeing it from my own academic point of view rather than yours, I'm afraid. I will come to it now without further hedging.' He leaned back in his chair and went on speaking. 'You recall the notch in the outline of the chiasma. Well, I believe that is the nerve itself, twisted out of position, kinked and pinched like a garden hose by bone fragments and the pressure of the metal fragment so that it is no longer capable of carrying impulses to the brain.'

'The blows on her temple—?' David asked.

'Yes. Those blows may have been just sufficient to alter the position of the bone fragments, or of the nerve itself, so as to enable the passage of a minimal amount of impulse to the brain – like the garden hose, movement could allow a little water to pass through but still hold back any significant flow, but once the twist is straightened the full volume of flow would be regained.'

They were all silent then, each of them considering the enormity of what they had heard.

'The eyes,' the Brig said at last. 'They are healthy?'

'Perfectly,' Ruby nodded.

'How could you find out – I mean, what steps would you take next?' David asked quietly.

'There is only one way. We would have to go to the site of the trauma.'

'Operate?' David asked again.

'Yes.'

'Open Debra's skull?' The horror of it showed only in his eyes.

'Yes,' Ruby nodded.

'Her head—' David's own flesh quailed in memory of the ruthless knife. He saw the lovely face mutilated and the pain in those blind eyes. 'Her face—' His voice shook now. 'No, I won't let you cut her. I won't let you ruin her, like they have me—'

'David!' The Brig's voice cracked like breaking ice, and David sank back in his chair.

'I understand how you feel,' Ruby spoke gently, his voice in contrast to the Brig's. 'But we will go in from behind the hairline, there will be no disfigurement. The scar will be covered by her hair when it grows out, and the incision will not be very large anyway—'

346

'I won't have her suffer more.' David was trying to control his voice, but the catch and break were still in it. 'She has suffered enough, can't you see that—'

'We are talking about giving her back her sight,' the Brig broke in again. His voice was hard and cold. 'A little pain is a small price to pay for that.'

'There will be very little pain, David. Less than an appendectomy.' Again they were silent, the two older men watching the younger in the agony of his decision.

'What are the chances?' David looked for help, wanting the decision made for him, wanting it taken out of his hands.

'That is impossible to say.' Ruby shook his head.

'Oh God, how can I judge if I don't know the odds?' David cried out.

'All right. Let me put it this way – there is a possibility, not probability, that she may regain a useful part of her sight.' Ruby chose his words with care. 'And there is a remote possibility that she may regain full vision or almost full vision.'

'That is the best that can happen.' David agreed. 'But what is the worst?'

'The worst that can happen is there will be no change. She will have undergone a deal of discomfort and pain to no avail.'

David jumped out of his chair and crossed to the windows. He stared out at the great sweep of bay where the tankers lay moored and the far hills of the Tygerberg rose smoky blue to the brilliant sky.

'You know what the choice must be, David.' The Brig was ruthless, allowing him no quarter, driving him on to meet his fate.

'All right,' David surrendered at last, and turned back to face them. 'But on one condition. One on which I insist. Debra must not be told that there is a chance of her regaining her sight—'

Ruby Friedman shook his head. 'She must be told.'

The Brig's moustache bristled fiercely. 'Why not? Why don't you want her to know?'

'You know why.' David answered without looking at him.

'How will you get her there – if you don't explain it to her?' Ruby asked.

'She has been having headaches – we'll tell her there is a growth – that you've discovered a growth – that it has to be removed. That's true, isn't it?'

'No.' Ruby shook his head. 'I couldn't tell her that. I can't deceive her.'

'Then I will tell her,' said David, his voice firm and steady now. 'And I will tell her when we discover the result after the operation. Good or bad. I will be the one who tells her – is that understood? Do we agree on that?'

And after a moment the two others nodded and murmured their agreement to the terms David had set.

D avid had the hotel chef prepare a picnic basket, and the service bar provided a cool bag with two bottles of champagne.

David craved for the feeling of height and space, but he needed also to be able to concentrate all his attention on Debra, so he reluctantly rejected the impulse to fly with her – and instead they took the cableway up the precipitous cliffs of Table Mountain, and from the top station they found a path along the plateau and followed it, hand in hand, to a lonely place upon the cliff's edge where they could sit together high above the city and the measureless spread of ocean.

The sounds of the city came up two thousand feet to them, tiny and disjointed, on freak gusts of the wind or bouncing from the soaring canyons of grey rock – the horn of an automobile, the clang of a locomotive shunting in the train yards, the cry of a muezzin calling the faithful of Islam to pray, and the distant shrilling of children released from the classroom – yet all these faint echoes of humanity seemed to enhance their aloneness and the breeze out of the south east was sweet and clean after the filthy city air.

They drank the wine together, sitting close while David gathered his resolve. He was about to speak when Debra forestalled him.

'It's good to be alive and in love, my darling,' she said. 'We are very lucky, you and I. Do you know that, David?'

He made a sound in his throat that could have been agreement, and his courage failed him.

'If you could, would you change anything?' he asked at last, and she laughed.

'Oh, sure. One is never absolutely content until and unless one is dead. I'd change many small things – but not the one big thing. You and I.'

'What would you change?'

'I would like to write better than I do, for one thing.'

They were silent again, sipping the wine.

'Sun is going down fast now,' he told her.

'Tell me,' she demanded, and he tried to find words for the colours, that flickered over the cloud banks and the way the ocean shimmered and dazzled with the last rays of gold and blood – and he knew he could never tell it to her. He stopped in the middle of a sentence.

'I saw Ruby Friedman today,' he said abruptly, unable to find a gentler approach, and she went still beside him in that special way of hers, frozen like a timid wild thing at the scent of some fearful predator.

'It's bad!' she said at last.

'Why do you say that?' he demanded quickly.

'Because you brought me here to tell me – and because you are afraid.'

'No,' David denied it.

'Yes. I can feel it now, very clearly. You are afraid for me.'

'It's not true,' David tried to reassure her. 'I'm a little worried, that's all.'

'Tell me,' she said.

'There is a small growth. It's not dangerous – yet. But they feel something should be done about it—' He stumbled through the explanation he had so carefully prepared, and when he ended she was silent for a moment.

'It is necessary, absolutely necessary?' she asked.

'Yes,' he told her, and she nodded, trusting him completely – then she smiled and squeezed his arm.

'Don't fret yourself, David, my darling. It will be all right. You'll see, they can't touch us. We live in a private place where they can't touch us.' Now it was she who was striving to comfort him.

'Of course it will be all right.' He hugged her to him roughly, slopping a little wine over the rim of his glass.

'When?' she asked.

'Tomorrow you will go in, and they'll do it the following morning.'

'So soon?'

'I thought it best to have it over with.'

'Yes. You are right.'

She sipped her wine, withdrawn, fearful, despite her brave show.

'They are going to cut my head open?'

'Yes,' he said, and she shuddered against him.

'There is no risk,' he said.

'No. I'm sure there isn't,' she agreed quickly.

He woke in the night with the instant knowledge that he was alone, that she was not curled warm and sleeping beside him.

Quickly he slipped from the bed and crossed to the bathroom. It was empty and he padded to the sitting-room of the suite and switched on the lights.

She heard the click of the switch and turned her head away, but not before he had seen the tears glowing on her cheeks like soft grey pearls. He went to her quickly.

'Darling,' he said.

'I couldn't sleep,' she said.

'That's all right.' He knelt before the couch on which she sat, but he did not touch her.

'I had a dream,' she said. 'There was a pool of clear water and you were swimming in it, looking up at me and calling to me. I saw your dear face clearly, beautiful and laughing—' David realized with a jolt in his guts that she had seen him in her dream as he had been, she had seen the beautiful dream-David, not the monstrous ravaged thing he was now. 'Then suddenly you began to sink, down, down, through the water, your face fading and receding—' Her voice caught and broke, and she was silent for a moment. 'It was a terrible dream, I cried out and tried to follow you, but I could not move and then you were gone down into the depths. The water turned dark and I woke with only the blackness in my head. Nothing but swirling mists of blackness.'

'It was only a dream,' he said.

'David,' she whispered. 'Tomorrow, if anything happens tomorrow—'

'Nothing will happen,' he almost snarled the denial, but she put out a hand to his face, finding his lips and touching them lightly to silence them.

'Whatever happens,' she said, 'remember how it was when we were happy. Remember that I loved you.'

The hospital of Groote Schuur sits on the lower slopes of Devil's Peak, a tall conical peak divided from the massif of Table Mountain by a deep saddle. Its summit is of grey rock and below it lie the dark pine forests and open grassy slopes of the great estate that Cecil John Rhodes left to the nation. Herds of deer and indigenous antelope feed quietly in the open places and the south-east wind feathers the crest with a flying pennant of cloud.

The hospital is a massive complex of brilliant white buildings, substantial and solid-looking blocks, all roofed in burnt red tiles.

Ruby Friedman had used all his pull to secure a private ward for Debra, and the sister in charge of the floor was expecting her. They took her from David and led her away, leaving him feeling bereft and lonely, but when he returned to visit her that evening she was sitting up in the bed in the soft cashmere bedjacket that David had given her and surrounded by banks of flowers which he had ordered.

'They smell wonderful,' she thanked him. 'It's like being in a garden.'

She wore a turban around her head and, with the serene golden eyes seeming focused on a distant vision, it gave her an exotic and mysterious air.

'They have shaved your head.' David felt a slide of dismay, he had not expected that she must also sacrifice that lustrous mane of black silk. It was the ultimate indignity, and she seemed to feel it also, for she did not answer him and instead told him brightly how well they were treating her, and what pains they were taking for her comfort. 'You'd think I was some sort of queen,' she laughed.

The Brig was with David, gruff and reserved and patently out of place in these surroundings. His presence cast restraint upon them and it was a relief when Ruby

Friedman arrived. Bustling and charming, he complimented Debra on the preparations she had undergone.

'Sister says that you are just fine, all nicely shaved and ready. Sorry, but you aren't allowed anything to eat or drink except the sleeping pill I've prescribed.'

'When do I go to theatre?'

'We've got you down bright and early. Eight o'clock tomorrow. I am tremendously pleased that Billy Cooper is the surgeon, we were very lucky to get him, but he owes me a favour or two. I will be assisting him, of course, and he'll have one of the best surgical teams in the world backing him up.'

'Ruby, you know how some women have their husbands with them when they are confined—'

'Yes.' Ruby looked uncertain, taken aback by the question.

'Well, couldn't David be there with me tomorrow? Couldn't we be together, for both our sakes, while it happens?'

'With all due respects, my dear, but you are not having a baby.'

'Couldn't you arrange for him to be there?' Debra pleaded, with eloquent eyes and an expression to break the hardest heart.

'I'm sorry,' Ruby shook his head. 'It's completely impossible—' Then he brightened. 'But I tell you what. I could get him into the students' room. It will be the next best thing, in fact he would have a better view of the proceedings than if he were in theatre. We have closed-circuit television relayed to the students' room and David could watch from there.'

'Oh, please!' Debra accepted immediately. 'I'd like to know he was close, and that we were in contact. We don't like being parted from each other, do we, my darling?' She smiled at where she thought he was, but he had moved aside and the smile missed him. It was a gesture that wrenched something within him.

'You will be there, David, won't you?' she asked, and though the idea of watching the knife at work was repellent to him, he forced himself to reply lightly.

'I'll be there,' and he almost added, 'always', but he cut off the word.

This early in the morning there were only two others in the small lecture-room with its double semi-circular rows of padded chairs about the small television screen, a plump woman student with a pretty face and shaggy-dog hairstyle and a tall young man with a pale complexion and bad teeth. They both wore their stethoscopes dangling with calculated nonchalance from the pockets of their white linen jackets. After the first startled glance they ignored David, and they spoke together in knowing medical jargon.

'The Coops doing an exploratory through the parietal.'

'That's the one I want to watch—'

The girl affected blue Gauloises cigarettes, rank and stinking in the confined room. David's eyes felt raw and gravelly for he had slept little during the night, and the smoke irritated them. He kept looking at his watch, and imagining what was happening to Debra during these last minutes – the undignified purging and cleansing of her body, the robing, and the needles of sedation and anti-sepsis.

The slow drag of minutes ended at last when the screen began to glow and hum, the image shimmered and strobed then settled down into a high view of the theatre. The set was in colour, and the green theatre gowns of the figures moving around the operating-table blended with the sub-dued theatre green walls. Height had foreshortened the robed members of the operating team and the muttered and disjointed conversation between the surgeon and his anaesthetist was picked up by the microphones.

'Are we ready there yet, Mike?'

David felt the sick sensation in the pit of his stomach, and he wished he had eaten breakfast. It might have filled the hollow place below his ribs.

'Right.' The surgeon's voice sharpened as he turned towards the microphone. 'Are we on telly?'

'Yes, Doctor,' the theatre sister answered him, and there was a note of resignation in the surgeon's voice as he spoke for his unseen audience.

'Very well, then. The patient is a twenty-six-year-old female. The symptoms are total loss of sight in both eyes, and the cause is suspected damage or constriction of the optic nerve in or near the optic chiasma. This is a surgical investigation of the site. The surgeon is Dr William Cooper, assisted by Dr Reuben Friedman.'

As he spoke, the camera moved in on the table and with a start of surprise David realized that he had been looking at Debra without knowing it. Her face and the lower part of her head were obscurred by the sterile drapes that covered all but the shaven round ball of her skull. It was inhuman-looking, egglike, painted with Savlon antiseptic that glistened in the bright, overhead lights.

'Scalpel please, Sister.'

David leaned forward tensely in his seat, and his hands tightened on the armrests, so the knuckles turned white, as Cooper made the first incision drawing the blade across the smooth skin. The flesh opened and immediately the tiny blood vessels began to dribble and spurt. Hands moved in the screen of the television, clad in rubber so that they were yellow and impersonal, but quick and sure.

An oval flap of skin and flesh was dissected free and was drawn back, exposing the gleaming bone beneath, and again David's flesh crawled as though with living things as the surgeon took up a drill that resembled exactly a carpenter's brace and bit. His voice continued its impersonal commentary, as he began to drill through the skull, cranking away at the handle as the gleaming steel bit swiftly through the bone. He pierced the skull with four round drill holes, each set at the corners of a square.

'Peri-osteal elevator, please, Sister.'

Again David's stomach clenched as the surgeon slid the gleaming steel introducer into one of the drill holes and manoeuvred it gently until its tip reappeared through the next hole in line. Using the introducer, a length of sharp steel wire saw was threaded through the two holes and lay along the inside of the skull. Cooper sawed this back and forth and it cut cleanly through the bone. Four times he repeated the procedure, cutting out the sides of the square, and when he at last lifted out the detached piece of bone he had opened a trapdoor into Debra's skull.

As he worked David's gorge had risen until it pressed in his throat, and he had felt the cold glistening sheen of nauseous sweat across his forehead, but now as the camera's eye peered through the opening he felt his wonder surmount his horror, for he could see the pale amorphous mass of matter, enclosed in its tough covering membrane of the dura mater that was Debra's brain. Deftly Cooper incised a flap in the dura.

'We have exposed now the frontal lobe, and it will be necessary to displace this to explore the base of the skull.'

Working swiftly, but with obvious care and skill, Cooper used a stainless steel retractor, shaped like a shoe horn, to slide under the mass of brain and to lift it aside. Debra's brain – staring at it, David seemed to be looking into the core of her being, it was vulnerable and exposed, everything that made her what she was. What part of that soft pale mass contained her writer's genius, he wondered, from which of its many soft folds and coils sprang the fruitful fountain of her imagination, where was her love for him buried, what soft and secret place triggered her laughter and where was the vale of her tears? Its fathomless mystery held him intent as he watched the retractor probe deeper and deeper through the opening, and slowly the camera moved in to peer into the gaping depths of Debra's skull.

Cooper opened the far end of the dura mater and commented on his progress.

'We have here the anterior ridge of the sphenoid sinus, note this as our point of access to the chiasma—'

David was aware of the changed tone of the surgeon's voice, the charging of tension as the disembodied hands moved slowly and expertly towards their goal.

'Now this is interesting, can we see this on the screen, please? Yes! There is very clearly a bone deformation here—'

The voice was pleased, and the two students beside David exclaimed and leaned closer. David could see soft wet tissue and hard bright surfaces deep in the bottom of the wound, and the necks of steel instruments crowding into it, like metallic bees into the stamen of a pink and yellow bloom. Cooper scratched through to the metal of the grenade fragment.

'Now here we have the foreign body, can we have a look at those X-ray plates again, Sister—'

The image cut quickly to the X-ray scanner, and again the students exclaimed. The girl puffed busily on her stinking Gauloise.

'Thank you.'

The image cut back to the operating field, and now David saw the dark speck of the grenade fragment lodged in the white bone.

'We will go for this, I think. Do you agree, Dr Friedman?'

'Yes, I think you should take it.'

Delicately the long slender steel insects worried the dark fragment, and at last with a grunt of satisfaction it came free of its niche, and Cooper drew it out carefully. David heard the metallic ping as it was dropped into a waiting dish.

'Good! Good!' Cooper gave himself a little encouragement as he plugged the hole left by the fragment with beeswax to prevent haemorrhage. 'Now we will trace out the optic nerves.'

They were two white worms, David saw them clearly, converging on their separate trails to meet and blend at the opening of the bony canal into which they disappeared.

'We have got extraneous bone-growth here, clearly associated with the foreign body we have just removed. It seems to have blocked off the canal and to have squeezed or severed the nerve. Suggestions, Dr Friedman?'

'I think we should excise that growth and try and ascertain just what damage we have to the nerve in that area.'

'Good. Yes, I agree. Sister, I will use a fine bone-nibbler to get in there.'

The swift selection and handling of the bright steel instruments again, and then Cooper was working on the white bone growth which grew in the shape of coral from a tropical sea. He nibbled at it with the keen steel, and carefully removed each piece from the field as it came away.

'What we have here is a bone splinter that was driven by the steel fragment into the canal. It is a large piece, and it must have been under considerable pressure, and it has consolidated itself here—'

He worked on carefully, and gradually the white worm of the nerve appeared from beneath the growth.

'Now, this is interesting.' Cooper's tone altered. 'Yes, look at this. Can we get a better view here, please?' The camera zoomed in a little closer, and the focus realigned. 'The nerve has been forced upwards, and flattened by pressure. The constriction is quite obvious, it has been pinched off – but it seems to be intact.'

Cooper lifted another large piece of bone aside, and now the nerve lay exposed over its full length.

'This is really remarkable. I expect that it is a one in a thousand chance, or one in a million. There appears to be no damage to the actual nerve, and yet the steel fragment passed so close to it that it must have touched it.'

Delicately, Cooper lifted the nerve with the blunt tip of a probe.

'Completely intact, but flattened by pressure. Yet I don't suspect any degree of atrophy, Dr Friedman?'

'I think we can confidently expect good recovery of function.' Despite the masked features, the triumphant attitude of the two men was easily recognized, and watching them, David felt his own emotions at war. With a weight upon his spirits he watched Cooper close up, replacing the portion of Debra's skull that he had removed, and once the flap of scalp was stitched back into place there was little external evidence of the extent and depth of their penetration. The image on the screen changed to another theatre where a small girl was to receive surgery for a massive hernia, and the fickle interest of the watching students changed with it.

David stood up and left the room. He rode up in the elevator and waited in the visitors' room on Debra's floor until the elevator doors opened again and two white-uniformed male nurses trundled Debra's stretcher down the corridor to her room. She was deadly pale, with dark bruised-looking eyes and lips, her head swathed in a turban of white bandages. There was a dull brown smear of blood on the sheets that covered her and a whiff of anaesthetic hung in the corridor after she was gone.

Ruby Friedman came then, changed from the theatre garb into an expensive light-weight grey mohair suit and a twenty-guinea Dior silk tie. He looked tanned and healthy, and mightily delighted with his achievement.

'You watched?' he demanded, and when David nodded he went on exuberantly, 'It was extraordinary.' He chuckled, and rubbed his hands together with glee.

'My God, something like this makes you feel good. Makes you feel that if you never do another thing in your life, it was still worthwhile.' He was unable to restrain himself any longer and he threw a playful punch at David's shoulder. 'Extraordinary,' he repeated, drawing it out into two words with relish, rolling the word around his tongue.

'When will you know?' David asked quietly.

'I know already, I'll stake my reputation on it!'

'She will be able to see as soon as she comes around from the anaesthetic?' David asked.

'Good Lord, no!' Ruby chuckled. 'That nerve has been pinched off for years, it's going to take time to recover.'

'How long?'

'It's like a leg that has gone to sleep when you sit wrongly. When the blood flows back in, it's still numb and tingling until the circulation is restored.'

'How long?' David repeated.

'Immediately she wakes, that nerve is going to start going crazy, sending all sorts of wild messages to the brain. She's going to see colours and shapes as though she is on a drug binge, and it's going to take time to settle down – two weeks to a month, I would guess – then it will clear, the nerve will have recovered its full and normal function and she will begin having real effective vision.'

'Two weeks,' David said, and he felt the relief of a condemned man hearing of his reprieve.

'You will tell her the good news, of course.' Ruby gave another buoyant chuckle, shaped up to punch David again and then controlled himself. 'What a wonderful gift you have been able to give her.'

'No,' David answered him. 'I won't tell her yet, I will find the right time later.'

'You will have to explain the initial vision she will experience, the colour and shape hallucinations, they will alarm her.'

'We will just tell her that it's the normal after-effect of the operation. Let her adjust to that before telling her.'

'David, I—' Ruby began seriously, but he was cut off by the savage blaze of blue in the eyes that watched him from the mask of scarred flesh.

'I will tell her!' The voice shook with such fury, that Ruby took a step backwards. 'That was the condition, I will tell her when I judge the time is ripe.'

O ut of the darkness a tiny amber light glowed, pale and far off, but she watched it split like a breeding amoeba and become two, and each of those split and split again until they filled the universe in a great shimmering field of stars. The light throbbed and pulsed, vibrant and triumphant, and it changed from amber to brightest purest white like the sparkle from a paragon diamond, then it turned to the blue of sunlight on a tropical ocean, to soft forest greens and desert golds – an endless cavalcade of colours, changing, blending, fading, flaring in splendour that held her captive.

Then the colours took shape, they spun like mighty Catherine wheels, and soared and exploded, showered down in rivers of flame that burst again into fresh cascades of light.

She was appalled by the dimensions of shape and colour that engulfed her, bewildered by the beauty of it and at last she could bear it no longer in silence and she cried out.

Instantly there was a hand in hers, a strong hard familiar hand, and his voice, dearly beloved, reassuring and firm.

'David,' she cried with relief.

'Quietly, my darling. You must rest.'

'David. David.' She heard the sob in her own voice as new torrents of colour poured over her, insupportable in their richness and variety, overwhelming in their depth and range.

'I'm here, my darling. I'm here.'

'What's happening to me, David? What's happening?'

'You are all right. The operation was a success. You are just fine.'

'Colours,' she cried. 'Filling my whole head. I've never known it like this.'

'It's the result of the operation. It shows that it was a success. They removed the growth.'

'I'm frightened, David.'

'No, my darling. There is nothing to be afraid of.'

'Hold me, David. Hold me safe.' And in the circle of his arms the fear abated, and slowly she learned to ride the oceanic waves and washes of colour, came gradually to accept and then at last to look upon them with wonder and with intense pleasure.

'It's beautiful, David. I'm not frightened any more, not with you holding me. It's wonderful.'

'Tell me what you see,' he said.

'I couldn't. It's impossible. I couldn't find the words.'

'Try!' he said.

David was alone in the suite, and it was after midnight when the call that he had placed to New York came through.

'This is Robert Dugan, to whom am I speaking?' Bobby's voice was crisp and businesslike.

'It's David Morgan.'

'Who?'

'Debra Mordecai's husband.'

'Well, hello there, David.' The agent's voice changed, becoming expansive. 'It's sure nice to talk to you. How is Debra?' It was obvious that Dugan's interest in David began and ended with his wife.

'That's why I am calling. She's had an operation and she's in hospital at the moment.'

'God! Not serious, is it?'

'She's going to be fine. She'll be up in a few days and ready for work in a couple of weeks.'

'Glad to hear it, David. That's great.'

'Look here, I want you to go ahead and set up that scriptwriting contract for *A Place of Our Own*.'

'She's going to do it?' Dugan's pleasure carried six thousand miles with no diminution.

'She'll do it now.'

'That's wonderful news, David.'

'Write her a good contract.'

'Depend on it, boyo. That little girl of yours is a hot property. Playing hard to get hasn't done her any harm, I tell you!'

'How long will the script job last?'

'They'll want her for six months,' Dugan guessed. 'The producer who will do it is making a movie in Rome right now. He'll probably want Debra to work with him there.'

'Good,' said David. 'She'll like Rome.'

'You coming with her, David?'

'No,' David answered carefully. 'No, she'll be coming on her own.'

'Will she be able to get by on her own?' Dugan sounded worried.

'From now on she'll be able to do everything on her own.'

'Hope you are right,' Dugan was dubious.

'I'm right.' David told him abruptly. 'One other thing. That lecture tour, is it still on?'

'They are beating the door down. Like I said, she's hotter than a pistol.'

'Set it up for after the script job.'

'Hey, David boy. This is the business. Now we are really cooking with gas. We are going to make your little girl into one very big piece of property.'

'Do that,' said David. 'Make her big. Keep her busy, you hear. Don't give her time to think.'

'I'll keep her busy.' Then as though he had detected something in David's voice. 'Is something bugging you, David? You got some little domestic problem going there, boy? You want to talk about it?'

'No, I don't want to talk about it. You just look after her. Look after her well.'

'I'll look after her,' Dugan's tone had sobered. 'And David—'

'What is it?'

'I'm sorry. Whatever it is, I'm sorry.'

'That's okay.' David had to end the conversation then, immediately. His hand was shaking so that he knocked the telephone from the table and the plastic cracked through. He left it lying and went out into the night. He walked alone through the sleeping city, until just before the morning he was weary enough to sleep.

The streams of colour settled to steady runs and calmly moving patterns, no longer the explosive bursts of brightness that had so alarmed her. After the grey shifting banks of blindness that had filled her head like dirty cotton wool for those long years, the new brightness and beauty served to buoy her spirits, and after the main discomfort of her head surgery had passed in the first few days, she was filled with a wondrous sense of well-being, a formless optimistic expectation, such as she had not experienced since she was a child anticipating the approach of a long-awaited holiday.

It was as though in some deep recess of her subconscious she was vaguely aware of the imminent return of her sight. However, the knowledge seemed not to have reached her conscious mind. She knew there was a change, she welcomed her release from the dark and sombre dungeons of nothingness into the new brightness, but she did not realize that there was more to come, that after colour and fantasy would follow shape and reality.

Each day David waited for her to say something that might show that she had realized that her sight was on the way back; he hoped for and at the same time dreaded this awareness – but it did not come.

He spent as much of each day with her as hospital routine would allow, and he hoarded each minute of it, doling out time like a miser paying coins from a diminishing hoard. Yet Debra's ebullient mood was infectious, and he could not help but laugh with her and share the warm excitement as she anticipated her release from the hospital and their return together to the sanctuary of Jabulani.

There were no doubts in her mind, no shadows across her happiness, and gradually David began to believe that it would last. That their happiness was immortal and that their love could survive any pressure placed upon it. It was so strong and fine when they were together now, carried along by Debra's bubbling enthusiasm, that surely she could regain her sight and weather the first shock of seeing him.

Yet he was not sure enough to tell her yet, there was plenty of time. Two weeks, Ruby Friedman had told him, two weeks before she would be able to see him and it was vitally important to David that he should extract every grain of happiness that was left to him in that time.

In the lonely nights he lay with the frantic scurryings of his brain keeping him from sleep. He remembered that the plastic surgeon had told him there was more they could do to make him less hideous. He could go back and submit to the knife once more, although his body cringed at the thought. Perhaps they could give Debra something less horrifying to look at.

The following day he braved the massed stares of hundreds of shoppers to visit Stuttafords Departmental Store in Adderley Street. The girl in the wig department, once she had recovered her poise, took him into a curtained-off cubicle and entered into the spirit of finding a wig to cover the domed cicatrice of his scalp.

David regarded the fine curly head of hair over the frozen ruins of his face, and for the first time ever he found himself laughing at it, although the effect of laughter was even more horrifying as the tight lipless mouth writhed like an animal in a trap.

'God!' he laughed. 'Frankenstein in drag!' and for the sales girl who had been fighting to control her emotions this was too much. She broke into hysterical giggles of embarrassment.

He wanted to tell Debra about it, making a joke of it and at the same time prepare her for her first sight of his face, but somehow he could not find the words. Another day passed with nothing accomplished, except a few last hours of warmth and happiness shared.

The following day Debra began to show the first signs of restlessness. 'When are they going to let me out, darling? I feel absolutely wonderful. It's ridiculous to lie in bed here. I want to get back to Jabulani – there is so much to do.' Then she giggled. 'And they've had me locked up here ten days now. I'm not used to convent life, and to be completely honest with you, my big lusty lover, I am climbing the wall—'

'We could lock the door,' David suggested.

'God, I married a genius,' Debra cried out delightedly, and then later, 'That's the first time it ever happened for me in Technicolor. I think I could get hooked on that.'

That evening Ruby Friedman and the Brig were waiting for him when he returned to his suite, and they came swiftly to the reason for their visit.

'You have already left it too long. Debra should have been told days ago,' the Brig told him sternly.

'He is right, David. You are being unfair to her. She must have time to come to terms, latitude for adjustment.'

'I'll tell her when I get the opportunity,' David muttered doggedly.

'When will that be?' the Brig demanded, the gold tooth glowing angrily in its furry nest.

'Soon.'

'David,' Ruby was placatory, 'it could happen at any time now. She has made strong and vigorous progress, it could happen much sooner than I expected.'

'I'll do it,' said David. 'Can't you stop pushing me? I said I'll do it – and I will. Just get off my back, won't you.'

'Right.' The Brig was brisk now. 'You've got until noon tomorrow. If you haven't told her by then, I'm going to do it.'

'You're a hard old bastard, aren't you,' David said bitterly, and anger paled the Brig's lips and they could see the effort he made to force it down.

'I understand your reluctance.' He spoke carefully. 'I sympathize. However, my first and only concern is for Debra. You are indulging yourself, David. You are wallowing in self-pity, but I am not going to allow that to hurt her more. She has had enough. No more delay. Tell her, and have done.'

'Yes,' David nodded, all the fight gone out of him. 'I will tell her.'

'When?' the Brig persisted.

'Tomorrow,' said David. 'I will tell her tomorrow morning.'

I t was a bright warm morning, and the garden below his room was gay with colour. David lingered over breakfast in his suite, and he read all of the morning papers from end to end, drawing out the moment to its utmost. He dressed with care afterwards, in a dark suit and a soft lilac shirt, then, when he was ready to leave, he surveyed his image in the full-length mirror of the dressing-room.

'It's been a long time – and I'm still not at ease with you,' he told the figure in the mirror. 'Let's pray that somebody loves you more than I do.'

The doorman had a cab ready for him under the portico, and he settled in the back seat with the leaden feeling in his stomach. The drive seemed much shorter this morning, and when he paid off the cab and climbed the steps to the main entrance of Groote Schuur, he glanced at his wristwatch. It was a few minutes after eleven o'clock. He was hardly aware of the curious glances as he crossed the lobby to the elevators.

The Brig was waiting for him in the visitors' room on Debra's floor. He came out into the corridor, tall and grim, and unfamiliar in his civilian clothes.

'What are you doing here?' David demanded, it was the ultimate intrusion and he resented it fiercely.

'I thought I might be of help.'

'Good on you!' said David sardonically, making no effort to hide his anger.

The Brig let the anger slide past him, not acknowledging it with either word or expression as he asked mildly, 'Would you like me to be with you?'

'No.' David turned away from him as he spoke. 'I can manage, thank you,' and he set off along the corridor.

'David!' the Brig called softly, and David hesitated and then turned back.

'What is it?' he asked.

For a long moment they stared at each other, then abruptly the Brig shook his head. 'No,' he said. 'It's nothing,' and watched the tall young man with the monstrous head turn and walk swiftly towards Debra's room. His footsteps echoed hollowly along the empty corridor, like the tread of a man upon the gallows steps.

The morning was warm with a light breeze off the sea. Debra sat in her chair by the open window, and the warm air wafted the scent of the pine forests to her. Resinous and clean-smelling, it mingled with the faint whiff of the sea and the kelp beds. She felt quiet and deeply contented, even though David was late this morning. She had spoken to Ruby Friedman when he made his rounds earlier, and he had teased her and hinted that she would be able to leave in a week or so, and the knowledge rounded out her happiness.

The warmth of the morning was drowsy, and she closed her eyes subduing the strong rich flow of colour into a lulling cocoon of soft shades which enfolded her, and she lay on the downy edges of sleep.

David found her like that, sitting in the deep chair with her legs curled sideways under her and her face side-lit by the reflected sunlight from the window. The turban of white bandages that swathed her head were crisp and fresh and her gown was white as a bride's, with cascades of filmy lace.

He stood before her chair studying her with care, her face was pale, but the dark bruises below her eyes had cleared and the set of her full lips was serene and peaceful.

With infinite tenderness he leaned forward and laid his open hand against her cheek. She stirred drowsily, and opened eyes that were honey brown and flecked with bright flakes of gold. They were beautiful, and vague, misty and sightless – then suddenly he saw them change, the look of them was sharp and aware. Her gaze focused, and steadied. She was looking at him – and seeing him.

Debra was roused from the warm edge of sleep by the touch upon her cheek, as light as the fall of an autumn leaf. She opened her eyes to soft golden clouds, then suddenly like the morning wind slashing away the sea mist, the clouds rolled open and she looked beyond to the monster's head that swam towards her, a colossal dis-embodied head that seemed must arise from the halls of hell itself, a head so riven with livid lines and set with the bestial, crudely worked features of one of the dark hosts, that she flung herself back in her chair, cringing away from the terror of it, and she lifted her hands to her face and she screamed.

David turned and ran from the room, slamming the door behind him, his feet pounded down the passage and the Brig heard him coming and stepped into the corridor.

'David!' He reached out a hand to him, to hold him back, but David struck out at him wildly, a blow that caught him in the chest throwing him back heavily against the wall. When he regained his balance, and staggered from the wall clutching his chest, David was gone. His frantic footsteps clattered up from the well of the stairs.

'David!' he called, his voice croaking. 'Wait!' But he was gone, his footsteps fading, and the Brig let him go. Instead he turned and hurried painfully down the corridor to where the hysterical sobs of his daughter rang from behind the closed door.

She looked up from her cupped hands when she heard the door open, and wonder dawned through the terror in her eyes.

'I can see you,' she whispered, 'I can see.'

He went to her quickly and took her in the protective circle of his arms.

'It's all right,' he told her awkwardly, 'it's going to be all right.'

She clung to him, stifling the last of her sobs.

'I had a dream,' she murmured, 'a terrible dream,' and she shuddered against him. Then suddenly she pulled away.

'David,' she cried, 'where is David? I must see him.'

The Brig stiffened, realizing that she had not recognized reality.

'I must see him,' she repeated, and he replied heavily, 'You have already seen him, my child.'

For many seconds she did not understand, and then slowly it came to her.

'David?' she whispered, her voice catching and breaking. 'That was David?'

The Brig nodded, watching her face for the revulsion and the horror.

'Oh dear God,' Debra's voice was fierce. 'What have I done? I screamed when I saw him. What have I done to him? I've driven him away.'

'So you still want to see him again?' the Brig asked.

'How can you say that?' Debra blazed at him. 'More than anything on this earth. You must know that!'

'Even the way he is now?'

'If you think that would make any difference to me – then you don't know me very well.' Her expression changed again, becoming concerned. 'Find him for me,' she ordered. 'Quickly, before he has a chance to do something stupid.'

'I don't know where he has gone,' the Brig answered, his own concern aroused by the possibility which Debra had hinted at.

'There is only one place he would go when he is hurt like this,' Debra told him. 'He will be in the sky.'

'Yes,' the Brig agreed readily.

'Get down to air traffic control, they'll let you speak to him.' The Brig turned for the door and Debra's voice urged him on.

'Find him for me, Daddy. Please find him for me.'

The Navajo seemed to come around on to a southerly heading under its own volition. It was only
when the sleek, rounded nose settled on course,
climbing steadily upwards towards the incredibly tall and
unsullied blue of the heavens, that David knew where he
was going.

Behind him, the solid flat-topped mountain with its
glistening wreaths of clouds fell away. This was the last of
the land, and ahead lay only the great barren wastes of ice
and cruel water.

David glanced at his fuel gauges. His vision was still
blurred, but he saw the needles registering a little over the
halfway mark on the dials.

Three hours' flying perhaps, and David felt a chill relief
that there was to be a term to his suffering. He saw clearly
then how it would end down there in the wilderness below
the shipping lanes. He would continue to bore for height,
climbing steadily until at last his engines starved and failed.
Then he would push the nose down into a vertical dive and
go in hard and fast, like the final suicide stoop of a maimed
and moribund eagle. It would be over swiftly, and the metal
fuselage would carry him down to a grave that could not be
as lonely as the desolation in which he now existed.

The radio crackled and hummed into life. He heard air
traffic snarl his call sign through the static crackle, and he
reached for the switch to kill the set – when the well-
remembered voice stayed his hand.

'David, this is the Brig.' The words and the tone in
which they were spoken transported him back to another
cockpit in another land.

'You disobeyed me once before. Don't do it again.'

David's mouth tightened into a thin colourless line and
again he reached for the switch. He knew they were
watching him on the radar plot, that they knew his course,
and that the Brig had guessed what he intended. Well,
there was nothing they could do about it.

'David,' the Brig's voice softened, and some sure instinct made him choose the only words to which David would listen. 'I have just spoken to Debra. She wants you desperately.'

David's hand hovered over the switch.

'Listen to me, David. She needs you – she will always need you.'

David blinked, for he felt tears scalding his eyes once more. His determination wavered.

'Come back, David. For her sake, come back.'

Out of the darkness of his soul, a light shone, a small light which grew and spread until it seemed to fill him with its shimmering brightness.

'David, this is the Brig.' Again it was the voice of the old warrior, hard and uncompromising. 'Return to base immediately.'

David grinned, and lifted the microphone to his mouth. He thumbed the transmit button, and spoke the old acknowledgement in Hebrew.

'*Beseder!* This is Bright Lance Leader, homeward bound,' and he brought the Navajo around steeply.

The mountain was blue and low on the horizon, and he let the nose sink gradually towards it. He knew that it would not be easy – that it would require all his courage and patience, but he knew that in the end it would be worth it all. Suddenly he needed desperately to be alone with Debra, in the peace of Jabulani.

MEN OF MEN

This book is for my wife, Danielle,
with all my love for ever

It had never been exposed to the light of day, not once in the 200 million years since it assumed its present form, and yet it seemed in itself to be a drop of distilled sunlight.

It had been conceived in heat as vast as that of the sun's surface, in those unholy depths below the earth's crust, in the molten magma that welled up from the earth's very core.

In those terrible temperatures all impurity had been burned from it, leaving only the unadulterated carbon atoms, and under pressures that would have crushed mountains these had been reduced in volume and packed to a density beyond that of any other substance in nature.

This tiny bubble of liquid carbon had been carried up in the slow subterranean river of molten lava through one of the weak spots in the earth's crust, and it had almost, but not quite, reached the surface before the laval flow faltered and finally stopped.

The lava cooled over the ensuing millennium, and it altered its form and became a mottled bluish rock, composed of gravelly fragments loosely cemented in a solid matrix. This formation was naturally unassociated with the country rock which surrounded it, and filled only a deep circular well whose mouth was shaped like a funnel almost a mile in diameter and whose tail descended sheer into the uncounted depths of the earth.

While the lava was cooling, the purged bubble of carbon was undergoing an even more marvellous transformation. It solidified into an eight-faced crystal of geometrical symmetry the size of a green fig, and so thoroughly had it

1

been purged of impurity in the hellish furnace of the earth's core that it was transparent and clear as the sun's own rays. So fierce and constant had been the pressures to which the single crystal had been subjected and so evenly had it cooled that there was no cracking or shearing within its body.

It was perfect, a thing of cold fire so white that it would appear electric blue in good light – but that fire had never been awakened, for it had been trapped in total darkness across the ages, and no single glimmer of light had ever probed its lucid depths. Yet for all those millions of years the sunlight had been no great distance away, a matter only of two hundred feet or less, a thin skin of earth when compared to the immense depths from whence its journey to the surface had begun.

Now, in the last wink of time, a mere few years out of all those millions, the intervening ground had steadily been chipped and whittled and hacked away by the puny, inefficient but persistent efforts of an antlike colony of living creatures.

The forebears of these creatures had not even existed upon this earth when that single pure crystal achieved its present form, but now with each day the disturbance caused by their metal tools set up faint vibrations within the rock that had been dormant so long; and each day those vibrations were stronger, as the layer between it and the surface shrank from two hundred feet to a hundred and then to fifty, from ten feet to two, until now only inches separated the crystal from the brilliant sunlight which would at last bring to life its slumbering fires.

M ajor Morris Zouga Ballantyne stood on the lip of the aerial ropeway high above the deep circular chasm where once a small hillock had risen above the flat and dreary landscape of the African continental shield.

Even in the fierce heat he wore a silk scarf at his throat, the tail of which was tucked into the buttoned front of his flannel shirt. Though recently washed and pressed with a heated stroking-iron, his shirt was indelibly stained to a dull reddish ochre colour.

It was the pigment of the African earth, red earth, almost like raw meat, where the iron-shod wheels of the wagons had cut it or the shovels of the diggers had turned the surface. Earth that rose in dense red dust clouds when the hot dry winds scoured it, or turned to bleeding glutinous red mud when the thunderstorms thrashed its surface.

Red was the colour of the diggings. It stained the hair of dogs and beasts of burden, it stained the clothing of the men and their beards and the skin of their arms, it stained their canvas tents and coated the corrugated iron shanties of the settlement.

Only in the gaping hole below where Zouga stood was the colour altered to the soft yellow of a thrush's breast.

The hole was almost a mile across, the rim of it nearly a perfect circle, and its bottom already two hundred feet deep in places. The men working down there were tiny insect-like figures, spiders perhaps, for only spiders could have spun the vast web that glittered in a silvery cloud over the entire excavation.

Zouga paused a moment to lift the wide-brimmed hat, its pointed peak stained by his own sweat and the blown red dust. Carefully he mopped the beads of sweat from the smooth paler skin along his hairline, and then inspected the damp red stain on the silk bandanna and grimaced with distaste.

His dense curling hair had been protected by the hat

from the fierce African sunlight and was still the colour of smoked wild honey, but his beard had been bleached to pale gold and the years had laced it with silver strands. His skin was dark also, baked like a crust of new bread, only the scar on his cheek was porcelain white where the elephant gun had burst so many years before.

There were little creases below his eyes from squinting in the sunlight at far horizons, and harsh lines cut his cheeks from the corner of his nose and ran down into the beard – lines of hardship and heartbreak. He looked down into the gaping pit below him and the green of his eyes clouded as he remembered the high hopes and bounding expectation that had brought him here – was it ten years before? It seemed like a day and an eternity.

He had first heard the name, Colesberg kopje, when he had stepped out of the bum-boat onto the beach at Rogger Bay below the vast square monolithic bulk of Table Mountain, and the sound of it had made his skin tingle and raised the hair at the nape of his neck.

'They have struck diamonds at Colesberg kopje, diamonds big as grapeshot and so thick they'll wear out the soles of your boots just walking across them!'

In a clairvoyant flash he had known that this was where his destiny would lead him. He knew that the two years he had just spent in old England, trying desperately to raise backing for his grand venture in the north, had been marking time for this moment.

The road to the north began in the diamond gravels of Colesberg kopje. He knew it with certainty as he heard the name.

He had one single wagon left, and a depleted span of draught oxen. Within forty-eight hours they were plodding through the deep sands that clogged the track across the Cape Flats, northwards six hundred miles to that kopje below the Vaal river.

The wagon carried all his possessions, and there were precious few of these. Twelve years following a grandiose dream had wasted his substance all away. The considerable royalties from the book that he had written after his travels to the unexplored lands below the Zambezi river, the gold and ivory that he had brought back from that remote interior, the ivory from four more hunting expeditions to that same haunting and yet sadly flawed paradise – all of it was gone. Thousands of pounds and twelve years of heart-break and frustration, until the splendid dream had become clouded and soured and all he had to show for it was a tattered scrap of parchment on which the ink was beginning to yellow and the folds were almost worn through so that it had to be glued to a backing sheet to hold it together.

That parchment was 'The Ballantyne Concession' title for one thousand years to all the mineral wealth of a huge tract of the wild African interior, a tract the size of France which he had cajoled from a savage black king. In that vast territory Zouga had panned red native gold from the outcropping quartz reef.

It was a rich land and all of it was his, but it needed capital, huge amounts of capital, to take possession of it and to win the treasures that lay below it. Half his adult life had been spent in a struggle to raise that capital – a fruitless struggle, for he had not yet found a single man of substance to share his vision and his dream with him. Finally, he had in desperation appealed to the British public. He had journeyed to London once more to promote the formation of the 'Central African Lands and Mining Co.' to exploit his concession.

He had designed and had printed a handsome brochure, extolling the riches of the land he had named Zambezia.

He had illustrated the pages with his own drawings of fine forests and grassy plains abounding with elephant and other game. He had included a facsimile of the original concession, with the great elephant seal of Mzilikazi, King of the Matabele, at its foot. And he had distributed the brochure throughout the British Isles.

He had travelled from Edinburgh to Bristol lecturing and holding public meetings, and he had backed up this campaign with full-page advertisements in *The Times* and other reputable newspapers.

However, the same newspapers that had accepted his advertising fees had ridiculed his claims, while the attention of the investing public was seduced by the flotations of the South American railway companies which unhappily coincided with Zouga's promotion. He had been left with the bill for printing and distribution of the brochure, the fees for advertising and for the lawyers and the expenses of his own travelling, and when he had paid them and his passage back to Africa there remained only a few hundred sovereigns from what had once been considerable wealth.

The wealth was gone, but the responsibilities remained. Zouga looked back from the head of the span of dappled black oxen.

Aletta sat on the wagon box. Her hair was still pale gold and silky in the sunlight, but her eyes were grave and the line of her lips no longer sweet and soft, as though she had set herself against the hardships that she knew lay ahead.

Looking at her now it seemed impossible that she had once been a pretty carefree butterfly of a girl, the pampered darling of a rich father, with no thought in her head beyond London fashion newly arrived on the mailship and the preparations for the next ball in the glittering social whirl of Cape society.

She had been attracted by the romance surrounding young Major Zouga Ballantyne. He was the traveller and adventurer in far places of the African continent. There was the legend of the great elephant hunter that surrounded him, the glamour of the book that he had recently published in London. All Cape Town society was agog with this young man and envied her his suit.

That had been many years ago, and the legend had tarnished.

Aletta's delicate breeding had not been equal to the rigours of the savage interior beyond the gentle and temperate airs of the Cape littoral – and the rough country and rougher peoples had appalled her. She had succumbed swiftly to the fevers and pestilences which had weakened her so that she suffered repeated miscarriages.

All her married life she seemed to be in childbed, or lost in the mists of malarial fever, or waiting interminably for the golden-bearded, godlike figure whom she worshipped to return from across an ocean or from the hot and unhealthy hinterland to which she could no longer follow him.

On this journey to the diamond fields, Zouga had taken it for granted that she would once again remain at her father's home at the Cape, to guard her failing health and to care for their two boys, fruit of the only pregnancies which she had succeeded in bringing to full term. However, she had suddenly shown an uncharacteristic determination, and none of his arguments to make her remain behind had prevailed. Perhaps she had some premonition of what was to follow – 'I have been alone too long,' she answered him, softly but stubbornly.

Ralph, the eldest boy, was old enough by then to ride ahead of the wagon with his father and take his shot at the springbuck herds which drifted like thin pale brown smoke across the scrubby plains of the wide Karroo. Already he sat his rugged little Basuto pony with the panache of a hussar and he shot like a man.

Jordan, the younger boy, would sometimes take his turn at leading the fore oxen of the span, or wander away from the wagons to chase a butterfly or pick a wild flower; but mostly he was content to sit beside his mother on the wagon box while she read aloud from a small leather-bound book of romantic poetry, his green eyes sparkling with the thrilling sound of the words that he was still too young properly to understand and the brilliant Karroo sunlight turning his golden curls into an angel's halo.

It was six hundred miles from Good Hope to the fields, a journey that took the family eight weeks. They camped each night on the open veld and the night sky was clear and cold and brilliant with white stars that shone like the diamonds that they were certain awaited them at the end of the journey.

Sitting beside the watch-fire with his two sons flanking him, Zouga would talk in that magnetic compelling tone that had the two small boys rigid with attention. He spun descriptions of great elephant hunts and ancient ruined cities, of graven idols and red native gold in the land to the north, the land to which he would one day take them.

Listening quietly from across the fire, wrapped in a shawl against the night chill, Aletta would find herself enchanted with the romantic dream, as she had been as a girl, and she wondered again at herself and the strange attraction of this intense golden-bearded man who was her husband of so many years and still so often seemed a stranger to her.

She listened as he told the boys how he would fill their caps with diamonds, fat glistening diamonds, and then at last they would set out on the final journey northwards.

She found herself believing it all again, though she had long ago experienced the first disillusion. He was so persuasive, so vital and strong and convincing, that the failures and the frustrations seemed of no account, only a temporary check on the destiny he had set for all of them.

The days rolled by at the leisurely pace of the wagon wheels and became weeks, weeks in which they travelled across a great sun-washed plain that was furrowed by steep dry watercourses and studded with the dense dark-green camel-thorn trees in whose branches hung the enormous communal nests of thousands of dry-land weaver birds, each nest the size of a haystack, growing until it snapped off the sturdy branch that supported it.

The monotonous line of the horizon was relieved by the occasional low hillock, the kopje of the African continent, and the track led them directly towards one of these.

Colesberg kopje. It was only weeks after they had arrived at it that Zouga heard the story of how the diamond hillock had been discovered.

A few miles north of Colesberg kopje the plain was broken by the bed of a wide shallow river, along whose banks the trees were taller and greener. The trek Boers had called it the Vaal river, which in the African Dutch taal means 'the grey river', the colour of its sluggish waters. From its bed and from the alluvial gravels of the flood plains along its course, a small colony of diamond diggers had for years been gleaning the odd sparkling stone.

It was dreary, back-breaking work and after the first rush of hopeful diggers only the hardiest had remained. These doughty souls had known for years that it was possible to pick up an occasional small diamond of inferior quality on the dry ground thirty miles south of the river, in fact the surly old Boer named De Beer who owned the ground in that area was selling licences to diamond claims on his property – although he favoured diggers of his own people and was notoriously prejudiced against granting 'briefies' to Englishmen.

For these reasons, and also for the more pleasant living conditions along the river, the diggers had not taken too much interest in the 'dry diggings' to the south.

Then one day a Hottentot servant of one of the river diggers rendered himself blind falling-down drunk with

Cape Smoke, the fierce Cape brandy, and while in that state accidentally set fire to his master's tent and burned it to the ground.

When he was once again sober, his master beat him with a sjambok whip of cured rhinoceros hide until he was once more unable to stand. When he recovered from his treatment, his master ordered him, still in disgrace, to go into the dry country 'and dig until you find a diamond'.

Chastened and still wobbly on his feet, the Hottentot had shouldered his shovel and pack and limped away. His master promptly forgot him, until he returned unannounced two weeks later and placed in his master's hand half a dozen fine white stones – the largest the size of the first joint of a lady's little finger.

'Where?' demanded Fleetwood Rawstorne, the single word all that he could choke through a throat suddenly parched and closed with excitement.

Minutes later, Fleetwood galloped furiously out of camp, a cartload of scrapings from the river bed left untreated and his diamond 'cradle' abandoned halfway through the process of concentrating the heavier diamondiferous gravel. Daniel, the Hottentot servant, hung from his stirrup leather, his bare feet kicking up little puffs of dust as they skimmed the dry earth, and the red woollen cap that was the insignia of Fleetwood's party blowing back from his bald head to flap like a flag beckoning others to follow.

Such behaviour instantly precipitated a wild panic amongst the fiercely competitive little community of diggers along the river. Within an hour a tall column of red dust rose above the flat dry land; a headlong column of horsemen flogged their mounts while behind them the Scotch carts rumbled and the less fortunate stumbled and slipped in the sandy footing as they ran the miles back southwards to old man De Beer's barren hard-scrabble little farm on which rose another bald stony little kopje, just like ten thousand others that studded the plains.

The kopje was that same day in the bleak, dry winter of 1871 named 'Colesberg' kopje, for Colesberg was Fleetwood Rawstorne's birthplace, and De Beer's New Rush came swarming out of the dusty sun-bleached distances towards it.

It was almost dark when Fleetwood reached the kopje, only just ahead of his followers. His horse was blown, lathered with sweat and white froth, but the Hottentot servant clung to the stirrup leather still.

Master and servant flung themselves from the heaving staggering animal and ran at the slope. Their scarlet caps bobbing above the scrub thorn could be seen from a half mile distance, and a hoarse excited cheer went up from the ragged column that pursued them.

On the crest of the hill, the Hottentot servant had burrowed a shaft ten feet into the hard earth, a tiny scratch when compared to what was to follow. Frantic with haste, casting fearful glances down the hillside at the horde that raced up towards him, Fleetwood drove the centre line of his claim pegs across the narrow mouth of the shallow prospect shaft.

Night fell over a battlefield on which brawny diggers cursed each other and swung punches and pick-handles to clear the ground and drive their own claim pegs. By noon the next day, when farmer De Beer rode across from his primitive two-roomed dwelling to begin writing out the 'briefies', which was taal for 'letters', the entire kopje was covered with claim pegs; even the flat plain for a quarter of a mile below the slopes was bristling with pegs.

Each claim was thirty feet square, its centre and corners marked with a sharpened wood stake cut from a camel-thorn branch. On payment of an annual fee of ten shillings to farmer De Beer, the digger received his written 'briefie' which entitled him to hold and work the claim in perpetuity.

Before nightfall that first day the lucky diggers who had

11

pegged the centre of the new rush had merely scratched the stony earth, but had turned up over forty stones of the first water; and already horsemen were away southwards carrying the word to the world that Colesberg kopje was a mountain of diamonds.

When Zouga Ballantyne's single wagon creaked the last few miles down the rutted red earth track towards Colesberg kopje, it was already half demolished, eaten away as though by the maggots in a rotten cheese, and men still swarmed over what remained. On the dusty plain below it were encamped almost ten thousand souls, black and brown and white. The smoke from their cooking fires blurred the high china-blue sky with dirty grey, and for miles in each direction the diggers had almost denuded the plain of the beautiful camel-thorn trees to feed those fires.

The settlement was strewn about under dirty weather-worn canvas, although already some sheets of the ubiquitous corrugated iron had been laboriously transported from the coast and knocked up into boxlike shanties. Some of these, with a fine sense of order, had been arranged in an approximation of a straight line, forming the first rudimentary streets.

These belonged to the 'kopje-wallopers', the previously nomadic diamond buyers who had until recently roamed the diggings, but who had now found it worth their while to set up permanent shop below the crumbling remains of Colesberg kopje. According to the infant diamond laws of the Boer Free State, each licensed buyer was obliged to display his name prominently. This they did in crudely lettered signs upon the little iron sweat-box offices, but most of them went further and flew a disproportionately large gaudy and fancifully designed flag from a mast on the roof to announce to the diggers that the incumbent was in office and ready to do business. The flags lent a carnival air to the settlement.

Zouga Ballantyne walked beside the offside lead ox of

his team, following one of the narrow meandering rutted tracks that ran through the settlement. Occasionally the team had to be swung to avoid the tailings that had spilled into the track from one of the recovery stations, or to avoid a deep morass formed by spilled sewerage and washings from the sorting tables.

The settlement was densely crowded upon itself – that was the first impression that struck Zouga. He was a man of the plains and savannah forests, accustomed to long uninterrupted horizons, and the crowding jarred upon his senses. The diggers lived within touching distance of each other, every man attempting to get as close to his claim as he could so that the gravel that he won from it would not have to be carried too far to the place where he would process it.

Zouga had hoped to find an open space upon which to outspan his wagon and erect the big bell tent, but there was no open space within a quarter of a mile of the kopje.

He glanced back at Aletta on the box. She was sitting very still, moving only as the wagon jolted, looking straight ahead as though oblivious of the almost naked men, many wearing merely a scrap of trade cloth about the loins, who milled the crunchy lumps of yellow gravel and then shovelled it into the waiting cradles. Swearing or singing as they worked, all of them oiled with their own sweat in the cruel white sunlight.

The filth appalled even Zouga, who had known the kraals of the Mashona in the north and had lived in a bushman settlement with the little creatures who never bathed in their entire lifetimes.

Civilized man generates particularly loathsome wastes, and it seemed that every square inch of the dusty red earth between the tents and the shanties of the settlement was covered with a litter of rusty bully beef tins, broken fragments of bottles and porcelain that glittered in the sunlight, a snowstorm of paper scraps, the decomposing corpses of stray kittens and unwanted dogs, the scrapings from the cooking pots, the excrement of those too lazy to dig a latrine in the hard earth and screen it with a thatch of the silvery Karroo grass, and all the other unidentifiable offal and castings with which ten thousand human beings without control or sanitary regulations had surrounded themselves.

Zouga caught Aletta's eyes and smiled at her reassuringly, but she did not return the smile. Her lips were set bravely, but her eyes were huge and brimming with tears that lapped at her lower lids.

They squeezed past a transport rider who had brought up a wagonload of goods from the coast, six hundred miles, and had set up shop from the tailboard of his wagon, displaying a sign on which he had chalked up a price list:

> Candles – £1 a pkt
> Whisky – £12 a case
> Soap – 5/- a piece

Zouga did not look back again at Aletta, the prices were twenty times higher than those prevailing at the coast. De Beer's New Rush was probably at that moment the most expensive spot on the surface of the globe. The remaining sovereigns in the wide leather money belt around Zouga's waist seemed suddenly feather light.

By noon that day they had found space to outspan the wagon on the periphery of the huge circular encampment. While Jan Cheroot, Zouga's Hottentot retainer, drove the cattle away to find grazing and water, Zouga hurriedly erected the heavy canvas tent, Aletta and the boys holding the guy ropes while he drove the pegs.

'You must eat,' Aletta mumbled, still not looking at him as she squatted over the smouldering cooking fire and stirred the cast iron stew pot that contained the remains of a springbuck that Ralph had shot three days before.

Zouga went to her, stooped and with his hands on her shoulders lifted her to her feet. She moved stiffly as an old woman, the long hard journey had taken a heavy toll of her frail body.

'It will be all right,' he told her, and still she would not look at him, perhaps she had heard that assurance too often. He cupped her chin and lifted her face, and the tears broke at last and slid down her cheeks, leaving little runnels through the red dust that powdered her skin. The tears angered Zouga unreasonably, as though they were an accusation. He dropped his hands and stepped back from her.

'I will be back before dark,' he told her harshly and, turning from her, he strode away towards the ruined silhouette of the Colesberg kopje which stood out starkly, even through the stinking miasma of smoke and dust that hovered over the camp.

Zouga might have been a wraith, a thing of air, invisible to human eyes. They hurried by him on the narrow track, or remained stooped over mill and cradle while he passed, without an inclination of head or even a casual glance, an entire community living for one thing only, completely absorbed and obsessed.

From experience Zouga knew there was one place where he might be able to establish human contact, and through it glean the information he so desperately needed. He was looking for a canteen that sold hard liquor.

Below the kopje there was an open space, the only one in the camp. It was roughly square in shape, bordered by shacks of canvas and iron, cluttered with the wagons of the transport riders.

Zouga selected one of the shacks that grandly announced itself as 'The London Hotel' and on the same board advertised:

Whisky 7/6. Best English Beer 5/- a schooner.

He was picking his way across the littered, rutted market square towards it when ragged cheers and a bellowed chorus of 'For he's a jolly good fellow' from the direction of the kopje checked him. A motley band of diggers came stamping through the dust carrying one of their number upon their shoulders, singing and yelling, their faces brick red with dust and excitement. They shouldered their way into the rickety bar ahead of Zouga, while from the other canteens and from the parked wagons men came running to find the cause of the excitement.

'What happened?' the question was yelled.

'Black Thomas pulled a monkey,' the reply was hurled back.

It was only later that Zouga learned the diggers' parlance. A 'monkey' was a diamond of fifty carats or more, while a 'pony' was that impossible diggers' dream, a stone of one hundred carats.

'Black Thomas pulled a *monkey*.' The reply was picked up and called across the square and through the encampment, and soon the crowd overflowed the rickety canteen so that the frothing schooners of beer had to be passed overhead to the men on the fringes.

The fortunate Black Thomas was hidden from Zouga's view in the crowd that pressed about him, everybody trying to draw close as though some of the man's luck might rub off onto them.

The kopje-wallopers heard the excitement, hastily lowered their flags and hurried across the square, gathering like carrion birds to the lion's kill. The first of them arrived breathless on the fringe of the revellers, hopping up and down for a glimpse of the man.

'Tell Black Thomas that Lion-heart Werner will make an open offer – pass it on to him.'

'Hey, Blackie, Lion-arse will go open.' The offer changed shape as it was yelled through the packed doorway. An

16

'open offer' was firm and the digger was free to tout the other buyers. If he received no higher bid for his diamond, he was entitled to return and close with the open offer.

Once again Black Thomas was raised by his fellows until he could see over their heads. He was a little gypsy-dark Welshman and his moustache was rimed with beer froth. His voice had the sweet Welsh lilt as he sang his defiance:

'Hear me, then, Lion-arse the robber, I would sooner—' what he proposed to do with his diamond made even the rough men about him blink and then guffaw with surprise ' – rather than let you get your thieving paws on it.'

His voice rang with the memory of a hundred humiliations and unfair bargains that had been forced upon him. Today Black Thomas with his 'monkey' was king of the diggings, and though his reign might be short, he was determined to reap all the sweets that it promised.

Zouga never laid eyes on that stone; he never saw Black Thomas again; for by noon the following day the little Welshman had sold his diamond, and sold too his 'briefies', and taken the long road south on the beginning of his journey home to a fairer, greener land.

Zouga waited in the press of hot sweat-stinking bodies that filled the canteen, choosing a man with care while he listened to the voices grow louder and the chaff coarser as the schooners went down.

He selected one who by his comportment and speech was a gentleman, and home-bred rather than colonial born. The man was drinking whisky, and when his glass was empty Zouga moved closer and ordered it refilled.

'Very decent of you, old man,' the man thanked him. He was in his twenties still and remarkably good-looking, with fair English skin and silky sideburns. 'The name is Pickering, Neville Pickering,' he said.

'Ballantyne – Zouga Ballantyne.' Zouga took the proffered hand and the man's expression altered.

'Good Lord, you are the elephant hunter.' Pickering raised his voice. 'I say, fellows, this is Zouga Ballantyne. You know, the one who wrote *Hunter's Odyssey*.'

Zouga doubted half of them could read, but the fact that he had written a book made him an object of wonder. He found the centre of interest had shifted from Black Thomas to himself.

It was after dark when he started back to the wagon. He had always had a strong head for liquor and there was a good moon, so he could pick his way through the ordure that littered the track.

He had spent a few sovereigns on liquor, but in return he had learned a great deal about the diggings. He had learned of the diggers' expectations and fears. He knew now the going price for 'briefies', the politics and economics of diamond pricing, the geological composition of the strike and a hundred other related facts. He had also made a friendship that would alter his whole life.

Although Aletta and the boys were already asleep in the wagon tent, Jan Cheroot, the little Hottentot, was waiting for him, squatting beside the watch-fire, a small gnome-like figure in the silver moonlight.

'There is no free water,' he told Zouga morosely. 'The river is a full day's trek away, and the thieving Boer who owns the wells sells water at the same price as they sell brandy in this hell-hole.' Jan Cheroot could be relied upon to know the going price of liquor ten minutes after arriving in a new town.

Zouga climbed into the wagon body, careful not to jolt the boys awake; but Aletta was lying rigidly in the narrow riempie bed. He lay down beside her and neither of them spoke for many minutes.

Then she whispered. 'You are determined to stay in this,' her voice checked, then went on with quiet vehemence, 'in this awful place.'

He did not reply, and in the cot behind the canvas

screen across the body of the wagon Jordan whimpered and then was silent. Zouga waited until he had settled before he replied.

'Today a Welshman named Black Thomas found a diamond. They say he has been offered twelve thousand pounds by one of the buyers.'

'A woman came to sell me a little goat's milk while you were away.' Aletta might not have heard him. 'She says there is camp fever here. A woman and two children have died already and others are sick.'

'A man can buy a good claim on the kopje for one thousand pounds.'

'I fear for the boys, Zouga,' Aletta whispered. 'Let us go back. We could give up this wandering gypsy life for every. Daddy has always wanted you to come into the business—'

Aletta's father was a rich Cape merchant, but Zouga shuddered in the darkness at the thought of a high desk in the dingy counting-room of Cartwright and Company.

'It is time the boys went to a good school, else they will grow up as savages. Please let us go back now, Zouga.'

'A week,' he said. 'Give me a week – we have come so far.'

'I do not think I can bear the flies and filth for another week.' She sighed and turned her back to him, careful not to touch him in the narrow cot.

The family doctor in Cape Town, who had attended Aletta's own birth, the birth of both boys and her numerous miscarriages, had warned them ominously.

'Another pregnancy could be your last, Aletta. I cannot be responsible for what may happen.' For the three years since then she had lain with her back to him, on those occasions when they had been able to share a bed.

Before dawn Zouga slipped out of the wagon while Aletta and the boys still slept. In the darkness before first light he stirred the ashes and drank a cup of coffee crouching over them. Then in the first rosy glow of dawn he joined the stream of carts and hurrying men that moved up for the day's assault on the hill.

In the strengthening light and rising heat and whirls of dust he moved from claim to claim, looking and assessing. He had long ago trained himself as an amateur geologist. He had read every book that he could find on the subject, often by candlelight on the lonely hunting veld; and on his infrequent returns home he had passed days and weeks in the Natural History Museum in London, much of the time in the Geological Section. He had trained his eye and sharpened his instinct for the lie of the rock formations and for the grain and weight and colour of a sample of reef.

At most of the claims his overtures were met with a shrug and a turned back, but one or two of the diggers remembered him as the 'elephant hunter' or the 'writer fellow' and used his visit as an excuse to lean on their shovels and talk for a few minutes.

'I've got two briefies,' a digger who introduced himself as Jock Danby told Zouga, 'but I call them The Devil's Own. With these two hands,' he held up his huge paws, the palms studded with raised calluses, the nails chipped away and black with dirt, 'with my own hands I've shifted fifteen thousand tons of stuff, and the biggest stone I've pulled is a two. That there,' he pointed to the adjoining claim, 'was Black Thomas's claim. Yesterday he pulled a monkey, a bloody fat stinking monkey, only two feet from my side peg. Christ! It's enough to break your heart.'

'Buy you a beer.' Zouga jerked his head towards the nearest canteen, and the man licked his lips then shook his head regretfully.

'My kid is hungry – you can see the ribs sticking out of the little bugger and I have to pay wages by noon tomorrow.' He indicated the dozen half-naked black tribes- men labouring with pick and bucket in the bottom of the neatly squared off excavation with him. 'These bastards cost me a fortune every day.'

Jock Danby spat on his callused palms and hefted the shovel, but Zouga cut in smoothly.

'They do say the strike will pinch out at the level of the plain.' At this point the kopje had been reduced to a mere twenty feet above the surrounding plain. 'What do you think?'

'Mister, it's bad luck to even talk like that.' Jock checked the swing of his shovel and scowled heavily up at Zouga on the roadway above him, but there was fear in his eyes.

'You ever thought of selling out?' Zouga asked him, and immediately Jock's fear faded to be replaced by a sly expression.

'Why, mister? You thinking of buying?' Jock straightened. 'Let me give you a little tip for free. Don't even think about it, not unless you got six thousand pounds to do the talking for you.'

He peered up at Zouga hopefully, and Zouga stared back at him without expression.

'Thank you for your time, sir, and for your sake I hope the gravel lasts.'

Zouga touched the wide brim of his hat and sauntered away. Jock Danby watched him go, then spat viciously on the yellow ground at his feet and swung the shovel at it as though it were a mortal enemy.

As he walked away Zouga felt a strange sense of elation. There was a time when he had lived by the turn of a card and the fall of a die, and he felt the gambler's instinct now. He knew the gravel would not pinch out. He knew it sank down, pure and rich into the depths. He knew it with a deep unshakable certainty, and he knew something else with equal certainty.

'The road to the north begins here.' He spoke aloud, and felt his blood thrill in his veins. 'This is where it begins.'

He felt the need to make an act of faith, of total affirmation, and he knew what it must be. The price of livestock on the diggings was vastly inflated, and his oxen were costing him a guinea a day to water. He knew how to close the road back.

By mid-afternoon he had sold the oxen: a hundred pounds a head, and five hundred for his wagon. Now he was committed, and he felt the currents of excitement coursing through his body as he paid the gold coin over the raw wooden counter of the tin shack that housed the branch of the Standard Bank.

The road back was cut. He was chancing it all on the yellow gravel and the road northwards.

'Zouga, you promised,' Aletta whispered when the buyer came to Zouga's camp to collect the oxen. 'You promised that in one week—' Then she fell silent when she saw his face. She knew that expression. She drew the two boys to her and held them close.

Jan Cheroot went to each of the animals in turn and whispered to them as tenderly as a lover, and his stare was reproachful as he turned to Zouga while the span was led away.

Neither man spoke, and at last Jan Cheroot dropped his gaze and walked away, a slight, bare-footed, bow-legged little gnome.

Zouga thought he had lost him, and he felt a rush of distress, for the little man was a friend, a teacher and a companion of twelve years. It was Jan Cheroot who had tracked his first elephant, and stood shoulder to shoulder with him as he shot it down. Together they had marched and ridden the breadth of a savage continent. They had drunk from the same bottle and eaten from the same pot at a thousand camp fires. Yet he could not bring himself to call him back. He knew that Jan Cheroot must make his own decision.

He need not have worried. When 'dop' time came that evening, Jan Cheroot was there to hold out his chipped enamel mug. Zouga smiled and, ignoring the line that measured his daily ration of brandy, he filled the mug to the brim.

'It was necessary, old friend,' he said, and Jan Cheroot nodded gravely. 'They were good beasts,' he said. 'But then I have had many fine beasts go from my life, four-legged and two-legged ones.' He tasted the raw spirit. 'After a little time and a dram or two, it does not matter so much.'

Aletta did not speak again until the boys were asleep in the tent.

'Selling the oxen and the wagon was your answer,' she said.

'It cost a guinea a day to water them, and the grazing has been eaten flat for miles about.'

'There have been three more deaths in the camp. I counted thirty wagons leaving today. It's a plague camp.'

'Yes.' Zouga nodded. 'Some of the claim holders are getting nervous. A claim that I was offered for eleven hundred pounds yesterday was sold for nine hundred today.'

'Zouga, it's not fair to me or the children,' she began, but he interrupted her.

'I can arrange a passage for you and the boys with a transport rider. He has sold his stock and he leaves in the next few days. He will take you back to Cape Town.'

They undressed in darkness and silence, and when Aletta followed him into the hard narrow cot the silence continued until he thought she had fallen asleep. Then he felt her hand, smooth and soft, touch his cheek lightly.

'I am sorry, my darling.' Her voice was as light as her touch, and her breath stirred his beard. 'I was so tired and depressed.'

He took her hand and held the tips of her fingers to his lips.

'I have been such a poor wife to you, always too sick and weak when you needed someone strong.' Timidly she let her body touch his. 'And now when I should be a comfort to you, I do nothing but snivel.'

'No,' he said. 'That's not true.' And yet over the years he had resented her often enough for just those reasons. He had felt like a man trying to run with shackles on his ankles.

'And yet I love you, Zouga. I loved you the first day I laid eyes on you, and I have never ceased to love you.'

'I love you too, Aletta,' he assured her, yet the words came automatically; and to make up for the lack of spontaneity, he placed his arm around her shoulders and she drew closer still and laid her cheek against his chest.

'I hate myself for being so weak and sickly,' she hesitated, 'for not being able to be a real wife any more.'

'Shh! Aletta, do not upset yourself.'

'I will be strong now – you will see.'

'You have always been strong, deep inside.'

'No, but I will be now. We shall find that capful of diamonds together, and afterwards we shall go north.' He did not reply, and it was she who spoke again. 'Zouga, I want you to make love to me – now.'

'Aletta, you know that is dangerous.'

'Now,' she repeated. 'Now, please.' And she took his hand down and placed it under the hem of her nightdress against the smooth warm skin of her inner thigh. She had never done that before, and Zouga found himself shocked but strangely aroused, and afterwards he was filled with a deep tenderness and compassion for her that he had not felt for many years.

When her breathing had become regular once more, she pulled his hands away gently and slipped out of the cot.

Leaning on one elbow he watched her light the candle and then kneel by the trunk that was lashed to the foot of the cot. She had plaited her hair with a ribbon in it, and her body was slim as a young girl's. The candlelight flattered her, smoothing out the lines of sickness and worry. He remembered how lovely she had been.

She lifted the lid of the trunk, took something from the

interior and brought it to him. It was a small cask with an ornate brass lock. The key was in the lock.

'Open it,' she said.

In the candlelight he saw that the cask contained two thick rolls of five-pound notes, each bound up with a scrap of ribbon, and a draw-string pouch of dark green velvet. He lifted out the pouch and it was heavy with gold coin.

'I was keeping it,' she whispered, 'for the day it was really needed. There is almost a thousand pounds there.'

'Where did you get this?'

'My father, on our wedding day. Take it, Zouga. Buy that claim with it. This time we will make it all right. This time is going to be all right.'

I n the morning the purchaser came to claim the wagon. He waited impatiently while the family moved their meagre possessions into the bell tent.

Once Zouga had removed the cots from the tented half of the wagon body he was able to lift the planking from the narrow compartment over the rear wheel truck. Here the heavier goods were stored to keep the vehicle's centre of gravity low. The spare trek chain, the lead for moulding into bullet, axe heads, a small anvil – and then Zouga's household god which he and Jan Cheroot strained to lift from its padded bed and lower to the ground beside the wagon.

Between them they carried it to the tent and set it upright against the far screen of the bell tent.

'I've lugged this rubbish from Matabeleland to Cape Town and back,' complained Jan Cheroot disgustedly as he stood back from the graven birdlike figure on its stone plinth.

Zouga smiled indulgently. The Hottentot had hated that ancient idol from the very first day they uncovered it together in the overgrown ruins of an ancient walled city, a city they had stumbled on while hunting elephant in that wild untamed land so far to the north.

'It's my good-luck charm,' Zouga smiled.

'What luck?' Jan Cheroot demanded bitterly. 'Is it luck to have to sell the oxen? Is it luck to live in a tent full of flies amongst a tribe of white savages?' Muttering and mumbling bitterly, Jan Cheroot stamped out of the tent and snatched up the halters of the two remaining horses to take them down to water.

Zouga paused for a moment in front of the statue. It stood almost as high as his head on its slim column of polished green soapstone. Atop the column crouched a stylized bird figure on the edge of flight. The cruel curve of the falcon beak fascinated Zouga, and in a habitual gesture he stroked the smooth stone and the blank eyes stared back at him inscrutably.

Zouga opened his lips to whisper to the bird, and at that moment Aletta stooped into the triangular opening of the tent and saw what he was doing.

Quickly, almost guiltily, Zouga dropped his hand and turned to face her. Aletta hated that stone image even more bitterly than did Jan Cheroot. Now she stood very still. Her arms were filled with a pile of neatly folded linen and clothing – but her eyes were troubled.

'Zouga, must we have that thing in here?'

'It takes up no room,' he told her lightly, and came to take her burden from her, place it on the truckle bed, and then turn back to take her in his arms.

'I will never forget what you did last night,' he told her, and felt the rigidity go out of her body. She swayed against him and lifted her face to his. Once again he felt his chest squeezed with compassion as he saw the lines of sickness and worry at the corners of her eyes and mouth, saw the grey patina of fatigue on her skin.

He bowed his head to kiss her lips, feeling awkward at

such unaccustomed demonstration of affection; but at that moment the two boys burst into the tent, raucous with laughter and excitement and dragging between them a stray puppy on a string, and Aletta broke hurriedly from Zouga's embrace and, flushing with embarrassment, adjusted her apron, beginning to scold her offspring fondly.

'Out with it! It's covered in fleas.'

'Oh please, Mama!'

'Out, I say!'

She watched Zouga set off into the sprawling settlement, striding down the dusty track with his shoulders squared and the old jaunty spring in his step, then she turned back to the cone of soiled canvas set on a bleak dry plain under the cruel blue African sky, and she sighed. The weariness came upon her again in waves.

In her girlhood there had been servants to perform the menial tasks of cooking and cleaning. She still had not mastered the smoky fluttering open flames of the camp fire, and already a fine red coating of dust had settled upon everything, even the surface of the goat's milk in its earthenware jug. With an enormous effort of will, she gathered her resolve and stooped determinedly into the tent.

Ralph had followed Jan Cheroot down to the wells to help with the horses. She knew that the two of them would not return until the next mealtime. They made an incongruous pair, the wizened little old man and the handsome reckless child already taller and more sturdy than his inseparable protector and tutor.

Jordan stayed with her. He was not yet ten years of age, but without his companionship she doubted that she could have borne the terrible journey across those bone-breaking miles, the burning dusty days and the frosty nights of aching cold.

Already the child could cook the simple camp dishes, and his unleavened bread and griddle scones were family favourites at every meal. She had taught him to read and write, and given to him her love of poetry and fine and beautiful things. He could already darn a torn shirt and wield the heavy coal-filled stroking-iron to smooth a shirt. His sweet piping tones and angelic beauty were constant sources of intense joy to her. She had grown his golden curls long for once, resisting her husband when he wanted to scissor them short as he had done Ralph's.

Jordan stood below her now, helping her to string a canvas screen across the tent that would divide the sleeping and living areas. She was suddenly compelled to lean down and touch those soft fine curls.

At the touch he smiled sweetly up at her, and abruptly her senses spun dizzily. She swayed wildly on the rickety cot, trying to keep her balance and, as she fell, Jordan struggled to hold and steady her. He did not have the strength and her weight bore them both to the ground.

Jordan's eyes were huge and swimming with horror. He helped her half crawl, half stagger back to the cot and collapse upon it.

Waves of heat and nausea and giddiness broke over her.

Zouga was the first customer at the office of the Standard Bank when the clerk opened the door onto Market Square. Once he had deposited the contents of Aletta's casket and the clerk had locked it in the big green iron safe against the far wall, Zouga had a balance of almost £2,500 to his credit.

That knowledge armed his resolve. He felt tall and powerful as he strode up the ramp of the central causeway.

The roadways were seven feet wide. The mining commissioner, after the lesson of the diggings at Bultfontein and Dutoitspan, had insisted that these access roads be left open to service the claims in the centre of the growing pit.

The workings were a mosaic of square platforms, each precisely thirty feet square. Some of the diggers, with more capital and better organization, were sinking their claims faster than others, so that the slower workers were isolated on towers of golden yellow earth, high above their neighbouring claims, while the fastest miners had sunk deep square shafts at the bottom of which toiled the naked black labourers.

For a man to move from one claim to another was already a laborious and often downright dangerous journey: crossing rickety board walks above the dizzying shaft of a deep claim, scrambling up high swaying rope ladders or down the steps of a pole ladder, lengths of native timber lashed together with cross-steps that creaked and gave with a man's weight.

Standing on the crumbling roadway with the workings gaping below him, Zouga wondered what would be the outcome if the strike continued to great depth. It already required a level head and strong stomach to chance the uneven pit, and he wondered again at man's determination to accumulate wealth against any odds, in the face of any danger.

He watched while from the bottom of the workings a leather bucket, brimming with broken lumps of the compacted yellow gravel, was hauled up, swinging at the end of a long rope, two sweating black men dipping and swinging over the windlass, their muscles swelling and subsiding in the bright sunlight.

The bucket reached the lip of the roadway, and they seized it, lugged it to the waiting cart with its patient pair of mules, and dumped the contents into the half-full body. Then one of them dropped the empty bucket over the side of the roadway to the waiting men fifty feet below. At hundreds of points along the fourteen causeways the same operation was being repeated, endlessly the loaded buckets came swinging up and were dropped back empty.

Occasionally, breaking the monotonous rhythm, the seam of a leather bucket would burst, showering the men below with jagged chunks of rock, or a worn rope would snap and, with warning shouts, the toilers at the bottom of the pit would hurl themselves aside to avoid the plunging missile.

There was an impatient humming excitement that seemed to embrace the entire workings. The urgent shouted commands between pit and roadway, the squeal of rope sheaves, the thudding jar of pick and swinging shovel, the rich lilting chorus of a gang of Basuto tribesmen singing as they worked, small wiry little mountaineers from the Dragon Range.

The white diggers, bullying and bustling, scrambled down the swaying ladderworks or stood over their gangs on the pit floor, hawk-eyed to forestall a 'pick-up': the possibility of a valuable diamond being exposed by a spade and swiftly palmed by one of the black workers, to be slipped into the mouth or other body opening at the first opportunity.

Illegal diamond selling and buying was already the plague of the diggers. In their eyes, every black man was a suspect. Only men with less than one quarter black blood were allowed to hold and work claims. This law made it easier to apportion blame, for a black face with a diamond in his possession was guilty without appeal. However, this law could not control the shady white men that hung around the diggings, ostensibly travelling salesmen, actors or proprietors of infamous drinking canteens but in reality all I.D.B., Illegal Diamond Buyers. The diggers hated them with a ferocity that sometimes boiled over in a night of rioting and beating and burning in which innocent merchants, as well as the guilty, lost all their possessions in the flames, while the mob of diggers danced about the burning shacks chanting: 'I.D.B.! I.D.B.!'

Zouga moved cautiously out along the crest of the

roadway, at times pushed perilously close to the edge by a passing cart laden with diamondiferous earth.

He reached the point above Jock Danby's claims from which he had spoken to the friendly digger the previous day.

The two claims were deserted, the leather bucket and rope coils abandoned, a pick handle standing upright with its point driven into the earth far below the level of the roadway.

There was a big bearded digger working the adjoining claim, and he scowled up in response to Zouga's hail.

'What you want?'

'I'm looking for Jock Danby.'

'Well, you are looking in the wrong place.'

The man turned and aimed a kick at the nearest labourer. 'Sebenza, you black monkey!'

'Where will I find him?'

'Other side of Market Square, behind the Lord Nelson.' The man answered off-handedly without turning his head.

The dusty pitted open square was as littered with filth as the rest of the settlement, and crowded with the wagons of the transport riders and the carts of farmers who had come in to sell milk or produce and of the water sellers, peddling the precious stuff by the bucket.

The Lord Nelson was a stained red dusty canvas over a wooden frame. Three of the previous night's drinkers were laid out like embalmed corpses in the narrow alley beside the canteen, while the single bar-room was already filling with the early morning customers.

A pariah dog sniffed the breath of one of the unconscious drunks, and recoiled with shock before slinking away to raid the open drum that served as a rubbish bin behind the shack.

Zouga stepped over the sprawling bodies and gingerly made his way into the noisome slum beyond. He had to make half a dozen further enquiries until he found Jock

Danby's hut. So obsessed were the diggers with their own race for the hidden glitter of wealth, and so transient the population of the diggings, that a man seemed to know only the names of his immediate neighbours. It was a community of strangers, every man caring only for himself, completely uninterested in the other human beings about him, except in as much as they could either hinder or help him in his quest for the bright stones.

Jock Danby's hut was hardly distinguishable from a thousand others. Two rooms built of adobe bricks and covered with thatch and tattered canvas. There was a lean-to at one end, with a smoking cooking fire on which stood a sooty black three-legged pot.

In the cluttered dusty yard stood the inevitable diamond sorting-table, a low structure with sturdy wooden legs, the top covered with a sheet of flat iron which was scoured shiny bright by the diamondiferous pebbles that had brushed over the surface. The wooden scrapers lay abandoned on the table top, and a heap of sieved and washed gravel formed a glittering pyramid in the centre of the table.

A two-wheeled cart stood in front of the main door of the hut, two somnolent donkeys still in the traces, flicking their ears at the swarming black cloud of flies. The cart was piled with lumps of yellow earth, but the yard was deserted.

Incongruously there were a few straggling scarlet geraniums growing in galvanized one-gallon syrup cans on each side of the doorway. There were also dainty lace curtains in the single window, so freshly washed that they had not yet turned ochre red with dust, nor become speckled with the excrement of the swarming flies.

The touch of a woman was unmistakable, and to confirm Zouga's guess there was the faint but harrowing sound of a woman weeping from the open doorway.

As Zouga hesitated in the yard, disconcerted by the

sounds of grief, a brawny figure filled the doorway and stood blinking in the sunlight, shading his eyes with a gnarled and dirt-ingrained hand.

'Who are you?' Jock Danby demanded, with unnecessary roughness.

'I spoke to you yesterday,' Zouga explained, 'up at the pit.'

'What do you want?' the digger demanded, showing no sign of recognition, his features screwed up in an expression of truculence and something else, some other emotion which Zouga did not immediately recognize.

'You spoke of selling your briefies,' Zouga reminded him.

Jock Danby's face seemed to swell and turn dark ugly red; the veins and cords stood out in his throat as he ducked his head down on the thickly muscled shoulders.

'You filthy bloody vulture,' he choked, and he came out into the sunlight with the heavy irresistible crabbing rush of a gut-shot buffalo bull.

He was taller than Zouga by a head, ten years younger and fifty pounds heavier. Taken completely by surprise, Zouga was a hundredth part of a second late in ducking and spinning away from the man's charge. A fist like a cannon ball smashed into his shoulder, a glancing blow but with the force to send Zouga reeling to sprawl on his back across the sorting-table, scattering diamondiferous gravel across the dusty yard.

Jock Danby charged again, his swollen face working, his eyes mad, his thick stained fingers hooked as they reached for Zouga's throat. Zouga jack-knifed his legs, drawing himself into a ball, tense as the arch in an adder's neck at the moment before it strikes, and he drove the heels of his boots into the man's chest.

The breath whistled out of Jock Danby's throat, and he stopped in mid-charge as though hit in the chest with a double charge of buckshot. His head and arms snapped forward, nerveless as a straw-man, and he flew backwards, crashing into the unbaked brick wall of the hut and beginning to slide down onto his knees.

Zouga bounded off the tabletop. His left arm was numb to the fingertips from the unexpected blow, but he was light on his feet as a dancer, and the quick rush of cold anger armed and strengthened him. He closed the gap between them with two swift strides and hooked Jock Danby, high in the side of his head just above and in front of his ear; the shock of the punch jarred his own teeth but sent the man spinning along the wall to slump on his knees in the red dust.

Jock Danby was stunned and his eyes were glazing over, but Zouga jerked him to his feet and propped him against the side of the cart, setting him up carefully for the next punch. His anger and outrage driving him on to revenge that unprovoked and senseless attack, Zouga shifted his weight, holding Jock Danby steady with his left hand and pulling back the right fist for a full-blooded swing.

Then he froze. He never threw the punch. Instead he stared incredulously. Jock Danby was blubbering like a child, his heavy shoulders shaking uncontrollably, tears greasing down the sunraddled cheeks into the dusty beard.

It was somehow shocking and embarrassing to see a man like this weep, and Zouga felt his anger swiftly extinguished. He dropped his fist and unclenched it at his side.

'Christ—' Jock Danby choked hoarsely. 'What kind of man are you to try and make a profit of another man's grief?'

Zouga stared at him, unable to answer the accusation.

'You must have smelt it, like a hyena or a fat bloody vulture.'

'I came to make you a fair offer – that's all,' Zouga replied stiffly. He took the handkerchief from his jacket pocket and handed it to Jock Danby. 'Wipe your face, man,' he ordered gruffly.

Jock smeared his tears and then studied the stained linen. 'You didn't know then?' he whispered. 'You didn't know about the boy?' He looked up and studied Zouga's face sharply and, seeing his answer, he handed back the handkerchief and shook his head like a spaniel shaking off the water from its ears, trying to steady his reeling senses. 'I'm sorry,' he grunted. 'I thought somehow you had learned about the boy – and come to buy me out.'

'I don't understand,' Zouga told him, and Jock Danby started for the door of the shack.

'Come,' he said, and led Zouga through the hot stuffy little front room. The chairs covered with dark green velvet were too bulky for the size of the room, and the family treasures – Bible and faded ancestral photographs, cheap cutlery and a porcelain dish commemorating the Queen's wedding to Prince Albert – were on display upon the central table.

In the door of the back room Zouga paused, and felt a sickening little lurch in the pit of his stomach. A woman knelt beside the bed. She had a shawl spread over head and shoulders. Her hands clasped before her face were roughened and reddened by the drudgery of labour over the diamond sorting-table.

She lifted her head and looked at Zouga in the doorway. She might once have been a pretty girl, but the sun had coarsened her skin and her eyes were swollen and reddened with grief. The wisps of hair that hung lankly from under the shawl were greasy and prematurely greyed.

After that one glance she lowered her head again and her lips moved silently as she prayed.

A child lay upon the bed, a boy no older than Jordan. His eyes were closed, his features very pale, bloodless as candlewax, but infinitely peaceful. He was dressed in a clean nightshirt, his limbs neatly arranged, the hands folded on his chest.

It took Zouga a full minute to realize that he was dead. 'The fever,' whispered Jock at Zouga's side. He broke off and stood dumb and massive as an ox awaiting the butcher's stroke.

Zouga took Jock Danby's cart down to Market Square and purchased a dozen rough-sawn planks of lumber, paying the transport rider's price without haggling.

In the dusty yard in front of Danby's shack he stripped to his shirtsleeves and planed the raw planks, while Jock sawed and shaped them. They worked in silence except for the whicker of plane and saw.

The rough coffin was ready before noon, but as Jock lifted his son's body into it Zouga caught the first whiff of corruption; it happens very swiftly in the African heat.

Jock's wife rode on the battered cart with the coffin and Zouga walked beside Jock Danby.

The fever was ravaging the camp. There were two other carts already at the burial ground, a mile beyond the last tents on the Transvaal road, each surrounded with a silent knot of mourners; and there were graves ready dug, and a grave-digger to demand his guinea.

On the way back from the burial ground Zouga stopped the cart in front of one of the canteens that fronted the market square, and with the remaining coins in his pocket he bought three bottles of Cape brandy.

He and Jock sat facing each other on the over-stuffed green velvet chairs, with an open bottle and two tumblers on the table between them. The tumblers were embossed with cheery gold letters:

Zouga half-filled the tumblers and pushed one across to Jock.

The big man studied the contents of the tumbler, holding it in his huge fists between his knees, hunching his shoulders and drooping his head.

'It was so quick,' he muttered. 'Yesterday evening he ran to meet the cart, and rode home on my shoulder.' He took a swallow of the dark liquor and shuddered. His voice was husky as he went on. 'He was so light. No meat on his little bones.'

They drank in unison.

'There was a jinx on me from the moment I drove my first peg on these bloody claims.' Jock shook his great shaggy head. 'I should have stayed on the river-diggings, like Alice told me.'

Outside the single lace-covered window the sun was already setting, a lurid red show through the dust clouds; and as the gloom gathered in the room, Alice Danby came through and placed a smoky hurricane lantern on the table between them and followed it with two bowls of Boer-meal porridge swimming in a thin and oily mutton stew. Then she disappeared silently into the back room and, from time to time during the long night, Zouga heard her gentle sobs through the thin dividing wall.

In the dawn Jock Danby lolled in the green velvet armchair, his shirt open to the navel and his hairy stomach bulging out of it. The third bottle was half empty.

'You are a gentleman,' Jock slurred unevenly. 'I don't mean a swell or a toff but a bloody gentleman, that's what you are.'

Zouga sat upright, grave and attentive; except for a slight reddening of his eyes he seemed totally unaffected by the night's drinking.

'I wouldn't want to wish the Devil's Own on a gentleman like you.'

Zouga said quietly, 'If you're going, you have to sell to someone.'

'They're jinxed, those two claims,' mumbled Jock. 'They've killed five men already, they've broken me, they've given me the worst year of my life. I've seen men on each side of me pull big stones; I've seen them become rich – while me—' he made a drunken gesture that encompassed the sordid little shack, 'look at me.'

The canvas that screened the connecting doorway was jerked aside and Alice Danby stood bareheaded beside her husband. It was evident by her drawn grey features that she had not slept either.

'Sell them,' she said. 'I cannot stay here another day. Sell them, sell everything – let's go, Jock, let's get away from this dreadful place. I cannot bear to spend another night here.'

The mining commissioner was a dour little magistrate appointed by President Brand of the fledgling Boer Free State, who laid claim to the diggings.

Brand was not the only one to have done so. Old Waterboer, the chief of the Griqua Bastaards, made cross claim to the arid plains where his people had lived for fifty years and more. In London, Lord Kimberley, Secretary of State for the Colonies, had only just awakened to the potential wealth of the diamond diggings, and for the first time was listening attentively to the pleas of the Imperialists to support old Nicholaas Waterboer's claim and take Griqualand into the sphere of British influence.

In the meantime the Free State mining commissioner was trying, with only qualified success, to maintain some order over the unruly diggers. Just as his roadways were crumbling into the surrounding pits on Colesberg kopje, so his authority was eroding before the onrush of events with the gathering of national interests and the emergence from obscurity of the first powerful figures as the financial aristocracy of the fields.

Zouga and Jock Danby found the commissioner bewailing his task over a liquid breakfast in the bar of the London Hotel and, supporting him by each elbow, they escorted him back across Market Square to his office.

By mid-morning that day, the commissioner had copied the details of the Devil's Own, claim Nos 141 and 142 held under perpetual quit-rent letter, from J. A. Danby, Esq. to Major M. Z. Ballantyne, and noted payment in full in the sum of £2,000 by cheque drawn on the Standard Bank.

An hour after noon, Zouga stood at the corner of Market Square, and watched the cart piled high with the green velvet armchairs and the brass bedstead pull away towards the northern corner of the square. Jock Danby led the team, and his wife sat thin and erect upon the load. Neither of them looked back at Zouga, and the moment they disappeared into the maze of narrow alleys and shanties Zouga turned towards the kopje.

Despite the night of sleep that he had missed, he felt no fatigue, and his step was so light that he almost ran out along the narrow causeway that intersected the jumble of claims and workings.

The Devil's Own were deserted, two forlorn patches of raw yellow earth, neatly squared off and littered with abandoned equipment. Jock Danby's black workers had gone, for there was always a desperate shortage of labourers on the diggings. When Jock had not mustered them the previous dawn they had simply wandered away to take daily hire with one of the other diggers.

Most of the mining gear left on the claims seemed worn out, the buckets on the point of bursting and the ropes furry as fat yellow caterpillars. Zouga would not trust them with his own weight.

Gingerly he climbed down the swaying ladder, his cautious movements alerting the diggers on the neighbouring claims that he was an outsider.

'Those are Jock Danby's briefies, man,' one of them shouted a challenge. 'You breaking the diggers' law. That's private ground. You better clear out – and bloody quick, at that.'

'I bought Jock out,' Zouga shouted back. 'He left town an hour ago.'

'How do I know that?'

'Why don't you go up to the commissioner's office?' Zouga asked. The challenger scowled up at him uncertainly, the level of his claim twenty feet below the Devil's Own.

Men had stopped work along the length of the irregular pit, others had lined the causeway high above, and there was an ugly mood on all of them – that was broken by a clear young voice speaking in the cadence and intonation of a refined English gentleman.

'Major Ballantyne – that is you, is it not?' And, peering up at the causeway, Zouga recognized Neville Pickering, his drinking companion from the first day in the London Hotel.

'It is indeed, Mr Pickering.'

'That's all right, fellows. I'll vouch for Major Ballantyne. He is the famous elephant hunter, don't you know?'

Almost immediately they lost interest and turned away to become absorbed once more in their own race to get the buckets of gravelly yellow stuff to the surface.

'Thank you,' Zouga called up to the man on the causeway above him.

'My pleasure, sir.' Pickering flashed a brilliant smile, touched the brim of his hat and sauntered away, a slim and elegant figure in the press of bearded dust-caked diggers.

Zouga was left alone, as alone in spirit as he had ever been in any of his wanderings across the vast African continent. He had spent almost the last penny he owned on these few square feet of yellow earth at the bottom of this hot and dusty pit. He had no men to help him work it, no experience, no capital – and he doubted that he would recognize an uncut diamond if he held one in the palm of his hand.

As suddenly as it had descended upon him, the gambler's elation, the premonition of good fortune that awaited him here evaporated. He was instantly overwhelmed by his own presumption and by the enormity of the gamble he was taking.

He had risked it all on claims that so far had not yielded a single good stone, the price of diamonds was plummeting, the 'pool goods', small splints of half a carat or less which formed the vast bulk of stones recovered, were fetching only five shillings each.

It was a wild chance, and his stomach slid sickeningly as he faced the consequences of failure.

The sun was almost directly overhead, burning down into the bottom of the workings; the air around him wavered with the heat and it came up through the leather of his boots to scorch the soles of his feet. He felt as though he were suffocating, as though he could not bear it another moment, as though he must scramble up out of this loathsome pit to where the air was cooler and sweeter.

He knew then he was afraid. It was an emotion to which he was not accustomed. He had stood down the charge of a wounded bull elephant, and taken his chance – man to man, steel to steel – on the frontiers of India and in the wild border wars of the Cape.

He was not accustomed to feeling fear, but the waves of panic rose up out of some dark place in his soul and he fought to control them. The sense of impending disaster crushed down upon him. Under his feet he could almost

41

feel the sterility of the baking earth, the barren earth which would cripple him at last, and destroy the dream which had been the fuel on which his life had run for all these years.

Was it all to end here in this hot and hellish pit?

He took a deep breath, and held it for a moment, fighting off the waves of blind panic, and slowly they receded, leaving him feeling weak and shaken as though from a heavy dose of malarial fever.

He went down on one knee and took a handful of the yellow stuff, sifting it through his fingers, and then examined the residue of dull and worthless pebbles. He let them drop and dusted his hand against his thigh.

He had beaten back the engulfing panic, but he was left with a terrible sense of despondency, and a weariness that ached in his bones so that he hardly had strength enough to climb the swaying rope ladder and his feet dragged and scuffed the ochre-red earth of the track, while around him the encampment swam and wavered in the heat and dust as he started back towards the outspan.

Above the hubbub of the camp a clear childish voice rang, and Zouga lifted the golden beard from his chest, his mood lightening as he recognized his son's sweet piping tones.

'Papa! Oh Papa!'

Jordan was racing towards him, wild abandon in every frantic pace, his arms pumping and his feet flying over the rutted track, while the mass of silken curls flew about his lovely face.

'Oh Papa, we have searched for you – all night, all day.'

'What is it, Jordan?' The child's distress alarmed Zouga afresh, and he started forward.

Jordan reached him and threw both arms about Zouga's waist, he pressed his face to Zouga's coat front so that his voice was muffled and he trembled like a frightened little wild animal.

'It's Mama! Something has happened to Mama! Something terrible has happened.'

The delirium of typhoid fever came upon Aletta in hot grey fog banks that blotted out reality and filled her head with phantoms and fantasies which cleared abruptly, leaving her too weak to sit upright, but with her senses enhanced so that her hot skin was hypersensitive to the touch of the clammy flannel against her face and the oppressive weight of her clothing threatened to smother her.

Her vision was sharp and the images enlarged as though seen through a fine reading glass. She could study each long curved eyelash that made up the dense fringe about Jordan's beautiful green eyes. She could see each individual pore in the satiny skin of his cheeks, could delight in the texture of his perfectly bowed lips that trembled now with his agitation and fear as he stooped over her.

She was lost in wonder at her son's beauty, and then the roaring started in her ears again and the beloved child's face receded, until she was looking at it down a long narrow tunnel through the roaring darkness.

She clung desperately to the image, but it began to turn, slowly at first like the wheel of a carriage, then faster still until Jordan's face blurred dizzily and she felt herself tumbling down into the humid darkness again like a leaf upon the roaring wind.

Again the darkness opened, a veil drawn aside in some deep place in her head, and with joy she sought the boy's face again – but instead she saw the falcon high above her.

It was the bird figure of the graven idol that had always been a part of her life since Zouga had come into it. At every cottage, at every outspan or room that they had called home for a day or a week or a month, that stone idol seemed to have been there with them, silent, implacable, heavy with a brooding and ancient malevolence. She had always hated that idol, had always sensed the aura of evil that surrounded it – but now her hatred and her fear could focus fully upon the stone bird that stood tall above the cot on which she lay.

She cursed it weakly, silently, lying on her back on the narrow cot, the robe she wore clinging damply to her skin with the fever sweat; and she mouthed her hatred at the stone image that towered above her on its polished green soapstone column. Again her vision narrowed, became concentrated so that the falcon head was her whole existence.

Then miraculously the blank stone eyes began to glow with a strange golden light; they revolved slowly in the sockets of the polished stone skull, and suddenly they were looking down at her. The pupils were black and glossy, alive and seeing – but cruel and so truly evil that she quailed in terror, staring up at the bird.

The curved stone beak opened, the tongue was sharp as an arrowhead, and from its tip was suspended a single perfect ruby drop of blood in which a star of light glowed – and Aletta knew it was the blood of the sacrifice. The darkness about the bird was filled with moving shadows, the wraiths of the sacrificial victims, the shades of the falcon-priests dead these thousand years, gathering again to reinforce the powers, gathering again to welcome her—

She screamed, again and again, her terror ringing insanely in her own ears – and then firm hands were shaking her gently, tenderly. Her vision cleared again, but not completely. Everything was dim and blurred, so she screwed up her eyes, still panting wildly from her screams.

'Ralph, is that you?' The strong dark features, already taking on the set of manhood, so different from the sweet angel face of his brother, were close above her.

'Don't take on so, Mama.'

'Ralphie, why is it so dark?' she mumbled.

'It's night time.'

'Where is Jordie?'

'He is asleep, Mama; he could not keep awake. I sent him to sleep.'

'Call Papa,' she whispered.

'Jan Cheroot is searching for him – he will come soon.'

'I'm cold.' She was trembling violently, and felt him draw the rough blanket up beneath her chin before she sank back into the darkness.

In the darkness she saw the shapes of men hurrying forward, pressing about her; she caught their urgency, the passion of their terrible purpose, and she saw their arms glint in the shadows, the flash of white steel, bared and honed for war. She heard the snick of breech-block, the rattle of bayonet in the scabbard, and here and there in the press she recognized a face, faces she had never seen before but which she recognized instantly with a clairvoyant flash of intuition. One was a man full grown, bearded, strong, who was her son – riding into war – and others, so many others; her blood, her flesh, her bones going forward in that awful expectant throng. She was consumed with terrible grief for them, but she could not weep. Instead, she lifted her eyes and saw the falcon on high, clear in the single brilliant shaft of sunshine that pierced the sombre and ominous clouds that rolled from horizon to horizon, the dun and terrible clouds of war.

The falcon hovered on outstretched pinions against the belly of the clouds, twisting the cruelly beautiful head to peer down, then the long pointed wings folded and the bird dropped in a stoop like a lightning bolt, the great talons reaching forward in the strike. She saw them hook into living flesh, saw the grimace on the face that she had never seen before but knew as deeply as she did her own.

And she screamed again. Then strong arms held her, the familiar beloved arms for which she had waited so long.

She looked up at him. The clear emerald eyes so close to hers, the powerful jut of his jawline half-masked by the full golden-streaked beard.

'Zouga,' she breathed.

'I am here, my love.'

The phantoms receded, the terrible nightmare world of her delirium was gone, and she found herself in a tent upon a dusty plain beneath a half-ruined hillock, and the bright African sunlight through the tent opening cut a stark slash of white light across the powdered red dust floor. She was mildly amazed by the swift transition from night to noon-day, from fantasy to reality, and her mouth and throat were filled with the dry chalk of terrible thirst.

'I am thirsty,' she whispered huskily.

He held the pitcher to her cracked lips, and the coolness and the sweetness of the liquid in her throat made her vision swim with delight.

But immediately afterwards, the memory of the nightmares assailed her and she darted a fearful glance across the tent at the silent statue. It seemed suddenly harmless, insignificant, the image blind and dumb, but a flicker of the night's terror remained.

'Beware the falcon,' she whispered, and she saw in his green eyes that he thought her words were still fever ravings. She wanted to convince him but she was terribly, deadly tired, and she closed her eyes and slept in his arms.

When she awoke, the sun's rays had mellowed to a glorious orange light that filled the whole tent and lit little stars in Zouga's beard and curls. She was filled with a deep sense of peace. His arms were so strong, so all-encompassing.

'Look after my babies,' she said softly, but very clearly, and then she died.

Aletta's grave was just another mound of red dirt in the long, neat row of freshly turned mounds.

After he had buried her, Zouga sent the boys back to the outspan with Jan Cheroot. Jordan was weeping inconsolably, his lovely face smudged with grief. Ralph sat behind his brother on the back of the gaunt bay gelding, holding the smaller child with both arms clasped about his waist. Ralph was silent, stoic, but his body was rigid with controlled emotion, and his eyes, the same clear deep green of his father's, smouldered with unexpressed grief.

Jan Cheroot led the bay, and the two boys seemed as frail and forlorn as swallows left on a fence rail long after the others had flown the oncoming winter.

Zouga stood beside the grave with military bearing, as expressionless as his elder son had been, but behind the handsome mask he was stunned by his own sorrow and pervading sense of guilt.

He wanted to speak aloud, to tell Aletta that he was sorry, that he knew that he was responsible for this lonely grave so far from her loving family and the beautiful forested mountains of Good Hope which she had loved so dearly. He wanted to ask for forgiveness for sacrificing her to a dream, an impossible grandiose dream. Yet he knew that words were futile and the red earth stopped Aletta's ears.

He stooped and with his bare hand dressed the mound where the earth had collapsed at one corner.

With the first diamond I will buy the headstone, he promised himself silently. The red earth had stained under his fingernails, little half-moons the colour of blood.

With a supreme effort he overcame his sense of futility, overcame the self-consciousness sufficiently to speak aloud to someone who could not hear.

'I will look after them, my dear,' he said. 'That is my last promise to you.'

'Jordie will not eat, Papa.' Ralph greeted him as he stooped into the tent, and Zouga felt the leap of alarm swamp his sorrow and his guilt. He strode to the cot on which the child lay, facing the canvas wall of the tent with his knees drawn up to his chest.

Jordan's skin was burning hot as the sun-scorched rocks that littered the plain outside the tent, and his silken cheeks smeared with tears were flushed a furious fever red.

By morning Ralph was feverish also, both boys tossing and muttering in delirium, their bodies hot as two little furnaces, the blankets sodden with their sweat and the tent reeking with the carrion stench of fever.

Ralph fought the fever.

'Ja, just look at him.' Jan Cheroot paused fondly in the act of sponging down the robust strong-boned body. 'He takes the sickness like an enemy, and struggles with it.'

Helping him, kneeling on the opposite side of the cot, Zouga felt the familiar glow of pride surface through his concern as he looked down at him. Already there were little smoky wisps of hair under Ralph's arms, and a darker explosion of curls at the base of his belly; and his penis was no longer the little wormlike appendage with a childish cap of wrinkled loose skin. His shoulders were squaring and filling with muscle, and his legs were straight and sturdy.

'He will be all right,' Jan Cheroot repeated, and Ralph thrashed out angrily in his delirium, his features scowling and dark with determination.

The two men drew the blanket up over him and turned to the other cot.

Jordan's long thick lashes fluttered like the wings of a beautiful butterfly, and he whimpered pitifully, unresisting as they stripped and sponged him. His little body was as sweetly formed as his features, but clad still in its puppy-fat so that his buttocks were round as apples and plump as a girl's; but his limbs were delicately boned and shapely, his feet and hands long and narrow and graceful.

'Mama,' he whimpered. 'I want my Mama.'

The two men nursed the boys, taking turns day and night, everything else neglected or forgotten, an hour snatched here to water and tend the horses, another hour for a hurried journey into the camp to purchase patent medicine from a transport rider or scramble for the few vegetables offered for sale on the farmers' carts. But diamonds were forgotten, never mentioned in the hot little tent where the struggle for life went on, and the Devil's Own claims were abandoned and deserted.

In forty-eight hours Ralph had regained consciousness, in three days he was sitting up unaided and wolfing his food, in six days they could no longer keep him in his cot.

Jordan rallied briefly on the second day, becoming lucid and demanding his mother fretfully, and then remembered that she was gone, began weeping again and immediately began to sink. His life teetered, the pendulum swinging erratically back and forth, but each time he fell back the presence of death grew stronger in the baking canvas tent, until its stench overpowered the odour of fever.

The flesh melted from his body, burned away by the fever, and his skin took on a pearly translucent sheen, so that it seemed in that uncertain light of dusk and early dawn that the very outline of the delicate bone structure showed through.

Jan Cheroot and Zouga nursed him in turns, one sleeping while the other watched – or, when neither could sleep, sitting together, seeking comfort and companionship from each other, trying to discount their helplessness in the face of onrushing death.

'He's young and strong,' they told each other. 'He will be all right also.'

And day after day Jordan sank lower, his cheekbones rising up out of his flesh, and his eyes receding into deep cavities the colour of old bruises.

Exhausted with guilt and sorrow, with helpless worry, Zouga left the tent each dawn before sunrise to be the first at Market Square – perhaps there was a transport rider freshly arrived with medicines in his chests, and certainly there would be Boer farmers with cabbages and onions and, if he was lucky, a few wizened and half-green tomatoes, all of which would be sold half an hour after dawn.

On the tenth morning, as Zouga hurried back to the tent, he paused for a moment at the entrance, frowning angrily. The falcon statue had been dragged from the tent, and there was a long furrow scraped by its base in the loose dust. It stood now at a careless angle, leaning against the trunk of the scraggy camel-thorn tree that gave meagre shade to the camp.

The branches of the tree were festooned with black ribbons of dried springbuck meat, with saddlery and trek gear – so that the statue seemed to be part of this litter. There was one of the camp's brown hens perched on the falcon's head, and it had dropped a long chalky smear of liquid excrement down the stone figure.

Still frowning, Zouga ducked into the tent. Jan Cheroot squatted beside Ralph's cot, and the two of them were deeply involved in a game of five stones, using polished pebbles of agate and quartz for the counters.

Jordan lay very still and pale, so that Zouga felt a lurch of dismay under his ribs. It was only when he stooped over the cot that he saw the rise and fall of Jordan's chest and caught the faint whisper of his breathing.

'Did you move the stone falcon?'

Jan Cheroot grunted without looking up from the shiny stones. 'It seemed to trouble Jordie. He woke up crying again – and kept calling to it.'

Zouga would have taken it further, but suddenly it did not seem worth the effort. He was so tired and dispirited. He would bring the statue back into the tent later, he decided.

'There are a few sweet potatoes – nothing else,' he grunted as he took up the vigil beside Jordan's cot.

Jan Cheroot made a stew of dried beans and mutton, and mashed this with the boiled potatoes. It was an unappetizing mess, but that evening, for the first time, Jordan did not roll his head away from the proffered spoon, and after that his recovery was startlingly swift.

He asked only once more after Aletta, when he and Zouga were alone in the tent.

'Has she gone to heaven, Papa?'

'Yes.' The certainty in Zouga's tone seemed to reassure him.

'Will she be one of God's angels?'

'Yes, Jordie, and from now on she will always be there – watching over you.'

The child thought about that seriously and then nodded contentedly, and the next day he seemed strong enough for Zouga to leave him in Ralph's charge while he and Jan Cheroot went up to the kopje and walked out along No. 6 Roadway to look down on the Devil's Own claims.

All the mining equipment, shovels and picks, buckets and ropes, sheave wheels and ladders had been stolen. At the prices the transport riders were charging it would cost a hundred guineas to replace them.

'We will need men,' Zouga said.

'What will you do when you have them?' Jan Cheroot asked.

'Dig the stuff out.'

'And then?' the little Hottentot demanded with a malicious gleam in his dark eyes, his features wrinkled as a sour windfallen apple. 'What do you then?' he insisted.

'I intend to find out,' Zouga replied grimly. 'We have wasted enough time here already.'

'My dear fellow,' Neville Pickering gave him that charming smile. 'I'm delighted that you asked. Had you not, then I should have offered. It's always a little problematic for a new chum to find his feet,' he coughed deferentially, and went on quickly, 'not that you are a new chum, by any means—'

That was a term usually reserved for the fresh-faced hopefuls newly arrived on the boat from 'home'. 'Home' was England, even those who were colonial born referred to it as 'home'.

'I'd bet a fiver to a pinch of giraffe dung that you know more about this country than any of us here.'

'African born,' Zouga admitted, 'on the Zouga river up north in Khama's land; accounts for the odd name – Zouga.'

'By Jove, didn't realize that, I must say!'

'Don't hold it against me.' Zouga smiled lightly, but he knew that there were many who would. Home born was vastly superior to colonial born. It was for that reason that he had insisted that Aletta should make the long sea voyage with him when it seemed that her pregnancies would reach full term. Both Ralph and Jordan had been born in the same house in south London, and both had arrived back at Good Hope before they were weaned. They were home born: that was his first gift to them.

Pickering glossed over the remark tactfully. He did not have to declare his own birth. He was an English gentleman, and nobody would ever mistake that.

'There are many parts of your book that fascinated me. I'll teach you what I know about sparklers if you'll answer my questions. Bargain?'

Over the days that followed they bombarded each other with questions, Zouga demanding every detail of the process of raising and sorting the yellow gravel from the deepening pit, while Pickering kept turning the conversation back to the land to the north, asking about the tribes and the gold reefs, about the rivers and mountains and the wild animals that swarmed upon the plains and in the lonely forests that Zouga had conjured up so vividly in *Hunter's Odyssey*.

Each morning an hour before the first light, Zouga would meet Pickering at the edge of the roadway above the workings. There would be an enamelled kettle bubbling on the brazier and they drank black coffee that was strong enough to stain the teeth, while around them in the gloom the black mine-workers gathered sleepily, still hugging their fur karosses over their shoulders, their voices muted but musical, their movements stiff and slow with sleepiness and the dawn chill.

At a hundred other points around the growing pit the gangs assembled, waiting for the light; and when it glimmered on the eastern horizon the men went swarming down into the workings, like columns of ants, along the boardwalks and down the swaying ladders, spreading out on the chequerboard of claims, the hubbub rising, the chant of tribesmen, the squeal of ropes, the hectoring shouts of the white overseers, and then the rattle of bucket-loads of yellow gravel into the waiting carts upon the roadway.

Pickering was working four claims, which he owned in partnership.

'My partner is down in Cape Town. Heaven knows when he will be back.'

Neville Pickering shrugged with that deceptively indolent air which he cultivated. 'You'll meet him one of these fine days, and it will be an experience – memorable but not necessarily enjoyable.'

It amused Zouga to see how Neville contrived to maintain his foppish elegance of dress, how he could walk the length of the No. 6 Roadway without the dust hazing the shine of his boots; how he could scramble across the ladderworks without dampening his shirt with sweat, or exchange a flurry of blows with a brawny digger who was encroaching on his claims without it seeming to affect the drape of his Norfolk jacket. His casual sauntering gait carried him from one end of the diggings to the other, at a pace which had Zouga stretching his own legs.

The four claims were not in a single block, but each separated from the others by a dozen or so intervening claims, and Pickering moved from one to the other co-ordinating the work, pulling a gang of half-naked black men from one claim and leading them across to another where the work had fallen behind.

Abruptly he was on the roadway, checking the loading of the carts, and then again, just as abruptly, at the fenced-off plot beyond Market Square where his black workers were rocking the cradles of gravel.

The diamond cradles were like giant versions of the old-fashioned baby cradles from which they took their name. Standing on their half-moon-shaped feet, a man on each side kept them swinging easily from side to side while a third worker shovelled the yellow gravel into the top deck of the cradle from the mound that the cart had dumped. The top deck was a coarse steel sieve, with inch and a half openings in the mesh.

As the cradle rocked rhythmically, the gravel tumbled and bounced across the sloping sieve, the finer stuff under one and a half inches in diameter dropping through onto the second deck of the cradle while the coarse pebbles and waste rolled over under the surveillance of the two cradle men, who watched for the highly unlikely flash of a diamond too big to fall through onto the second deck.

A diamond more than one and a half inches across would be the fortune-maker, the finder's passport to great wealth, the almost impossible 'pony' of the diggers' dreams, a stone heavier than one hundred carats.

On the second deck the mesh was much finer, half-inch square, and a yellow dust blew away like smoke as the cradle agitated it, while on the third deck the mesh was finer still, allowing only the worthless tailings to drop to waste, stuff smaller than the crystals of refined sugar.

From the third deck the gravel was gathered with reverential care, and this was washed in a tub of precious water, every drop of which had been transported thirty miles from the Vaal river.

The gravel was washed in a circular sieve of the No. 3 mesh, the finest of all. The worker agitating and dipping over the tub, muddy to the elbows. Finally the contents of the sieve, cleansed of mud, were dumped onto the flat metal surface of the sorting-table, and the sorters began picking over it with the flat wooden blades of their scrapers.

Women were far away the best sorters, they had the patience, the manual dexterity and the fine eye for colour and texture that was needed. The married diggers kept their wives and daughters at the sorting-table from the minute the mellow morning light was strong enough until the dusk faded each evening.

Pickering was not lucky enough to have women working his tables, but the Africans he had were carefully trained, although never trusted.

'You would never credit what they do with a good stone to try and get away with it. I smile sometimes at what the Duchess would think if she knew that the shiner hanging around her neck had been up the tail end of a big black Basuto,' Pickering chuckled. 'Come, I'll show you what to look for.'

The wiry little black sorter at the head of the table advertised his superior status by his European finery, embroidered waistcoat and Derby hat, but his feet were bare and he carried his snuff-horn in the pierced lobe of his ear. He vacated his seat at the table cheerfully, and Neville Pickering took up the scraper and began to sift through the gravel, a few pebbles at a time.

'There!' he grunted suddenly. 'Your first wild diamond,

old man! Take a good look at it, and let's hope it isn't your last.'

Zouga was surprised. It was not what he had expected, and then his surprise was replaced immediately by disappointment. It was a drab little chip of stone, barely the size of one of the sand fleas which swarmed in the red dust of the camp.

It lacked the fire and flash that Zouga had expected, and its colour was a dingy yellow: the colour of champagne perhaps, but without that wine's sparkle.

'Are you sure?' Zouga asked. 'It doesn't look like a diamond to me. How can you tell?'

'It's a splint-chip, probably a piece of a larger stone. It will go ten points, that's a tenth part of a carat, and we will be lucky to get five shillings for it, but it will pay the wages of one of my men for a week.'

'How do you tell the difference between that – and those?' Zouga indicated the mound of gravel in the centre of the table, still wet from the washing-tub, glistening in a thousand different shades of red and gold, anthracite black and flesh pinks, the gaudy show of diamondiferous gravel.

'It's the soapiness,' Pickering explained, 'the soap texture. You will train your eye to it soon, don't bother about the colour – look for the soap.' He took the stone in the teeth of a pair of wooden tweezers and turned it in the sunlight. 'A diamond is unwettable, it repels water; so in the wet gravel it stands out, and the difference is that soapy look.'

Neville proffered the stone. 'There, I tell you what, you keep it as a gift, your first diamond.'

They had been hunting for nearly ten days now, and had gradually moved farther and farther north.

Twice they had sighted quarry, small groups, but each time the quarry had scattered at the first approach.

Zouga was getting desperate. His claims were lying abandoned in the New Rush workings, the level of the surrounding claims would be sinking swiftly, making his more difficult to work and every day increasing the danger of rock slide. Those claims had already killed five men. Jock Danby had warned him.

He was lying now, belly down, on a tiny rocky kopje fifty miles north of the Vaal river, eighty miles from New Rush, and he was still not certain when he could finish this business and turn southwards again.

Jan Cheroot and the two boys were farther down the slope with the horses, holding them in a shallow ravine that was choked with scrub thorn. Jordan's girlish tones carried to where Zouga sat, blending with the cries of circling birds, and Zouga lowered the binoculars to rest his eyes and to listen to his son's voice.

He had worried about taking the boy on this rough journey, especially so soon after that bout of camp fever, but there had been no alternative, no safe place to leave him. Once again Jordan's stamina had belied his delicate looks. He had ridden hard and kept up well with his brother, at the same time recovering the flesh that the fever had burned from his body; and in the last days the deathly pallor of his skin had been gilded to velvety peach.

Thinking about Jordan led directly to memories of Aletta, memories still so filled with sorrow and raw guilt that he could not bear them and he lifted the binoculars again and raked the plain, seeking distraction. He found it with relief.

There was unusual movement far out on the wide plain. Through the lens Zouga picked up a herd of a hundred wildebeest, the 'wild cattle' of the Boers. These ungainly animals, with their mournful Roman noses and scraggly beards, were the clowns of the veld. They chased each other in aimless circles, nose to earth and heels kicking at the sky, then abruptly they ceased this lunatic cavorting and stood snorting at one another with wild-eyed expressions of amazement.

Beyond them Zouga caught a flicker of other movement: until that moment it had been hidden by the dust kicked up by the splayed wildebeest hooves. Carefully he adjusted the bevelled focus ring of his binoculars, and the heat mirage trembled and melted before his gaze, turning the movement into a serpentine wriggle that seemed to float above the plain on a lake of silver shimmering water.

'Ostriches!' he thought disgustedly. The distant shapes seemed to wriggle like long black tadpoles in the watery wavering mirage of distance. The long-legged birds seemed to float free of the earth, blooming miraculously in the tortured air above the plain. Zouga tried to count them, but they changed shape and coagulated into a dark wavering mass, their plumed backs bobbing.

Suddenly Zouga sat up. He dropped the binoculars and polished the lens with the tail of the silk bandanna around his throat, then quickly lifted them to his eyes again. The grotesque dark shapes had separated, the lumpy wriggling bodies fined down, the elongated legs had assumed normal proportions.

'Men!' whispered Zouga, and counted them eagerly, as eagerly as he had ever made a first sighting of the huge ivory-carrying grey bull elephants in the hunting veld. He reached eleven before another layer of heated air intervened and altered the distant man-shapes to grotesque unsteady monsters once again.

Zouga slung the binoculars over his shoulder and went down the slope with the loose scree rolling under his boots. Jan Cheroot and the boys lay in the bottom of the ravine on their saddle blankets, their saddles propped behind them as bolsters.

Zouga slid down the bank and landed between them before they had returned from the fairyland that Jan Cheroot had been spinning for them.

'A good bunch,' he told Jan Cheroot.

Zouga reached down and withdrew the short Martini-Henry carbine from the leather bucket of Ralph's saddle. He levered the breech-block down and checked the weapon was empty.

'We aren't after springbuck. Don't you load until either Jan Cheroot or I tell you,' he ordered sternly.

Jordan was still too little to handle the heavy rifle, but he rode well enough to make the encircling sweep with which they would try to close the net.

'Remember, Jordie, that you stay close enough to Jan Cheroot to hear what he tells you,' Zouga told him, glancing up at the sun as he did so.

It was well past noon; he would have to move fairly soon – for if they could not surround the little band of black men at the first attempt, if they did not achieve surprise, then it would be the old time-consuming business of spooring them down individually. So far attempts at doing so had always been interrupted by the sudden African nightfall.

'Saddle up,' Zouga ordered, and they scrambled to their horses.

Zouga swung up onto the bay gelding and glared sternly at Ralph.

'Now you do what you are told – or I'll warm your tail feathers for you, young man.'

He swung the horse's head and pointed it down the ravine, while behind his back Ralph grinned at Jan Cheroot conspiratorially, his face flushed with excitement, and the little Hottentot closed one eyelid briefly but kept his flat wrinkled oriental features expressionless.

Zouga had chosen the kopje with care; from it a ravine meandered out across the plain in an approximate east to west direction – and he followed it now, slouching in the saddle to keep his head below the level of the banks and keeping the gelding down to a walk so as not to raise dust.

After half a mile he removed the wide-brimmed hat from his head and raised himself cautiously in the stirrups until his eyes were just above the bank, and he darted a quick glance into the north and then immediately ducked down again.

'Station here,' he told Ralph. 'And don't move until I do.'

They moved on down the ravine, while Zouga placed Jan Cheroot and Jordan side by side in a bend of the ravine where the bank had collapsed and formed an easy ramp up which they could launch their charge.

'Keep Jordie close,' Zouga cautioned Jan Cheroot, and swung the gelding around with the saddlery creaking as the animal turned in the narrow gut of the ravine; then Zouga trotted back until he was in the centre of the waiting line, and there he halted and contained his impatience, glancing up repeatedly at the lowering sun.

There would probably not be another chance for many days, and each day was vital for those untended claims. Zouga jerked the rifle from the leather bucket at his knee, selected a cartridge from the bandolier around his waist and slipped it into the breech. Then he returned the weapon uncocked to the bucket. It was merely a precaution, but he had no means of knowing what manner of men those approaching figures were.

Even if their intentions were peaceable, and their ultimate object identical to Zouga's own, yet they would be armed and nervous, so nervous that they had avoided the road from the north and were travelling over the open veld. They were in company for defence, and Zouga knew they would have been harassed often along the way, by black men and white: the black men trying to rob and cheat them of their meagre possessions, the white men of something infinitely more valuable, their right to contract their labour to the highest bidder.

On the day that Zouga thanked Neville Pickering for his tuition and began preparing to work the Devil's Own claims for his personal account, he had faced the problem that was already wracking the entire sub-continent.

Only black men could stand the conditions of physical labour in the diggings. Only black men would work for a wage that made the diggings profitable, and even that beggarly wage was many times more than the Boer farmers of the surrounding backveld republics could afford to pay.

The diamond diggings had denuded the countryside of labourers for five hundred miles around; and the Boers resented that as fiercely as they resented the nest of adventurers and fortune seekers that the diggings supported.

The diamonds had caused an upheaval in the Boers' traditional way of life; not only were the miners threatening the supply of cheap labour, which only just allowed a diligent and frugal farmer to eke out a living for himself and his family from the savage land, but the diggers were doing something else that from the Boer point of view was unforgivable, that went against all their deeply held beliefs and threatened not just their livelihood but their very physical existence.

The diamond diggers were paying the black tribesmen with *guns*. The Boers had fought the tribes at Blood River and Mosega, they had stood to the laager in ten thousand threatening dawns, the favourite hour of attack. They had seen the smoke rising from their burning homesteads and crops, they had ridden out on commando on the spoor of their stolen herds, and they had buried the pale corpses of their children, the blood drained from the frail bodies through the gaping and terrible wounds of the assegai.

They had buried them at Weenen – the Place of Weeping – and at other accursed and abandoned grave sites across the land.

The payment of black men with guns went against every one of their instincts; it flew full in the face of their laws and offended the memories of their dead heroes.

For these reasons Boer commandos from the little backveld republics were sweeping the land and patrolling the lonely roads from the north to try and prevent the tribesmen reaching the diggings and instead press them to work upon the land.

However, five shillings a week and a musket at the end of a three years' contract were a lure that brought the tribesmen, on foot, against a hundred hazards, on a journey of hundreds of miles, daring the commandos and all else, to reach the diggings.

They came in their hundreds, but still not enough of them arrived to fill those hungry diamond pits. In vain Zouga and Jan Cheroot had ridden the workings. Every black man was signed on contract, and jealously guarded by his employer.

Zouga had told Jan Cheroot, 'We'll offer seven shillings and sixpence a week.'

They signed five men that same day at the higher wage, and the next day there were a dozen deserters waiting outside Zouga's camp, eager for the new coin.

Before Zouga could sign them, Neville Pickering sauntered up. 'Official visit, old man,' he murmured apologetically. 'As a member of the jolly old Diggers' Committee, I have to tell you the rate is five shillings not seven and six.'

When Zouga opened his mouth to protest, Pickering smiled easily and held up his hand.

'No, Major. I'm sorry. It's five shillings, and not a penny more.'

Zouga was already in no doubt about the sweeping

powers of the Diggers' Committee. An edict from the elected body was enforced firstly by a warning, then a beating, and finally by the full aggression of the entire community of diggers which could end in a burning or even a lynching.

'What do I do for a gang, then?' Zouga demanded.

'You do what we all do; you go out and find a gang, before another digger or a Boer commando grabs them.'

'I might have to go as far north as the Shashi river,' Zouga snapped sarcastically, and Pickering nodded in agreement.

'Yes, you might.'

Zouga smiled thinly at the memory of his first lesson in digger labour relations, and now he settled his hat firmly and gathered up his reins.

'All right,' he muttered, 'let's go recruiting!' And he put his heels into the gelding's flanks and went lunging up the bank of the ravine onto the open plain.

The tribesmen were five hundred yards dead ahead, and he counted swiftly: sixteen of them. If he could take them all he could start back for New Rush in tomorrow's dawn. Sixteen men were sufficient to work the Devil's Own, and at that moment they had, for Zouga, the same value as a fifty-carat diamond. They were in single file, moving swiftly, the trotting gait of the fighting impis of Zulu, no women or children with them.

'Good,' grunted Zouga as the gelding stretched out under him, and he held him back in an easy canter as he glanced right.

Jan Cheroot was tearing across the plain, Jordan plugging along in his dust fifty strides behind. At this distance Jordan did not look like a child; they might have been a pair of armed riders, and Jan Cheroot was swinging wide, trying to get behind the little group of men, pinning them before they scattered, pinning them long enough for Zouga to get within hail.

Zouga glanced left and scowled as he saw that Ralph was at full gallop, leaning low over his horse's neck, brandishing the Martini-Henry rifle – and Zouga hoped it was still unloaded, wished that he had specially ordered Ralph not to show the rifle, and yet even in that moment of anger he experienced a little prickle of pride as he watched his son ride; the boy was born to the saddle.

Zouga checked the gelding again, bringing him down to a trot, giving his flank men time to complete the circle, and at the same time trying to reduce the dramatic effect of his approach. He knew that they would appear to the tribesmen to be an armed commando, their intentions warlike, and he tried to soften this by lifting his hat and waving it over his head.

Then suddenly Jan Cheroot was reining in, gesturing to Jordan to do the same. They had got behind the band, and opposite them, facing them across the wide circle, Ralph was wheeling his filly and bringing her up sharply on her hind legs, rearing and shaking out her mane theatrically.

In the centre the tribesmen had moved swiftly, and with the concerted action of trained fighting men.

They had dropped the rolled bundles of sleeping-mat, cooking-pot and leather grain bag that they had been carrying on their heads, and they had bunched into a defensive circle shoulder to shoulder, war shield overlapping war shield, while above them the steel of their assegais flicked little pinpricks of sunlight.

They did not wear the full regalia of their fighting regiments, the kilts of monkey tails, the cloaks of desert fox furs, the tall headdress of ostrich and widow-bird feathers, they were travelling with weapons only; but the shields they presented to the approaching horseman and the glint of steel told Zouga all he wanted to know. The shields gave the tribe its name, the Matabele – the people of the long shields.

The little group of men who stood impassively in the sunlight and watched Zouga ride up were the finest warriors that Africa had ever spawned. Yet they were almost five hundred miles south of the borders of Matabeleland.

'I set for a covey of partridge,' Zouga smiled to himself, 'and I have trapped a brood of eagles.'

A hundred yards from the ring of shields, Zouga reined in; but the gelding, infected by the tension, fidgeted under him.

The long shields were made of dappled black and white oxhide, every regiment of the Matabele carried a distinctive shield.

Zouga knew that black dappled with white was the regimental colour of the Inyati, the Buffaloes Regiment, and again he felt a twist of nostalgia.

Once the induna who commanded the Inyati had been a friend; they had travelled together across the mimosa-clad plains of Matabeleland; they had hunted together and shared the comfort of the same camp fires. It was all so long ago, on his first visit to the land below the Zambezi river, but Zouga was carried back so vividly that it required an effort of will to shake off the memory.

He lifted his right hand, fingers spread in the universal gesture of goodwill.

'Warriors of Matabele, I see you,' he called to them, speaking their language as fluently as one of them, the words returning to his tongue readily.

He saw the small stir behind the war-shields, the shift of heads with which they greeted his words.

'Jordan!' Zouga called, and the child circled out and reined in his pony at Zouga's side. Now the difference in size between man and boy was apparent.

'See, warriors of King Lobengula, my son rides with me.' No man took his children to war. The ring of shields sank a few inches so Zouga could see the dark and watchful eyes of the men behind them; but as Zouga pushed the gelding a few paces forward, the shields were immediately lifted again defensively.

'What news of Gandang, induna of the Inyati Regiment, Gandang who is as my brother?' Zouga called again persuasively.

At the mention of the name one of the warriors could no longer contain himself, swept aside his shield and stepped from the ring of spears.

'Who calls Gandang brother?' he demanded in a clear firm voice, a young voice, yet with the timbre and inflection of one used to authority.

'I am Bakela, the Fist,' Zouga gave his Matabele name, and he realized that the warrior facing him was still a youth, barely older than Ralph. But he was lean and straight, narrow in the hips and with muscle in the shoulder and arms built up in the games of war. Zouga guessed he had probably already killed his man, washed his spear in blood.

Now he crossed the open ground towards Zouga, his stride lithe, his legs long and shapely beneath the short leather kilt.

'Bakela,' he said, as he stopped a dozen paces from the gelding's head. 'Bakela.' He smiled, a brilliant show of white even teeth in the broad and handsome Nguni face. 'That is a name I took with the first draught of my mother's milk, for I am Bazo, the Axe, son of the same Gandang whom you call brother, and who remembers you as an old and trusted friend. I know you by the scar on your cheek and the gold in your beard. I greet you, Bakela.'

Zouga swung down off the gelding, leaving the rifle in the saddle scabbard, and, grinning broadly, went to clasp the youth's upper arms in an affectionate salute.

Then, turning with his fists on his hips, still smiling, Zouga shouted to Ralph. 'Go and see if you can shoot a springbuck, or better even, a wildebeest; we'll need plenty of meat for tonight.'

Ralph let out a whoop at the command, and provoked the filly with his heels, forcing her to rear again and then come down in full run, mane flying, hooves pounding as she bore away. Without being ordered, Jan Cheroot shook his bony mare into a canter and followed the flying filly.

The two riders returned in the dusk, and the hunt had gone well. They had found rare quarry, a bull eland so old that his neck and shoulders had turned blue with age and the swinging dewlap almost swept the dusty earth between his stubby forelegs.

He was as big as a prize stud bull, with a chest round as a brandy cask of Limousine oak, and Zouga guessed he would weigh not much under a ton, for he was fat and sleek; there would be a tubful of rich white lard in the chest cavity, and thick layers of yellow fat beneath the glossy hide. He was a prize indeed, and the little band of Matabele drummed their assegai against the hide shields and shouted with delight when they saw him.

The bull snorted at the hubbub and broke into a lumbering gallop, trying to break away, but Ralph swung the filly to head him off and within a hundred yards the bull changed the gallop for a short-winded trot and allowed himself to be turned back towards the group of waiting men.

Ralph reined in the filly, kicked his feet from the stirrups and jumped easily to the earth, throwing up the carbine as he landed cat-like on his toes and seeming to fire in the same instant.

The bull's head flinched at the shot, blinking the huge shining eyes convulsively as the bullet slammed into his skull between them, and he collapsed with a meaty thud that seemed to tremble in the earth.

The Matabele streamed out like a pack of wild dogs,

swarming over the mountainous carcass, using the razor edge of their war-assegai as butchers' knives, going for the tidbits, the tripes and the liver, the heart and the sweet white fat.

The Matabele gorged on fat eland meat, grilling the tripes over the coals, threading garlands of liver and fat and succulent heart onto wet white mimosa twigs from which they had peeled the bark, so that the melting fat sizzled and bubbled over the layers of meat.

'We have killed no game since we left the forests,' Bazo explained their ravenous appetites. Though the desert teemed with springbuck herds, they were not the type of game that a man on foot, armed only with a stabbing spear, could run down easily.

'Without meat a man's belly is like a war drum, full of nothing except noise and wind.'

'You are far from the land of the Matabele,' Zouga agreed. 'No Matabele has been this far south since the old king took the tribe north across the Limpopo, and in that time even Gandang, your father, was a child.'

'We are the first to make this journey,' Bazo agreed proudly. 'We are the point of the spear.'

In the firelight the warriors about him looked up and their expressions echoed his pride in their achievement. They were all youths, the eldest only a few years older than Bazo, not one of them over nineteen years of age.

'Where does this long journey take you?' Zouga asked.

'To a wonderful place in the south from which a man returns with great treasures.'

'What manner of treasures?' Zouga asked again.

'These.' Bazo reached across the circle to where Ralph leaned against his saddle, using it as a pillow, and Bazo touched the polished wooden butt of the Martini-Henry that protruded from the gun bucket.

'*Isibamu* – guns!' said Bazo.

'Guns?' Zouga asked. 'A Matabele *indoda* with a gun?' His voice mildly derisive. 'Is not the assegai the weapon of the true warrior?'

Bazo looked uncomfortable for a moment and then recovered his aplomb.

'The old ways are not always the best,' he said. 'The old men tell us that they are, so that young men will consider them wise.' And the Matabele in the circle about the fire nodded and made little sounds of agreement.

Although he was certainly the youngest of the group, Bazo was clearly their leader. Son of Gandang, he was therefore the nephew of King Lobengula, grandson of old King Mzilikazi himself. His noble birth assured him preference, but it was clear that he was quick and clever also.

'To earn the guns you covet a man must work hard, in a deep pit in the earth,' Zouga said. 'He must milk himself of his sweat by the calabash-full every day for three years, before he is paid with a gun.'

'We have heard these things,' Bazo nodded.

'Then you shall have your guns, each of you a fine gun, at the end of three years. I, Bakela, the Fist, give you my word on it.'

I t was a custom of the diggings, a ceremony of initiation, that when a gang of raw tribesmen arrived at New Rush the established black labourers would rush to line each side of the track, most of them dressed in cast-off European finery as a badge of their sophistication.

They would jeer their newly arrived brethren:

'Behold, the baboons have come down from the hills.'

'Nay! Baboons are cunning; these cannot be baboons.' And they pelted the newcomers with pieces of filth as well as insults.

Bazo's group were the first Matabele to reach the diggings. The Matabele language is almost identical to that of Zululand, and very closely associated to the Southern Xhosa. Bazo understood every word of the banter, and he gave a quiet but grim order to his little group.

His men dropped their sleeping-mats and the long shields rattled one against the other, the broad bright assegais whispered in the sunlight as they were bared, and the taunts and derisive laughter dried on the instant, to be replaced with expressions of astonishment and real dismay.

'*Manje!* Now!' hissed Bazo. The ring of shields exploded outwards, and the crowd fled before it in disordered panic.

From the back of the gelding, Zouga had a grandstand view of the charge, and he had no illusions as to the danger of the moment. Even such a tiny war party of Matabele *amadoda* on the rampage through the camp could cause chaos and frightful slaughter amongst the unarmed black labourers.

'Bazo! Kawulisa! Stop them!' he roared, spurring across the front of the murderous rank of rawhide shields and steel.

The erstwhile tormentors ran with their heads twisted backwards, yelling with terror and eyes popping. They knocked each other down and the fallen grovelled in the dust. A portly black man, dressed in grubby duck breeches many sizes too small and a frock coat many sizes too large, ran into the side of one of the shacks lining the track, the home of one of the less affluent diggers, and the canvas wall burst open before the power of his run, the thatch roof collapsed on top of the fugitive, covering him completely with a haystack of dried grass and probably saving his life – for the point of a Matabele assegai had been inches from the straining seam of his bulging breeches at the moment the shack collapsed.

Bazo gave a single blast on the buckhorn whistle that hung on a thong at his throat, and the spearmen froze. The charge stopped dead on the instant, and the Matabele trotted back to where they had dropped their baggage, all of them grinning with delight; as they formed up again, Bazo sang the first line of the Inyati regimental war chant in a high ringing voice:

> 'See the war shields black as midnight,
> white as the high storm clouds at noon—'

And the men behind him came crashing in with the chorus:

> 'Black as the Inyati bull, white as the egrets
> that he carries upon his back—'

The entry of the little band of warriors to the New Rush diggings became a triumphal procession. Riding at their head Zouga felt like a Roman emperor.

Yet not one of the young warriors had ever swung a pick or hefted a shovel. Jan Cheroot had to place the tools in their hands, positioning their fingers correctly on the handles, all the while muttering his disdain of such ignorance. However, they had the knack of it within minutes, and the velvety black muscles, forged in war and the training for war, changed the mundane tools into lethal weapons; they attacked the yellow earth as though it were a mortal adversary.

Confronted with a wheelbarrow for the first time, two of them lifted it bodily and walked away with it and its contents. When Ralph demonstrated the correct use of the vehicle, their wonder and delight was childlike, and Bazo told them smugly: 'I promised you many wonders, did I not?'

They were a highly disciplined group of young men, accustomed since childhood firstly to the strict structure of family life in the kraals and then from puberty to the communal training and teamwork of the fighting regiments.

They were also fiercely competitive, delighting in any challenge to pit their strength or skill against one another.

Zouga, knowing all these things, organized them in four teams of four men, each named after a bird – the Cranes, the Hawks, the Shrikes and the Khorhaans – and each week the team with the best performance in lashing the gravel was entitled to wear the feathers of their adopted bird in their hair and to a double ration of meat and mealie-meal and *twala*, the African beer fermented from millet grain. They turned the work into a game.

There were some small adjustments to be made. The Matabele were cattle-men, their whole lives devoted to raising, protecting and enlarging their herds, even if these expansions were often at the expense of their less warlike neighbours. Their staple diet was beef and *maas*, the calabash-soured milk of the Nguni.

Beef was an expensive item on the diggings, and it was with patent distaste that they sampled the greasy stringy mutton that Zouga provided. However, hard physical labour builds appetites, and within days they were eating this new diet if not with relish at least without complaint.

Within those same few days the labour was apportioned and each man learned his task.

Jan Cheroot could not be inveigled down into the workings.

'Ek is nie 'n meerkat nie,' he told Zouga loftily, reverting to the bastard Dutch of Cape Colony. 'I am not a mongoose; I do not live in a hole in the ground.'

Zouga needed a trusted man on the sorting-tables, and that was where Jan Cheroot presided. Squatting like a yellow idol over the glittering piles of washed gravel, the triangular shape of his face was emphasized by the scraggy little beard on the point of his chin – by the high oriental cheekbones and slanted eyes, each in their spider-web of wrinkles.

He was quick to pick out the soapy sheen of the noble stones in the piles of dross, but there was another pair of eyes sharper and quicker. Traditionally the women made the best sorters, but little Jordan proved immediately to have an uncanny talent at picking out diamonds, no matter what their size or colour.

The child picked the very first stone from the very first sieveful. It was a minute stone, twenty points, a fifth part of a carat, and the colour was a dark cognac brown, so that Zouga doubted its integrity. But when be showed it to one of the kopje-wallopers, it was a veritable diamond and the buyer offered him three shillings for it.

After that nobody questioned Jordan, instead a doubtful stone was passed to him for judgement. Within a week he was the Devil's Own chief sorter.

He sat opposite Jan Cheroot at the low metal table, almost the same size as the Hottentot. He wore a huge sombrero of plaited maize stalks to protect his delicate peachlike skin from the sun, and he sorted the gravel as though it were a game of which he never tired. Competing with Jan Cheroot avidly, a high-pitched shriek of excitement signalled each discovery, and his neat little hands flew over the gravel like those of a pianist over the ivory keyboard.

Zouga had found a woman to give both Ralph and Jordan their lessons. The wife of a Lutheran preacher, she was a plump-breasted, sweet-faced woman with iron-grey hair swept up into an enormous bun at the back of her head. Mrs Gander was the only schoolmistress within five hundred miles, and for a few hours each morning she gave a small group of diggers' children their reading, writing and arithmetic in the little galvanized-iron church at the back of Market Square.

It was a daily ritual to which Ralph had to be driven by his father's threats, and to which Jordan hurried with the same enthusiasm as he did to the sorting-table after school was out. With his angelic looks, and the intense interest in the written word that Aletta had germinated in him, Jordan was instantly Mrs Gander's darling.

She made no effort to conceal her preference. She called him 'Jordie-dear' and gave to him the task of wiping clean the blackboard, which immediately made it an honour for which the dozen other children in the class would have scratched out his lovely densely-lashed angel eyes.

There was a pair of twins in Mrs Gander's class. The tough sons of a tough out-of-luck digger from the Australian opal fields, they were a matched pair, with shaven heads to inhibit the breeding of lice, bare-footed, for their father was working a poor claim on the eastern edge of the diggings, their braces supporting patched canvas breeches over faded and frayed shirts. Henry and Douglas Stewart made a formidable pair, acting in complete concert, quick with a cruel jibe too soft for Mrs Gander to hear or a crafty jab with the elbow or a tug of the hair too quick for her to see.

Jordan was natural prey. 'Jordie-girl' they christened him, and his soft curls felt good between their fingers, and his tears were enormously satisfying – especially when they realized that Jordan for some strange reason of pride would not appeal to his big brother for protection.

'Y ou tell Goosie-Gander that I've a belly ache,' Ralph instructed Jordan. 'And that Papa says I am too sick to come to class.'

'Where are you going?' Jordan demanded. 'What are you going to do?'

'I'm going to the nest – I think the chicks may be ready.' Ralph had discovered a lanner falcon's nest on the top ledge of a rocky kopje five miles out on the Cape road. He was planning to take the chicks and train them as hunting falcons. Ralph always had exciting plans; it was one of the many reasons why Jordan adored him.

'Oh, let me come with you. Please, Ralph.'

'You're still just a baby, Jordie.'

'I'm nearly eleven.'

'You're only just ten,' Ralph corrected him loftily, and from experience Jordan knew there was no profit in arguing.

Jordan delivered Ralph's lie for him in such sweet piping tones and with such a guileless flutter of the long lashes, that it never occurred to Mrs Gander to doubt it, and the Stewart twins exchanged a quick glance of complete accord.

There was a latrine at the back of the church, a sentry box of corrugated iron, a boxwood seat with an oval cut from it suspended over a galvanized steel bucket. The heat in the tiny room was ovenlike and the contents of the bucket ripened swiftly. The twins trapped Jordan there in the mid-morning break.

They had hold of an ankle each and were standing on the wooden seat, the hole between them, and Jordan was dangling upside down, clinging desperately to the box-wood seat as they tried to force his head and shoulders through the opening and into the brimming bucket.

'Stamp on his fingers,' Douglas panted. Jordan had offered unexpected opposition. Douglas had a red scratch down his neck, and they had had to pry Jordan's jaws open to release their grip on Henry's thumb. The injuries had changed the mood of the twins. They had started out with laughter, spiteful laughter, but laughter all the same; now they were angry and vicious, their self-esteem smarting as much as their injuries.

'Shut up, you little sissy,' blurted Henry, as he obeyed his brother and brought down his horny heel on Jordan's white knuckles. Jordan's shrieks of agony and horror and terror reverberated in the tiny iron shed as he kicked and fought.

Against their combined strength, Jordan's wildest efforts were ineffectual. His fingernails scratched white splinters from the wooden seat, and his shrieks mounted hysterically, but his head was forced down. The stench was suffocating, the disgust choked his throat and strangled his cries.

At the moment that he felt the cold wet filth soaking into his golden curls the door of the shed was wrenched open and Mrs Gander's motherly bulk filled the opening.

For a moment she stared incredulously, and then she began to swell with outrage. Her right arm, muscled from kneading bread and pounding wet washing, flew out in a round open-handed blow that knocked both twins flying into a corner of the latrine – and she gathered Jordan up, holding him at arms' length. With her flushed face wrinkling at the smell of his soaked curls, she rushed out with him, shouting to her husband to bring a bucket of precious water and a bar of the yellow and blue mottled soap.

Half an hour later Jordan reeked of carbolic soap and his curls were fluffing out again as the sun dried them into a shining halo, and from behind the closed doors of the vestry the yells of pain emitted by the twins were punctuated by the clap of the Reverend Gander's Malacca cane walking stick as his wife urged him on to greater endeavour.

Around the whittled remains of Colesberg kopje had grown up a miniature range of man-made hillocks. These were the tailings from the diamond cradles, dumped haphazardly on the open ground beyond the settlement. Some of these artificial hills were already twenty feet high, and they formed a wasteland where no tree nor blade of grass grew. A maze of narrow footpaths laced the area, made by the daily pilgrimage of hundreds of black workers to the pit.

The shortcut between the Lutheran church and Zouga's camp followed one of these footpaths, and in the heat-hushed hour of noon, the labourers were still in the workings and the hills were deserted. The sun directly overhead threw only narrow black strips of shade below the mounds of loose gravel as Jordan hurried along the dusty path, his eyes still red-rimmed with weeping the tears of humiliation and stinging from the foam of carbolic soap.

'Hello Jordie-girl.' Jordan recognized the voice instantly, and it stopped him dead, blinking his swimming eyes in the sunlight, peering up at the summit of one of the gravel mounds beside the path.

One of the twins stood silhouetted against the pale blue noon sky. His thumbs hooked into his braces, his shaven head thrust forward, his eyes with their thin colourless lashes as vicious as those of a ferret.

'You told, Jordie-girlie,' the twin accused flatly.

'I never told,' Jordan denied, his voice squeaking uncertainly.

'You screamed. That's the same as telling – and now you are going to scream again, but this time there isn't going to be anyone to hear you, Jordie-girl.'

Jordan spun around, and in the same movement he was running with all the desperation and speed of a gazelle pursued by a hunting cheetah; but he had not gone a dozen frantic paces when the second twin slid down the sloping bank, the gravel hissing around his bare feet, full into the narrow pathway ahead of Jordan, his arms spread in welcome, his mouth twisted into a grin of anticipation.

They had laid the trap with care. They had caught him in a narrow place, where the gravel banks were highest, and behind him the first twin slid adroitly down to block the path, keeping his balance on the little avalanche of rolling gravel under his bare feet until he hit the level pathway.

'Jordie-dear,' called one twin.

'Jordie-girl,' echoed the other, and they closed from each side, slowly, tantalizing themselves, so that Henry giggled almost breathlessly.

'Little girls shouldn't tell tales.'

'I'm not a girl,' whispered Jordan, backing away from him.

'Then you shouldn't have curls; only girls have curls.' Douglas groped in his pocket and brought out a bone-handled clasp knife. He opened the blade with his teeth.

'We are going to turn you into a boy, Jordie-girl.'

'Then we are going to teach you not to tell tales.' Henry brought out his hand from behind his back. He had cut a camel-thorn branch, and stripped the bunches of lacy leaves, but not the thorns. 'We are going to do the same to you as old Goosey-Gander did to us. Fifteen cuts each. That's thirty for you, Jordie-girl.'

Jordan's gaze fastened on the branch with sickened fascination. It was twice as thick as a man's thumb, more a club than a cane, and the thorns were half an inch long, each on a little raised knob of rough black bark. Henry swung it in an experimental cut and it hissed like an adder.

The sound galvanized Jordan, he whirled and flew at the high bank of gravel beside him; it slid treacherously under his feet so that he had to use his hands to claw his way towards the summit.

Behind him the twins yipped with excitement, like the hunting call of a pack of wild dogs, and they raced after him, scrambling up the soft collapsing bank.

Their weight buried them at each pace above the ankles, so that Jordan, lighter and buoyant with terror, reached the top of the bank ahead of them, and he raced silent and white-faced across the flattened table of the summit, opening the gap further.

Henry snatched up a stone as he ran, a lump of quartz as big as his own fist, and he used his own momentum to hurl it. It flew an inch past Jordan's ear, and he flinched and whimpered, losing his balance, stumbled at the far edge of the dump, and went tumbling down the steep slope.

'Stop him,' yipped Douglas, and launched himself over the edge.

At the bottom Jordan rolled to his feet, dusty and wildly dishevelled, his curls bushed out and dangling in his eyes. He wasted a second, glancing about desperately, and then darted away along the narrow footpath through the gut of the pass between the gravel dumps.

'Catch him. Don't let him get away.' The twins yelled at each other, panting with laughter, like two cats with a mouse, and here on the flat their longer legs quickly narrowed Jordan's lead.

He heard their bare feet slapping on hard earth in a broken rhythm close behind him, and he twisted his head back over his shoulder, almost blinded with his own sweat and dancing curls, his breath sobbing, his skin white as bone china and his huge brimming eyes seeming to fill his whole face.

Henry steadied himself, poised with his right arm held back at full stretch and then he threw the thorn stick, cartwheeling it low over the ground so that it slammed into the back of Jordan's knees, the thorns ripping the soft bare skin, raising deep parallel scratches as though from the slash of a cat's claws.

Jordan's legs folded under him and he went down, sliding on his belly, the wind driven from his lungs as he hit the baked earth of the pathway. Before he could raise himself, Douglas landed with all his weight between Jordan's shoulder blades and shoved his face, cheek down, against the ground, while Henry snatched up the thorn branch and danced about them, looking for an opening, the branch held in both hands above his head.

'His hair first,' gasped Douglas, choking with laughter and his own excitement. 'Hold his head.'

Henry dropped the cane and stooped over Jordan, grabbing a double handful of the fine curls and leaning back against it with all his weight so that Jordan's neck was stretched out. Douglas was still perched between Jordan's shoulder blades. Pinning him against the earth and brandishing the open clasp knife, he told his twin, 'Hold him still.' The fine golden hair was stretched like the strings of a violin and Douglas hacked at it.

It came away in tufts in Henry's fists, some of it cut through, some of it torn out at the roots, like feathers from the carcass of a slaughtered chicken, and he threw it high in the air, shouting with laughter as it sparkled in the sunlight.

'Now you will be a boy!'

All the resistance went out of Jordan. He lay crushed against the earth, shaken only by his own sobs, and Henry grabbed another handful of his curls.

'Cut closer,' he ordered his twin, and then shrieked with shock and pain.

The thin tapered end of a rhinoceros-hide riding whip curled with a snap around the seat of Henry's breeches, over the fresh bruises raised by the Reverend Gander's Malacca cane, and Henry shot erect clutching at his own buttocks with both hands and hopping up and down on the same spot.

A hand closed on the collar of his shirt and he was yanked into the air and held suspended, kicking, a foot above the ground, still clutching the seat of his breeches that felt as though they were filled with live coals.

His brother looked up from his seat on Jordan's back. In the excitement of tormenting the smaller boy, neither of the twins had heard or seen the horseman. He had walked his horse around the bend in the footpath between the gravel heaps and come across the squirming yelling knot of small bodies in the middle of the path. He recognized the twins immediately; they had earned quick notoriety on the diggings, and it had taken only another second to guess the cause of the commotion, to understand who were the attackers and who the victim.

Douglas was quick to realize the changed circumstances as he looked up at his twin, dangling like a man on the gallows from the horseman's fist. He scrambled to his feet and darted away, but the horseman turned his mount with his heels and, like a polo player, cut backhanded with the long rhino-hide sjambok, and the agony of it paralysed Douglas. But for the thick canvas breeches it would have opened his skin.

Before he could begin to run again the horseman stooped in the saddle, seized his upper arm and lifted him easily. On each side of the horse, the twins wriggled and whimpered with the sting of the lash and the rider looked down at them thoughtfully.

'I know you two,' he told them quietly. 'You are the Stewart brats, the ones who drove old Jacob's mule into the barbed wire.'

'Please, sir, please,' blubbered Douglas.

'Keep quiet, boy,' said the rider evenly. 'You are the ones that cut the reins on De Kock's wagon. That cost your daddy a penny, and the Diggers' Committee would like to know who set fire to Carlo's tent then—'

'It weren't us, Mister,' Henry pleaded. It was clear they both knew who their captor was, and that they were truly afraid of him.

Jordan crawled to his knees and peered up at his rescuer. He must be somebody very important – perhaps even a member of the committee he had mentioned. Even in his distress Jordan was awed by that possibility. Ralph had explained to him that a committee member was something between a policeman, a prince and the ogre of the fairy tales which their mother used to read to them.

Now this fabulous being looked down at Jordan as he knelt in the pathway, with his cheek smeared with dust and tears, his shirt torn and the buttons dangling on their threads, while the backs of his knees were criss-crossed with bloody welts.

'This little one is half your size,' the horseman said. His eyes were blue, a strange electric blue – the eyes of a poet – or of a fanatic.

'It was just a game, sir,' mumbled Henry; the collar of his shirt was twisted up under his ear.

'We didn't mean nothing, Mister.'

The horseman transferred that glowing blue gaze from Jordan to the two wriggling bodies in his hands.

'A game, was it?' he asked. 'Well, next time I catch you playing your games, you and your father had better have a story for the committee, do you hear me?'

He shook them roughly. 'Do you understand me clearly?'

'Yes, sir—'

'So you enjoy games, do you? Well then, here is a new one, and we shall play it every time you so much as lay a finger on a child smaller than you are.'

He dropped them unexpectedly to earth, and before the twins could recover their balance had cut left and right with the sjambok, starting them away at a run, and then he cantered easily along behind them for a hundred yards or so, leaning from the saddle to flick the whip at the back of their legs to keep them at their best speed. Then abruptly he let them go and wheeled the horse, cantering back to where Jordan stood trembling and pale in the pathway.

'If you are going to fight, then one at a time is the best policy, young man,' said the rider and stepped down easily from the stirrup and threw the reins over his shoulder as he squatted on his haunches facing Jordan.

'Now where does it hurt most?' he asked.

It was suddenly terribly important to Jordan that he did not appear a baby. He gulped noisily as he fought his tears, and the man seemed to understand.

'Good fellow,' he nodded. 'That's the spirit.' And he drew a cotton handkerchief from his pocket and wiped away the muddy tears.

'What's your name?'

'Jordie – Jordan,' he corrected himself and sniffed noisily.

'How old are you, Jordan?'

'Almost eleven, sir.'

The sting of his injuries and of his humiliation began to recede, to be replaced by a warm flood of gratitude towards his rescuer.

'Spit!' ordered the horseman, proffering the handkerchief, and Jordan obeyed, dampening a corner of the cloth with his saliva.

The man turned him with a hand on his shoulder, and with the handkerchief cleaned the bloody lines on his legs. It was perfunctory treatment, and the man's touch was masculine and ungentle, but Jordan was powerfully reminded of his mother by the attention, and that empty place inside him ached so that he almost began weeping again. He held back the tears, and twisted his neck to watch the man work on his injured legs.

The fingers were square and powerful, but a little unco-ordinated. The nails were big and strong and even, cut short, with a pearly translucent lustre. The back of his hands were covered with fine golden hairs that caught the sun.

The man glanced up from his task at Jordan. His face was fair, the skin was smooth-shaven and unblemished except for the small fine moustache. His lips were full, high-coloured, sensual. His nose was large, but not too large for the big round head and the thick waves of light-brown hair.

He was young, probably ten years older than Jordan, though he had such a powerful presence, such a sense of maturity and of power seemed to invest him, that he appeared much older.

Yet there was something else about him that seemed to contradict the first appearance. The high colour in his lips and cheeks was not the flush of health and the open air life. It was a shade hectic, and though the skin was unlined, there were the subtle marks of suffering and pain at the corners of his eyes and mouth, while behind that penetrating gaze, that compelling intensity, there was a tragic shadow, a sense of sadness that was perhaps only readily apparent to the uncomplicated view of a child.

For a moment the man and the boy looked into each other's eyes, and something twisted almost painfully deep in Jordan's soul, a sweet pang – gratitude, puppy love, compassion, hero-worship – it was all of those and something else for which he would never have words.

Then the man stood; he was tall and big built, over six foot in his riding boots, and Jordan only reached as high as his ribs.

'Who is your father, Jordan?' And Jordan was grateful that he did not use the diminutive. The rider nodded at his reply.

'Yes,' he said. 'I have heard of him. The elephant hunter. Well, then, we had best get you home.'

He stepped up into the stirrup and from the saddle reached down, took Jordan by the arm and swung him up onto the horse's rump. Jordan sat sideways, and as the horse started forward, he put both arms round the rider's waist to balance himself.

Jan Cheroot came hurrying from the sorting-table as they trotted into Zouga's camp, and when the rider reined in, he reached up and lifted Jordan down.

'He has been in a fight,' the rider told Jan Cheroot. 'Put a little iodine on his cuts, and he'll be all right. The boy has spirit.'

Jan Cheroot was obsequious, almost cringing, far from his usual acerbic and cynical self. He seemed to be rendered speechless by the direct and startling gaze of the big man on the rangy horse. He held Jordan with one hand and with the other lifted the old regimental cap from his head and held it against his chest, nodding in servile agreement with the orders the man gave him.

The rider transferred his steady gaze back to Jordan, and for the first time he smiled.

'Next time pick on somebody your own size, Jordan,' he advised, took up the reins and trotted out of the camp without looking back.

'You know who that was, Jordie?' Jan Cheroot asked portentously, staring after the rider and not waiting for Jordan's reply. 'That's the big boss of the Diggers' Committee, that's the most important man on New Rush, Jordie—' he paused theatrically, and then announced, 'That's Mr Rhodes.'

'Mr Rhodes.' Jordan repeated the name to himself, 'Mr Rhodes.' It had a heroic sound to it, like some of the poetry that his mother had read to him. He knew that something important had just happened in his life.

Every member of Zouga's family found his place in the work, almost as though a special niche had been reserved for each of them: Jan Cheroot and Jordan at the sorting-table, the Matabele *amadoda* in the open diggings, and, naturally there was only one place for Ralph – in the diggings with them.

So they found the stones; they won them from the tiny squares of ground in the depths of the growing pit, and carried them to the surface in the swinging buckets, and carted them out along the rotten crumbling roadways which each day became more dangerous and they washed and sieved them, until at last Jan Cheroot or Jordie could pounce upon them on the sorting-table.

Then in the evening there might be three or four of Zouga's Matabele workmen waiting under the camel-thorn tree beside Zouga's tent.

'Let me see,' Zouga would grunt, and with a deal of showmanship the man would unknot a scrap of grubby cloth to display a chip of stone or a small transparent crystal.

These were the 'pick-ups' from the claims. As the Matabele handled the stuff, shovelling it and emptying the leather buckets, a glitter or shine of a pebble might catch their eye – and there was a reward for a diamond 'picked-up' and handed in.

Most of these 'pick-ups' were not veritable diamonds, for they took anything that sparkled, or anything pretty and unusually coloured. They brought in agate and quartz, feldspar and rock crystal, jasper and zircons – and once in a while a diamond; and then for each diamond, large or small, clear or discoloured, Zouga would hand over a golden sovereign from his dwindling hoard and add the diamond to the contents of the little chamois leather drawstring bag that he carried buttoned into his breast pocket, and which was under his pillow when he slept at night.

Then each Saturday morning, while Jan Cheroot and the two boys gathered around the camp table under the camel-thorn tree beside the tent, Zouga would carefully tip the contents of the leather bag onto a sheet of clean white paper, and they examined and discussed the week's recovery; and always Zouga tried to cover his disappointment, tried to ignore the nauseating bite of worry in his guts as he looked at the tiny, discoloured and flawed diamonds which the Devil's Own so reluctantly yielded up.

Then with the chamois bag buttoned into his pocket once again, his riding boots freshly waxed and polished by Ralph, his frayed shirt collar neatly darned and the buttons replaced by Jordan, and the gelding curried to a gloss by Jan Cheroot, Zouga would ride into the settlement, putting on the best face he could muster, smoking a cigar to show how little he really needed the money, and he would hitch the gelding at the door of the first diamond-buyer's galvanized iron shack.

'The Devil's Own.' The first kopje-walloper was a Hollander, and his accent was difficult to understand, but Zouga's brave show did not deceive him, and he sucked his teeth and shook his head dismally over Zouga's offering. 'The Devil's Own,' he repeated. 'It killed five men, and broke three others. Jocky Danby was lucky to get out at the price you paid him.'

'What's your offer?' Zouga asked quietly, and the buyer prodded the scattering of tiny stones.

'You want to see a real diamond?' he asked, and without waiting for Zouga's reply, swivelled his chair and opened the iron safe on the wall behind his desk.

Reverently he unfolded a square of white paper and displayed the beautiful flashing crystal, almost the size of a ripe acorn.

'Fifty-eight carats,' he whispered, and Zouga stared at it with the sour acid of envy in the back of his throat. 'I bought it yesterday.'

'How much?' he asked, hating himself for the weakness.

'Six thousand pounds!' said the buyer and carefully refolded the paper, placed the diamond back in the safe, locked the thick iron door, hung the key on his watch chain and glanced at Zouga's stones.

'Forty pounds,' he said off-handedly.

'The lot?' Zouga asked quietly. He had sixteen men to pay and feed and he needed new rope, and he would have to pay the piratical prices of the transport riders for it.

'The price of pool goods is right down.' The buyer shrugged. 'Every digger south of the Vaal is bringing in rubbish like this.'

Zouga refilled the bag and stood up.

'I made you that price as a favour,' warned the buyer. 'If you come back later, it will be thirty pounds.'

'I'll take that chance.' Zouga touched the brim of his hat and strode out into the sunlight.

The second buyer he visited poured the diamonds into the bowl of the diamond balance and then carefully added weights to the other arm until the scale was in balance.

'You should have stuck to elephant hunting,' he said, as he wrote down the weights and made his calculations in a leather notebook. 'The diamond market is flooded. There is a limit to the number of rich ladies who want to hang baubles round their necks, and here on the Vaal diggings we have mined more stones in a few years than were found in the six thousand years before that.'

'They are using them in watch movements, and tools for cutting glass and steel,' Zouga said quietly.

'A fad,' the buyer waved his hands in dismissal. 'Diamonds are finished. I'll give you fifty-five pounds for this lot and that's generous.'

One morning Zouga found Ralph working side by side with Bazo in the bottom of the pit, swinging the pick in rhythm with the Matabele chant. He stood there watching for a few minutes, saw the shape of mature muscle emerging from the soft flesh of childhood, saw the breadth of shoulder. Ralph's belly was greyhound slim and the cloth of his breeches, that were suddenly many sizes too small, strained over neat round buttocks as he stooped to break the point of the pick from the compacted yellow earth.

'Ralph,' he called him at last.

'Yes, Papa.' His throat was greasy with sweat, and it had cut little runnels down through the dust that coated his upper body, fat glistening drops clung in the little nest of fine dark curls that had abruptly appeared in the centre of his chest.

'Put your shirt on,' Zouga ordered.

'Why?' Ralph looked surprised.

'Because you are an Englishman. By God's grace and, if necessary, the strength of my right arm you are going to be a gentleman as well.'

So Ralph worked booted and buttoned to the throat beside the naked Matabele, and he earned firstly their respect and then their affection and friendship.

From the first day when they had met in the open veld, the Matabele had been impressed with his horsemanship, and with the marksmanship which had brought down the old eland bull. Now they began to accept him amongst them, first in the patronizing manner of elder brothers, then gradually on more and more equal terms, until Ralph was competing with them in all they did, their work and their sport. He was not yet as tall or strong as the Matabele, so he won very seldom; and when he failed or was beaten, he scowled until his face darkened and the heavy brows met above the big nose.

'A good sportsman knows how to lose graciously,' Zouga told him.

'I don't want to be a sportsman, I don't want to learn how to lose,' Ralph replied. 'I want to learn how to win.' And he threw himself back at the task with fiercely renewed determination.

It seemed that his strength grew with each day in the diggings, the puppy fat was burned away, and he made that final spurt to his full height without outstripping his strength. And he learned how to win.

He began to win the contests with Bazo at lashing

gravel, frenziedly filling bucket after huge leather bucket so that the yellow dust flew in choking clouds. He won one of the dangerous races down the ladderworks from the roadway to the bottom of the pit, scorching his palms on the ropes and swinging out over the drop to pass another man on the reverse side of the ladder, using the pole of a gantry to cross a deep void between two claims, running across it upright, like a tight-rope walker, without looking at his feet or the hundred-foot drop beneath him. Even Bazo shook his head and said 'Hau!' which is an exclamation of deep amazement, and Ralph stood panting in the bottom of the pit, looking up at Bazo, and shouted with triumphant laughter.

Then Ralph learned to use the fighting sticks the hard way – for this was the game the Matabele had played since their first day as herd boys in the veld. Before he mastered the art of the sticks he had, perforce, to learn how to staunch a bleeding cut in his own scalp inflicted by Bazo's stick by plugging it with a handful of dust snatched in the midst of the contest.

A week short of his sixteenth birthday, Ralph beat Bazo for the first time. They fought behind the thatched beehive huts that the Matabele had built on the open veld beyond Zouga's camp.

It started light-heartedly, Bazo the instructor, hectoring his pupil, executing the weaving steps of the traditional combat with indolent grace like a sleepy black panther, a fighting stick held in each hand and flourished with studied artistry of movement to form a fluid screen from which a vicious cutting attack could be launched with either hand.

Ralph turned to face him so that they revolved smoothly as a balanced wheel, like a pair of trained dancers, and when they taunted each other Ralph's repartee was in fluent and colloquial Matabele. He was stripped to the waistband of his riding breeches, and his torso, which had at Zouga's orders been so long protected from the sun, was creamy pale; only his arms and the deep V at his throat were sun dark.

'I once had a pet baboon,' Bazo told him. 'It was an albino baboon, white as the moon, and so stupid it never learned even a simple trick. That baboon reminds me of somebody, though I cannot think who.'

Ralph smiled with his lips only, exposing square white teeth, but the black brows were joined above his nose. 'I am only surprised that a Matabele thought he could teach a baboon – surely it should be the other way around.'

Bazo jumped back and hooted, beginning the *giya* – the challenge dance of the warrior – leaping high and making the kerries sing in the air until they blurred like the wings of a sunbird in flight.

'Let us see if your sticks are as quick as your tongue,' he shouted; and then suddenly he was attacking, the song of the fighting sticks rising to a shriek as he cut for Ralph's knee, the shriek ending with a crack like a rifle shot as Ralph caught it on his guard; and instantly Bazo cut with the other hand, for the elbow and – crack – again as Ralph warded off the blow with his own kerrie.

The sticks clattered against each other in a rising tempo, and the circle of Matabele watchers encouraged them with the deep drawn-out 'Jee!' as a stroke was skilfully countered and turned into a hissing riposte to be countered in its turn.

Bazo broke first, jumping back with a light sheen of sweat turning his muscles to black velvet, his chest swelling and subsiding, his chuckle only slightly hoarse.

There should be a pause now, as the combatants circled each other again, in that stylized shuffling dance, trading light insults, catching breath, stooping to dry their hands in the dust to improve their grip on the sticks – but, not this time, for as Bazo broke and jumped back and for an instant dropped his right hand, so Ralph went in.

Even the pretence of a smile was gone from Ralph's

mouth. His jaw was clenched, lumps of muscles knotted with determination beneath his ears. Bazo's right guard had dropped, and his attention had switched to the audience of Matabele faces, for whose benefit he was already composing the next jibe.

'Jee!' They shouted encouragement and warning, and Bazo tried desperately to raise his guard and swivel to face the unexpected attack. He managed a touch of stick against stick, just enough to cushion the blow, otherwise it would have broken bone. Ralph's kerrie smashed into the point of his shoulder, and abruptly it was no longer a game.

The blow to Bazo's shoulder raised a welt as thick as a finger across the muscle, and almost paralysed the arm to the fingertips. So as he caught Ralph's next cut he felt the kerrie jerk and turn in his numb fingers, almost breaking his grip, and the shock of it was transferred into the abused muscle so that he grunted involuntarily, a little grunt of agony that seemed only to goad Ralph.

His sun-dark features were a mask of fighting fury, his eyes cold and green, and little droplets of sweat flew from his long black hair with the force of every blow that he swung.

The Matabele had never seen him like this, but they recognized the killing madness, for they had themselves all been in battle and killed, and it infected them so that they danced and stamped with excitement and spurred Ralph with their voices.

'Jee!' they sang, and Bazo fell back, giving ground to Ralph's attack as the sticks cracked and rattled. His mouth was wide open now as he gasped for air and his throat was a deep pink cavern. Blood ran in a thin shining slick down behind his ear, spreading over his straining throat and then onto his right shoulder like a mantle. A glancing blow above his eye had not opened the flesh, but had formed a blister of black blood as large as a walnut under the skin. It hung from Bazo's forehead like some bizarre bloodsucking leech, and still the blows hissed and cracked about him, thick as tropical rain, falling on his guard so that the shock was carried through arm and shoulder and jarred his head upon the thick black column of his neck.

Then another blow went through and the ivory flash of Bazo's teeth was dulled with a film of blood that snaked down from one nostril into his mouth, and another blow went through, on the line of his thigh, the swelling rising instantaneously, the skin stretched glossy and black, and almost crippled Bazo who was pinned by the injured leg – and Ralph was still attacking, instinctively swinging him against the bad leg so that Bazo was slow and clumsy in the turn, and again one of Ralph's sticks fluted and thumped into rubbery muscle and Bazo reeled and almost went down, recovering with an immense effort, his counter-stroke loose and lacking power, so that Ralph spurned it aside and used his point.

He drove the end of his right-hand kerrie through Bazo's guard, using it as though it were a sword rather than a club, and Bazo was not ready for it. With all Ralph's weight behind it, the kerrie tore into Bazo's belly muscles, up under the heavy ribcage, and the Matabele doubled over the blow, one kerrie flying from his hand the other dropping to dangle uselessly at his side.

He dropped on his knees, head bowed to expose the back of his neck, the knuckles of his spine standing out between the ridges of hard black muscle.

Ralph's eyes were fastened on the unprotected neck, and they were glazed over with the same soapy sheen as an uncut diamond, his movements too swift to be anything but instinctive. He threw the kerrie on high and shifted his weight from the back foot to the leading foot, and all his strength flowed into his back and shoulders as he went into the killing stroke.

'Jee!' roared the watchers, themselves carried beyond the frontiers of sanity on the hot wave of fighting madness, crowding forward for the death.

Ralph froze like that, right arm high, his entire body arched like a drawn bow, the fallen Matabele at his feet – and then slowly the tension went out of his limbs and he shook his head with the fumbling uncertainty of a man awaking from a nightmare. He looked about him with stunned disbelief, blinking his eyes as though to clear them of that opaque glittering madness, and suddenly his legs were trembling, unable to hold his weight. He sank down in front of Bazo, knelt facing him and put out one arm and wrapped it around the Matabele's neck, and laid his cheek against Bazo's.

'God,' he whispered. 'Oh God – I nearly killed you.'

Their blood and their sweat mingled, and both of them were pumping for air, their chests heaving, their bodies racked for the precious stuff.

'Never teach an albino baboon a trick,' Bazo spoke at last, his voice was husky and unsteady. 'He might learn it a little too well.'

Then they were dragged to their feet by the laughing, hooting Matabele and carried to the nearest hut.

Ralph drank first from the calabash of gruel – thick bubbling millet beer – and then handed it across to Bazo.

Bazo washed the blood from his mouth and spat it on the ground, then he drank with his head tilted back, a dozen deep swallows before he lowered the gourd and looked at Ralph.

For a moment they were grave, green eyes holding the gaze of smouldering black, and then suddenly they were both laughing, great gusts of shaking uncontrolled laughter, so that the men that squatted in the circle about them began to chuckle also, and then to laugh with them.

Still laughing, Bazo leaned across and gripped Ralph's

right forearm briefly. 'I am your man,' he said, through his laughter, and through the blood in his mouth.

When Zouga stepped off the ladder in the bottom level of the Devil's Own, the heat was already enough to bring out a dark patch of sweat between the shoulder blades of his blue flannel shirt. He lifted his hat to mop the dewdrops along his hairline and then paused and frowned quickly.

'Ralph!' he snapped, and his son sank the pickhead into the yellow gravel, let it stand like that and then straightened with his hands on his hips.

'Just what do you think you are doing?' Zouga demanded.

'I've worked out a new way of doing it,' Ralph told him. 'First Bazo's gang breaks rock, then Wengi comes along behind and—'

'You know what I'm talking about.' Zouga cut in impatiently. 'It's Monday; you are supposed to be at school.'

'I'm sixteen now,' Ralph told him. 'And besides, I know how to read and to write.'

'Don't you think you might have mentioned your decision,' Zouga asked with deceptive mildness, 'if only in passing?'

'You were busy, Papa, I didn't want to worry you with something so unimportant. You've got enough to worry about without that.'

Zouga hesitated. Was that just his usual clever twisting, or did Ralph truly realize how finely stretched they were, just how much Zouga truly did have to worry about?

Ralph sensed his advantage. 'We need every pair of hands we can get, and these are free.' He held them up, and Zouga noticed for the first time that they were powerful and broad with yellow calluses on the palms.

'Just what is this new idea of yours?' Zouga's scowl smoothed away, and Ralph grinned as he realized that he was no longer a schoolboy; and he began to explain, gesturing with spread hands while Zouga nodded.

'All right,' he said at last. 'It makes sense. We'll try it.'

Zouga turned and walked away, and Ralph spat on his hands and shouted in Matabele.

'Come on, you are not a bunch of women hoeing for yams; let's break ground.'

On Claim No. 183 an American digger named Calvin Hine hit an enrichment, a tiny pocket, and in a single bucket he took out two hundred and sixteen diamonds, the biggest over twenty carats. In a stroke he was transformed from a ragged, bearded sun-blackened beggar grovelling in the yellow dust into a rich man.

Calvin was there that night when Diamond Lil climbed up onto the wooden counter of her grog-shop, with her ostrich feathers swirling and her sequins aglitter in the lamplight. She asked in cockney that chimed like Bow Bells:

'Will some sporting gent name me a price for these fancy goods?' and squeezed out her own big round breasts between painted red fingertips, so that they bulged over the top of her crimson velvet bodice, the skin smoother than the velvet and the big pink coin of a nipple coming up like the dawn over the horizon of her neckline.

'Come on, dearies, one night of paradise, one little glimpse of heaven, me loves.'

'Tenner, Lil darling. Ten iron men,' shouted a digger at the back of the bar, and Lil turned and flipped up the back of her skirts at him.

'Shame on you, for a mean little man,' she chided him over her white shoulder; and the laced and beribboned pantaloons beneath her rustling skirts had no crotch to them, so for a fleeting part of a second they saw what she was selling, and bellowed like trek-oxen five days in the desert when they smell the waterhole.

'Lil, my beauty.' Calvin climbed unsteadily onto the packing case that acted as a table. He had been drinking since noon when he left the kopje-walloper's office. 'Lily, the moon of my soul,' he crooned, 'every night for a year and more I dreamed of this moment.'

He dug into the back pocket of his coat and held up a fistful of crumpled five-pound notes.

'I don't know how much that is,' he blurted, 'but it's yours.'

For a moment Lily's plucked and pencilled eyebrows contracted as she made a rapid calculation of the proffered wad of banknotes; and then she smiled so that the tiny diamond set in her front tooth sparkled like the evening star.

'You beautiful boy,' she sang. 'Tonight I am your bride. Take me in your arms, my lover.'

The next day someone took a thirty carat stone on the eastern section, a lovely white stone of the first water, and the day after that a huge champagne-coloured diamond came from Neville Pickering's block.

'You'll be leaving now?' Zouga asked him when they met on the roadway above the Devil's Own, and he hoped that the envy did not show in his smile.

'No.' Pickering shook his head, and answered with his own charming sunny smile. 'I always bet on a winning streak. My partner and I are staying in the game.'

It seemed that the diamond god was intent on showering sudden largesse on the New Rush, and a fever of expectation and excitement gripped them all so that the great pit at noon sounded like a hive of wild bees when the acacia forests are in yellow bloom. Three great finds in three days; nobody had seen it happen before.

At night around the camp fires, and in the lantern-lit grog-shops and canteens, the wild theories were aired by dusty diggers drunk on bad liquor and reborn hope.

'It's a stratal enrichment,' pontificated one. 'It's a layer of fat babies right across the kopje. You mark my words, somebody will take a pony before the week is out.'

'Hell no,' argued another. 'The stones are lying in potholes. Some lucky bastard is going to scoop the pot again, like Calvin's two one six or Pickering's monkey.'

Thursday night of the crazy week it rained. Here on the fringes of the Kalahari desert the rainfall was less than twenty inches a year. They had almost half of that on that single night.

The rain was a slanting curtain of silver arrow shafts in the brilliant crackling blue flare of the lighting. The clouds piled to the heavens banged against one another like fighting bulls, mountainous in the lightning bursts, and the thunder jarred the earth while the rain hissed down.

In the dawn it was still raining, and at another time the diggers might have stayed out of the pit and waited for it to dry out. But not on this day, not with the fierce excitement that gripped the entire settlement. That day nothing would keep them out of the pit.

The diggings were greasy with yellow mud. The lowest claims were knee deep with the insidious clinging stuff. It coated the bare legs of the black workmen to the thigh; it built up in mud bricks on the boots of the white overseers, weighing them down like convicts shackled to a ball and chain.

The thick red mud on the roadways clogged the wheels of the gravel carts and had to be prised clear with the point of a crowbar. They shovelled the slush into the buckets and as they were hoisted the thin watery mud cascaded down on the men below, so that it was no longer possible to tell black man from white behind their slick and glistening yellow masks.

What none of the men in the workings realized was that, apart from the discomfort and filth that the downpour of the night's thunderstorms had brought to the pit, they had created a less obvious but infinitely graver change in the riddled remains of Colesberg kopje.

The rushing rivulets had found a fissure at the neck of No. 6 Roadway and had poured into it, carving and cutting and weakening; and the slimy yellow mud had hidden the deep vertical cracks in the hundred-foot high earthen embankment.

There were sixteen mule carts crowded onto the causeway, most of them fully laden with the first load of the morning, the drivers swearing at each other, the long trek whips firing explosively as they tried to clear a path to get their load out to the waiting cradles.

Down on the Devil's Own the Matabele teams were working side by side, but the icy sting of the rain on bare shoulders and backs slowed the swing of the picks, and at each forward pace they slithered and slipped in the treacherous footing. The work chant sounded like a dirge; Zouga snarled at them to keep them moving, and the mood was ugly.

Up on the roadway an overladen gravel cart began to slide sideways in the mud, and the wheeler mule was pulled down on his knees, unable to hold it. The off wheel dropped over the edge, and the cart sagged drunkenly and then hung out over the pit. The team slewed across the narrow causeway in tangled traces while the unequal weight of gravel snapped the outer axle of the cart. Zouga's cart was directly behind the stranded team, facing in the same direction, and Ralph jumped down off the driver's seat and shouted furiously.

'You damned fool – you've jammed us in.'

'You cheeky puppy,' the driver of the bogged-down vehicle yelled back. 'You need a lick of the whip across your backside.'

Immediately half a dozen diggers were joining in, taking sides, shouting advice or abuse.

'Cut the traces, get those bloody animals off the roadway.'

'Dump the gravel out, you're overloaded.'

'You don't touch my rig,' yelled the driver of the stricken cart. Ralph had drawn the sheath knife from his belt and run forward.

'That's the ticket, Ralph.'

'That little blighter needs a lesson.'

Men and vehicles and mud-smeared beasts formed an angry, unstable knot at the top of the high earthen wall. In the bottom of the diggings, Zouga threw his head back and cupped his hands to his mouth.

'Ralph!' he bellowed. He could see how dangerous the tangle had become. Tempers were flaring; he could sense how close they were to mortal danger as fighting men lost control of panicking animals.

In the uproar Zouga's voice was almost drowned, and if Ralph heard him, he gave no sign of doing so. He was kneeling beside the downed wheel mule, hacking at the thongs of the traces with his sheath knife.

'Get away from there,' howled the driver, and reared back, the long trek whip flying out high above his shoulders and then snaking forward, twenty feet long, whispering like the wing of a wild duck in flight.

Ralph saw it, and ducked behind the mule's heavy barrel-like body; the lash exploded in the air like a bursting grenade, and the mule lunged wildly, swinging the dissel-boom of the cart across the causeway so that the broken axle collapsed before the snapping of the half-severed leather thongs allowed the mule to regain its feet and then gallop away down the muddy track to firmer ground.

Ralph leaned out and ran to his own team. He called to his wheeler mule, 'Pull, Bishop!' The wheels sucked and farted in the mud as Ralph drove them at the narrow gap, the stranded cart on one side, sprawled half across the track, on the other the sheer unguarded drop into the open workings.

'Ha, Rosie!' Ralph grabbed the bridle of the lead mule and, running at her head, guided her into the gap.

'Ralph, damn you!' Zouga roared. 'Stop! Do you hear me, stop!'

But he was a helpless spectator. It would take five minutes or longer to reach the causeway across the complicated system of ladderworks and board walks. There was nothing he could do to prevent the developing tragedy.

The infuriated owner of the stranded cart was still on the body of the vehicle, brandishing his long whip and howling with anger and frustration. He was not a big man, an inch or so shorter than Ralph – but heavy in the shoulder and the belly, not flabby fat but work-braided muscle, and his hands on the stock of the whip were rough as oak bark, baked by the sun and scoured by gravel and the haft of pick and shovel.

'I'll settle your account, you little bugger,' he shouted, and again threw back the whip; again Ralph ducked under the flailing lash, but it caught the sleeve of his faded and patched shirt, splitting the rotted material and opening the skin of Ralph's upper arm in a thin red razor cut from which the bright blood bloomed instantly.

Rising from his crouch in the mud, Ralph placed one hand on the wheel mule's withers and used his own impetus and the leverage of his arm to leap high in the air. It was a trick that Jan Cheroot had taught him, the way a good teamsman crosses from one side of the span to another. In mid-air Ralph tucked his legs and swung his body, vaulting cleanly over the mules' backs and landing on the far side of the team alongside the leading wheel. His next jump carried him onto the truck of the cart, and with the same movement he had snatched his own long trek whip from its slot beside the brake handle.

The handle was ten feet long, and the tapered lash another twenty. A skilled teamsman could cut a fly off the tip of the lead mule's ear with the lash, and Jan Cheroot had trained Ralph: he was good with the whip, very good.

Ralph's lips were a thin chalky white line, his eyes green and furious. The sting of the whip had driven him into murderous, unthinking rage.

'Ralph!' Zouga shouted vainly. He had seen his son like this before. It frightened him. 'Ralph! Stop!'

Standing high on the cart bed Ralph shot the lash out to full stretch behind him. It was an easy graceful movement like a salmon fisherman putting up the fly, and in the same action he brought the tip of the whip stock forward, all wrist and shoulders, and the lash whined and reached out to the other driver.

It cut him like a sword stroke, from breast to belt buckle, and only the heavy wet oilskin he wore protected him from serious injury. The torn fabric flapped about his body, and the rain diluted the dribble of blood from the shallow wound.

Ralph's mules swung from the crack of the whip, and the off wheel hooked that of the stranded cart, locking both vehicles hopelessly in the soft mud.

Ralph was too close now to the other driver to stretch the lash, and he reversed the whip stock, using it like a club, and swung it at the man's head.

Below them in the diggings, the Matabele were encouraging their favourite with the fighting 'Jee!' and it goaded Ralph. He was quicker than the other driver, nimble to avoid his swinging stock, using his own like the fighting sticks with which he had trained so assiduously.

The mules were panicked by the uproar, the crack of

whips, the Matabele war chant, the shrieked insults and the bellow of the watchers.

Rosie reared and cut with her fore-hooves, whinnying hysterically, and her team mate lunged and struggled against the jammed off wheel.

Bishop shirked the yoke, turned from it; his hind legs scrabbled on the crumbling edge of the causeway and he went over, hanging in the tangle of reins and chains, kicking and pawing at the air and shrieking wildly.

Then quite gently, like a sleeper awaking from deep slumber, the yellow earthen causeway shook itself.

The movement started below the wheels of the locked carts and the trampling hooves of the terrified mules – and then it rippled along the embankment to the neck where it joined the rim of the pit – and at that point a deep vertical crack opened miraculously in the muddy yellow wall. It opened with only a soft wet sound like an infant suckling at the breast, but it silenced the shouting, chanting men who watched.

Suddenly the only sound in the open diggings was the rustle of the falling rain and the shrieks of the dangling mule. On the cart Ralph stood poised like a Greek statue of an athlete, the whip stock thrown back, the cords in his throat relaxing, the insane rage in his green eyes clearing to leave a bemused expression of disbelief; for beneath his feet the earth was moving.

'Ralph!' This time Zouga's voice reached him clearly, and he looked down into the pit, saw their faces, the shock, the terror upon them.

'Run!' shouted Zouga, and the urgency galvanized Ralph. 'Get off the roadway.'

Ralph threw the whip aside and jumped down off the cart. The sheath knife in his hand again.

The rein that held Bishop, the big grey mule, was stretched tight as an iron bar. It parted cleanly to the touch of the blade and the mule dropped free, twisting in the air so that the men below scattered away, and the heavy body smacked into the mud. Then the beast scrambled to its feet and stood trembling miserably, belly deep in the yellow mud that had saved it.

The earth trembled like jelly under Ralph's feet as he hacked at the traces that held the other three mules and the moment they were free of the trapped cart he drove them ahead of him along the causeway, yelling them into a gallop. The yellow mud shook and tilted as the cracks yawned open, and the entire causeway began to sag.

'Run, you bloody fool,' Ralph panted at the man he had been fighting, as he stood in the rain and looked about him, the tattered oilskins dangling about his legs, his expression bewildered.

'Come on, run,' and Ralph grabbed his arm and dragged him after the galloping mule team.

One after another the gantries that lined the roadway, some of them with the huge buckets still hanging from the sheaves, began to topple over into the pit, the timber crackling and twisting, the ropes tangling and snapping like strands of cotton.

Ahead of Ralph the three yoked mules reached firm ground and galloped away, whisking their tails and kicking out skittishly at relief from their burden.

The causeway tilted and sagged, so that suddenly Ralph seemed to be running up a steep hill. The driver beside him missed his footing and went down on his knees, and then as he started to slide backwards he threw himself face down and spread his arm as though to hug the earth.

'Get up.' Ralph checked his own run, and stood over him.

Behind them the earth growled like a voracious animal, moving gravel grinding upon itself; and there were still fourteen carts out on the collapsing causeway. Half a dozen of the drivers had abandoned their teams and were running back along the trembling, sagging roadway, but they had left it too late. They stopped in a little group. Some of them fell flat and clung to the earth. One turned and leapt boldly from the edge into the gaping pit.

He plunged into the mud, and three black workers seized him and dragged him to safety, a broken leg twisting and slithering over the mud behind him.

One of the laden carts, with four mules in the traces, toppled over and, as it hit the bottom of the diggings, the weight of gravel shattered it to ragged splinters of raw white wood, and a shaggy black mule impaled on the disselboom screamed with shockingly human agony and kicked wildly. tearing out its own entrails from the gaping wound in its flank.

Ralph stooped and dragged the driver to his feet, pulling him up the steepening incline, but the man was semi-paralysed by terror and hampered by the flapping tails of his heavy oilskins.

The centre of the roadway cracked through abruptly and a hundred feet of it collapsed sideways with a swift rumbling rush, hurling carts and animals into the pit as though from some gigantic catapult.

Ralph glanced once over his shoulder at the terrifying carnage and saw that the whole roadway was going, starting from that centre point and running swiftly towards him, a breaking wave of soft yellow earth seeming to be of some thick and viscid fluid, breaking with that grinding whisper.

'Come on,' Ralph grunted at the man on his arm, and suddenly the earth beneath their feet lunged the other way, throwing them forward towards the rim of the pit – and safety.

They went forward with a rush, the driver clutching at Ralph's shoulder for support. A dozen paces to go to firm ground, and Ralph did not look back again. The hideous sounds from the pit were unnerving, and he sensed that another glimpse of that onrushing wave of collapsing earth might paralyse his own legs.

'Come on,' he gasped. 'We'll make it – almost there. Come on!' And as he said it the earth opened in front of their feet as though from a giant's axe stroke. It opened with a smacking sound, as of kissing lips, and the mouth of it was sheer, eighty feet deep and three feet across, but in the brief seconds that they tottered on the edge it gaped wider, six feet, eight feet, and the causeway tilted sideways – the final convulsion.

'Jump!' said Ralph. 'Jump for it, man.' And he shoved the driver at it, forcing him at that frightful crack that seemed to split the earth to its very core.

The man stumbled off balance, his arms waving wildly for control, and then he made a clumsy scrambling leap out over the drop. The torn oilskins tangled with his limbs and fluttered about his head. He hit the far lip of the crack with his chest, his legs hanging into the drop and kicking hopelessly, and clawed at the muddy lip. But there was no purchase and inexorably he began to slide backwards.

Ralph knew there was no chance of making a run-up to the jump. He had to take it from a standstill, and it was gaping wider with every second, ten feet or more now – and the quivering bank of collapsing earth was an unstable platform.

He sank on one knee, steadied himself with a clenched fist against the earth, and then straightened his legs and body in a sudden burst of energy like a released coilspring, jumping high because the causeway had already sagged below the level of the rim.

The power of that leap surprised even Ralph; he cleared the driver's wriggling body and landed deep, on firm and rock-steady ground, stumbled with his own forward impetus and then ran on half a dozen paces.

Behind him the driver wailed and slid back a few inches,

and around his spread fingers opened a mesh of smaller cracks, running parallel to the gaping sheer line. Ralph spun and ran back. He threw himself flat and reached for the driver's wrist. It was greasy with mud, slippery as a freshly netted trout, and he knew he could not hold him for long.

Over the driver's head Ralph stared down into the diggings. He watched the final collapse of the causeway, a massive rush of earth, some of it liquid mud, mixed with huge chunks of compacted gravel that ground together like the jaws of some mindless monster, crushing and smothering men and animals between them.

The entire No. 6 Roadway was gone, and across the floor of the pit, deep dark cracks spread out like a grotesque spider's web.

In the bottom of the diggings the figures of men seemed frail and insectlike, their cries feeble and without consequence, their pathetic scurrying without purpose.

Ralph suddenly recognized his father. He alone was standing firm, his head thrown back, and even across that dizzy space Ralph could feel the strength of his gaze.

'Hold on, boy!' Zouga's voice carried faintly above the pandemonium. 'They're coming. Hold on!'

But under Ralph's belly the earth whispered and shrugged impatiently and the driver's weight pulled him another inch towards the drop.

'Hold on, Ralph!'

Across that aching breathless space Zouga was reaching out with both hands, a gesture that was more eloquent than any words – a gesture of suffering and helpless love.

Then suddenly Ralph felt rough hands seize the ankles of his muddy boots, the shouts of many men behind him, the rasp of a hairy manila rope against his cheek, the noose dangling in front of his face – and with a huge surge of relief he saw the dangling driver thrust his free arm through the noose and saw it drawn tight.

Ralph could let the muddy wrist slip from his grip, and he crawled back from the edge.

He looked down at his father. It was too far for either of them to see the expression on each other's face.

For a moment longer Zouga stared up at him. Then he turned away abruptly, his stride businesslike, his gestures imperative as he ordered his Matabele forward to the rescue work.

T he rescue went on all that day. For once every digger on New Rush was united by a common purpose.

The Diggers' Committee closed the workings and ordered every man out of the unaffected areas. The five other roadways that had not collapsed were declared out of bounds to all traffic and they stood high and menacing in the silver clouds of drifting rain.

On the churned and collapsed remnants of No. 6 Roadway the rescuers swarmed. These were the men who had been trapped on the floor by the severed ladderworks and the fallen system of gantries.

There were no members of the Committee in the No. 6 area, and Zouga Ballantyne with his natural air of authority was quickly accepted as the leader. He had marked the position of the gravel carts and drivers on the roadway at the moment of the cave-in, and he split the available men into gangs and set them to digging where he guessed men and vehicles were buried. They attacked the treacherous shapeless mass of earth with a passion which was a mixture of hatred and stale fear, an expression of their own relief at having escaped that smothering, entombing yellow cascade.

For the first hour they dug men out alive, some miraculously protected by an overturned cart or the body of a dead mule. One of these survivors rose shakily to his feet unaided when the earth was shovelled away, and the rescuers cheered him with a kind of wild hysteria.

Three mules had survived the drop (one of these was Zouga's old grey Bishop) but others were fearfully mutilated by the wrecked carts. Someone lowered a pistol and a packet of cartridges from the ground level and Zouga slipped and slid from one team to the other and shot the unfortunate beasts as they lay screaming and kicking in the mud.

While this was going on there were teams of men busy above them at ground level. Under the direction of the Diggers' Committee they were rigging rope ladders and a makeshift gantry to bring up the dead and the injured. By noon that day they could begin taking the injured out, strapped to six-by-three timber boards and hoisted on the new gantry, swaying up the high wall of the pit.

Then they began to find the dead men.

The last of the missing men was locked like a foetus into the cold muddy womb of the earth. Zouga and Bazo stooped shoulder to shoulder into the mouth of the excavation, seized the limp wrist that protruded from the bank and, straining together, freed the corpse. It came out in a rush of slippery mud, like the moment of birth, but the man's limbs were convulsed in rigor mortis and his eye sockets packed with mud. Other hands lifted the corpse and carried it away, and Zouga flexed his back and groaned. Cold and weariness had tied knots in his muscles.

'We are not finished yet,' he said, and the young Matabele nodded.

'What is there still to do?' he asked simply, and Zouga felt a rush of gratitude and affection towards him. He placed his hand on Bazo's shoulder and for a moment they considered each other gravely, then Bazo asked again, 'What must be done?'

'The roadway is gone. There will be no work on these

claims – not for a long time,' Zouga explained, his voice dulled and his hand dropping wearily from Bazo's shoulder. 'If we leave any tools or equipment down here, they will be stolen.'

They had lost the gravel cart, the hoist with its iron sheave wheels and valuable rope, and the gravel buckets.

Zouga sighed, and the fatigue swept over him like a cold dark wave. There was no money to replace those essentials. 'We must save what we can from the vultures.'

Bazo called to his men in their own language and led them along the shapeless bank of broken earth from which protruded shattered pieces of equipment and tangles of sodden rope, to the deserted Devil's Own claims.

The fallen roadway had buried the eastern corner of No. 142, but the rest of the claims were clear. However, a pressure crack had opened in a deep zigzag across the floor and some of Zouga's equipment had fallen into it and lay half submerged in muddy water.

Bazo clambered down into the fissure and groped for the mess of rope and tools, passing it up to the Matabele on the bank above his head. Here Zouga supervised them as they tied the tools into bundles and then staggered away with them to the high eastern bank, there to wait their turn for the single functioning gantry to hoist the bundles out to ground level.

As they worked the last pale rays of the sun pierced the mass of low cloud and struck down into the huge man-made pit.

In the bottom of the fissure Bazo found the last missing pick, passed it up, and then leaned against the bank to rest for a few moments. He felt that he no longer had the strength to climb out of the deep crack. The cold had numbed his legs and softened his skin until it was wrinkled and water-logged like that of a drowned man. He shivered and laid his forehead on his arm, bracing himself against the bank of yellow earth. He felt that if he closed his eyes he would fall asleep on his feet.

He kept them open with an effort, and stared at the earth in front of his face. A trickle of rainwater was still running down from the level above his head; it had cut a narrow runnel a few inches wide and deep. Most of the mud had settled out of this little streamlet, and it was almost clear, only slightly milked with colour.

At one point in its trickle down the mud wall it had encountered an obstacle, and was pouring over it, forming a little plume of running water.

Suddenly Bazo was thirsty. His throat was rough and dry. He leaned forward, and let the trickle flow over his lips and tongue, and then slurped a mouthful.

The watery sun touched the bank, and a strange brilliant light flared inches from Bazo's face. It came pouring up, powerful and pure and dancing white, from the tiny freshet from which he was drinking.

He stared at it dully, and slowly it dawned upon him that the obstruction over which the water was pouring was something embedded in the gravel bank, something that glowed and flickered as the random beam of sunlight played upon it, something that seemed to change shape and substance through the trickling yellow-tinged waters.

He touched it with his forefinger, and the cold water ran down his forearm and dripped from his elbow. He tried to work it loose, but it was firmly implanted, and soapy-feeling in his raw numb fingers so that he could not get a fair grip upon it.

He took the buckhorn whistle from around his neck and used the point to prise the pretty fiery object loose, and it dropped heavily into the raw pink palm of his hand, almost filling it.

It was a stone, but a stone such as he had never seen before. He held it under the trickle of rainwater, and with his thumb rubbed off the clinging mud until it was clean. Then he looked at it again, turning it curiously in the weak sunlight.

Until Bazo had arrived at New Rush he had never thought about rocks and stones as being different from one another, any more than one drop of water differed from another or one cloud in the sky was more valuable or useful than the others. The Matabele language did not differentiate between a granite pebble and a diamond, they were both simply '*imitshe*'. Only the white men's maniacal obsession with stones had made him look at them afresh.

In all these months he had spent toiling in the diggings, he had seen many strange things and learned much of the white men and their ways. At first he had not been able to believe the extraordinary value they placed on the most trivial items. That a single pebble could be exchanged for six hundred head of prime cattle seemed some grotesque madman's dream, but at last he had seen that it was true and he and his little band of *amadoda* had become fanatical gatherers of pebbles. Every sparkling or coloured stone they had pounced upon like magpies and carried proudly to Bakela for their reward.

This initial enthusiasm had swiftly waned, for there was neither logic nor system in the white man's mind. The showiest stones were discarded contemptuously. Lovely shiny red and blue pebbles, some of them shot through with different colours like ceramic beads, Bakela handed back to them with a grunt and a shake of the head. While occasionally, very occasionally, he would select some dull and uninteresting little chip and hand the delighted finder a gold coin.

At first, payment in coin had confused the Matabele, but they learned fast. Those little metal discs could be exchanged in their turn for anything a man desired, as long as he had enough of them he could have a gun, or a horse, a woman or a fine ox.

112

Bakela had tried to explain to Bazo and his Matabele how to recognize the stones for which he would pay a red gold coin. Firstly, they were small, never much bigger than the seed of the camel-thorn tree.

Bazo considered the stone in his palm. It was huge; he could barely close his fingers over it. The stones that Bakela wanted were usually of a certain shape, a regular shape with eight sides, one for every finger less the thumbs. This huge stone was not so shaped. It had one clean side, as though cut through with a knife blade, and the rest of it was rounded and polished to a strange soapy sheen.

Bazo held it under the trickle of rainwater again, and when he brought it out the film of water that covered the surface instantly coagulated into little droplets and shrank away, leaving the stone dry and glittering.

That was strange, Bazo decided, but the stone was the wrong colour. Bakela had explained that they must look for pale lemon, or glossy grey, even brown colour. This stone was like looking into a clear pool in the mountains. He could see the shape of his own hand through it, and it was full of stars of moving light that hurled little darts of sunlight into his eyes as he turned it curiously. No, it was too big and much too pretty to be of value, Bazo decided.

'Bazo! *Checha!*' Bakela was calling him. 'Come on, let's go where we can eat and sleep.'

Bazo dropped the stone into the leather pouch at his waist and scrambled up out of the open fissure. Already the file of Matabele workers led by Zouga were plodding away through the mud, each of them bowed under a bundle of spades or picks, one of the big leather buckets or a coil of sodden muddy rope.

'He has the lives of six men on his hands. I was there, I saw it all happen. He drove his team into Mark Sanderson's gravel bucky.' The accuser was a tall digger with a huge shaggy head of greying hair, heavy shoulders and heavier paunch. He was working himself up into a boil of righteous indignation, and Zouga saw that it was infectious, the crowd was beginning to growl and surge restlessly around the wagon body.

The New Rush Diggers' Committee was in public session. Ten minutes previously they had formed themselves into a Board of Enquiry into the cave-in of No. 6 Roadway.

A wagon had been dragged into the centre of Market Square to provide a platform for their deliberations, and around it was a solid packed crowd of diggers from the No. 6 Section. Since the cave-in, they had not been able to get back into the diggings to work their claims and they had just come from the mass funeral of the six men that had been crushed to death by the treacherous yellow gravel. Most of them had begun the wake for their mates and were carrying uncorked green bottles.

Mixed with the diggers were all the loafers of New Rush, the transport riders and merchants; even the kopje-wallopers had closed their offices for the meeting. This was something that affected all their futures directly.

'Let's have a look at the little blighter,' somebody yelled out at the back of the crowd, and there was a menacing growl of agreement.

'Right, let's see him.'

Zouga stood beside the tall back wheel of the wagon, hemmed in by the press of bodies, and he glanced at Ralph who stood at his shoulder. He no longer had to look down at his son, their eyes were on a level.

'I'll go up and face them,' Ralph whispered huskily. Under the dark tan, his skin was grey and his eyes dark green and worried. He knew as well as Zouga did how grave was his position: he was to be tried by a mob that was angry and vindictive and mostly filled with cheap liquor.

The collapse of the roadway had destroyed the value of their claims. They could no longer get the gravel out; their claims were isolated, cut off from ground level, and they were spoiling to place the blame and extract vengeance. That vengeance would be brutal.

Ralph put one hand on the spokes of the wagon wheel, ready to climb up onto the wagon body where the dozen members of the Committee were already waiting.

'Ralph.' Zouga stopped him with a hand on his arm. 'Wait here.'

'Papa—' Ralph began to protest quietly, the fear still dark in his eyes.

'Stay,' Zouga repeated softly, and vaulted up onto the wagon body lightly.

He nodded briefly to the members of the Committee and then turned to face the mob. He was bare-headed, his beard catching the sunlight and jutting aggressively as he placed his clenched fists on his hips and set his feet easily apart.

'Gentlemen,' he said, and his voice carried clearly to the last row of the crowd, 'my son is only sixteen years old. I am here to answer for him.'

'If he's old enough to kill six men, then he's old enough to face the music himself.'

'He killed nobody,' Zouga answered coldly. 'If you look to place the blame, then put it on the rain. Go down to the pit, and you will see where it undercut the bank.'

'He started fighting,' the shaggy-headed accuser bellowed. 'I saw him use his whip on Mark Sanderson.'

'There is a fight on one of the causeways every hour of every day,' Zouga shot at him. 'I've seen you throwing punches out there, and getting your arse whipped at that.'

There was a ripple of laughter, a lightening of the mood, and Zouga took his advantage.

'In the name of all that's holy, gentlemen, there is not one of us here who does not protect his rights. My son was doing that, against a man older and stronger than himself, and if he's guilty for that, then so are all of you.'

They liked that, liked being told they were tough and independent, proud of being hard fighters and hard livers.

'Are you telling me that one boy with a trek whip brought down the No. 6 causeway all on his own? If so, then I'm proud that boy is my son.'

They laughed again, and on the wagon behind Zouga the tall blond untidily dressed man with the cleft chin and pale blue eyes smiled thoughtfully and murmured to the Committee member beside him.

'He's good, Pickling,' using Neville Pickering's familiar nickname. 'He talks as well as he writes, and that's well enough.'

'No, gentlemen,' Zouga changed pace. 'That causeway was a death-trap, ready to go off before the first gravel bucky went out on it Friday morning. The collapse was nobody's fault; we had just dug too deep, and there was too much rain.'

Heads were nodding now, their expressions concerned and grave as Zouga went on.

'We are too deep on the New Rush, and unless we work out a new system of getting the stuff out of our claims, then there are going to be a lot more dead men for us to bury.'

Zouga glanced down as one of the diggers shouldered his way through the crowd and climbed up onto the disselboom of the wagon.

'Now you pay attention, you bunch of dirt-hounds,' he yelled.

'The chair acknowledges Mister Sanderson,' Neville Pickering murmured sarcastically.

'Thanking you, Guv.' The digger lifted his battered Derby hat, finery that he had donned especially for this meeting, then turned and scowled at the crowd. 'This nipper of Zouga Ballantyne's is going to be a bad one to mess with, and a good one to have at your side when things get hard.' Still scowling, he turned and called to Ralph. 'You come up here, young Ballantyne.'

Still pale and worried, Ralph hung back, but rough hands pushed him forward and hoisted him onto the wagon.

The digger had to reach up to put his arm around Ralph's shoulder.

'This boy could have let me drop into the pit like a rotten tomato, and squash the same way when I hit the bottom.' He made a vaguely obscene squelching sound with his lips to illustrate his own demise. 'He could have run and left me, but he didn't.'

'That's 'cause he's young and stupid,' someone called. 'If he had any sense he'd have given you a shove, you miserable bastard.'

There was a hubbub of cheers and hooted derision.

'I'm going to buy this boy a drink,' announced Sanderson belligerently.

'That will be some sort of record. You ain't never bought nobody a drink yet.'

Sanderson ignored them haughtily. 'Just as soon as he turns eighteen, I'm going to buy him a drink.'

The meeting started to break up in a storm of friendly catcalls and laughter, the diggers streaming away across the square to the canteens.

It was obvious to even the most bloody-minded of them that there wasn't going to be a lynching, and hardly any of them bothered to wait for the Committee's verdict. It was more important to get a good place at the bar.

'Which doesn't mean we approve of your behaviour, young man,' Pickering told Ralph severely. 'This isn't Bultfontein or Dutoitspan. Here on New Rush we try to set an example to the other diggings. In future, do try and behave like a gentleman. I mean fists are one thing, but whips—' He raised one eyebrow disdainfully and turned to Zouga. 'If you have any ideas about how we are going to work the No. 6 area now that the causeway has gone, we'd like to hear them, Major Ballantyne.'

Hendrick Naaiman would have called himself a 'Bastaard', and would have used the term with a deep sense of pride. However, the British Foreign Office had found the word awkward, possibly the double 'A' in the spelling offended the proper order of official correspondence and treaties, especially if one of those treaties should ever be laid for signature before Queen Victoria. So the nation was now referred to as Griqua, and the land on which New Rush stood was renamed Griqualand West, a definition which made it easier for Whitehall to champion old Nicholaas Waterboer, the Bastaard captain's claim to the area, over that of the Boer presidents of the backveld republics which also claimed the area as part of their dominions.

It was remarkable how before the discovery of the bright stones nobody, and especially not Great Britain, had shown the slightest interest in this desolate and arid plain, no matter what it was called.

In Hendrick Naaiman's veins flowed the rich intermingled blood of numerous peoples.

Its basis was that of the Hottentot, the sturdy golden-skinned, dark-eyed people who had met the first Portuguese circumnavigators of the globe when they stepped onto the gleaming white beach sands of Good Hope.

Added to the Hottentot was the blood of the captured yellow bushman girls. Tiny doll-like creatures whose buttery yellow skins and dainty triangular faces with orientally slanted eyes and flattened pug features were only part of their attraction. To a people who regarded a large female posterior as a mark of beauty, the buttocks of the bushmen girls were irresistible, a bountiful double bulge that stood out behind them like the hump of a camel – and in the arid deserts of the Kalahari served the same purpose.

To this blood mixture was added the contribution of outcast Fingo and Pondo tribesmen, fugitives from the wiles of their own cruel chiefs and merciless witchdoctors, and Malayan slaves, escaped from their Dutch burgher masters, who had found their way through the secret passes of the mountains that defended the Cape of Good Hope like the turreted walls of a great castle. They also joined the bands of wandering Griquas on the vast plains of the interior.

This blood mixture was compounded with that of little English girls, orphaned survivors of shipwrecked East India men that had perished on the treacherous rocks scoured by the Agulhas current, and taken to wife at puberty by their darker-skinned rescuers. And there was other northern blood, that of British seamen, pressed into the Royal Navy's service in the time of Napoleon's wars and desperate to exchange that harsh duty even for the life of deserter in such a wild and desert land as Southern Africa. Others had fled into the same wilderness, escaped convicts from the transport ships that had called at Good Hope to reprovision for the long eastern leg of the voyage to Australia and penal settlement of Botany Bay.

Then came travelling Jewish pedlars, Scottish missionaries taking God's injunction 'Be fruitful' as their text for the day – riders on commando, collecting slaves and taking others of the traditional spoils of war in a dusty donga or behind a thorn bush under the inscrutable African sky. The old hunters had passed this way at the century's turn, and had paused in their pursuit of the great elephant herds to take on more tender game at closer range.

These were Hendrick Naaiman's ancestors. He was a Bastaard and proud of it. He had dark gypsy ringlets that dangled to the collar of his tanned buckskin jacket. His teeth were square and strong and starred with tiny white specks from drinking the lime-rich waters of the Karroo wells since childhood.

His eyes were black as tarpits, and his toffee-coloured skin thickly sown with the darker coin-like scars of small-pox, for his white ancestors had bestowed upon the tribe many of the other virtues of civilization: gunpowder, alcohol and more than one variety of the pox.

Despite the scarring, Hendrick was a handsome man, tall, broad shouldered, with long powerful legs, flashing black eyes and a sunny smile. He squatted across the fire from Bazo now, with his wide-brimmed hat still on his head; the ostrich feathers nodded and swirled above the flat crown as he gestured widely, laughing and talking persuasively.

'Only the ant-bear and the meercat dig in the earth for no reward more than a mouthful of insects.' Naaiman spoke in fluent Zulu, which was close enough to their own tongue for the Matabele to follow him readily. 'Do these hairy white-faced creatures own all the earth and everything upon and beneath it? Are they then some kind of magical creature, some god from the heavens that they can say to you "I own every stone in the earth, every drop of water in the—"' Hendrick paused, for he was about to say oceans, but he knew that his audience had never seen the sea, '" – every drop of water in the rivers and lakes."'

Hendrick shook his head so that the ringlets danced on his cheeks. 'I tell you then to see how, when the sun burns away their skin, the red meat that shows through is the same coloured meat as yours or mine. If you think them gods, then smell their breath in the morning or watch them squatting over the latrine pit. They do it the same way as you or me, my friends.'

The circle of black men listened fascinated, for they had never heard ideas like these expressed aloud.

'They have guns,' Bazo pointed out, and Hendrick laughed derisively.

'Guns,' he repeated, and patted the Enfield in his own lap. 'I have a gun, and when you finish your contract you also will have a gun. Then we are gods also, you and me. Then we own the stones and the rivers also.'

Cunningly Hendrick used 'we' and 'ours', not 'me' and

'mine', although he despised these naked black savages as heartily as did any of the other bigots on New Rush.

Bazo took the stopper from his snuff-horn and poured a little of the fine red powder onto the pink palm of his hand, a palm still riven and scabbed from the rescue in No. 6 Section, and he closed one nostril with his thumb and with the other sniffed the powder deep, left and right, and then sat back blinking deliciously at the ecstatic tears before passing the snuff-horn on to Kamuza, his cousin, who sat beside him.

Hendrick Naaiman waited with the patience of a man of old Africa, waited for the snuff-horn to complete the circle and come into his own hands. He took a pinch in each nostril and threw back his head to sneeze into the fire, then settled into silence again, waiting for Bazo to speak.

The Matabele frowned into the living coals, watching the devils form and fade, the figures and faces of strange men and beasts, the spirits of the flames – and he wished they had counsel for him.

At last he lifted his gaze to the man across the fire, once again studying the laced velskoen on his feet, the breeches of fine corduroy, the Sheffield-steel knife on his brass-studded belt, the embroidered waistcoat of beautiful thread and velvet and the flaming silk at his throat.

He was without doubt an important man, and a rogue. Bazo did not trust him. He could almost smell the deceit and cunning upon him.

'Why does a great chief, a man of worth, like yourself, come to tell us these things?'

'Bazo, son of Gandang,' Hendrick intoned, his voice becoming deep and laden with portent, 'I dreamed a dream last night. I dreamed that under the floor of your hut lie buried certain stones.'

For a moment the eyes of every Matabele warrior swivelled from Hendrick's face to the mud-plastered floor at the back of the low, smoky thatched hut, the darkest area of the circular room, and Hendrick suppressed the smile that crowded his lips.

Treasure was always buried under the floor of the hut, where a man could spread his sleeping-mat over it at night and guard it even in his sleep. It had not been difficult to guess where, the only question had been whether or not the gang of Matabele had yet learned the value of diamonds and begun gathering their own, as every other gang on the diggings was doing. Those furtive, guilty glances were his answer, but he let no trace of satisfaction show as he went on quietly.

'In my dream I saw that you were cheated, that when you took the stones to the white man, Bakela, he gave you a single gold coin with the head of the white queen upon it.' Hendrick's broad handsome face darkened with melancholy. 'My friend, I come to warn you. To save you from being cheated. To tell you that there is a man who will pay you the true value of your stones, and that you will have a fine new gun, a horse with a saddle, a bag of gold coins; whatever you desire will be yours.'

'Who is this man?' Bazo asked cautiously, and Hendrick spread his arms and for the first time smiled.

'It is me, Hendrick Naaiman, your friend.'

'How much will you give? How many white queens for these stones?'

Hendrick shrugged. 'I must see these stones. But one thing I promise, it will be many, many times more than the single coin that Bakela will give you.'

Again Bazo was silent.

'I have a stone,' he admitted at last. 'But I do not know if it has the spirit you seek, for it is a strange stone, like none other we have ever seen.'

'Let me see it, my old friend,' Hendrick whispered encouragingly. 'I will give you the advice of a father to his favourite son.'

122

Bazo took the snuff-horn and turned it over and over between his fingers, the muscles in his shoulders and arms bulged and subsided and his smooth regular features, knitted now in thought, seemed to be carved from the wood of the wild ebony.

'Go,' he said at last. 'Return when the moon sets. Come alone, without a gun, without a knife. And know you that one of my brothers will stand always at your back ready to drive the blade of his assegai out of your breastbone if you so much as think a treacherous thought.'

When Hendrick Naaiman crawled through the low doorway again it was past midnight; the fire had sunk to a puddle of ruddy ash, the smoke swirled like grey phantoms in the light of the bull's-eye lantern he carried, and the naked blades of the short broad stabbing spears flickered blue and deadly in the shadows.

He could smell the nervous sweat of the men that wielded those dreadful weapons, and the vulture wings of death seemed to rustle in the dark recesses of the hut. Hendrick knew how close that dark presence could crowd about him, for frightened men are dangerous men. It was part of his trade, this ever-present threat of death, but he could never accustom himself to it, and he heard the quaver in his own voice as he greeted Bazo.

The young Matabele sat as he had last seen him, facing the single door of the hut, his back protected by the thick mud wall and his assegai at his side, the shaft ready to his hand.

'Sit,' he instructed the Griqua, and Hendrick squatted opposite him.

Bazo nodded to two of his men and they slipped away as silently as hunting leopards to stand guard in the starlight, while two others knelt at Hendrick's back, their assegais in their right hand, the points merely inches from his cringing spine.

There was the weird 'woo woo' call of a nightjar out in the starlight, clearly the signal for which Bazo waited; one of his Matabele assuring him that they were unobserved. Hendrick Naaiman nodded in approval, the young Matabele was clever and careful.

Now Bazo lifted into his lap a small cloth-wrapped package on which fresh earth still clung in little yellow balls. He unwrapped it swiftly and, leaning forward across the smouldering fire, placed the contents in Hendrick's cupped hands.

The big Griqua sat paralysed like that, his cupped hands before his face, his dark pock-marked features frozen in an expression of disbelief, of utter astonishment. Then his hands began to tremble slightly; and quickly he placed the huge glittering stone on the hard-packed mud floor as though it had burned his fingers, but his tar-dark eyes seemed to bulge from their deep sockets as he stared at it still.

Nobody spoke or moved for almost a minute, and then Hendrick shook himself as though he were waking from deep sleep, but his eyes never left that stone.

'It is too big,' he whispered in English. 'It cannot be.'

Then suddenly he was hasty; he snatched up the stone and dipped it and his hand wrist-deep into the calabash of drinking water which stood beside the fire; then, holding it up in the lantern light, he watched the great stone shed water as though it had been greased, as though it were the feather of a wild goose.

'By my daughter's virgin blood,' he whispered again, and the men watching him stirred darkly into the shadows. His emotions had infected them with restless excitement.

Hendrick reached for the side pocket of his buckskin

coat, and immediately the point of the assegai pricked the soft skin behind his ear.

'Tell him!' Hendrick blurted, and Bazo shook his head. The prick of steel ceased and Hendrick took from his pocket a shard of curved dark green glass, part of a shattered champagne bottle discarded in the veld behind one of the grog-shops.

Hendrick set it firmly on the floor of the hut, pressing the sharp points of glass into the clay. Then he closely examined the stone for a moment. One plane of the crystal had sheared through cleanly, leaving a sharp ridge around the rim, and the curved upper surface fitted neatly into Hendrick's cupped hand.

He placed the sharp ridge of the stone against the polished dark green curve of the broken bottle, then pressed down with the full strength of his right forearm and began to draw the edge across the glass. There was a thin abrasive screech that set his big white-starred teeth on edge, and behind the moving edge of the glittering stone a deep white groove appeared in the green glass, the stone had cut it as a hot knife cuts cheese.

Reverently the Griqua placed the stone in front of him, on the bare floor, and it seemed to be moving as the light played within its limpid depths, turned to magical stars of mauve and green and flaming crimson.

His voice had dried, his throat cleaved closed, he could barely breathe for iron bands of avarice had bound his chest, but his eyes glittered like a wolf in the firelight.

Hendrick Naaiman knew diamonds as a jockey knows fine horse flesh or a tailor the feel of good tweed cloth between his fingers. Diamonds were his salt, his bread, his very breath, and he knew that before him on the swept mud floor of this smoky little thatched hut lay something that would one day repose in the treasure house of the palace of some great king.

It was a living legend already: something that only a king could buy, something whose value, when converted to gold pounds or dollars, would stun even a rich man.

'Has this stone the spirit you seek?' Bazo asked quietly, and Hendrick swallowed before he could talk.

'I will give you five hundred gold queens for this stone,' he answered, and his voice was hoarse, ragged as though he were in pain.

His words struck the dark group of Matabele the way the east wind off the sea strikes the forests of Tzikhama, so that they swayed and rustled with the shock.

'Five hundred,' repeated Hendrick Naaiman. 'Which will buy you fifty guns or many fine cattle.'

'Give the stone to me,' Bazo ordered, and when Hendrick hesitated, the assegai pricked him again so that he started violently.

Bazo took the stone and stared at it broodingly, then he sighed.

'This is a heavy matter,' he said. 'I must think on it. Go now and return tomorrow at the same time. I will have an answer for you then.'

Long after the Griqua left, the silence persisted in the darkened hut, broken at last by Kamuza.

'Five hundred gold pieces,' he said. 'I long to see the hills of Matopos again; I long for the sweet milk of my father's herds again. With five hundred gold queens we could leave this place.'

'Do you know what the white men do to people who steal these stones?' Bazo asked softly.

'Not their stones. The Bastaard told us—'

'No matter what the yellow Bastaard told you, you will be a very dead Matabele if the white men catch you.'

'One man they burned alive in his hut. They say he smelled like a roasting joint of warthog meat,' one of the others murmured.

126

'Another they tied by his heels and dragged behind a galloping horse as far as the river. When they were finished, he no longer looked like a man at all.'

They thought about these atrocities a while, not shocked by them for they had seen men burned alive before. On one of the cattle raids to the east of Matabeleland their own regiment had chased two hundred Mashona men and women and children into the maze of caves that honeycombed the kopjes above their village.

It would have been a tedious task to hunt them out of the dark belly of the hills, so they had packed every entrance to the underground passages with branches of mopani trees and then put in fire. At the end some of the Mashona had run out through the flames, living torches of shrieking flame.

'Fire is a bad way to die,' said Kamuza, and uncorked his own snuff-horn.

'And five hundred pieces is a great deal of gold,' one of his friends answered him across the fire.

'Does a son steal the calves from his father's herd?' Bazo asked them, and now they were shocked indeed. To the Matabele the great herds of cattle were the nation's wealth, and the harsh laws and penalties that governed the management of the herds they had learned as part of their existence as '*mujiba*', the apprenticeship as herd boys which every Matabele boy must serve.

'It is death even to squirt the milk of another man's cow into your mouth,' Bazo reminded them; and they all remembered how they had taken that chance at least once in the solitude of the bush, spurting it directly from the teat so that it dribbled down their chins onto their naked chests – risking their lives for a mouthful of warm sweet milk and the respect of their peers.

'It is not a calf,' Kamuza reminded, 'but a single little stone.'

'Gandang, who is my father, looks upon the white man Bakela as a brother. If I take anything from Bakela, then it is as taking from my own father.'

'If you take this stone to Bakela he will give you a single coin. If you take it to the Bastaard he will give you five hundred.'

'It is a heavy matter,' Bazo agreed. 'I will think on it.' And long after all the others had curled on their reed sleeping-mats under the karosses of fur, he sat alone over the dying fire with the great diamond burning coldly in his right hand.

Three men rode into Zouga's camp that Monday morning, and Zouga stooped out of his tent to meet them, standing bareheaded in the sunlight.

Neville Pickering led the party, and as he stepped down from the stirrup, he said, 'I hope we do not disturb you, Major, but I'd like you to meet some friends of mine.'

'I know Mr Hayes.' Zouga shook the hand of the lanky Texan engineer and then turned to the third man.

'And of course I know Mr Rhodes by sight and reputation.'

Rhodes' hand was cool, the skin dry and the knuckles large and bony. It had the feel of strength, although his grip was quick and light. Zouga found the pale blue eyes on a level with his. The man was tall, and startlingly young, he could be very little older than twenty, young to have earned such a formidable reputation.

'Mr Rhodes.' Nobody, not even Pickering, used his Christian name. It was said he even signed his letters to his own mother 'Your affectionate son, C. J. Rhodes'.

'Major Ballantyne.' Zouga was startled again, for Rhodes had a slight voice, pitched high and with a breathless quality. 'I am delighted to meet you at last. Of course, I have read your book, and there are many questions I should like to ask you.'

'Jordan, take the horses,' Zouga called, and began to lead his guests towards the scant shade of the camel-thorn tree. But Rhodes paused as Jordan scurried from the tent, obedient to his father's order.

'Good morning, young Jordan,' he said, and the child stopped abruptly and stared up at him speechlessly, beginning to blush a deep pink with transparent hero-worship, overcome at being recognized and addressed by name.

'I see you have taken to reading rather than fisticuffs now.'

In his haste Jordan still carried a book in his hand. Rhodes stooped and took it from him.

'Good Lord—' he said, 'Plutarch! You have cultivated taste for one so young.'

'It's a fascinating book, sir.'

'Indeed it is, one of my favourites. Have you yet read Gibbon?'

'No, sir,' Jordan whispered shyly, the blush subsiding to leave him only faintly pink. 'I do not know where I could find a copy.'

'I will lend you one, when you have finished this.' He handed the battered dog-eared copy of Plutarch's *Lives* back to Jordan. 'Do you know where my camp is?'

'Oh, yes, Mr Rhodes.'

Every day of his life Jordan made a detour on his way back from his lessons in the church, a detour that passed the tented and thatched camp where Pickering and Rhodes kept a bachelor mess, and Jordan passed with dragging footsteps. Twice he had glimpsed his idol at a distance and each time overcome with shyness had scampered away.

'Good. Call in when you are ready for it.' For a moment longer he studied the angelic child, and then turned and followed the other men to the shade of the tree.

There were empty packing cases and logs to sit on, and

the four men arranged themselves in a casual circle. Zouga was relieved that it was too early to offer his guests liquor. He had barely sufficient money to buy food for his family, let alone to afford whisky, and he guessed that a bottle would not last long in this company; all three guests were drinking men.

They sipped coffee and swapped the news of the settlement for a few minutes before Pickering brought up the real business of their visit.

'There are only two schemes we have come up with to get the No. 6 area back to work,' he said. 'The first is the ramp—'

'I'm against that,' Rhodes said brusquely, impatiently. 'Within months we'll be back at the same problem – just too damned deep!'

'I would agree with Mr Rhodes,' said Hayes, the engineer. 'At best it would be only a temporary measure. Then the ramp itself would start collapsing.'

'Major Ballantyne's idea is the only one worth considering,' Rhodes cut in, and Zouga was struck forcibly by the man's manner of cutting through unnecessary discussion and getting to the core of a problem. 'The idea of building stagings on the rim of the workings, and running wires to the floor of the diggings is the only one that will beat the problem of depth. Hayes, here, has done some drawings.'

The engineer unrolled the plans he carried, spread them on the dusty earth at his feet and anchored the corners with diamondiferous pebbles from Zouga's tailing dump which had spilled into and was threatening to engulf the entire camp.

'I have considered a cantilever design.' Hayes began to explain the drawings in crisp technical terms, and the others moved their seats closer and bowed over the plans. 'We will have to use hand winches, and perhaps horse whims, until we can get a steam engine to do the haulage.'

They discussed it quietly, asking penetrating questions

and, when the answers were obscure, cutting them down with sharp minds and quick words. There was no waste of words, no repetitions, no drawn-out discussion and the work went swiftly.

The stagings would be tall scaffoldings built on the edge of the pit, and they would house the haulage winches.

'We will have to use steel hawsers. Manila will never do the job,' Hayes told them. 'There will have to be a single wire to each individual claim. A lot of wire.'

'How long to get it out?'

'Two months to Cape Town.'

'How much is this going to cost?' Zouga asked the questions which had been burning his lips all morning.

'More than any of us can afford,' smiled Pickering. A man with a thousand guineas in his pocket was a rich man on New Rush in these days.

'What we cannot afford is not to do it,' Rhodes answered him without a smile.

'What about those diggers who cannot afford their share of the stagings?' Zouga persisted, and Rhodes shrugged.

'Either they find the money, or they will not have a wire down to their claims. From now on it's going to take capital to work a claim on New Rush.'

'Those who haven't got it will have to sell out – it's as easy as that.'

'Since the cave-in the price of claims in the No. 6 has dropped to £100,' Zouga said. 'Anybody who sells now is going to take a hell of a knock.'

'And anybody who buys at £100 is going to make a killing,' Rhodes answered him, and lifted his pale blue eyes from Hayes' plans, and for a moment held Zouga's gaze significantly. He was giving advice, Zouga realized, but what impressed Zouga was the strength and determination behind that level gaze. He no longer wondered why somebody so young commanded such widespread respect on the diggings.

'Are we all agreed, then?' he asked.

With less than twenty pounds cash in the world and his claims cut off eighty feet below ground level and partially covered by the earth fall of the roadway, Zouga hesitated.

'Major Ballantyne.' They were all looking at him. 'Are you in?'

'Yes,' he nodded firmly. 'Count me in.' He would find the money, somewhere, somehow.

They all relaxed, and Pickering chuckled. 'It's never easy to play it all on one card.' He understood.

'Pickling, didn't I hear your saddle-bag clink when you dismounted?' Rhodes asked, and Pickering laughed again and went to fetch the bottle.

'Cordon Argent,' he said as he pulled the cork. 'The right juice for such an occasion, gentlemen.'

They swished the coffee grounds from their mugs and held them out for a dram of the cognac.

'The No. 6 stagings – fast may they rise and long may they stand!' Pickering gave them the toast, and they drank together.

Hayes wiped his whiskers with the back of his hand and stood up. 'I'll have the quantities ready to send off on the noon coach tomorrow,' he said, and hurried to his mount. Men who worked for Rhodes were always in a hurry. But neither Pickering or Rhodes moved to follow him.

Instead, Rhodes stretched out his long legs in the stained white cricket flannels and crossed his dusty riding boots at the ankles, at the same time offering his coffee mug to Pickering.

'I'll be damned if we don't have something else to celebrate this day,' he said as Pickering glugged cognac into their mugs.

'The Imperial Factor,' Pickering suggested.

'The Imperial Factor,' Rhodes agreed, and when he smiled the cleft in his smooth chin deepened and the melancholy line of his full lips under the fair moustache relaxed. 'Even this awful creature Gladstone has not been able to halt the march of Empire northwards through Africa. The Foreign Office has moved at last. The Griquas are to be recognized as British subjects, and Waterboer's request has been granted. Griqualand West is to become part of Cape Colony, and of the Empire. We have Lord Kimberley's assurance on it.'

'That's wonderful news,' Zouga interrupted.

'You think so?' The pale blue eyes sought and held Zouga's.

'I know it to be so,' Zouga told him. 'There is only one way to bring peace and civilization to Africa and that is under the Union Jack.'

Immediately there was a relaxation of the relationship between the three men, an unspoken accord, so that even without moving they seemed to have drawn closer, and their talk was easier, more intimate.

'We are the first nation in the world and anything less than our total duty is unworthy of us,' Zouga went on, and Rhodes nodded. 'We destroyed the slave trade on this continent; that was only a beginning. When you have seen the conditions that still exist, the savagery and barbarism, to the north of us, only then can you appreciate how deep that duty still is.'

'Tell me about the hinterland,' Rhodes demanded in that thin, almost querulous voice that so ill-suited his big loose-knit frame.

'The hinterland.' It was an unusual term, but it stuck like a burr, and Zouga heard himself use it as he described that wilderness through which he had travelled and hunted and prospected.

Rhodes sat on a log of firewood, the shaggy leonine head sunk forward, brooding and silent, only his eyes quick and attentive, listening with an almost religious fervour, rousing himself every few minutes, lifting his head to ask a question and then letting it sink again to the answer.

Zouga spoke of the wide slow rivers that ran in their deep valleys where the cream of tartar trees grew upon the banks and in the green shallows herds of hippopotamus challenged the traveller with gaping pink mouths and curved white tusks.

He described the deadly malarial swamps, vast stands of papyrus reeds swaying like dancers from horizon to horizon, where the sky pressed down, smothering the world under a heavy blue blanket sodden with steamy vapours, and he told of the relief of climbing the steep rocky escarpments to the cool high plateau of golden grasslands.

With words he showed them the vast and empty spaces, the plains dotted with moving herds of wild game, the cool green forests of standing timber, the streams of sweet water, crystal cold, from which a man could water his herds or his homestead.

He talked of vanished kingdoms of long dead kings, the Mambo and the Monomatapa, who had built cities of massive grey stone and left them to the smothering vines – their idols thrown down and shattered, the foundations of the walls menaced by the twisted grey python roots of the wild fig trees which found the joints in the stonework and forced them inexorably apart.

He told them of the square mine shafts that these vanished people had driven into the matrix and then abandoned, leaving the gold-bearing quartz where they had piled it before they fled.

'Visible gold,' he told them, 'thick as butter in the reef. Lying out there in the bush.'

He spoke of the people, the remnants of the subjects of the Monomatapa, their glories long past, decimated by war. He told them of the conquerors, the Matabele, the cruel legions from the south, calling the subservient tribes 'cattle' and, contemptuously, 'Mashona – eaters of dirt', taking them as slaves, killing them as sport, to prove their manhood, or merely on the king's whim.

He described the wealth of the Matabele, their uncount-able herds of cattle, thousands upon tens of thousands of fine beasts, glossy hump-backed bulls whose blood lines ran back to Egypt and the land between the Tigris and Euphrates, big rangy animals with widespread horns and hides of every colour from unrelieved black to purest white.

He told them of deep and secret caverns in the hills where the priests of the vanished kings still conducted their mysteries and sustained the oracle, weaving a gossamer net of witchcraft and magic which enfolded even their proud and arrogant Matabele overlords.

Then, as the day wasted away and the sun began to set behind a flaming curtain of red dust, Zouga told them of the kraals of the Matabele, the impis trained into the most merciless killing machine Africa had ever brought forth, racing barefoot into battle behind their tall rawhide shields, the plumes nodding and streaming from their dark heads and the dazzle of their assegais lighting the plains as the stars light the night sky.

'How would you fight them, Ballantyne?' Rhodes fired the question harshly, and it checked Zouga in full lyrical flow. They stared at each other for a moment, but a moment that was fraught with portent, a moment in which the lives of many thousands – black men and white – teetered in the balance. Then slowly the arm of the balance came down on one side, and the destiny of a continent moved, like a fiery planet shifting its orbit through the universe.

'I would thrust for the heart,' Zouga said, suddenly his eyes cold and green, 'a small mobile force of mounted men—'

'How many men?'

And suddenly they were talking war as the sun fell below the dusty mauve and purple plain, leaving the sinister shadows to draw in around the little group under the camel-thorn tree.

Jan Cheroot threw logs on the fire and they sat on in the ruddy wavering light and the talk was of gold and of war, diamonds and gold and war, Empire and war, and their words conjured columns of armed and mounted men from the night, dark phantoms riding into the future.

Suddenly Zouga checked in the middle of a sentence, his expression changed as though he had seen a ghost or recognized an old implacable enemy in the shadows under the camel-thorn tree.

'What is it, Ballantyne?' Rhodes asked sharply, swivelling the big untidy head to follow the direction of Zouga's gaze.

Against the bole of the thorn tree stood the tall green soapstone bird-statue. Unnoticed until now, hidden by the welter of harness and loose equipment that festooned the branches around it, some trick of the flames, the fall and flare of one of the burning logs, had illuminated it with sudden and dramatic firelight.

It stood taller than the seated men, seeming to preside over their counsels, listening to and directing the talk of gold and of blood. The falcon head, timeless as evil itself, as ancient as the hills of the far land from which it had been hewn, stared back at Zouga with sightless, yet somehow all-seeing, blank eyes, the cruel curve of the beak seemed on the point of opening to emit the falcon's hunting cry – or to bury itself in living flesh. To Zouga it seemed that in the darkness above the statue the words of the prophecy, spoken so long ago in that deep cavern of the Matopos hills by the beautiful naked witch who was the *Umlimo* of Monomatapa, still persisted, hovering in the shadows like living things:

The stone falcons will fly afar. There shall be no peace in the kingdoms of the Mambos or the Monomatapas until they return. For the white eagle will war with the black bull until the stone falcons return to roost.

In his memory Zouga heard the words again, spoken by that silken voice, and they seemed to echo against the dome of his skull and fill the drums of his ears.

'What is it, my dear fellow?' Pickering repeated the question and something slithered along Zouga's spine and crawled upon the skin of his forearms so that the hair came erect and he had to shudder to free himself of it.

'Nothing,' he answered, huskily. 'It's nothing; a grey goose walked over my grave.' But he stared still at the statue and Rhodes followed his gaze.

'By Jove. Isn't that the bird you wrote about in the book?' Rhodes sprang to his feet.

Eagerly he strode to where it stood and paused before it for a long silent moment before he reached out and touched the head.

'What an extraordinary piece of work,' he said softly, and went down on one knee to examine the shark-tooth pattern that was carved into the plinth. In that attitude he seemed like a worshipper, a priest conducting some weird rite before the idol.

Again Zouga felt that superstitious flutter of nerves crawl like insects upon his skin, and to break the mood he called loudly for Jan Cheroot to bring a lantern.

In the lantern's beam they scrutinized the polished greenish stone, and as Rhodes ran his big large-knuckled hand over it his expression was rapt, the gaze of those strange pale eyes remote, like a poet hearing words in his head.

Long after Pickering and Zouga had returned to their seats by the log fire, Rhodes stood alone under the camel-thorn tree with the falcon – and when at last he left it to join them once more, his tone was brittle with accusation.

'That thing is a treasure, Ballantyne. It is unforgivable to leave it lying out under a tree.'

'It's lain in worse conditions for hundreds, perhaps thousands of years,' Zouga replied drily.

'You are right.' Rhodes sighed, his attention straying back to the bird. 'It's yours to do with as you wish.' And then, impulsively, 'I wish to purchase it from you. Name a price.'

'It's not for sale,' Zouga told him.

'Five hundred pounds,' said Rhodes.

The sum startled Zouga, but his reply was immediate.

'No.'

'A thousand.'

'I say,' Pickering intervened. 'You can pick up ten claims in No. 6 Section for that.'

Rhodes did not glance at him, but he nodded. 'Yes, you could, or Major Ballantyne could pay for his share of the new stagings with a thousand pounds.'

A thousand pounds. Zouga felt himself tempted. A thousand pounds would see him clear.

'No.' He shook his head. 'I'm sorry.' He felt he had to explain. 'It has become the household god, my personal good-luck symbol.'

'Good luck!' snorted Jan Cheroot from across the fire, and all three of them turned their heads in his direction. None of them noticed him sitting on the edge of the shadows like a wizened little yellow gnome.

'Good luck!' the Hottentot repeated scornfully. 'Since we picked up that verdamned bird we haven't seen a day's good luck.' He spat into the fire, and his phlegm sizzled and exploded in a little puff of steam. 'That bird has put blisters on our feet and rubbed the skin from our backs, it has broken the axles of our wagons and lamed our horses. It has brought us fever, and sickness and death. Miss Aletta died looking at that bird, and Jordie would have followed her if I hadn't thrown the verdamned thing out.'

'That's nonsense,' Zouga snapped sharply. 'That's an old Hottentot maid's superstition.'

'Ja,' Jan Cheroot challenged him hotly. 'Is it an old

138

Hottentot superstition that we are sitting in the dust of this hell-hole, swatting flies and rubbing empty bellies? Is it superstition that all around us they are pulling fat diamonds and we find only the droppings and manure? Is it superstition that the earth has fallen on our claims, and that it nearly swallowed Ralph? Is that your good luck that you boast the bird brings you, Master Zouga? If it is, then hear the words of old Jan Cheroot and take the thousand pounds that Mr Rhodes offers you; take it with both hands, and thank him for getting rid of that – that—' Jan Cheroot ran out of words and glared across the fire at the birdshape under the thorn tree.

'Damn me,' Pickering smiled. 'But you nag like a wife.'

None of them were surprised at the familiar address between servant and master. In Africa relationships like this were common; the servant considering himself to be part of the family with a voice in the affairs of the family, and his claim was accepted by all.

'Jan Cheroot has hated the idol since the day we discovered it.'

'Tell me about that day, Jan Cheroot,' ordered Rhodes brusquely; and Jan Cheroot puffed up visibly with self-importance. There were few things he enjoyed more than an important and attentive audience and a good story to tell them. While he made a show of packing his clay pipe with black Magaliesberg shag tobacco and lighting it with an ember from the fire, the two boys crept out of the tent drawn by the prospect of a story. They glanced cautiously at Zouga and, when he made no move to send them back, they were emboldened.

Jordie sat next to Jan Cheroot and leaned his curly golden head against the Hottentot's shoulder, while Ralph came diffidently to sit with the men beside the fire.

'We had been one year in the bush,' Jan Cheroot began, 'one year without seeing a civilized man, one year trekking and hunting—' And the boys settled down with delicious anticipation. They had heard the story a hundred times before and enjoyed each telling more than the last.

'We had killed two hundred great elephant since leaving the Zambezi river, and we had fought bad men and savages. Our porters had mostly deserted or died of disease and wild animals, our provisions were long finished, no salt, no tea, no medicine and little gunpowder. Our clothes were rags, our boots worn through and repaired with the wet hide of buffalo.

'It had been a killing journey, over mountains with no passes and rivers with no names, and ordinary men would long ago have fallen and the birds would have picked their bones white. Even we were tired and sick and we were lost. Around us, as far as our eyes could see, there was nothing but wild hills and bad bush through which only the buffalo could pass.'

'And you needed honey for your strength,' Jordie burst out, unable to contain himself, and knowing the story word perfect. 'Otherwise you would have died in the bush.'

'And we needed honey for our strength or we would have died in the bush,' Jan Cheroot agreed solemnly.

'Out of the bush came a little brown honey guide, and he sang thus—' Jan Cheroot imitated the high-pitched burring call and fluttered his fingers in an uncanny imitation of the bird. '"Come!" he called to us. "Come, follow me, and I will lead you to the hive."'

'But he wasn't a real honey-bird, was he, Jan Cheroot?' Jordie cried excitedly.

'No, Jordie, he wasn't a real honey-bird.'

'And you followed him!'

'And we followed him for many days through bad country. Even when Master Zouga, your father, would have turned back, old Jan Cheroot was firm. We must go on, I told him, for by this time I, who have a deep knowledge and understanding of ghosts and spirits, realized that this

140

was not a real honey-bird but a hobgoblin in the guise of a bird.'

Zouga smiled softly. He remembered the incident differently. They had followed the bird for some hours, and it was Jan Cheroot who had lost interest in the hunt and had to be prodded and cajoled to continue.

'Then suddenly—' Jan Cheroot paused and flung out both hands theatrically, ' – before our eyes, a wall of grey stone rose out of the bush. A wall so high it was like a mountain. With my axe I chopped away the vines and found a great gateway, guarded by fierce spirits—'

'Spirits?' Zouga smiled.

'They were invisible to ordinary eyes,' Jan Cheroot explained loftily. 'And I put them to flight with a magical sign.'

Zouga winked at Pickering, but Jan Cheroot ignored their smiles.

'Beyond the gateway was a temple yard, in which lay the falcon statues, cast down, some of them shattered, but all of them covered with heaps of gold, mountains of gold.'

Zouga sighed. 'Fifty pounds weight to be exact. Fragments and tiny pieces which we had to sift from the soil. How I wish it had been a mountain.'

'We gathered the gold from where it lay, and we took up that statue on our shoulders and carried it one thousand miles—'

'Complaining every step of the way,' Zouga pointed out.

' – Until we reached Cape Town again.'

It was after midnight when Jan Cheroot brought the saddled horses to the camp fire, and as Rhodes took the reins he paused in the act of mounting.

'Tell me, Major, this land to the north, this Zambezia as you call it in your book – what is it that keeps you from it? What are you doing here?'

'I need money,' Zouga told him simply. 'And somehow I know that the road to the north begins here. The money to take and hold Zambezia will come from the workings of New Rush.'

'I like a man who thinks big, a man who counts not in ones and twos but in tens of thousands,' Rhodes nodded approval.

'At this moment I count my fortune in ones and twos.'

'We could change that.' Rhodes shot a pale piercing glance towards the bird carving, but Zouga chuckled and shook his head.

'I would like first refusal,' Rhodes persisted.

'If I sell, it will be to you,' Zouga agreed, and Rhodes stepped up in the stirrup, swung a leg over the horse's rump, settled in the saddle and rode out of the camp.

Pickering edged his mount closer to Zouga and leaned down from the saddle to tell him seriously:

'He will have it from you – in the end he will have it.'

'I think not.' Zouga shook his head.

But Pickering smiled. 'He always gets what he sets his heart on. Always.'

He saluted Zouga with the hand that held the reins and then started his horse into a canter and followed Rhodes out onto the dusty starlit track.

'Give the stone to the yellow man,' Kamuza urged quietly. 'Five hundred gold queens, and we will return to our own people with treasures. Your father, the induna of Inyati, will be pleased, even the king will call us to the great kraal at Thabas Indunas for audience. We will become important men.'

'I do not trust the Bastaard.'

'Do not trust him. Trust only the yellow coins he brings.'

'I do not like his eyes. They are cold and he hisses like a yellow cobra when he speaks.'

They were silent then, a circle of dark figures in the smoky hut, squatting around the diamond as it lay on the clay floor and flickered with weird lights in the reflection of the fire.

They had argued since the sunset had released them from their labours. They had argued over the meal of stringy mutton with its rind of greasy fat and maize porridge baked until it was stiff as cake.

They had argued over the snuff-horn and beer pot, and now it was late. Soon, very soon, there would be a scratching at the door of the hut as the Bastaard came for his answer.

'The stone is not ours to sell. It belongs to Bakela. Does a son sell the calves from his father's herds?'

Kamuza made a clucking sound of exasperation. 'Surely it is against law and custom to steal from the tribe, from the elders of the tribe, but Bakela is not Matabele. He is *buni*, white man, it is not wrong doing to take from him any more than it is against law and custom to send the assegai through the heart of a Mashona dog, or to mount his wife in sport, or to take the cattle of a Tswana and put fire into his kraal to hear his children squeal. Those are natural and right things for a man to do.'

'Bakela is my father, the stone is his calf, given into my care.'

'He will give you a single coin,' Kamuza lamented, and Bazo seemed not to hear him.

He picked up the diamond again and turned it in his hand.

'It is a large stone,' he mused aloud, 'a very large stone.' He held it to his eye and looked into the stone as though it were a mountain pool, and he watched with awe the fires and shapes move within it.

Still holding it to his eye, he said, 'If I bring my father a newborn calf, he will be happy and give me a reward. But if I bring him one hundred calves how much greater will be his joy, and one hundred times greater the reward that he will give me.'

He lowered the stone and gave a series of orders that sent his men hurrying out into the night, to return immediately with the tools Bazo had sent them to fetch.

Then in silence they watched him make his preparations.

Firstly he spread a kaross of silver jackal pelts on the earth floor and then in the centre of the fur he placed a small steel anvil at which he had watched Zouga shaping horse-shoes and working the iron hoops to repair the wagon wheels.

On the anvil Bazo placed the diamond, and then he threw aside his cloak so that he stood stark naked in the firelight, tall and lean and hard, his belly muscles standing up in concentric ridges under the dark satiny skin and the wide rangy shoulders overdeveloped by practice with shield and spear.

With his legs braced wide, he stood over the anvil, and hefted the sweat-polished handle of the pick, feeling the balance and weight of the steel head that had become so familiar.

Bazo narrowed his eyes, measuring his stroke, and then he reared back with the pick almost touching the thatched roof. He drove his body weight into the stroke, and the steel pick head came hissing down from on high.

The point caught the diamond exactly on the high centre of its curved upper surface, and the great stone exploded as though a bucketful of mountain water had been dashed to the earth. The sparkling drops, the shattered fragments, the glowing chips of priceless crystal, seemed to fill the whole hut with a burst of sunlight.

They pattered against the thatched walls, stung the naked skins of the watching Matabele, kicked little puffs of grey ash as they fell into the fire, and scattered on the lustrous fur of the silver jackal kaross, shining there like live fish in the net.

'Son of the Great Snake,' hooted Kamuza joyously. 'We are rich men.' And the laughing Matabele flung themselves into the task of gathering up the fragments.

They picked them from the ashes, swept them up from the earthen floor, shook them out of the jackal skin kaross – and piled them into Bazo's cupped hand until it was filled to overflowing. Even then they missed some of the tiny chips that had fallen into the dust or the fire and were lost for ever.

'You are a wise man,' Kamuza told Bazo with unaffected admiration. 'Bakela has his stones – a hundred calves – and we will have more coins than the yellow Bastaard would give us.'

T here was no work in the collapsed No. 6 Section, no need to rise before dawn, so the sun was clear of the horizon when Zouga strode out of the tent, clinching his belt as he joined Jan Cheroot and the two boys under the camel-thorn tree.

The table was a packing-case, the lid stained with candle grease and spilled coffee, and breakfast was maize-meal porridge in chipped enamel bowls, unsweetened, for the price of sugar had recently risen to a pound a pound on the diamond fields.

Zouga's eyes were red-rimmed, for he had slept little the previous night, but had lain awake worrying and scheming, going over and over in his mind every detail of the plans for the new staging – and coming back each time to the most important detail, the one for which there seemed to be no solution: the cost, the enormous cost of it all.

The two boys saw his face, recognized his mood, and were immediately silent, applying themselves with

145

complete absorption to the unappetizing grey gruel in their bowls.

A shadow fell across the group, and Zouga looked up irritably, squinting into the early sunlight with the spoon half raised to his lips. 'What is it, Bazo?'

'Pick-ups, Bakela.' The tall young Matabele used the English words. 'Pick-ups.' Zouga grunted.

'Let me see it.' Zouga was immediately uninterested. Almost certainly it would be a worthless chip of quartz or rock crystal. But Bazo placed a small bundle wrapped in a dirty scrap of cloth beside Zouga's bowl.

'Well, open it,' Zouga ordered; and Bazo picked the knot, and spread the cloth.

'Glass!' thought Zouga disgustedly. There was almost a handful of it, chips and pieces, the biggest not much bigger than the head of a wax Vesta.

'Glass!' and he made the gesture of sweeping it away, and then stayed his hand as the sunlight fell on the pile and a shaft of it pricked his eyes in a rainbow burst of colours.

Slowly, disbelievingly, he changed the gesture of dismissal and reached hesitantly, almost reverently for the glittering heap, but Jordan forestalled him.

With a shriek of joy the child's small graceful fingers danced over the pile.

'Diamonds, Papa,' he screamed. 'They are diamonds, real diamonds.'

'Are you sure, Jordie?' Zouga asked the question unnecessarily, his voice hoarse, realizing it was too good to be true. There must be many hundreds of precious stones in the pile, small, very small, but of what superb colour, white, ice-white, seeming to crackle like lightning they were so bright.

Still hesitantly Zouga took one of the largest stones from Jordan's fingers.

'Are you sure, Jordie?' he repeated.

'They are diamonds, Papa. All of them.'

Zouga's last doubts faded, to be replaced immediately by a deeper uncertainty.

'Bazo,' he said. 'There are so many—' And then something else puzzled him. Quickly he picked out twenty of the largest stones and stood them in a row across the top of the packing case.

'The same colour, they are all the same colour, exactly!'

Zouga shook his head, frowning, confused; and then suddenly the shadows in his eyes cleared.

'Oh my God,' he whispered, and slowly all blood drained from his face, leaving the skin dirty yellow like a man ten days gone in malaria fever.

'The same; they are all the same. The breaks are clean and fresh.'

Slowly he lifted his eyes to Bazo's face.

'Bazo, how big—' his voice roughened and dried, so that he had to clear his throat, 'how big was the stone before – before you cracked it?'

'This big.' Bazo clenched and showed his fist. 'With my pick I made it into many stones, for you, Bakela, knowing how you value many stones.'

Zouga's voice was still a husky whisper. 'I will kill you,' he said in English. 'For this, I will kill you.'

The scar across his cheek turned slowly into an ugly inflamed weal, the stigmata of his rage, and now he was shaking, his lips trembling as he rose slowly to his feet.

'I will kill you.' His voice rose to a bellow, and Jordan shrieked again, this time with terror. He had never seen his father like this before; there was a terrifying maniacal quality about him.

'That was the stone I was waiting for, you bastard, you black bastard, that was it. That was the key to the north.'

Zouga snatched the Martini-Henry rifle from where it leaned against the bole of the camel-thorn tree beside the falcon carving. The steel clashed and snickered as he pumped a cartridge into the chamber and in the same moment swung up the barrel.

'I'm going to kill you,' be roared, and then checked.

Ralph had jumped to his feet, and now he faced his father, stepping forward until the muzzle of the loaded and fully cocked rifle almost touched the entwined brass snakes of his belt buckle.

'You will have to kill me first, Papa,' he said. He was as pale as Zouga, his eyes the same deep haunted green.

'Get out of the way.' Zouga's voice sank into that croaking, husky whisper and Ralph could not answer him, but he shook his head, his heavy jaw clenched so determinedly that his teeth grated audibly.

'I warn you, stand aside,' Zouga choked, and they stood confronting each other, both trembling with tension and outrage.

Then the muzzle of the heavy rifle wavered in Zouga's hands, lowered slowly until it pointed to the dusty red earth between the toes of Ralph's boots.

The silence went on for many seconds; then Zouga took a full breath and the barrel of his chest swelled under the faded blue flannel shirt.

With a gesture of utter frustration he hurled the rifle against the treetrunk and the butt snapped through. Then he sank back into his seat at the packing-case table and his golden head sank slowly into his hands.

'Get out.' All the fire and fury had gone from his voice; it was quiet and hopeless. 'Get out, all of you.'

Zouga sat on alone under the thorn tree. He felt burned out with emotion and anger, empty and blackened and devastated within, like the veld after fire has swept through it.

When at last he lifted his head the first thing he saw was the falcon squatting opposite him on its greenstone plinth. It seemed to be smiling, a cruel and sardonic twist to the predator's beak, but when he stared at it Zouga saw that it was merely a trick of shadow and sunlight through the thorn branches.

The kopje-walloper was a small man, with legs so short that his polished high-heeled boots did not touch the floor when he sat on the swivel piano stool behind his desk.

The desk filled most of the tiny galvanized-iron hut, and it was furnace-hot in the room; the heat quivered and danced down from the roof. On the raw deal planks of the desk stood the accoutrements of the kopje-walloper's trade. The whisky bottle and shot-glasses to mellow the man with stones to sell; the sheet of white paper on which to examine the goods for colour; the wooden tweezers, the jeweller's eye-glass, the balance and scales, and the cheque book.

The cheque book was the size of a family Bible, each cheque form embossed in gold leaf and printed in multi-colours, the border depicting choirs of heavenly angels, sea nymphs riding in half clam shells drawn by teams of leaping dolphins, the Queen as Britannia with helmet, shield and trident, twisting cornucopia from which poured the treasures of Empire and a dozen other patriotic symbols of Victorian might.

The cheque book was by far the most impressive item in the hut, not excepting the buyer's flowing silk Ascot tie and the yellow spats that covered his boots. It was unlikely that a digger would be able to refuse payment offered in such flamboyant style.

'How much, Mr Werner?' Zouga asked.

Werner had swiftly sorted the glittering heap of diamond chips into separate piles, grading them by size alone for each stone was of the same fine white colour.

The smallest stones were three points, three hundredth parts of a carat, barely bigger than a grain of beach sand, the largest was almost a carat.

Now Werner laid aside his tweezers and ran his hand through his dark locks.

'Have another whisky,' he murmured, and when Zouga refused, 'Well, me, I'm having one now.'

He poured both glasses full to the brim, and despite Zouga's frown pushed one across to him.

'How much?' Zouga persisted.

'The weight?' Werner sipped the whisky and smacked his thick liver-coloured lips. 'Ninety-six carats, all told. What a diamond it must have been. We will never see the likes again—'

'How much in cash?'

'Major, I would have offered you fifty thousand pounds, if that had been a single stone.'

Zouga winced and blinked his eyes closed for an instant, as though he had been slapped across the face with an open hand.

With fifty thousand pounds he could have taken Zambezia – money for men, horses and guns, money for wagons and bullock teams, machinery to mine the reef and mill the gold, money for the farms, the seed and implements. He opened his eyes again.

'Damn you, I'm not interested in what might have been,' he whispered. 'Just tell me how much you will pay for that.'

'Two thousand pounds; that's my top price, and it's not an "open" offer.'

The stone had splintered into almost two hundred chips. That meant a 'pick-up' payment to Bazo of that many sovereigns. Zouga would intensely resent having to make that payment, but he owed it and he would make it. Of what remained after paying Bazo, at least a thousand would go for his share of the new stagings on the No. 6 Section.

Eight hundred left, and it cost him a hundred a week to work his claims, so he had won himself two months. Sixty days, instead of a land. Sixty days instead of a hundred thousand square miles of rich land.

'I'll take it,' he said quietly, picked up the whisky glass and drained it. It burned away the bitter taste at the back of his throat.

Ralph's bird was a lanner, one of the true members of the family *Falco*, long-winged and perfect for hunting the open plains of Griqualand. At last, after many attempts, he had found her and taken her for his own, a falcon and therefore bigger than the male bird, which was not a falcon but a tercel or, in the case of a lanner, a 'lanneret'.

She was 'eyas', the falconers' term for a wild bird taken at the nest when almost full-fledged. Ralph had climbed to the nest high on the top branches of a giant acacia and brought the bird down in his shirt, bleeding where she had raked him with her talons across his belly.

Bazo had helped him fashion the hood and jesses of soft glove leather for the proud head, but it was Ralph who walked her on his hand, hour after hour, day after day, stroking and gentling her, calling her 'darling' and 'beauty' and 'lovely' until she would eat from his fist and greet him with a soft 'Kweet! Kweet!' of recognition when she saw him. Then he introduced her to the lure of stuffed pigeon feathers, teaching her to hit it as he swung it on its long cord.

Finally, in the traditional ritual of the falconer, he sat up all night with the bird on his fist and a candle burning beside him. He sat with her in the trial of wills which would prove his domination over her, staring into her fierce yellow eyes, in the candlelight, hour after hour, outlasting her until the lids closed over her eyes and she slept perched upon his fist and Ralph had won. Then at last he could hunt her.

Jordan loved the bird for her beauty, and once she was trained Ralph occasionally let him carry her and stroke the hot sleek plumage under his gentle fingers. It was Jordan who found her name. He took it from Plutarch's *Lives*, which he was re-reading, and so the falcon was named Scipio, but Jordan accompanied the hunt only once, disgracing himself irretrievably by bursting into tears at the moment of the kill. Ralph never invited him again.

The same rains that had undermined the No. 6 causeway had flooded every depression and vlei for a hundred miles around the New Rush diggings. Slowly, in the hot dry months since that deluge, the shallower pools and swamps had dried out; but five miles south on the Cape Road, halfway to the low line of blue Magersfontein hills, there was still a wide body of open water, and already reed-beds had grown up around its perimeter and colonies of scarlet and ebony bishop birds had woven their hanging basket nests on the nodding reed staffs. Amongst the reeds Ralph and Bazo built their blind.

They drew the long, leafy fronds down over their own heads, careful not to slice their hands on the razor-edged leaves; the fluffy white silks snowed down on them from the laden seed heads of the reeds, and they plaited the roof of stems in place, concealing themselves from the open sky.

Ralph scooped a handful of black mud and smeared it over his face. He knew that his white face turned upwards would shine like a mirror, catching the eye of even a high-flighted bird.

'You should have been born Matabele, then you would not need mud.' Bazo chuckled as he watched him, and Ralph made an obscene sign at him with his fingers before they settled down to wait.

It was fascinating to see how Scipio, blind under the leather hood, could still pick up the beat of approaching wings long before the men could see or hear them, and they were alerted by the set of her head and the anticipatory stretch of her talons.

'Not yet, darling,' Ralph whispered. 'Soon now, darling.'

Then Bazo whistled sharply and pointed with his chin.

Across the swamp, still two miles out, very high against the empty sky, Ralph saw them. There were three of them, big black wings curving on the downbeat in that characteristic unhurried, weighty action.

'Here they come, my love,' Ralph murmured to Scipio, and touched the russet-dappled breast with his lips and felt the beat of the fierce heart against his face.

'God, but they are big,' Ralph murmured, and the tiny shapely body on his arm was feather light. He had never flown her against geese before, and he was torn with doubts.

The V-shaped flight of geese went far out across the swamp in a leisurely descending circle and then they were coming back, low, flying into the sun. It was perfect. Scipio would have the sun behind her when she towered, and Ralph thrust his doubts aside.

He slipped the soft leather hood off Scipio's beautiful dove-grey head, and the yellow eyes opened like full moons, focusing swiftly. She shook out her feathers, swelling in size for a moment, puffing out her breast – until she saw the thick black skein of geese against the sky, and her plumage flattened, going sleek and polished, steely in the early sunlight, and she crouched forward on Ralph's wrist.

Turning with her to follow the flight of the geese, Ralph could feel the rapier points of her talons through the cuff of his leather gauntlet and sense the tension of the small neat body. She seemed to vibrate like a violin's strings as the bow is drawn lightly across them.

With his free hand he broke the quick-release knot that secured the jesses to Scipio's leg.

'Hunt!' he cried, and launched her, throwing her clear of the reed; and she went on high like a javelin, towering swiftly for the sun on wings shaped like the wicked blades of a pair of fighting knives.

The geese saw her instantly, and stalled back on great wings that were suddenly ungainly with shock. Their tight V-formation broke up as each bird turned away – two of them rising, driving hard for height while the third bird swung north again towards the river, dropped height steeply to pick up the speed he had lost in the initial stall of shock, and then levelled out low and winged hard, neck outstretched, webbed feet tucked up under his tail.

Scipio was still towering, going up on wings that blurred with speed and turned to golden discs in the early slanting sunlight.

Her tactics were those of the instinctive killer. She needed every inch of height that she could achieve. She needed it to exchange for speed when she began her stoop, her body weight was many times lighter than the huge birds she was hunting, and she had to kill with shock and speed.

Even as she went up her head was twisted to the side, watching, judging, as the game scattered away below her.

'Don't duck, my sweeting,' Ralph called to her.

There was very real danger of it, for though Scipio was hungry to hunt, she had never been flown against birds such as these. Geese were not her natural prey; nature had not equipped her for the shock of binding to something so massive.

As she climbed so the difference in size of hunter and hunted was emphasized; and then abruptly Scipio was at the height she judged sufficient and she hovered, ten beats of Ralph's own heart as he watched her standing in the air.

She was daunted, the game was too big, she was going to duck.

'Hunt, darling, hunt!' he called to her and she seemed to have heard him. She screamed that terrible death cry of the falcon, high and shrill and fierce, and then she folded her wings and dropped into her stoop.

'She's taking the low bird,' Ralph shouted his triumph; she was not going to duck, she had selected the goose that had dropped close to earth and was now crossing her front at an acute angle.

'There is the liver of a lion in that small body.' Bazo's voice was full of wonder as he stared upwards at the tiny deadly dart that fell against the blue.

They could hear the wind hissing through her half-cocked wings, see the infinitesimal movements of her tip feathers with which she controlled that terrible headlong plunge.

The goose flogged at the air, heavy, massive, black flashed with frosty white, its panic evident in every beat of its frantic wings.

The speed with which Scipio closed was chilling. Ralph felt the hair on the nape of his neck come erect as though an icy wind had touched him as Scipio reached forward with her steely talons.

This was the moment for which he and the bird had worked and trained so long. The supreme moment of the kill – an involuntary cry burst from his throat, a primeval and animal sound, as Scipio bound to the great goose and the sound of the hit was like a single beat of a bass drum that seemed to shake the very air about Ralph's head.

The goose's spread wings spun like the spokes of a wheel, and a burst of black feathers filled the air as though a shrapnel shell had been fired from a heavy cannon; and then the goose's body collapsed under the shock, one wing snapped and trailed down the sky as it fell, the long serpentine goose neck was arched back in the convulsion of death, and Scipio was bound to the gigantic black body, her talons locked deep into the still frantically beating heart. The impetus of Scipio's stoop had shattered bone in the big body and burst the pulsing blood vessels around the goose's heart.

Ralph started to run, whooping with excitement, and Bazo was at his shoulder, laughing, head thrown back, watching the birds fall, leaving a tracery of feathers like the plume of a comet in the sky behind them.

A hawk binds to its prey, from the moment of strike unto the earth. A falcon does not. Scipio should break, and let the goose fall, but she had not; she was still locked in, and Ralph felt the first frost of worry cool his excitement. Had his bird broken bone, or otherwise injured herself in that frightful impact?

'Beauty!' he called to her. 'Unbind! Unbind!' She could be caught under the heavy goose and crushed against the earth. It was not her way to hold on all the way in.

'Unbind!' he screamed again, and saw her flutter, stabbing at the air with those sharp-bladed wings. She was stunned, and the earth rushed up at her.

Then suddenly she lunged, unbinding, breaking loose from her kill, hovering, letting the goose go on to thud into the rocky earth beyond the swamp, only then sinking, dainty and poised, and settling again upon the humped black carcass. Ralph felt his chest choked with pride and love for her courage and her beauty.

'Kweet,' Scipio called, when she saw Ralph. 'Kweet,' the recognition call, and she left the prize that she had risked her life to take and came readily to Ralph's hand.

He stooped over her, his eyes burning with pride, and kissed her lovely head.

'I won't make you do it again,' he whispered. 'I just had to see if you could do it – but I won't ever make you do it again.'

Ralph fed the goose's head to Scipio, and she tore it to pieces with her curved beak, between each morsel pausing to stare at Ralph.

'The bird loves you,' Bazo looked up from the fire over which he was roasting chunks of fat goose, the grease dripping onto the coals and frizzling sharply. Ralph smiled, lifted the bird and kissed its bloody beak.

'And I love her.'

'You and the bird have the same spirit. Kamuza and I have spoken of it often.'

'Nothing is as brave as my Scipio.'

Bazo shook his head. 'Do you remember the day that Bakela would have killed me? In the moment that he took the gun to me he was mad, mad to the point of killing.'

Ralph's expression changed. It was many months since he had intervened to save the young Matabele from the wrath of his father.

'I have not spoken of it before.' Bazo held Ralph's eyes steadily. 'It is not the kind of matter about which a man chatters like a woman at the water-hole. We will probably never speak of it again, you and I, but know you that it will never be forgotten—' Bazo paused, and then he said it solemnly. 'I shall remember, Henshaw.'

Ralph understood immediately. 'Henshaw, the hawk.' The Matabele had given him a praise name, a thing not lightly done, a mark of enormous respect. His father was Bakela, the Fist, and now he was Henshaw, the Hawk, named for the brave and beautiful bird upon his wrist.

'I shall remember, Henshaw, my brother,' repeated Bazo, the Axe. 'I shall remember.'

Zouga was never entirely sure why he kept the rendezvous; certainly it was not merely because Jan Cheroot urged him to do so, nor the fact that the payment of £2,000 for the shattered chips of the great Ballantyne diamond had not lasted him as long as he had hoped, nor that the cost of the new stagings was rising all the time. His share looked to be more like two thousand than a thousand pounds. Sometimes in his least charitable moods Zouga suspected that Pickering and Rhodes and some other members of the committee were content to see the costs of the stagings rise and the pressure begin to squeeze out the smaller diggers. The going price of claims in the collapsed No. 6 Section continued to drop as the cost of the stagings rose; and somebody was buying, if not Rhodes and his partners, then it must be Beit or Werner, or even the newcomer, Barnato.

Perhaps Zouga kept the rendezvous to distract himself from these grave problems, perhaps he was merely intrigued by the mystery that surrounded it all, but when he looked at himself honestly it was more likely the prospect of profit. The whole affair reeked of profit, and Zouga was a desperate man. He had very little left to sell apart from the claims themselves. To sell the claims was to abandon his dream. He was ready to explore any other path, to take any risks, rather than that.

'There is a man who wishes to speak with you.' Jan Cheroot's words had started it, and something in his tone made Zouga look up sharply. They had been together many years and there was little they did not know of each other's moods and meanings.

'That is simple enough,' Zouga had told him. 'Send him to the camp.'

'He wishes to speak secretly, at a place where no other eyes will be watching.'

'That sounds like the way of a rogue,' Zouga frowned. 'What is the man's name?'

'I do not know his name,' Jan Cheroot admitted, and then when he saw Zouga's expression, he explained. 'He sent a child with a message.'

'Then send the child back to him, whoever he is. Tell him he will find me here every evening, and anything he has to discuss I will be pleased to listen to in the privacy of my tent.'

'As you wish,' Jan Cheroot grunted, and the wrinkles on his face deepened so that he looked like a pickled walnut. 'Then we will continue to eat maize porridge.' And they did not discuss it again, not for many weeks, but the worm was planted and it gnawed away at Zouga until he was the one who asked.

'Jan Cheroot, what of your nameless friend? What was his reply?'

'He sent word that it was not possible to help a man who refused to help himself,' Jan Cheroot told him airily. 'And it is clear to all the world that we have no need of help. Look at your fine clothes, it is the fashion now to have the buttocks hanging out of the pants.'

Zouga smiled at the hyperbole, for his breeches were neatly patched. Jordan had seen to that.

'And look at me,' Jan Cheroot went on. 'What reason do I have for complaint? I was paid a year ago, wasn't I?'

'Six months ago,' Zouga corrected him.

'I cannot remember,' Jan Cheroot sulked. 'The same way I have forgotten what beef tastes like.'

'When the stagings are completed—' Zouga began, and Jan Cheroot snorted.

'They are more likely to fall on our heads. At least then we won't have to worry about being hungry.'

Serious defects had shown up in the design of the stagings. They had been unable to support the weight of cable. The cables between them weighed over three hundred tons and they had to be stretched to sufficient tension to carry the gravel buckies without sagging excessively.

The very first day of operation the stagings at the north end of the section gave under the strain. Two winches tore loose and the wires fell twanging and snaking into the diggings. There had been a gravel bucky on the rope, carrying five black workmen down to the floor of the workings to begin re-opening the long deserted claims. They screamed the whole way down as the bucky spun and twisted, throwing them clear, and the tangle of snapping silver cables caught them up like the tentacles of some voracious sea-monster.

It took the rest of the day to bring out the fearfully mutilated bodies, and the Diggers' Committee closed the No. 6 Section again while modifications were made to reinforce the stagings.

The No. 6 Section was still closed.

Zouga had one bottle of Cape brandy left which he had been saving, but now he fetched it from his locker, pulled the cork with his teeth and poured into their two mugs.

He and Jan Cheroot drank in moody silence for a while, and then Zouga sighed.

'Tell your friend I will meet him,' he said.

P ale dust chalked the sky above the plain, so that the distances drifted away, dreamlike and insubstantial, to an indefinite horizon.

There was no living thing, no bird nor vulture in the milky blue sky, no ripple of flocks nor smoky drift of springbuck herds through the low scrub.

In this loneliness the little cluster of buildings stood forlorn, long deserted, roofs sagging and the adobe plaster falling from the walls in chunks exposing the unsawn timber frames beneath.

Zouga touched the reins and brought the gelding down to a walk, while he slouched in the saddle, riding with long stirrups and the disinterested mien of a man on a long and boring journey – but his eyes under the brim of the wide hat were quick and restless.

He was uncomfortably aware of the empty rifle scabbard under his right knee.

'Unarmed.' The invitation had been unequivocal. 'You will be watched.'

The man had chosen an ideal rendezvous. There was no approach to this deserted farmhouse except across miles of bare veld, no cover higher than a man's knee – and it was good shooting light, with the sun in the west. Zouga shifted his weight restlessly in the saddle, and the big ungainly Colt revolver under his coat dug into his side, a pain he did not resent – although the comfort it gave him was illusory. A man with a rifle could pick his shot and take his time as Zouga rode in.

The sheep kraal was part of the homestead, unplastered stone walls, and there was a well in front of the house, again with a stone coping. Beside the well lay the remains of a wagon, three wheels and the disselboom missing, the paint dried and cracked away, the weed growing up through the wagon bed.

Zouga touched the gelding's neck and he stopped beside the wagon. He dismounted swiftly, dropping off on the side farthest from the building, using the horse as cover, and while he made a show of adjusting the girth, he studied the empty building again.

The windows were dark empty holes, like missing teeth, and there could be an unseen marksman standing well back in the gloomy interior. The front door was blanched by the sun; Zouga could see the light through the cracks. It banged aimlessly and unrhythmically in the wind, and the wind hooted and moaned in the eaves and through the empty windows.

Behind the gelding's body Zouga loosened the revolver in his belt, making certain that it was ready to hand. He tied the gelding's reins to the wagon body with a slippery knot that would come undone at a tug, and then he consciously steeled himself, drew breath and squared his shoulders and stepped out from behind the horse.

He began to walk towards the front door, but his right hand was on his hip, under the tail of his jacket, almost touching the checkered grip of the revolver.

He reached the doorway, keeping clear of the entrance, and then flattened his back against the wall.

With faint surprise he realized that his breathing was rough, as though he had been running. Then another surprise – he was enjoying his own fear, the feeling of heightened sensitivity of his skin, the enhanced clarity of vision, the singing of the adrenalin in his blood, the nervous tension of his sinew and muscle, the awareness of being alive in the threat of death. He had been too long without this stimulant.

He placed one hand on the sill of the window and vaulted through it lightly, dropping to the earthen floor as he landed and rolling swiftly to his feet again in the corner, facing the room. It was small and empty, bunches of dusty cobwebs hung from the rafters, and the floor was scattered with the white-flecked droppings of gecko lizards.

Zouga moved down the wall, keeping his back covered, and stepped through into the second room. The kagel fireplace was blackened with soot, and the smell of dead ash caught in his throat. He looked through the open doorway into the sunlit sheep kraal beyond. There was a riderless horse tethered in the angle of the wall. A grey, dappled quarters, uncropped dark mane and full tail almost sweeping the ground. The rifle scabbard on the saddle was empty, and Zouga's nerves fizzed. The unknown rider must have the gun with him.

Zouga loosed the long barrel of the Colt revolver in his belt, peering out into the sunlight.

'Keep your hand away from that gun.' The voice came

from behind him, from the empty front room through which Zouga had just passed. 'Don't draw it, and don't turn around.'

The voice was quiet, controlled and very close. Zouga obeyed it, standing awkwardly with his right hand under his coat, and he felt the touch of steel between his shoulder blades. It had been well done; the man had been lying outside, had let him walk through the house and then had come in behind him.

'Now very slowly bring out the gun and put it on the floor between your feet. Very slowly, please, Major Ballantyne. I don't want to have to kill you, but if I hear the hammer cocked I will – believe me, I will.'

Slowly Zouga freed the heavy pistol and stooped to place it on the littered kitchen floor. He glanced back between his own legs and saw the man's feet. He was wearing velskoen of tanned kudu hide and leather leggings, big feet, big man, strong legs.

Zouga straightened up, holding his hands well away from his body.

'You should not have brought a gun, Major. That is very distrustful of you, and dangerous for both of us.' He could hear the relief in the man's tone, and the voice was familiar, he searched his memory. That strange accent, where had he heard it? The footsteps retreated across the kitchen.

'Slowly now, Major, very slowly, you may turn around.'

The man stood in the gloom of the soot-darkened walls, but the shaft of sunlight from the high window fell on his hands and the weapon they held.

It was a shotgun. Both big fancy hammers were at full cock, and the man's fingers were hooked around the triggers.

'You!' said Zouga.

'Yes, Major, me!' The pockmarked Griqua Bastaard smiled at him, white teeth in the darkly handsome face and the gypsy ringlets dangling to his collar. 'Hendrick Naaiman, at your service, once again.'

'If you are buying cattle, it's a hell of a way to do business.' The Griqua was the one who had bought Zouga's bullock team, the money he had used to buy the Devil's Own.

'No, Major, this time I am selling.' And then sharply, 'No, Major, do not move, and keep your hands there, where I can see them. I have loaded with Big Loopers – lion-shot, Major. At this range it will cut you in half.'

Zouga lifted his hands away from his sides.

'What are you selling?'

'Wealth, Major, a new way of life for you, and for me.'

Zouga smiled bleakly, sarcastically.

'I am truly grateful for your kindness, Naaiman.'

'Please call me Hendrick, Major – if we are to be partners.'

'We are?' Zouga inclined his head gravely. 'I am honoured.'

'You see, you have something I need and I have something you need.'

'Go on.'

'You have two excellent claims, they are truly excellent claims in all except they yield very few diamonds.'

Zouga felt the scar on his cheek heating up, but he kept his expression neutral.

'And as you know, Major, my ancestry, the touch of the tarbrush, I think is the polite term, or more succinctly my kaffir blood, precludes me from owning claims.'

They were silent then, regarding each other warily across the darkened kitchen. Zouga had abandoned any idea of going for the shotgun. He was starting to become intrigued by the articulate and persuasive voice of the tall Griqua.

'For that reason I cannot sell you my claims, not even at gunpoint,' Zouga said quietly.

'No, no, you do not understand. You have the claims but no diamonds, while I have no claims but—'

Hendrick drew a drawstring tobacco bag from his inner pocket and dangled it by its string from his forefinger.

' – But I have diamonds.' He finished the sentence and tossed the bag across the room.

Instinctively Zouga reached out one hand and caught it. The bag crunched in his hands like a bag of humbugs, bringing back childhood memories. He held it, staring still at Hendrick Naaiman.

'Open it, please, Major.'

Slowly Zouga obeyed, pulling open the mouth of the cloth bag, and then peered into it.

The light was bad, but in the bag something gleamed like the coils of a sleeping serpent.

Zouga felt the diamond thrill close its fist upon his chest. It never failed, he thought, always that choking feeling when the stones shine.

He tipped the bag and spilled a small rush of uncut diamonds into his hand. He counted them quickly; there were eight of them altogether.

One was a canary bright stone, twenty carats if it was a point. Two thousand pounds' worth, Zouga estimated.

'These are just samples of my wares, Major, a week's takings.'

There was another perfect eight-sided crystal, slick and soapy silver-grey, bigger than the yellow diamond, at least three thousand pounds' worth.

Another of the stones was a symmetrical triangular shape, like those throat lozenges that tasted of liquorice, more childhood memories. A clear silver stone, limpid and lovely. Zouga picked it up between thumb and forefinger and held it to the light of the high window.

'These are I.D.B?' he asked.

'Dirty words, Major; they offend my delicate breeding. Do not concern yourself further with where they come from, or how I get them. Just be certain that there will be more, many more, every week there will be a parcel of first-water stones.'

'Every week?' Zouga asked, and heard the greed in his own voice.

'Every week,' Hendrick agreed, watching Zouga's expression, and he knew the fly had touched the sticky strands of his web. He let the barrel of the shotgun sag towards the mud floor, and he smiled that flashing flamboyant smile. 'Every week you will have a parcel like this to seed into your own cradle, to throw out on your own sorting-table.'

There was another stone in his palm. At first Zouga had thought it to be black boart, the almost worthless industrial diamond; but his heart bounced suddenly as the poor light caught it and he saw the deep emerald colour flash from its heart. His fingers trembled slightly as he lifted it.

'Yes, Major.' Hendrick Naaiman nodded approval. 'You have a good eye; that's a green dragon.'

A freak stone, a green diamond, a 'fancy' in the parlance of the kopje-wallopers. There were fancy diamonds the colour of rubies, or sapphires or topaz, and fancies commanded whatever the trade would bear. It was not impossible that this green dragon would fetch ten thousand pounds, and end up in the crown jewels of an emperor.

'You said partners?' Zouga asked softly.

'Yes, partners,' Hendrick nodded. 'I will find the stones. Let me give you an example. I paid three hundred to one of my men for that green dragon. You put it across your table and register it from the Devil's Own—'

Zouga was staring at him fixedly, hungrily, his hands still trembling, and Hendrick stepped towards him confidently.

' – You should get four thousand pounds for a stone like that, a profit of three thousand seven hundred; and we share that fifty-fifty, because I am not a greedy man. Equal partners, Major, eighteen fifty for you and eighteen fifty for me.'

Zouga poured the glittering stones into his left hand. His eyes had not left Hendrick Naaiman's lips.

'What do you say, Major? Equal partners.' Hendrick transferred the shotgun to his left hand and reached out with his right.

'Equal partners,' he repeated. 'Let's shake hands on it.'

Slowly Zouga stretched out his own right hand, fingers open, palm upwards. And then, as their fingers touched, he hurled the handful of diamonds into Hendrick Naaiman's face. All Zouga's strength was behind the throw, all his anger at being so sorely tempted, all his outrage at this devilish assault upon his own self-esteem.

The diamonds tore into Hendrick Naaiman's flesh, one sharp-sided crystal ripped open his smooth olive-skinned forehead above the right eye, another sliced his lip.

Involuntarily Hendrick threw up his hands, lifting the shotgun muzzle high before his face as he staggered back from this unexpected assault, but at the same instant his right hand closed over the pistol grip and his forefinger hooked for the triggers. The gun was still at full cock, each barrel loaded with lion-shot. Hendrick started to drop the muzzles, pointing for Zouga's belly.

Zouga grabbed the barrel six inches below the gaping muzzles and forced the gun upwards, grasping with his left hand for Hendrick's right wrist. The big Griqua jerked backwards with both arms, and Zouga made no effort to resist him; instead he lunged forward, thrusting the gun into Hendrick's own face. The blue steel barrels cracked against his cheekbone, and Hendrick gasped at the blow and reeled backwards. Zouga drove at him again, forcing him into the soot-blackened wall so that he grunted with pain, pinned there for a moment with the shotgun pointing at the roof. In these seconds Zouga reached with his left hand, hooked his thumb through the trigger guard and jerked back against the triggers.

Both barrels fired simultaneously.

The burst of gunfire in the tiny confined kitchen was deafening. The bright orange muzzle flashes lit the gloom like a lightning strike, and the charges of shot crashed through the rotten roof, blowing gaping holes through which the sun shot long bright shafts of light.

The massive recoil of the double-shotted gun drove the butt back into Hendrick's own belly, and he doubled over with a gasp of shock and agony.

The gun was empty, harmless. Zouga let it go and dived full length across the dusty floor. At full stretch his fingers touched the cool checkered grip of the ugly black Colt revolver. As he fumbled for it desperately, he heard the light crunch of footsteps across the earthen floor behind him, and rolled right, flicking over on his back without raising his head.

Hendrick was over him, the empty shotgun raised above his head with both hands like an executioner's axe, and he had already launched the stroke. The gun swung down in a wide arc, the blue steel glittering sullenly in the gloom and the hiss of it like the sound of a goose's wing. Zouga rolled again flipping his body aside. But the butt of the shotgun caught him.

It was only a touch, high in the shoulder, but it jerked his head so that his teeth clashed in his skull, and his right arm was instantly nerveless, numb from his shoulder to fingertips. The Colt revolver went flying from his grip, spinning away across the kitchen floor until it hit the far wall.

Instantly Hendrick turned to chase the pistol, and Zouga kicked out at the back of his knee, landing solidly with the heel of his boot. Hendrick's leg folded under the blow, and he would have gone down but the wall was there to hold him. He fell against it, pinned for a moment by his crippled leg, and Zouga rolled to his feet.

He stabbed with his good left hand, feeling the solid shock of the Griqua's jawbone under his fist. Then again Zouga caught him with the left and heard the gristle in the beaky nose give with a crunch like chewing on a ripe apple, and the fresh blood from Hendrick's nostrils gave him a fierce joy.

He was going to beat this man to a bleeding pulp.

'Wait!' Hendrick shouted. 'Please! Don't hit me again.'

The appeal was so frantic, the terror on the Griqua's bloody face so pitiful, that even in his own cold killing anger, Zouga checked.

He stepped back and lowered his hands, and the Griqua hurled the empty shotgun at Zouga's face. It was completely unexpected, Zouga was off-guard, and even as he started to duck, Zouga knew it was too late, and he hated himself for a fool.

It felt as though somebody had slammed a door behind Zouga's eyes, and his vision was suddenly narrowed and dimmed with blood. He hurled himself forward, and dived again for the revolver. He got a hand on the barrel, and as he touched it the full weight of Hendrick's charging body crashed into his back, driving him into a heap against the doorjamb. But he still had a grip on the pistol barrel, and he struck out blindly using it like a club.

He felt the steel butt sock into flesh, and he hit again and again, some of the blows dying in the air, others thudding into the floor, but others cracking against bone.

He was sobbing and panting, blinded by his own blood, and for seconds he did not realize that Hendrick no longer clutched and tore at him.

Zouga shrank back against the wall and wiped the blood from his eyes. Then he peered like an old man through the red film. Hendrick was beside him. He was on his back, his arms flung wide as a crucifix and the blood snored and bubbled from his nostrils. He lay very still, his breathing the only sign of life.

Zouga lowered the pistol, and used the wall to hoist himself to his feet. He stood there swaying, his head hanging, the pistol dangling from his hand that was suddenly so weak that he could barely support its weight.

'Master Zouga!' Jan Cheroot dashed into the yard, panting from his run, carrying the Lee-Enfield rifle at high port across his chest, sweat streaking down from under his brimless pillbox infantry cap and his face crumpling with dismay as he saw Zouga's bloody torn face.

'You took your time,' Zouga accused him huskily, still clinging to the door for support. He had left Jan Cheroot with the rifle hidden in a ravine half a mile out across the dusty plain.

'I started running as soon as I heard the shots.'

Zouga realized that the fight had lasted only a few minutes, as long as it takes a man to run half a mile. Jan Cheroot unslung the water-bottle from his shoulder and tried to wash a little of the blood from Zouga's face.

'Leave that.' Zouga pulled away brusquely. 'See if there is a rope in the Bastaard's saddle bags, something to tie him, a knee halter, anything.'

There was a coil of braided rawhide rope on the pommel of the grey mare's saddle. Jan Cheroot hurried back with it and then paused in the door of the derelict shanty.

'I know him.' He stared at Hendrick Naaiman's bloody snoring face. 'I think I know him, but you made such a mess of him.'

'Tie him,' Zouga whispered, and drank from the water bottle. Then he unwound the silk scarf from around his throat and wetted it from the bottle before tenderly wiping away the blood and dust from his cuts and scratches.

The worst injury was in his hairline, where the breech of the broken shotgun had caught him; by the feel of it, it needed to be stitched.

Jan Cheroot was muttering insults and abuse at Hendrick Naaiman as he worked.

'You yellow snake.' He rolled the Griqua onto his back. 'You got shoes on your feet and pants covering your black arse, and you think you are a gentleman.'

He pulled Hendrick's arms up behind him and trussed them, quickly and expertly, at wrist and elbow.

'You'd give a vulture a bad name.' Jan Cheroot looped the rawhide around his ankles and pulled it up tight. 'Even the hyenas wouldn't eat dung alongside of you, my beauty.'

Zouga capped the water bottle and picked up the empty tobacco bag. Then he hunted for the diamonds. They had been kicked and scattered about the kitchen. The eighth and last was the green dragon, dark and inconspicuous in one gloomy corner.

Zouga tossed the bag to Jan Cheroot, and he whistled as he peered into it.

'I.D.B.,' he muttered, his wrinkled brown face puckering into a sculpture of pure avarice. 'The yellow snake was I.D.B.'

'He wanted us to run those stones across our sorting-tables.'

'What shares?' Jan Cheroot demanded, playing with the stones.

'Half shares.'

'That's a good deal. We could be rich in six months and get out of this god-damned and blasted desert for ever.'

Abruptly Zouga snatched the bag back again. He had been through the temptation once already.

'Get his horse,' he ordered angrily.

They hoisted the Griqua's inert body and threw it over the grey's saddle. As Jan Cheroot was tying the Griqua to the horse, Hendrick kicked his legs weakly and tried to raise his head, twisting his neck to peer blearily at Zouga.

'Major,' he croaked, only half conscious. 'Major, let me explain. You don't understand.'

'Shut your mouth,' Zouga growled at him.

'Major. I am not a thief, let me explain about those diamonds.'

'I told you to hold your mouth,' Zouga warned, and wrenched the Griqua's jaw open, roughly digging his thumbs into the sallow bloody cheeks; then he thrust the bag of diamonds into his slack mouth.

'Choke on your bloody diamonds, you thieving, treacherous bastard,' he told him grimly as he bound the man's mouth closed with his scarf, jamming the bag in place, while Hendrick squawked and rolled his eyes, jerking his head from side to side, his cries muffled and his spittle soaking the gay band of silk.

'That will keep you quiet until we get you in front of the Committee.'

Jan Cheroot sat up behind the trussed Griqua on the grey's back and followed Zouga on the gelding.

He sucked his teeth mournfully, sighed and shook his head.

'What a waste!' he grumbled just loud enough for Zouga to hear. 'That bag would take us back to the north.'

He rolled his eyes sideways at Zouga, but there was no reaction.

'The Committee is going to see this yellow bastard lynched anyway. He is as good as vulture breakfast already—'

Hendrick wriggled helplessly and snuffled through his swollen nose.

' – If we just did the job for them, nice and quietly, a bullet in the head, and leave him for his brothers and sisters, the jackals and the hyena, man, nobody will ever know.'

He glanced hopefully at Zouga again. 'What's in that bag will take us north again, as far as we want to go.'

Zouga kicked the gelding into a canter, and ahead of them the iron roofs and dusty tent cones of New Rush glowed ruddily in the slanting rays of the sunset. Jan Cheroot sighed, swatted the double-laden grey across the quarters and followed Zouga into the camp.

Pickering and Rhodes messed with a few other bachelor diggers directly beyond Market Square, at the edge of the main tailing dumps. There were two good spreading acacias to give them shade, and they had planted a hedge of milkbush around the cluster of iron huts and walled shanties.

Every member of the mess owned good claims and was recovering stones; he had to do so to afford the mess bills for champagne and old cognac that seemed to form the group's staple diet. One of them was the younger son of a belted earl, another was a baronet in his own right, although merely of the Irish aristocracy. Most of them were members of the Diggers' Committee, and their style had earned the group the title of 'The Swells'.

When Zouga rode into their camp, half a dozen of the Swells were lounging under the acacia trees, dining on Veuve Cliquot champagne, although the sun was still above the horizon, and wrangling amiably over the heavy wagers that they were placing against how many flies would settle on the sugar lumps that each had on the camp table in front of him.

Pickering looked up, his fair open features for once puckered in astonishment, as Zouga rode into the camp.

'Gentlemen,' Zouga announced grimly. 'I have something for you.'

He leaned out of his saddle and cut the thongs that secured Hendrick Naaiman's heels to the saddle girth of the grey mare, and then tipped him off the horse, letting him fall head-first into the dust in front of the seated group of Diggers' Committee members.

'I.D.B.,' Zouga told them, as they stared at him.

Pickering moved first. He jumped to his feet.

'Where are the diamonds, Major?' he asked.

'In his mouth.'

Pickering went down on one knee next to the Griqua, and he undid the scarf.

He worked the saliva-drenched bag out of Hendrick's broken mouth, and poured the contents onto the camp table amongst the flies and sugar lumps and champagne bottles.

'Eight,' Rhodes counted them swiftly, and looked immensely relieved. 'They are all there.'

'I told you not to worry. I bet fifty guineas on them all being there. Don't forget it.'

Pickering smiled at Rhodes and turned back to the Griqua, who was flapping around in the dust like a trussed chicken.

Pickering helped him solicitously to his feet.

'My dear fellow,' he asked. 'Are you all right?'

'He nearly killed me,' Hendrick bleated bitterly. 'He's a madman!'

'I told you to be careful,' Pickering agreed. 'He's not a man to trifle with.' He patted the Griqua's back. 'Well done, Hendrick; you did a good job.'

Then Pickering turned to Zouga. 'We owe you a little apology, Major.' He spread his hands and smiled winningly.

Zouga had been staring at him, unable to speak, his face so pale that his scratches and gouges stood out lividly. But now the scar under his eyes began to glow and he found his voice.

'A trap!' he whispered. 'You set a trap for me.'

'We had to be sure of you,' Rhodes explained reasonably. 'We had to know what kind of man you really were before we got you onto the Diggers' Committee.'

'You swine,' Zouga husked. 'You arrogant swine.'

'You came out of it with flying colours, sir,' Rhodes told him stiffly. He was not accustomed to being addressed in those terms.

'If I had fallen for your trap, what would you have done?'

Rhodes shrugged his heavy shoulders. 'The question doesn't arise. You acted like a true English gentleman.'

'You will never know how close it was,' Zouga told him.

'Oh yes, I do. Most of us here have been tested.'

Zouga turned to Pickering. 'What would have happened, a lynching party?'

'Oh, my dear fellow, probably nothing so theatrical. You just might have slipped on the roadway and taken a tumble into the diggings, or had the misfortune to be standing under a gravel bucky when the rope parted.' He laughed merrily, and the men at the table laughed with him.

'You need a glass of Charlie Champers, Major, or something stronger perhaps.'

'Do join us, sir,' cried another, making room for him at the table. 'An honour to drink with a gentleman.'

'Come along, Major.' Pickering smiled. 'I'll send for the quack to see to that cut on your head.'

Then Pickering stopped and his expression changed.

Zouga had kicked his feet loose from the stirrups and jumped down to face him. They were of an even height, both big men, and the group at the camp table was instantly enchanted. This would be more diverting than watching bluebottles settling on sugar lumps.

'By gad, he's going to bang Pickling's head.'

'Or Pickling his.'

'Ten guineas the elephant hunter to win.'

'I don't approve of brawling,' murmured Rhodes, 'but I'll take Pickling for ten.'

'I say, the other horse has run a fair chase already. I do think you might offer some odds.'

Pickering's smile had turned frosty, and he was on his toes, his fists clenched, and his guard half raised.

Zouga dropped his own guard and turned disgustedly to the group under the acacia.

'I've provided you with enough amusement for one day,'

he told them coldly. 'You can take your bloody diamonds, and your damned Committee and you can—'

There was a burst of clapping and laughing cheers to cover Zouga's outburst. Zouga swung back onto the gelding's back and kicked him into a gallop, and the ironical applause followed him out of the camp.

'I hope we haven't lost him.' Pickering lowered his fists and stared after Zouga. 'God knows, we need honest men.'

'Oh, don't worry,' Rhodes told him. 'Give him time to simmer down and then we'll square him.'

'Henshaw.' Bazo held the woven reed basket on his lap and peered into it mournfully.

'Henshaw, she is not ready to fight again so soon.'

They sat in a circle about the cooking fire in the centre of the thatched beehive. Ralph felt more at home here than in the tent under the camel-thorn tree. Here he was with friends, the closest friends he had ever known in his nomadic life, and here also he was beyond the severe and unrelenting surveillance of his father.

Ralph dipped into the communal three-legged black pot with his left hand and scooped up a little of the stiff fluffy white maize porridge. While he rolled it into a ball between his fingers he argued with the Matabele princeling opposite him.

'If it were you to decide, she would never fight again,' Ralph told him, and dipped the maize ball into the flavouring of mutton gravy and wild herbs.

'Her new leg is not strong enough yet,' Bazo shook his head.

Ralph popped the morsel and chewed as he talked. 'The leg is hard and bright as a knife.'

Bazo puffed out his cheeks and looked even more lugubrious, and on her perch in the shadows behind him Scipio, the falcon, shook out her feathers and 'kweeted' softly as though in sympathy with him.

Bazo's decision, although heavily influenced by Ralph's arguments and by the urgings of the other young Matabele, would be final. For it was Bazo who had made the original capture of the animal under discussion.

'Every night that she does not fight, we, your brothers, are the poorer,' Kamuza came in to support Ralph. 'Henshaw is right. She is fierce as a lioness and ready to earn us all many gold queens.'

'Already you speak and think like a white man,' Bazo replied loftily. 'The yellow coins fill your head day and night.'

'What other reason for that,' Kamuza shuddered slightly as he pointed at the basket, 'that thing. If it stings you, the spear of your manhood will shrivel like a rotten fruit until it is no bigger than the finger of a new born baby.'

'What a shrivelling that would be,' Ralph chuckled. 'Like a bull hippopotamus shrivelling into a striped field mouse.'

Bazo grinned and made the gesture of placing the tiny basket on Kamuza's lap. 'Come, let her suckle a little to give her strength for the conflict,' he suggested, and the circle exploded with a roar of delighted laughter at Kamuza's patent horror as he yelled and leapt violently away.

The noisy jeers covered their own uneasiness at the close proximity of the basket, and they were immediately silent as Bazo cautiously lifted the lid.

They craned forward with sickly fascination, and in the bottom of the basket something dark and furry and big as a rat stirred.

'Hau! Inkosikazi!' Bazo greeted it, and the creature reared up on its multiple legs, raising the front pair defensively, and the rows of eyes glittered in the softly wavering firelight. Bazo lifted his own right hand to return the salute of long hairy legs.

'I see you also, Inkosikazi.'

Bazo had named her Inkosikazi, the queen, for, as he explained to Ralph, 'She is right royal in her rage, and as thirsty for blood as a Matabele queen.'

He and Ralph had been unloading timber baulks at the eastern end of the new stagings, and as one load had swung upwards in the slings the great spider had come out from its nest between the sawn planks, and, raising its swollen velvety abdomen, had scampered over Ralph's arm and leapt ten feet to the ground.

The spider was the size of a dinner plate when its legs were extended. Its hirsute appearance and its extraordinary jumping prowess had given the species the common name of baboon spider.

'Get him, Bazo!' Ralph yelled from the top of the loaded wagon.

For now that Griqualand West and the New Rush diggings were part of Cape Colony and the British Empire there had been changes.

New Rush had been re-named Kimberley, after Lord Kimberley, the Colonial Secretary in London, and the town of Kimberley was starting to enjoy the benefits of British civilization and Victorian morality, amongst which was the total ban on cock fighting which was strictly enforced by the new administrator. The diggers, always eager for distraction, had not taken long to find an alternative sport. Spider fighting was the rage of the diggings.

'Don't let him get away!' Ralph vaulted down from the wagon, ripping off his shirt, but Bazo was quicker. He whipped the loincloth from his waist and flared it at the spider like a matador caping the bull, bringing the huge arachnid to bay on its hind legs, threatening him with its waving arms, then, naked and triumphant, Bazo had flipped the cloth over it and swiftly bundled it into a bag.

Now he slowly but deliberately extended his own hand into the basket, and the spider raised itself higher, the wolflike mandibles chewing menacingly, and between them the single curved red fang rising from its shallow sheath, a pale droplet of venom shining upon the needlesharp tip.

There was not even the sound of breathing in the dark hut, and the soft tick and rustle of the ashes sounded deafening in the silence as they watched Bazo's open hand draw closer and closer to the creature.

Then he touched it with his fingertips and began to stroke the soft furry carapace. Slowly the spider subsided from her threatening posture, and the watchers sighed and began to breathe again.

Inkosikazi had fought five times, and five times she had killed, although in the last conflict against another huge and ferocious female she had lost one of her legs, chewed through at the elbow joint. That had been almost three months previously; but the severed limb had now regenerated itself, and the new leg was lighter coloured than the others like the fresh shoots on a rose bush.

Slowly Bazo turned his hand palm upwards and the spider scuttled up into it and crouched there, filling it completely without extending her many jointed legs.

'A queen,' he said, 'a veritable queen.' And then, frowning, he told her, 'Henshaw would like to see you fight again.' He glanced up at Ralph, and there was a mischievous twist to his full lips.

'Go to Henshaw and tell him if you will fight or no.' And he offered the spider to Ralph.

Ralph felt the crawling of the tiny feet of horror across his skin as he stared at the spider crouching like a hairy toad before his face.

'Come, Henshaw,' Bazo smiled. 'Talk to her.'

It was a challenge, and the watchers stirred with

anticipation. If the challenge was not taken up, then their mockery would be merciless. Ralph tried to force himself to move, but his loathing was a cold nauseating lump under his ribs, and the sheen of sweat on his forehead was suddenly glacially cold.

Bazo was still smiling, but the challenge in his direct gaze was slowly changing to taunting disdain. With an enormous effort Ralph raised his hand, and at the movement the spider lifted itself and the soft bloated abdomen seemed to pulse softly, obscenely.

Only one person had ever handled Inkosikazi, and her reaction to a strange touch was totally unpredictable; but Ralph forced himself to reach out towards her.

Slowly his fingertips drew closer, six inches, two inches from the hairy body, and then the spider sprang. It launched itself in a high parabola, and landed on Ralph's shoulder.

The circle of watchers broke up in comic panic, yelling with terror and falling over one another to reach the single low doorway. Only Bazo and Ralph had not moved. Ralph sat with his hand still extended and the spider squatted massively on his shoulder. Infinitely slowly Ralph cocked his head and peered down at it, and it began to move; lifting the long bristled legs with a chilling daintiness, it crept sideways into the hollow of Ralph's neck – so that he could no longer see it but suddenly he felt the sharp points of its feet scratching the soft of his throat.

There was a horrified yell locked in the back of Ralph's throat, but he kept it there with a total effort of will. The spider climbed his chin and hung upside down for a moment like a huge hairy bat, and Ralph did not move.

Instead he lifted his gaze and held that of the Matabele opposite him. The mockery was gone from Bazo's eyes, and behind him the other watchers drew closer, fascinated and fearful. Perhaps for a minute they sat like that, and then Ralph lifted his hand. The gesture was so calm, so controlled, that the spider showed only perfunctory symptoms of alarm, and then quite willingly scuttled onto the inviting fingers and Ralph transferred her gently back into her basket.

Ralph wanted to leap up and run out into the darkness, to be alone while he vomited up his horror, but he forced himself to sit and stare impassively at Bazo until the Matabele lowered his eyes.

'She will fight,' he said softly. 'As you wish, Henshaw, she will fight again tomorrow.' And he closed the lid of the basket.

Inkosikazi had not fought for almost three months, and the punters, always fickle, had forgotten her. Other champions had emerged in her absence and commanded the fanatic loyalty of their followers. They gathered four deep around the handlers, trying to peer into the baskets and assess the fighting mettle of the caged creatures, as they waited for the first bout of the afternoon.

Although lantern-lit contests were held each evening behind Diamond Lil's canteen, Sunday afternoon was the main event of the week when every digger in Kimberley was free to crowd the western corner of Market Square and pick his fancy.

The arena was a square wooden structure, six feet by six and three deep, covered by a sheet of clear glass. This sheet of glass was the largest in Griqualand; originally intended as a display window for a ladies' dress shop on Main Street, it had miraculously survived the long wagon journey from the coast – and was now probably one of the most cherished items in Kimberley. Without it the sport would die, and Sunday afternoons would be tedium indeed.

The sheet of glass and the wooden arena were owned by a one-time kopje-walloper who had found there was more money in spiders than in diamonds. Ownership of the glass gave him a monopoly of the game and allowed him to charge a cruel entrance fee, and take a lion's share of the winnings.

Half a dozen wagons had been drawn up in a square around the arena to make grandstand accommodation for the crowds. The canteens around the square provided al-fresco service, their waiters staggering under trays laden with foaming schooners of beer to quench the raging thirsts that men had built up during a week in the pit.

The female population had doubled and re-doubled since Kimberley had become part of the Empire, and the ladies used the occasion to show off a pretty hat and a nicely sculptured ankle. Their delighted squeals of horror when the fighting spiders were released into the arena added to the feverish air of excitement.

In one of the alleys that led into the square, Ralph and his Matabele were huddled in solemn discussion.

'I do not know what that name means,' Bazo was protesting to Ralph.

'It is the name of a dangerous woman, who danced so beautifully that when she asked for it the king cut off a man's head and gave it to her.'

They all looked impressed. It was the kind of story which appealed to a Matabele.

'What is the name again?' Bazo asked thoughtfully.

'Salome—'

'But why cannot she fight under her real name?' Bazo glanced down at the basket under his arm. 'Why must we change Inkosikazi's name for this fight? It is not a good omen.'

Ralph looked exasperated. 'If we use that name they will know it is the same Inkosikazi who has already killed five times. If we call her Salome, why, one spider looks like another. They will not recognize her. They will believe her to be unblooded, and we shall win more money.'

'That is a good reason,' Kamuza cut in, and Bazo ignored him.

'Who found this name?' Bazo insisted.

'Jordie. He found it in the big book.' That decided it. Bazo had vast respect for the lovely gentle boy and his knowledge of books.

'Salome.' He nodded. 'It is agreed, but only for today.'

'Good.' Ralph rubbed his palms together briskly. 'Now where is the money?' And they all looked to Kamuza. He was the treasurer of the group. In their years of unbroken labour the gang of young Matabele had accumulated a hoard of gold and silver coin, for to their wages they had added the bounty on 'pick-ups'. Then of course there were the considerable winnings from Inkosikazi's previous bouts.

Kamuza kept this treasure buried under the floor of the communal hut, but he had reluctantly exhumed part of it the evening before, and now he produced a soft furry white bag, made from tanned scrotal skin of a springbuck ram, and reluctantly counted out coins into Ralph's hand. No white bookmaker would accept a wager from a black man, so Ralph was frontman for the Matabele syndicate.

'Make a book,' Kamuza said, and Ralph scribbled a receipt for sixteen sovereigns on a page of his notebook, tore it out and handed it to Kamuza, who examined it minutely. He trusted Ralph without question. He could not read, but the rituals of European commerce fascinated Kamuza and he had seen white men passing slips of paper whenever they exchanged coin.

'Good.' He tucked the receipt into the springbuckskin wallet.

'I have four gold queens of my own.' Ralph displayed his life savings. 'I will pay my share of the entrance fee and bet the rest of it.'

'May the gods go with us all, Henshaw,' said Bazo, and handed Ralph the precious little basket.

Ralph adjusted his cap to an angle that would hide as

much of his face as possible. It was unlikely that his father would be amongst the crowd, and if he was, the cap would hardly disguise his firstborn sufficiently for him not to be recognized – so the gesture was instinctive, as was his fear of his father's wrath.

'I will wait here for the money,' Kamuza told him.

'If she wins,' Ralph agreed.

'She will win,' said Bazo darkly. 'Would that I could serve her with my own hands.'

There was no law to prevent a black man entering a fancy in the lists, but none of them had ever done so. The niceties of this complex society were unwritten but understood by all.

Ralph slipped out of the alley and mingled with the crowd, working his way through the press until he was on the outskirts of the group of handlers, each of them with his woven basket, as they waited to enter their fancy.

'Ah, young Ballantyne.' Chaim Cohen looked up from his register, the wire-rimmed spectacles on the end of his nose, sweating jovially in the dust and blazing sun. 'Haven't seen you in some time.'

'Didn't have a fancy, Mr Cohen. Caught a new one now,' Ralph lied glibly.

'What happened to – what did you call her, some kaffir name?'

'She died. Lost a leg and died after her last fight.'

'What is your new lady's name?'

'Salome, sir.'

'Salome it is, then. That will be two pounds, young Ballantyne.' The coins disappeared with uncanny speed into the enlarged pocket that Cohen had sewn into the inside of his long frock coat, and with relief Ralph sidled into the crowd, trying to lose himself until the draw was announced.

He found a place near the tailboard of one of the

wagons, where he was partly concealed and from where he could watch the ladies in the crowd. Some of them were young and pretty, and they knew it. Every few minutes one would pass close enough to Ralph for him to hear the frou-frou of her petticoats and to smell her, for the heat brought out the subtle musk of womankind that was emphasized and not concealed by the sweet reek of French perfume. It seemed to catch in Ralph's throat, too poignant to breathe, and there was a hollow aching place at the base of his belly and weird thoughts in his head.

The fruity smell of cognac suddenly blotted out that French perfume and a hoarse voice close to his ear put the imaginings to flight.

'You are fighting a new fancy, I see, young Ballantyne.'

'Yes, sir. That's right, sir, Mr Lennox.'

Mr Barry Lennox was a big man, a brawler with a reputation for quick fists that was respected as far as the river workings. He was a plunger, who had bet a thousand guineas on a single cock fight, and won. That was in the days before civilization had reached the diggings, but now he chanced as much on the spider fights. He was a rich man by the standards of New Rush, for he owned eighteen claims in the No. 4 Roadway block. He had the red-veined cheeks and husky voice of the heavy drinker, but what intrigued Ralph most about this man was that he employed three young women, not one but three women to keep house for him. One was a pretty pug-faced daffodil-yellow Griqua girl, another a bold-eyed Portuguese mulatto from Mozambique, and the third a mulberry black Basuto with haunches on her like a brood mare. Whenever Ralph thought about this dusky trio, which was often, his imagination conjured up a garden of forbidden delights.

Of course, neither Ralph's father nor any other member of the Committee would acknowledge Lennox's existence and cut him elaborately on the street. Lennox's application to join the Kimberley Club had been met with a record-breaking fifty-six black balls. But Ralph removed his cap respectfully now, as Lennox asked throatily:

'What happened to Inkosikazi? I made a bundle on her.'

'She died, Mr Lennox. Old age, I suppose.'

'Baboon spiders live nearly twenty years and more,' Lennox grunted. 'Let's have a look at your new lady.'

'I don't like to unsettle her – not just before a bout, sir.'

'Does your daddy know where you spend your Sunday afternoons, young Ballantyne?'

'All right, sir.' Ralph capitulated swiftly and lifted the lid of the basket a crack. Lennox cocked a bloodshot but knowledgeable eye at it.

'That looks like a strong left front – new grown.'

'No, sir. Well, it might be. Caught her just the other day. Don't know her history, Mr Lennox.'

'Boy, you wouldn't be running a ringer, would you! 'Fess up now.' Lennox looked sternly into Ralph's eyes, and Ralph dropped them.

'You don't want to go up before the Diggers' Committee, do you? The shame you would bring on your daddy. It might break his heart.'

It might not break Zouga Ballantyne's heart, but it would certainly break Ralph's head.

Miserably Ralph shook his head. 'Very well then, Mr Lennox. It's Inkosikazi, she grew a new leg. I thought I'd get better odds – but, I'll withdraw her now. I'll go tell Mr Cohen I lied.'

Barry Lennox leaned so close that his lips touched Ralph's ear and the smell of fine old cognac on his breath almost overpowered him.

'You don't do anything so stupid, Ralph, my lad. You fight your fancy, and if she wins there will be a special treat for you. That's promise. Barry Lennox will see you right – and then some. Now, if you will excuse me, I've got some business to attend to.' Lennox twirled his cane and drove a wedge into the crowd with his bow-fronted belly.

Chaim Cohen climbed up onto the disselboom of the nearest wagon to the arena and began chalking up the draw on a greenruled board, and the bookmakers craned for the matchings and then began calling their odds for each bout.

'Threes on Mr Gladstone in the first.'

'Dreadnought even money. Buttercup fives in the second.'

Ralph waited as bout after bout was drawn, and each time that Inkosikazi's name was omitted his nerves stretched tighter. There were only ten bouts, and Mr Cohen had finished chalking the ninth already.

'Bout No. 10,' he called as he wrote. 'This is a biblical match, gentlemen and ladies, a diamondiferous bout straight out of the Old Testament.' Chaim Cohen used the adjective 'diamondiferous' to describe anything from a thoroughbred horse to a fifteen-year-old whisky. 'A pure diamondiferous match, the one and only, the great and deadly, Goliath!' There was a burst of applause and whistles of approval. Goliath was the champion spider of the diamond fields, with twelve straight kills to her credit. 'Matched against your favourite is a pretty little newcomer, Salome!'

The name was greeted with indifference as the punters scrambled to get money onto the champion.

'I'm giving tens on Salome,' called one desperate bookie as he tried to stem the flow of wagers. They were taking Goliath at odds on, and Ralph shared his distress.

Leaden-footed he traipsed back to the alleyway. Kamuza had heard the draw announced.

'Give us back the sixteen queens,' he greeted Ralph; but the demand stung Bazo:

'Inkosikazi will drink her blood—'

'The other is a giant—'

'Inkosikazi is quick, fast as a mamba, brave as a honey badger.' Bazo chose the most fearless and indomitable fighters of the veld as comparisons for his fancy.

They argued while the sudden roar of voices from the Square signalled the beginning of the first bout, and the squeals of the ladies told that the kill had been swiftly made.

They argued fiercely, Bazo becoming so agitated that he could no longer sit still. He leapt up and began to *giya*, the challenge dance of the Matabele warrior preparing for battle.

'Thus Inkosikazi sprang, and thus she drove her assegai into the chest of Nelo,' Bazo shouted, as he imitated the death stroke of his fancy; but the Matabele always found difficulty in pronouncing the letter 'R', and the Roman Emperor's was mutilated in the recounting of the battle.

'You must decide,' Ralph broke in on his heroics, and Bazo abruptly ended his *giya* and looked at Kamuza.

In matters of money Kamuza was without question the leader of the group, just as Bazo was in all else.

'Henshaw,' Kamuza asked gravely. 'Are you risking your four queens against this monster?'

'Inkosikazi is risking her life,' Ralph replied, without hesitation. 'And I am risking my money for her.'

'So be it, then. We will follow you.'

There were only minutes left before the tenth bout of the afternoon. Already Chaim Cohen was upending his schooner of beer and, considerably refreshed, wiping the froth from his whiskers. At any moment he would climb back onto the wagon and call for the handlers to bring their fighters to the arena for the final bout.

Ralph still had five sovereigns to place.

'You said twelves,' he argued desperately with the ferret-eyed bookmaker in the flowing Ascot tie.

'If you are betting your own fancy, then it's tens.'

'That's welshing.'

'Life is all a welsh,' the bookie shrugged. 'Take it or leave it.'

'All right, I'll take it.' Ralph snatched the slip and pushed towards the circle of wagons, and once again found his way blocked by the grand belly of Barry Lennox.

'Are you betting her yourself?'

'With everything I've got, sir.'

'That's all I wanted to know, Ralph me boy.' And he strode to the nearest bookmaker, pulling his purse from his hip pocket just as Chaim Cohen crowed from his perch on the wagon.

'Lovely ladies and sporting gentlemen! The tenth and final bout of the day! The mighty Goliath meets the dancing lady Salome!'

Goliath crabbed into the glass-topped arena. Her four pairs of legs undulated sinuously so that her progress was stately and deliberate.

She was a huge beast, newly moulted, for her chintyl armoured covering was a lustrous coppery colour and the long hairs that covered her abdomen and legs were burnished like newly spun gold wire. She left a double necklace of tiny stippled footprints in the swept sand of the arena floor, and the crowd cheered her. Their inhibitions had long been lost in the primeval conflicts in the little arena, and most of them had been drinking since noon: there was a peculiar ring of ferocity and cruelty in their voices.

'Kill her!' screamed a pretty blonde girl with gold ringlets and flowers in her hat. 'Rip her to pieces!' Her face flushed feverishly and her eyes were glittering.

'All right, Mr Ballantyne. Put your fancy in,' Chaim Cohen commanded, raising his voice to be heard above the uproar. But Ralph delayed a few seconds longer, letting the other spider complete its circuit and face away from his side of the cage. Then he lifted the sliding door and tapped the basket to rouse Inkosikazi.

She crawled forward cautiously, lifting her abdomen clear of the sand, stepping on the spiked toes of her ranked legs, and then freezing as she saw her adversary across the cage. Her multiple jewelled eyes were sparkling like chips of black diamond.

Goliath sensed her presence and leaped high, turned in the air and landed facing her. The two spiders confronted each other across the smoothly swept floor of white river sand – and only now was the difference in their sizes apparent. Goliath was enormous, swelling in rage, the long silken mane of burnished hair rising like the quills of a porcupine to enhance her size as she began to dance her challenge to her smaller adversary.

Immediately Inkosikazi replied to the challenge, raising and lowering her abdomen in time to the rhythmic swaying of her carapace, lifting her legs in pairs and weaving them with an awful grace, like the many-armed Hindu god, Shiva.

An utter silence had fallen on the watchers as they strained to catch every nuance of this stylized dance of death – and then a lust-choked roar burst from them as Goliath sprang.

She exploded into flight, soaring with her talons fully extended, clearing the length of the arena without effort and landing precisely where Inkosikazi had stood a thousandth part of a second before. Inkosikazi had evaded that flashing leap with a bouncing side jump of her own, and now she faced the huge enraged creature and danced her defiance.

The dazzling agility of these great spiders was the essential attraction that drew such a following of eager spectators. There was no preliminary bracing or crouching to herald one of those swallowlight bounds. The spiders fired themselves like bullets, suddenly and unerringly at their rival, and reacted as swiftly to the counter-attack. Then between each onslaught that mesmeric and chilling dance resumed.

'Jee! Jee!' The tightly drawn silence was interrupted by the chilling, killing cry of a Matabele warrior.

'Jee! Jee!' The deep hissing chorus that had carried a black wave of naked bodies across a continent, a wave crested by the plumes of the war bonnets and lit by the glitter of the bright silver assegais.

Bazo had not been able to skulk in the alley beyond the square. He had edged forward into the crowd until he reached the wagons, but as the conflict mounted, so had his warrior passions. He thrust forward through the packed ranks and now he was in the forefront, and he could not contain himself further.

'Jee! Jee!' He hissed his battle cry, and Ralph found himself echoing it.

Inkosikazi was fighting instinctively, reacting mindlessly to the presence of another female in deadly sexual rivalry. It was the waving arms of the gigantic female across the cage which infuriated her, and it was mere coincidence that her first attacking leap was synchronized with the war chant.

Twice she launched herself, and twice Goliath gave her ground. And then on her third leap Inkosikazi vaulted too high and touched the glass roof of the arena. The impact broke the perfect parabola of her flight, and she fell short and out of balance, scrabbling frantically in the fine white sand as Goliath saw her chance and flew in for the kill.

The men howled with cruel glee, the women trilled with delicious horror as the two huge furry bodies came together chest to chest and entangled each other's limbs in a hideous octopus embrace.

The impetus of Goliath's leap sent them rolling across the arena like an india-rubber ball, until they struck the far wall and wrestled in a flurry of serpentine limbs. Both their long hooked fangs were fully erect, and they slashed at each other with their hairy wolf mouths, the needle points of the fangs striking the impenetrable shiny armour of carapace and jointed legs, glancing off the polished surface and leaving minute dribbles of colourless honey-thick venom on each other's chests.

Instinctively they were holding their vulnerable abdomens clear, while straining to tear from the embrace for a chance to strike into the soft skin of the other. They came up on their hind legs and wrestled together, and immediately Goliath's weight began to take effect.

With a sharp crackling sound, like a walnut in the jaw of a silver nutcracker, one of Inkosikazi's legs was torn bodily from the joint of her carapace, and she jerked convulsively, contracting her soft belly in a dreadful spasm.

'Kill her! Rip her to pieces!' screamed the pretty blonde girl, and tore at her perfumed silk handkerchief, shredding it between her fingers. Her face was swollen and inflamed and her eyes wild.

Goliath shifted the grip of her many legs, groping for a soft spot into which to plunge the jerking red fang.

'Jee! Jee!' sang Bazo, his eyes bloodshot with passion, and Inkosikazi strained with all her remaining legs to break the grip that was slowly smothering her under the huge hairy body. Again there was that grisly crackling, one of her front legs broke off in a little spurt of body juices, and instinctively Goliath lifted the severed limb to her mouth.

The distraction was sufficient, and Inkosikazi tore herself

free and bounded halfway across the arena, landing in an unbalanced sprawl, her body fluids oozing from the leg stumps, but gathering herself swiftly. Goliath was still worrying the severed legs, the smell of her opponent's blood enrapturing her so that she mouthed the twitching limbs, striking at them with her fang, her full attention upon them – and Inkosikazi rebounded like a rubber ball thrown against a brick wall.

She dropped lightly onto Goliath's broad furry back, locked in with her remaining legs, and then plunged the long blood-red fang into Goliath's abdomen, her head pumping as she forced a steady gush of poison into the bloated body.

Goliath's body arched, her long jointed legs straightened into an agonized rictus, and the balloon of her belly spasmed and convulsed as the venom pulsed into her. Crouched upon her back like some grotesque incubus, Inkosikazi squirted in the fatal fluid until the bigger creature's limbs wilted and crumpled under her and her belly sagged gradually to the white sand of the arena.

In the roaring consternation of disappointed punters and squeaks of women, both loathing and gloating at the same time, Ralph and Bazo rushed together and embraced with whoops of triumph. In the glassed arena Inkosikazi slowly withdrew the long curved hypodermic fang. Her venom not only paralysed and killed but also liquefied the body tissue of her prey. Her jaws opened and then locked into the jelly-soft passive body beneath her, and her own abdomen began to swell and subside as she sucked her vanquished adversary's fluids from her – while she still lived.

Ralph broke from the embrace of Bazo's thickly muscled arms.

'Get her out of the cage,' he told him. 'I'll go and get the money.'

Bazo bore the basket high on the return from the

conflict. His bare-chested Matabele ran behind him, in that floating stylized gait, half dance, half trot, and they brandished their fighting sticks and sang the praise song which Kamuza had composed in Inkosikazi's honour:

> 'See with your thousand eyes,
> Hold hard with many arms of steel,
> Kiss with your long red assegai,
> Taste the blood, is it not richer
> than the milk of Mzilikazi's herds?
> Taste the blood, is it not sweeter
> than the wild honey in the comb?
> Bayete! Bayete!
> Royal greetings, Black Queen,
> Loyal greetings, Great Queen.'

Ralph dearly wanted to run with them in that triumphant procession, but he knew what his father would say if he heard that his son had joined such a barbaric display through the dusty streets, past the very portals of the Kimberley Club where Zouga Ballantyne was almost certainly passing his Sunday afternoon.

Ralph followed them in a fashion that better suited Zouga's idea of how a young English gentleman should comport himself, but his cap was on the back of his head, his hands were thrust deeply into pockets jingling the gold coin, and there was a beatific grin on his face. The smile broadened further as a familiar big-gutted figure rolled out through the doors of Diamond Lil's canteen.

'Mr Ballantyne,' bellowed Barry Lennox across the street. 'Mr Ballantyne, will you do me the very great honour of taking a glass with me?'

'Enchanted indeed, sir.' Ralph felt cocky enough to reply facetiously, and Lennox guffawed and flung an arm around Ralph's shoulders and led him into the canteen.

Ralph looked about him quickly; it was the first time he

had ever entered a place such as this. He hoped to see naked women dancing on the tables and gamblers in flowered waistcoats fanning open hands full of aces and kings and sweeping up pots of gold sovereigns.

The only partially nude figure was that of Charlie, the undertaker, snoring on the sawdust floor with his shirt open to his hairy belly button; and the gamblers were all familiar faces, men beside whom Ralph worked every day on the stagings or in the pit. They were dressed in their work clothes and the cards were dog-eared and greasy and the pot was a small pile of copper and worn silver.

'Ralph,' said one of them, looking up. 'Your daddy know where you are?'

'Does yours?' Ralph shot back, the cockiness unabated. 'And do you know *who* he is?'

There was a hoot of laughter from the others, and the man grinned good-naturedly. 'Damn me, but the boy has a sharp enough tongue.'

'Give my sporting friend a beer,' Lennox told the barman, and he looked dubious.

'How old is your sporting friend?'

'He will be forty years old on one of his future birthdays. However, sir, I consider that question to be a direct slur on my sporting friend's honour. I have broken jaws that asked less impertinent questions.'

'Two beers coming up, Mr Lennox.'

Barry Lennox and Ralph saluted each other with the schooners, and Lennox gave them a toast.

'To a lady of our mutual acquaintance, bless her bright eyes and all her lovely legs.'

The beer was faintly warm and tasted like soap and quinine, but Ralph forced down a mouthful and smacked his lips appreciatively. He would have much preferred a cool green bottle of ginger beer with a pop up marble in the neck.

'Cigar?' Lennox opened his silver case, and Ralph

hesitated only a moment, then selected one of the thick Havanas and bit off the end in a faithful imitation of Zouga Ballantyne.

He sucked from the Vesta that Lennox held for him, and cautiously held the smoke in his mouth. That was the last draw he took, and after that he used the cigar like a conductor's baton, waving it airily and creating about himself a cloud of perfumed blue without actually touching it to his lips again. Somehow he was able to impart the impression of swagger while standing at the rough-sawn bar counter.

' – I mean, anybody knows the classic Zulu battle tactics. They wait for bad ground and thick bush, there are few soldiers who use cover and defilade the way they do.' Ralph sipped his beer and waved his cigar as he discussed Lord Chelmsford's current campaign against the Zulu King Cetewayo. The views he was expressing were those of Zouga Ballantyne, learned by heart and unadulterated; so though his listeners winked and nudged at his pretensions, they could not fault his logic. 'The device of decoying Chelmsford's flying column out of the camp and then doubling back to destroy the base with its depleted defences is as old as Chaka Zulu himself. Chelmsford was at fault, there, no doubt on it.'

There was a gloomy shaking of heads, as there always was when anyone mentioned the catastrophic reversal of British arms that Chelmsford had been manoeuvred into at the Hill of the Little Hand, Isandhlwana, across the Buffalo River in Zululand.

The corpses of seven hundred British dead, militia and regular regiments, had already lain for six months on the bleak grassland below the little hill. Lord Chelmsford had abandoned the field, and his dead lay where they had fallen, their bellies ripped open by Zulu assegais to allow their souls to escape, the litter of wagons and broken equipment scattered about them, their flesh taken off the bone by vulture and jackal and hyena.

The thought of leaving British soldiers unburied on the battlefield seemed to threaten the very foundation of the greatest empire the world had ever known.

'Chelmsford must retake the field,' said one of the men at the bar.

'No, sir,' Ralph shook his head firmly. 'That will be inviting another disaster for a sentimental gesture.'

'What do you propose, Mr Ballantyne?' the man asked sarcastically.

'A page from the Boer book.' Ralph had an audience of grown men listening to him – perhaps not with respect, but at least with attention. This was heady stuff, even though the ideas were his father's, and Ralph threw in an oath. 'By God, those fellows know how to fight the tribes. Mounted men as a screen around a column of wagons that can be thrown into laager within minutes. Go for the heart of the Zulu nation – their cattle herds – pull the impis into the open, make them come in across good shooting ground against the laagered wagons—' Ralph did not finish his plan of battle; abruptly he lost his sequence of ideas and began to stutter like an idiot, a blush darkening his tanned, handsome young face.

Barry Lennox followed the direction of Ralph's gaze, and then he grinned delightedly.

Diamond Lil had entered the canteen through the rear door. It was six o'clock in the evening and an hour before she had risen, stretching and yawning like a sleepy leopard, from the brass bed in the darkened room behind the canteen.

A servant had filled the enamelled hip bath with buckets of steaming water, and Lil had poured in a vial of perfume before stepping into the bath and settling luxuriously into the fragrant water, shouting for her canteen manager.

She listened attentively, a small frown cracking the perfect pale skin of her forehead, as he recited the figures of the previous night's take, his eyes averted from the white skin of her shoulders and the tight pink-tipped bosom that peeked through the hot suds. Then she had dismissed him with a wave of her hand and stepped naked from the bath, glowing pinkly from the hot water, her steam-damp hair dangling down the sleek white body. She poured a little gin into a coloured Venetian glass and sipped it neat as she started the powdering and the painting, rolling her eyes at herself in the mirror, practising her professional smile with the tiny diamond twinkling in the centre of the wide display of white teeth, then, at last, considering herself levelly and appraisingly.

She was twenty-three years old, and she had come a long hard way from the house in Mayfair where Madame Hortense had sold her maidenhood to an elderly Whig minister of state for one hundred guineas. She had been thirteen years old then, only ten years ago, but it seemed like a dozen lifetimes.

The house in Mayfair was truly the only home she had ever known, and she often thought back with nostalgia to those days. Madame Hortense had treated her more like a daughter than a house girl. There was always a pretty bonnet or a new dress on her birthday and at Christmas, and she had had special privileges. Lil would ever be grateful for what she learned about men and money and power from Hortense.

Then one Saturday evening a half dozen young officers from a famous cavalry regiment, celebrating their orders for foreign service, had visited the house in Mayfair. Amongst them was a young captain, dashing, rich and beautiful; he saw Lil across the salon the moment he entered. Ten days later Lil had sailed with him for India on the Peninsular and Orient mailship, while Madame Hortense wept on the quay and waved until the ship cleared the pool of London and disappeared beyond the first bend of the river. Forty days later Lil found herself abandoned by her protector.

From an upper window of the Mount Nelson Hotel in Cape Town she watched her cavalry captain's ship clear Table Bay for Calcutta, her sorrow at parting alleviated by the luxurious surroundings in which her protector had left her. Lil shrugged off her grief, drank a glass of gin, bathed and re-painted her face, then sent for the manager.

'I cannot pay my bill,' she told him and, taking his hand, led him unprotestingly into the bedroom of her suite.

'Madame, may I give you some advice?' he asked a little later as he retied his Ascot and shrugged into his waistcoat.

'Good advice is always welcome, sir.'

'There is a place called New Rush five hundred miles north of here and there are five thousand diggers there, each with a pocket full of diamonds.'

Now Lil entered her canteen. It was still early for a Sunday. It was one of the things she had learned from Madame Hortense, always be there long before you are expected. It keeps clients satisfied and employees honest.

Quickly she checked her clientele. It was the usual Sunday afternoon crowd. It would be better soon. She stooped and counted the bottles under the bar counter, examining the wax seals to make certain they had not been tampered with.

'Never be greedy, darling,' Hortense had taught her. 'Water the beer, they expect that, but keep good whisky.'

She straightened and opened the huge ornate cash register with a chime of bells, making certain that it flagged the correct price, and then touched the line of gold sovereigns in their special slotted drawer. The metal had a marvellous feel under her fingertips, and she picked up a coin as though merely to feel the weight and take pleasure from it. Gold was the only thing in all the world she trusted. Her barman was watching her in the mirror as he swabbed the counter top; she pretended to replace the sovereign in its slot, letting it clink and then palmed it smoothly and closed the drawer of the register. The barman was new. It would be interesting to see if he covered the shortage or reported it, little things like that had made her rich at the age of twenty-three.

She glanced up into the mirror, once again appraising her own face and shoulders in the less flattering sunlight that streamed into the canteen. Her eyes were sharp as a stropped razor, but the skin around them was clear and fresh as rose petals without the first sign of wrinkling.

'You will wear well, my dear,' Hortense had told her, 'if you use the gin and don't let it use you.' She had been right, Lil decided. She looked as she had when she was sixteen years old.

She shifted her gaze from her own face, and swept the canteen. The mirror was imperfect, and the silvering was beginning to go in dark spots, slightly distorting the young face that was watching her intently. Her gaze flicked over it, and then came back.

The boy was blushing as he studied her avidly, that was the only thing that had caught her attention. Now when she looked at him again she realized he was probably under-age, and she already had trouble with the Committee. He wore a boy's cloth cap on the back of his head and he was very obviously still growing, his Norfolk jacket straining around the sturdy arms and across the shoulders.

Too young and certainly penniless. She had to get him out fast, and she turned quickly, her fists on her hips, her blond head cocked aggressively.

'Good afternoon, Miss Lil.' Ralph was stunned by his own audacity at addressing this heavenly presence directly. 'I was about to buy my friends a round of drinks. We should be honoured if you would take a glass with us, ma'am.' Ralph slapped the counter with a sovereign, and Lil uncocked her head and raised one hand from her hip to touch her hair.

'I like a big spending gent.' She flashed the little diamond in her front tooth at him and nodded to the barman. He would pour from her special bottle labelled Booth's Gin but filled with rain water from the galvanized tank beside the backdoor.

Suddenly she realized that the boy was bonny, with a strong jaw and good white teeth. Now that his blush had subsided, his skin was clear and smooth as her own, and his eyes a penetrating emerald green. And the eagerness and freshness that he exuded was so different from that of the hairy diggers, caked with red dirt and smelling like goats, that formed her usual clientele.

Let the boy pay for his round of drinks, and there would be time to get rid of him after that. In the meantime his transparent adoration was amusing and flattering.

'Lil, me darling.' Barry Lennox leaned across the counter and she did not flinch from his breath. 'Give me your pearl-like little ear.'

Smiling her bright smile she held her ear to his lips, and cupped her hand in an exaggerated pantomime of secrecy.

'Are you working tonight, Lil?'

'I'm always ready for a quick rattle of the dice with you, my sweet. You want to go right now or finish your drink?'

'No, darling, not me. How would you like to be first to put the saddle on an unbroken colt?'

Her eyes flicked to Ralph's face again, and her hard bright smile softened thoughtfully. He was a lovely boy, and for the first time since her cavalryman had left her in Cape Town she felt the prickle of her loins and bitter sweet catch in her throat, so that she did not trust her voice entirely.

'It's still early, Lil, and business isn't good this time on Sunday, Lil dearie.' Barry Lennox wheedled and chuckled beerily at the same time. 'He is a pretty boy, and I should charge you for the pleasure, but I'll just let you make me a special price instead.'

Lil's throat cleared instantly and the languid expression disappeared. Her reply was crisp.

'I'll not charge you school fees, Barry Lennox, just the usual ten guineas.'

Lennox shook his head. 'You are a hard one, Lil. I'll send him to you, love. But just one thing, make it good, make it something that he will remember if he lives a hundred years.'

'I don't teach you to dig diamonds, Barry Lennox,' she said, and without looking back swept from the canteen. They heard the door of her bedroom bang, and Ralph stared after her in dismay – but Barry Lennox put an arm around his shoulders and as he talked quietly, punctuating each sentence with a throaty lewd chuckle, all the colour fled from Ralph's face.

'Come in.' Her voice reminded Ralph of the gentle contented cooing that the plump wild pigeons made at sunset in the top branch of the camel-thorn tree above Zouga's camp.

With his hand on the brass doorknob, he lifted his feet one at a time and polished the toe-cap of his boots against the back of his trouser leg. He had doused his head under the tap of the rainwater tank and combed his hair while it was still wet, sleeking it away from his forehead, and the droplets had run down his neck, turning the dust on his darned shirt collar into damp red mud.

He glanced down at his hand on the doorknob, saw the black rinds under his finger nails and lifted it quickly to his mouth, trying desperately to pick out the dirt with his eye tooth.

'Come in!' The command was repeated; but this time there was no cooing of pigeons, but a sharp imperious command, and Ralph lunged for the door handle. There was no resistance, the door flew open, and Ralph went with it. He entered Diamond Lil's boudoir like a cavalry charge, tripped on the frayed edge of a cheap oriental carpet and sprawled headlong across the brass bed.

There was a Chinese lacquer screen across one corner of the small violently furnished room, and over the top of it rose Diamond Lil's magnificently sculptured blonde coiffure.

'Oh,' she said sweetly, the sharp slanted eyes widening with amusement. 'Are you going to start without me then, darling?'

Ralph scrambled untidily to his feet like a puppy with oversized paws and stood to attention in the middle of the floor, holding his cloth cap to his stomach with both hands.

From behind the screen came the most evocative sounds he had ever heard. The rustle of lace and cloth, the clink of china and the gurgle of water poured from a jug. The lacquer screen was ornamented with oriental figures, women bathing in a willow-screened pool with a waterfall in the background. The women were all naked, and the artist had lingered on their physical charms. Ralph felt his ears and neck heating again – and hated himself for it.

He wished he had kept the cigar, as a proof of his manhood. He wished that he had worn a fresh shirt, he wished – but then there was no further time for wishing.

Lil stepped out from behind the screen. She was bare-footed, and her toes were chubby and rosy pink like those of a little girl.

'I have seen you on the street, Mr Ballantyne,' Lil told him quietly. 'And I have admired your manly disposition. I am so glad we have had an opportunity to meet.'

The words worked a miracle. Ralph felt himself growing in stature, the trembling in his legs stilled and they felt strong and sure under him.

'Do you like my robe?' Lil asked, and took the long skirts in her hands, turning to make them flare.

Ralph nodded dumbly, his new-found strength had not yet reached his tongue, but his eyes were wide and feverish.

She came to him and without her heels she stood only as high as his shoulder. 'Let me help you with your coat.' And when he was in his shirtsleeves, she said, 'Come and sit on the sofa.' She took his hand and led him across the room.

'Do you like me, Mr Ballantyne?'

At last he could speak, 'Oh yes. Oh yes!'

'May I call you Ralph? I feel I know you so well.'

Very early one January morning long ago she had left the Mayfair house, and reached the deserted park where it had snowed during the night. The snow lay white and smooth and unmarked. She left the gravelled path, and the snow crumbled like sugar under her feet. When she looked back her tiny footprints were strung out across the unblemished snow, as though she were the first and only woman in the world. It gave her an extraordinary feeling of her own importance. Now as she lay on the wide bedstead beside the lad, she experienced that same feeling.

He was not a lad, but she thought of him as that. His body was fully matured, but his innocence made him as vulnerable as an unweaned infant, and his body was like the snow which no other feet had trodden.

The sun had stained his throat in a deep V down onto his chest, but the skin of his chest and flat belly were the lustrous white of watered marble or of freshly fallen snow. She touched it with her lips and when his little dusty rose nipples puckered and started her own skin crawling deliciously, she took his hands. His palms were rough and callused from work on the stagings and in the pit. The fingernails were torn and cracked, with ingrained dirt beneath them. But it was honest dirt, and the hands were shapely, long and graceful. She had learned to judge men by the shape of their hands, and now she lifted Ralph's to her lips and kissed them lightly, watching his eyes as she did so.

Then slowly she took his hands down and cupped them over her own soft breasts. She felt the rough skin rasp her own nipples, and they popped out like full moons, pale pink and tense.

'You like that, Ralph?'

She asked that same question five times, and the last time was when the room was almost dark and he was convulsed and shaking within the circle of her arms and her pliant thighs, drenched with his own sweet young sweat, and breathing in little choking sobs.

'You like that, Ralph?' And his reply was broken and ragged:

'Oh yes. Oh yes, Miss Lil.'

Suddenly she was sad. The snow was trodden, the magic was passing, just as the power she had wielded was transitory.

She had not cried in ten long hard years, not since that first evening in the Mayfair house, but now she was shocked to find the constriction in her throat and the burning behind her eyes.

'What is there to cry for?' she wondered desolately. 'It's far too late for tears.'

She rolled Ralph expertly onto his back, his body limp and unresisting – and for a moment she stared at him hatefully. He had touched something in her which had hurt unbearably. Then the hating passed and there was only the sadness.

She kissed him once more, softly and regretfully.

'You must go now, Ralph,' she said.

He lingered at the door, with his jacket over his arm and his cap in his hand.

'I will come and see you again, Lily.'

She formed a bow with her lips and painted them with

quick deft strokes before she replied, but while she worked she was watching him in the mirror.

He was altered already, she saw. He stood four-square, his shoulders wide and his neat young head proud on the column of his sun-tanned neck. The sweet diffidence was gone, the appealing shyness evaporated. An hour before he would have said:

'Please can I come and see you again, Miss Lil.'

She smiled at him in the mirror, that bright burnished smile, and the diamond in her tooth winked sardonically.

'You come any time, dearie – any time you have saved ten guineas.'

I t was only surprising that the full report of Ralph's foray into the lilac fields of Venus took so long to reach Zouga, for Barry Lennox had repeated the story with zest and embroidery to anyone who would listen, and the chaff and banter had flown like a Kalahari dust-storm every evening in Diamond Lil's canteen.

'Gentlemen, you are speaking about the eldest son of one of the pillars of Kimberley Society,' Lil admonished them saucily. 'Remember that Major Ballantyne is not only a member of the Kimberley Club, but a respected ornament of the Diggers' Committee.' She knew that one of them would soon succumb to the temptation to take the story to Zouga Ballantyne. 'I would love to hear what that cold-bellied, stuck-up prig will say when he hears,' she told herself secretly. 'Even the iced water in his veins will boil.'

'Whores and whore masters,' said Zouga. He stood on the wide verandah, in the shade of the thatched roof which had replaced the original tent of the first camp.

Ralph stood below him in the sunlight, blinking up at his father.

'Perhaps you have no respect for your family, for the

name of Ballantyne – but do you have none for yourself and for your own body?'

Zouga was barring the front door to the cottage of raw unbaked brick. He was bare-headed, so that his thick dark-gold hair shone like a war helmet and his neatly-cropped beard emphasized the jut of his heavy jaw, and the long black tapered hippohide kurbash whip hung from his right hand, touching the floor at the toe of his riding boot.

'Do you have an answer?' Zouga's tone was quiet, and deadly cold.

Ralph was still dusty as a miller from the pit. The dust was thick and red in his hair, and outlined the curl of his nostrils and ran like tears from the corners of his eyes. He wiped his forehead on his shirtsleeve, an excuse to break the gaze of his father's eyes, and then examined the muddy smear with attention.

'Answer me,' Zouga's voice did not alter. 'Give me a reason – just one reason why I should not throw you out of this home – for ever.'

Jordan could bear it no longer, the thought of losing Ralph overcame his terror of his father's wrath.

He ran down the length of the verandah, and seized the arm that held the whip.

'Papa! Please, Papa – don't send him away.'

Without glancing at Jordan, Zouga lashed out and the blow caught Jordan across the chest and hurled him back against the verandah wall.

'Jordie did nothing,' said Ralph, as quietly as his father had spoken.

'Oh, you do have a tongue?' Zouga asked.

'Get out of it, Jordie,' Ralph ordered. 'This is not your business.'

'Stay where you are, Jordan.' Zouga still did not look at him, his gaze was riveted on Ralph's face. 'Stay here and learn about whores and the kind of men who lust after them.'

Jordan was stricken, his face like last night's camp-fire ashes, his lips dry and white as bone. He knew what they were talking about – for he had listened while Bazo and Ralph wove their fantasies aloud, and with his interest piqued, he had questioned Jan Cheroot furtively – and the replies had disgusted and terrified him.

'Not like animals, Jan Cheroot, surely not like dogs or goats.'

Jordan's questions to Jan Cheroot had been generalized – men and women, not any person he knew or loved or respected. It had taken him days fully to appreciate Jan Cheroot's reply, and then the terrible realization had struck – all men and women, his father who epitomized for him all that was noble and strong and right, his mother, that sweet and gentle being who was already a fading wraithlike memory – not them, surely not them.

He had been physically sickened, vomiting and wracked by excruciating bowel cramps so that Zouga had dosed him with sulphur and treacle molasses.

Now they were talking about that thing, that thing so dreadful that he had tried to purge his memory of it. Now the two most important people in his world were talking about it openly, using words he had only seen in print and which had even then shamed him. They were mouthing those words and the air was full of shame and hatred and revulsion.

'You have wallowed like a pig where a thousand other pigs have wallowed before you, in the fetid cesspool between that scarlet whore's thighs.'

Jordan crept away along the wall, and reached the corner of the stoep. He could go no further.

'If you were not ashamed to muck in that trough, did you not give a thought to what those other rutting boars had left there for you?'

His father's words conjured up vivid images in Jordan's

mind. His stomach heaved, and he covered his mouth with his hand.

'The sickness a harlot carries there is the curse of God upon venery and lust. If you could only see them in the pox hospital at Greenwich, raving idiots with their brains eaten half away by the disease, drooling from empty mouths, their teeth rotted out, their noses fallen into black festering holes, blind eyes rolling in their crazed skulls—'

Jordan doubled over, and sicked up on his own rawhide boots.

'Stop it,' said Ralph. 'You have made Jordie sick.'

'I have made him sick?' Zouga asked quietly. 'It is you who would make any decent person sick.'

Zouga came down the steps into the dusty yard, and he swung the whip, cutting the air with it, across and back and the lash fluted sharply.

Ralph stood his ground, and now his chin was up defiantly.

'If you take that whip to me, Papa – I shall defend myself.'

'You challenge me,' Zouga stopped.

'You only use a whip on an animal.'

'Yes,' Zouga nodded. 'An animal – that's why I take it to you.'

'Papa, I warn you.'

Gravely Zouga inclined his head and considered the young man before him. 'Very well. You claim to be a man, make good that claim.' Zouga tossed the hippohide whip casually onto the verandah, and then turned back to his son.

Ralph was prepared, his weight balanced on the balls of his feet, although his hands were held low before him, they were balled into fists.

He never saw it. For a moment he thought that someone else had used a club on him from behind. The crack of it seemed to explode under the dome of his skull. He reeled backwards, his nose felt numb and at the same time swollen horribly. There was a tickling warmth on his upper lip and dumbly he licked it. It tasted of coppery salt, and he wiped at it with the back of his hand and then stared at the smear of blood on the back of his wrist.

His rage came on him with startling ferocity, as though a beast had pounced upon his back, a black beast that goaded him with its claws. He heard the beast growl in his ears, not recognizing his own voice, and then he rushed forward.

His father's face was in front of him, handsome, grave and cold, and he swung his fist at it with all his strength, wanting to feel the flesh crush under his knuckles, the gristle of that arrogant beaked nose break and crackle, the teeth snap out of that unforgiving mouth.

His fist spun through air, meeting no check, swinging high about the level of his own head, and the blow died there, the sinews of his shoulder wrenched by the unexpected travel of his arm.

Again that burst of sound in his skull, his teeth jarring, his head snapping back, his vision starring momentarily into pinpoints of light and areas of deep echoing black, and then clearing again so that his father's face floated back towards him.

Until that instant the only feelings he had ever had for Zouga were respect and fear and a weighty monumental love, but suddenly from some deep place in his soul rose a raging unholy hatred.

He hated him for a hundred humiliations and punishments, he hated him for the checks and frustrations with which he filled each precious day of Ralph's life, he hated him for the reverence and deep respect in which other men held him, for the example that he knew he would be expected to follow faithfully all his life and doubted that he could. He hated him for the enormous load of duty and devotion he owed him and which he knew he could never discharge. He hated him for the love he had stolen from him, the love his mother had given unstintingly to his father and which he wanted all for himself. He hated him because his mother was dead, and his father had not prevented her going.

But most of all he hated him because he had taken something which had been wonderful and made it filthy, had taken a magical moment and made him ashamed of it, sick and dirty ashamed.

He rushed back at Zouga, swinging wildly with both fists meeting only air, and the blows that landed on his own head and face sounded as though somebody far away was chopping down a tree with a steel axe.

Zouga fell away neatly before each charge, swaying his head back or to the side, deflecting a blow with his arms, ducking carefully under a flying fist, and counter-punching only with his left hand, flicking it in with deceptive lightness, for at each shot Ralph's head snapped backwards sharply and the blood from his nose and his swollen lips slowly turned his face into a running red mess.

'Stop it, oh please stop it!' Jordan crouched against the verandah wall with the yellow vomit staining his shirt front. 'Please stop it!'

He wanted to cover his face with his hands, to blot out the violence and the blood and the terrible black hatred – but he could not. He was locked in an awful fascination, watching every stinging cruel blow, every droplet of flung blood from his brother's face.

Like a corrida bull Ralph came up short at last, and stood with his feet wide apart, his knees giving like reeds overweighted with dew, trying feebly to shake the blackness from his head and the blood from his eyes, his fists bunched up still but too heavy and weak to lift above his waist, his chest heaving for air, swaying and catching his balance every few seconds with an uncontrolled stagger, peering blindly about him for his tormentor.

'Here,' said Zouga quietly, and Ralph lurched towards the voice and Zouga used his right hand for the first time. He chopped him cleanly under the ear, a short measured blow, and Ralph flopped face forward into the dust and snored into it, blowing little red puffs with each breath.

Jordan flew down the steps and dropped to his knees beside his brother, turning his head to one side so he could breathe freely and dabbing ineffectually at the blood with his fingers.

'Jan Cheroot,' Zouga called. He was breathing deeply but slowly; there was colour in his cheeks above his beard, and he touched a few beads of perspiration on his forehead with the kerchief from around his throat.

'Jan Cheroot!' he called again irritably, and this time the little Hottentot roused himself and hurried down the steps.

'Get a bucket of water,' Zouga told him.

Jan Cheroot dashed the contents of a gallon bucket into Ralph's face, washing away the bloody mask, and Ralph gasped and snorted and tried to crawl to his knees.

Jan Cheroot dropped the bucket and grabbed his arm; Jordan stooped and got his head under Ralph's other armpit and between them they lifted him to his feet.

They were both much smaller than Ralph and he hung between them like a dirty blanket on a washline, with the mixture of water and blood dripping to form pale pink rosettes on his shirt front.

Zouga lit a cheroot, studied the ash to be sure it was drawing evenly, then replaced it between his teeth.

He stepped up to his eldest son. With his thumb he pulled down each lower eyelid in turn and peered into his pupils, then grunted with satisfaction. He studied the cut in Ralph's eyebrow, then took his nose between his fingers and moved it gently from side to side to check it for damage, then finally he pulled back Ralph's lip and inspected his teeth for chips or breakage and stepped back.

'Jan Cheroot, take him down to Jameson's surgery. Ask Doc to stitch that eye and give him a handful of mercury pills for the pox.'

Jan Cheroot started to lead Ralph away but Zouga went on, 'Then on your way back stop at Barnato's Gymnasium and sign him up for a course of boxing lessons. He'll have to learn to fight a bit better than that or he's going to get his head beaten in even before he dies of the clap.'

O n the way back from Market Square Jan Cheroot and Ralph walked with their heads together, talking seriously.

'Why do you think they call him Bakela, the Fist?' Jan Cheroot asked, and Ralph grimaced painfully.

His face was lumpy and the colour was coming up in his bruises, deep plum and cloudy blue like summer thunderclouds. The horsehair stitches stuck up stiffly out of his eyebrow and lip, and the cuts were soft-scabbed like cranberry jam.

Jan Cheroot grinned and clucked with sympathy, and then asked the question that had burned his tongue since first he had learned the cause of Zouga's wrath.

'So how did you like your first taste of pink sugar?'

The question stopped Ralph in his tracks while he considered it seriously, then he answered without moving his damaged lip.

'It was bloody marvellous,' he said.

Jan Cheroot giggled and hugged himself with delight. 'Now you listen to me, boy, and you listen good. I love your daddy, we been together so many years I can't count, and when he tells you something you can believe it –

nearly every time. But me, I have never in my life passed up a chance for a slice of that warm stuff – never once, old or young or in between, ugly as a monkey or so pretty it would break your heart, whenever it was offered and lots of times when it wasn't, old Jan Cheroot grabbed it, boy.'

'And it never killed you.' Ralph supplied the summation.

'I guess I would have died without it.'

Ralph started walking again. 'I hope Bazo will fight his fancy again next Sunday. I'm going to need ten guineas pretty badly by then.'

The moon was lipping the horizon, putting the stars to pale shame. It was still a few days short of full, but on the stoep of Zouga's cottage it was light enough to read the headlines of a crumpled copy of the *Diamond Fields Advertiser* that lay beside Zouga's empty riempie chair.

The only sounds were the distant baying of a moon-crazy hound, and the flirt of bats' wings as they spun high parabolas in the moonlight or came fluttering in under the overhang of the verandah roof to pick a moth from the air. The front door was stopped wide open to allow the night's cool to penetrate the inner rooms of the cottage. Jordan crept through it timidly.

He was bare-footed, and the old flannel shirt he wore as a nightdress was one of Zouga's cast-offs. The tails flapped around his bare knees as he moved down the verandah and stopped before the tall falcon-headed carving that stood on its pedestal at the end of the covered stoep.

The slanting moonlight lit the graven bird image from the side, leaving half of it in black mysterious shadow.

Jordan stopped before the image. The clay floor was cold

on his bare soles, and he shivered not entirely from the cold, and looked about him surreptitiously.

Zouga's camp slept, that deep pre-dawn sleep.

Jordan's curls, bushed wildly from the pillow, sparkled like a halo in the moonlight, and his eyes were in shadow, dark holes like those of a skull. All night he had lain rigid in his narrow bed and listened to his brother's heavy breathing through his swollen nose.

Lack of sleep made Jordan feel light-headed and fey. He opened the little twist of newspaper which he had hidden under his pillow when he went to bed.

It contained half a handful of rice and a thin slice of cold roasted lamb. He laid it at the foot of the soapstone column, and stepped back.

Once more he looked about him to make sure that he was alone and unobserved. Then he sank down to his bare knees with the book held against his chest, and bowed his head.

The book was bound in blue leather with gold leaf titling on its spine: *Religions of the American Indians*.

'I greet you, Panes,' Jordan whispered, his swollen eyelids tightly closed.

'The Indians of California, the Acagchemem tribe adore the great buzzard Panes.' The book Jordan held to his breast had become far and away the most precious of all his possessions. He did not like to remember how he had obtained it. It was the only thing he had ever stolen in his life, but he had been forgiven for that sin. He had prayed to the goddess and been forgiven.

'The Panes was a woman, a young and beautiful woman, who had run off into the mountains and been changed into a bird by the god Chinigchinich.'

Jordan knew with all his being whom this description depicted. His mother had been young and beautiful, and she had run away to the black mountain of Death without him.

Now he opened the book and bowed his head over it. It was not light enough to read the fine print of the text, but Jordan knew the invocation to the goddess by heart.

'Why did you run away?' he whispered. 'You would have been better with us. Are we not the ones who love you? It was better that you stayed, for now you are Panes. If we make you a sacrifice of rice and meat, will you not come back to us? See the sacrifice we set for you, great Panes.'

The morning wind stirred, and Jordan heard the branch of the camel-thorn scrape upon the roof before the wind touched him. It was a warm, soft wind, and it ruffled his hair.

Jordan clenched his eyes even tighter, and the little insects of awe crawled upon his skin. The goddess had many ways of showing her presence. This was the first time she had come as a soft warm wind.

'Oh great Panes, I don't want to wallow in filth like Ralph. I don't ever want to smell the trough where a thousand pigs have wallowed. I don't want to go mad, and have my teeth rot out of my mouth.' He whispered softly but ardently, and then the tears began to squeeze out from between his lids.

'Please save me, great Panes.' He poured out all his horror and disgust to the sacred bird-woman. 'They were hitting each other. They were hating each other, and the blood, oh the blood—'

At last he was silent, head bowed, shivering, and then he rose to his bare feet, and for the first time looked at the image.

The bird stared back at him stonily, but Jordan cocked his lovely golden head as though he were listening, and the moonlight silvered his skin.

He turned, still clutching the book, and crept back along the verandah. As he turned the far corner there was a furry rush of dark bodies out of the shadows, and the soft squeals of the bush rats as they squabbled over the sacrifice.

Jordan pushed open the door of the kitchen and it smelled of woodsmoke and curry powder and carbolic soap.

He stooped to the ashbox of the black iron stove, and when he blew lightly through the grating the ashes glowed.

He pushed a long wax taper through the bars and blew again and a little blue flame popped into life. He carried it carefully across the kitchen, sheltering it with his cupped hand, and transferred the flame to the stump of candle in the neck of the dark green champagne bottle. Then he blew out the taper and placed the bottle on the scrubbed yellow deal table and stepped back.

For a few seconds longer he hesitated, then he took the skirts of the faded and patched nightshirt, lifted them as high as his shoulders and looked down at his body.

The puppy fat had disappeared from his belly and hips. His navel was a dark eye in the flat clean plain of his trunk, and his legs were gracefully shaped. His buttocks lean and tight, like immature fruit.

His body was smooth and hairless except for the golden wisps at the juncture of his legs. It was not yet thick enough to curl, and was sparse and fine as silk thread freshly spun upon the cocoon.

From the centre of this cloudy web his penis hung down limply. It had grown alarmingly in the last few months, and in Jordan's horrified imagination, he foresaw the day when it would be thick and heavy as his arm, a huge shameful burden to carry through life.

At this moment it looked so soft and white and innocent, but when he woke in the mornings it was hard as bone, hot and throbbing with a sinfully pleasurable ache.

That was bad, but in these last weeks that terrible swelling and stiffening had come upon him at the most unexpected times: at the dinner table with his father seated

217

opposite him, in the schoolroom when the new school-mistress had leaned over him to correct his spelling, seated at the sorting-table beside Jan Cheroot, on the gelding's back when the friction of the saddle had triggered it, and that awful stiff thing had thrust out the front of his breeches.

He took it in his hand now and it seemed helpless and soft as a newborn kitten, but he was not deceived. He stroked it softly back and forth and instantly he felt it change shape between his fingers. He released it quickly.

The joint of mutton that the family had dined off the previous evening stood on the deal table, under a steel mesh fly-cover. Jordan lifted the cover, and the leg was hacked down to the bone.

His father's hunting knife lay beside the cold joint. The handle was stag-horn and the blade was nine inches long, sweeping up to a dagger point, and the white mutton fat had congealed upon the blade.

Jordan picked up the knife in his right hand.

The previous evening he had watched his father flicking the edge of the blade across the long steel. It always fascinated him, because Zouga held the razor edge towards his own fingers as he worked.

The proof of his father's expertise with the steel was the way in which the heavy knife seemed to glide effortlessly through the meat of the joint. It was wickedly sharp.

Jordan looked down again at that long white thing that stuck out of his body. The loose skin at the tip was half retracted so that the pink acorn pushed out from beneath it.

He tucked the tail of his shirt under his chin to free both hands and seized himself at the root, enclosing within the circle of his fingers the wrinkled bag with its tender marbles of flesh, and he pulled it out, stretching it out like the neck of the condemned man upon the headsman's block, while with the other hand he brought the knife down and laid the blade against his own belly, just above the fine golden fluff of pubic hair.

The blade was so cold that he gasped, and the mutton fat left a little greasy smear on his belly. He took a long breath to steel himself, and then slowly began to draw the blade downwards, to free himself for ever of that shameful wormlike growth.

'Jordie, what are you doing?' The voice from the doorway behind him startled him so that he cried out aloud. He threw the knife onto the table and at the same time dropped the shirt to cover himself.

'Jordie!'

He turned swiftly, breathing in sharp little gasps, and Ralph came towards him from the kitchen door. He wore only a pair of baggy shorts, and there were goose-bumps on the smooth bare skin of his chest from the pre-dawn chill.

'What were you doing?' he repeated.

'Nothing. I wasn't doing anything.' Jordan shook his head wildly.

'You were whacking your old winker, weren't you?' Ralph accused and grinned. 'You dirty little bugger.'

Jordan let out a choking sob and fled past him to the door, and Ralph chuckled and shook his head.

Then he picked up the stag-handled knife and cut a thick slab of mutton off the joint, dipped the blade into the stone pot and smeared a gob of yellow mustard over the meat, and munched it as he went about building up the fire in the stove and setting the coffee water to boil.

The following Sunday afternoon on the white sand of the fighting arena, Inkosikazi, the spider, died an agonizing death in the ghastly embrace of a smaller more agile adversary.

Bazo mourned her as he would a lover, and Kamuza sang the dirge with him just as sadly, for the Matabele syndicate had lost twenty sovereigns with her passing.

The return from Market Square to Zouga's camp resembled Napoleon's retreat from Moscow, headed by Ralph and Bazo bearing between them the basket and its sorry contents.

Opposite Diamond Lil's canteen, Ralph halted the cortege for a moment and wistfully contemplated the painted windows across the street, and listened for a moment to the sounds of laughter from beyond the green door – imagining that he could distinguish Lil's tinkling chimes.

When they reached the thatched beehive communal hut, Kamuza passed Ralph the clay pot of bubbling millet beer.

'How much did you lose, Henshaw?'

'Everything,' Ralph replied tragically. The very reason for living.' He took a long swallow of the thick gruel-like beer.

'That is bad; only a foolish man keeps all his cows in the same kraal.'

'Kamuza, your words are always a great solace,' Ralph told him bitterly. 'But I am unworthy of such wisdom. Keep those treasures for yourself alone.'

Kamuza looked smug and turned to Bazo. 'Now you know why I would not lay fifty gold queens, as you bid me.'

Bazo shot a glance at Ralph, and they acted together.

Ralph draped a seemingly brotherly arm over Kamuza's shoulders, but it was a steely yoke that held him helpless, and with the other hand he pulled open the front of Kamuza's loincloth – and Bazo scooped the soft furry carcass of the great spider out of the basket and dropped it into the opening.

As Ralph released him, Kamuza went up into the air,

rearing like an unbroken stallion feeling the saddle and spur for the first time, whinnying wildly with horror, beating at his own loins with both hands.

If Ralph had not caught him, Bazo, in a shaking paralysis of mirth, might have fallen into the fire in the centre of the hut.

K amuza had been gone almost three years.
When Bazo and the other Matabele had signed their contracts for a third period, Kamuza alone had asked Bakela to 'Bala Isitupa', to write off the contract as complete, and he had taken the road north back to Matabeleland.

Bazo had missed him deeply. He had missed the spiked tongue and shrewd acerbic counsel. He had missed Kamuza's intuitive understanding of the white man's ways of thinking, ways which Bazo still found unfathomable.

Even though Henshaw was his friend, had worked at Bazo's shoulder for all those long years, though they had hawked and hunted together, dipped into the same baking of maize porridge and drunk from the lip of the same beer-pot – though Henshaw spoke his language so easily that sitting in the darkness when the fire had burned down to embers it might have been a young Matabele buck talking, so faithfully did Henshaw echo the deep cadence of the north, so complete was his command of the colloquial, so poetic the imagery he used – yet Henshaw would never be Matabele as Kamuza was Matabele, could never be brother as Kamuza was, had never shared the initiation rites with Bazo as Kamuza had, had never formed the 'horns of the bull' with him as the impi closed for the kill, and had never driven the assegai deep and seen the bright blood fly as Kamuza had.

Thus Bazo was filled with joy when he heard the word.

'Kamuza is amongst us again.'

Bazo heard it first whispered by another Matabele as they formed a line at the gate of the security compound.

'Kamuza comes as the king's man,' they whispered around the watch-fires, and there was respect, even fear, in their voices. 'Kamuza wears the headring now.'

Many young Matabele had come to work at *Umgodi Kakulu*, 'The Big Hole', these last few years, and each month more came down the long and weary road from the north, small bands of ten or twenty, sometimes only in pairs, or threes and occasionally even a man travelling alone.

How many had reached Kimberley? There was nobody to keep a tally, a thousand certainly, two thousand perhaps, and each of them had been given the road southwards by the great black elephant, each of them had the king's permission to journey beyond the borders of Matabeleland, for without it they would have been speared to death by the bright assegais of the impis that guarded every road to and from the king's great kraal at Thabas Indunas – the Hills of the Chiefs.

Even in exile these young Matabele formed a close-knit tribal association. Each newcomer from the north carried tidings, long messages from fathers and indunas, repeated verbatim with every nuance of the original. Just as every Matabele who left the diamond fields, whether he had worked out his three-year contract or was bored and homesick or had fallen foul of the white man's complicated and senseless laws and was deserting, carried back with him messages and instructions that he had committed to the phenomenal memory of a people who did not have the written word.

Now the word passed swiftly from Matabele to Matabele.

'Kamuza is here.'

Kamuza had never warranted such attention before. He had been one amongst a thousand; but now he had returned as the king's man, and they lowered their voices when they spoke his name.

Bazo looked for him each day, searching the faces on the high stagings and on the running skips. He lay sleepless on his mat beside the cooling watch-fire, listening for Kamuza's whisper in the darkness.

He waited for many days and many nights, and then suddenly Kamuza was there, stooping through the low entrance and greeting Bazo.

'I see you, Bazo, son of Gandang.'

Bazo stifled his joy and replied calmly.

'I see you also, Kamuza.'

And they made a place for Kamuza in the circle, not pressing him too closely, giving him space, for now Kamuza wore the simple black tiara upon his close-cropped pate, the badge of the Councillor, the induna of the king of Matabeleland.

They called him 'Baba', a term of great respect, and even Bazo clapped his hands softly in greeting and passed him the beer pot.

Only after Kamuza had refreshed himself could Bazo begin to ask the questions of home, disguising his eagerness behind measured tones and an expression of calm dignity.

Kamuza was no longer a youth, neither of them were; the years had sped away and they were both in the full flowering of their manhood. Kamuza's features were sharper than the true Matabele of Zanzi blood, the old blood from Zululand, for his was mixed with Tswana, the less warlike but shrewd and cunning peoples of King Khama. Kamuza's grandmother had been captured as a maiden, still short of puberty, by one of King Mzilikazi's raiding impis, and taken to wife by the induna who commanded her captors. From her Kamuza had inherited his mulberry black skin and the Egyptian slant of his eyes, the narrow nostrils and the thin and knowing twist of his lips.

There were very few Matabele who could still trace their bloodline back to the pure Zanzi, to the line of Chaka and Dingaan, the Zulus, the Sons of Heaven, and Bazo was one of those. Yet it was Kamuza who wore the ring of the induna on his head now.

In the time of Mzilikazi, a man would have the hoar frost of wisdom and age powdering his hair, and the cowtails bound about his elbows and knees would proclaim his deeds in battle to the world before the king ordered him to take the *isicoco*. Then his wives would plait and twist the headring into his own hair and cement it permanently into place with gum and clay and ox blood, a permanent halo of honour that entitled the wearer to his seat on the Council of the Matabele nation.

However, the old times were changing. More cunning than fierce, Lobengula, son of Mzilikazi, looked for cunning in those about him. Mzilikazi had been a warrior and lived by the white flash of the assegai. Lobengula, though he had blooded his spear, had never been a warrior, and he scorned the warriors' simpleness of thought and directness of action. As his father's greybeards faltered, he replaced them with men who thought as swiftly as the old ones had stabbed.

He had no patience with the old men's preoccupation with a world that was passing, and he sought out the young ones with clear fresh eyes, men who could see with him the dark clouds gathering on the southern borders like the soaring thunderheads of high summer.

Men who could sense the change and terrible events which his wizards and his own divinations warned him would soon rush down upon him like the fires that sweep the papyrus beds of the Zambezi swamps at the end of the dry season.

Lobengula, the great Black Elephant, whose very tread shakes the earth's foundations, and whose voice splits the skies, was choosing young men with eyes to see and ears to hear.

Thus Kamuza now wore the *isicoco* of the induna and, as he spoke over the fire in his dry whisper, his slanted eyes black and bright as those of a mamba in the firelight, men listened – and listened with great attention.

It was a measure of the gravity of the news he carried from the north that Kamuza began the council – the *indaba* – with a recital of the history of the Matabele nation. Each of them had heard it first with their mother's breast in their mouths, had drunk it in with her milk, but they listened now as avidly as then, reinforcing their memories so that when the time came they would be able to repeat it perfectly in each detail to their own children, that the story might never be lost.

The history began with Mzilikazi, war chief of the impis of Zulu, warrior without peer, beloved comrade and trusted intimate of King Chaka himself. It told of the black sickness of King Chaka, driven mad with grief at the death of his mother Nandi, the Sweet One. Chaka ordering the year of mourning in which no man might sow seed, on pain of death; in which the milk from the cows must be thrown upon the earth, on pain of death; in which no man might lie with his woman, on pain of death.

Mad Chaka brooded in his great hut and looked for cause to strike down all around him, even the most trusted, even the most beloved.

So it was that Chaka's messengers came to Mzilikazi, the young war chieftain. They found him in the field with his impis about him, five thousand of Zululand's bravest and finest, all of them still hot from battle, driving before them the spoils they had taken – the captured herds, the young and comely girls roped neck to neck.

The king's messengers wore the long tail feathers of the stately blue cranes in their headdress, token of their solemn mission.

'The king accuses the induna Mzilikazi,' began the first messenger, and looking into his arrogant face Mzilikazi

225

knew that he looked upon the face of death. 'The king accuses Mzilikazi of stealing the king's share of the spoils of war.'

Then the second messenger spoke, and his words were an echo of the king's black madness, so that the words of King Chaka stood in the air above Mzilikazi's impis the way that the vultures circle above the battlefields on wide and motionless pinions.

If the sentence of death had been upon him alone, Mzilikazi might have gone to his king and met it with courage and dignity. But his five thousand fighting men were doomed also, and Mzilikazi called them his children.

So Mzilikazi reached out and seized the king's messengers, and for a moment the earth seemed to lurch in its courses, for to touch those who wore the blue crane feathers was to touch the person of the king himself. With the razor edge of his assegai, Mzilikazi slashed the blue feathers from their heads, and threw them into the faces of the grovelling messengers.

'That is my reply to Chaka – who is no longer my king.'

Thus began the great exodus towards the north and, seated over the watch-fire, Kamuza, the king's man, related it all again.

He told the battle honours of Mzilikazi, the renegade. He told how Chaka sent his most famous impis after the fleeing five thousand, and how Mzilikazi met them in the classic battle tactics of the Nguni, how he waited for them in the bad ground.

Kamuza told how Mzilikazi threw the 'horns of the bull' around the impis of Chaka, and how his young men shouted '*Ngi dhla!* I have eaten!' as they drove in the steel; and the listeners in the dark hut murmured and moved restlessly, and their eyes shone and their spear hands twitched.

When it was over, the survivors of Chaka's shattered impi came to Mzilikazi and, on their knees, swore allegiance to him, to Mzilikazi who was no longer a renegade, but a little king.

Kamuza told how the little king marched north with his swollen impi, and how he defeated other little kings and became a great king.

Kamuza told how after Chaka was murdered by his brothers, Dingaan, the new leader of the Zulu nation, did not dare to send out more impis to pursue Mzilikazi. So Mzilikazi flourished, and like a ravaging lion he ate up the tribes. Their warriors swelled his fighting impis, and his Zanzi, the pure-blooded Zulu, bred upon the bellies of the captured maidens and the Matabele became a nation and Mzilikazi became a black emperor whose domain over-shadowed even that of Chaka.

The men about the fire listened and felt their hearts swell with pride.

Then Kamuza told how the *buni*, the strange white men, crossed the river in their little wagons and outspanned upon the land that Mzilikazi had won with the assegai. Then Mzilikazi paraded his impis, and they danced with their war plumes aflutter, and their long shields clashing as they passed before him.

After he had reviewed the might of his nation, Mzilikazi took the little ceremonial spear of his kingship, and he poised before his impis and then hurled the toy-like weapon towards the banks of the Gariep river on which the white men had outspanned their wagons.

They took them in the hour before dawn, at the time of the horns, when the horns of the cattle can first be seen against the lightening sky. The front ranks of racing black warriors received the first volley of the long muzzle-loading guns, absorbing it as though it were a handful of pebbles thrown into a stormy black sea.

Then they stabbed the bearded men as they worked frantically with powderhorn and ramrod. They stabbed the white women as they ran from the wagons in their nightdresses, trying to carry the second gun to their men. They snatched the infants from their cradles on the wagonbed, and dashed out their brains against the tall iron-shod wheels of the wagons.

Oh, it was a rare feast that they set for Mzilikazi's chickens, the grotesque naked-headed vultures. They believed it was an ending – but it was only a beginning, for the Matabele were about to learn of the persistence and the dour courage of these strange pale people.

The next wave of white men came out of the south, and when they found the abandoned wagons and the jackal-chewed bones on the banks of the Gariep, theirs was a fury such as the Matabele had never encountered in all their wars.

So the *buni* met the impis on the open ground, refusing to be drawn into the ravines and thorn scrub. They came in pitifully small squadrons on shaggy ponies to dismount and discharge their volleys in a thunder of blue powder smoke. Then they went up into the saddle to wheel away from under the wall of charging rawhide shields, and reload and circle back to let loose the thunder again into the mass of half-naked bodies glistening with oil and sweat.

The *buni* built fortresses on the open plain, fortresses with their wagons' bodies which they lashed wheel to wheel; and they let the impis come to die upon the wooden walls of the fortress, while their womenfolk stood close behind them to take the gun while the barrel was still hot and pass up the second gun, charged and primed.

Then when the impis drew back, mauled and shaken, the wagons uncoiled from their circle, like a slow but deadly puffadder, and crawled forward towards the kraal of Mzilikazi. And the dreadful horsemen galloped ahead of them, firing and circling, firing and circling.

Sadly Mzilikazi counted his dead and the price was too high, the red mud through which the iron-shod wheels churned was puddled with the blood of Zanzi, the blood of Heaven.

So he called his nation, and the herd boys brought in the herds, and the women rolled the sleeping-mats, and the little girls balanced the clay cooking-pots upon their heads, and Mzilikazi put fire into his kraals and led the Matabele nation away. A vast throng of people and animals were guarded by the depleted impis, while the white men on their sturdy ponies drove them and pointed them the way the sheepdog works the flock. Mzilikazi led them northwards until they crossed the great river into a new land.

'Now the white birds are gathering again,' Kamuza told the young men about the watch fire. 'Each day they come up the road to Thabas Indunas, and they bring their tawdry gifts and the little green bottles of madness. Their words are sweet as honey on the tongue, but they catch in the throat of those who try to swallow them as though they were the green bile of the crocodile.'

'What is it they seek from the king?' Bazo asked the question for all those who listened, and Kamuza shrugged.

'This one asks for the right to hunt elephant and take the teeth, this one asks for the young girls to be sent to his wagon, another wants to tell the nation of a strange white god that has three heads, another wishes to dig a hole and look for the yellow iron, yet another wishes to buy cattle. One says he wants only this, and another only that, but they want it all. These people are consumed by a hunger that can never be appeased, they burn with a thirst that can never be assuaged. They want everything they see, and even that is never enough for them. They take the very earth, but that is not enough, so they tear it open like a man tearing a child from the mother's womb. They take the rivers, and that is not enough, so they build walls across them and turn them into lakes. They ride after the elephant herds and shoot them down, not just one or two, not just the big bulls, but all of them – the breeding cows and the calves with ivory no longer than your finger. Everything they see they take; and they see everything, for they are always moving and searching and looking.'

'Lobengula must eat them up,' Bazo said. 'He must eat them up as Mzilikazi his father would have eaten them.'

'Hau!' Kamuza smiled his thin twisted smile. 'Such wisdom from my brother. He recalls how Mzilikazi ate the white men on the banks of the Gariep, and lost a land. Listen to Bazo, my children. He counsels the King Lobengula to throw the war spear and loose his impis as Cetewayo the King of Zulu did at the Hill of the Little Hand. How many Englishmen did Cetewayo slay? There was no counting, for their red jackets lay one upon the other like the snows of the Dragon Mountains when the sunset turns them to fire, and their blood fed the land so that the grass still grows greener and thicker and sweeter upon the slopes of the Little Hand to this day. Oh a fine killing, my children, a great and beautiful stabbing – and afterwards Cetewayo paid for it with the spear of his kingship. He paid for it with his royal herds, he paid for it with the liver and heart of his young men, with the grassy hills of Zululand. For after the avengers had made the great slaughter at Ulundi they took it all, and they placed chains of iron upon Cetewayo's wrists and ankles and they chained his indunas and his war captains and led them away. Now Bazo, the wise, would have you know what a good bargain King Cetewayo made, and he urges Lobengula to make the same bargain with these white men.'

Bazo's expression remained grave and dignified while Kamuza chided and mocked him but he twisted the snuff-horn between his fingers and once he glanced to the dark corner of the thatched hut where the long war shields and the broad assegai were stacked.

But when Kamuza finished, Bazo shook his head. 'No

one here dares counsel the king; we are his dogs only. No one here doubts the might and resolve of the white men, we who live each day with their strange and wonderful ways. All we ask is this: what is the king's word? Tell us what Lobengula wishes – for to hear is to obey.'

Kamuza nodded. 'Hear then the king's voice, for the king has travelled with all his senior indunas – Babiaan and Somabula and Gandang – all the indunas of the house of Kumalo – they have gone into the hills of Matopos to the place of the Umlimo—'

A superstitious tremor shook the group, a little shiver as though the name of the wizard of the Matopos had crawled upon their skins like the sickle-winged tsetse fly.

'The Umlimo has given the oracle,' Kamuza told them, and then was silent, the pause theatrical, to pique their attention, to dramatize the effect of his next words.

'On the first day the Umlimo repeated the ancient prophecy, the words that have come down from the time of Monomatapa. On the first day the Umlimo spoke thus:

"The stone falcons will fly afar. There shall be no peace in the kingdoms of the Mambos or the Monomatapas until they return. For the white eagle will war with the black bull until the stone falcons return to roost."'

They had all of them heard the prophecy before, but now it had a new and sinister impact.

'The king has pondered the ancient prophecy, and he says thus: "The white birds are gathering. Eagle and vulture – all of them white, they roost already upon the roof of my kraal."'

'What is the meaning of the stone falcons?' one of his listeners asked.

'The stone falcons are the bird gods that the ancient ones left at the burial place of the old kings, Zimbabwe.'

'How will stone birds fly?'

'One has flown already,' Bazo answered this time. 'One of the stone falcons stands close by us now. It stands under the roof of Bakela, the Fist. It was he who took the falcon, and carried it away.'

'When the other birds fly, then war will sweep over Matabeleland,' Kamuza affirmed. 'But listen now to the oracle of the Umlimo.' And their questions were stilled.

'On the second day the Umlimo prophesied thus:

"When the midnight sky turns to noon, and the stars shine on the hills – then the fist will hold the blade to the throat of the black bull."

'This was the prophecy of the second day.'

Again they were silent as they pondered the words then, mystified, they looked to Kamuza for the meaning of the prophecy.

'Lobengula, the Black Elephant, alone understands the meaning of the prophecy of the second day. Is he not versed in the mysteries of the wizards? Did he not pass his childhood in the caves and secret places of the wizards? Thus says Lobengula. "This is not yet the time to explain the words of the Umlimo to my children, for they are momentous words indeed, and there will be a time for the nation to understand."'

Bazo nodded and passed his snuff-horn. Kamuza took it and drew the red powder up into his nostrils with two sharp inhalations of breath and, watching him, Bazo did not dare to voice his own suspicion that perhaps Lobengula, the mighty thunder of the skies, was as mystified by the prophecy of the second day as was the little group around the fire.

'Was this all the oracle?' Bazo asked instead, and Kamuza shook his head.

'On the third day the Umlimo prophesied for the last time:

"Sting the mamba with his own venom, pull down the lion with his own claws, deceive the clever chacma baboon with his own trickery."

'This was the prophecy of the third and final day.'

'Does the king intend that we, his humble cattle, should know the meaning of the prophecy of the third day?'

'Thus spoke Lobengula: "We the Matabele cannot prevail until we arm ourselves as our adversary is armed, until we gather to ourselves the strength that is found only in the yellow coins and shining stones. For it is these things which have made the white man strong."'

Nobody interrupted the silence that followed, for they all sensed that there was more to come.

'Thus the king summoned me to the royal kraal and bid me carry his word to all the Matabele who live beyond the borders of the king's domains. For thus spoke the king: "Bring me guns to answer the smoke of the white man's guns. Bring me diamonds and bring me the yellow coins that I may grow as strong as the white Queen who lives beyond the sea. For then her soldiers will not dare to come against me."'

Bazo replied for them all. 'Let Lobengula know that what he requires of us he shall have. Guns he shall have, for it is part of our contract with the white man. Each of us will carry a gun when we return to Matabeleland, some of us who have worked out two *Isitupa* will carry two guns when we return. Some of us will bring three guns.'

'That is known,' Kamuza nodded.

'Lobengula will have gold coins, for we are paid in coin, and what we bring home to Thabas Indunas belongs to the king.'

'That is right and proper.'

'But diamonds?' Bazo asked. 'The diamonds belong to the white man. They are fierce for them as a lioness is

233

fierce for her cubs. How are we to bring diamonds to the king?'

'Listen to me,' whispered Kamuza. 'There will be no more "pick-ups". When one of you turns up the shine of a diamond in the yellow gravel, then that diamond belongs to Lobengula.'

'It is against the law.'

'Against the white man's law only, not against the law of Lobengula, who is your king.'

'To hear is to obey,' Bazo grunted, but he thought of Bakela, the Fist, who was his father, and Henshaw, the Hawk, who was his brother, and he did not relish stealing the stones for which they laboured as hard as Bazo did himself.

'Not only in the pit,' Kamuza went on. 'Each of you will watch for the chance on the sorting-tables, you, Donsela—' He picked out a Matabele across the fire from him, a young man with a deep intelligent brow and strong jaw. 'You have been chosen to work in the new grease house.'

'The tables are guarded,' Donsela replied. 'They are covered with a steel screen.'

They had all of them heard Donsela speak of the marvel of the new grease house.

Once again the ingenuity of the white men had put the diamond's unique qualities to his own advantage. The diamond was unwetable, shedding moisture like the body-feathers of a goose. So while wet gravel would roll across a steel table smeared with thick yellow grease, the dry diamond would stick fast.

The pipeline from the Vaal river had at last reached Kimberley, and this water supply was augmented by the subterranean water pumped up from the depths of the vast excavation. There was water enough now to wash the gravel, instead of laboriously dry-sorting it, water enough to wash the sieved gravel over the slanting grease tables.

The diamonds stuck like fat little blisters, half embedded in the grease, ready to be scraped off with a steel spatula at the end of each shift.

'There is a steel screen over the tables,' Donsela repeated, and Kamuza smiled and passed him a thin reed, cut from the riverbank. On the tip of the reed was a little lump of beeswax.

'The reed will pass through the mesh of the screen,' Kamuza told him. 'The diamond will stick more firmly to the wax than to the grease.'

Donsela examined the reed cautiously. 'Last week a Basuto was found with a stone. That same day he fell from the skip as they were bringing him out of the pit. Men who steal stones have accidents. Those accidents always kill them.'

'A warrior's duty is to die for his king,' Kamuza told him drily. 'Do not let the overseer catch you, and pick out only the biggest and brightest stones.'

In the three years between Kamuza's departure from Kimberley and his abrupt return, Ralph had reached his full growth. Only months short of his twenty-first birthday, he stood as tall as Zouga; but unlike his father, he was clean-shaven except for the thick dark moustache which he allowed to curl down at the corners of his mouth.

At rare intervals he was still able to gather together the ten gold sovereigns necessary to keep his surreptitious friendship with Diamond Lil alive. Then suddenly that was no longer relevant, for Ralph fell in love.

It happened in the street outside that exclusive institution, already the most famous in Africa south of the equator, membership of which conferred enormous prestige and a semi-mystical entrée to the elite band of men who wielded the growing wealth and burgeoning power of the diamond fields.

Yet the Kimberley Club was merely a single-storeyed wood-and-iron building as drab as any on the diggings. True it boasted a billiard room with a full-sized table, a picket fence of ornate cast iron and a stained-glass front door – but it was situated in the noisiest street just off Market Square, and it enjoyed its fair share of the flies and the all-pervading red dust.

It was mid-morning and Ralph was bringing one of the gravel carts back from the blacksmith who had replaced the iron tyres on the wooden-spoked wheels.

There was a stir in the street ahead of him. He saw men run from the canteens and kopje-wallopers' offices, most of them bareheaded and in shirtsleeves.

A vehicle came bowling out of the Square – an extra-ordinary vehicle, light and fast, with high narrow wheels, so cunningly sprung that it seemed to float behind the pair that drew it. They were matched, a strange pale brazen colour, softer than the colour of honey, and their manes were white blond.

Both horses were martingaled to force them to arch their necks, and the long combed platinum manes flew like the battle colours of a famous regiment.

The driver, either by chance, but more probably by skill, had them leading with their off fores in perfect unison, and their gait was an exaggerated trot in which they threw their forehooves so high that they seemed almost to touch the shining heads as they nodded to the rhythm of their run.

Ralph was stabbed by such a pang of envy that it was a physical pain. He had never seen anything so beautiful as those pale glistening animals and the vehicle that they drew – until he raised his eyes to the driver.

She wore a tricorn hat of midnight blue, set at a jaunty angle over one eyebrow. Her eyebrows were jet black, narrow and exquisitely arched over huge drop-shaped eyes.

As she came up to the plodding gravel cart she barely

lifted the gloved hand that held the reins, and the plunging pair of pale horses swerved neatly and the elegant vehicle flashed past so close that, had he dared, Ralph might have reached up and touched one of those slim ankles in its high-buttoned patent leather boot which just showed under the tailored skirt of moiré taffeta.

Then she dropped her hand again, and the matched pair swung the carriage in neatly before the wrought-iron gate of the Kimberley Club and stopped, shaking out their manes fretfully and stamping their forefeet.

'Bazo, take them,' Ralph called urgently. 'Go on to the stagings. I'll follow you.'

Then he darted across the street and reached up to seize the head of the nearest thoroughbred.

He was only just in time, for half a dozen other loiterers had raced him to it. Ralph removed his cap and looked up at the woman on the buttoned leather seat of the carriage. She glanced down at him and fleetingly smiled her thanks, and Ralph saw that her eyes were the same midnight blue as the hat on her head. Those eyes touched him for only an instant and then went back to the stained-glass front door of the club, but Ralph felt a physical shock from her gaze like a blow in the chest, so that he could not catch his breath.

Ralph was aware of voices, men's voices, from the direction of the club, but he could not tear his eyes from that lovely face. He was absorbing each fine detail, the braid of her hair, the colour of freshly-washed coal, thick as the tail of a lioness, which dropped from under the hat over her shoulder and hung to her waist. The fine peppering of dark freckles high on her cheekbones seemed to emphasize the purity of the rest of her skin. Her small pointed ears were set at an alert listening angle which gave a peculiar vivacity to her face. The dark V of the widow's peak below the brim of her hat pointed up the depth of forehead. Her nose was narrow and straight with elegantly flared nostrils that gave her expression an hauteur that was instantly belied when she smiled, as she was smiling now, but not at Ralph.

She was smiling at the group of men who came out onto the porch of the club, chatting animatedly as they adjusted their hats.

'A splendid lunch, sir.' The only stranger to Ralph in the group thanked his host and then led them down the short walk to the street.

He was a tall, well-proportioned man. His dress was sober. The cut was not English but he wore it with a dash that made the dark colours appear flamboyant.

He wore a dark patch over one eye, and it gave him a piratical air. His beard was trimmed to a point, and touched with silver.

'He is at least forty years old,' Ralph thought, bitterly, as he realized that the woman was smiling directly at this man.

At his right hand was a small neat figure, a man with an unremarkable face and thin receding hair, a small moustache of indeterminate colour – but eyes so intelligent and humorous that they altered the man's appearance – made it striking and interesting.

'Ah, Ralph,' this man murmured, as he noticed the young man standing at the horse's head; but Ralph could not meet his eyes.

Doctor Leander Starr Jameson was an intimate friend of his father's, and privy to Ralph's shame and disgrace. It was he who had administered the mercury tablets, and washed them down with a stern admonition to avoid in future the snares of harlotry. For a moment Ralph wondered if the doctor would impart his vile secret to the lovely lady on the seat of the carriage – and the thought burned his soul like hoar frost.

On the bearded man's other hand was Mr Rhodes, big and serious, his dress untidy, the knot of his tie slipping and his breeches baggy, but with that sense of determination and certainty about him that always awed Ralph.

Behind them all followed the stooped scholarly figure of Alfred Beit, like Mr Rhodes' shadow.

The four men paused in a group beside the carriage, and the tall stranger reached up and took the woman's hand.

He touched her fingers to his lips.

'Gentlemen, may I present my wife, Mrs St John.' The big man's accent was unmistakable, even Ralph recognized the soft drawl that emanated from the Southern States of America.

However, it was the title the man used and not the accent which struck like a fiery dart into Ralph's breast.

' – Mrs St John, my wife – Mrs St John.'

While Ralph stood rigid at the horse's head, destroyed by his adoration which he now knew was hopeless, the group ignored him and the men made their bows.

'Louise, my dear, this is Mr Rhodes of whom you have heard so much—'

The formal phrases might have been spoken in a foreign language as far as Ralph was affected by them. Her name was Louise, and she was married. That is all that he understood.

General St John climbed up beside his wife. He moved lithely for such a big man, and one so old, Ralph conceded reluctantly, and hated him anew for that. St John took the reins from Louise's gloved hand, lifted his hat to the three men and started the horses. Ralph had to jump back to avoid being knocked down, and Louise was talking animatedly to the General. Neither of them glanced at Ralph again, and the carriage whirled away, down the street.

Ralph stared after it wistfully.

Jordan decorated the borders of the menus with roman-ticized scenes of the diggings: the stagings soaring above the gaping pit, heroic figures working on the walls of yellow earth, a sorter at his table – and at the head of the sheet a man's cupped hands overflowing with uncut diamonds – and he coloured the illustrations with water paints.

'What's Velouté de la Nouvelle Ruée?' Ralph asked.

'Soup New Rush,' Jordie told him without looking up from his artistic labours.

'What's going to be in it?'

'Marrow bones and pearl barley.'

'And what's Quartier de Chevreuil Diamant Bleu?'

'Haunch of springbuck in the style of a blue diamond.'

'I don't know why we can't just speak English,' Ralph complained. 'What's the style of a blue diamond, anyway?'

'Lard the haunch with bacon fat, marinade it in olive oil and cognac with wild garlic, and then bake it in a pie crust.'

Ralph swallowed his saliva. Jordan's culinary skills were always a source of delight to him.

'All right – I'll eat it.'

Jordan licked his brush, leaving a streak of Prussian blue on his tongue, and then looked up at his brother.

'You are going to serve it, not eat it—' Jordan paused portentously, 'Mr Rhodes is coming to lunch,' as though that explained it all.

'Well, if I'm not good enough to sit at the same table as your famous Mr Rhodes – I'll be damned if I'll play waiter. You can get Donsela. For a shilling Donsela will spill soup on Mr Rhodes, for a shilling Donsela would throw soup on King Lobengula himself. I'm going to bribe him.'

However, in the end curiosity and Jordan's promise of the leftovers prevailed and Ralph dressed himself in the ridiculous monkey-jacket that Jordan had designed and tailored for him and carried the tray of Velouté out on the wide verandah of Zouga's camp – and there nearly dropped it.

'Madame, you remind me of the heroine from Mr Longfellow's poem,' Neville Pickering complimented Louise St John, and she smiled back at him from her seat at the centre of the luncheon table.

'Thank you, sir.'

Her jacket was in pale creamy buckskin with tasselled sleeves, and the bodice was crusted with bright-coloured beads in bold geometrical patterns. Louise had parted her thick black hair in the centre, braided a blue ribbon into each of the thick tresses, bound them with a band about her forehead, and then let them hang onto her bosom. The soft tanned buckskin was divided into ankle-length culottes, and her boots were also of soft beaded leather.

Louise was the only woman at the long trestle table on the open verandah of Zouga's camp. The men seated on each side of her were already emerging as the most influential subjects on this continent of an omnipotent queen. Like the men that another English queen had sent out to the corners of the earth, these were the new Elizabethans, most of them already rich – all of them restless and consumed with their lust for power, for wealth, for land. Each with a separate dream that he would follow relentlessly all his life, every one of them driving, ruthless men.

Ballantyne. Beit. Jameson. Rhodes. Robinson. The list of names read like a roll-call for a regiment of filibusters, and yet here they were listening to a discourse on women's fashion as though it were a company report on tonnage treated and cartage recovered.

Only Zouga Ballantyne was not smiling. The woman offended Zouga. Her beauty was too flamboyant, her colouring too vivid. Zouga preferred the pale gold blonde hair and the complexion of sugared cream and strawberries. An Englishman's idea of beauty.

This woman's dress was outrageous, the styling of her hair pretentious. Her gaze was too direct, her eyes too blue, her conversation too easy and her style of address too familiar. Of course American women had the reputation of affecting masculine manners, but Zouga found himself wishing that Louise St John had kept those manners on the other side of the Atlantic Ocean where they belonged.

It was enough that she had galloped into his camp ahead of her husband, riding astride, and dismounted by freeing both of her narrow booted feet from the stirrups and vaulting lightly to the ground; but then she had come up onto the stoep with an assured stride and smile, her right hand out like a man, and without waiting for her husband to introduce them had said: 'You must be Zouga Ballantyne. I'd recognize you anywhere by Mungo's description of you.'

Her hand was narrow, the skin warm but dry, but the grip of her fingers was unfemininely firm, the grip of a skilled horsewoman.

These leisurely Sunday luncheons at Zouga's camp were his one extravagance, and they had become one of the traditions of Kimberley, when excellent fare and good liquor and the company of intelligent men made for memorable afternoons.

Women were very seldom invited to these gatherings, and Louise St John would not have been there if Zouga had been able to have her husband come alone, but Mungo St John had replied pointedly to the invitation, 'General *and Mrs St John* have pleasure in accepting.'

The friendship between St John and Zouga had begun many years previously, and he was the kind of man whom Zouga could admire: a man like himself, hard and determined, one who lived by his own code without compromise. One who expected no preference nor favour, but whose triumphs were of his own engineering and whose disasters were met with fortitude, without plea or excuse, even when occasioned by cruel circumstances beyond his control.

In the late 'fifties St John had built up a commercial empire, a fleet of trading vessels which had carried the black ivory of slaves from the African continent to that of North America. Legend was that in three voyages, in the course of a single period of twelve months, across the notorious middle passage of the Atlantic, he had transported almost two million dollars' worth of slaves, and with those profits he had acquired vast estates in Louisiana.

It was at this time that Zouga had first met him. Zouga had travelled as a passenger on St John's magnificent clipper *Huron* out of the Port of Bristol in southern England to the Cape of Good Hope. The irony of that voyage had been that Zouga at the time had not been aware that St John was engaged in the trade, and Zouga had been accompanied on the voyage by his only sister, Robyn Ballantyne, a medical missionary whose declared goal in life was the extinction of the trade on the African continent.

When Robyn Ballantyne had discovered that St John was not sailing to Africa to barter beads and copper wire for ivory and ostrich feathers, for gumcopal and alluvial gold dust from the kingdom of Monomatapa, but was seeking richer, living black cargo, her hatred was rendered more implacable by her shame at having travelled in company with such a man.

It was Robyn Ballantyne who had called up the avenging spectre of the Royal Navy. She had been the chief instrument in delivering St John and his beautiful clipper *Huron*, with her cargo of five hundred prime slaves, to the gunboats of the British anti-slavery squadron.

St John, as was his right as an American captain, had resisted the British boarders, and in the savage action that followed, half his crew had been killed or maimed and his lovely ship so badly mauled that she had to be towed into Table Bay by her captors.

Though after imprisonment in Cape Town castle, the British governor had finally released St John and allowed him to sail away, still his cargo of slaves were seized and released from their chains, and the African coast was closed for ever to his ships.

It was then that Zouga had lost contact with him; but after Zouga's book *A Hunter's Odyssey* had been published, St John had written to him care of his London publishers, Messrs Rowland Ward, and since then they had corresponded at irregular intervals. Indeed it was Zouga's description of the diamond fields in one of these letters that was responsible for St John's presence here now.

Through the exchange of letters Zouga had been able to follow St John's career, and he learned how after his release from the Cape Town castle, St John had returned to Fairfields, his cotton and sugar estates near Baton Rouge, only weeks before the first cannon shots were fired at Fort Sumter.

Louisiana had voted for secession from the Union, and when the war began, Mungo raised his own force of irregular cavalry and led them in a brilliant series of hit-and-run raids against the supply lines and rear bases of the Federal army. So successful were these depredations that the northerners christened him 'Murdering Mungo', declared him an outlaw and placed a reward of fifty thousand dollars on his head. Promoted to major-general, he was later struck in the left eye by a red-hot splinter of shrapnel and dragged over a mile when his horse bolted. By the time he was discharged from the hospital, Vicksburg had fallen. Recognizing this as a fatal stab in the heart of the Confederacy, he had limped back along the empty road to Fairfields.

The reek of fermenting sugar juices mingled with that of charred flesh was more revolting than any battlefield

Mungo had ever smelled. Four colonnades stood above the ashes of his homestead, like monuments to all his dreams.

Now, all these years later, St John had come up the road from Good Hope, driving a pair of magnificent pale gold horses with flowing white manes that he called 'Palaminos', a long black cigar between his white teeth, an eagle gleam in his single eye and this strangely disturbing woman on the seat of the phaeton beside him.

St John's first act in Kimberley had been to walk into the office of the Standard Bank on Market Square and present a letter of credit to the flabbergasted clerk. The letter of credit was on heavy, expensive paper, the printing embossed in rose and gold, the wax seal that of Messrs Coutts and Co. in the Strand, and the sum for which it was drawn was half a million of sterling.

St John had drawn a modest hundred pounds against that formidable total, and taken rooms for himself and his wife at the Craven Hotel, Kimberley's most fashionable and comfortable.

When he recovered from his shock, the bank clerk had excitedly begun to spread the news. There was an American general on the fields who disposed of a half million pounds in cash.

The following noon St John had casually accepted an invitation to lunch at the Kimberley Club and smiled indulgently as his name was proposed for membership by Mr C. J. Rhodes and seconded by Dr Leander Starr Jameson. There were men, rich and influential men, who had tried in vain since the foundation of the Club to obtain membership.

St John was smiling that same indulgent smile now as he leaned back in his chair, twisting the stem of his champagne glass between his fingers and watching the other guests at the table fawning over his wife.

Even Mr Rhodes, who was famous for his immunity to female wiles, and who usually bluntly terminated any frivolous conversation, was responding to her artless questions and chuckling at her sallies.

With an effort, Zouga tore his own attention from Louise and tuned to Mungo St John. Quite pointedly he changed the discussion from the split skirts which allowed his wife to ride astride to Mungo's own doings since their last meeting.

The reason for the change of subject was not missed by Louise. She shot a sharp speculative glance at Zouga, but then smiled graciously and relapsed into dutiful silence while the conversation became at last serious and important.

St John had been in Canada and Australia, and without being specific they all understood that both journeys had been rewarding, for St John spoke of wheat and opals and wool and gold, and they listened avidly, shooting their questions like arrows and nodding to the deft replies, until at last St John ended: 'Well, then I heard from my dear friend Zouga what you gentlemen have been doing here, and thought it was time to come and have a look.'

Almost on cue Ralph came down the verandah carrying the scrubbed carving board with its cargo of roasted venison enclosed in a crisp brown envelope of pastry. The company applauded with exclamations of delight and approbation.

Zouga stood up to carve the roast and while he stropped the hunting knife against steel, he glanced at Ralph who still lingered on the verandah.

'Are you feeling well?' he asked out of the side of his mouth, and Ralph roused himself, tearing his adoring gaze from Louise St John.

'Oh yes, Papa, I'm fine.'

'You don't look fine. You look as if you have a belly ache. Better get Jan Cheroot to give you a dose of sulphur and treacle.'

Jan Cheroot, dressed in his old regimental jacket with burnished buttons and his scarlet cap set at a rakish angle, brought in fresh bottles of champagne, the buckets packed with crushed white ice.

'Ice!' Louise clapped her hands with delight. 'I never expected such sophistication here.'

'Oh, we lack very little, ma'am,' Rhodes assured her. 'My ice-making factory has been in operation for a year or more. In a year or so the railway line will reach Kimberley and then we shall become a city, a real city.'

'And all this on woman's vanity.' Louise shook her long black tresses in mock dismay. 'A lady's baubles, a city built on engagement rings!'

Despite Zouga's best efforts, the focus of attention had shifted again. They were all hanging on her words with that slightly bemused expression which overcomes even the most sensible of men when he looks at a beautiful woman.

'Beautiful woman.' It was the first time Zouga had acknowledged that fact, even to himself, and for some reason it increased his resentment of her.

'Do you know, Mr Rhodes,' she leaned across the table confidentially, 'I have been here for five days now – and although I have searched the sidewalks diligently, I have not seen a single diamond – and I was assured the streets of Kimberley were paved with diamonds.'

They all laughed, more heartily than the witticism warranted, and Rhodes murmured a few words to Pickering before turning back to Louise.

'We shall do what we can to remedy that, Mrs St John,' and while he spoke Pickering scrawled a note and then summoned one of the coloured grooms who was lolling and smoking in the shade of the camel-thorn tree.

'Major, may I borrow one of your champagne buckets?' Pickering asked, and when Zouga agreed, he handed the empty bucket and the note to the groom.

Zouga was carving seconds off the roast when the groom returned. He was followed by a nondescript white man with an uncertain seat on his placid steed. He came up onto the verandah carrying the bucket as though it were filled with Mr Alfred Nobel's new-fangled blasting gelatine.

He placed the bucket on the table in front of Rhodes with a timid flourish, and then seemed to disappear from sight. With his thin colourless hair and myopic eyes behind pebble-lens wire-rimmed spectacles, his dark jacket shiny with wear at elbows and cuffs, he blended like a chameleon with his background.

'Where is young Jordan?' Rhodes asked. 'That boy loves diamonds as much as any of us do.'

Jordan came from the kitchen in his apron and with his colour high from the heat of his stove. He greeted Rhodes shyly.

'Ladies and Gentlemen, Mr Jordan Ballantyne is not only the finest chef on the diggings – but he is also one of the best diamond sorters that we have.' Rhodes was expansive as few of them had ever seen him. 'Come and stand by me, Jordan, where you can have a good view.'

When Jordan was beside his chair, Rhodes tipped the bucket carefully and even Zouga heard himself gasp with shock, while Louise St John cried out aloud.

The bucket was filled to the brim with uncut diamonds, and now they cascaded onto the white tablecloth in a sullenly glowing pyramid from which random darts of light sped to astound the eye.

'All right, Jordan. Tell us something about them,' Rhodes invited. And the boy stooped over the fabulous pile of treasure, his long tapered fingers flying lightly over the stones, spreading and sorting them into piles. While he worked he talked, and his voice was as lovely as his face, low and melodious. Fluently he explained the shapes of the crystals, pointed out the flaws in one, placed two side by side to compare the colours, twisting one to the light to bring up its smouldering fires.

Zouga was puzzled. This little act was too theatrical to be Rhodes' usual style, and he would never go to such lengths to impress a woman, even a beautiful one; for by jumbling up a bucket of stones he had given his own sorters many days of extra work. Every one of those stones would have to be re-graded and appraised and returned to its own little white envelope.

'Here is a perfect stone,' Jordan picked a diamond the size of a green pea. 'Look at that colour, blue as a bolt of lightning and as full of fire.'

Rhodes took it from him, considered it a moment, holding it between thumb and forefinger, then he leaned across the table and placed it before Louise St John.

'Madam, your first diamond. I sincerely hope not your last,' said Rhodes.

'Mr Rhodes, I cannot accept such a generous gift,' said Louise, her eyes wide with delight, and she turned to Mungo St John. 'Can I?'

'If I agreed with you, you would never forgive me,' Mungo St John murmured, and Louise turned back to Rhodes.

'Mr Rhodes, my husband insists, and I can find no words to express my gratitude.'

Zouga watched the scene attentively; there was so much happening here, so many nuances, so many undercurrents.

It was on the surface merely a demonstration of the remarkable effect that these bright hard pebbles had upon a woman. That was their true value, perhaps their only value. When he looked at Louise St John's face he could see that it was not avarice that lit it so, but a mystical emotion not far removed from love – the love of a living thing, a child, a horse, a man, a warming thing to watch.

Quite suddenly Zouga found himself wishing that he had been the author of such joy. That it had been he and not Rhodes who had made the gift which had transformed her, and it took a moment for him to free himself of that desire, so that he almost missed the glance that Rhodes shot beyond the woman's face.

Suddenly it was clear to Zouga. Rhodes was not baiting for the woman; he was fishing for the man. That display of treasure was for Mungo St John, the man with half a million sterling to dispose of.

Rhodes needed capital. When a man sets out to buy up every single claim on the Kimberley field, and when he is in a desperate hurry to do it, he must always be starved of capital. Rhodes' ambition was no secret. Zouga himself had been present at the long bar of the Kimberley Club when Rhodes had made the declaration of his intent.

'There is only one way to stabilize the price of the goods—' Rhodes' euphemism for diamonds – 'and that is an orderly, centralized marketing policy. There is only one way to stop the stealing of goods by the I.D.B., and that is through the institution of a rigorous security screen; and there is only one way to achieve both these objects, and that is to have every claim on the fields owned by one company.' Everyone listening to him had known who Rhodes intended that the head of that company should be.

That had been a year previously, and now the bucket of diamonds on Zouga's luncheon table was proof of how far Rhodes had made good his threat and had eaten up the field. Already he was more than halfway towards his goal, but he had been forced to take in partners and still he was short of capital, desperately short.

For the serious obstacle that stood between him and complete ownership of the field was Barney Barnato's company. He would need millions – literally millions of sterling – for that final step.

So the reason for the little charade was clear to Zouga now, and he was about to turn his head to study General Mungo St John's reaction to it when the tableau at the far end of the table struck him forcibly.

The untidily dressed young man, heavy in the shoulders, hunched forward in his chair, unruly curling hair spilling over onto the broad forehead above the florid meaty face, thick arms and square powerful hands enclosing a glittering mound of treasure. At his shoulder the slim and graceful figure of the boy with the bright and lovely face, and behind them both, towering above them, holding them both in its thrall, the graven statue of the falcon god.

Zouga shivered, touched for the first time in the presence of the falcon by a superstitious chill. For the first time he was aware of the sense of evil that the old Hottentot had immediately detected in the statue's stony eyes. For one horrifying instant Zouga was convinced that the bird was about to spread its sharp blade-shaped wings and hold them like a possessive canopy over the two human figures beneath it – and then the moment was past. The tableau broke up.

Rhodes was sweeping the gems back into the bucket, talking quietly to Jordan.

'Are you still studying the book of Mr Pitman's shorthand that I sent you, Jordan?'

'Yes, Mr Rhodes.'

'Good – you'll find it of great value one day.'

The boy understood the dismissal and slipped away down the verandah to his kitchen, while Rhodes casually handed the bucket of diamonds to his clerk and addressed General St John directly.

'In the section of the workings that we own we are recovering an average of ten carats to each ton of gravel that we process, to that we must add at least another two carats a ton which is being stolen by the labourers between the pit floor and the grading room. As our security system becomes more efficient and as we have better laws to control the I.D.B. we can expect to eliminate that wastage—' Rhodes was talking in that high-pitched voice so incongruous in such a big man, gesturing with strong square hands, persuasive and articulate. Reeling off figures for production costs and anticipated recovery, the expectations of profits on tonnage worked, returns on capital outlaid, he was addressing himself to one man only, the erect bearded figure with the black eye-patch, yet his manner was so persuasive that every one of them was listening with full attention, even Louise St John.

Zouga glanced at her and saw that she was concentrating on the confusing jumble of figures, and that she seemed to be able to absorb them. She proved that immediately.

'Mr Rhodes, you said earlier that working costs on the No. 9 Section were ten shillings and sixpence; now you use a new figure – twelve shillings?' She challenged unexpectedly, and Rhodes paused, gave a little nod of recognition for her perception before he replied.

'At the deeper levels the costs rise. Ten and six is our present cost, twelve shillings our projected cost for twelve months hence.' His voice had a new note of respect. 'I am flattered that you have followed my discourse so closely, madam.' Then he turned back to St John. 'From this you will see, General, that the returns on capital invested are about the best you will find anywhere: ten per cent is certain, fifteen per cent is possible.'

St John had been holding an unlit cigar between his teeth; now he removed it and stared hard at Rhodes with his single eye.

'So far, Mr Rhodes, you have not mentioned the blue.'

'The blue.' Every single one of them at the long table froze.

'The blue.' It was as if St John had spoken a gross obscenity, shocking them all into silence.

'The blue' was the main reason why Rhodes was hungry for capital.

'The blue' was the reason why the banks were calling on all diggers who had borrowed against the collateral of their claims to reduce their overdrafts by fifty per cent; and

Rhodes had borrowed a million pounds to finance his attempt to acquire every single claim on the New Rush field. As he had acquired each block, Rhodes had immediately used it as security to borrow money to buy the next block, pyramiding loan upon loan, debt upon debt.

Zouga was one of the few who so far had resisted Rhodes' advances, resisted with pain and heart-searching an offer of £5,000 for his claims on the Devil's Own. The offer had been made six months before, before those dreaded words 'the blue' were whispered in the inner sanctum of the long bar of the Kimberley Club.

Nobody would offer Zouga £5,000 for his claims now. On the contrary, a week after he first heard those two dreaded words, the manager of the Standard Bank had sent a note asking him to call.

'Major Ballantyne, in view of recent developments, the bank has been forced to review the value of collateral securing our clients' overdrafts. We have calculated the present market value of your claims as five hundred pounds each.'

'That's ridiculous, sir.'

'Major, the blue has shown on the claims of the Orphen Company.' The bank manager did not have to elaborate. The Orphen block was only separated from the Devil's Own by a dozen intervening claims. 'I don't enjoy doing this, Major, but I must ask you to reduce your overdraft to one thousand pounds.'

'The blue' was the reason why many of the town's merchants were running down their stocks, preparing themselves to pull out.

'The blue' was the reason why many of the transport riders were re-routing their wagons to the new goldfields at Pilgrims' Rest.

'What is the blue?' asked Louise St John, and when none of the others spoke, Zouga's duty as host placed the burden of reply upon him.

'The blue is the diggers' name for a type of rock formation, Mrs St John. A volcanic conglomerate, dark blue in colour and very hard – too hard to work easily.' Zouga picked up his champagne glass, sipped the yellow wine and then studied the rising pinpricks of bubbles.

'Is that all?' Louise asked quietly.

'It has zircons in it, small zircons the size of sugar grains, but there is no market for zircons,' Zouga went on grudgingly.

'What is the significance of this – blue?' Louise persisted.

Zouga paused to pick his words with care.

'The diamondiferous earth is a friable yellow gravel – friable means crumbling.'

'Thank you,' Louise smiled without rancour. 'I do know the word.'

'Well then, on some of the deeper claims in the northern section the yellow gravel has pinched out, and we have come up short against this hard blue floor, hard as marble and just as sterile.'

'That hasn't been proved,' Rhodes cut in sharply, and Zouga inclined his head in acceptance.

'No, it hasn't been proved, but that is what we all fear. That we have come to the end. That the fields are worked out.'

They were all silent then, contemplating that terrifying eventuality.

'When will you know for certain?' Mungo St John asked. 'When will you know that this blue ground underlies the entire field, and that there are no diamonds in it?'

'It will be many months still before the shallower claims can be worked down to the level of those that have run into the blue,' Rhodes answered. 'Then if we do find it covers the whole field, we will have to drive pot-holes through it to make sure that it is not a thin layer, and that the yellow gravel does not recur below it.'

254

'I see,' St John nodded. 'It seems that I was fortunate to delay my visit to Kimberley until after this blue ground was encountered, or I might have found myself the owner of a mountain of blue marble and no diamonds.'

'You have always been a fortunate man, Mungo.' Louise flashed a smile at him, and he replied to it gravely.

'You, my dear, are the greatest of all my good fortunes.'

With obvious relief the company abandoned the subject of the dreaded blue ground and turned to lighter topics. Only Rhodes did not join them, but sat silent and brooding at the head of the long table.

Though Zouga smiled and nodded at the repartee, he also was distracted by the talk of lurking disaster, and his thoughts were a barrier between him and the company, so that Louise St John had to repeat his name to gain his attention.

'Is that possible, Major Ballantyne?'

Zouga roused himself and turned to her. 'Forgive me, Mrs St John. Will you repeat the question?'

Louise was not accustomed to having a man's thoughts wander when she was talking to him. This cold and correct Englishman was truly beginning to irritate her, and she found herself wanting to shock some natural reaction out of him. She had thought of including a man's word, one of Mungo's soldier's words, in her conversation, but good sense warned her that he would merely raise an eyebrow at such gaucherie. She had thought of ignoring him, but intuition warned her that he would probably welcome that treatment. The best course open to her was to direct her queries at him and force him to recognize her existence, and let it nettle him.

'I was led to understand that you were the Chairman of the Kimberley Sporting Club?'

'I have that honour,' Zouga agreed.

'I have heard also that your steeplechases or point-to-point races – I am never quite sure of your British terminology – are the most popular diversions on the diamond fields.'

Zouga shook his head and smiled. 'I'm not sure of the terminology myself. They certainly are not steeplechases, we are critically short of steeples out here, and they are not point-to-point exactly, for we throw in a little rifle drill. So, we prefer to call them rough rides. A fairly accurate description, I think.'

'I thought to enter one of my horses – in a rough ride,' Louise said.

'We would welcome your participation,' Zouga agreed. 'I could prepare a list of our better riders from which you could choose.'

'I prefer to ride myself,' Louise shook her head.

'I am afraid that would not be possible, Mrs St John.'

'Why not?'

'Because you are a woman.'

Her expression gave Zouga his first truly satisfying moments in her company. She had turned waxen pale so that the freckles stood out boldly on her cheeks and her eyes glowed a lighter, brighter, angry blue.

Zouga waited for her retort, but she sensed his anticipation and, with a huge effort, denied him the satisfaction. Instead she turned to her husband.

'It's after three o'clock. It has been a very pleasant luncheon, but I should like to return to the hotel now.' She stood up quickly, and Mungo St John shrugged resignedly and stood up beside her.

'Please do not let us break up this delightful gathering.' His smile and his tone asked their indulgence for a womanly whim.

The groom brought her horse to her and she caressed its pale silken muzzle. Then she gathered the reins, looked up at the group of men on the stoep, held Zouga's eye for a moment, before deliberately turning away.

She placed one neat gloved hand on the stallion's withers where the long white mane rose into the crest of the shoulders, and then in the next instant she was seated on the broad and powerful back, her small feet thrust deeply into the silver-starred Mexican-type stirrups.

Zouga was astounded. He had never seen a woman vault to the saddle. Usually it took a groom to hold the head and another to form a bridge of linked fingers to boost her to the height of the horse's back.

Louise St John had gone up so lightly and easily that she might have flown, and the movement of her left hand that made the stallion rear was only apparent to someone looking for it.

The huge horse went up on its hind legs, walking backwards in a circle, cutting at the air with its fore-hooves, until it faced the five-foot barbed-wire fence that marked the division between Zouga's camp and the public road.

Then Louise moved her hand again and the stallion dropped into a dead run, straight at the fence.

The watching men exclaimed in alarm for the stallion had a bare twenty strides to build up momentum for the jump, yet he flew at it with his pink nostrils flaring and the serpentine veins beneath the burnished skin of his cheeks swelling with the pumping of the great heart.

Louise's thick black braids were flung out tautly behind her head by the power of the stallion's acceleration, and then she lifted him into the jump with her knees and her hands.

For an instant of time the horse and the tiny figure upon its back seemed to hang suspended against the pale blue of the sky, the horse with its forefeet drawn up beneath its noble head and the woman rising in the saddle to cushion the shock of take-off and landing – and then they were over.

The stallion landed neatly, with his rider in perfect

balance, and the golden body flowed smoothly into the continuation of his run.

There was a soft involuntary sigh from the group on the verandah, and Zouga felt a surge of relief as powerful as the driving leap of the stallion. He had had a mental image of the woman caught up in the bloody strands of barbed wire, like a wild bird in the trapper's net, with torn body and broken wings.

Zouga stood on top of the central stagings. He was as high above the level of the plain as a three-storey building, and from his vantage point he could see as far north as the Vaal river. The dark-green stain of the lusher scrub and grass along its course looked like cloud shadow upon the dust-pale earth, but there were no clouds in the high vault of the sky, and the brutal sun threw stark shadows below the high stagings, geometrical patterns that parodied in two-dimensional plan the intricate structure of timber and iron and steel wire. The stagings clung perilously to the sheer precipice that fell into the depths.

It was as though a gigantic meteor had ploughed into the yellow earth, gouging this bowl-shaped dish through the earth's crust. In the deepest sections it was almost two hundred feet deep already, and each spadeful of gravel had been dug out by hand, lifted to the surface and laboriously picked over before being discarded in the mountainous waste dumps. It was a monument to the persistence of those antlike creatures that swarmed down there on the pit floor.

Zouga wiped the black grease off his hands with a wad of cotton waste, and nodded to the Matabele winchman who threw in the gear lever of the steam winch.

Once again the numbing clatter hammered against

Zouga's skull and the slender thread of shining steel cable slithered in over the drums. The winch and steam boiler had cost Zouga over a thousand pounds, the entire winnings of an unusually productive week's labour when Jordan had picked eleven good diamonds off the sorting-table. That week's recovery had been one of the false promises that the Devil's Own had whispered to him, like an unfaithful wife.

Zouga moved to the front of the stagings to escape the painful sound of the winch. He was on an unguarded wooden balcony with the drop sucking seductively at him, but he ignored it.

He had ten minutes to rest now, the time that it took the gravel skip to travel up from the claims to the surface. He could see it lifting off the floor below like a fat spider creeping up its individual silken thread towards him, still too deep for him to recognize for certain the human figure riding on the enormous steel bucket.

Zouga lit a cheroot, and it tasted of engine grease from his fingers. He looked down again, and decided that instead of an ant's nest the pit reminded him more of a beehive. Even at these deep levels the precise shape of each claim had been maintained, and the geometrical shapes were like the individual cells in a honeycomb.

'If only mine would yield a little more honey,' he thought.

The skip was close enough now for there to be no doubt of the tall young figure standing casually on the lip of the steel bucket, balancing easily with both hands on his hips as the drop grew steadily deeper under him.

It was a matter of pride amongst the younger diggers to ride the skip in the most casual or spectacular manner possible. Zouga had forbidden Ralph to dance on the skip, a fad that had been started by a young Scot who had once danced between the floor and the stagings, accompanying himself on the bagpipes.

Ralph drew steadily closer, rising up through the glistening web of steel cables that hung over the pit like a silver cloud. Hundreds of cables, one for each individual claim, every strand polished by the pulley wheels, by the friction over the winding drums, until they caught the sunlight and shimmered into a silver mist that hung like an aura over the pit – ethereal and lovely, hiding the harsh reality of that gouged raw earth, with its dangers and disappointments.

While he waited for the skip to reach him, Zouga cast his mind back to that first day when he had led the single oxen into the sprawling encampment with Aletta on the wagon box beside him, and they had looked up at the riddled and torn kopje.

So much earth had been moved since then, so many men had died in this terrible pit where that kopje had once stood and so many dreams had perished with them.

Zouga lifted the wide-brimmed hat. Carefully he mopped the beads of sweat from the smoother paler skin along his hairline, and then he inspected the damp red stain on the silk bandanna and grimaced with distaste. It looked like blood.

He re-knotted the silk about his throat, still peering down into the depths, and his eyes clouded with disenchantment as he remembered the high hopes and bounding expectation that he had brought with him on that day – was it really ten years ago? It seemed like a day and an eternity.

He had found himself dreaming, the random events from those lost years replaying through his mind, the sorrows and the joys magnified by his imaginings and by the passage of time.

Then, after a few minutes, Zouga roused himself. Dreaming was an old man's vice. The past was beyond regret; today was all that counted. He straightened his shoulders and looked down at Ralph in the swinging skip. Something jarred him, scattering the last of his dreams.

The skip was riding differently, it did not have the accustomed weight to it, he could not yet make out the heaped yellow gravel, which, despite his orders, Ralph usually over-loaded high above the steel sides of the skip.

It was empty, and Ralph was alone. He was coming up without the Matabele gang to help run the skip over the bars and up-end its burden of gravel into the chute, down which it would be carried to the waiting cart.

Zouga cupped his hands to his mouth to shout an enquiry – but the words stayed in his throat.

Ralph was close enough now for Zouga to see the expression on his face. It was tragic, stricken with some terrible emotion.

Zouga lowered his hands and stared at his son in dread anticipation. The skip hit the end bars with an iron clash and the winchman threw out the gear lever, expertly braking the steel skip against the bars.

Ralph jumped lightly across the narrow gap onto the platform, and stood there, still staring at Zouga.

'What is it, my boy?' Zouga asked quietly, fearfully – and for answer Ralph turned away and glanced down into the empty body of the skip.

Zouga stepped up beside him, and followed his glance. He saw that he had been mistaken – the skip was not empty.

'It has taken us all morning to hack that out of the east face,' Ralph told him.

It looked like a roughly cut gravestone, before the inscription was chiselled in, as wide as the stretch of a man's arms and imperfectly squared up, the marks of the steel wedges and pickaxe still fresh upon it.

'We broke three pick handles on it,' Ralph went on grimly, 'and we only got it out because there was a natural fracture line that we could crack open with wedges.'

Zouga stared at the ugly cube of stone, not wanting to believe what it was, trying to close his ears against his son's voice.

'Underneath it's the same, solid, hard as a whore's heart, no faults, no cracks.'

The lump of stone was a dull ugly mottled thing, across which the steel tools had left paler weals and furrows.

'Sixteen of us,' Ralph went on. 'We worked on it all morning.' He opened his hands, and showed them palms upwards. The horny yellow calluses had been torn open, the raw flesh beneath was mushy and caked with dust and earth. 'All morning we broke our hearts and our picks on it – and that bloody little chip weighs less than half a ton.'

Slowly Zouga stooped over the edge of the skip and touched the stone. It was as cold as his heart felt – and its colour was dark mottled blue.

'The blue,' Ralph confirmed quietly. 'We have hit the blue.'

'Dynamite or blasting gelatine,' Ralph said. 'That's the only way we'll ever move it.'

He was stripped to the waist, a polish of sweat on his arms, and little drops of it hanging like dew in the thick hair of his chest.

The tombstone of blue marble lay at his feet, and Ralph rested on the shaft of the sledgehammer. The blows he had swung at the rock had raised bursts of sparks and tiny puffs of white dust that stung their nostrils like pepper – but had not cracked the rock through.

'We cannot blast in the pit,' Zouga said tiredly. 'Can you imagine two hundred diggers firing away dynamite, every one doing it when and how he wanted?' He shook his head.

'There is no other way,' Ralph said. 'No other way to get it out.'

'And if you do get it out?' Jordan asked from the verandah where he had stood without speaking for the past hour.

'What do you mean?' Zouga demanded. He could hear the strain in his own voice, and knew how close his anger and frustration were to the surface.

'What will you do with it when you do get it out?' Jordan persisted, and they all stared at the awful blue lump.

'There are no diamonds in that stuff.' Jordan said it for them.

'How do we know that?' Ralph snapped at him, his voice rough and ugly with the same tension that gripped Zouga.

'I know it,' Jordan said flatly. 'I can sense it – just look at it. It's hard and bleak and bare.'

Nobody replied to that, and Jordan shook his curls regretfully. 'Even if there were diamonds in it, how would you free them from the blue? You can't smash them out with sledgehammers. You'd end up with diamond dust.'

'Ralph,' Zouga turned away from Jordan, 'this stuff, this blue – it's only on the east face, isn't it?'

'So far.' Ralph nodded. 'But—'

'I want you to cover up the east face,' Zouga told him bluntly. 'Shovel gravel over the exposed rock. Nobody else must see it. Nobody else must know.'

Ralph nodded, and Zouga went on, 'We will keep on raising the yellow gravel from the other sections as though nothing has happened; and nobody, not one of you, is to say a word about – about us having struck the blue.' He looked directly at Jordan. 'Do you understand, not a word to anybody.'

Zouga sat easily in the saddle, riding with the long stirrups of a Boer hunter or of a born colonial.

He knew that Rhodes was leaving in the next few weeks, to keep his term at Oxford University. Perhaps his imminent departure would make his judgement hasty.

'Let's hope so, anyway.' And his mount flicked his ears back to listen to his voice.

'Steady, old man.' Zouga touched his withers, feeling a quick twist of guilt at his intentions. He knew he was going to try and sell faulty goods, and he steeled himself against his own conscience.

He touched his mount's flank with his knee and turned him off the rutted dusty track through the break in the milkwood fence and into Rhodes' camp.

Rhodes sat with his back to the mud wall of the shack, a mug in his hand, the big shaggy leonine head cocked to something that Pickering was saying.

The talk of the diggings was that he was already a multimillionaire, at least on paper, and Zouga had seen the champagne bucket of uncut diamonds poured out onto his lunch table. Yet here Rhodes was sitting on a soap box in the dusty yard, dressed in shabby ill-fitting clothes, drinking from a chipped enamel mug.

Zouga dropped his reins and his horse stopped obediently, and when he slipped off its back there was no need for him to tether it. It would stand as long as Zouga wanted it to.

He crossed the yard towards the small group of men, and Zouga smiled to himself. Rhodes' mug might be chipped – but it contained a twenty-year-old cognac. Rhodes' seat might be a soapbox, but he sat it as though it were a throne, and the men that sat around him like courtiers or supplicants were all rich and powerful men, the new aristocracy of the diggings.

One of these rose now and came to meet Zouga, laughing lightly and brandishing a rolled newspaper.

'By gad, Major, they say you need only speak of the devil.' He clapped Zouga's shoulder. 'I hope you are taking this assault on our masculine pride as seriously as we are – and have come to offer to champion our cause.'

'I don't understand.' Zouga's protest was lost in the laughter and friendly pummelling as they came to crowd around him. Only Rhodes had not left his seat against the wall, but even he was smiling.

'Let him read it for himself, Pickling,' Rhodes suggested mildly, and Pickering handed Zouga the news sheet with a flourish.

It was a copy of the *Diamond Fields Advertiser* – so newly printed that the ink smudged beneath Zouga's fingers.

'Front page,' said Pickering gleefully. 'The headline.'

GAUNTLET THROWN DOWN
LADY INSULTED
SEEKS SATISFACTION

This morning your editor was privileged to receive a visit from a beautiful and distinguished visitor to Kimberley. Mrs Louise St John is the wife of a hero of the American Civil War, and in her own right a noted equestrienne.

Her stallion 'Shooting Star' is a remarkable example of the recently developed American breed known as Palamino. He is a former Louisiana champion of the breed, and quite one of the most magnificent animals ever to be seen on the Diamond Fields.

Mrs St John attempted to enter her mount in the regular point-to-point meetings organized by the Kimberley Sporting Club – but was informed by Major Ballantyne, the Club President, that she was barred from riding—

Zouga skipped quickly over the next few paragraphs:

'Simply because I happen to be a woman . . .
Insufferable masculine arrogance.'

He smiled and shook his head.

'Challenge the good major to ride against me over any
course of his choice for any purse he stipulates.'

Now Zouga laughed delightedly, and tossed the paper back
to Pickering.

'The lady has good bottom', he admitted, 'in both senses
of the word.'

'I will lend you King Chaka,' Beit promised. He was a
strong hunter, English and Arab blood, from one of the
famous Cape studs. Beit had paid three hundred guineas
for him.

Zouga shook his head and shot an affectionate glance at
his own hunting horse standing across the yard. 'That
won't be necessary, I shan't be riding.'

There was a howl of jovial protest from them all.

'By God, Ballantyne, you can't let us down.'

'This damned vixen will say you funked it, old man.'

'My wife will crow for a week – you'll ruin my marriage.'

Zouga held up his hands. 'I'm sorry, gentlemen. This is
merely a bit of female nonsense – and you can quote me.'

'You won't ride, then?'

'Certainly not.' Zouga was smiling, but his voice had a
brittle edge. 'I have more serious matters to concern me.'

'You are right, of course.' Rhodes' piping voice stilled
them all into respectful silence. 'That pale brute is a flying
devil and the lady rides like a witch – we have all seen
that.'

The scar on Zouga's cheek turned pale pink, and there
was a sudden green glint in his eye; but the smile stayed on
his lips.

'That fancy high-stepper moves well on the flat, I grant

you, but over the course I would choose he would be lucky to finish, let alone win.'

'You'll ride then?' They were clamouring again immediately.

'No, gentlemen. That's my final word.'

L
ong after the others had left, the three of them sat on: Pickering, Rhodes and Zouga. The sun had set, and just the orange glow of the fire lit their faces. The first bottle of cognac was empty and Pickering had opened another. Now Rhodes was staring into his mug, and he spoke without lifting his eyes.

'So, Major, at last you are ready to sell, and I ask myself a question, a simple little question – why?'

Zouga did not reply, and after a moment Rhodes lifted his head.

'Why, Major?' he repeated. 'Why now suddenly?'

Zouga found that the lie he had prepared would not come to his lips. He was dumb, but he held the gaze of those pale blue eyes – and it was Rhodes who broke the silence.

'I have trusted very few men in my life,' and involuntarily his eyes flickered to Pickering and then back to Zouga, 'but now, Major, you are one of them.'

He picked up the cognac bottle and spilled a little of the honey-dark liquor into Zouga's mug.

'Once you were offered a hundred thousand pounds in illicit diamonds – and you couldn't bring yourself to take them.' Rhodes was speaking so softly that Zouga had to lean forward to catch the words. 'Yesterday your son brought up the first hunk of blue ground from the Devil's Own – and still you could not bring yourself to lie.'

'You knew!' Zouga whispered, and Rhodes nodded and then sighed.

'By God, I wish I knew more like you.' He shook the big curling head and his voice was become brusque and businesslike. 'Once I offered you five thousand pounds for your claims. All right, I will make the same price—' and he lifted one meaty hand to still Zouga. 'Wait! Listen to the rest of it, before you thank me. The bird goes with the claims.'

'What?' For a moment Zouga did not understand.

'The stone bird, the statue. It becomes part of the deal.'

'Damn it!' Zouga half rose from the log on which he was sitting.

'Wait!' Rhodes stopped him again. 'Listen – before you refuse,' and Zouga sank back. 'You'll ride for it.'

Zouga shook his head, not understanding.

'You'll ride against this woman, St John, on her terms, and if you win you keep the claims and the bird and my five thousand.'

The silence stretched out for a full minute – and then Zouga asked with a harsh gravelly sound in the back of his throat:

'And if I lose?'

'You yourself have said there is little chance of that,' Rhodes reminded him.

'And if I lose?' Zouga persisted.

'Then you leave these fields as you came – with nothing.'

Zouga looked away to the horse standing at the edge of the shadows. He had named him Tom, after a friend, the old hunter who had first told Zouga about the land to the north and how to reach it, Tom Harkness, now dead these many years.

The horse was part of Zouga's dream of the north, the mount that would carry him back to Zambezia. Zouga had selected him with more care than a man usually gives to choosing his wife – and beauty was the last thing he looked for.

Tom was a mixture of many bloodlines, the wide nostrils

and big chest of the Arab for staying power, the sturdy legs and sure feet of the Basuto, the canny eye and hammer head of a wild Mustang, the heart and strength of an English hunter. However, Tom was a drab unrelieved dun-colour. His coat was long and thick, brushed but not curried, protection from the night frost and the noon sun, from flying pebbles thrown by frantic hooves of the quarry in a stern chase or from the rip of red-tipped 'wait-a-bit' thorns.

Tom had proved that the intelligent gleam in his eye was no illusion. He learned swiftly and well. He learned to stand when the reins were dropped on his neck, giving his rider both hands for the rifle, and he remained stone-still while gunfire crashed about his head, only the twitching of his ears signalling his consternation.

When Zouga took him out into the open veld to continue his training, Tom displayed nimble feet on the rocky slopes of the kopje and a buffalo skin through the thorn bush; he learned to hunt, and seemed to enjoy it the way a good polo pony revels in the crack of the bamboo root and the riotous chase.

He seemed instinctively to understand stalking, keeping his own body between Zouga and the game, angling off his approach, never heading directly at the quarry, and the herds of springbuck let the seemingly riderless horse walk up into easy rifle shot. Then Tom would carry the freshly killed carcass on his back, without shying and fussing about the blood.

Tom was ugly, with a Roman nose, ears a little too long, legs a little too short, and he ran with an awkward hump-backed gait – which he could keep up all day, over any ground.

He was an incorrigible thief. Jordan's vegetable garden had to be fenced, but still Tom left tufts of his drab hair on the spikes of the barbed wire. He had a trick of plucking the carrots out of the ground with a delicate grip between his square white teeth, and then knocking the earth off them against his forehooves.

He learned to push open the kitchen window and reach the fresh loaves of bread that were cooling on the marble sink, and once when Jan Cheroot left the door to the storeroom off the latch, Tom got in and ate half a bag of sugar – at twenty shillings a pound.

However, he would follow like a dog, and when ordered he would stand for hours – and Zouga, who was not sentimental about animals, had come to love him.

Zouga looked back from the horse to the young man across the log fire.

'Agreed,' he said without emphasis. 'Do we need to have further witnesses?'

'I don't think so, Major,' said Rhodes. 'Do you?'

'At the gun the competitor will ride out to the first flag—' Neville Pickering was the steward-in-chief, and his voice through the speaking trumpet carried to every member of the huge Sunday crowd that spilled out across the dry veld below the Magersfontein hills.

'At the first red flag they will fire upon the standing targets. When they have demolished all four targets to the satisfaction of the stewards, they will be free to round the second yellow flag, and thereafter to return to the finish line.' He pointed to the twin poles each with its crown of coloured bunting. 'The first rider to pass between them will be declared the winner.'

Pickering paused and drew fresh breath before going on.

'Are there any questions?'

'Would you recite the rules, please, Mr Pickering,' Louise St John called. She looked like a child on the great glistening pale stallion's back. She was walking him in circles, leaning forward to pat his neck for the crowds had made him nervous. He was chewing the light snaffle and sweating in dark patches on the rippling muscled shoulders.

'There are no other rules, ma'am.' Pickering answered her loudly enough for those at the back of the crowd to hear.

'No rules – barging and fouling?'

'There are no fouls, ma'am,' Pickering replied. 'Though if one of you deliberately shoots an opponent, he or she might have to face criminal charges, but not disqualification.'

Louise turned her head towards the figure on the front seat of the high-wheeled phaeton which was parked beyond the course markers. Her face was pale, the freckles standing out on her cheeks; and her head was bared so that the thick dark braid of hair thumped against her shoulder.

Mungo St John smiled back at her over the heads of the crowd, and shrugged slightly, so that Louise was forced to turn back to Pickering.

'Very well, then,' she agreed. 'But the stake. We have not agreed the stake.'

'Major Ballantyne,' Pickering called to where Zouga stood at Tom's head. 'You have laid out the course. Now will you be good enough to name the stake.'

Then a strange thing happened. For the first time since Zouga had met her, Louise St John was uncertain of herself. Nobody else seemed to notice it, perhaps it was merely that Zouga had become highly receptive to every shade of her voice and expression. But he was certain that he saw something dark move in the blue depths of her eyes, like the shadow of a shark beneath the surface of the sea, and she took a pinch of her soft lower lip between her white teeth and again she glanced almost furtively at Mungo St John.

It was not Zouga's imagination. Mungo St John did not return Louise's glance with his usual amused indulgence. He was looking at Zouga and under his calm was a small undercurrent of unease, like an eddy at highwater when the tide turns.

Zouga raised his voice so that it would carry to St John.

'Firstly, the loser will publish at his or her own expense upon the front page of the *Advertiser* in terms dictated by the winner, an acknowledgement of defeat.'

'A composition I shall enjoy.' Louise had swiftly recovered her poise. 'And what else, Major?'

'A payment by the loser to a charity of the winner's choice of,' Zouga paused, and both man and woman watched his face with outward calm, 'of the sum of one shilling!'

'Done!'

There was a slightly jarring note in Louise's laugh, relief perhaps, and though Mungo St John's expression did not alter, the tension went out of his shoulders.

'Mrs St John. You are under starter's orders,' Pickering called through his speaking trumpet. 'Be so good as to bring your mount under control.'

'He is under perfect control, sir,' she called back, and Shooting Star put his head down and lashed out with both back hooves towards the crowd.

'If he is under control, Missus, then so is my mother-in-law,' called a wag, and there was a hoot of laughter.

'On the count of three then,' Pickering intoned, his voice hollow and solemn through the trumpet. 'One.'

Shooting Star backed up against the crowd, and they scattered as he bucked.

'Two.'

He went into a tortured high-stepping circle, so tight that his nose almost touched the toe of Louise's boot in the fancy silver stirrup.

'And three.' Louise lifted her left hand. Shooting Star came smoothly out of the circle, for the first time facing the start line, beginning to pace towards it majestically, and the pistol shot was a brief blurt of sound which sent the stallion sweeping away with an irresistible rush that made the slight figure on his wide back seem vulnerable and childlike.

There was no horse on the diamond fields that could match that first blazing burst of speed, the gap between the two horses opened, but not so dramatically as the watchers had expected. Tom's awkward gallop took him over the ground at surprising speed, and he was not following directly in Shooting Star's tracks.

'She's going wide, Thomas,' Zouga told him with satisfaction, and Tom cocked his ears back to listen. 'They aren't going to chance the river. Well, we didn't really think they would, did we?'

Directly ahead of Zouga the river started a lazy series of loops, symmetrical hairpin turns, winding back upon itself like a dying python.

Zouga had placed the red flag so that the direct line would cross the river-bed twice, and like most southern African rivers the banks were sheer, dropping ten feet to the dry sand and isolated rocky pools strung along the course. Each crossing was a trap in which a horse could break a leg and a rider his neck.

The alternative to the crossings was to ride wide, taking a circuit out beyond the meandering river course; but that almost doubled the distance to run to the first flag.

Already Shooting Star was a distant flying shape far out on the right, showing at intervals through gaps in the thorn scrub, marked by a little pale feather of dust flung up by his hooves.

'Here we are,' said Zouga, and under Tom's ugly Roman nose the ground opened abruptly.

Zouga gave him a slack rein, and Tom hardly checked on the brink of the steep clay bank. He sat down, and skidded over the edge on his fat round haunches, his forelegs sticking out stiffly ahead of him, and they tobogganed down into the river bed and hit the sand in a scrambling tangle; and then Tom was up and lunging for the far bank, going half up before the dried clay crumbled under his hooves and they slid back again, Tom stiff-legged and trembling with exertion.

Zouga circled him once in the clinging white sand, and then put him to the bank again, and he went up in a determined series of buck-jumps, shifting his weight before the clay could break under his hooves, and they flew out over the top and were running again, the next bend of the river a quarter of a mile ahead.

At the next crossings Tom had the knack of it and they went down the bank and out the other side without a check. Under Tom's hooves the grass exploded into a whirl of noisy wings, and, with a wild harsh cry that would have panicked another horse, a big black-bellied bustard shot up into the air. Tom rolled a disdainful eye at the bird, steadied and gathered himself on the river bank of the last crossing and went down into it in a slide of dust and rolling pebbles.

As they came up the far bank the red flag was two hundred paces dead ahead.

Zouga swivelled in the saddle and looked out on his right hand.

'Good for you, Tom,' he called. 'You've made a mile on them.'

Far out across the plain, the golden horse was just swinging wide of the last bend of the river, and Louise was bent low on his neck, pushing him at reckless speed over the rough going.

'If she rides like that for a shilling—' Zouga broke off, and himself leaned into the rhythm of Tom's gallop. A mile was such a slim margin, and the stakes he was riding for were enormous. His fortune, his dream – nay his very existence – was at stake.

'Go, Thomas, go!' Zouga whispered grimly into the long

furry ears, and Tom stabbed at the earth with his awkward hump-backed gait.

Zouga did not look back again; he knew the stallion was bearing down on them, fast, too fast, but Zouga dismissed them from his attention and slid the carbine from the leather boot at his knee and opened the breech, checking the load.

The targets were white china soup plates, the range two hundred yards, extreme range after a gallop like this. The stewards were waving their hats to guide him up to the firing line.

'This way, Major.'

Zouga dropped the reins as he reached the low barrier of thorn branches that marked the firing line, and Tom came up short. He swung up the carbine, and fired as the butt slapped into his shoulder. One of the far-off specks of white burst and vanished. He cranked another round into the chamber, and glanced over his shoulder. The stallion was still half a mile away, but coming on with a war drum of hooves.

Zouga fired again, but Tom was blowing between his knees, heaving with the effort of the wild gallop.

'Damn it to hell.'

Haste would be fatal now, but his fingers fumbled the reload and a shiny brass cartridge slipped and struck his boot before it fell into the sand. He thrust another into the breech, took a long slow breath, and judged Tom's movements beneath him.

The rifle jumped against his shoulder, and the acrid plume of gunsmoke blew into his face. The second target exploded.

'Two down, Major,' one of the stewards shouted, and then as he fired again, 'Three down – one to go!'

Then beside Zouga the golden stallion came plunging to a halt, coming back low on glossy bunched quarters.

Louise vaulted from his back in a swirl of beaded buckskin skirts. There was a flash of the silky skin of her upper calf above the boot, and the back of a dimpled knee. Even in the press of the moment, he found the pale beautiful flesh disturbing enough to spoil his aim – and he swore as his next shot flew wide.

Louise was shooting the latest model of the legendary '73 Winchester repeater, the original polished brass frame replaced by blued steel, and Zouga knew that the modern centre-fire ammunition drove the heavy lead bullet with amazing power and accuracy.

She threw the stallion's rein over her left shoulder, and braced herself to fire from a standing position, leaning forward to absorb the recoil of the Winchester, and let her first shot fly.

She shot in the American style, throwing the rifle to her shoulder and firing in the same movement, not holding her aim nor giving the barrel time to wander. It was fine shooting.

'One hit to Mrs St John,' yelled the steward. But the crash of the shot had startled Shooting Star and he reared wildly and backed off on his hind legs, heaving at the reins that were looped over Louise's shoulder, jerking her over backwards so that her second shot flew in a long spurt of powder smoke towards the sky; and then she was down on her back, being dragged away, her skirts tangled about her legs, and the Winchester rifle was flung from her hand.

The stallion came down on his forelegs again. One hoof, sharp as a woodman's axe, grazed the tender spot at the nape of Louise's neck, just below the thick plait of dark hair, leaving an angry pink blaze on the pale skin but not breaking it.

Zouga felt the sweat on his throat turn so cold that he could not swallow. He swung Tom around to head off the stallion.

For unholy seconds Louise's body was hidden by flying

dust and trampling hooves; Zouga tried to shout to her to let the horse go, but his voice had choked, and then abruptly Louise was on her knees.

She was facing Shooting Star, clinging stubbornly to his reins with both hands, and when he reared again she used his strength to let him boost her to her feet.

'Steady!' she called to him. 'Steady, I tell you.'

She was dusty and a tendril of dark hair had escaped the plait and hung into her eyes, but she was safe and very angry. Her voice crackled like breaking ice. Zouga's relief was immediate, but he mocked her as he swung Tom back to the firing line for his last target.

'I advise you to have that animal properly trained, madam.'

'To hell with you, Major Ballantyne!' she told him in the same tone as she had quelled her mount. Somehow the oath on her lips was not shocking at all, but strangely titillating.

Zouga gave Tom a few seconds to settle and regulate his breathing, and then swung up the rifle, held a full bead on the distant white speck and touched off the shot.

'Four hits – you are free to ride on, Major,' shouted the steward.

Louise was dragging Shooting Star by the reins to a wild plum tree, a tree with low and sturdy branches. Swiftly she lashed the stallion's reins to a branch, and now she was running back holding her skirts up to just below the knee, and the stewards gawked at her ankles in the tight-fitting buttoned boots.

She snatched the Winchester from a clump of sansevieria and ran up towards the firing line, reloading as she came. Zouga could see that there were little blisters of perspiration across her forehead, and knew that she was badly shaken, for when she threw up the rifle she held the shot and the heavy weapon wavered unsteadily.

She lowered it, and her shoulders were trembling. She

took two long deep breaths and then lifted the Winchester again, firing on the toss up.

'Hit!' yelled the steward.

Louise's lower lip was quivering and she bit down on it fiercely, and shot again.

Zouga slid the carbine back into its leather scabbard, touched the brim of his helmet to Louise in a cavalier salute. 'Good shooting, ma'am.'

He turned Tom's head away from the firing line.

As they reached the wild plum, Zouga leaned out from the saddle. Louise had tied Shooting Star's reins to the branch with a slippery fisherman, it was a sailor's knot, a quick-release knot for a fast getaway.

Zouga twitched the loose end and the knot fell apart, then he slapped Shooting Star across the cheek with his open hand. 'Go on,' he said. 'Get out of it!'

The stallion jerked his head, found that he was free and kicked his heels high.

Zouga looked back as he reached the next low fold in the plain.

The stallion was grazing head down, but even at that distance it was apparent that he was keeping a wary eye on the lonely figure that ran after him in hampering skirts. As soon as Louise came within arm's length of his bridle, he tossed up his head and trotted away to the next clump of grass, leaving her blundering behind.

'Come, Tom.' He turned away, trying not to let his conscience trouble him. There were no rules, any ruse was acceptable, but it still felt bad – until he reminded himself of the stakes. A shilling against all he owned – and he set Tom to run in earnest.

Another mile and he glanced back, just in time to see Shooting Star and his rider come over the rise. They seemed to fly clear of the earth, borne along by the floating carpet of their own dust.

'Run! Tom! Run!' Zouga swept the hat off his head and

slapped it against Tom's neck, goading him to his best speed.

Within another half mile Tom's shoulders were hot and slick with salt sweat. Ropes of saliva spilled from the corners of his lips and splattered onto Zouga's boots – but the yellow flag was in sight.

'Not far,' Zouga called to him anxiously. 'We must beat them to the flag.'

He looked back. He could not believe they were so close.

The stallion's head was driving like a hammer to each stride, and his neck and shoulders were black with sweat. She had pushed him fearfully. Louise was driving him with her arms and the rhythmic force of her body. Her hair was a wild tangle about her face, and her eyes were a blaze of blue.

Yet as she came up to them she straightened in the saddle, her chin lifted high, and she looked at Zouga coldly, expressionlessly, the way a queen might glance at an urchin running at the wheel of her coach.

Zouga lifted his right hand to salute her achievement. It had been a tremendous run, to make up so much ground. He was turned slightly towards her – and her expression of cold disinterest lulled him for the vital instant that it took her to bring Shooting Star level with Tom's shoulder.

Zouga never saw the command, probably the toe of her boot on the far side of Shooting Star's heaving chest; he had certainly not expected a show horse to have learned the low tricks of a polo pony. Shooting Star's huge sweat-streaked shoulder crashed into Tom, taking him in the short ribs with a force that drove the air out of him in a belching grunt, and as he was spun aside Tom chopped desperately to keep from falling, twisting and dropping to his knees, his nose on the ground, too tired and taken too unawares to meet the power of that ferocious barge.

Zouga lost a stirrup and was thrown onto Tom's neck.

He clung desperately, feeling the saddle shift under the unequal transfer of weight; then Tom heaved again and Zouga went over, landing on his shoulders and the back of his neck.

He seemed to strike solid rock and blackness crushed down from the dome of his skull. When it cleared, he was standing again, swaying like a drunk, blinking uncertainly after the pounding stallion as he pulled away towards the last flag.

Zouga pulled Tom to his feet, and checked swiftly for strained sinew or broken bone, then threw himself back into the saddle.

'We're not beat yet,' he told Tom. 'There are still the thorns.'

Far ahead Shooting Star was making the turn around the last flag. From there Louise was free to make her way back to the finish line any way she wanted, but there were still the thorns.

Tom was winded, his chest shuddering with the effort of each laboured breath, and they reached the flag in an awkward jarring trot and made the turn. Ahead of them the thorns stretched in a solid green barrier. This was the last obstacle – and beyond it was a clear run to the finish.

A rider had a choice: go through the thorn, or ride wide.

'Which way did she go?' Zouga shouted at the stewards below the flag as he went past.

'She's gone for the gap,' one of them yelled back, and then Zouga saw the little feather of dust a mile or more out on the right subsiding only slowly as the stallion sped away.

The thorn barrier petered out on the rocky slopes of the Magersfontein hills, and there was an open gap below the steep ironstone cliffs – that was where the stallion was aimed.

Grimly Zouga swung Tom around the flag and pointed him directly at the thorns. This route was almost two miles shorter, but he would need every inch of it. Yet he stopped Tom when they reached the edge of the thorns and let him breathe as he untied the heavy greatcoat from the pommel of his saddle and shrugged into it. He buttoned it high at the throat and felt the sweat burst out on his forehead as he pulled on the leather gauntlets to protect his hands.

'Let's go,' he whispered, and lay flat on Tom's neck, as they crashed into the thorn.

The red-tipped hooked points of the thorns skidded over Zouga's thick felt hat with a rasping tearing sound, and tugged at the shoulders and skirts of the greatcoat.

The brush grew as high as a mounted man's head, the sturdy trunks just far enough apart to let a horse pass, but the barbed branches intertwined and exacted a cruel toll. However, Tom kept going, swinging and chopping from side to side; he dodged between the white barked trunks, ducking his head under the branches, his ears flat against his skull and his eyes closed to slits, maintaining just the right amount of momentum to snap the thorns off their triangular bases and showering both himself and Zouga with a confetti of feathery green leaves. Every few seconds he snorted at the sting of thorn that had penetrated his tough shaggy hide.

Shooting Star's burnished skin was so thin and finely bred that the network of veins and arteries showed through it. The thorns would have ripped it to bloody tatters.

Zouga felt blood trickling down his own neck from where a thorn had nicked his ear, but he crouched lower and let Tom pick his own way through. 'Poor Tom,' he encouraged him. 'Poor brave Tom.' The horse whickered with the pain of the stinging red needles, but did not check his stride. Yet his breathing was easier now, the slower gait had helped him; and the sweat was drying in salty white crystals on his shoulders.

Then abruptly they burst out of the thorn onto the open plain. Zouga tore off the leather gauntlets and threw them away. He ripped at the buttons of the greatcoat and let it fly away, flapping like a great black crow in the wind of Tom's gallop – and then he stood high in the stirrups and shaded his eyes with the brim of his hat.

Swiftly he searched the open ground, but it was empty as far as the tiny specks of colour in the distance: women's dresses and the gay bunting that marked the finish. His heart bounded with relief, and under him Tom lunged into a clumsy gallop.

Still standing in the stirrups, Zouga looked towards the line of hills out on his right hand, and he saw them.

The stallion had turned the far end of the thorn barrier where it ran into the hills and was coming down the rocky slope towards the level ground in a dangerous scramble.

The tiny figure on his back was being thrown about brutally. One instant she seemed to be on his neck, the next she was flung back onto his haunches, as Shooting Star plunged and heaved to keep his balance.

'We have them now, Tom. There it is. There is the line, right under you nose.' Zouga pointed his head. 'They cannot catch us now. Go, old man, go!'

Tom's hooves cracked on the hard earth like the beat of a joyous drummer. The crossing of the thorns had been cruel work, but it had rested him and he was pushing hard now.

''Ware hole!' Zouga called to him, and Tom flicked his ears reproachfully. He had seen it before Zouga had, and he jinked around the burrow neatly, while the heads of the curious little ground squirrels bobbed out of the earth as they passed.

The ground was rotten with their warrens, but Tom barely checked his gallop, swinging to avoid the mounds of freshly-turned earth, or occasionally stretching out to step over an entrance hole.

The ground squirrels were almost indistinguishable from their northern cousins, except for the stripe down their furry backs and their terrestrial habit. They stood on their hind legs, like small groups of spectators at the entrance of each warren, their expressions comically astonished and their long bushy tails curled over their backs as Tom pounded past them.

Zouga looked over his shoulder. Shooting Star was off the steep slope of the hills, down onto the open plain, and it was apparent that he was burning the last reserves of his great strength, coming on in a blazing run, driving out with his forelegs, and then bunching up his sweat-drenched hindquarters to hurl himself into the next stride. Louise was pushing him with her arms, like a washerwoman working over the scrubbing board, but she was too far behind for Zouga to see the expression on her face.

Much too far behind, half a mile behind – and there was less than a mile to run to the line of gaily coloured bunting that marked the finish.

Zouga could clearly see the crowds on each side of the posts, thick as bees at the entrance to the hive, and others were running for the wagons to join them.

He could hear the faint pop of gunfire, see the little spurts of gunsmoke jumping up above the heads of the crowd as his supporters fired into the air in jubilation.

Soon he would hear their voices, catch the sound of their cheers, even above the beat of Tom's hooves.

It was all over. He had won. He had won back his claims, the cherished image of the falcon god – and the five thousand pounds with which he could take his family away to a new life. He had taken on the gods of chance and won.

He had only one regret – that the courage of the horse and rider behind him had been in vain. Careful not to unbalance Tom's heavy unlovely gallop, he looked back under his own arm.

By God, she had not yet accepted defeat. She was driving with all her strength and all her heart, pushing the great horse as hard as she pushed herself, coming on so swiftly that Zouga glanced uneasily over Tom's pricked ears to reassure himself as to the proximity of the finish line. No, there was no chance – even at that tremendous speed – Shooting Star could never catch them.

Already he could hear the voices of the crowd, make out their individual faces, even recognize Pickering, the chief steward, on his seat on the wagon, and beside him Rhodes' unmistakable bulk and the mop of unruly hair. With him to witness it, Zouga's triumph was complete.

He turned for the last time to look back at Shooting Star – just in time to see him fall. It had been much too fast, too uncontrolled, that wild gallop across ground rotten with squirrel warrens. Shooting Star's front legs went from under him. Zouga imagined he could hear the bone break, like the crack of a pistol shot, and the huge horse went down from full gallop, shoulder first, neck twisted around in an agonized contortion like that of a dying flamingo; dust flew up in a cloud, blanketing them, and above it the stallion's hooves kicked spasmodically, convulsively, and then sagged.

The pale beige dust cloud drifted aside, revealing the tragic tangle of horse and rider. Shooting Star lay on his side and, as Zouga reined in and swung Tom's nose back the way he had come, the great stallion made a feeble effort to lift his head off the ground and then let it fall back weakly.

Louise's body had been flung clear. She lay curled like a sleeping child on the bare earth, very still, very small.

'Ha, Tom, ha!' Zouga urged him to greater speed. He was shocked at the sense of utter desolation that assailed him as he galloped back to where she lay. There was something so final, so terribly chilling in her stillness, in the complete relaxation, the lifelessness of that tiny crumpled body.

'Please God,' Zouga spoke aloud, his throat seared by dust and thirst and dread. 'Please don't let it be.'

He imagined the lovely delicate neck twisted at an impossible angle against the shattered vertebrae. He imagined the awful bloodless depression in the delicate dome of her skull; he imagined those huge dark eyes, open and staring, the inner glow fading – he imagined, oh God, he imagined – Then he was kicking his feet clear of the stirrups and jumping down even while Tom was at full gallop, stumbling to keep his balance and then running to where she lay.

Louise uncurled her body and rolled lightly to her feet.

'Come, darling, up darling,' she called to Shooting Star, as she ran to him. The stallion lunged once, twice and then he was standing, head up.

'What a clever darling,' Louise laughed, but with the huskiness of excitement and the tremor of heart-breaking exertion in the sound of it.

She did not have the strength left to vault for the saddle, and for a moment she hopped with one foot in the stirrup before she could find the energy to swing her other leg up over Shooting Star's back, while Zouga stood and gaped at her.

From the saddle she looked down at Zouga. 'Playing dead is an old Blackfoot Indian's trick, Major.'

Louise swung the stallion's head towards the finish line.

'Let's see you run the last lap on equal terms,' she challenged, and Shooting Star jumped away at full gallop.

For a moment Zouga could not bring himself to believe that she had taught the stallion to fall so convincingly, and to lie so still. Then suddenly his concern for her safety, the desolate feeling of believing her dead or maimed turned to fury and outrage.

As he ran back to where Tom stood, he yelled after her.

'Madam, you are a cheat — may God forgive you for that.'

She turned in the saddle and waved gaily. 'Sir, you are gullible, but I will forgive you for that.'

And Shooting Star bore her away towards the finish at a pace that poor Tom could never match.

Zouga Ballantyne was drunk. It was the first time in the twenty-two years they had been together that Jan Cheroot had seen him so.

He sat very erect on the high-backed deal chair, and his face above the beard had a strange waxen look to it. His eyes were glazed over with the same soapy sheen of uncut diamonds. The third bottle of Cape Brandy stood on the green baize of the table between them, and as Zouga fumbled for it, he knocked it over. The spirit glugged loudly from the mouth, and soaked into the cloth.

Jan Cheroot snatched it upright, with a shocked oath.

'Man, if you want to lose the Devil's Own, I don't mind — but, when you spill the brandy — that's another thing.'

Jan Cheroot stumbled a little over the words; they had been drinking since an hour before sundown.

'What am I going to tell the boys?' mumbled Zouga.

'Tell them that they are on holiday — for the first time in ten years. We are all on holiday.'

Jan Cheroot poured brandy into Zouga's mug, and pushed it closer to his hand. Then he poured a good dram into his own, thought about it for a moment, and added as much again.

'I have lost everything, Old Jan.'

'Ja,' Jan Cheroot said cheerfully. 'And that was not very much, was it.'

'I have lost the claims.'

'Good.' Jan Cheroot nodded. 'For ten years those

double-damned squares of dirt ate our souls away – and starved us while they were doing it.'

'I have lost the bird.'

'Good again!' Jan Cheroot swigged his brandy, and smacked his lips with appreciation. 'Let Mr Rhodes have his share of bad luck now. That bird will finish him, as it nearly finished us. Send it to him as soon as you can, and thank God to be rid of it.'

Slowly Zouga lowered his face into his hands, covering his eyes and his mouth – so that his voice was muffled.

'Jan Cheroot. It's all over. For me the road to the north is closed. My dream is finished. It's all been for nothing.'

The bibulous grin faded slowly and Jan Cheroot's yellow face puckered with deep compassion.

'It is not finished – you are still young and strong – with two strong sons.'

'We shall lose them too – soon, very soon.'

'Then you will have me, old friend, like it has always been.'

Zouga lifted his head out of his hands and stared at the little Hottentot.

'What are we going to do, Jan Cheroot?'

'We are going to finish this bottle and then open another,' Jan Cheroot told him firmly.

In the morning they loaded the soapstone idol into the gravel cart, and laid it on a bed of straw; then Zouga spread a stained and tattered tarpaulin over it and Jordan helped him rope it down.

Neither of them spoke – until they were finished, and then Jordan whispered so softly that Zouga barely caught the words.

'You can't let it go, Papa.' And Zouga turned to look at his younger son, truly seeing him for the first time in many years.

With a small shock he realized that Jordan was a man. In imitation of Ralph perhaps, he also had grown a moustache. It was a dense coppery gold, and accentuated the gentle line of his mouth – yet, if anything, the man was more beautiful than the child had been.

'Is there no way we can keep it?' Jordan persisted, with a thin edge of desperation in his voice, and Zouga went on staring at him. How old was he now? Over nineteen years, and yesterday he had been a baby – little Jordie. Everything was changed.

Zouga turned away from him, and placed his hand on the tarpaulin-wrapped burden in the bottom of the cart.

'No, Jordan. It was a wager – a matter of honour.'

'But, Mama—' Jordan started and then broke off abruptly as Zouga looked back at him sharply.

'What about Aletta?' he demanded, and Jordan looked away and flushed, bringing up the colour under the velvety skin of his cheeks.

'Nothing,' he said quickly, and went to the head of the lead mule. 'I will take the bird to Mr Rhodes,' he volunteered, and Zouga nodded immediately, relieved that he would be spared this painful duty.

'Ask him when he will be free to sign the transfer of the claims.'

Zouga touched the wrapped statue again as though in farewell and then he pulled his hand away, went up the steps onto the verandah and into the bungalow without looking back.

Jordan led the mules out into the rutted road and swung them towards the settlement. He walked bare-headed in the sunlight. He was tall and slim and he moved with a peculiar grace, stepping lightly and lithely in the soft red dust. His chin was up, his eyes focused far ahead, with the dreaming, yet all-seeing, gaze of a poet.

Men and women, especially women, looked after him as

he passed and their expressions softened, but Jordan walked on as though he were alone on a deserted street.

Though his lips never moved, the words of the invocation to the goddess Panes kept running through his mind.

' – Why did you run away? You would have been better with us—' So many times he had called to the goddess, the words were part of his very existence. 'Will you not come back to us, great Panes?'

The goddess was going – and Jordan did not believe he could support the agony of it. Statue, goddess and mother were all one in his mind, his last link with Aletta. Aletta who had become Panes.

He felt desolate, bereaved as though of his dearest love, and when he reached the milkwood fence of Rhodes' camp, he stopped and wild fancies seized him. He would take the goddess, run with her into the wilderness, hide her in some distant cave. His heart bounded. No, he would take her back to the ancient ruined city from which she had come, that far place in the north from which his father had stolen her, where she would be safe.

Then with a plunge of his spirits and a slide of despair in his guts he knew that these were childish dreamings and that he was no longer a child.

With a light touch on the lead mule's bridle, he guided her into the camp, and Rhodes was standing at the front door of his bungalow, bareheaded and in shirtsleeves. He was talking quietly, urgently to a man below the stoep. Jordan recognized him as one of the Central Diamond Company overseers.

When Rhodes looked up and saw Jordan, he dismissed the overseer with a curt word and a nod.

'Jordan,' Rhodes' greeting was grave, perhaps he sensed the mood of the young man before him, 'you have brought it?'

When Jordan nodded, he turned back to the waiting overseer.

'Bring four of your best men,' he ordered. 'I want this cart unloaded – and carefully. It's a valuable work of art.'

He watched keenly as they untied the ropes that held the tarpaulin in place, but cocked the large curly head when Jordan spoke.

'If we have to lose it, then I'm glad it's you that it goes to, Mr Rhodes.'

'The bird means something to you also, Jordan?'

'Everything,' Jordan said simply, and then caught himself; that sounded ridiculous. Mr Rhodes would think him strange. 'I mean, it has been in my family since before I was born. I don't really know what it will be like without that goddess. I don't really want to think about losing it.'

'You don't have to lose it, Jordan.'

Jordan looked at him, unable to bring himself to ask the meaning.

'You can follow the goddess, Jordan.'

'Please don't tease me, Mr Rhodes.'

'You are bright and willing, you have studied Pitman's shorthand, and you have an excellent pen,' Rhodes said. 'I need a secretary – somebody who knows and loves diamonds as I do. Somebody whom I feel easy with. Somebody I know and whom I like. Somebody I can trust.'

Jordan felt a vast soaring rush of joy, something sharper, brighter and more poignant than he had ever known before. He could not speak; he stood rooted and stared into the pale blue and beautiful eyes of the man whom he had worshipped for so many years.

'Well, Jordan, I am offering you the position. Do you want it?'

'Yes,' Jordan said softly. 'More than anything on earth, Mr Rhodes.'

'Good, then your first task is to find a place to set up the bird.'

The white overseer had pulled the tarpaulin aside to

expose the statue, and the sheet hung down over the side of the cart.

'Easy now,' he shouted at the gang of black labourers. 'Get a rope on it. Don't drop it. Watch that end, damn you.'

They swarmed over the statue, too many of them for the job, getting in one another's way – and Jordan's heady joy at Rhodes' offer was submerged in a quick stab of concern for the safety of the bird.

He started forward to set the ropes himself, but at that moment there was the clatter of hooves and Neville Pickering rode into the yard. He was astride his mare, a highly bred and finely mettled bay, and he reined her down to a walk.

He shot a glance at Jordan, and his face clouded for an instant – a quick show of irritation, or of something else. With a sudden intuitive flash Jordan realized that Pickering resented his presence here.

Then as quickly as it had come the shadow passed from Pickering's handsome features and he smiled that sunny charming smile of his and looked down at the statue in the cart.

'What have we here?' His tone was gay, his manner carefree and relaxed. As always he was elegantly dressed, the drape of broadcloth showing off his broad shoulders, the tooled leather belt emphasizing his narrow waist, as the polished half boots did the length and shape of his legs. The low-crowned, broad-brimmed hat was cocked forward over one eye, and he was smiling.

'Oh, the bird.' He looked up at Rhodes on the stoep of the bungalow. 'So you have it at last, as you said you would. I should congratulate you.'

The day had been still and too hot, it would change soon. The wind would come out of the south and the temperature would plunge, but until then the only movements of air were the sudden little dust devils that sprang out of nowhere, small but violent whirlwinds that lifted a high churning vortex of dust and dry grass and dead leaves a hundred or more feet into the still sky as they sped in a wildly erratic course across the plain, and then just as suddenly collapsed and disintegrated into nothingness again.

One of these dust devils rose now, on the open ground beyond the milkwood hedge. It tore a dense red cloud of spinning dust off the surface of the road, then swerved abruptly and raced into the yard of Rhodes' camp. Jordan felt his heart gripped in a cold vice of superstitious dread.

'Panes!' The cry was silent in his head. 'Great Panes!'

He knew what that wind was, he knew the presence of the goddess – for how many times had she come to his invocation? Suddenly the whole yard was filled with the swirling torrents of dust, and the wind battered them. It flew into Jordan's face, so that he must slit his eyes against it. It flung his soft shiny curls into his face, and it flattened his shirt against his chest and his lean flat belly.

The broad-brimmed hat sailed from Pickering's head, the tails of his coat flogged into the small of his back and he lifted one hand to protect his face from the stinging sand and sharp pieces of twig and grass.

Then the wind got under the ragged old tarpaulin, and filled it with a crack like a ship's mainsail gybing onto the opposite tack.

The harsh canvas lashed the bay mare's head, and she reared up on her back legs, whinnying shrilly with panic.

So high she went that Jordan thought she would go over on her back, and through the red raging curtain of dust, he jumped to catch her head; but he was an instant too late. Pickering had one hand to his face, and the mare's leap took him off balance; he went over backwards out of the saddle, and he hit hard earth with the back of his neck and one shoulder.

The rushing sound of the whirlwind, the grunt of air

driven from Pickering's lungs and the meaty thump of his fall almost covered the tiny snapping sound of bone breaking somewhere deep in his body.

Then the mare came down from her high prancing dance, and she flattened immediately into full gallop. She flew at the gateway in the milkwood hedge, and Pickering was dragged after her, his ankle trapped in the steel of the stirrup, his body slithering and bouncing loosely across the earth.

As the mare swerved to take the gap in the hedge, Pickering was flung into the hedge, and the white thorns, each as long as a man's forefinger, were driven into his flesh like needles.

Then he was plucked away, out into the open ground, sledging over rocky earth, striking and flattening the small wiry bushes as the mare jumped them, his body totally relaxed and his arms flung out behind him.

One moment the back of his head was slapping against the earth, and the next his ankle had twisted in the stirrup and he was face down, the skin being smeared from his cheeks and forehead by the harsh abrasive earth.

Jordan found himself racing after him, his breath sobbing with horror – calling to the mare.

'Whoa, girl! Steady, girl!'

But she was maddened, firstly terrified by the wind and the flirt of canvas into her face, and now by the unfamiliar weight that dragged and slithered at her heels. She reached the slope of the trailing dumps and swerved again, and this time, mercifully, the stirrup leather parted with a twang. Freed of her burden, the mare galloped away down the pathway between the dumps.

Jordan dropped on his knees beside Pickering's inert crumpled body. He lay face down; the expensive broadcloth was ripped and dusty, the boots scuffed through to white leather beneath.

Gently, supporting his head in cupped hands, Jordan

rolled him onto his back, turning his face out of the dust so that he could breathe. Pickering's face was a bloodied mask, caked with dust, a flap of white skin hanging off his cheek – but his eyes were wide open.

Despite the complete deathlike relaxation of his arms and body, Pickering was fully conscious. His eyes swivelled to Jordan's face, and his lips moved.

'Jordie,' he whispered. 'I can't feel anything, nothing at all. Numb – my hands, my feet, my whole body numb.'

They carried him back in a blanket, a man at each corner, and laid him gently on the narrow iron-framed cot in the bedroom next door to Rhodes' own room.

Dr Jameson came within the hour, and he nodded when he saw how Jordan had bathed and dressed his injuries and the arrangements he had made for his comfort.

'Good. Who taught you?' But he did not wait for an answer. 'Here!' he said. 'I'll need your help.' And he handed Jordan his bag, shrugged out of his jacket and rolled his sleeves.

'Get out,' he said to Rhodes. 'You'll be in the way here.'

It took Jameson only minutes to make certain that the paralysis below the neck was complete, and then he looked up at Jordan, making sure that he was out of sight of Pickering's alert, fever-bright eyes, and he shook his head curtly.

'I'll be a minute,' he said. 'I must speak with Mr Rhodes.'

'Jordie,' Pickering whispered painfully, the moment Jameson left the room, and Jordan stooped to his lips. 'It's my neck – it's broken.'

'No.'

'Be quiet. Listen.' Pickering frowned at the interruption. 'I think I always knew – that it would be you. One way or the other, it would be you—'

He broke off, fresh sweat blistered on his forehead, but he made another terrible effort to speak. 'I thought I hated you. But not any more – not now. There is not enough time left for hate.'

He did not speak again, not that night, nor the following day. But at dusk when the heat in the tiny iron-walled room abated a little, he opened his eyes again and looked up at Rhodes. It was frightening to see how low he had sunk. The fine bones of forehead and cheeks seemed to gleam through the translucent skin, and his eyes had receded into dark bruised cavities.

Rhodes leaned his great shaggy head over him until his ear touched Pickering's dry white lips. The whisper was so light, like a dead leaf blown softly across a roof at midnight, and Jordan could not hear the words, but Rhodes clenched his lids closed over his pale blue eyes as though in mortal anguish.

'Yes,' he answered, almost as softly as the dying man. 'Yes, I know, Pickling.'

When Rhodes opened his eyes again they were flooded with bright tears, and his colour was a frightening mottled purple.

'He's dead, Jordan,' he choked, and put one hand on his own chest, pressing hard as though to calm the beat of his swollen heart.

Then quite slowly, deliberately, he lowered his head again, and kissed the broken, torn lips of the man on the iron-framed cot.

Zouga thought the voice was part of his dream – so sweet, so low, and yet tremulous and filled with some dreadful appeal. Then he was awake, and the voice was still calling, and now there was a light tap on the window above the head of his bed.

'I'm coming,' Zouga answered, as low as he was called. He did not have to ask who it was.

He dressed swiftly, in total darkness, instinct warning him not to light a candle, and he carried his boots in his hand as he stepped out onto the stoep of the cottage.

The height of the moon told him that it was after midnight, but he barely glanced at it before turning to the figure that leaned against the wall beside the door.

'Are you alone?' he demanded softly. There was something in the way the figure slumped that frightened him.

'Yes.' The distress, the pain, were clear in her voice now that they were so close.

'You should not have come here – not alone, Mrs St John.'

'There was nobody else to turn to.'

'Where is Mungo? Where is your husband?'

'He is in trouble – terrible, terrible trouble.'

'Where is he?'

'I left him out beyond the Cape crossroad.'

For a moment her voice choked on her, and then it came out with a forceful rush.

'He's hurt. Wounded, badly wounded.'

Her voice had risen, so that she might rouse Jan Cheroot and the boys. Zouga took her arm to calm and quieten her, and immediately she fell against him. The feel of her body shocked him, but he could not pull away.

'I'm afraid, Zouga. I'm afraid he might die.' It was the first time she had used his given name.

'What happened?'

'Oh God!' She was weeping now, clinging to him, and he realized how hard-pressed she was. He slipped his arm around her waist and led her down the verandah.

In the kitchen he seated her on one of the hard deal chairs, and then lit the candle. He was shocked again when he saw her face. She was pale and shaking, her hair in wild disorder, a smear of dirt on one cheek and her eyes red-rimmed and bloodshot.

He poured coffee from the blue enamel pot at the back of the stove. It was thick as molasses. He added a dram of brandy to it.

'Drink it.'

She shuddered and gasped at the potent black brew, but it seemed to steady her a little.

'I didn't want him to go. I tried to stop him. I was sick of it. I told him I couldn't take it any more, the cheating and lying. The shame and the running—'

'You aren't making sense,' he told her brusquely, and she took a deep breath and started again.

'Mungo went to meet a man tonight. The man was going to bring him a parcel of diamonds, a parcel of diamonds worth one hundred thousand pounds. And Mungo was going to buy them for two thousand.'

Zouga's face set grimly, and he sat down opposite her and stared at her. His expression intimidated her.

'Oh God, Zouga. I know. I hated it too. I have lived with it so long, but he promised me that this would be the last time.'

'Go on,' Zouga commanded.

'But he didn't have two thousand, Zouga. We are almost broke – a few pounds is all that we have left.'

This time Zouga could not contain himself and he broke in.

'The letter of credit, half a million pounds—'

'Forged,' she said quietly.

'Go on.'

'He didn't have the money to pay for the diamonds – and I knew what he was going to do. I tried to stop him, I swear it to you.'

'I believe you.'

'He arranged to meet this man tonight – at a place out on the Cape road.'

'Do you know the man's name?'

'I'm not sure. I think so.' She passed her hand over her eyes. 'He is a coloured man, a Griqua, Henry – no, Hendrick Somebody—'

'Hendrick Naaiman?'

'Yes. Naaiman, that's it.'

'He's an I.D.B. trap.'

'Police?'

'Yes, police.'

'Oh sweet God, it's even worse than I thought.'

'What happened?' Zouga insisted.

'Mungo made me wait for him at the crossroads and he went to the rendezvous alone. He said he needed to protect himself – he took his pistol. He went on my horse – on Shooting Star, and then I heard the gunfire.'

She took another gulp of the coffee and coughed at the burn of it.

'He came back. He had been shot, and so had Shooting Star. They couldn't go any further, neither of them. They were both hard hit, Zouga. I hid them near the road and I came to you.'

Zouga's voice was harsh. 'Did Mungo kill him?'

'I don't know, Zouga. Mungo says the other man fired first and he only tried to protect himself.'

'Mungo tried to hold him up and take the diamonds, without paying for them,' Zouga guessed. 'But Naaiman is a dangerous man.'

'There were four empty cartridges in Mungo's pistol, but I don't know what happened to the policeman. I only know that Mungo escaped, but he is hurt very badly.'

'Now keep quiet and rest for a while.' He stood up and paced up and down the kitchen, his bare feet making no sound, his hands clasped at the small of the back.

Louise St John watched him anxiously, almost fearfully, until he stopped abruptly and turned to her.

'We both know what I should do. Your husband is I.D.B.; he is a thief and by now he is probably a murderer.'

'He is also your friend,' she said simply. 'And he is very badly wounded.'

He resumed his pacing, but now he was muttering to himself, troubled and scowling, and Louise twisted her fingers in her lap.

'Very well,' he said at last. 'I'll help you to get him away.'

'Oh, Major Ballantyne – Zouga—'

He silenced her with a frown. 'Don't waste time talking. We'll need bandages, laudanum, food—' He was ticking off a list on his fingers. 'You can't go like that. They'll be watching for a woman. Jordan's cast-off clothes will fit you well enough – breeches, cap and coat—'

Zouga walked at the flank of the mule, and the gravel cart was loaded with bales of thatching grass.

Louise lay silently in the hollow between two bales, with another ready to pull over herself if the cart was stopped.

The iron-shod wheels crunched in the sand, but the night dew had damped down the dust. The lantern on the tailboard of the cart swung and jiggled to the motion.

They had just passed the last house on the Cape road, and were drawing level with the cemetery when there was the dust-muffled beat of hooves from behind them and Louise only just had time to drop down and cover herself before a small group of riders swept out of the darkness and overtook them.

As they galloped through the arc of lantern light, Zouga saw they were all armed. He stooped and lowered his chin into the collar of his greatcoat and the woollen cap was pulled low over his eyes. One of the riders pulled up his horse and shouted to Zouga.

'Hey, you! Have you seen anybody on this road tonight?'

'*Niemand nie!*' Nobody!' Zouga answered in the taal, and the sound of the guttural dialect reassured the man.

He wheeled his horse and galloped on after his companions.

When the sound of hooves had died away Zouga spoke quietly.

'That means that Naaiman got away to spread the word. Unless he dies of his wounds later, it's not murder.'

'Please God,' Louise whispered.

'It also means that you cannot try to get out on either the Cape road or the road to the Transvaal. They will be watched.'

'Which way can we go?'

'If I were you I would take the track north, it goes to Kuruman. There is a mission station there – it's run by my grandfather. His name is Doctor Moffat. He will give you shelter, and Mungo will need a doctor. Then when Mungo is strong enough, you can try to reach German or Portuguese territory and get out through Lüderitz Bay or Lourenço Marques.'

Neither of them spoke for a long time as Zouga trudged on beside the mule, and Louise crawled out to sit on the bench of the cart. It was she who broke the silence.

'I am so tired of running. We seem to have run out of lands, America, Canada, Australia, we cannot go back to any of them.'

'You could go home to France,' Zouga said, 'to your sons.'

Louise's head jerked up. 'Why do you say that?'

'When Mungo and I first met he told me about you, his wife – that you were of a noble French family. He told me that you and he had three sons.'

Louise's chin sank onto her chest and Jordan's cloth cap covered her eyes.

'I have no sons,' she said. 'But oh how I pray that one day I may have. I belong to a noble family, yes – but not French. My grandmother was the daughter of Hawk Flies Lightly, the Blackfoot War Chief.'

'I don't understand, Mungo told me—'

'He told you about the woman who is his wife, Madame Solange de Montijo St John.'

Louise was silent again, and Zouga had to ask:

'She is dead?'

'Their marriage was unhappy. No, she is not dead. She returned with their three sons to France at the beginning of the Civil War. He has not seen her since.'

'Then she and Mungo are,' Zouga hesitated over the unsavoury word, 'divorced?'

'She is a Catholic,' Louise replied simply; and it was fully five minutes before either of them spoke again.

'Yes,' Louise said. 'What you are thinking is correct. Mungo and I are not married; we could not be.'

'It's not my business,' Zouga murmured, and yet what she had said did not shock him. He felt instead a strange lightness of spirit, a kind of glowing joy.

'It's a relief to speak completely honestly,' she explained. 'After all the lies. Somehow it had to be you, Zouga. I could never have admitted all this to anybody else.'

'Do you love him?' Zouga's voice was rough-edged, brusque.

'Once I loved him completely, without restraint, wildly – madly.'

'And now?'

'I do not know – there have been so many lies, so much shame, so much to hide.'

'Why do you stay with him, Louise?'

'Because now he needs me.'

'I understand that.' His voice was gentler. He did understand, he truly did. 'Duty is a harsh and unforgiving master. And yet you have a duty to yourself also.'

The mules plodded on in the darkness, and the swinging lantern did not light the face of the woman on the bench, but once she sighed, and it was a sound to twist Zouga's heart.

'Louise,' he spoke at last. 'I am not doing this for Mungo, even a friendship cannot condone deliberate robbery and premeditated murder.'

She did not reply.

'Many times you must have seen the way I have looked at you – for, God knows, I could not help myself.'

Still she was silent.

'You did know,' he insisted. 'You, as a woman, must know how I feel.'

'Yes,' she said at last.

'When I thought you were married to a friend, it was hopeless. Now, at least, I can tell you how I feel.'

'Zouga, please don't.'

'I would do anything you asked me to – even protect a murderer, that is how I feel for you.'

'Zouga—'

'I have never known anybody so beautiful and bright and brave—'

'I am not any of those things—'

'I could put you and Mungo on the road to Kuruman and then go back to Kimberley and tell the diamond police where to find you. They would take Mungo, and then you would be free.'

'You could,' she agreed. 'But you never would. Both of us are tied, Zouga, by our own peculiar sense of duty and of honour.'

'Louise—'

'We have arrived,' she said, with patent relief. 'The crossroads. Turn off the road here.'

From the bench she guided him as he threaded the cart through the scattered bush and the high wheels bumped over rock and rough ground. A quarter of a mile from the road there stood a massive camel-thorn tree, silver and high as a hill in the moonlight. Beneath its spread branches the moon shadow was black and impenetrable.

From the darkness a hoarse voice challenged.

'Stand where you are! Don't come any closer.'

'Mungo, it's me and Zouga is with me.'

Louise jumped down from the cart, lifted the lantern off its bracket and went forward, stooping under the branches. Zouga tethered the mules and then followed her. Louise was kneeling beside Mungo St John. He lay on a saddle blanket, propped on the silver ornamented Mexican saddle.

'Thank you for coming,' he greeted Zouga, and his voice was ragged with pain.

'How badly are you hit?'

'Badly enough,' he admitted. 'Do you have a cheroot?'

Zouga lit one from the lantern and handed it to him. Louise was unwrapping the torn strips of shirt and petticoat that were bound about his chest.

'Shotgun?' Zouga asked tersely.

'No, thank God,' Mungo said. 'Pistol.'

'You are lucky,' Zouga grunted. 'Naaiman's usual style is a sawed-off shotgun. He would have blown you in half.'

'You know him – Naaiman?'

'He's a police trap.'

'Police,' Mungo whispered. 'Oh God.'

'Yes,' Zouga nodded. 'You are in trouble.'

'I didn't know.'

'Does it really matter?' Zouga asked. 'You planned an I.D.B. switch, and you knew you might have to kill a man.'

'Don't preach to me, Zouga.'

'All right.' Zouga squatted next to Louise as she exposed the wound in Mungo's back. 'It looks as though it missed the lymph.'

Between them they lifted Mungo into a sitting position.

'Through and through,' Zouga murmured, as he saw the exit wound in Mungo's back. 'And it looks as though it missed the lung. You are luckier than you'll ever know.'

'One stayed in,' Mungo St John contradicted him, and reached down to his own leg. His breeches had been split down the leg, and now he pulled the bloodstained cloth aside to reveal a strip of pale thigh in the centre of which was another vicious little round opening from which fluid wept like blackcurrant juice.

'The bullet is still in,' Mungo repeated.

'Bone?' Zouga asked.

'No.' St John shook his head. 'I don't think so. I was still able to walk on it.'

'There is no chance of trying to cut the bullet out. Louise knows where she can find a doctor, and I have told her how to get there.'

'Louise?' Mungo asked with a sardonic twist of his lips.

She did not look up, concentrating on the task of painting the skin around the wounds with iodine.

Mungo was staring at Zouga, his single eye gleaming, and Zouga felt the scar on his cheek throb and he did not trouble to hide his anger.

'You don't think I am doing this for you,' he demanded. 'I hate I.D.B. as much as any digger on the workings, and I'm not that complacent about deliberate robbery and murder.' And he took the pistol from the blanket where it lay at Mungo's side.

He checked the load as he walked to where Shooting Star stood, head down in the moonlight beyond the camel-thorn tree.

The stallion lifted his head, and blew a fluttery breath through his nostrils as Zouga approached; then he shifted his weight awkwardly and painfully on three legs.

'There, boy. Easy, boy.' Zouga ran his hands down the animal's flank. It was sticky with drying blood, and Shooting Star whickered as he touched the wound.

Behind the ribs, bullet hole, and Zouga sniffed at it quickly. The bullet had pierced the bowel or the intestines – he could smell it.

Zouga went down on one knee and gently felt the foreleg that the stallion was favouring. He found the damage, another bullet wound. It had struck a few inches above the fetlock and the bone was shattered. Yet the horse had carried Mungo, a big heavy man, and it had brought him many miles. The agony must have been dreadful, but the stallion's great heart had carried them through.

Zouga shrugged off his greatcoat and wrapped it around the pistol in his right hand. A shot could alert the searching bands on the not too distant road.

'There, boy,' Zouga whispered, and touched the muzzle to the forehead between the horse's eyes.

The cloth muffled the shot. It was a dull blurt of sound, and the stallion dropped heavily on his side and never even kicked.

Louise was still bowed over Mungo, tying the knots in the bandage, but Zouga saw that her eyes were bright with tears in the moonlight.

'Thank you,' she whispered. 'I couldn't have done it myself.'

Zouga helped her lift Mungo to the cart. Mungo's breath whistled in his chest and the sweat of agony drenched his shirt and smelled rancid and gamey.

They settled him into the nest of thatching grass and spread a screen of it over him. Then Zouga led the mules on over the veld until they struck the track that led northwards towards the Vaal river, and beyond it Kuruman and the vast Kalahari Desert.

'Travel at night, and hobble the mules to graze during the day,' Zouga told her. 'There is more than enough meal and biltong; but you will have to spare the coffee and sugar.'

'Words cannot thank you enough,' she whispered.

'Don't attempt the main drift of the Vaal.'

'Somehow I know that this is not goodbye.' She seemed not to have heard the advice. 'And when we meet again—' she broke off.

'Go on,' he said, but she shook her head and took the reins from his hand and led the mules onto the track.

The cart seemed to merge into the night, and the wheels made no sound in the thick pale sand. Zouga stood staring after them, long after they had disappeared – and then Louise came back.

She came silent as a wraith, running with a kind of terrible desperation, the long tresses of hair had fallen out from under the cap and were streaming down her back. Her face was pale and stricken in the moonlight.

The grip of her arms about his neck was fierce, almost painful, and her mouth was shockingly hot and wet as it spread over his. But the taste of it he would never forget, and her sharp white teeth crushed his lips.

For seconds only they clung to each other, while Zouga thought his heart would burst; then she tore herself from his arms, and with neither a word nor a backward glance, she flew into the night – and was gone.

Ten days after Neville Pickering's funeral, Zouga signed the transfer deeds to the Devil's Own claims, and watched while one of Rhodes' secretaries registered them in favour of the Central Diamond Company. Then he walked out into the cold.

For the first time in living memory it was snowing over the diamond fields. Big soft flakes came twisting down like feathers from a shimmering white egret struck by birdshot.

The snowflakes vanished as they touched the earth, but the cold was a vindictive presence and Zouga's breath steamed in the air and condensed on his beard as he trudged up to the workings to watch the shift come off the Devil's Own claims for the last time. As he walked he tried to compose the words to tell Ralph that this was the last shift.

They were coming up in the skip. Zouga could make out Ralph, for he was the only man who wore a coat. The other men with him were almost naked.

Once again Zouga wondered idly that the men had not rebelled against the harsh measures of the new Diamond Trade Act, enforced by Colonel John Fry of the recently recruited Diamond Police, and aimed at stamping out I.D.B. on the fields.

Nowadays the black workers were compounded behind barbed wire; there were new curfew regulations to keep them in the compounds after nightfall; and there were spot searches and checks of the compounds, of men on the streets even during daylight, and body searches of each shift coming out of the pit.

Even the diggers, or at least a few of them, had protested at the most draconian of John Fry's new regulations. All black workers had been forced to go into the pit stark naked, so that they would not be able to hide stones in their clothing.

John Fry had been amazed when Zouga and a dozen other diggers had demanded to see him.

'Good Lord, Ballantyne, but they are a bunch of naked savages anyway. Modesty, forsooth!'

In the end, with the co-operation of Rhodes, they had forced him to compromise.

Grudgingly Fry had allowed every worker a strip of seamless cotton 'limbo' to cover himself.

Thus Bazo and his Matabele wore only a strip of loincloth each as they rode up beside Ralph in the skip. The wind threw an icy noose about them, and Bazo shivered as goose-bumps rose upon the smooth dark skin of his chest and upper arms.

Above him stood Ralph Ballantyne, balancing easily on the rim of the steel skip, ignoring the wind and the deadly drop below him.

Ralph glanced down at Bazo crouching below the side

of the steel bucket, and on impulse slipped the scrap of stained canvas off his own shoulders. Under it Ralph wore an old tweed jacket and dusty cardigan. He dropped the canvas over Bazo's neck.

'It's against the white man's law,' Bazo demurred, and made as if to shrug it off.

'There are no police in this skip,' Ralph grunted, and Bazo hesitated a moment and then crouched lower and gratefully pulled the canvas over his head and shoulders.

Ralph took the butt of a half-smoked cheroot from his breast pocket, and carefully reshaped it between his fingers; the dead ash flaked away on the wind and wafted down into the yawning depths below. He lit the butt and drew the smoke down deeply, exhaled and drew again, held the smoke and passed the butt to Bazo.

'You are not only cold, but you are unhappy,' Ralph said, and Bazo did not answer. He cupped the stubby cheroot in both hands and drew carefully upon it.

'Is it Donsela?' Ralph asked. 'He knew the law, Bazo. He knows what the law says of those who steal the stones.'

'It was a small stone,' murmured Bazo, the words and blue smoke mingled on his lips. 'And fifteen years is a long time.'

'He is alive,' Ralph pointed out and took the cheroot that Bazo passed back to him. 'In the old days before the Diamond Trade Act, he would be dead by now.'

'He might as well be dead,' Bazo whispered bitterly. 'They say that men work like animals, chained like monkeys, on the breakwater wall at Cape Town harbour.'

He drew again on the cheroot and it burned down with a fierce little glow that scorched his fingers. He crushed it out on the workhardened calluses of his palm and let the shreds of tobacco blow away.

'And you, Henshaw – are you then so happy?' he asked quietly, and Ralph shrugged.

'Happy? Who is happy?'

'Is not this pit' – with a gesture Bazo took in the mighty excavation over which they dangled – 'is not this your prison, does it not hold you as surely as the chains that hold Donsela as he places the rocks on the breakwater over the sea?'

They had almost reached the high stagings and Bazo slipped off his canvas covering before he could be spotted by one of the black constables who patrolled the area inside the new security fences.

'You ask me if I am unhappy.' Bazo stood up, and did not look at Ralph's face. 'I was thinking of the land in which I am a prince of the House of Kumalo. In that land the calves I tended as a boy have grown into bulls and have bred calves which I have never seen. Once I knew every beast in my father's herds, fifteen thousand head of prime cattle, and I knew each of them, the season of its birth, the twist of its horns and the markings of its hide.'

Bazo sighed and came to stand beside Ralph on the rim of the skip. They were of a height, two tall young men, well formed, and each, in the manner of his race, comely.

'Ten times I have not been with my impi when it danced the Festival of Fresh Fruits, ten times I did not witness my king throw the war-spear and send us out on the red road.'

Bazo's sombre mood deepened, and his voice sank lower.

'Boys have grown to men since I left, and some of them wear the cowtails of valour on their legs and arms.' Bazo glanced down at his own naked body with its single dirty rag at the waist. 'Little girls have grown into maidens, with ripe bellies, ready to be claimed by the warriors who have won the honour on the red road of war.' And both of them thought of the lonely nights when the phantoms came to haunt them. Then Bazo folded his arms across his wide chest and went on.

'I think of my father, and I wonder if the snows of age have yet settled upon his head. Every man of my tribe that comes down the road from the north brings me the words of Juba, the Dove, who is my mother. She has twelve sons, but I am the first and the eldest of them.'

'Why have you stayed so long?' Ralph asked harshly.

'Why have you stayed so long, Henshaw?' The young Matabele challenged him quietly, and Ralph had no answer.

'Have you found fame and riches in this hole?' Again they both glanced down into the pit, and from this height the off-shift waiting to come up in the skips were like columns of safari ants.

'Do you have a woman with hair as long and pale as the winter grass to give you comfort in the night, Henshaw? Do you have the music of your sons' laughter to cheer you, Henshaw? What keeps you here?'

Ralph lifted his eyes and stared at Bazo, but before he could find an answer the skip came level with the platform on the first ramp of the stagings. The jerk brought Ralph back to reality and he waved to his father on the platform above them.

The roar of the steam winch subsided. The skip slowed and Bazo led the party of Matabele workers onto the ramp. Ralph saw them all clear before he jumped across the narrow gap to the wooden platform and felt it tremble under the combined weight of twenty men.

Ralph signalled again. Then the winch growled, and the steel cable squealed in its sheaves. The heavy-laden skip ran on until it hit the striker blocks. Ralph and Bazo drove the jumper bars under it, and threw their full weight on them. The skip tipped over, and the load of gravel went roaring down the chute into the waiting cart.

Ralph looked up to see his father's encouraging smile and to hear his shouted congratulations.

'Well done, boy! Two hundred tons today!'

But the staging was deserted. Zouga had gone.

Zouga had packed a single chest, the chest that had belonged to Aletta and which had come up with her from the Cape. Now it was going back, and it was almost all that was going back.

Zouga put Aletta's Bible in the bottom of the chest, and with it her diary and the trinket box which contained the remaining pieces of her jewellery. The more valuable pieces had long ago been sold, to support the dying dream.

Over these few mementoes he packed his own diaries and maps, and his books. When he came to the bundled pile of his unfinished manuscript, he paused to weigh it in his hand.

'Perhaps I shall find time to finish it now,' he murmured, and laid it gently in the chest.

On top of that went his clothing, and there was so little of that – four shirts, a spare pair of boots – barely an armful.

The chest was only half-full, and he carried it easily down the steps into the yard. That was all that he was taking – the rest of it, the meagre furnishings of the bungalow he had sold to one of the auctioneers in Market Square. Ten pounds the lot. As Rhodes had predicted, he was leaving as he had come.

'Where is Ralph?' he demanded of Jan Cheroot, and the little Hottentot paused in chaining the cooking-pot and black iron kettle onto the tailboard of the cart.

'Perhaps he stopped at Diamond Lil's. The boy has got a right to his thirst – he worked hard enough for it.'

Zouga let it pass, and instead ran an appraising eye over the cart. It was the newest and strongest of the three vehicles he owned. One cart had gone with Louise St John, and she had taken the best mules – but this rig would get them back to Cape Town, even under the additional burden that he was planning to put into it.

Jan Cheroot ambled across to Zouga and took the other handle of the chest, ready to boost it up into the body of the cart.

'Wait,' Zouga told him. 'That first.' And he pointed to the roughly-hewn block of blue mottled rock that lay below the camel-thorn tree.

'My mother—' Jan Cheroot gaped. 'This I don't believe. In twenty-two years I've seen you do some stupid crazy things—'

Zouga strode across to the block of blue ground that Ralph had brought up from the Devil's Own and put his foot on it. 'We'll hoist it up with the block and tackle.' He glanced at the sturdy branch above his head from which the sheave block and manila rope hung. 'And we'll back the cart up under it.'

'That's it!' Jan Cheroot sat down on the chest and folded his arms. 'This time I refuse. Once before I broke my back for you, but that was when I was young and stupid.'

'Come on, Jan Cheroot, you are wasting time.'

'What do you want with that – piece of ugly bloody stone? With another piece of thundering nonsense.'

'I have lost the bird – I need a household god.'

'I have heard of someone putting up a monument to a brave man, or a great battle – but to put up a stone to stupidity,' Jan Cheroot mourned.

'Back the cart up.'

'I refuse – this time I refuse. I won't do it. Not for anything. Not for any price.'

'When we get it loaded – you can have a bottle of Smoke all to yourself to celebrate.'

Jan Cheroot sighed, and stood up. 'That's my price.' He shook his head and came across to stand beside Zouga. He glared at the block of blue stone venomously. 'But don't expect me to like it.'

Zouga chuckled, for the first time in weeks, and in an unusual display of affection he put one arm around Jan Cheroot's shoulders.

'Now that you have something to hate again – just think how happy it will make you,' he said.

'Y ou have been drinking,' Zouga said, and Ralph tossed his hat into the corner and agreed.

'Yes, I have had a beer or two.' He went to the black iron stove and warmed his hands. 'I would have had more – if I had had the money.'

'I have been waiting for you,' Zouga went on, and Ralph turned back to him truculently.

'I give you every hour of my day, Papa – let me have a little time at the end of it.'

'I have something of great importance to tell you,' Zouga nodded to the deal chair facing him. 'Sit down, Ralph.'

Zouga rubbed his eyes with forefinger and thumb as he collected his words. He had tried so often in the last days to find an easy way to tell Ralph that it was over, that they were destitute, that all that toil and heartbreak had been in vain – but there was no easy way. There were only the stark hard words of reality.

He dropped his hand, and looked at his son, and then slowly and carefully he told him, and when he had finished he waited for Ralph to speak. Ralph had not moved during the long recital, and now he stared at Zouga stonily.

Zouga was forced to speak again. 'We shall leave in the morning. Jan Cheroot and I have loaded the No. 2 wagon and we shall need all the mules, double team – it's a long haul.'

Again he waited, but there was still no reaction.

'You will be wondering where we are going and what we shall do. Well, once we get back to the Cape we still have the Harkness cottage.'

'You gambled it all.' Ralph spoke at last. 'Without telling me. You – you, who are always preaching to me about gambling, and honesty.'

'Ralph!'

'It wasn't yours, it belonged to all of us.'

'You are drunk,' Zouga said flatly.

'All these years I have listened to your promises. We shall go north, Ralph.' He mimicked Zouga with a sudden savagery in his tone. 'It's for all of us, Ralph. It's yours to share. There is a land waiting for us, Ralph. It will be yours as well as mine, Ralph.'

'It's not over – I still have the concession. When we get back to Cape Town—'

'You, not me.' Ralph's voice was flat, angry. 'You go back to Cape Town. Go dream your old man's dreams. I am sick of them.'

'You dare to use that tone to me?'

'Yes, I dare. And by God, I'll dare more than that. I'll dare what you are too weak or afraid to dare—'

'You insolent and stupid puppy!'

'You toothless old dog!'

Zouga threw himself half across the table, and his right arm lashed out. He caught Ralph open-handed across the face, and the crack of palm on flesh was stunning as a pistol shot.

Ralph's head snapped back, and then slowly he brought it upright again. 'That,' he said, 'is the last time you will strike me, ever.' He stood up and strode towards the door, and there he turned. 'Go dream your dreams – I will go live mine out.'

'Go then,' said Zouga, and the scar on his cheek was glassy and white as ice. 'Go and be damned to you.'

'Remember I took nothing with me, Papa, not even your blessing,' said Ralph, and stepped out into the night.

B azo woke instantly at the touch on his cheek, and reached for the assegai at his side, his eyes wide in the faint glow of the ashes. A hand closed on his wrist, holding his spear hand from the weapon, and a voice spoke softly above him.

'Do you remember the road to Matabeleland, O Prince of Kumalo?'

It took Bazo a moment to gather his wits from where sleep had scattered them.

'I remember every running ford and every green hill, every sweet watering place along the way,' he whispered back, 'as clearly as I remember my father's voice and my mother's laughter.'

'Roll up your sleeping-mat, Bazo, the Axe, and show me the road,' said Ralph.

D iamond Lil did not smile so readily these days, not since the tooth that held the diamond had turned a dingy grey as the root died, and began to ache until Lil wept with the little explosion of agony against the top of her skull. The travelling dentist from the Cape had pulled the tooth and drained the virulent abscess beneath it.

Relief had been immediate, but it left a black gap in her smile.

She had put on flesh also, the consequence of good food and those little nips of gin which bolstered her day. Her breasts, always generous, had lost their individual definition and the cleavage that showed above the richly embroidered bodice was no longer a deeply sculptured crevasse but a thin line where abundant flesh packed against flesh.

The hand that held the bone china teacup was pudgy and dimpled over the knuckles, the rings that adorned each plump little finger had sunk into the flesh, but the diamonds and rubies and emeralds sparkled in a royal show of Lil's wealth.

Her hair was still lustrous gold, and crimped into long dangling ringlets with the hot-iron. Her skin was still smooth and rich as Devon cream, except around the eyes where it was just beginning to crack into little spider-webs of lines.

She sat at the corner of the verandah, on the second floor above the street, where the eaves of the roof were of intricate white wrought-iron mouldings, pretty as Madeira lace. Although there were other double-storeyed buildings in Kimberley these days, not even the offices of the Central Diamond Company across the wide unpaved street boasted such affluent adornment.

Lil's chair was high-backed, and magnificently carved in dark red teak by oriental craftsmen, inlaid with mother-of-pearl and ivory and carried across the eastern oceans by the tall ships of the now long departed Dutch East India Company. It had cost her two hundred pounds, but from this throne she could watch every movement on the main thoroughfares that fed into Market Square, could sense the pulse of the diamond city, could check each coming and going, the scurry of a buyer with a good scent in his nostrils, the swagger of a digger who had turned up a bright one. She could watch the front of the four canteens around the square, all of which she now owned, and judge the volume of trade going through their doors.

Similarly, she could glance to her left, down De Beers Road to the red-brick cottage behind its white picket fence and discreet sign, 'French Dressmakers. Haute Couture. Six Continental Seamstresses. Specialities for individual tastes.' Business was always brisk there – from noon to midnight. Her girls seldom lasted the pace for more than six months or so – before taking the coach southward again, exhausted but considerably richer.

Lil herself worked her old trade only occasionally, perhaps once or twice a week with a favoured 'regular', just for old times' sake, and because it got her blood going and made her sleep better at night. There was too much else that required her constant attention.

Now she poured fresh tea from the rococo silver pot into the pretty bone china cups, hand-painted with pink roses and golden butterflies.

'How many spoons?' she asked.

Ralph sat on the cane-back chair opposite her. He smelled of shaving soap and cheap eau-de-Cologne. His chin shone with a burnish given it by the cut-throat razor, and his shirt was so crisply ironed and starched that it crackled at each movement.

Lil studied him speculatively over the rim of her tea cup.

'Does the good major know your plans?' she asked quietly, and Ralph shook his head. Lil thought on that a while and it gave her a ripple of pleasure to have the son of a foundation member of the Kimberley Club sitting on her verandah. Son of one of the Kimberley gentlemen who would not greet her on the street, who had returned her donation towards the new hospital, who had not even replied to her invitation to attend the stone-laying ceremony of her new building – oh, the list of humiliations was too long to recite now.

'Why did you not go to your father?' she asked instead.

'My father is not a rich man.' Ralph would not say any more, too loyal to explain that Zouga was destitute, that he would soon leave Kimberley with a cartload of his meagre possessions. He did not want Lil to know that he and his father had turned from each other with harsh words.

Lil studied his face for a moment, then picked up the handwritten sheet of cheap notepaper from the tea tray and glanced down the list and the figures.

'Nine hundred pounds for oxen?'

'A full span of the biggest and best animals,' Ralph explained. 'The road to the Shashi river is sand veld, heavy going. I want to be able to haul a full load, eight thousand pounds weight.'

'Trade goods – fifteen thousand.' She looked up at him again.

'Guns, powder, brandy, beads and limbo cloth.'

'What type of guns?'

'Tower muskets. Five pounds ten shillings each.'

Lil shook her head. 'They have seen the breech-loaders. Your muskets won't have much pull.'

'I can't afford breech-loaders, and I wouldn't know where to find a load.'

'Ralph dearie, I could hire a bunch of Whitechapel hags to run my dressmakers' shop and I could get them cheap. But I don't. I pick them young and fresh and pretty. If you think small, your profits are small. Don't be cheap, Ralph darling, never be cheap.' She poured a little gin from the silver flask into the empty teacup before she went on. 'I can get Martini-Henry rifles but they will cost us fifteen hundred more.' Lil reached across and dipped her pen in the ink-well, then scratched out and re-wrote the figure.

'Brandy?'

'Cape Smoke in twenty-gallon casks.'

'I have heard that Lobengula likes Courvoisier cognac, and his sister Ningi drinks only Piper-Heidsieck champagne.'

'Another five hundred pounds – at least,' Ralph mourned.

'Three hundred,' Lil corrected the list. 'I can get it at wholesale prices. Now, ammunition – ten thousand rounds?'

'I'll need at least a thousand for my own account, and the rest to trade with the rifles.'

'If Lobengula gives you permission to hunt elephant,' Lil corrected.

'My grandfather is one of his oldest friends; my Aunty Robyn and her husband have been at Khami River Mission for almost twenty years.'

'Yes, I know that you have friends at court.' Lil pursed her lips approvingly. 'But I have heard that the elephant have been shot out across the whole of Matabeleland.'

'The herds have been driven into the fly belt on the Zambezi.'

'You cannot take horses into the fly and hunting elephant on foot in the fly is not work for a white man.'

'My father hunted on foot, and anyway I cannot afford a horse.'

'All right,' she agreed reluctantly, and made a tick on the sheet.

They worked on for an hour longer, going down the list item by item – and then starting again at the head and going over it all once more, Lil ticking and scratching with the pen – fining it down by ten pounds here and a hundred there, until at last she tossed the pen onto the tea tray, and then poured a little more gin into her tea cup and sipped it with a genteel flourish, her little finger raised, the spirit slurping softly through the gap in the front of her teeth.

'All right,' she said again.

'Does that mean you will lend me the money?'

'Yes.'

'I don't know what to say.' He leaned towards her, young and glowing and eager. 'Lil, I just don't—'

'Then don't say anything until you have heard my terms.' She smiled thinly, without lifting her upper lip. 'Twenty per cent per annum interest on the loan.'

'Twenty per cent!' he gasped. 'In God's name – that's usury, Lily!'

'Exactly,' she told him primly. 'But let me finish. Twenty per cent interest and half the profits.'

'And half, Lil – that's not usury, that's highway robbery.'

'Right again,' she agreed. 'At least you are bright enough to recognize it.'

'Can't we just—' he started desperately.

'No, we cannot. Those are my terms.' And Ralph remembered Scipio, his falcon, with her beautiful pouting breast and fierce cold eyes.

'I accept,' he said, and though she did not smile with her lips, her eyes were suddenly soft and merry.

'Partners,' she murmured, and placed her plump white hand on his forearm. His muscles were lean and sinewy, the skin brick-coloured from the sun. She stroked it slowly, sensually.

'It only remains to seal our bargain,' she told Ralph. 'Come!' She slid her hand down his arm and twined her fingers into his.

She led him through the stained-glass doors, and when she drew the velvet corded curtains it was cool and dark in the room. She turned back to him and reached up to unbutton his shirt at the throat. He stood still while she worked her way down slowly to his belt buckle, and then she placed one hand, palm down, upon his naked right breast.

'Ralph,' her voice was a husky tremor. 'I want you to do something for me.'

'What is it?' he asked, and she stood on her tiptoes, placed her lips against his ear and told him in a whisper. She felt him begin to pull back from under her hand.

'Partners?' she asked, and he hesitated a moment longer and then stooped and picked her up, one arm behind her knees, and carried her to the wide brass bed with the patchwork quilt.

'You will find it less arduous than hunting elephant on foot in the fly,' she told him, and it was dark enough in the room for her not to worry about the missing tooth.

She lifted her arms above her head, opened her mouth and chuckled in delicious anticipation.

'The good thing about life, dearie, is that you can have whatever you want, just as long as you are willing to pay the price,' she told him, still chuckling.

'These are not bullocks,' Bazo told Ralph. 'Each one is the son of a snake mated with the ghost of a Mashona dog.'

They were all strong oxen, big-boned, heavy in the shoulder, with wide straight horns for strength and even yellow teeth – hand-picked by Bazo, who was a Matabele and loved cattle, had lived with the great herds since he was old enough to toddle after the calves.

However, Bazo was not a trek man. He had never worked an eighteen-foot wagon, with an eight-thousand-pound load aboard. He had never tried to put twenty-four trek oxen into the traces.

The entire Matabele nation owned only a pair of wheeled vehicles, and those belonged to King Lobengula. To Bazo cattle were a store of wealth, a source of meat and milk – they were not draught animals. The closest that either he or Ralph had ever come to putting a team into the traces was working the little two-wheel gravel carts.

Ralph had assumed that the oxen he had purchased were trained and amiable, but within minutes of his and Bazo's first attempt to get them into span, the animals sensed their incompetence and became as spooky and wild as hunted buffalo.

It took two hours of wild chasing across the bleak grasslands beyond the town limits, two hours of running and cursing and whip-cracking to bring the bullocks together and get the yokes upon their necks. Half of them were badly winded by then and promptly lay down, and the others backed out and turned their great horned heads towards the load, tangling the trek chain and plunging the entire span into chaos.

The excitement had brought out most of the loafers and idlers from the canteens on Market Square, though they had enough forethought to bring their bottles with them. They formed an appreciative and jovial audience, greeting each new effort by Bazo and Ralph with delighted guffaws and facetious advice.

Bazo wiped the sweat from his face and chest, and looked broodingly down the dusty road to town.

'Soon Bakela will hear of this and come to see our disgrace,' he said.

Ralph had not seen his father since that stormy night, but he had visited Jordan in his tiny office next door to Mr Rhodes in the magnificent new Central Diamond Company building on De Beers Street.

Perhaps Zouga Ballantyne had not yet recovered from the shock of being deserted by both his sons, but Jordan said that he had not yet left for Cape Town.

The thought of his father witnessing this humiliating scene brought dark blood to Ralph's face, and he fired the long trek whip, at least that was one trick he had learned, and bellowed at the span.

'Nkosana!' There was a salutation at the level of Ralph's elbow, the mild tone belied by the mocking title.

'Nkosi' was a chief, and 'Nkosana' was the condescending diminutive – usually reserved for a little white boy, an untried child.

Ralph turned and glared at the speaker, who went on to explain in the same condescending tone. 'Only one beast in ten will pull in front.' He pointed out one of the oxen. 'That one there is a lead ox. Any man who knows oxen can see that with both his eyes closed.'

He was a little black gnome, not as tall as Ralph's shoulder. His face was wrinkled and lined like that of a very old man, his eyes were mere slits in the merry smiling folds – but his cap of woolly hair and his little goatee beard were unmarred by a single strand of grey, and his teeth were even and white, the teeth of a man in his full flowering.

On his head was the polished black ring of the induna, and about his waist was a kilt of wild cat tails. Over that he wore a threadbare military-type tunic from which all insignia and buttons had been stripped, leaving small punctures in the fabric, some of which had enlarged into rents from which the lining peaked coyly. In the pierced lobe of one ear, he carried an ivory snuff-box, and in the other lobe a snuff spoon of the same material and a toothpick of porcupine quill. The language he used was very close to Matabele, but it preserved the ancient intonation and classic word structures of Zululand.

So when Ralph asked 'Zulu?' the question was redundant, and the little man shot a contemptuous glance at Bazo.

'Pure Zulu, not the treacherous house of Kumalo, of the traitor Mzilikazi who denied a king and whose blood is now so watered by Venda and Tswana and Mashona that they can no longer tell you if an ox grows horns on its head or on its testicles.'

Bazo bridled instantly. 'Hark!' He cocked his head. 'Do I hear a small baboon barking his boasts from the top of the kopjes?'

The little Zulu grinned at him mirthlessly, and took the stock whip from Ralph's sweaty hands. Then he walked to the tangled span with a jaunty step.

He touched the big black ox on the neck. 'Hau, Sathan!' he greeted him, and at the same time baptized him 'Devil'.

The great ox rolled one eye at him, seemed to recognize his assurance and immediately quietened. The little Zulu loosed him and took him forward, talking to him easily in a bizarre mixture of Zulu, English and the Cape Dutch taal, and chained him into the lead position.

He went back quickly and pulled the red ox out of the tangle by the rein about his horns.

'Dutchman—' he named him, for no good reason. 'Come, you red thunder!'

And he put him into the lead file beside Sathan and called to them quietly.

'*Donsa*, Sathan, pull. *Pakamisa*, Dutchman, pick up the chain!' Obediently the pair of bullocks straightened their forelegs and leaned forward against the yoke – and a miracle happened. The long heavy silver chain from the disselboom came up straight and hard as an iron bar, and those animals on the ground were forced to lunge up onto their feet, those that had backed out were pulled into the span, horns and heads pointing forward. In that moment Ralph learned the single most important rule of the open road, keep the chain straight and true, and all else is possible.

Now the little Zulu moved with a deceptively casual air along the double rank of bullocks, touching and talking and wheedling.

'Hey! Fransman, I can see by your wise and beautiful eyes that you were born to the wheel!' And the sturdy black and white beast was led back to his position at the off-wheel.

It took ten minutes, and then the Zulu put the long lash into the air. It hissed like a black mamba and then snaked forward over the ears of the team, not touching a single hair as it fired explosively. The heavy wagon jolted, the white canvas tent that covered the rear half of the long body shook like the unfurling mainsail of a tall ship and then it was rolling away smoothly.

The Zulu crinkled his eyes at Ralph and called a question. '*Yapi*? Where? Which way?'

'*Yakato!*' North!' Ralph shouted back joyously, and despite himself Bazo snatched up his war shield and assegai and whirled into a frenzied challenge dance, leaping and stabbing at a host of imaginary enemies, shouting defiance and ecstasy to all the world.

The road to the Vaal river was the first leg of the journey, and the ruts were axle deep, and red soil raw as a fresh wound, the dust a fog in the windless air through which it was just possible to make out the horns of the two wheeler bullocks. The dust hid from Ralph his parting view of the sprawling town, and its high stagings above the gaping hole which had been his home and his prison for so many years, and by the time that the other traffic on the road had thinned sufficiently for the dust cloud to settle, they had made five miles and the stagings might have been merely a distant line of dead thorn trees silhouetted against the sunset.

The little Zulu called to his boy who led the front oxen, and the child swung them off the road, and the high rear wheels bumped out of the ruts and then crunched through crisp winter grass as the wagon rolled towards a spreading umbrella-shaped acacia which would give them shelter and firewood for the night.

Walking at the front wheel Ralph pondered the two unexpected additions to his company.

The child had come out of the curtain of red dust, naked except for the little flap of his *mutsha* in front, and with the roll of sleeping-mat and the cooking-pot balanced upon his head.

He had placed these meagre possessions on the tailboard of the wagon and then, at a nod and a word from the Zulu, had taken the lead rein and plodded solemnly ahead of the span, his bare feet sinking ankle-deep in the powder dust.

Ralph wondered how old he was, and decided he could not be more than ten years of age.

'What is his name?' he asked the Zulu.

'A name?' The little man shrugged. 'It is not important. Call him Umfaan – the Boy.'

'And what is your name?' Ralph went on, but the little driver suddenly had urgent business at the head of the span and perhaps the dust had clogged his ears for he did not seem to hear the question.

Ralph had to ask the question again, after the outspan, when the Zulu was squatting beside the cooking fire watching Umfaan stir the maize-meal in the black pot.

'What is your name?' And the Zulu smiled as though at a secret thought, and then he said:

'A name can be dangerous, it can hover over a man like a vulture and mark him for death. Before the soldiers came to the royal kraal at Ulundi, I was called one thing—'

Ralph stirred uncomfortably at the reference to the battle that had ended the Zulu War. The tattered tunic that the Zulu wore had once been the same dark blue as that of the Natal police uniform and one of those rents in the faded cloth might have been made by the stabbing blade. Lord Chelmsford had sent the Zulu king and most of his indunas in chains to the island of St Helena, where another emperor had died in captivity. However, some of his fighting chiefs had escaped from Zululand and now wandered homeless exiles across the vast continent. The driver wore the headring of an induna.

' – It was a name which men once spoke carefully, but I have not heard it for so long now that I have forgotten it,' the Zulu went on, and again Ralph wondered if there was a legend still alive amongst the defeated Zulu of a little induna, smaller than the tall warriors he commanded and wizened far beyond his years, who had led them in that terrible charge into the English camp below the Hill of the Little Hand.

In the firelight Ralph studied the Zulu's tunic again, and

he told himself that it was unlikely that it had been taken from the corpse of an Englishman on that grisly field; yet he shivered briefly although the night was warm.

'Now you have forgotten that name?' he encouraged, and the Zulu crinkled his eyes again.

'Now I am called Isazi, the Wise One, for reasons that should be clear even to a Matabele.'

Across the fire Bazo snorted disdainfully, then stood and walked out of the firelight, into the darkness where the jackals piped plaintively.

'My name is Henshaw,' Ralph told him. 'Will you stay with me and drive my wagon all the way?'

'Why not, Little Hawk?'

'You do not ask where I am going.'

'I need a road.' Isazi shrugged. 'The one to the north is no longer or harder than the road to the south.'

The jackal yipped again, but much closer this time, and Bazo paused, changed the assegai to his right hand, and answered the cry, cupping his palm over his mouth to give resonance to the sound; and then he moved on to where a small stone kopje shone in the moonlight like a pile of silver bullion.

'Bazo.' The greeting was a whisper, soft as the night wind in the pale grass, and a shadow stepped from amongst the moon shadows at the base of the kopje.

'Kamuza, my brother.' Bazo went to him and embraced him, open hands upon his shoulders.

'I have a stone in my belly, heavy with sorrow at this parting.'

'We will share the road again – one day, we will drink from the beer pot and fight with our shoulders touching—' Kamuza answered him quietly. 'But now we are both upon the king's business.'

Kamuza slipped the thongs that held his kilt in place, and it sagged heavily to his knees, leaving him naked.

'Hurry,' he said. 'I must return before the curfew bell.' Since the Diamond Trade Act, blacks were not allowed on the streets of Kimberley once the curfew bell had rung.

'You were not marked by the police?' Bazo asked, as he removed his own kilt and changed it with Kamuza.

'They are everywhere, like pepper ticks in the new spring grass,' Kamuza grunted. 'But I was not followed.'

Bazo weighed the fur kilt in both hands while Kamuza swiftly belted the replacement about his own waist.

'Show me,' Bazo said, and Kamuza took the kilt back from his hands and spread it on one of the flat moon-washed boulders.

He picked at the knotted thong that doubled the waistband, and as it came undone he opened the secret pouch of soft tanned leather, crusted with ceramic trade beads. The pouch ran the full length of the wide waistband, the opening concealed by the decorative beadwork, and the interior of the long pouch was divided into cells, like a wasp's nest.

In each stitched leather cell nestled a large pebble that glistened with a slick soapy sheen in the moonlight.

'Count them,' Kamuza instructed. 'Let us agree on the number – and let Lobengula, the great Black Elephant, count the same number into his mighty hands when you lay the belt before him at the kraal of GuBulawayo, the place of killing.'

Bazo touched each diamond with his fingertip, his lips moving silently. '*Amashumi amatatu!*'

'Thirty,' Kamuza repeated. 'It is agreed.'

And they were all large clean stones, the smallest the size of the first joint of a man's little finger.

Bazo tied the kilt about his waist, the fleecy tails of the bat-eared fox dangling to his knees.

'It looks well upon you,' Kamuza nodded, and then went

on. 'Tell Lobengula, the Great Elephant, that I am his dog and I grovel in the dirt at his feet. Tell him that there will be more of the yellow coins and the bright stones. Tell him that his children labour each day in the pit – and there will be more, many more. Every man who takes the road north will bring him riches.' Kamuza stepped forward and laid his right hand on Bazo's shoulder.

'Go in peace, Bazo the Axe.'

'Stay in peace, my brother, and may the days disappear like raindrops into the desert sand until we smile upon each other once more.'

Isazi put the span to its first real test in the drift of the Vaal river.

The grey waters were barely flowing, but they covered the hubs of the tall iron-shod rear wheels, and the bottom was broken waterworn rock that clanked and rolled under pressure, threatening to jam the wheels and denying purchase to the driving hooves of the span.

Yet they ran the wagon through under load, leaning into the yokes, noses down almost touching the surface of the river, and the wagon tent jolting and rocking behind them.

Until, under the steep cut up the far bank, the rear wheels stuck and the wagon bed tilted alarmingly. Then Isazi showed his expertise. He swung the team wide, giving them a run at it, and when he called to his leaders and burst the air asunder with the thirty-foot lash that tapered to the thickness of twine they went in stiff-legged, jerked her clear, and took the load out of the river bed at a canter, while Isazi pranced and sang their praises and even Umfaan smiled.

Ralph ordered an early outspan under the tall trees on the far bank, for there was good grass and unlimited water, and the next leg of the road to his grandfather Moffat's mission station was a hundred and twenty miles, hard and dry going all the way.

'See, Little Hawk,' Isazi was still rapturous over the performance of his span. 'See how clever they are. They pick a good patch of grass and eat it up; they do not wander from patch to patch, wasting their time and strength, as lesser beasts might do. Soon they will settle with the cud, and in the morning they will be strong and rested. Each of them is a prince among cattle!'

'From tomorrow we begin night marches,' Ralph ordered, and Isazi's smile faded and he looked severe.

'I had already made that decision,' he said sternly, 'but where did you ever hear of night marching, Little Hawk? It is a trick of the wise ones.'

'Count me amongst them then, Isazi,' Ralph told him solemnly, and walked out of camp to find a place upon the riverbank from which to enjoy the sunset.

Here the banks of the Vaal were churned into mounds and irregular hollows, the old river workings, picked over by the first diggers and now abandoned and overgrown. It was a mass burial ground of men's dreams, and looking upon it Ralph's high spirits that had buoyed this first day's trek upon the open road began to evaporate.

It was the first day in his life that Ralph had been free and completely his own man. Walking at the wheel of his own wagon, he had woven dreams of fortune. He had imagined his wagons – fifty, a hundred – carrying his cargoes across the continent. He had seen them coming south again, loaded with ivory and bars of yellow gold. He had seen in his mind's eye the wide lands, the herds of elephant, the masses of native cattle, the riches that lay out there in the north beckoning to him, warbling the siren call in his ears.

He had been carried so high that now as his spirits turned they fell as low. He looked at the deserted diggings on the banks across the river, the vain scratchings where other men had attempted to turn this great brown slumbering giant of a continent to their own account.

Then suddenly he felt very small and lonely, and afraid. His thoughts turned to his father, and his spirits plunged lower still as he recalled the last words he had spoken.

'Go then! Go and be damned to you.'

That was not the way he had wanted it. Zouga Ballantyne had been the central figure in his life until that day. A colossus who overshadowed each of his actions, each of his thoughts.

Much as he had chafed under the shackles that his duty to his father had placed upon him, much as he had resented every one of his decisions being made for him, each of his actions ordered, yet now he felt as though the greater part of himself had been removed by some drastic surgery of the soul.

Until this moment he had not really thought of losing his father, he had not let the memory of their brutal parting cut him too deeply. Now suddenly this dirty slow river was the barrier between him and the life he had known. There was no going back – now or ever. He had lost his father and his brother and Jan Cheroot and he was alone and lonely. He felt the acid tears scald his eyelids.

His vision wavered, played him tricks, for across the wide river course, on the far bank was the figure of a horseman.

The horseman slouched easily in the saddle, one hand on his hip, the elbow cocked; and the set of the head upon the broad shoulders was unmistakable.

Slowly Ralph came to his feet, staring in disbelief, and then suddenly he was running and sliding down the sheer bank and splashing waist deep through the grey waters of the ford. Zouga swung down from Tom's back and ran forward to meet Ralph as he came up the bank.

Then both of them stopped and stared at each other.

They had not embraced since the night of Aletta's funeral, and they could not bring themselves to do so now, though longing was naked in the eyes of both of them.

'I could not let you go, not like that,' said Zouga, but Ralph had no reply, for his throat had closed.

'It is time for you to go out on your own,' Zouga nodded his golden beard. 'Past time. You are like an eaglet that has outgrown the nest. I realized that before you did, Ralph, but I did not want it to be. That is why I spoke so cruelly.'

Zouga picked up Tom's reins and the pony nudged him affectionately. Zouga stroked his velvety muzzle.

'There are two parting gifts that I have for you.' He placed the reins in Ralph's hand. 'That is one,' he said evenly, but the green shadows in his eyes betrayed how dearly that gesture had cost him. 'The other is in Tom's saddle-bag. It's a book of notes. Read them at your leisure. You may find them of interest – even of value.'

Still Ralph could not speak. He held the reins awkwardly, and blinked back the stinging under his eyelids.

'There is one other small gift, but it has no real value. It is only my blessing.'

'That is all that I really wanted,' whispered Ralph.

It was six hundred miles to the Shashi river, to the border of Matabeleland.

Isazi inspanned at dusk each evening and they trekked through the cool of the night. When the moon went down and it was utterly dark, then Umfaan threw the lead rein over Dutchman's head, and the big black ox put his nose down and stayed on the track, like a hunting dog on the spoor, until the first glimmering of dawn signalled the outspan.

During a good night's trek they made fifteen miles – but

when the going was heavy with sand they might make only five miles.

During the days, while the cattle grazed or chewed the cud in the shade, Ralph saddled up Tom and, with Bazo running beside his stirrup, they hunted.

They found herds of buffalo along the banks of the Zouga river, the river on whose bank Ralph's father had been born, big herds, two hundred beasts together.

The herd bulls were huge, bovine and bald with age, their backs crusted with the mud from the wallow, the spread of their armoured heads wider than the stretch of a man's arms, the tips of the polished black horns rising into symmetrical crescents like the points of the sickle moon, while the bosses above their broad foreheads were massively crenellated.

They ran them down, and Tom loved those wild flying chases every bit as much as his rider.

They chased the ghostly grey gemsbuck over the smoking red dunes, and in the thorn country they hunted the stilt-legged giraffe and sent their grotesque but stately bodies plunging and sliding to earth with the crack of rifle fire, the long graceful necks twisting in the agony of death like that of a swan.

They baited with the carcasses of zebra, and the coppery red Kalahari lions came to the taint of blood, and Tom stood down their charge. Though he trembled and snorted and rolled his eyes at the shockingly offensive cat smell, he stood for the shot which Ralph took from the saddle, aiming between the fierce yellow eyes or into the gape of rose-pink jaws starred with white fangs.

Thus, fifty days out from Kimberley they came at last to the Shashi river, and when they had made the crossing Bazo was on his native soil. He put on his war plumes and carrying his shield on his shoulder he walked with a new spring and joy in his stride as he led Ralph to a hilltop from which to survey the way ahead.

'See how the hills shine,' Bazo whispered with an almost religious fervour. And it was true. In the early sunlight the granite tops gleamed like precious jewels. Soft, dreaming, ruby, delicate sapphires and glossy pearl shaded like a peacock tail into a fanfare of colour.

The hills rolled away, rising gradually towards the high central plateau ahead of them, and the valleys were clad with virgin forest.

'You never saw such trees on the plains around Kimberley,' Bazo challenged him, and Ralph nodded. They stood on soaring trunks, some scaled like the crocodile, others white and smooth as though moulded from potter's clay, their tops sailing in traceries of green high above the open glades of yellow grass.

'See, the buffalo herds – thick as cattle.'

There was other game. There were small family groups of grey kudo, pale as ghosts, trumpet-eared, the bulls carrying the burden of their long black corkscrew horns with studied grace.

There were clouds of red impala antelope upon the woven silk carpet of golden grasses. There were the darkly massive statues of the rhinoceros seemingly graven from the solid granite of the hills, and there were the noblest antelope of all, the sable antelope, black and imperial as the name implied, the long horns curved and cruel as Saladin's scimitar, the belly blazing white, the neck of the herd bull arched haughtily as he led his lighter-coloured females out of the open glade into the cool green sanctuary of the forest.

'Is it not beautiful, Henshaw?' Bazo asked.

'It is beautiful.'

There was the same awe in Ralph's voice, and a strange unformed longing in his throat, a wanting that he knew could never be satisfied – and suddenly he understood his own father's obsession with this fair land: 'My north,' as Zouga called it.

'My north,' Ralph whispered, and then, thinking of his father, the next question came immediately to mind.

'Elephant – *Indhlovu*? There are no elephant, Bazo. Where are the herds?'

'Ask Bakela – your own father,' Bazo grunted. 'He was the first to come for them with the gun, but others followed him, many others. When Gandang, my father, son of Mzilikazi the Destroyer, half brother of the great black bull Lobengula, when he crossed the Shashi as a child on his mother's hip, the elephant herds were black as midnight upon the land and their teeth shone like the stars. Now we will find their bones growing like white lilies in the forest.'

In the last hours of daylight, when Bazo and Isazi and Umfaan still slept to fortify themselves for the long night's trek, Ralph took the leather-bound notebook out of Tom's saddle-bag.

By now the pages were dog-eared and grubby from the constant perusal to which Ralph had subjected it. It was the gift that Zouga Ballantyne had given him on the bank of the Vaal river, and the inside cover was inscribed:

> To my son Ralph.
> May these few notes guide your feet
> northwards, and may they inspire you to
> dare what I have not dared
> > Zouga Ballantyne

The first twenty pages were filled with hand-drawn sketch maps of those areas of the land between the Zambezi and the Limpopo and the Shashi rivers over which Zouga, and before him the old hunter Tom Harkness, had travelled.

Often the map was headed by the notation:

> Copied from the original map drawn by Tom Harkness in 1851.

Ralph recognized the unique value of this information, but there was more. Page 21 of the notebook bore a terse explanation in Zouga's precise spiky hand:

> In the winter of 1860 while on trek from Tete on the Zambezi River, to King Mzilikazi's town at Thabas Indunas I slew 216 elephant. Lacking porters or wagons I had perforce to cache the ivory along my route.
>
> During my later expeditions to Zambezia, I was able to recover the bulk of this treasure.
>
> There remain fifteen separate caches, containing eighty-four good tusks, which I was for various reasons unable to reach.
>
> Here follows a list of these caches with directions and navigational notes to reach them:

And on page 22 the list began:

> Cache made 16 September 1860.
>   Position by sun sight and dead reckoning:
>   30° 55′ E.   17° 45′ S.
> A granite kopje which I named Mount Hampden. The largest for many miles in any direction. Distinct peak with three turrets. On the northern face between two large *ficus natalensis* trees there is a rock fissure. 18 large tusks total weight 426 pounds placed in fissure and covered with small boulders.

The current price of ivory was twenty-two shillings and sixpence the pound, and Ralph had added the total weights of the ivory still lying out in the veld. It exceeded three thousand pounds: a great fortune waiting merely to be picked up and loaded on his wagon.

Still that was not all. The final entry in the notebook read:

In my book *A Hunter's Odyssey* I described my discovery of the deserted city which the tribes call 'ZIMBABWE', a name which can be translated as 'The Graveyard of the Kings'.

I described how I was able to glean fragments of gold from the inner courtyards of the walled ruins, a little over 50 lbs weight of the metal in all. I also carried away with me one of the ancient bird-like statues. A souvenir which has been with me from that time until very recently.

It is possible that there is precious metal which I overlooked, and certainly there remain within the walled enclosures six more bird carvings which I was unable to bring away.

In *Hunter's Odyssey* I deliberately refrained from giving the location of the ancient ruin. As far as I know, it has not been rediscovered by any other white man – while a superstitious taboo forbids any African to venture into the area.

Thus there is every reason to believe the statues lie where last I laid eyes upon them.

Bearing in mind that my chronometer had not been checked for many months when these observations were made, I now give you the position of the city as calculated by myself at that time.

The ruins lie on the same longitude as the kopje which I named Mount Hampden on 30° 55' E. – but 175 miles farther south at 20° 0' S.

There followed a detailed description of the route that Zouga had taken to reach Zimbabwe, and then the notes ended with this statement:

Mr Rhodes offered the sum of £1,000 for the statue which I rescued.

The following noon Ralph took the brass sextant from its travel-battered wooden case. He had bid ten shillings for it at one of the Saturday auctions in the Market Square of Kimberley – and Zouga had checked its accuracy against his own instrument and showed Ralph how to shoot an 'apparent local noon' to establish his latitude. Ralph had no chronometer to fix a longitude, but he could guess at it from his proximity to the confluence of the Shashi and Macloutsi rivers.

Half an hour's work with *Brown's Nautical Almanac* gave him an approximate position to compare with the one that his father had given in the notes for Zimbabwe.

'Less than one hundred and fifty miles,' he muttered to himself, still squatting over his father's map, but staring eastwards.

'Six thousand pounds just lying there,' Ralph said quietly, and shook his head in wonder. It was a sum difficult to imagine.

He packed away the sextant, rolled the map and went to join the slumbering trio beneath the wagon for what remained of the drowsy afternoon.

R alph woke to a stentorian challenge that seemed to echo off the granite cliffs above the camp.

'Who dares take the king's road? Who chances the wrath of Lobengula?'

Ralph scrambled out from under the wagon. The day was almost gone, the sun flamed in the top branches of the forest, and the chill of evening prickled his bare chest. He stared about him wildly, but some instinct warned him not to reach for the loaded rifle propped against the rear wheel of the wagon. Below the trees the shadows were alive, blackness moved on blackness, dusky rank on rank.

'Stand forth, white man,' the voice commanded. 'Speak

your business – lest the white spears of Lobengula turn to red.'

The speaker stepped forward, out of the forest to the edge of the camp. Behind him the ring of dappled black and white war-shields overlapped, edge to edge in an unbroken circle surrounding the entire outspan, the 'bull's horns' of the Matabele fighting formations.

There were many hundreds of warriors in that deadly circle, and the broad stabbing spears were held in an underhand grip so that the silver blades pointed forward at belly height between the shields.

Above each shield the frothy white ostrich-feather headdress trembled and swayed in the small evening breeze, the only movement in that silent multitude.

The man who had broken the ranks was one of the most impressive figures that Ralph had ever seen. The high crown of ostrich feathers turned him into a towering giant. The breadth of his chest was enhanced by the flowering bunches of white cowtails that he wore on his upper arms. Each separate tail had been awarded him by his king for an act of valour – and he wore them not only on his arms but around his knees also.

His broad intelligent face was lightly seamed by the passage of the years, as though by the chisel of a skilled carpenter, forming a frame for the dark penetrating sparkle of his eyes; yet his chest was covered with the elastic muscle of a man only just reaching his prime and his lean belly rippled with the same muscle as he moved forward.

His legs were long and straight under the kilt of black spotted civet tails, and the war-rattles bound about his ankles rustled softly at each pace.

'I come in peace,' Ralph called, hearing the catch in his own voice.

'Peace is a word that sits as lightly on the tongue as the sunbird sits upon the open flower, and as lightly does it fly.'

There was movement beside Ralph, and Bazo came from his bed under the wagon.

'Baba!' Bazo said reverently, and clapped his hands softly at the level of his face. 'I see you Baba! The sun has been dark all these years, but now it shines again, my father.'

The tall warrior started, took a swift pace forward, and for an instant a wonderful smile bloomed upon the sculptured ebony of his face; then he checked himself, and drew himself up to his full height again, his expression grave – but the feathers of his headdress trembled and there was a light in his tar-bright eyes that he could not extinguish. Still clapping his hands, stooping with respect, Bazo went forward and knelt on one knee.

'Gandang, son of Mzilikazi – your eldest son – Bazo the Axe, brings you the greetings and the duty of his heart.'

Gandang looked down at his son, and at that moment nothing else existed for him in all the world.

'Baba, I ask your blessing.'

Gandang placed his open hand on the short cropped fleecy cap of the young man's head.

'You have my blessing,' he said quietly, but the hand lingered, the gesture of blessing became a caress, and then slowly and reluctantly Gandang withdrew the hand.

'Rise up, my son.'

Bazo was as tall as his father, and for a quiet moment they looked steadily into each other's eyes. Then Gandang turned, and flirted his war-shield, a gesture of dismissal, and instantly the still and silent ring of warriors turned their own shields edge on, so that they seemed to fold like a woman's fan, and with miraculous swiftness they split into small platoons and disappeared into the forest.

Within seconds it seemed as though they had never been. Only Gandang and his son still remained at the edge of the camp, and then they too turned and slipped away like two shadows thrown by the moving branches of the mopani trees.

Isazi came out from under the wagon, naked except for the sheath of hollowed gourd covering the head of his penis, and he spat in the fire with a thoughtful and philosophical air.

'Chaka was too soft,' he said. 'He should have followed the traitor Mzilikazi, and taught him good manners. The Matabele are upstart bastards, with no breeding and less respect.'

'Would a Zulu induna have acted that way?' Ralph asked him, as he reached for his shirt.

'No,' Isazi admitted. 'He would certainly have stabbed us all to death. But he would have done so with greater respect and better manners.'

'What do we do now?' Ralph asked.

'We wait,' said Isazi. 'While that vaunting dandy, who should wear the induna headring not on his forehead but around his neck like the collar of a dog, decides what should become of us.' Isazi spat in the fire again, this time with contempt. 'We may have long to wait – a Matabele thinks at the same speed as a chameleon runs.' And he crawled back under the wagon and pulled the kaross over his head.

In the night the cooking fires from the camp of the Matabele impi down the valley glowed amber and russet on the tops of the mopani, and every time the fickle night wind shifted, the deep melodious sound of their singing carried down to Ralph's outspan.

In the grey dawn Bazo appeared again, as silently as he had disappeared.

'My father, Gandang, induna of the Inyati Regiment, summons you to *indaba*, Henshaw.'

Ralph bridled immediately. He could almost hear his father's voice. 'Remember always that you are an Englishman, my boy, and as such you are a direct representative of your Queen in this land.'

The reply rose swiftly to Ralph's lips: 'If he wants to

see me, tell him to come to me.' But he held the words back.

Gandang was an induna of two thousand, the equivalent of a general. He was a son of an emperor and half-brother of a king, the equivalent of an English duke, and this was the soil of Matabeleland on which Ralph was an intruder.

'Tell your father I will come directly.' And he went to fetch a fresh shirt and the spare pair of boots, which he had taught Umfaan to polish.

'You are Henshaw, the son of Bakela,' Gandang sat on a low stool, intricately carved from a single piece of ebony. Ralph had been offered no seat, and he squatted down on his heels. 'And Bakela is a man.' And there was a murmur of assent and a rustle of plumes as the massed ranks of warriors about them stirred.

'Tshedi is your great-grandfather, and in the king's name has given you the road to GuBulawayo. Tshedi has the right to do so – for he is Lobengula's friend and he was Mzilikazi's friend before that.'

Ralph made no reply. He realized that these statements about his great-grandfather, old Dr Moffat, whose Matabele name was Tshedi, were for the waiting warriors rather than for himself. Gandang was explaining his decision to his impi.

'But for what reason do you take the road to the king's kraal?'

'I come to see this fair land of which my father has told me.'

'Is that all?' Gandang asked.

'No, I come also to trade – and if the king is kind enough to give me his word, then I wish to hunt the elephant.'

Gandang did not smile, but there was a sparkle in his dark eyes. 'It is not for me to ask which you desire most, Henshaw. The view from a hilltop – or a wagonload of ivory.'

Ralph suppressed his own smile, and remained silent.

'Tell me, son of Bakela, what goods do you bring with you to trade?'

'I have twenty bales of the finest beads and cloth.'

Gandang made a gesture of disinterest. 'Women's fripperies,' he said.

'I have fifty cases of liquor – of the kind preferred by King Lobengula and his royal sister Ningi.'

This time the line of Gandang's mouth thinned and hardened. 'If it were my word on it, I would force those fifty cases of poison down your own throat.' His voice was almost a whisper, but then he spoke again in a natural tone. 'Yet Lobengula, the Great Elephant, will welcome your load.' And then he was silent and yet expectant. Ralph realized that Bazo would have reported to his father every detail of his little caravan.

'I have guns,' he said simply, and suddenly there was an intense hunger in Gandang's expression. His eyes narrowed slightly and his lips parted.

'Sting the mamba with his own venom,' he whispered, and beside him Bazo started. It was the Umlimo's prophecy that his father had repeated, and he wondered that Gandang could have uttered it in the presence of one who was not Matabele.

'I do not understand,' Ralph said.

'No matter.' Gandang waved it away with a graceful pink-palmed hand. 'Tell me, Henshaw. Are these guns of yours of the kind that swallow a round ball through the mouth and place the life of the man that fires them in more danger than the man who stands in front?'

Ralph smiled at the description of the ancient trade muskets, many of which had survived Wellington's Iberian campaign and some of which had seen action at Bull Run and Gettysburg before being shipped out to Africa in trade; the barrel worn paper thin, the priming pan and hammer mechanism so badly abused that each shot fired threatened to tear the head off any marksman bold enough to press the trigger.

'These guns are the finest,' he replied.

'With twisting snakes in the barrel?' Gandang asked, and it took Ralph a moment to recognize the allusion to the rifling in the barrel.

He nodded. 'And the barrel opens to take the bullet.'

'Bring me one of these guns,' Gandang ordered.

'The price of each is one large tusk of ivory,' Ralph told him, and Gandang stared at him impassively for a moment longer. Then he smiled for the first time – but the smile was sharp as the edge of his stabbing spear.

'Now,' he said. 'I truly believe that you have come to Matabeleland to see how tall stand the trees.'

'I am leaving you now, Henshaw,' Bazo said, without lifting his eyes from the thick yellow tusk that he had brought from his father in payment for the rifle.

'We knew it was not for ever,' Ralph answered him.

'The bond between us is for ever,' Bazo replied, 'but now I must go to join my regiment. My father will leave ten of his men to escort and guide you to GuBulawayo – where King Lobengula awaits you.'

'Is Lobengula not at Thabas Indunas, the Hills of the Chiefs?' Ralph asked.

'It is the same kraal, in the days of Mzilikazi it was Thabas Indunas, but now Lobengula has changed the name to GuBulawayo, the Place of Killing.'

'I see,' Ralph nodded, and then waited for it was clear that Bazo had more to say.

'Henshaw. You did not hear me say this – but the ten warriors who will go with you to the king's kraal are not only for your protection. Do not look too closely at the stones and rocks along the road, and do not dig a hole,

344

even to bury your own excrement, else Lobengula will hear of it and believe that you are searching for the shiny pebbles and yellow metal. That is death.'

'I understand.'

'Henshaw, while you are in Matabeleland, give up your habit of travelling at night. Only magicians and sorcerers go abroad in the darkness, mounted on the backs of the hyena. The king will hear of it – and that is death.'

'Yes.'

'Do not hunt the hippopotamus. They are the king's beasts. To kill one – is death.'

'I understand.'

'When you enter the presence of the king, be sure that your head is always below that of the Great Elephant, even if you must crawl on your belly.'

'You have told me this already.'

'I will tell you again,' Bazo nodded. 'And I will tell you once more that the maidens of Matabeleland are the most beautiful in all the world. They light a raging fire in a man's loins, but to take one of them without the king's word is death for both man and maiden.'

For an hour they squatted opposite each other, occasionally taking a little snuff or passing one of Ralph's cheap black cheroots back and forth, but always with Bazo talking and Ralph listening.

Bazo spoke quietly, insistently, reciting the names of the most powerful indunas, the governors of each of Matabeleland's military provinces, listing those who had the king's ear and should be treated with care, explaining how a man should conduct himself so as not to give offence, advising how much tribute each would ask and finally accept, trying to give it all to Ralph in these last minutes, and then finally glancing up at the sky.

'It is time.' He stood. 'Go in peace, Henshaw.' And he walked out of Ralph's camp without looking back.

As Ralph's wagon, with its escort of warriors, climbed out of the low veld, so the heat abated. The air was so sweet and clean that it made Ralph feel as though the blood sparkled and fizzed in his veins.

Isazi was infected by the same elation. He composed new verses to sing to his bullocks, lauding their strength and beauty, and occasionally he slipped in a reference to a 'feathered baboon' or some other fanciful and unlovely creature, while rolling his eyes significantly in the direction of the bodyguard of Matabele warriors that preceded the wagon.

The forests thinned as they climbed, becoming open woodlands of shapely mimosa trees, the paper-thin bark peeling away to reveal the clear smooth underbark, and the branches loaded with the fluffy yellow flower heads. The grass cloaked the undulating earth, thick and sweet, so that the bullocks fleshed out after the enervating heat of the lowlands, and they stepped out with a new will against the yoke.

This was cattle country, the heartland of the Matabele, and they began to encounter the herds. Huge assemblies of multi-coloured animals, red and white and black and all the combinations of those colours. Smaller than the big Cape bullocks, but sturdy and agile as wild game, the bulls with the hump and heavy dewlap of their Egyptian forebears.

Isazi looked at them covetously, and came back to Ralph at the forewheel of the wagon to say:

'Such were the herds of Zululand, before the soldiers came.'

'There must be hundreds of thousands, and they would be worth twenty pounds a head.'

'Will you never learn, Little Hawk?' Isazi still returned to the diminutive when one of Ralph's stupidities exasperated him. 'A man cannot place a value on a fine breeding cow or a beautiful woman in little round coins.'

'Yet, as a Zulu you pay for a wife.'

'Yes, Little Hawk.' Isazi's voice was weary with Ralph's obtuse arguments. 'A Zulu pays for a wife; but he pays in cattle, not in coin, which is what I have been telling you all along.' And he ended the discussion with a thunderous clap of his long trek whip.

Small family kraals dotted the wide savannahs, each built around its own cattle stockade and fortified against predators – or against marauders. As they passed the settlements of thatched beehive-shaped huts, the little naked herd boys scampered to alert the kraals, and then the women came out, bare-legged and naked-breasted, balancing the clay pots and hollowed gourds upon their heads, an exercise that gave them a stately dignity of movement.

Then Ralph's bodyguard of warriors from Gandang's regiment paused to refresh themselves on the tart and bubbling millet beer or on the delicious soured milk, thick as yoghurt. The young women examined Ralph with bold and curious eyes. Totally unaware that he spoke the language, they speculated about him in such intimate terms that his ears turned bright red, and he challenged them:

'It is easy to speak the lion's name and question his size and his strength when he is hidden in the long grass, but will you be so brave when he raises himself in his rage to confront you face to face?'

The silence, stunned and incredulous, lasted only a second, then they covered their mouths and shrieked with delighted laughter, before the bravest came to wheedle coquettishly for a strip of ribbon or a handful of pretty beads.

As they drew closer to the stronghold of Lobengula, so they passed the great regimental kraals. Each of them was fifty miles from its neighbours, a day's travel at the rate of a marching impi, the ground-devouring trot that they could maintain for hour after hour.

Here there was no exchange of greeting and banter. The warriors came swarming from the kraal like bees from a disturbed hive, and they lined each side of the track and settled into a deathly stillness, watching Ralph's wagon pass in total silence. There was a blankness in their eyes, the inscrutable gaze with which the lion watches his prey before he begins the stalk.

Ralph passed between the massed ranks at a measured walk, sitting very upright on Tom's back, without deigning to glance left or right at the silent menacing ranks; but when they had passed out into the open grasslands again, his shirt was wet under the arms and between his shoulder blades, and there was a catch in his breathing and a chill in the pit of his belly.

The Khami was one of the last wide rivers to cross before reaching the king's kraal at GuBulawayo.

As soon as Ralph saw the denser and greener growth of mimosa trees that marked the river course, he threw the saddle on Tom's back and trotted ahead to survey the drift.

Ports had been cut into the steep sides of the river banks to enable a wagon to enter the watercourse, and the sandbank between two tranquil green pools had been corduroyed with carefully selected branches, cut to length and laid side by side across the softer going to prevent the narrow ironshod wheels from sinking.

Whoever had travelled this road ahead of Ralph had saved him a great deal of trouble. Ralph knee-haltered Tom on a patch of good grass and went down into the river bed to check the crossing. It was obviously many months since the last wagon had crossed, and Ralph worked his way slowly over the corduroyed pathway, repairing the damage that time had wrought, kicking the dried branches back into place and refilling the hollows scooped by water and wind beneath them.

It was furnace-hot in the river bed and the white sand bounced the sun's rays back at him so that by the time he reached the far bank he was sweating heavily, and he threw himself down in the shade of one of the trees and wiped his face and arms with his scarf moistened in the waters of the river pool.

Quite suddenly he was aware of being watched, and he scrambled quickly to his feet. There was someone standing on the bank above him at the head of the roadway.

With a shock of disbelief, he realized that it was a girl – a white girl, and she was dressed all in white: a loose cotton shift that reached to her ankle just above her bare feet. It was caught in at the waist with a ribbon of blue, and she was so slim that Ralph felt he could lift her with one hand.

The dress was buttoned with mother of pearl to the throat and the sleeves reached to her elbows; but the cotton had been washed, ironed and bleached so often that it seemed to have less substance than gossamer, and the light was behind her.

Ralph could clearly see the outline of her legs under the skirt, and it shocked him again so his breathing tripped. Her legs were long and so delicately shaped that he had to exercise his will to tear his eyes from them. With his heart still pounding he looked at her face.

It was pale as bone china, and seemed almost translucent, so that he thought he could see the sheen of fragile bone beneath the skin.

Her hair was pale shining silver blonde, brushed into a fine cascade that flowed over her shoulders, and shimmered and shook with each breath that lifted the tiny girlish breasts under the thin cotton.

There were flowers on her brow, and a garland of them over her shoulders, and about the brim of the wide straw hat that she held in her hands at the level of her narrow hips – and Ralph felt a sense of unreality. The flowers were roses. The girl and the flowers seemed not to belong in this wilderness but in some gentle and cultivated English garden.

She came down the cutting; her bare feet were silent and seemed to glide over the sandy earth. Her eyes were huge and luminous blue in her pale face, and she was smiling. It was the sweetest smile that Ralph had ever seen, and yet it was neither shy nor simpering.

While Ralph still stood, self-conscious and gawking, the girl lifted her slim smooth arms and stood on tiptoe to kiss him full upon the mouth. Her lips were cool and soft, delicate as the rose petals at her brow.

'Oh Ralph, we are so glad to see you. Nobody has talked of anything else since first we heard that you were upon the road.'

'Who – who are you?' Ralph blurted, his surprise and embarrassment making him boorish; but she seemed unaffected by the gauche question.

'Salina,' she said, and slipped her hand into the crook of his elbow to lead him up the bank. 'Salina Codrington.'

'I don't understand.' He pulled against the hand so that she had to turn to face him again.

'Salina—' she repeated, laughing now, and her laughter was warm and sweet as her smile. 'I'm Salina Codrington.' And then when it was apparent that the name meant nothing, 'I'm your cousin, Ralph. My mother is your father's sister – Robyn Codrington – but she was Robyn Ballantyne.'

'Good God!' Ralph stared at her. 'I didn't know Aunt Robyn had a daughter.'

'I suppose not. Uncle Zouga never was a good correspondent.' But suddenly the smile was no longer on Salina's lips, and Ralph remembered abruptly that he had never taken the trouble to unravel the tangled skein of family history, except to comprehend vaguely that there was ill-feeling and unsettled scores between Zouga and his Aunt Robyn. Then it came back to him, he had overheard his father recalling bitterly how Robyn had taken unfair advantage by publishing her own version of their joint expedition to the Zambezi months before Zouga's *Hunter's Odyssey* – thereby robbing Zouga of his fair share of critical acclaim, and royalties.

Ralph's touching on the family enmities must account for Salina's quick change of mood, but it was fleeting. She took his arm again, and was smiling as they came up the bank.

'Not one daughter, Ralph. We Codringtons will not let you off so lightly. There are a whole tribe of us, four of us, all girls.' And she stopped, lifted the straw hat to shade her eyes and looked down the winding overgrown track that meandered away across the grassy savannah. 'Oh dear!' she exclaimed. 'I came ahead to warn you – and I was only just in time!'

Down the track towards them pelted three small figures, jostling one another for advantage, their faint squeaks of excitement gaining rapidly in volume, long hair flying wildly, fluttering skirts of faded and patched cloth lifted high above the knees so that bare legs flashed, faces freckled and flushed, contorted with exertion and excitement and recrimination.

'Salina! You promised to wait!'

They bore down on where Ralph stood with the lovely blonde girl on his arm.

'Good God!' Ralph whispered again, and Salina squeezed his elbow.

'That's the second time that you have used the Lord's name, Cousin Ralph. Please don't.' So that was the reason for her faint displeasure.

'Oh – I'm terribly sorry.' And he remembered too late that Salina's parents were pious missionaries. 'I didn't mean—' Again he was thick-tongued, for suddenly this girl's good opinion was the most important thing in all the world. 'I won't do it again. I promise'.

'Thank you,' she said softly, and before either of them could speak again they were surrounded by what appeared to be an ocean of small females, every one of whom was bobbing up and down with remarkable rapidity, competing vocally for Ralph's attention and at the same time shrieking accusations at their eldest sister.

'You cheated, Salina. You told us—'

'Ralph, Cousin Ralph, I'm Victoria, the eldest twin.'

'Cousin Ralph, we prayed God to speed you to us.'

Salina clapped her hands, and there was a barely noticeable reduction in the volume of sound.

'In order of age!' she said calmly.

'You *always* say that because you are the eldest!'

Salina ignored the protest and picked out a dark-haired child with a hand on her shoulder.

'This is Catherine.' She drew her forward to face Ralph. 'Cathy is fourteen.'

'And a half, almost fifteen,' said Cathy, and her manner changed with this declaration, becoming lady-like and controlled.

She was thin, and as flat-chested as a boy, but the young body gave the immediate impression of strength and suppleness. Her nose and cheeks were peppered with freckles, but the mouth was full and frank, her eyes the same Ballantyne green as Ralph's own, and her thick dark

352

brows were a frame for their bright intelligent gleam. Her chin was a little too large, as was her nose, but they had a determined set and thrust. Her thick dark hair was plaited and piled on top of her head, leaving her ears exposed, small and pointed and lying flat against her head.

'Welcome to Khami, Ralph,' she said evenly, and bobbed a small curtsey, holding her skirts up as she had obviously been coached; and Ralph realized that the skirt was made of old flour bags that had been stitched together and dyed a muddy green. The lettering still showed through: 'Cape Flour Mills'.

Then Cathy reached up and kissed him quickly, and it left a little wet spot on Ralph's lips. Kissing was obviously the accepted family salutation, and Ralph glanced with trepidation at the eager but grubby faces of the twins.

'I'm Victoria, the eldest.'

'And I'm Elizabeth, but if you call me "baby", I shall hate you, Cousin Ralph.'

'You won't hate anybody,' Salina said, and Elizabeth hurled herself at Ralph's neck, got a fair grip and hung on as she plastered her mouth to Ralph's.

'I was teasing, Ralph. I shall love you,' she whispered fiercely. 'Always! Always!'

'Me!' howled Victoria indignantly. 'I'm older than Lizzie. Me first.'

Salina led them with that gliding walk which did not move her shoulders and barely ruffled the white-gold curtain of her hair, and every once in a while she turned to smile at Ralph, and he thought he had never seen anything so lovely.

The twins each had hold of one of Ralph's hands, and they gabbled out all the things they had saved up for weeks to tell him, and skipped to keep pace with his stride. Cathy came up behind them all, leading Tom. She and the pony had formed an immediate accord.

'Oh, he's beautiful, Ralph,' she had said and kissed Tom's velvety muzzle.

'We don't have a horse,' Victoria explained. 'Daddy is a man of God, and men of God are too poor to have horses.'

The small party straggled over the first low rise beyond the river, and Salina stopped and pointed down into the shallow basin ahead of them.

'Khami!' she said simply, and all of them looked to Ralph for approbation.

There was a notch in the next line of granite hills, a natural divide and shed for underground water, which accounted for the spread of lush grass that carpeted the valley.

Like chickens under the hen, the small huddle of buildings crouched beneath the hills. They were neatly laid out, thatched with yellow grass and painted dazzlingly white with burnt limewash. The largest building had a wooden cross set proudly on the ridge of the roof.

'Daddy and Mummy built the church with their own hands. King Silly Cat would not allow any of his people to help them,' Victoria explained.

'Silly Cat?' Ralph asked, puzzled.

'King Mzilikazi,' Salina translated. 'You know Mama does not like you using fun names for the kings, Vicky,' she rebuked the child mildly; but Victoria was shaking Ralph's hand excitedly and pointing to a distant figure in the valley below them.

'Daddy!' shrieked the twins in unison. 'There's Daddy!'

He was working in the precise geometrically laid out gardens below the church, a lanky figure whose shoulders remained stooped even when he stood upright and looked towards them, stabbed his spade into the earth and came striding up the hill.

'Ralph!' He swept off the sweatstained hat, and he was bald – like a monk, with just a fringe of silky hair forming a halo around his pate at the level of his ears. It was immediately apparent from whom Salina had inherited her glorious white-gold tresses.

'Ralph,' the man repeated, and he wiped his right hand on the seat of his pants and then held it out. Despite the stoop, he was as tall as Ralph, his face deeply tanned, his bald dome as shiny as if it had been waxed and polished, his eyes pale blue as a summer sky, washed out by heat haze; but his smile was like Salina's – calm and tranquil, so that as he took the hand Ralph realized that this was the most contented and deeply happy man he had ever met in his life.

'I'm Clinton Codrington,' he said. 'And I suppose I must count as your uncle, though goodness knows I do not feel that old.'

'I would have known you anywhere, sir,' said Ralph.

'Would you indeed?'

'I have read Aunt Robyn's books, and I have always admired your exploits as a Royal Naval officer.'

'Oh dear.' Clinton shook his head in mock dismay. 'I thought to have left that all far behind me.'

'You were one of the most illustrious and courageous officers in the African anti-slavery squadron, sir.' Ralph's eyes shone with a still boyish hero worship.

'Your Aunt Robyn's account suffered a dreadful list to port, I'm afraid.'

'Daddy is the bravest man in the world,' Victoria declared stoutly, and she released Ralph's hand and ran to her father.

Clinton Codrington gathered her up and held her on his hip.

'And yours, young lady, is probably the most unbiased opinion in Matabeleland,' he chuckled, and Ralph was suddenly sharply jealous of this palpable aura of deep affection and love which welded the little group, from which he felt himself excluded. It was something beyond his experience, something he had never missed until that moment. Somehow Salina seemed to sense his pang of melancholy, and she took the hand that Victoria had relinquished.

'Come,' she said. 'Mama will be waiting. And there is one thing you will soon learn, Ralph. In this family, nobody keeps Mama waiting.'

They went down towards the church, passing between the beds of growing vegetables.

'You didn't bring any seed?' Clinton asked, and when Ralph shook his head, 'Well, how were you to know?' and he went on to point out with pride his flourishing crops. 'Maize, potatoes, beans, tomatoes do particularly well here.'

'We divide it this way,' Cathy told Ralph, teasing her father. 'One for the bugs, two for the baboons, three for the bushbuck – and one for Daddy.'

'Be good to all God's creatures.' Clinton reached out to ruffle her dark hair, and Ralph realized that these gentle people were always touching and kissing one another. He had never experienced anything like it.

Squatting patiently on the shady side against the wall of the church were twenty or more Matabele of all ages and sexes, from a skeleton-thin ancient with a completely white cap of wool on his bowed head and both his eyes turned to blind orbs of milky jelly by tropical ophthalmia to a new-born infant held against its mother's milk-swollen breasts with its tiny dark face screwed up with the terrible colic of infant dysentery.

Catherine tethered Tom beside the church door, and they all trooped into the cool interior, insulated by thatch and thick walls of unbaked brick from the outside heat. The church smelled of homemade soap, and of iodine. The pews of rough-hewn timber had been pushed aside to make way for an operating table of the same material.

There was a girl at work over the table, but as they came in she tied the last knot in a bandage and dismissed her semi-naked black patient with a word and a pat – then, wiping her hands on a clean but threadbare cloth, she came down the aisle of the church towards them.

Ralph was certain that she was Cathy's twin, for though she was a little taller, she was as slim and as flat-chested; her hair had the same dark brown colouring, though shot through with tones of russet and chestnut, her skin the same youthful lustre, and her nose and chin the same forceful size and thrust.

Then as she came closer, Ralph realized that he had been mistaken and that she was older than Cathy, perhaps even older than Salina, but not much.

'Hello, Ralph,' the girl said. 'I'm your Aunt Robyn.' Ralph felt the blasphemy of surprise leap to his lips again, but conscious of Salina's hand in his he suppressed it.

'You are so young,' he said instead.

'Bless you for that,' she laughed. 'You turn a prettier compliment than your daddy ever did.' She was the only one who made no effort to kiss him; instead she turned to the twins.

'Right!' she said. 'I want ten pages of copperplate written out before Evensong – and I don't want to see a single blot.'

'Oh Mama! Ralph—'

'Ralph has been your excuse for two weeks. Go – or you will eat in the kitchen hut tonight.'

Then, to Cathy: 'Have you finished the ironing, young lady?'

'Not yet, Mama.' Cathy followed the twins.

'Salina, you're baking.'

'Yes, Mama.'

Then there were three of them alone in the little church, and Robyn ran a professional eye over her nephew.

'Well, Zouga has bred a likely boy,' she gave her opinion. 'But I never expected anything else.'

'How did you all know I was coming?' Ralph voiced his bewilderment at last.

'Grandpa Moffat sent a runner when you left Kuruman, and Induna Gandang passed here two weeks ago on his way to King Lobengula's kraal. His eldest son was with him, and Bazo's mother is an old friend of mine.'

'I see.'

'Nothing moves in Matabeleland but the whole nation knows of it immediately,' Clinton explained.

'Now, Ralph, how is your father? I was terribly distressed to hear of the death of Aletta, your mother. She was a lovely person, so good and gentle. I wrote to Zouga, but he never replied.'

Robyn seemed determined to catch up on the doings of a decade in the first ten minutes, and her questions were quick and incisive; but Clinton soon excused himself and left the two of them alone in the little church to return to his gardens.

Ralph replied dutifully to all her questions, while he reassessed his first impression of his aunt. Youthful she looked, but childlike she was not. Now at last he could understand the remarkable achievements of this forceful woman. How she had enrolled at a famous London hospital, one which would never accept a female on its student body, by impersonating a man. Dressed in breeches, she had kept her terms and been granted her doctorate when she was twenty-one years of age. The scandal which attended the discovery that a female had invaded an exclusive male preserve had rocked all England.

Then she had accompanied Zouga to Africa, equal partners in the expedition to find their father Fuller Ballantyne, who had been missing in the unexplored interior for eight years. When she and Zouga had fallen out over the conduct of the expedition, she had pushed on, a white woman alone with only primitive black tribesmen as companions, and achieved the main object of the expedition on her own.

Her book describing the expedition, entitled *Africa in My Blood*, had been a publishing phenomenon and had sold almost a quarter of a million copies – three times as many as Zouga Ballantyne's *A Hunter's Odyssey* published six months later.

Robyn had signed over all her royalties from the book to The London Missionary Society, and that august body had been so delighted by the donation that they had reinstated her as a society officer, had ordained her husband as her assistant, and had approved her heading a mission to Matabeleland.

Her two subsequent publications had not enjoyed the same success as the first. *The Sick African*, a practical study of tropical medicine, had contained ludicrous theories that had earned her the derision of her medical peers – she had even dared to suggest that malarial fever was not caused by breathing the foul night airs of tropical swamps, when this fact had been known since the time of Hippocrates.

Then her further account of her life as a medical missionary, *Blind Faith*, had been too homely in style and too prejudiced in championing the indigenous tribes. She had firmly embraced the beliefs of Jean-Jacques Rousseau and had added her own refinements to them. Her round condemnation of all settlers, hunters, prospectors and traders, and of their treatment of the noble savages, had been too salty for her European readers.

Indeed, scandal and contention seemed to follow Robyn Codrington as vultures and jackals follow the lion, and at each new provocation all her previous adventures would be recalled:

What decent female missionary would provoke men

sufficiently to make them fight a bloody duel over her? Robyn Ballantyne had.

What God-fearing lady would sail aboard a notorious slaver, unchaperoned and with only slavers for company? Robyn Ballantyne had.

What lady would choose for her husband a man who had been court martialled, stripped of his naval rank and imprisoned for piracy and dereliction of duty? Robyn Codrington had.

What loyal subject of the Queen would hail the terrible reversal of British arms at Isandhlwana, the bloody death of hundreds of Englishmen at the hands of the savage Zulus, as a judgement of God – Robyn Codrington had, in a letter to the *Evening Standard*.

Who, other than Robyn Codrington, would write to Lord Kimberley demanding that half the profits of the diamond fields that bore his name should go to the Griqua captain, Nicholaas Waterboer?

Only Robyn Codrington would demand of Paulus Kruger, the newly-elected President of the little Transvaal Republic, that he return to Lobengula, King of the Matabele, the land below the Cashan mountains from which the Boer commandos had driven Mzilikazi, his father.

She spared no one. Nothing was sacred to her except her God, whom she treated rather like a senior partner in the business of running Africa.

Her enemies, and they were legion, hated her fiercely, and her friends loved her with equal passion. It was impossible to be unmoved by her, and Ralph found himself fascinated as she sat beside him on the church pew and subjected him to an exhaustive catechism that covered every aspect of his life and that of the family.

'You have a brother,' she seemed to know it all. 'Jordan? That is his name, isn't it? Tell me about him.' It was a command.

'Oh, Jordie is everybody's favourite; everybody loves him.'

Ralph had never met anybody like her. He doubted he could ever bring himself to like her, she was far too prickly. That was the exact word to describe her, but he would never doubt her strength and her determination.

Clinton Codrington came back into the church as the light outside was mellowing into late afternoon.

'My dear, you really must let the poor fellow go now.' He turned to Ralph. 'Your wagon has come up. I showed your driver where to outspan. He seems a first-rate chap, I must say.'

'You will sleep in the guest house,' Robyn announced as she stood.

'Cathy has taken your soiled clothes from the wagon, and she has washed and ironed them,' Clinton went on.

'You will want to put on a fresh shirt before Evensong,' Robyn told him. 'We shall not begin the service until you return.'

He had liked it better on the open road, Ralph thought sourly; then he had made his own decisions as to when he made his ablutions, as to how he dressed and where he spent his evenings – but he went to change his shirt as he was bidden.

The distaff side of the Codrington family filled the front pew. Clinton Codrington faced them from the pulpit. Ralph was between the twins; there had been a brief but ferocious competition between Victoria and Elizabeth to decide who should sit closest to him.

Apart from the family, there was nobody else in the church, and Victoria saw his glance and explained to Ralph in a penetrating whisper, 'King Ben won't let any of his people come to our church.'

'King Lobengula,' Salina corrected her sweetly, 'not King Ben.'

Despite the full attendance, Clinton delayed the commencement of the evening service, finding and losing his place in the Book of Common Prayer half a dozen times – and glancing repeatedly towards the rear of the tiny church.

From this quarter there was a sudden commotion. A small retinue of Matabele women had arrived outside the church. Clearly they were servants, house slaves and ladies-in-waiting to the imposing female figure in their midst. She dismissed them with a royal gesture and came in through the doors of the church. Every one of the Codringtons turned their heads and their faces lit with pleasure.

The way in which this matron paced majestically down the aisle left not a doubt as to her high breeding and her place in the aristocracy of Matabeleland. She wore bangles and bracelets of beaten red copper, strings of highly prized *sam-sam* beads that only a chief would afford. Her cloak was of beautifully tanned leather, ornamented with feathers of the blue jay and worked with designs of chipped ostrich shell.

'I see you, Nomusa,' she declared.

Her huge naked breasts shone with an ointment of fat and red clay; they pushed out ponderously from under her tanned cloak and dangled weightily to the level of her navel.

Her arms were thick as a grown man's thigh, her thighs as thick as his waist. There were rolls of fat around her belly, and her face was a black full moon, the glossy skin stretched tightly over her abundant flesh. Her merry eyes sparkled from between creases of fat, and her teeth flashed like the sunlit surface of a lake as she smiled. All this size was evidence to the world of her station, of her amazing beauty, of her fecundity. It was also unassailable proof of the high regard of her husband, of his prosperity and importance in the councils of Matabeleland.

'I see you, Girlchild of Mercy,' she smiled at Robyn.

'I see you, Juba, the little dove.' Robyn answered her.

'I am not a Christian,' Juba intoned. 'Let no evil one bear false tidings to Lobengula, the Black and Mighty Elephant.'

'If you say so, Juba,' Robyn answered primly, and Juba pinioned her in a vast embrace while at the same time she called to Clinton in the pulpit.

'I see you also, Hlopi. I see you, White Head! But do not be deceived by my presence here, I am not a Christian.' She drew an elephantine breath and went on, 'I come merely to greet old friends – not to sing hymns and worship your God. Also I warn you, Hlopi, that if you read the story tonight of a man called the Rock who denied his God three times before the call of the cock, I shall be displeased.'

'I shall not read that story,' Clinton answered. 'For by now you should know it by heart.'

'Very well, Hlopi, then let the singing begin.' And led by Juba in a startlingly clear and beautiful soprano, the entire Codrington family rollicked into the first verse of 'Onward Christian Soldiers' – which Robyn had translated into the Matabele vernacular.

After the service Juba bore down on Ralph.

'You are Henshaw?' she demanded.

'Nkosikazi!' Ralph agreed, and Juba inclined her head to acknowledge the correct style of address to the senior wife of a great chief that Ralph had employed.

'Then you are the one whom Bazo, my first-born son, calls brother,' Juba said. 'You are very skinny and very white, Little Hawk – but if you are Bazo's brother, then you are my son.'

'You do me great honour, Umame!' Ralph said, and Juba took him in those mammoth arms. She smelled of clarified fat, and ochre and wood-smoke, but the embrace was

363

strangely comforting, not at all unlike the feeling, only half remembered, that he had once experienced in Aletta's arms.

The twins knelt side-by-side at the low truckle cot, both in long nightdresses, their hands clasped before their eyes which were so tightly closed that they seemed to be in pain.

Salina, also in her nightdress, stood over them to supervise the last prayer of the day.

'Gentle Jesus meek and mild—'

Cathy was already in her own bed, hair ribboned for the night, writing the day's entry in her diary by the light of the guttering candle made from buffalo fat and cloth wick.

'Pity my simplicity—' gabbled the twins, at such a speed that it came out as, 'Pretty mice, and pretty me!'

Arriving at the 'Amen' in a dead heat, the twins leaped into the bed that they shared, pulled the blanket to their chins and watched with fascination as Salina began to brush her hair, one hundred strokes with each hand, so that it rippled and flamed with white fire in the candlelight. Then she came to kiss them, blew out the candle, and the thongs of her bed squeaked from across the small thatched hut as she climbed into it.

'Lina?' whispered Victoria.

'Vicky, go to sleep.'

'Just one question, please.'

'All right then, just one.'

'Does God allow a girl to marry her own cousin?'

The silence that followed the question seemed to hum in the darkened bedroom like a copper telegraph wire struck by a sword.

Cathy broke the silence.

'Yes, Vicky,' she answered quietly. 'God does allow it.

Read the Table of Kindred and Affinity on the last page of your prayer book.'

The silence was contemplative now.

'Lina?'

'Lizzie, go to sleep.'

'You allowed Vicky to ask a question.'

'All right then, just one.'

'Does God get cross if you pray for something just for yourself – not for Daddy or Mama or your sisters, but just for you alone?'

'I don't think so,' Salina's voice was becoming drowsy. 'He might not give it to you but I don't think He will be cross. *Now* go to sleep, both of you.'

Cathy lay very still, on her back with her hands clenched at her sides, staring at the lighter oblong across the hut where the moon defined the single window.

'Please God,' she prayed. 'Let him look at me the way he looks at Salina, just once. Please.'

'What do you think of Zouga's boy?' Robyn took Clinton's arm as they stood together on the darkened stoep and looked out at the star-pricked black velvet curtain of the African night.

'He's a powerful lad – and I don't mean merely muscle.' Clinton took his pipe from between his teeth and peered into the bowl. 'His wagon is loaded with cases, long wooden cases from which the markings have been burned with a hot iron.'

'Guns?' Robyn asked.

'I think so.'

'There is no law against trading guns north of the Limpopo,' Robyn reminded him. 'And Lobengula needs all the power he can get to defend himself.'

'Still, guns! I mean, it does go against the grain.' Clinton sucked at his pipe, and each puff of smoke he exhaled was denser and ranker. They were both silent for a while.

'He has a hard and ruthless streak, like his father,' Robyn judged at last.

'A man needs that to survive in this land.'

Robyn shivered suddenly, and hugged her own arms.

'Are you cold?' Clinton was immediately solicitous.

'No. A grey goose walked over my grave.'

'Let's go off to bed.'

'A moment longer, Clinton. The night is so beautiful.'

Clinton put his arm about her shoulders.

'Sometimes I am so happy that it frightens me,' he said. 'So much happiness cannot go on for ever.'

His words seemed to precipitate the thick but formless dread that had hung over Robyn all this day like the pall of smoke above the winter bush fires. It weighed her down with the premonition that something had changed in all their lives.

'May God save us all,' she whispered.

'Amen to that,' said Clinton as softly, and took her in out of the night.

The interior of the thatched hall was domed and darkened, so that the patterns of latticed branches and lovingly knotted bark rope disappeared into the gloom above their heads like the arches of a medieval cathedral.

The only light was from the small fire on the clay hearth in the centre of the floor. One of the king's wives threw another handful of dried herbs upon it and oily blue tendrils of smoke twisted upwards towards the unseen roof.

Across the fire, on a low platform of dried clay covered with a thick mattress of furs, silver-backed jackal and blue monkey, bat-eared fox and spotted civet, sat the king.

He was a mountainous figure, stark naked, and his skin polished with fat so that he gleamed like an enormous Buddha carved from a solid block of washed anthracite. His head was round as a cannon ball, surmounted by the induna's ring. His arms were massive, bulging with muscle and fat, but the hands in his lap were strangely dainty, narrow across the pink palms, with long tapered fingers.

His trunk was thickened, his breasts pendulous. All this was flesh which he had carefully cultivated. The beer pots and beef dishes stood close at hand. The thick millet beer bubbled softly and the cuts of beef each had a thick rind of yellow fat. Every few minutes one of his wives responded to a nod or a small movement of one graceful hand by proffering a dish. Weight and size were the mark of a king. Not for nothing was Lobengula called the Great Black Elephant of Matabeleland.

His manner was slow, imbued with the vast dignity of his size and rank. Yet his eyes were thoughtful and deeply intelligent, his features despite the burden of fat which blurred them were handsome, lacking outward traits of the hideous cruelties which any Matabele king had to make part of his life.

'My people expect me to be strong and harsh. There are always those who look for the smallest weakness in me – as the young lions watch the black-maned leader of the pride,' Mzilikazi had explained to his son. 'See how my chickens follow me to be fed.' He had pointed with the toy spear of kingship at the high wheel of tiny specks turning slowly in the sky above the hills of Thabas Indunas. 'When my vultures desert me, I will be as dust.'

Lobengula, his son, had learned the lesson well – but it had not brutalized him. Indeed, there was a line to his mouth that was almost diffident, and a shadow behind the light of intelligence in his eyes that was hesitant, the confusion of a man tugged at by too many currents and winds – a man caught up by his destiny, and uncertain as to how he could break away from its remorseless toils.

Lobengula had never expected to take up his father's spear of kingship. He was never the heir apparent, there had been older brothers from mothers of higher rank and nobler blood.

He stared now across the fire at the man that squatted there. A magnificent warrior, his body tempered to black steel by long marches and savage warfare, his understanding and compassion expanded by close and intimate daily contact with common men, his courage and loyalty proven to all the world ten thousand times so there could be no doubts, not even in his own midnight watches, which is the time of doubts – and Lobengula found himself longing to rid himself of this fearsome burden of kingship and place it on the other man's shoulders. He found himself wishing for that quiet and secret cave in the Matopos hills where he had known the only happy days of his life.

The man opposite him was a half-brother; his blood line, like that of Lobengula himself, reaching back unsullied to the Zanzi of Zululand. He was a prince of the House of Kumalo, wise and brave and untroubled by doubts.

'Such a one should have been king,' Lobengula thought, and his love for his half-brother choked his throat so that he coughed. He moved one little finger, and a wife held the beer pot to his lips and he swallowed once and then signed for it to be taken away.

'I see you, Gandang.' His voice was throaty and low, the sadness still in it for he knew that he could not escape that way. He felt like a man on a solitary journey through the forest where the lions are hunting. His recognition released Gandang from his respectful silence. The induna clapped his hands softly and began to recite his half-brother's ritual praises, and Lobengula's mind wandered back across the years.

His earliest memory was of the road, the hard road up from the south – driven by the mounted men dressed all in brown, riding brown ponies. He remembered the popping sound of the guns, which he learned only later to fear, and the smell of gunsmoke, spicy and sour as the wind brought it down to where he clung to his mother, and he remembered the wailing of the women as they mourned the dead.

He remembered the heat and the dust, trotting naked as a puppy at his mother's heels. How tall she had seemed, the muscles of her back gleaming with sweat, and Ningi, his sister, in the sling upon her hip, clinging to one of his mother's fat jostling breasts with mouth and tiny determined fists.

He remembered toiling up the stony hills with his father's single wagon rolling and pitching along ahead of them. On it rode Mzilikazi's senior wife, and her son Nkulumane, three years older than Lobengula and heir apparent to the kingship of the Matabele. They were the only ones who did not walk.

He remembered how his mother's back had withered, the beautiful gleaming skin becoming loose and baggy, the ribcage beginning to show through as the famine wasted her substance, and Ningi screaming with hunger as the rich creamy flow from her teats dried up.

This was where the memory of Saala began; it was mixed up at first with the shouting and singing as a band of raiding Matabele returned to the fleeing column. He had first seen Saala in the firelight, as the warriors slaughtered the captured cattle, and Lobengula could almost still feel the hot grease and the bloody juices of the beef running down his chin and dripping onto his naked chest as they feasted, breaking the long days and months of starvation on cattle taken from the white men, the *buni*.

Once his belly was bulging tightly with meat, Lobengula had joined the circle of curious Matabele princelings and princesses who surrounded the captives; but he had stood back from the teasing and jeering and prodding of the other children.

Saala was the eldest of the two little girls. It was only long afterwards that Lobengula learned that her name was Sarah, but even now he could not pronounce that sound. The Matabele raiding party had surprised a small caravan of Boer wagons, and had killed everybody except these two small white children.

Her whiteness was the first thing that had struck Lobengula. How white her face was in the firelight, as white as an egret's wing, and she had not wept as her younger sister wept.

After that the memories grew stronger, Saala walking ahead of him as the slow column wound through thick thorn forest. Saala taking the infant Ningi from his mother when she slipped and fell with weakness in the black mud of the swamps while the mosquitoes formed a dark whining cloud over them.

Exactly where Saala's little sister died, Lobengula could not recall. It might have been in the swamps. They left her small naked white body unburied, and the column marched on.

At last Lobengula's own mother fell and could not rise again, and with her last strength handed little Ningi to Saala; then she curled up quietly and died. All the weak ones died like that, and their infants died with them, for no other women would take the orphans, for each of them had her own infants to care for.

However, Saala strapped little Ningi on her own thin white back in the way that the Matabele carry their babies, then she took Lobengula's hand in hers and they toiled on after the fleeing nation.

By now Saala's clothing had long ago fallen off her thin white body, and she was as the other Matabele girls who had not yet reached puberty, completely naked. She had half forgotten her own language, and spoke only the language of the tribe. The sun had darkened her skin, and the soles of her bare feet had grown a thick covering, hard as rhinoceros skin, so she could march over razor flint and needle thorns.

Lobengula came to love Saala, transferring everything he had ever felt for his mother to her, and she stole extra food for him and protected him from the bullying of his older brothers – from Nkulumane the cruel one, and from Nkulumane's mother, who hated all that might one day stand in the way of her son's claim to the kingship of the Matabele.

Then the Matabele crossed the Limpopo, the River of Crocodiles, and the land beyond was fair, thick with game and running with sweet rivers. The wandering nation followed Mzilikazi into the magical hills of the Matopos. There on a lonely hilltop the king met the wizard of the Matopos, face to face.

Mzilikazi saw fire spring up at the Umlimo's bidding, and he heard the spirits speak from the very air about the Umlimo, a hundred different voices – voice of infant and crone, of man and of beast, the cry of the fish eagle, the snarl of the leopard – and from that day the Umlimo had the reverence and superstitious awe of the king and all his people.

The Umlimo pointed the way north again, and as the Matabele emerged from the broken hills of the Matopos, they saw spread before them a beautiful land, rich with grass and tall trees.

'This is my land,' said Mzilikazi, and built his kraal under the Hills of the Indunas.

However, the Matabele had lost nearly all their cattle and many of the women and children had died on that cruel journey northwards.

At Thabas Indunas Mzilikazi left his senior wife, mother of Nkulumane, as his regent, and he took five thousand of his finest warriors and went out against the tribes – for women and for cattle.

He went westwards into the land ruled by great Khama, and there was no word from him. The seasons came and changed, the rains followed the long dryness, the heat followed the frosts, and still there was no word of Mzilikazi.

Slowly the strict order of Matabele society began to break up, for the regent, Mzilikazi's senior wife, was unrestrained in her intercourses, and she rutted shamelessly with her lovers.

Some of the lesser wives followed her example, and then the common people took sexual licence, the youths, unblooded and without the royal permission to go into the women, lay in wait for the young girls on the path to the water-hole, and dragged them giggling into the bushes.

With the code of morality broken, other vices followed. The remaining cattle – the breeding herds – were slaughtered, and the feasting went on for months. Looseness and drunkenness swept through the nation like a plague, and in the midst of this debauchery, one of the Matabele patrols captured a little yellow Bushman who had wandered in out of the west, and the Bushman had momentous tidings.

'Mzilikazi is dead,' he told his captors. 'I have thrust my own fingers into the stab wound in his heart, and watched the hyena wolfing down his flesh and cracking his bones.'

The senior wife had her guards boil clay pots of water, and pour them over the Bushman until his flesh fell off his bones and he died, which is fitting treatment for one who brings news of the death of a king. Then she called the indunas into council, and urged them to proclaim Nkulu-mane king in place of his dead father. However, none of the indunas were fools. One whispered to the other, 'It would take more than a Tswana dog to kill Mzilikazi.'

While they procrastinated and talked, the senior wife grew wild with impatience and sent for the executioners, determined now that there would be no rival for her son. Saala was playing outside the queen's hut, moulding little clay oxen and figures of men and women for Ningi. Through the thatched wall she heard the queen giving her orders to the Black Ones. Frantic with terror for the safety of Lobengula, Saala ran to the other royal mothers.

'The Black Ones are coming for the royal sons. You must hide them.'

Then Saala left little Ningi, now weaned and strong, with one of the royal women who was barren and childless.

'Look after her,' she whispered, and ran out into the grasslands.

Lobengula was by now ten years of age, and was tending what remained of the royal herds: the duty of every Matabele boy, the essential service through which he learned the secrets of the veld and the ways of cattle, the nation's treasure.

Saala found him bringing in the herd to water. He was naked except for the little flap of leather over his loins, and armed only with two short fighting sticks with which he was expected to drive off any predator and to hold his own in competition with the other herd boys.

Holding hands again, the Matabele princeling and the little white girl fled, and instinctively they turned southwards, back the way they had come.

They lived on roots and berries, on the eggs of wild birds and the flesh of the iguana lizards. They competed with the jackals and vultures for the remains of the lion kill – and sometimes they went hungry, but at last they found themselves in the maze of the Matopos Hills where the Black Ones would not follow them. They slept under the single kaross that Saala had brought with her, and the nights crackled with frost so they slept in each other's arms, clinging together for warmth.

Early one morning the old man found them thus. He

was thin and mad-looking, with strange charms and magical objects about his neck, and the children were terrified of him.

Saala pushed Lobengula behind her, and with a show of false courage faced the wizard.

'This is Lobengula. Favourite son of Mzilikazi,' she declared stoutly. 'Who harms him, harms the king.'

The old man rolled his mad eyes, and drooled horribly as he grinned with toothless gums. Then suddenly the air was full of the sound of ghost voices – and Saala screamed and Lobengula wailed with terror, and they clung to each other pitifully.

The wizard led the children, chastened, shivering and weeping, through secret passages and over precipitous trails, deeper and deeper into the hills, until at last they came to the caves which honeycombed the rock.

Here the old man began the instruction of the boy who would be king. He taught him many of the mysteries, but not how to control the ghost voices, nor how to throw fire by pointing his finger, nor how to see the future in a calabash of mountain water.

Here in the caves of the Matopos, Lobengula learned the scope and power of the magical order. He learned how the little wizards, the witchdoctors, were spread across the land, performing the small rites, making rain and giving charms for fertility and childbirth, smelling out the evildoers, and sending back their reports to the cave in the Matopos.

Here the grand wizards, of which the old man was one, worked the great magics, called up the spirits of their ancestors, and looked into the mists of time to see what the future would bring. Above them all was the Umlimo. It was a name only for Lobengula, Umlimo, a name that even after he had lived five years in the cave could still make him shiver and sweat.

Then when he was sixteen, the mad old wizard took

him to the cave of the Umlimo. And the Umlimo was a woman, a beautiful woman.

What Lobengula saw in the cave of the Umlimo he would never speak about, not even to Saala, but when he came back from the cave there was a sadness in his eyes, and the weight of knowledge seemed to bow his young shoulders.

There was a furious thunderstorm the night of Lobengula's return, and the blue lightning clanged upon the anvil of the hills with strokes that tortured their eardrums as they lay together under the kaross. Then it was that the little orphan white girl made the boy into a man, the princeling into a king; and when her term was run she gave him a son who was the colour of the early morning sunlight on the yellow winter grass, and Lobengula knew happiness for the only time in his life.

In their joy they paid little attention to tidings which the mad old wizard brought to their cave.

He told them how Mzilikazi, great with plunder, fat with cattle, had come back to Thabas Indunas, arriving suddenly with the blood barely dried on the spears of his impi, and red rage in his heart.

At Mzilikazi's nod the Black Ones gathered all those who had acted as if the king were dead. Some they hurled from the cliff of execution, some they pegged down upon the sandbanks of the river where the crocodiles sunned themselves, others they skewered with bamboo spikes through the secret openings of their bodies.

But when the mother of Nkulumane was led before the king, she wept so and tore her own flesh with her nails while she called on all the spirits of the dead to witness how faithful she had been to Mzilikazi in his absence, how constant had been her belief in his eventual safe return and how during his absence she had guarded the other royal sons from the Black Ones and had even sent Lobengula into the wilderness to save him that Mzilikazi, who at the bottom was only a man, believed her. However, the others died in their hundreds, victims of the king's wrath, and the nation rejoiced for the king had returned and the good old days were back.

Through all this Lobengula and Saala and their little yellow son stayed on in the cave of the Matopos and knew happiness.

Far away in the south below the Limpopo river, a Hottentot elephant hunter stopped to water his horse at the well beside a Boer homestead that stood not far from the battlefield where the Boer horsemen had long ago first defeated Mzilikazi before driving him out of this country.

'I saw a curious thing,' said the Hottentot to the big, solemn, bearded man who was his host. 'In the southern hills of Matabeleland, I saw a white woman, full grown and naked. She was shy as a wild buck and ran into the rocky ground where I could not follow her.'

Two months later, when the Boer farmer took his family into the service of Nachtmaal in the new church at Rustenberg, he repeated the strange story which the Hottentot hunter had brought from the north. Someone recalled the story of the massacre of the Van Heerden family, and the two little girls, Sarah and Hannah, taken by the murderous plundering savages.

Then Hendrik Potgieter, that doughty trekker and kaffir-fighter, stood up in the pulpit, and thundered:

'The heathen have a Christian woman as captive!' And the words offended much that the congregation held dear: God and their womankind.

'Commando!' roared Hendrik Potgieter. 'I call commando!'

The women filled the powder-horns and poured the lead into the bullet moulds, and the men picked out their best horses and elected Potgieter as their leader.

Not all of it was for God and womankind; for one

whispered to another, 'Even if there is no white woman, I have heard that there are fine new herds in Matabeleland.'

Then the old wizard came to Lobengula's cave and rolled his eyes and cackled.

'The *buni* have crossed the river of crocodiles, riding on the backs of strange beasts. Many men, many men!'

Instinctively Lobengula knew why the Boer commando was coming, and he knew also what to do about it.

'Stay here, with the child,' he ordered Saala. 'I am going to my father's kraal, and I will lead his impis back here.'

But Saala was a woman, with a woman's curiosity, and blood called to blood. Vaguely she remembered that these strange white men had once been her kin.

When Lobengula had gone north to Thabas Indunas, she slung the baby on her back and crept out of the cave. At first the distant sound of gunfire guided her, for the Boer commando was living off the abundant herds of wild game. Then later she heard the shout of voices, and the whicker of horses, sounds that awakened a terrible nostalgia in her breast.

She crept closer and closer to the bivouac, with all the stealth of a wild animal, closer still until she could clearly see the tall sun-bronzed men, dressed to throat and wrists in brown homespun, the white-brimmed felt hats on their heads – closer still until she could hear their voices lifted in praise of their God as they sang their hymns around the camp fire.

She recognized the words, and memories flooded back to her. She was no longer Saala but Sarah, and she rose from her place of hiding to go down to her people. Then she looked down at her body – and she saw that she was naked. She looked at the child on her hip – and saw that it was yellow, and its features were neither hers nor yet those of its Matabele father.

The awareness of sin came upon her, as it had done to Eve in another Paradise, and Sarah was ashamed.

She crept away, and in the dawn she stood on the top of one of those soaring granite precipices that rend the Matopos hills.

She kissed her baby and then holding the little mite to her breast she stepped out into the void.

Lobengula found them at the bottom of the cliff. He found them before the vultures did, and they were still together, Sarah's grasp on the infant had not faltered during the long plunge from the top of the precipice.

Strangely, both she and the child seemed to be merely sleeping – quiet and at peace.

At the memory Lobengula sighed now, and returned his gaze to his half-brother, the Induna Gandang who still sat across him from the fire.

If only he had been able to escape the prophecy of the Umlimo – for she had foreseen this destiny for him:

Your name is Lobengula, the one who drives like the wind. Yet the winds will drive you, high as an eagle. Lobengula will hold the spear of Mzilikazi. Yet again the winds will drive you, down, down, down, and your nation with you.

Those were the words of that strange and beautiful woman of the cave, and already the first part of the prophecy had held true.

Mzilikazi, the mighty warrior, had died like an old woman – riddled with arthritis and dropsy and gout and liquor – in his royal hut.

His widows had wrapped him in the skin of a freshly-killed bull, and sat mourning over him for twelve days: until his remains were almost liquid with putrefaction in the summer heat.

After the mourning the regiments had carried his corpse into the Matopos Hills, the Sacred Hills, and they had seated Mzilikazi in the cave of the king. They placed all his possessions about him: his assegais, his guns, his ivory; even his wagon was taken down and the pieces piled in the crevices of the cave.

Then masons closed the opening with blocks of granite, and after the feasting and dancing the indunas of Matabele met to decide who would succeed Mzilikazi as king.

The argument and counter-argument lasted many weeks, until the indunas led by the princes of Kumalo returned into the Matopos bearing rich gifts to the cave of the Umlimo.

'Give us a king!' they pleaded.

'The one who drives like the wind!' replied the Umlimo, but Lobengula had fled, trying even at the last moment to escape his destiny.

The border impis captured him, and led him back to Thabas Indunas like a criminal to judgement. The indunas came to him one by one, and swore their allegiance and loyalty unto death.

'Black Bull of Matabele, The Thunderer! The Great Elephant. The one whose tread shakes the earth.'

Nkulumane was the first of his brothers to crawl before him, and Nkulumane's mother, the senior wife of Mzilikazi, followed her son on her knees.

Lobengula turned to the Black Ones who stood behind him, like hounds on the leash.

'I do not wish to look upon their faces again.'

It was Lobengula's first command, spoken like a true king, and the Black Ones took mother and son into the cattle stockade and twisted their necks, quickly and mercifully.

'He will be a great king,' the people told one another delightedly. 'Like his father.'

But Lobengula had never known happiness again. Now with a shudder he threw off the terrible burden of the past, and his voice was a deep but melodious bass.

'Rise up, Gandang my brother. Your countenance warms me like a watch-fire in the frosty night.'

They spoke then, easily and intimately, trusted companions of a lifetime, until at last Gandang passed the Martini-Henry rifle to his king and Lobengula held it in his lap and rubbed the cold blued metal of the block with one forefinger and then held the finger to his nose to smell the fresh grease.

'Sting the mamba with his own venom,' he murmured. 'This is the fang of the mamba.'

'The lad, Henshaw, son of Bakela, has a wagon filled with these.'

'Then he will be welcome,' Lobengula nodded. 'But now let me hear all this from the mouth of your own son. Bring him to me.'

Bazo lay face down on the hard clay floor of the king's hut, and he chanted the ritual praises with a catch in his throat, and brave as he was, he sweated with fear in the king's presence.

'Rise up, Bazo the Axe,' Lobengula broke in impatiently. 'Come closer.'

Bazo crept forward on all fours, and he offered the beaded kilt. Lobengula spilled the diamonds from it into a glowing puddle and he stirred them with his finger.

'There are prettier stones than these in every river bed of my land,' he said. 'These are ugly.'

'The *buni* are mad for them. No other stone will satisfy them, but for these their hunger is so great that they will kill any who stand in their way.'

'Tear the lion with his own claws.' Lobengula repeated the prophecy of the Umlimo and then went on, 'Are these ugly little stones the claws of the lion? Then, if they are, let all men see how Lobengula is ready with claws.'

And he clapped his hands for his wives to come to him.

The royal hut was crowded now, rank upon rank of squatting men faced the low platform on which Lobengula lay. Every man of them except Bazo wore the headring of the induna, and their names were the rolls of glory of the Matabele nation.

There was Somabula, the lion-hearted old warrior, and beside him Babiaan, royal prince of Kumalo, and all the others. Their ranks were silent and attentive, their faces grave in the light of the fire which had been built up and whose flames leapt almost to the high-domed roof of the king's hut.

They were watching the king.

Lobengula lay on his back on the built-up platform beyond the fire. There was a low carved headrest under the nape of his neck. Only the tip of his penis was covered by the dried and hollowed-out gourd, otherwise he was stark naked. His great belly was mountainous and his limbs were like tree trunks.

Four of his wives squatted about him in a circle, each of them with a calabash of rendered white beef fat beside her. They anointed the king, smearing the fat thickly over his body from his throat to his ankles. Then when it was done they rose silently, and stooped out through the opening in the back of the hut which led to the women's quarters.

Singing softly, shuffling and swaying to the song, another file of younger wives began to wind into the hut; each of them carried upon her head a beer pot of fired clay; but these pots were not filled with the bubbling millet beer.

The wives knelt on each side of the king, and at a word from the senior wife they dipped into the clay pots and each of them came out with a large uncut diamond in her fingers. They began sticking the stones on the king's skin, and the thick coating of grease held them in the patterns that they built up to ornament Lobengula's gleaming limbs. They worked swiftly, for they had done this before, and under their fingers Lobengula was transformed. He became a creature of mythology: half man, half glittering scaled fish.

The diamonds caught the beam of the fire, and sent it spinning against the thatched walls and high roof, darting insects of golden light that flashed in the eyes of the watchers and dazzled them so that they grunted with amazement, and their voices went up like a choir in praise of their king.

At last the work was done and the wives crept away and left Lobengula lying on the thick soft furs, covered from throat to wrist to ankle in a silver burning coat of mail, each link of which was a priceless diamond; and as the king's chest and belly rose and subsided to the tide of his breathing, so this immense treasure burned and flamed.

'Indunas of Matabele, Princes of Kumalo, hail your King.'

'*Bayete! Bayete!*' The royal salute burst from their throats. '*Bayete!*'

Then the silence was complete but expectant, for it had become the king's custom that after this ritual display of the contents of the nation's treasury, he would dispense honours and rewards.

'Bazo,' Lobengula's voice was sonorous. 'Stand forward!'

The young man rose from his lowly position in the rearmost rank.

'*Bayete, Nkosi.*'

'Bazo, you have pleased me. I grant you a boon. What shall it be? Speak!'

'I crave only that the king should know the depth of my duty and love for him. Set me a task, I pray you, and if it should be fierce and hard and bloody, my heart and my mouth will sing the king's praises for ever.'

'On Chaka's royal buttocks, your pup is hungry for glory.' Lobengula looked to Gandang in the front rank of indunas. 'And he shames all those who ask for trinkets and cattle and women.'

He thought a moment, and then chuckled.

'In the direction of the sunrise, two days' march beyond the forests of Somabula, on a high hilltop lives a Mashona dog who deems himself such a great magician and rain-maker that he is beyond the king's arm. His name is Pemba.' And there was a hiss of indrawn breath from the squatting ranks of elders. Three times in the past season the king had sent impis to Pemba's hilltop, and three times they had returned empty-handed. The name Pemba mocked them all. 'Take fifty men from your old regiment, Little Axe, and fetch Pemba's head so that I can see his insolent smile with my own eyes.'

'*Bayete!*' Bazo's joy carried him in a single bound over the grey heads of the indunas. He landed lightly in the space before the fire and he whirled into the *giya*, the challenge dance:

> 'Thus will I stab the traitor dog –
> and thus will I rip out the bellies of his sons—'

The indunas grinned and nodded indulgently, but their smiles were tinged with regret for the fury and passion of their youth which had long ago cooled in their own breasts.

Lobengula sat on the bench of his wagon. It was a big twenty-four-foot four-wheeler built in Cape Town from good English oak, but it still showed all the marks of punishment from its long trek up from the south.

It had not moved in many years, so the grass had grown up through the wheel spokes and around the axle shafts. The canvas of the tent was bleached bone white and crusted with the dung of the hens which roosted on the hoops of the tent framework, but the canvas protected Lobengula from the sun and the seat on the box elevated his head above the level of his courtiers and guards and children and wives and supplicants who crowded the enclosed stockade.

The wagon was Lobengula's throne, and the open stockade his audience chamber. Because there would be white men and women in his audience, he had donned his European finery for this occasion. The long coat encrusted with gold lace had once belonged to a Portuguese diplomat. The lace was tarnished and one epaulette was missing, and the front could not be buttoned over the king's noble belly, not by twelve inches, and the cuffs reached only halfway down his forearms.

The toy spear of kingship, the haft of red wild mahogany and the blade of brightest silver, was in his right hand, and he used it to summon a young boy from out of the crush.

The child was shaking with terror, and his voice so tremulous that Lobengula had to lean forward to hear him.

'I waited until the leopard entered the goat house; then I crept up and closed the door and I barricaded it with stones.'

'How did you kill the beast?' Lobengula demanded.

'I stabbed him through the chinks in the wall with my father's assegai.'

The boy crept forward and laid the lustrous gold and black dappled skin at Lobengula's feet.

'Take your choice of three cows from my royal herds, little one, and drive them to your father's kraal and tell him that the king has given you a praise name. From this day you will be known as "The one who stares into the eyes of the leopard".'

The boy's voice cracked in an adolescent squeak as he backed away gabbling the praises.

Next was a Hollander, a big arrogant white man with a querulous voice.

'I have waited three weeks for the king to decide—'

This was translated for Lobengula, and he mused aloud.

'See how red the man's face becomes when he is angry, like the wattles on the head of the black vulture. Tell him that the king does not count days, perhaps he will have to wait as long again, who knows?' And he dismissed him with a flirt of the spear.

Lobengula took a pull from the bottle of champagne that stood on the wagon seat beside him. The wine fizzed and spilled onto the front of his gold-frogged jacket. Then suddenly his face lit into a beatific smile, but his voice was carping and querulous.

'I sent for you yesterday, Nomusa, Girlchild of Mercy. I am in great pain; why did you not come sooner?'

'An eagle flies, a cheetah runs, but I am limited to the pace of a mule, oh King,' said Robyn Codrington, as she picked her way through the offal that littered the earthen floor of the stockade, and with the fly switch in her hand cleared a path through the crowd towards the wagon, even dealing a stinging cut to one of the king's black-cloaked executioners.

'Out of my way, eater of human flesh,' she told him primly. 'Be gone, child stabber.' And the man leaped aside nimbly and scowled after her.

'What is it, Lobengula?' she asked as she reached the wagon. 'What ails you this time?'

'My feet are filled with burning coals.'

'Gout,' Robyn said as she touched the grotesquely swollen appendages. 'You drink too much beer, oh King, you drink too much brandy and champagne.' She opened her bag.

'You would have me die of thirst. You are not well named, Nomusa; there is no pity in your heart.'

'Nor yours, Lobengula,' Robyn snapped. 'They tell me you have sent another impi to murder the people of Pemba.'

'He is only a Mashona,' Lobengula chuckled. 'Save your sympathy for a king whose stomach feels as though it is filled with sharp stones.'

'Indigestion,' Robyn scolded. 'Gluttony killed your father, and it is killing you.'

'Now you would starve me also. You want me to be a skinny little man of no consequence.'

'A thin live one or a fat dead one,' Robyn told him. 'Open your mouth.'

Lobengula choked on the draught, and rolled his eyes theatrically.

'The pain is better than the taste of your medicine.'

'I will leave you five of these pills. Eat one when your feet swell and the pain becomes fierce.'

'Twenty,' said Lobengula. 'A box full. I, Lobengula, King of Matabele, command it. Leave me a box of these little white pills.'

'Five,' said Robyn firmly. 'Or you will eat them all at one time, as you did before.'

The king rocked with gargantuan laughter, and almost fell from the wagon seat.

'I think I will command you to leave those little white huts of yours at Khami, and come to live closer to me.'

'I should not obey.'

'That's why I do not command it,' Lobengula agreed, with another shout of laughter.

'This kraal is a disgrace, the dirt, the flies—'

'A few old bones and a little dog shit never killed a Matabele,' the king told her, and then was serious and motioned her closer, dropping his voice so that only she could hear.

'The Dutchman with the red face, you know he wishes to build a trade post at the ford of the Hunyani river—'

'The man is a cheat. The goods he brings are shoddy, and he will deceive your people.'

'A runner has brought this book.' He handed the folded and wafered sheet to Robyn. 'Read it for me.'

'It is from Sir Francis Good. He wishes—' For almost an hour, whispering hoarsely so that no other could hear,

Lobengula consulted Robyn on fifty different matters ranging from the British Commissioner's letter to the menstrual problems of his youngest wife. Then at last he said, 'Your coming is like the first sweet rain at the end of the long dry. Is there aught I can do for your happiness?'

'You can let your people come to worship in my church.'

This time the king's chuckle was rueful. 'Nomusa, you are as persistent as the termites that gnaw away the poles of my hut.' He frowned with thought and then smiled again. 'Very well, I will let you take one of my people – as long as it is a woman, the wife of an induna of royal blood, and the mother of twelve sons. If you can find one of my people who meets all those conditions, you may take her and splash water on her and make your sign on her forehead; and she may sing songs to your three white gods if she so wishes.'

This time Robyn had to answer his sly and mischievous grin. 'You are a cruel man, Lobengula, and you eat and drink too much. But I love you.'

'And I love you also, Nomusa.'

'Then I will ask one more favour.'

'Ask it,' he commanded.

'There is a lad, son of my brother—'

'Henshaw.'

'The king knows all.'

'What of this boy?'

'Will the king listen to his petition?'

'Send him to me.'

Even from where he stood Bazo could see that the grain bins were overflowing with corn that had been sun-dried still on the cob. There was enough to feed an army, he decided bitterly. There was no chance of starving them out.

The grain bins were cylindrical in shape, their walls of plaited green saplings plastered with clay and cow dung. They stood on stilts of mopani poles to allow the air to circulate below them, and to keep out bush rats and other vermin.

They were perched on the very edge of the precipice.

'The dog has brought good rains to his own fields,' murmured Zama, Bazo's lieutenant. 'He is fat with corn. Perhaps he is a rain-doctor as he claims.'

'Water,' Bazo mused, staring up the sheer cliff. Beyond the grain bins he could make out the thatched roofs of the tribal huts. 'Can we drive them out with thirst?' he asked advice, for Zama had been a member of one of the previous abortive raids upon the stronghold.

'The three other indunas tried that at first,' Zama pointed out. 'But then one of the Mashona that they captured told them that there is a running spring from which they draw all the water they wish.'

The sun was beyond the summit of the hill, so Bazo squinted his eyes against it. 'There is lush green growth there—' He pointed to a narrow gulley that cleft the top of the cliff like an axe stroke but was choked with growth. 'That would be it.'

As if to confirm his words the tiny distant figure of a girl appeared suddenly out of the gulley. She was foreshortened by her height above them, and the ledge along which she climbed was not apparent from where they stood.

She had a calabash gourd balanced on her head, with green leaves stuffed into its mouth to stop the water splashing out of it as she moved.

She disappeared over the top of the cliff.

'So,' grunted Bazo. 'We must climb up to them.'

'It would be easier to fly,' Zama grunted. 'That rock would daunt a baboon – or a klipspringer.'

The rock was pearly grey and marble smooth. There were streaks of lichen dashed across it, green and blue and red, like dry paint on an artist's palette.

'Come,' Bazo ordered, and they began a slow measured circuit of the hill – and as they went so the armed guards on the clifftop above kept pace with them, watching every move they made, and if they approached too close to the foot of the cliff, a hail of rocks fell upon them, striking sparks from the scree slope and caroming viciously past their heads, forcing them to shelve their dignity as they retired in haste.

'It is always the Mashona way,' Zama grumbled. 'Stones instead of spears.'

In places the cliff was riven by vertical cracks, yet none of these reached from base to crest, none of them offered a route to the summit. Bazo looked for a place that had been polished by the paws of wild baboon or marked by the hooves of the tiny little chamois-like klipspringer which might reveal a way up the rock face, but there was none. The cliff girded the entire hill, and transformed it into a fortress.

'There!' Zama pointed to a tiny irregularity in the face. 'That is where two warriors of the swimmers' impi tried to force a road to the top. They climbed as far as that little bush.' It grew in a crack in the face a hundred feet from the base of the cliff. 'And there the ledge narrowed and gave out. They could not go on, nor could they return. They hung there two days and three nights until their strength failed and they fell, one after the other, to be crushed like beetles on the rocks here where we stand.'

They went on, and as the sun was setting they came back to where they had started – the bivouac below the ladderway. Pemba's people had built a ladder of long straight mopani poles, bound together with bark rope, and they had used it to span the lowest point in the cliff – a place where a deep gully descended from the summit to within fifty feet of the surrounding plain. Like a drawbridge, the massive ladder was cunningly counter-weighted with round ironstone boulders, so that it had only to be drawn up on its ropes – as it was now – and the mountain stronghold was impregnable.

When the sun set, Bazo was still leaning on his long shield staring up the cliff, seemingly oblivious to the faint shouted insults of the Mashona that just reached him in the evening silence.

'Pustules on Lobengula's fat buttocks.'

'Puppies of the rabid dog Lobengula.'

'Dried turds of the spavined Matabele elephant.'

Only when it was too dark to make out the top of the cliff did Bazo turn away – but even then he sat late beside the watch-fire, and rolled into his kaross only after the rise of the big white star over the top of the kopje.

Even then his sleep was troubled with dreams. He dreamed of water, of streams and lakes and waterfalls.

He woke again before light and checked that his sentries were alert before he slipped from the camp and under cover of the darkness crept up to the base of the cliff – at the point directly below the gulley choked with green growth where they had seen the girl carry water the day before.

Bazo heard the liquid chuckling, and his spirits soared. Guided by the sound he groped through the darkness, and found the spring in the base of the cliff. It filled a small natural basin of grey rock and then overflowed to waste itself again in the dry earth of the plain. Bazo scooped a handful and it was icy cold and sweet on his tongue. The fountain came splashing out of a dark rent in the rock face. Bazo explored it in the short time that was left before the strengthening light threatened to expose him to the sentries on the cliff above.

'Up,' Bazo shouted as he strode into the bivouac. 'All of you, up!' And his men came off their sleeping-mats, leopard swift and with the stabbing spears in their fists.

'What is it?' Zama hissed.

'We are going to dance,' Bazo told them, and they looked from one to the other in amazed disbelief.

On the north side of the kopje, farthest from the spring in the rock cliff and from the long ladder drawbridge, they danced. While they danced, all Pemba's people lined the clifftop to watch them, first in puzzled silence and then yelling with ribald laughter, hurling down taunts and stones.

'I count four hundred – without the children,' Zama panted, as he stamped and leaped and stabbed at the air.

'There will be enough for each of us,' Bazo agreed, and pirouetted with his shield high over his head.

They danced until the sun was high and then Bazo led them back to the camp, and when he stretched out on his mat and fell instantly asleep, his warriors looked at Zama with exasperation, but Zama could only shrug and turn his eyes to the sky.

An hour before sunset Bazo woke. He ate a little maize cake and drank a small gourd of sour milk, then he called for Zama and spoke quietly with him until it was almost dark.

Zama listened and nodded and his eyes shone, and while he talked, Bazo was honing the silver blade of his assegai until the light twinkled like tiny stars along its cutting edge.

At dark Bazo rose to his feet, handed his long dappled war shield to Zama and, armed only with his assegai, strode out of the bivouac. At the spring in the base of the cliff, Bazo shed his kilt and cloak and headdress. He rolled them into a bundle and hid them in a rock crevice. Then stark naked with only his assegai tied to his back by a leather thong, he waded across the pool. The reflection of the stars on its surface exploded into chips of light.

The water cascaded over him from the fountain in the cliff and he shuddered and gasped with the cold and then reached up into the dark rocky opening, found a finger-hold, drew a deep breath, and then pulled himself upwards.

With a solid black jet of water racing over his head, he held his breath and wriggled frantically up into the hole in the cliff. The force of water opposed him, and it required all his strength to go against it. Inch by inch, his chest throbbing for air, he fought his way upwards – and then just when he knew he would have to let himself be washed back into the pool, his head broke out – and he could breathe.

He sucked air desperately, wedging shoulders and knees against the smooth water-polished rock to hold himself in the torrent. It was utterly dark, not the faintest glimmering of starlight, and the darkness seemed to have physical weight that threatened to crush him.

He reached as high as he could and found another smooth fingerhold, and with all the strength of his arms gained another few feet, rested a moment, and then reached up again. The rock was like glass, and in places coated with a thick beard of algae, slippery as an eel's skin. The cold was a terrible living thing that invaded his body. His bones ached and his fingers were so numbed that he could barely take his holds.

The water tore at him, battering his shoulders, forcing its way into his nose and mouth and ears, filling his head with its angry animal roaring. Still he went up in the irregular twisting tunnel, sometimes horizontal, wriggling forward on his belly, the roof cracking his skull if he lifted his head too quickly to find the few precious inches of air trapped beneath it. Mostly the tunnel climbed vertically, and he wedged with knees and elbows to hold himself against the cascade, while his skin, softened with water, was smeared and torn away in slabs against the stone; but the inches became yards, and the minutes became hours, and still he went up.

Then the tunnel narrowed so sharply that he was trapped, cold slippery rock at each shoulder and hard heavy rock cramming down between his shoulderblades. He could not go on, nor could he go back. He was trapped in the rocky maw of the mountain, and he screamed with terror, but his voice was lost in the thunder of water and the water gushed into his throat.

He fought with the last of his drowning, desperate strength, and suddenly he kicked himself forward into a narrow cavern where he could breathe again, and where the water swirled into little back-eddies so that he could rest a few moments from its drag.

Even while he coughed and choked on his flooded lungs, he realized that he had lost his assegai, and he groped for it until he felt the tug of the thong on his shoulder; there was still something tied to the other end. Hand over hand he drew in the thong and then his fingers closed on the familiar shaft and he sobbed with relief and pressed his lips to the beloved steel.

It took time for him to realize that the air in the tiny cavern was sweet, and he felt it moving like a lover's fingers on his skin, warm and soft – warmth, that was what made his heart soar. Warmth from the outside world, beyond this icy roaring tomb of water. He found the shaft down which the torrent was sucking air from the surface, and from somewhere came the strength to attempt it. He climbed slowly, agonizingly, and suddenly there was a white prick of light ahead of him, distorted by racing black water.

He thrust his head forward, and the night wind struck his cheek, and he smelled woodsmoke and grass and earth redolent of the lingering warmth of the sun, and the great white star stood in the night sky high above his head. That dreadful passage had connected the fountain at the base of the cliff to the one high above.

He did not have the strength to drag himself more than a few feet from the fountainhead, and there under a bush on the soft bed of leaf mould he lay and panted like a dog.

He must have drifted into an exhausted and cold-drugged sleep, for he woke with a start. The sky had paled. He could just see the branches of the bush above his head outlined against it. He dragged himself out, and he found that he ached down to the bones of his spine and his skinned elbows and knees burned even at the touch of the dawn wind.

There was a narrow path, well marked by many feet from the fountainhead up the last few feet of the cliff, and as he stepped out onto it he looked down and saw far below him the moonsilver forest and the tiny sparks that were the watch-fires of his own bivouac. As he moved, he felt his muscles easing and unknotting, felt the blood recharging his limbs.

Although he was ready for one, there was no sentry at the top of the path, and he peered out cautiously from behind the stone portals of the gully onto the tranquil village.

'By Chaka's teeth, they sleep like fat and lazy dogs,' Bazo thought grimly. The doors were all tightly closed, and smoke oozed from every chink in the walls. They were half suffocating themselves to keep out the mosquitoes. He could hear a man coughing hoarsely in the nearest hut.

He was about to slip out from behind his rocky screen when faint movement in the gloom between the huts made him sink gently down again. A dark figure scurried directly towards where he hid. He shifted his grip on the assegai, but only a few paces from him the figure stopped.

It was swathed in a skin cloak against the pre-dawn chill, hunched up like an old woman, until it straightened and threw off the cloak. Bazo felt his breath hiss up his throat and he bit down to stop it reaching his lips.

The naked girl was in that lovely tender stage just past puberty, on the very brink of full womanhood. There were the last vulnerable vestiges of childhood in the plump little buttocks and in the kitten awkward way she stood with toes turned slightly inwards. She was naked and the first light touched her sable skin with a lemon glow. Then she turned her head.

She had a long slender neck and the neat little head balanced perfectly upon it. The dome of her skull was covered with an intricate pattern of closely woven plaits. Her forehead was high and smooth, her cheekbones vaulted in the Egyptian way, her lips chiselled into perfect sweeps, symmetrical as the wings of a beautiful butterfly, and the light glinted briefly in her huge slanted eyes as she looked about her.

Then she squatted briefly and her water tinkled against the earth. It was a sound that unaccountably filled Bazo's chest with a swollen tender feeling, for the act was so innocent and so natural.

She stood, and in the instant before she covered her head once more with the cloak, he had one more glimpse of her face. He knew then that he had never seen anything so beautiful in all his life – and he stared after her as she hurried back between the huts with a peculiar aching hunger consuming his very being.

It took him many minutes to rouse himself, and then as he crept forward he found that, hard as he tried, he could not drive the girl's image from his mind. The pathway that led from the village to the ladder drawbridge was unmistakable. It was broad and its surface beaten smooth. There were walls of worked stone on each side of it behind which the defenders could meet any thrust up the path. There were piles of stones at intervals along its course, placed ready to be hurled down at anybody attempting to force the ladder or fight their way up the path.

The pathway dropped steeply into the gully, and then ended on a wide level stone platform. The light was stronger now and Bazo could see that there were sentries here; two of them stood on the lip watching the plain fifty feet below the platform, guarding the massive counterbalanced ladder. Farther back four other guards squatted around a small smoky fire, and Bazo's saliva flooded as he smelled the roasting maize cakes. The men were talking in the low sleepy tones of men who had stood a long watch, and their backs were turned to the gully, for they would never expect an enemy to come from that direction.

Bazo crept closer. There was another pile of rocks at the corner of the platform, ready for the guards to hurl down the cliff. Bazo crawled into the shadows behind it.

He did not have long to wait. Very faintly on the morning wind he heard the singing. Zama had begun the dance below the cliff. The song was the fighting hymn of his regiment, and Bazo's blood thrilled in his veins. He felt the divine madness begin. It was a feeling that other lesser men got only from the hemp pipe.

He felt the sweat break on his skin, and the madness mount from his belly to his heart – felt the blood swell in his throat, felt his eyes burn and bulge.

The guards had left the fire now and crowded the edge of the cliff, peering downwards, laughing and pointing.

'Hear Lobengula's puppies yap!'

'Look at them dance like virgins at the Festival of First Fruits!'

The signal Bazo had agreed with Zama was the moment the battle song ended, but he could barely contain himself that long.

He rose from his crouch, and his muscles twitched, his head jerked like that of a maniac, and in the dawn light his eyes were glazed like shards of ceramic pottery, the red rage of the berserker. At that instant the distant song ended.

Bazo's cry froze the men on the edge of the cliff, it was the bellow of a heart-struck buffalo bull, the screech of the stooping eagle.

In the paralysed moment before they could turn, Bazo struck them. He charged with outstretched arms and swept four of them away into the void. They twisted and turned in the air as they fell, and they screamed the whole way down on a high receding note that was cut off abruptly at the end.

Bazo's charge had been so headlong that he almost followed them over the brink; for a giddy moment he tottered there, and then he caught his balance and spun to strike underhand at one of the survivors. The blade went into the man's belly and out the other side, cleaving his bowels and his kidneys, and crunching through his backbone; and when Bazo jerked the steel clear, the life blood sprayed hotly onto his forearm and his chest. The last sentry ran, silently and desperately, for the pathway, and Bazo let him go.

Bazo bounded along the edge of the cliff and reached the point where the top of the ladder was secured. The ropes that held it were of twisted and plaited bark, reinforced with liana and leather thongs. They were thick as Bazo's arm, and he changed his grip on the assegai to a chopping stroke.

The ropes popped and crackled as he hacked through them. He grunted at each stroke, slitting his eyes against the flying chips of wood and bark.

Behind him he heard the babble of many voices on the pathway. The sentry would call them down like hunting dogs – but Bazo scorned to turn until the work was done. One rope gave, and the massive unwieldy ladder sagged and twisted. He cut again, reversing his grip to swing back-handed, and the other ropes went.

The ladder swung outwards and downwards, gathering momentum, and the timbers crackled and squealed, drowning out the voices of the men coming down behind him. The bottom of the ladder struck the scree below the cliff with a shattering crash, and some of the uprights snapped under the impact. The head of the ladder was still secured at Bazo's feet, and the whole twisted mess hung down like the rigging of a dismasted ship.

Bazo stood long enough to watch Zama lead his warriors swarming up the dangling tangle of rope and timber. Then he turned.

They were coming down the pathway, a solid phalanx of black bodies and sparkling weapons; but their advance was hesitant enough for Bazo to race forward and reach the narrow gap in the wall before the leaders did. With solid rock to guard his flanks, he laughed at them, and it was a sound to stop them dead, those in front pushing back and those behind struggling forward.

One of them threw a long spear and it clashed sparks from the wall at the level of Bazo's head. He drove forward and stabbed into the press of bodies caught in the narrow gut between the stone walls. The screams and moans goaded him – and the blood from the gaping wounds splattered his face and sprayed into his open mouth, a ghastly draught that maddened him further. They broke and fled, leaving four of their number writhing and twisting on the pathway.

Bazo glanced behind him. None of his Matabele had reached the head of the ladder yet. He looked back up the pathway and saw that the real men were coming.

These would be the picked warriors, the best spearmen – there was no mistaking their superiority over the rabble that Bazo had just scattered; they were bigger and more powerful in body, their expressions grim and determined, and their formation ordered and controlled.

They came down in massed ranks to where Bazo stood,

their shields raised, their spears poised, and at their head danced a skinny wizened old man with a face ravaged by some terrible disease, his nose and ears rotted away and his cheeks and forehead covered with silver white blotches.

He was hung about the waist and neck with the accoutrements of his magical trade, and he shrieked and gibbered like an enraged ape.

'Kill the Matabele dog.'

Bazo was naked, without a shield, but he hefted the assegai and stood to meet them and their horrid master and he laughed again, the wild joyous laughter of a man who was living a lifetime in his last few seconds.

'Bazo!' The cry reached him, even through his rage, and he turned.

Zama had crawled onto the platform, blown from that long scrambling climb up the swinging twisted ladder. He rose on his knees and sent the great dappled shield skimming across the platform. Like a falcon coming to the lure it settled on Bazo's shoulder, and Bazo laughed and went springing forward.

His assegai drove through the wizard's rotting flesh as though it were soft as a boiled yam, and Pemba screeched one last time.

'Bazo, wait! Leave some of them for us!' The shouts of his fifty Matabele behind him, as they scrambled onto the platform, and then Zama's muscled shoulder was touching his as they locked shields and swept the pathway, the way the flash floods of summer scour the dry riverbeds.

It was a beautiful stabbing, a glory which men would sing about. The assegais seemed to hold their keen edge no matter how often they were buried and the spear arms never tired despite the heavy work. The line of Matabele swept the hilltop from end to end, roaring their frustration when the last of Pemba's men threw down their spears and leapt out over the cliff, grudging them that easy death for the assegais were still thirsty and the madness was still on them.

Then they turned and went back through the village, ransacking the huts, throwing a toddling infant high and catching it on the point as it fell, or sending the steel full length out between the withered dugs of some scurrying crone, for the divine madness does not pass swiftly.

With his shoulder, Bazo smashed open another hut, and Zama leaped in at his side, both of them were painted from throat to knee with red running crimson, their contorted faces hideous, blood-glutted masks. Someone tried to escape from the dark interior of the hut.

'Mine!' roared Zama and sped his long steel, and the low early sun struck a ray through the open doorway, sparkling on Zama's assegai and falling in the same instant on the huge slanted terrified eyes and high Egyptian cheekbones of the girl he was killing.

Zama's steel clashed against Bazo's great shield and was deflected past the girl's cheek by the width of a finger, so that the stroke died in the air. Before Zama could strike again Bazo stood over the girl, spreading the shield over her the way a heron covers its chick with a wing, and he snarled at Zama like a leopard whose cub is menaced.

After the first weary day of the return march, while the long file of roped captives was settling exhausted and miserable beneath the grove of msasa trees, Bazo strode down the line and stopped beside the girl.

'You!' he said, and with a careless stroke of his assegai severed the thong at her neck. 'Cook my meal!'

While she worked over the fire, Bazo joked loudly with Zama and his men, trying to prevent his eyes from straying from their faces. He ate what she cooked without showing either pleasure or displeasure, while she knelt at a respectful distance and watched every mouthful he took.

Then suddenly when he had finished eating, she came gliding to his side with that disconcerting silent grace, and she lifted the bunch of wilted leaves from the swollen and crusted spear wound in Bazo's flank. It was an impertinence, and he lifted his hand to strike her – and then let the hand fall. She had not flinched and her manner was assured and competent.

She cleaned the wound with deft fingers and then she unstoppered two of the little buck-horn containers that she wore on her belt and with the powder they contained made a poultice. It burned like fire for a few seconds, but then felt much easier.

Bazo made no acknowledgement, but when one of his Matabele came to rope her back with the other captives, Bazo frowned, and the man passed her by.

When Bazo lay on his sleeping-mat, she curled like a puppy at his feet. He was ready for her to try to escape once the camp settled, but after midnight she had not stirred and he fell asleep.

In the hour before dawn when he rose to check the sentries, there was frost on the grass, and he heard the girl's teeth chattering softly. He dropped his fur regimental cloak over her as he passed and she cuddled down into it quickly.

When he called for the day's march to begin, she had his bedding roll and cooking-pot balanced on her head, and a dozen times during the march, Bazo had to go back along the winding column for no reason that he could explain to Zama, and each time his steps slowed as he came up behind the girl, and he watched the play of muscle down her back, the roll of her plump black buttocks and the joggle of her glossy sable breasts. But when she turned her head and smiled shyly at him, his hauteur was frosty and he stalked back to the head of the column.

That night he permitted himself a nod of approval at the first taste of her cooking, and when she dressed the wound, he said, 'The heat has gone from it.'

She did not lift her eyes.

'Who taught you this skill?' he insisted.

'Pemba, the wizard,' she whispered.

'Why?'

'I was his apprentice.'

'Why you?'

'I have the gift.'

'So then, little witch, make me an oracle,' Bazo laughed, and she lifted her head and he looked into those disconcerting slanted tar-bright eyes.

'Do not scoff, lord.'

'*Nkosi* – lord,' she called him, but Bazo stopped laughing, and felt the spirits tickle the hair at the nape of his neck. That night, when he heard her shiver, he opened a fold of his kaross and she crept into it.

Bazo feigned sleep, but his body was tense and he was aware of each tiny movement that the girl made as she settled to sleep. It would have been so easy to reach out and hold her down with his arm across her chest while he forced his knee between hers. The thought made him twitch and grunt.

'Lord?' she whispered. 'Something troubles you.'

'What is your name?' he asked, for want of a reply, and found that he was whispering also.

'Tanase.'

'Tanase.' He measured it on his tongue, and it fitted well enough, although he recognized it was a Rozwi name, one of the splinter tribes of the Mashona, and he did not know the meaning.

'I know your name – everyone speaks it with respect,' she said. 'Bazo, the Axe.'

'I killed your master, Pemba. I struck him down with my own hand.' He did not know what compelled him to say that.

'I know,' she whispered.

'Do you hate me for that, little witch?'

'I praise you for that!' Her voice shook with quiet vehemence, and her hip touched his under the kaross.

'Praise? Did you not love Pemba as a dog loves its master?'

'I hated him, and when I foresaw his death in the magic calabash, I was filled with joy.'

'You saw his death?'

'I saw his death – as I saw your face, long before you came to take me.'

Bazo shuddered involuntarily, and she felt it.

'You are cold, lord.' She pressed a little closer to him. Her flesh was hot and soft, he felt his own flesh respond to its touch.

'Why did you hate Pemba?'

'He was evil beyond the telling. The things he forced me to do I will never forget.'

'He used your body?' There was a rough edge to Bazo's question.

'Not even Pemba would dare tamper with the body of one of the chosen ones, for to tear the veil of maidenhood is to destroy the gift.'

'The gift?'

'The gift of foresight which the likes of Pemba value so highly.'

'What then did he force upon you?'

'Dark things, midnight things, torture not of the body but of the spirit.'

Now it was her turn to shudder, and she turned towards him and clung to his broad smooth chest, hiding her face against it so that her voice was muffled and he could hardly catch her next words.

'I did not wish to be chosen, I hate and fear what still lies ahead of me if I follow that road.'

'Pemba is dead.'

'You do not understand. Pemba was but a little wizard, already he had taught me almost all he knew. Then I would have been called by the one whose name I dare not speak aloud. That call will still come – and I shall not be able to deny it.'

'You are under my protection.'

'There is only one way you can protect me, Bazo Lord.'

'How?'

'Make me worthless to them. Destroy this gift which is such a terrible burden.'

'How?'

'As you destroyed Pemba with the stabbing spear of steel, destroy it with your great spear of flesh, tear my veil and let this thing pass from me.'

She felt him, hot and fierce, pressing against her, and her body seemed to melt and become pliant and yielding.

'Ah yes, Lord. Make me as other women, so that I may feel your noble belly on mine in the nights, that I may feel your son kick in my womb and tug at my breast when I give him suck.'

'All these things you will have, Tanase.' Bazo's voice was hoarse with his wanting. 'When we reach GuBulawayo the king will reward me, and give me leave to go in to the women, and take a wife.'

'Lord, it is dangerous to wait.'

'I will not rut on you like a slave girl. You will be the first and senior of all my wives.'

'Lord—'

'Enough, Tanase, tempt me no further, for what you feel, hard though it may be, is not stone but flesh only.'

'*Nkosi*, you do not know the power of the wizards. Save me from them.'

'I know the law and custom of Matabele, and that is all a man should know and heed.'

Bazo's scout came in at a dead run, the sweat snaking down his back and chest, and he shouted his report the moment he came up to the head of the column.

Bazo whirled and barked three sharp orders. Immediately the column closed up, and the captives were forced to squat with a dozen warriors standing guard over them. The rest of the Matabele formed up behind Bazo and he led them away at that gait between a trot and a run which lifted the dust to their knees.

Bazo picked his ambush with an unerring eye. He chose a place where broken ground and thick bush allowed only one passage through, and the single horseman rode into it. The long shields were suddenly all around him, fencing him in as his dun-coloured pony snorted and skittered.

The rifle was half-way drawn from the leather boot at the horseman's knee when Bazo stopped him with a shout.

'Too late for that. You were dead, and the jackals feasting already. You grow careless, despite all that I taught you, Henshaw.'

Ralph let the rifle slide back into its scabbard, and he threw up his hands, pleasure and chagrin warring on his face.

'Shake any tree and a Matabele falls out of it.' His voice was mock-mournful, and he swung down off Tom's sturdy back and strode to meet Bazo.

'I expected to see the induna's ring on your forehead already, oh mighty slayer of Mashona,' he laughed as they embraced.

'Soon, Little Hawk, very soon. But you, I thought your wagon would be heavy with ivory—'

'Done, Little Axe, already done.' Ralph stepped back and looked at him. In the months since they had parted, both men had changed.

In Bazo there remained no trace of the young mine labourer who had worked his shifts in the pit and eaten

Zouga Ballantyne's rations. Here was a warrior and a prince, tall and plumed and proud.

Ralph was no longer the callow lad, his every action ordered by his father. Instead he was a grown man, with a jaunty lift to his chin and a self-assured set to his shoulder. Yet though his clothes were travel-worn and stained the training of Zouga Ballantyne still showed, for they were recently washed and his jaws had been clean shaven that very morning. They looked at each other and the affection between them was tempered and hardened with respect.

'I shot a young buffalo cow, not two hours ago.'

'Yes,' Bazo nodded. 'It was the shot which brought us.'

'Then I am glad of it. The buffalo meat is fat, and there is enough even for a hungry Matabele.'

Bazo glanced at the sun. 'Though I am in haste, on the king's business, my prisoners are in need of rest. We will help you eat your buffalo, Henshaw, but in the dawn we will go on.'

'Then there is much to talk about – and little time to do so.'

There was the pop of a trek-whip, and Bazo glanced beyond Ralph's shoulder to see the oxen come plodding between the trees and the wagon lurching and wallowing behind them.

'You still keep bad company,' Bazo scolded with a grin as he recognized Umfaan at the head of the span and Isazi, the little Zulu, on the flank, 'but the load you carry is welcome.'

From the wagon box hung the raw quarters and shoulders of the freshly-butchered buffalo carcass.

'We have not tasted fresh meat since we left the king's kraal.'

Ralph and Bazo sat at a separate fire apart from their retinues, where they could talk freely.

'The king agreed to buy the guns and bottles that I carried up from Kimberley,' Ralph told Bazo, 'and he paid me generously.'

He did not go on to describe to Bazo the currency in which be had been paid. He did not describe his own astonishment when Lobengula had offered him an uncut diamond, a big bright first-water stone.

His surprise had immediately been tempered by conscience; he had no doubts about where that stone had come from. His conscience lasted about as long as his surprise, and he haggled with gusto, forcing up the price to six stones, which he had picked with an eye trained by many years on the diggings. He knew they would be worth £10,000 when he got them back to civilization.

Thus in a single stroke he had paid for the wagon and team, his entire debt to Diamond Lil – interest and all – and was already many thousands of pounds in profit.

'Then I asked Lobengula to let me hunt elephant, and he laughed and said I was too young and that the elephant would eat me up. He kept me waiting outside his kraal for ten days.'

'If he kept you such a short time, then you have found favour with the king,' Bazo interrupted. 'Some white men have waited from the beginning of the dry season to the middle of the wet, merely for permission to take the road out of Matabeleland.'

'Ten days was long enough for me,' Ralph grunted. 'But when I asked him in which part of his lands I was allowed to hunt, he laughed again and said, "The elephant will be in so little danger from you, Little Hawk, that you may go where you wish, and kill as many as are stupid or lame enough to let you."'

Bazo chuckled delightedly. 'And how many lame stupid elephant have you found so far, Henshaw?'

'I have fifty good tusks in the wagon already.'

'Fifty!' Bazo's chuckles died and he stared at Ralph in amazement; then he stood up and crossed to the wagon. He untied one of the straps and lifted the canvas cover to peer in at the load, while Isazi looked up from his cooking fire, frowned and called to Ralph.

'This boy's great-grandfather, Mashobane, was a thief, his grandfather, Mzilikazi was a traitor – you have every reason to trust him with our ivory, Henshaw.'

Bazo did not look at him, but glanced up into the trees. 'The monkeys hereabout make a frightful chatter,' he murmured, and then came back to Ralph.

'Fine tusks!' he admitted. 'Like the ones the hunters took when I was still a child.'

Ralph did not tell him that most of those in the wagon were taken even before that time. He had discovered all but two of the caches that his father had bequeathed to him.

The ivory had dried out – lost almost a quarter of its green weight; but most of it was still in good condition, and would fetch the market price once he got it to the railhead.

Though Ralph had hunted diligently for his own elephant whilst he sought out Zouga's ancient dumps, he had had little success. He had killed five, only one of which was a bull and whose green tusks had weighed just over sixty pounds. The others had been small female ivory, barely worth taking.

The great herds that Zouga had described in *A Hunter's Odyssey* no longer existed. Since those days there had been many hunters, some of them inspired by Zouga's own writing. Boer and Briton, Hottentot and German, they had hunted and harried the huge grey beasts and left their white bones piled on the veld and in the forest.

'Yes, they are good tusks,' Ralph nodded. 'And my wagon is heavy laden now. I am on the road back to the king's kraal to ask him for permission to leave Matabeleland and go back to Kimberley.'

'Then when you have gone, we will see you no more,' Bazo said quietly. 'You will be like the other white men who come to Matabeleland. You will take what you want, and never come back.'

Ralph laughed. 'No, old friend, I will be back. I do not have everything I wish, not yet. I will come back with more wagons, perhaps six wagons, all loaded with trade goods. I will set up trading posts from the Shashi river to the Zambezi.'

'You will be a rich man, Henshaw. I am sure of it,' Bazo agreed. 'But rich men are not always happy men. This I have remarked often. Is there nothing else in Matabeleland for you but ivory and gold and diamonds?'

Ralph's expression changed. 'How did you know that?' he demanded.

'I asked, I did not know,' Bazo denied, still smiling. 'Though I do not have to throw the bones or look in the magic calabash to know it is a woman – you have suddenly the look of a dog that smells the bitch. Tell me, Henshaw, who is she and when will you take her to wife?' Then he laughed aloud. 'You have not yet asked her father? Or you have asked and he has refused?'

'It is not a matter for laughter,' Ralph said stiffly, and with an effort Bazo wiped the mirth from his face, though it twinkled still in his eyes.

'Forgive one who loves you as a brother, I did not know it was such a heavy matter.' And at last he managed to match Ralph's portentous expression, while he waited for him to speak again.

'Once, long ago, while we rode up in the skip, you spoke of a woman with hair as white and fine as the winter grass,' Ralph said at last, and Bazo nodded.

'It is she, Bazo. I have found her.'

'She wants you as much as you want her?' Bazo said

firmly. 'If she does not, then she is so stupid that she does not deserve you.'

'I haven't asked her yet,' Ralph admitted.

'Do not ask her, tell her, and then ask her father. Show the father your tusks of ivory; that will settle the matter.'

'You are right, Bazo,' Ralph looked dubious. 'It will be that simple.' And then softly in English, so that Bazo could not understand. 'God knows what I shall do if it is not. I don't think I can live without her.'

If he did not follow the words, Bazo understood the sense and the mood. He sighed, and his eyes strayed to Tanase at the cooking fire.

'They are so soft and weak, but they wound more deeply than the sharpest steel.'

Ralph followed his eyes, and then suddenly his own expression cleared and it was his turn to guffaw and reach across to slap Bazo's shoulder.

'Now I recognize the look you spoke of earlier, the dog with the smell of the bitch in his nostrils.'

'It is not a matter for laughter,' said Bazo, haughtily.

Long after the last gnawed buffalo bone was thrown upon the fire and the last beer pot emptied; long after the Matabele warriors had tired of singing the song of Pemba, the ode to their own prowess and courage on the hill of the wizard, and rolled into their sleeping karosses; long after the last captive girl had ceased wailing, Bazo and Ralph sat on beside their own fire – and the drone of their voices and the munch of the oxen chewing the cud were the only sounds in the camp.

It was as though every last moment was precious to them for both sensed that when they met again they would be changed, and perhaps the world with them.

They relived their youth, remembering Scipio, the

falcon, and Inkosikazi, the great spider; they smiled at the stinging memory of the fighting sticks, and Bakela's wrath when Bazo gave him the shattered diamond; they talked of Jordan and Jan Cheroot and Kamuza and all the others – until at last reluctantly Bazo rose.

'I will be gone before the sun, Henshaw,' he said.

'Go in peace, Bazo – and enjoy the honours that await you and the woman you have won.'

When Bazo reached his sleeping-mat, the girl was already wrapped in his kaross.

As soon as Bazo lay down beside her, she reached for him. She was as hot as though she was in high fever – her body burning and her skin dry. Silent sobs racked her and her grip was fierce.

'What is it, Tanase?' He was shocked and alarmed.

'A vision. A terrible vision.'

'A dream.' He was relieved. 'It was only a dream.'

'It was a vision,' she denied. 'Oh, Bazo, will you not take this terrible gift from me, before it destroys us both?'

He held her and could not answer her; her distress moved him deeply, but he was helpless to alleviate it.

After a while she was quiet, and he thought that she slept, but then she suddenly whispered.

'It was a terrible vision, Bazo Lord – and it will haunt me unto my grave.'

He did not answer, but he felt the superstitious chill in his guts.

'I saw you high upon a tree—' She broke off, and another single sob hit her like a blow. 'The white man, the one you call Henshaw, the Hawk – do not trust him.'

'He is as my brother, and like a brother I love him.'

'Then why did he not weep, Bazo, why did he not weep when he looked up at you upon the tree?'

Salina Codrington rolled out her pastry with long and expert strokes of the pin. The sleeves of her blouse were rolled high and she was floury to the elbows. Little blobs of pastry stuck to her hands and fingers.

The thatched ceiling of the kitchen at Khami Mission Station was sooty from the open iron stove, and the smell of the dough was yeasty and warm.

A single skein of white-gold hair had escaped the ribbon and now tickled her nose and chin. Salina pursed her lips and blew it away; it floated like gossamer and then gently settled across her face again, but she did not change the rhythm of the rolling-pin.

Ralph thought that little gesture the most poignant he had ever witnessed, but then everything she did fascinated him – even the way she cocked her head and smiled at him as he slouched against the jamb of the kitchen door.

Her smile was so gentle, so unaffected, that his chest squeezed again, and his voice sounded choked in his own ears.

'I am leaving tomorrow.'

'Yes,' Salina nodded. 'We shall all miss you dreadfully.'

'This is the first chance I have had to speak to you alone, without the monsters—'

'Oh Ralph, that's an unkind, if totally accurate, description of my darling sisters.' Her laughter had a surprising timbre and depth to it. 'If you wanted to speak to me, you should have asked.'

'I'm asking now, Salina.'

'And we are alone.'

'Will you not stop still for a moment?'

'The baking will spoil, but I can listen well enough while I work.'

Ralph shifted his feet, and hunched his shoulders uncertainly. It was not as he had planned it. It was going to be a feat of timing and dexterity to sweep her up in arms all covered with flour and dough and with a heavy rolling-pin clutched in her hands.

'Salina, you are the most beautiful girl – woman – I mean, lady, that I have ever seen.'

'That's kind, but untrue, Ralph. I do have a mirror, you know.'

'It's true, I swear—'

'Please don't swear, Ralph. In any event, there are much more important things in life than physical beauty – kindness, and goodness and understanding, for instance.'

'Oh yes, and you have all those.'

Suddenly Salina stopped in mid stroke, and she stared at him with an expression of dawning consternation.

'Ralph,' she whispered. 'Cousin Ralph—'

'Cousin I may be,' he was stammering slightly in his rush to have it all said, 'but I love you, Salina, I loved you from the first moment I saw you at the river.'

'Oh Ralph, my poor dear Ralph.' Consternation was mingled now with compassion.

'I would never have spoken, not before – but now, after this expedition I have some substance. I will be able to pay off my debts, and when I come back I will have my own wagons. I am not yet rich, but I will be.'

'If only I had known. Oh Ralph, if only I had suspected, I would have been able to—'

But he was gabbling it out now.

'I love you, Salina, oh how dearly I love you, and I want you to marry me.'

She came to him then, and her eyes filled with blue tears that trembled on her lower lids.

'Oh dear Ralph. I am so sorry. I would have given anything to save you from hurt. If only I had known.'

He stopped then, bewildered. 'You will not – does that mean you will not marry me?' The bewilderment faded, and his jaw thrust out and his mouth hardened. 'But why not, I will give you everything, I will cherish and—'

'Ralph.' She touched his lips, and left a little dab of flour upon them. 'Hush, Ralph, hush.'

'But, Salina, I love you! Don't you understand?'

'Yes, I do. But, dear Ralph, I don't love you!'

Cathy and the twins went as far as the river with Ralph. Vicky and Lizzie rode, two up, on Tom's back. They rode astride, with their skirts up around their thighs, and squealed with delight every few seconds, until Ralph thought his eardrums would split, and he scowled moodily ahead – not replying to Cathy's questions and comments as she skipped along beside him, until the spring went out of her step and she, too, fell silent.

The bank of the Khami river was where they would part. All of them knew that, without speaking about it. And when they reached it Isazi had already taken the wagon through the drift. The iron-shod wheels had left deep scars in the far bank. He would be an hour or so ahead. They stopped on the near bank and now even the twins were silent. Ralph looked back along the track, lifting his hat and shading his eyes with the brim against the early sunlight.

'Salina isn't coming then?' he said flatly.

'She's got a belly ache,' said Vicky. 'She told me so.'

'If you ask me, it's more like the curse of Eve,' said Lizzie airily.

'That's rude,' Cathy said. 'And only silly little girls talk about things they don't understand.'

Lizzie looked chastened, and Vicky assumed a virtuous air of innocence.

'Now both of you say goodbye to Cousin Ralph.'

'I love you, Cousin Ralph,' said Vicky, and had to be prised off him like a leech.

'I love you, Cousin Ralph.'

Lizzie had counted the kisses that Vicky had bestowed on him, and she went for a new world record, a noble attempt, but frustrated by Cathy.

'Now, scat,' Cathy told them. 'Go, both of you.'

'Cathy is crying,' said Lizzie, and both twins were immediately entranced.

'I am not,' said Cathy furiously.

'Oh yes you are,' said Vicky.

'I have something in my eye.'

'Both eyes?' asked Lizzie sceptically.

'I warn you,' Cathy told them. They knew that expression of old, and reluctantly they retired just out of range. Cathy turned her back to them so they missed half of what followed.

'They are right.' Her whisper was as blurred as her eyes. 'I am crying, Ralph. I hate so to see you go.'

Ralph had not truly looked at her, not ever, his eyes had been for Salina alone, but now her frank admission touched him and he saw her for the first time.

He had thought her a child, but he had been wrong, he realized suddenly. It was the thick dark eyebrows and the firm chin that gave strength to her face, so that he sensed that anything that made her cry was deeply felt. Surely she had not been so tall when first he met her almost a year before. Now the top of her head reached his chin.

The freckles on her cheeks kept her young, but her nose was set in the shape of maturity and the gaze of her green eyes below the arched brows, though flooded now with tears, was too wise and steady for childhood.

She still wore the muddy green dress of sewn flour sacks, but its fit had altered. Now it was baggy at the waist, while at the same time it was too tight across her chest. Yet it could not suppress the thrust of young firm breasts, and the seams strained across hips that he remembered being as narrow and bony as a boy's.

415

'You will come back, Ralph? Unless you promise, I cannot let you go.'

'I promise,' he said, and suddenly the pain of rejection by Salina, which he had thought might destroy him, was just supportable.

'I will pray for you each day until you do,' Cathy said, and came to kiss him. She no longer felt skinny and awkward in his arms, and Ralph was suddenly very aware of the softness of her against his chest – and lower.

Her mouth had a taste like chewing a stalk of green spring grass. Her lips formed a pillow for his. He had no burning desire to break the embrace, and Cathy also seemed content to let it persist. The pain of unrequited love ebbed a little more to be replaced by a warm and comforting sensation, a most pleasant glow, until with a shock Ralph realized two things.

Firstly, the twins were an avid audience, their eyes enormous and their grins impudent. Secondly, that the pleasant glow which had suffused him had its source considerably lower than his broken heart, and was accompanied by more tangible changes that must soon become apparent to the fresh young innocent in his arms.

He almost shoved her away, and vaulted up onto Tom's back with unnecessary violence. However, when he looked down at Cathy again, the tide of green tears in her eyes had receded and been replaced by a look of satisfaction, a knowingness that proved beyond doubt what he had just come to realize, that she was no longer a child.

'How long?' she asked.

'Not before the end of the rains,' he told her. 'Six or seven months from now.' And suddenly that seemed to Ralph to be a very long time indeed.

'Anyway,' she said. 'I have your promise.'

On the far bank of the river he looked back. The twins had lost interest and started home. They were racing each other down the track, skirts and plaits flying – but Cathy still stood staring after him. Now she lifted her hand and waved. She kept waving until horse and rider disappeared amongst the trees.

Then she sat down on a log beside the track. The sun made its noon and then sank into the misty smoke of the bush fires that blued the horizon and turned to a soft red orb that she could look at directly without paining her eyes.

In the gloaming a leopard sawed and hacked harshly from the dense dark riverine forest nearby. Cathy shivered and stood up. She cast one last lingering glance across the wide river bed and then at last she turned for home.

B azo could not sleep; hours ago he had left his sleeping-mat and come to squat by the fire in the centre of the hut. The others had not even stirred when he moved, Zama and Kamuza and Mondane, those who would accompany him tomorrow.

Their finery was piled beside their recumbent figures. The cloaks of feathers and furs and beads, the headdresses and kilts – the regalia reserved for only the most grave and momentous occasions – like the Festival of the First Fruits, or a personal report to the king, or, again, the ceremony for which they had gathered and which would start at the dawn of the morrow.

Bazo looked at them now, and his chest felt congested with his joy, joy so intense that it sang in his ears and fizzed in his blood. Joy even more intense in that these his companions of the years, with whom he had shared boyhood and youth and now manhood, would be there again at one of the most important days of his life.

Now Bazo sat alone at the fire while his companions snored and muttered in sleep, and he took each coin of his good fortune and, like a miser counting his treasure, fondled it with his mind, turning each memory over and gloating upon it.

He lived again every moment of his triumph when the lines of captive women had filed before Lobengula and piled the spoils in front of his wagon, the bars and coils of red copper, the axe heads, the leather bags of salt, the clay pots full of beads, for Pemba had been a famous wizard and had gathered his tribute from a host of fearful clients.

Lobengula had smiled when he saw his treasure, for that was what had been at the root of his feud with Pemba. The king was not above the jealousies of common men. When Lobengula smiled, all his indunas smiled in sympathy and made those little clucking sounds of approval.

Bazo remembered how the king had called him forward, and smiled again when Bazo emptied the bag he carried over his shoulder, and the wizard's head, which by then was in an advanced state of decomposition, had rolled to the forewheel of the wagon and grinned up at Lobengula with ruined lips drawn back from uneven teeth stained by the hemp pipe.

A troop of the gaunt, mange-ridden pariah dogs that skulked about the king's kraal had come to snarl and squabble over the morsel, and when one of the black-cloaked executioners would have scattered them with blows of his knobkerrie, the king restrained him.

'The poor beasts are hungry, let them be.' And he turned back to Bazo. 'Tell me how it was done.'

Bazo relived in his mind every word with which he had described the expedition, and while he told it he had begun to *giya*, to dance and sing the ode to Pemba which he had composed:

'Like a mole in the earth's gut
Bazo found the secret way—'

He sang, and in the front row of the senior indunas, Gandang, his father, sat grave and proud.

> 'Like the blind catfish
> that live in the caves of Sinoia
> Bazo swam through darkness—'

Then as the verses of the song mentioned them, Zama and his warriors sprang forward to whirl and dance at his side.

> 'Like the black mamba from under a stone
> Zama milked death from his silver fang—'

When the triumph dance was over, they threw themselves face down on the earth in front of the wagon.

'Bazo, son of Gandang, go out and choose two hundred head from the royal herds,' said Lobengula.

'*Bayete!*' shouted Bazo, still panting from the dance.

'Bazo, son of Gandang – you who commanded fifty so skilfully – now I give you one thousand to command.'

'*Nkosi!* Lord!'

'You will command the levy of young men waiting now at the royal kraal on the Shangani river. I give you the insignia for your new regiment. Your shields will be red, your kilts the tails of the genet cat, your plumes the wing feathers of the marabou stork, and your headband the fur of the burrowing mole,' Lobengula intoned, and then paused. 'The name of your regiment will be Izimvukuzane Ezembintaba – the moles that burrow under a mountain.'

'*Nkosi kakhula!* Great King!' Bazo roared.

'Now Bazo, rise up and go into the women to choose yourself a wife. Be sure that she is virtuous and fruitful, and let her first duty be to set the headring of the induna on your brow.'

'*Indhlovu! Ngi ya bonga!* Great Elephant, I praise you!'

Sitting his solitary watch by the fire, Bazo remembered every word, every change of tone, every pause and emphasis that the king had used to heap his honours upon him. He sighed with contentment and placed another log upon the fire, carefully so as not to wake his companions, and the sparks floated up through the opening in the highest point of the domed roof.

Then a distant sound interrupted his reverie; it was the single whoop of a hyena, not an unusual sound except that it was the first time that he had heard it since nightfall. On every other night the hideous cries of these loathsome animals began when they crept from their burrows at dusk and continued until sunrise.

They haunted the small woody copse beyond the cattle enclosure that all the inhabitants of Gandang's kraal used as a communal open-air latrine. They hyena cleansed the area of excrement during the hours of darkness. For this reason, Gandang's people tolerated the presence of an animal that they usually abhorred with a superstitious dread.

So tonight the single whooping cry at midnight drew attention to the silence that had preceded it. Bazo listened a few seconds longer and then let his thoughts stray to the morrow.

After the king, Gandang was one of the three most important personages in Matabeleland – only Somabula and Babiaan were his peers, so that a marriage at his kraal would have been a momentous event even if it were not his eldest son – himself a newly appointed induna of one thousand – who was to be the bridegroom.

Juba, senior wife of Gandang, and mother of Bazo the bridegroom, had supervised the brew of beer, watching with an expert eye for the bloom of yeast on the germinating sorghum, testing with her own plump finger the temperature of the ground meal gruel as it was malted, judging the addition of the final booster of yeast and then standing over the matrons as they strained the brewing through woven bamboo sieves into the huge black clay beer-pots. Now there were a thousand pots each holding half a gallon of her famous brew, ready to greet the guests as they arrived at Gandang's kraal. There would be a thousand invited guests.

Lobengula and his retinue were already on the road; they were sleeping tonight at the regimental kraal of the Intemba regiment, only five miles distant, and they would arrive before noon.

Somabula was with the king, while Babiaan was coming in from his kraal in the east with a hundred warriors in his bodyguard. Nomusa and Hlopi were coming from the mission station at Khami as Juba's special guests, and they were bringing all their daughters with them.

Gandang had picked fifty fat bullocks from his herds, and the bridegroom and his young companions would begin to slaughter and butcher them in the dawn – while the unmarried girls took the bride down to the river pool, bathed her and then anointed her with fat and clay until she glistened in the early sunlight. Then they would deck her with wild flowers.

The hyena called again much closer this time, sounding as if it were right outside the stockade – and then a strange thing happened. The single cry was answered by a chorus, as though a great multitude of the huge shaggy spotted dog-like beasts had surrounded Gandang's kraal.

Bazo started up from the fire in astonishment. He had never heard anything to equal this – there must be a hundred or more of the ungainly animals out there. He could imagine them, their high shoulders sloping down to meagre hindquarters, the flat snake-like heads held low as though the weight of massive underslung jaw and yellow carnassial teeth was too heavy for the neck.

One hundred at least, he could almost smell their breath

as they opened those iron jaws, capable of crunching the thigh bone of a bull buffalo to splinters. They would reek of long-dead carrion and excrement and other filth, but it was the sound of their voices that chilled Bazo's guts and started the march of ghost feet along his spine.

It was as though all the souls of the dead had risen from their graves to clamour outside Gandang's stockade. They whooped and howled, beginning in a low moan and rising sharply in key.

'Oooh – wee!'

They shrieked like the ghost of a Mashona feeling again the steel cleave his breast, and the terrible cries woke the echoes amongst the kopjes along the river.

Almost humanly, they giggled, and they laughed – that maniacal and mirthless laughter. The peals of fiendish laughter mingled with the tormented shrieks, and then with them were the cries of the kraal's watchmen, the screeches of the waking women in their huts, the shouts of the men, still half-asleep, as they scrambled for their weapons.

'Do not go out,' Kamuza shouted across the hut as Bazo sprang to the door with his shield on his shoulder and his assegai in his right hand. 'Do not go into the dark, this is a witchcraft. Those are not animals out there.'

His words stopped Bazo at the threshold. There was nothing of flesh and blood he would not face, but this—

The fiendish chorus reached a climax, and then abruptly ceased. The silence that followed was even more chilling, and Bazo shrank away from the door. His companions crouched on their sleeping-mats, weapons in their hands, their eyes wide and white in the firelight – but not one of them moved towards the door.

All of Gandang's kraal was awake now, but silent, waiting, the women creeping away into the farthest recesses of their huts and covering their heads with their fur karosses, the men frozen with superstitious terror.

The silence lasted the time it would take for a man to run the full circle of the stockade, and then was broken by the call of a single hyena, the same whooping cry, starting low and rising to a shriek. The head of every one of the warriors in Bazo's hut lifted, and they all stared upwards to the roof and the star-pricked sky above it – for that was from where the ghostly cry emanated – from the very air high above Gandang's kraal.

'Sorcery.' Kamuza's voice shook, and Bazo choked down on the wail of terror that rose in his own throat.

As the animal cry died in the night, there was only one other sound. The voice of a young girl, raised in terrible distress.

'Bazo! Help me, Bazo!'

It was the only thing that could have roused him. Bazo shook himself like a dog that leaps from water to land, throwing off the terror that paralysed him.

'Do not go!' Kamuza yelled, after him. 'It is not the girl, it is a witch voice.'

But Bazo tore the locking bar from the door.

He saw her immediately. Tanase raced towards him from the women's quarters, from Juba's own great hut where she had been passing the last night before her nuptials.

Her dark naked body was without substance, like a moon shadow as she sped to him. Bazo leaped towards her, and they met in front of the main gate of the stockade, and Tanase clung to him.

No other person had left the huts; the kraal was deserted, the fearful silence oppressive. Bazo lifted his shield to cover both himself and the girl – and instinctively he turned to face the gateway. It was only then that he realized that the gate was open.

He tried to retreat towards the hut, taking the girl with him, but she was rigid in his arms, rooted to the earth like the stump of a wild ebony tree – and his own strength was sapped by terror.

'Bazo,' Tanase whispered. 'It is them, they have come.'

As she spoke the watch-fire beside the gate, which had long ago burned down to ash and charred logs, suddenly burst into flame once again. The flames sprang higher than a man's head, roaring like a waterfall, and the stockade and gateway were lit brightly by the yellow dancing light. Beyond the open gateway, at the very edge of the firelight stood a human figure. It was the figure of a very old man, with stick-like limbs and bowed back; his cap of hair was white as the salt from the Makarikari pan; his skin was grey and dusty with age. The whites of his eyes flashed as they squinted and rolled upwards into his skull, and glassy strings of spittle dribbled from his toothless mouth onto his chest, wetting the dry parchment skin through which each skeletal rib stood out clearly.

His voice was a quavering ancient squeal.

'Tanase!' he called. 'Tanase, daughter of the spirits.'

In the firelight all life went out of Tanase's eyes; they became blank.

'Do not heed—' Bazo croaked, but a bluish sheen appeared over Tanase's eyeballs like the nictitating membrane that covers the eye of a shark or the cataract of tropical ophthalmia, and blindly her head turned towards the spectral figure beyond the gates.

'Tanase, your destiny calls you!'

She broke out of Bazo's arms. It seemed to require no effort. He could not hold her. Her strength was superhuman.

She began to walk towards the gateway, and when Bazo tried to follow her, he found he could not lift a foot. He dropped his shield, and it clattered on the hard earth, but Tanase did not look back. She walked with a floating grace, light as river mist towards the ancient stooped figure.

'Tanase!' Bazo's voice was a despairing cry, and he fell upon his knees, yearning after her.

The old man held out one hand, and Tanase took it,

and as she did so, the watch-fire died down as abruptly as it had flared, and the darkness beyond the gateway was instantly impenetrable.

'Tanase!' whispered Bazo, his arms outstretched – and far away, down by the river the hyena called one last time.

The twins came pelting into the church, tumbling over each other with eagerness to be the first to tell.

'Mama! Mama!—'

'Vicky, I saw first, let me!'

Robyn Codrington looked up from the black body stretched on the table and quelled them with a frown.

'Ladies don't push.'

They came up in a parody of demureness, but hopping with impatience.

'Very well, Vicky. What is it?'

They began together, and Robyn stopped them again.

'I said Vicky.'

And Victoria puffed up importantly.

'There is someone coming.'

'From Thabas Indunas?' Robyn asked.

'No, Mama, from the south.'

'It's probably one of the king's messengers.'

'No, Mama, it's a white man on a horse.'

Robyn's interest quickened; she would never have admitted even to herself how often the isolation palled. A white traveller would mean news, perhaps letters, stores and supplies, or even the most precious of all, books. Failing those treasures there would be the mere mental stimulation of a strange face and of conversation and ideas.

She was tempted to leave the patient on the table, it was not a serious burn, but she checked herself.

'Tell Papa I shall come directly,' she said, and the twins

fled, jammed in the doorway for a moment, and then popped through like a cork from a champagne bottle.

By the time Robyn had finished dressing the burn, dismissed the patient, washed her hands and hurried out onto the porch of the church – the stranger was coming up the hill.

Clinton was leading the mule on which he was mounted. It was a big strong-looking grey animal, so the rider looked small and slim upon the broad back. He was a lad, dressed in an old tweed jacket and a boy's cloth cap. The twins danced on each side of the mule, and Clinton at its head was looking back over his shoulder, listening to something that the stranger was saying.

'Who is it, Mama?' Salina came out of the kitchen and called across the yard.

'We shall find out in a moment.'

Clinton led the mule to the porch, and the rider's head was on a level with Robyn's.

'Dr Ballantyne, your grandfather, Dr Moffat, sent me to you, I have letters and gifts from him for you.'

With a start Robyn realized that under the patched tweed coat and cap was a woman – and even in that moment of surprise she was aware that it was an extraordinarily handsome woman, younger than Robyn herself, not much over thirty years of age, with steady, dark eyes and almost Mongolian cheekbones.

She jumped down from the mule with the agility of an expert horsewoman, and came up the steps of the porch to seize Robyn's hands. Her grip was firm as a man's, and her expression was intense.

'My husband is ill and suffering. Dr Moffat says you are the only one who can help him. Will you do it? Oh please, will you?'

'I am a doctor.' Robyn gently twisted her fingers out of the other woman's painful grip – but it was not that which troubled her – there was something too intense, too passionate about her. 'I am a doctor, and I could never refuse to help anyone who is suffering. Of course, I shall do whatever I can.'

'Do you promise that?' the woman insisted, and Robyn bridled slightly.

'I have said I will help, there is no need to promise.'

'Oh, thank you.' The woman smiled with relief.

'Where is your husband?'

'Not far behind. I rode ahead to warn you – and to make sure that you would help us.'

'What is it that ails your husband?'

'Dr Moffat has explained it all in a letter. He sent gifts for you also.' The woman was evasive, turning away from Robyn's scrutiny and running back to the mule.

From the saddle-bags she lifted down two packages, wrapped in oilskin to protect them against the elements and bound up with rawhide thongs. They were so heavy and bulky that Clinton took them from her and carried them into the church.

'You are tired,' Robyn said. 'I am sorry I cannot offer you coffee, we used the last a month ago – but a glass of lemonade?'

'No.' The woman shook her head decidedly. 'I shall go back immediately, to be with my husband – but we shall arrive before nightfall.'

She ran back, and vaulted lightly to the mule's back. None of them had ever seen a woman do that.

'Thank you,' she repeated, and then trotted out of the yard, back down the hill.

Clinton came out of the church and put one arm around Robyn's shoulders.

'What a very beautiful and unusual woman,' he said, and Robyn nodded. That was one of the things that had troubled her. Robyn mistrusted beautiful women.

'What is her name?' she asked.

'I didn't have a chance to ask.'

'You were too busy looking, perhaps,' Robyn suggested tartly, and wriggled out from under his arm and went back into the church, while Clinton stared after her with a rueful expression.

After a moment he made a move as if to follow her – but then sighed and shook his head. It was always as well to let Robyn come round on her own, coaxing only angered her even more unreasonably.

I n the quiet of the church Robyn untied the first package, and unpacked the contents onto the table.

There were five heavy bottles with glass stoppers, and she read the labels as she lifted out each one.

'Carbolic Acid.'

'Alum.'

'Quicksilver.'

'Iodine.'

And then the fifth bottle was labelled:

'Trichloromethane.'

'Bless you, Grandfather.' She smiled delightedly – but still she unstoppered the last bottle and sniffed cautiously at the mouth to confirm her good fortune.

The pungent sweet odour was unmistakable. Chloroform was to her more precious than her own life's blood; she would gladly have exchanged drop for drop.

Her own last supply had been exhausted months before and the London Missionary Society was as parsimonious as ever with its stores. She wished she had retained just a few hundred guineas of her enormous book royalties to enable her to purchase her own medicines rather than having to plead for them with the secretary in London by a correspondence which often took twelve months each way.

Sometimes, in a flagrantly unchristian manner, she wished she could have that bloodless myopic little man at her side when she removed an eye damaged by a blow with a knobkerrie and hanging out of its socket onto a black cheek, or when she went for a Caesarean section – all without anaesthetic.

She hugged the bottle to her chest for a moment.

'Darling Grandfather,' she repeated, then as reverently as if it were the fabulous Kohinoor diamond, she set the bottle of colourless but precious fluid aside, and turned to the second package.

A roll of newspapers – *The Cape Times* and *The Diamond Fields Advertiser*. In the weeks ahead every column would be read and re-read, down to the announcements of auction sales and the legal notices; then the newsprint itself would be used for a dozen domestic chores. Under the newspaper – books, wonderful fat leather-bound books.

'Bless you, Robert Moffat.'

She lifted out a translation of Ibsen's *An Enemy of the People*. She admired the Norwegian for his insight into the human mind, and the muted poetry of his prose. Robert Louis Stevenson's *Virginibus Puerisque*; the title made her pause. She had four virgins in her household, and she intended maintaining that happy condition without allowing any inflammatory literature to thwart her. She flipped through the book. Despite the dubious title, it was merely a collection of essays – and the man was a good Calvinistic Scot. It might just do to let the girls read it, but she would vet it first.

Then there was Mark Twain's *Tom Sawyer*. Here she was less sanguine. She had heard of this American's frivolous and irreverent attitude towards adolescence, industry and filial duty. She would read it carefully before letting it anywhere near Salina or Catherine. Reluctantly she left the other books for future study and turned to her grandfather's letter.

There were many pages, written with sooty home-made ink, and the script was shaky and wavering. She skimmed swiftly through the salutations and the personal news until she reached the middle of the second page:

Robyn, they say a doctor buries his mistakes: blatantly untrue. I send mine to you. The patient who delivers this letter should long ago have sought the sanctuary of a modern hospital, such as that at Kimberley.

This he has steadfastly refused to do. His reasons are his own, and I have not pried. However, the fact that for over a year now he has had a pistol ball lodged in his body may point to his motives.

Twice I have cut for this foreign body, but at 87 years of age my eyes are not as bright nor my hand as steady as yours. Each time I have failed and I fear that I have done more harm than good.

I know that you have interest and skill in treatment of this type of injury, as so you should, for you have been provided by young Lobengula's warriors with endless opportunity to practise your technique. I recall with admiration your inspired reintroduction of the spoon of Diokles, after nearly 2,000 years, which you designed from the contemporary description by Celsus – and your successful removal of barbed arrowheads with it.

Thus I send you one more subject on which to demonstrate your art – and with him my last bottle of Chloroform; for the poor fellow – whatever his sins – has suffered enough under my knife.

The letter left her with a sense of foreboding – as did the woman who had delivered it. She folded the letter and thrust it into the pocket of her skirt as she left the church and hurried across the yard.

'Cathy,' she called. 'Where is that girl! She must set the guest-house to rights.'

'She's gone to it already, Mama.' Salina looked up as she stormed into the kitchen.

'Then where is your father?'

Within an hour the mission station was prepared to receive guests, and buzzing with anticipation; but they had to wait until mid-afternoon before a two-wheeled cart of unusually high and heavy construction appeared over the rise before the river. It was drawn by a pair of mules.

The entire family assembled on the front porch of the main building, and all of them had changed their clothing, while the girls had also brushed and dressed their hair with ribbons. A dozen times the twins had to be cautioned for improper comments and unrestrained behaviour, but finally the cart wheeled into the yard.

The woman had put her mule into the traces and now she walked beside the wheel of the cart, which reached almost as high as her head. There was a coloured servant in ragged cast-off clothes leading the mules, and over the body of the cart was rigged a makeshift sunshade of saplings and stained canvas.

Below the porch the cart stopped, and all of them craned forward as a man's head and upper body appeared above its side. He was laid on a straw mattress on the floor of the cart, and now he lifted himself on one elbow.

He was a gaunt wasted figure; the flesh seemed to have melted from the big bones of his shoulders. His cheeks had fallen in and turned a muddy yellow, the hand on the side of the cart was bony, and the veins were roped under the skin like blue serpents. His hair bushed wildly about his head, coarse dark hair that was shot through with strands of dead white. He had not shaved in days; thick stubble covered his jaws and was salted with the same white as his hair. One eye was sunk into a bruised cavity, and it had that feverish glitter that Robyn recognized instantly. It was the look of mortal illness.

The other eye was covered by a black piratical patch. There was something dreadfully familiar about the big aquiline nose and the wide mouth – yet it was only when he smiled that old mocking yet somehow tender smile that she had never forgotten that Robyn reeled backwards, one hand flying to her mouth too late to stop her cry.

She caught for support at one of the mopani poles that held the roof.

'Mama, are you all right?' But Robyn pushed Salina's hands away and went on staring at the man in the cart.

Only one memory out of so many rose up like a freak wave out of a storm-swept sea to overwhelm her. She saw again that dark bush of curls, devoid only of its silver lacing, bowing to her naked bosom. She saw above her the beamed roof of the great cabin in the stern-quarters of the slave ship *Huron*, and she remembered as she had a thousand times in the twenty years since then – that pain. The deep splitting incursion that rocked her. Four child-births since then had not eradicated the memory of it, the agony of passing from maiden to woman.

Her senses wavered, there was a rushing in her ears, she was going to fall, but then Clinton's voice steadied her. The hard fierce tone of it which she had not heard in years.

'You!' he said.

As Clinton drew himself erect, the years seemed to fall away from him. He was once again tall and lithe, stiff with anger as the young Royal Naval officer who had come up onto the slaver's quarter-deck with pistols and a naval cutlass on his hip to confront this same man.

Still clinging to the verandah pole, Robyn remembered the words he had spoken then in that same fierce tone:

'Captain Mungo St John, your reputation precedes you, sir. The first trader ever to transport more than three thousand souls across the middle passage in a single twelve-month period – I'd give five years' pay to have the hatches off your holds, sir.'

Robyn remembered then how it had taken another year for Clinton to get his wish, when off Good Hope he had

432

come back onto *Huron*'s decks, boarding her over the stern in the cannon smoke with his fighting seamen at his back, and how this action had cost him more than a mere five years' pay. He had been court martialled and cashiered from the Royal Navy and imprisoned for it.

'You dare to come here, to us.' Clinton was pale with rage; his blue eyes, so gentle for so long, were bleak and hating. 'You, you cruel and bloody slaver, you dare to come here.'

Mungo St John was still smiling, taunting him with that smile and the glitter in his single eye, but his voice was low and rough with his suffering.

'And you, you kind and sainted Christian gentleman, do you dare to turn me away?'

Clinton flinched as though he had been struck across the face, and he took a step backwards. Slowly the litheness and youth went out of his stance, his shoulders slumped into their habitual stoop. He shook his bald head uncertainly, and then instinctively he turned towards Robyn.

With a huge effort Robyn gathered herself, pushed away from the supporting pole. Despite the turmoil of her emotions she managed to keep her expression neutral.

'Dr Ballantyne,' Louise St John came to the steps of the verandah. She took the cap from her head, and the thick black plait tumbled out from under it.

'I find it difficult to beg,' she said. 'But I am begging now.'

'That is not necessary, madam. I gave you my word.' Robyn turned away. 'Clinton, please help Mrs St John to put this patient into the bed in the guest-house.'

'Yes, dear.'

'I shall be there directly to make an examination.'

'Thank you, Doctor, oh thank you.' Robyn ignored Louise, but when she had followed the mule cart across the yard to the guest-hut, she turned to face her daughters.

'None of you – not even you, Salina – will go near the

guest-house while that man is here. You will not speak to him or the woman, you will not answer if they speak to you. You will do your best to avoid seeing either of them, and if you do by error find yourself in their presence, you will leave immediately.'

The twins were quivering with excitement, their eyes shone, and even their ears seemed to be pink and pricked like those of a pair of young bunny rabbits. They could not remember a day so wildly exciting.

'Why?' gasped Vicky, forgetting herself sufficiently in this incredible series of events to question her mother's order. For a moment it seemed that she would have to pay for the impertinence with a box on one pink ear, but Robyn's hand dropped back to her side.

'Because—' Robyn said softly, ' – because he is the devil – the very devil.'

H e was propped on the iron cot, with a bolster under his shoulders, and Louise rose from the other cot as Robyn entered the guest-hut carrying her bag.

'Madam, will you kindly wait outside,' Robyn ordered brusquely and, not deigning to see if she would obey, Robyn placed her bag on the chair beside his cot. Behind her the latch on the door clicked.

Mungo St John wore only a pair of baggy white trousers from which one leg had been hacked off high in the thigh. Like his face, his body was wasted by sickness, but there was still the width of shoulder and the solidity of bone that she remembered so well. His belly had sunk in like that of a greyhound, and his ribs stood out in a rack above it, but his skin retained the texture and silkiness of a far younger man, while the body hair that was crimped into curls upon his chest was not marred with silver as was his beard and the hair upon his head.

'Hello, Robyn,' he said.

'I will speak to you only when it is absolutely necessary for your treatment, and you will do the same,' she said, without looking at his face.

She started with the wounds in his flank and back – bullet wounds, she realized, but through and through – and completely healed. Then with a little start she noticed the other old, long-healed scar just below the bullet wound.

She recognized the little white pricks of the suture which had closed the knife-cut. Her own work was distinctive, there was nobody who could throw down those even and precise knotted sutures as she could, and before she realized what she was doing she touched the old hardened cicatrice.

'Yes,' Mungo nodded. 'Camacho made that.'

She jerked her hand away. Mungo had taken that knife-cut when he had intervened to protect her from the Portuguese slaver. He had saved her life that night.

'Do you remember this also?' Mungo asked, and showed her the pock mark on his forearm. That was where she had inoculated him when smallpox had swept through *Huron*.

'Do you remember?' Mungo insisted softly, but she kept her face averted and her lips compressed in a thin hard line as she lifted the dressing from his upper leg.

Then the horror showed on her face. Her grandfather's uneven knife strokes had lacerated the leg from knee to groin, where he had probed and searched for the ball, and his crude stitches had cobbled it all back together like a man repacking a valise in haste.

'Bad?' Mungo asked.

'It's a mess,' she said, and then hated herself for unbending that far, and by inference criticizing her grandfather's work.

435

The flesh of the leg had that unhealthy putty colour, and there was ulceration in the wounds, that awful slough-ing of tissue that hinted at the corruption beneath.

Her grandfather had left drains in the wounds, thick black horse hairs that stuck stiffly out between the stitches. She drew one now, and Mungo gasped but did not flinch. A weak little trickle of watery pus followed the hair out. She stooped and sniffed it and grimaced. This was not the rich creamy pus that the ancients had called '*pus bonum et laudabile*'. From the stink of it, gangrene was not far off. She felt a little icy splinter of dread, and immediately wondered at it; surely there were no feelings left in her for this man.

'Tell me how it happened.'

'That, doctor, is my business.'

'Dirty business, I have no doubt,' she snapped. 'And I want no lurid account of it, but if I am to locate the ball I must know where you were in relationship to the weapon that was fired at you, the type of weapon, the weight and charge—'

'Of course,' he said quickly. 'Your grandfather did not bother to enquire.'

'Leave my grandfather out of it.'

'The man used a pistol; it looked like a single-action Remington army model, in which case the ball would be .44, of lead, cone-shaped, weight one fifty grains, and driven by black powder.'

'Low penetration, break up of the ball if it hit bone,' she muttered.

'The man was lying on the ground, about twenty-five paces distant, and I was in the act of dismounting from my horse, this leg raised—'

'He was ahead of you.'

'Slightly ahead and on my right hand.'

Robyn nodded. 'This will hurt.' And ten minutes later she stood back and called, 'Mrs St John.'

As soon as Louise entered, she said, 'I shall operate as soon as the light is good enough tomorrow morning. I shall need your assistance. I warn you now that even if I am successful, your husband will not recover full use of the leg. He will always have a pronounced limp.'

'And if you are unsuccessful?'

'The degeneration will accelerate, mortification and gangrene—'

'You are frank, doctor,' Louise whispered.

'Yes,' Robyn agreed. 'I always am.'

Robyn could not sleep, but she reminded herself that she seldom could on the eve of an operation under anaesthetic. Chloroform was such an unpredictable substance, the margins of safety were frighteningly narrow, overdosage, too high a concentration or inadequate oxygenation, would lead to primary collapse with fatal depression of the heart, lungs, liver and kidneys.

She lay beside Clinton in the darkness and ran through a mental list of her preparations for the morrow, and set her mind on the procedures she must adopt. Firstly she must re-open and find the source of the mortification. She moved and Clinton stirred beside her and muttered in his sleep. She froze and waited for him to settle.

The distraction altered the direction of her thoughts, and she found she was thinking about the man and not the patient. For a while she tried to prevent it, and then gave in.

She remembered him on his quarter-deck, the white linen shirt open to the throat and his chest hair curling out of the V, his head thrown back to hail the masthead, the thick dark mane of his hair rippling in the wind.

Then suddenly she remembered that morning when she slipped out of her cabin and stepped out onto *Huron's* main-deck. He had been under the deck pump, while two seamen worked the handles, and clear sea water hissed over him as he stood naked under the jet. She remembered his body and the way he smiled at her without attempting to cover it from her gaze. Then abruptly she remembered his eyes, those flecked yellow eyes above her in the gloom of the cabin, eyes like those of a leopard.

She moved again, and this time Clinton came half awake. He said her name and threw one arm across her at the level of her waist. For a while she lay quiescent under his arm and then slowly she reached down and drew up the hem of her nightdress. She took Clinton's wrist lightly and guided his hand downwards. She felt him come fully awake, heard his breathing change and his hand went on without her insistence.

Long ago she had learned, painfully, that there were limits to the restraint that she could exercise over her unruly sensuality. So now she closed her eyes, relaxed her limbs and let her imagination run unchecked.

She drank only a cup of the hot coffee substitute that she had concocted of roasted sorghum and wild honey – and while she did so she composed her mind by glancing through her notes.

She always found comfort in Celsus' injunctions, somehow the fact that they were written around the time of Christ made them more poignant.

Now a surgeon, the *chirurgus*, should be youthful or at any rate closer to youth than age, with a strong and steady hand that never trembles, ready to use left hand as well as right, with vision sharp and clear and spirit undaunted . . .

Then there was Galen, the surgeon of the gladiators, the Roman who had stored all his experience in twenty-two volumes. Robyn had read them in the original Greek, and extracted the pearls of his genius, which she had used with great success in treating the gladiatorial-type wounds of Lobengula's young men. Though she had substituted alum for corn, iodine for pigeon dung, and carbolic acid for lamp black and oil in the fight against inflammation and mortification.

The kind of trauma that faced her now as she bowed over the long table in the church was much like those described by Galen, though caused by a different projectile. Mungo St John's hoarse, muffled breathing was the only sound in the quiet church. Robyn tested the depth of his coma by pricking his finger with a probe, and then immediately lifted the mask of plaited bamboo and lint from his nose and mouth.

Then she listened to his breathing as it eased, and found herself examining his face as she had not been able to while he was conscious. He was still a handsome man, despite the missing eye and marks of pain and of advancing age etched into his face. Louise St John had borrowed Clinton's straight razor the previous day. Mungo St John was clean-shaven now, and suddenly she realized that the new lines in his face and the silver wings above his temples accentuated the power of the man, while at the same time the relaxation of his mouth gave him a childlike innocence which made the breath catch in her throat.

Clinton looked across at her, and she turned her face away quickly before he could see her expression.

'Are you ready, madam?' Robyn made her voice cold and businesslike, and Louise nodded. She was very pale, the fine freckles standing out in sharp contrast on her cheeks and the bridge of her nose.

Still Robyn hesitated. She knew that she was squandering

the moments during which the chloroform was having its blessed effect, but she was seized by a terrible dread. For the first time in her life she was afraid to wield the knife, and a thought transfixed her.

'If you once love a man, can you ever cease entirely to do so?'

She dared not look again at Mungo St John's sleeping face; she felt she must turn and run from the church.

'Are you unwell, doctor?' Louise St John's concern steeled her. She would not let this woman suspect weakness in her.

The leg was painted dark yellow brown with tincture of iodine. It looked like a rotten banana. She snipped her grandfather's stitches and the wound fell open. She saw the depth of the ulceration, and knew from dreadful experience that a wound like this would never heal, even by second intention. Her main task was not to find the pistol ball but to repair this damage.

She went in deeper, down past the thick pulsing snake of the femoral artery, down to the bone, the bared femur, and again she felt her spirits quail. The bone was mal-formed, yellow and cheesy.

She guessed at the cause, this was where the pistol ball had struck and been deflected away. It had struck a long splinter of bone off the femur, and she picked something out of the dead stinking tissue with the forceps and held it up to the light from the window.

It was a flake of black lead. She dropped it into the bucket under the table and bent once more over the open chasm in Mungo's flesh. There was hardly any blood, a few drops only from the stitches, and the rest of it was slimy yellow matter smelling like a corpse.

She knew the risks of attempting to remove this decom-posing tissue surgically; she had tried it before – and killed in the process. It was drastic treatment which only a very strong man could survive, yet if she closed up, the macabre spectre of gangrene lurked close at hand.

She took up the scraper and it rasped over the exposed bone of the femur. Stinking pus welled up from out of the bone itself. Osteomyelitis, the mortification of the bony tissue. She worked at it grimly, the scraper was the only sound in the room until Louise St John choked.

'Madam, if you are going to throw up – please leave,' Robyn told her, without looking up.

'I shall be all right,' Louise whispered.

'Then use the swab as I instructed you,' Robyn snapped.

The rotten bone came away, curling off the blade in little yellow whorls like wood shavings from the carpenter's plane, until Robyn reached the porous core – and at last clean bright blood came up through it like wine from a sea sponge that had been squeezed, and the bone around the hole was hard and white as china.

Robyn sighed with relief, and at the same moment Mungo groaned and would have twitched the leg if Clinton had not been holding it at the ankle. Swiftly Robyn replaced the little bamboo basket over his nose and mouth then let a few drops of chloroform fall on the lint covering.

She cut away the rotten ulcerations, working perilously close to the artery and the white cord of the femoral nerve. She found more pockets of sepsis around the sutures with which her grandfather had closed the blood vessels. She cleaned these out and carefully cut away dead tissue.

There was blood now, plenty of it, but clean bright blood. Robyn had reached the most critical stage of the reparative surgery. She knew that there was still infection amongst the healthy tissue and as soon as she closed the wound it would blossom again.

She had mixed the antiseptic the night before, one part of carbolic acid to one hundred parts of rainwater. With this she washed out the open pit in Mungo's leg, and the astringent action of the mixture dried up the weeping blood from the vessels too small to tie off.

She could come out now, and sew up. She had left foreign bodies in before, and often they stabilized and became encysted, causing the patient little further discomfort, but instinct warned her not to do so this time.

She glanced at Clinton's big silver hunter watch, which he had placed beside her instrument case where she could see it readily. She had been in for twenty-five minutes, and experience had taught her that the longer she stayed in the greater the danger of primary or secondary collapse.

She looked up at Louise St John. She was still very pale, but the sweat of nausea had dried on her forehead. She had grit, Robyn conceded grudgingly, and that was one thing she could admire – much more than her exotic beauty.

'Madam, I am about to go after the ball now,' she said. 'I shall only have time for one attempt.'

She knew from Lister's writing and her own observation how risky it was to use her bare hands in a wound – but that risk was preferable to leading with a sharp instrument into the nest of veins, arteries and nerves in the groin.

She had guessed the location of the ball by the restricted movement of the femur within its pelvic socket, and by the focus of intense pain when she had palpated the area while Mungo was conscious. She probed with her forefinger, boldly up into the tissue above the raw scraped area of the bone. The direction of the shot, from ahead and upwards, must be on this line.

She met resistance and tried again, and then again. Suddenly her finger slid into a narrow canal in the hot meat of his thigh, right in to its full length, and then at the very limit of her reach she touched something hard. It could have been the head of the femur or the lower ridge of pelvic bone – but she took up the scalpel.

A fine needle jet of blood from a severed blood vessel

sprayed her cheek and forehead before she could twist it closed, and she could hear Louise gagging again, but her hands with the swab barely shook as she wiped away the blood so that Robyn could cut again – and there was a rush of thick creamy yellow matter out of the cut like a dam burst by muddy flood waters. In the flood were little chips and fragments of shattered metal, rotting threads of woollen cloth and other detritus.

'Praise God!' whispered Robyn, and brought her hand out, dripping with the reeking yellow discharge, but with the distorted, misshapen lump of bluish lead held firmly between thumb and forefinger.

The twins had long ago discovered the literary treasure trove that Robyn kept in the locked cupboard against the far wall of her bedroom. Of course, they could only visit it when their parents and elder sisters were fully occupied elsewhere – for instance when King Ben had summoned them to GuBulawayo and Salina was cooking and Cathy was painting or reading.

Then they could sneak into the bedroom and push the chair against the wall so that Vicky standing on Lizzie's shoulders could reach the key.

There were more than fifty books in the cupboard. The great majority unfortunately contained no illustrations. These had proved unrewarding, as the twins' efforts at deciphering the text had been shipwrecked on too many rock-hard words; at other times, just when it was becoming intensely interesting, they would encounter a solid slab of foreign language which they suspected was either Latin or Greek.

The twins avoided these tomes, but the ones with pictures were a forbidden delight, greatly enhanced by danger and guilt. There was even one that had drawings of the inside of women, with and without a baby *in situ*, and another of the baby in the process of emerging.

However, their perennial favourite was the one they called 'The Devil Book' – for there was an illustration on each facing page vivid, lifelike and explicit, of souls in torment and the devils who attended them. The artist who had interpreted this edition of Dante's *Inferno* had dwelt ghoulishly on decapitation and disembowelment, on red-hot irons and hooks, lolling tongues and bulging eyes. Even the briefest stolen perusal of this masterpiece was enough to ensure that the twins would spend most of the following night clinging together in their bed, shivering with delicious terror.

However, this particular visit to the forbidden cupboard was in the interest of scientific research, otherwise they would never have taken the risk while Robyn Ballantyne was actually at Khami Mission.

They chose the time of morning clinic when Mama would certainly be in the church attending her patients, when Daddy would be mucking out the sties, and Salina and Cathy at their chores.

The raid went with the precision of repeated rehearsal. They left their open readers on the dining-room table, and were down the verandah and had the key within the time it takes to draw a long breath.

Lizzie took guard at the window from where she could cover kitchen, the church and the pigsties – while Vicky got the cupboard open and the 'Devil Book' out and open at the correct page.

'See!' she whispered. 'I told you so.'

There he was – Satan, Lucifer, King of the Underworld – and Vicky had been right. He did not have horns. All the lesser demons had horns, but not the Devil, not the very Devil himself. What he did have was a tail, a magnificent tail with a point like the blade of a Matabele assegai upon the end of it.

'He's got a beard in this picture,' Lizzie pointed out, reluctant to abandon her position.

'He probably shaved it off – to fool us,' Vicky told her. 'Now look!' She took a pin out of her hair and used the black round tip to cover one of Lucifer's eyes. Immediately the resemblance was undeniable, the thick dark curls, the broad forehead, the beaked nose and the piercing eye under arched brow, and the smile, the same satanically mocking smile.

Lizzie shuddered luxuriously. Vicky was right, it was him all right.

'Kitty Cat!' Vicky hissed a warning. Salina was coming out of the kitchen, and they had the book back on its shelf, the cupboard locked, the key back in its hiding-place, and were once more seated at the table poring over their readers by the time that Salina had crossed the yard and looked in upon them.

'Good.' She smiled at them tenderly, they were such an angelic pair – sometimes. 'Good girls,' she said, and went back towards the kitchen.

'Where does he put it?' Lizzie asked softly, without looking up from her reader.

'What?'

'His tail.'

'Watch!' Vicky ordered. 'And I'll show you.'

Napoleon, the aged yellow mongrel, was sleeping in the patch of sunlight on the verandah. He had a ridge down his back, and grey hair around his muzzle. Every few minutes a dream of rabbits and guineafowl made his back legs gallop spasmodically and he would puff off an evil-smelling fart of excitement.

'Bad dog!' Vicky said loudly. 'Napoleon, you are a bad, bad dog!'

Napoleon sprang to his feet, appalled by this unjust accusation, and wriggled his entire body ingratiatingly, while his upper lip lifted in a simpering sycophantic grin. At the same time his long whippy tail disappeared between his legs and curled up under his belly.

'That's how he tucks it away. Just like Napoleon,' Vicky announced.

'How do you know?'

'If you look carefully, you can see the bulge where it comes out in front of him.'

They worked on distractedly for a few seconds, then Lizzie could not restrain herself further.

'Do you think we could see his tail?'

'How?'

'What if we—' Halfway through propounding her scheme, Lizzie faltered. Even she realized that it would be impossible to modify the latrine, drilling a peephole through the back wall, without being apprehended; and their motives could never be convincingly explained, especially not to Mama.

'Anyway,' Vicky quashed the plan effectively, 'Devils are probably like fairies, they just don't go.'

Silence fell again. Obviously relieved that nobody had followed up the original accusation, Napoleon re-composed himself to his dreams, and it seemed the project was abandoned – until Vicky looked up with a determined gleam in her eyes.

'We are going to ask him.'

'But,' stammered Lizzie, 'but Mama forbade us to talk to him—' She knew her protest to be unavailing; that gleam in Vicky's eye was familiar.

Ten days after she had removed the pistol ball, Robyn came down to the guest-house with a crutch carved from mopani wood.

'My husband made it for you,' she told Mungo St John. 'And you are going to use it every day from now on.'

The first day Mungo managed one halting circuit of the yard, and at the end of it he was pale and sweating. Robyn checked the leg and the stitches had all held, but the muscles of the thigh had withered and contracted, pulling the leg an inch shorter than the other. The next morning she was there to watch him at exercise. He moved more easily.

After fifteen days she removed the last catgut stitches, and though the scar was raised and thickened, a livid purplish red, yet there was no indication of mortification. It looked as though it had healed by first intention – the drastic use of strong antiseptic on living tissue seemed to have been justified.

After five weeks, Mungo abandoned the crutch in favour of a stout stick, and took the footpath that girded the kopje behind the Khami Mission.

Each day he walked farther and stayed out longer. It was a relief to be away from the bitter arguments with Louise which punctuated the long periods of her icy withdrawal.

He had found a viewpoint beyond the sharp northern ridge of the kopje, a natural platform and bench of dark serpentine rock under the spreading branches of a lovely old leadwood tree, where he could sit and brood out over the gently undulating grassland to the far blue silhouette of hills that marked the site of Lobengula's kraal.

His instinct warned him that there was an opportunity there. It was the instinct and the awareness of the cruising shark which could detect the presence of prey at distances and depths beyond the range of other senses. His instinct had seldom failed him, and there had been a time when he had seized every opportunity with boldness, with the ruthless application of all his skills and all his strength.

Sitting under the leadwood, his hands upon the head of the cane and his chin upon his hands, he cast his mind back to his triumphs: to the great ships that he had won and sailed to the ends of the oceans and brought back laden with treasures, with tea and coffee and spices or holds filled with black slaves. He remembered the rich fertile lands to which he had held title, and the sweet smell of sugar-cane fields when the harvest was being cut. He remembered piles of gold coins, carriages and beautiful horses – and women.

So many women, too many women perhaps; for they were the cause of his present low condition.

He let himself think of Louise at last. She had been a fire in his blood, which grew fiercer the more often he tried to slake it, and she had weakened him, distracted him, diverted him from his ruthless purpose of old.

She had been the daughter of one of his overseers on Fairfields, his vast Louisiana estate. When she was sixteen years of age he had allowed her to exercise his wife's Palamino horses; when she was seventeen he arranged for her to move into the big house as companion and maid to his wife and when she was eighteen he had raped her.

His wife was in the next-door bedroom, suffering from one of her black headaches, and he had torn Louise's clothes off her body, possessed by a madness that he had never known before. She had fought him with the savagery of one of her Blackfoot Indian ancestors, but in some perverse fashion her resistance maddened him as much as the glimpses of her hard young flesh, as it was revealed a gleaming flash at a time.

She had clawed red lines down his chest, and bitten him until he bled, but through it all she had not uttered a word or a sound, although a single scream would have brought her mistress or the house servants running.

In the end, he had borne her down onto the thick white pelt of a polar bear in the middle of the floor, naked except for the tatters of her petticoats hanging from her long fine legs, and with his full weight he had spread her and entered her.

Only then had she made any sound, she had gripped him with the same atavistic savagery, legs and arms encircling him, and she had whispered hoarsely, brokenly. 'I love you, I have always loved you, I shall always love you.'

When the armies of the North had marched against them, and his wife had fled with the children to her native France, Louise had stayed with him. When she could she had been in the field with him, and when she could not she had waited for him, filling in the days and most of the nights nursing the wounded at the Confederate Hospital in Galveston, and there she had nursed him when he was brought in half-blinded and terribly hurt from the battle-field.

She had been with him when he went back to Fairfields for the last time, and shared his desolation at the burnt fields and ruined buildings, and she had been at his side ever since. Perhaps if she had not, things would have been different now, for she had weakened him; she had dulled the edge of his resolve.

So many times he had smelled out the opportunities – the chances for the coup which would restore it all, and each time she had caused him to waver.

'I could never respect you again,' she had said once. 'Not if you did that.'

'I never suspected you were capable of that, Mungo. It's wrong, morally wrong.'

Gradually it had changed, until sometimes, after another abortive attempt to restore his fortunes, she would look at him with a coldness – a kind of icy contempt.

'Why do you not leave me?' he had challenged her then.

'Because I love you,' she had replied. 'And, oh, sometimes how I wish I did not.'

In Perth, when he had forced her to bait the trap for him, luring in the intended victim – she had for the first time rebelled. She herself had ridden to warn the man, and they had been forced to run again, shipping out on a little trading schooner only an hour or so ahead of the constables with the warrant for Mungo's arrest.

He had never trusted her again, although he had never been able to make the decision to desert her. He found that he needed her still. At Cape Town a letter had finally caught up with Mungo. It was one of five copies sent out by his brother-in-law, the Duc de Montijo, a copy to each of the addresses that Mungo had occupied in the years since his wife had left him. Solange, his wife, had taken a chill while out riding and had died five days later of pneumonia. Her children were in the care of the Duc, being educated with his own, and the Duc hinted that he would resist any attempt by Mungo St John to assume custody.

At last Mungo was free to make good his promise to Louise, the solemn promise he had made to her as they knelt hand in hand before the altar in London's church of St Martin-in-the-Fields. He had sworn in the sight of God that just as soon as he was able to do so, he would marry Louise.

Mungo had read through his brother-in-law's letter three times, and then held it in the flame of the candle. He had crushed the ashes to powder, and never mentioned the letter or its news to Louise. She had gone on believing that he was married, and their relationship had limped on, sickening and staling.

Yet still she could influence him even when she was not physically present. At the dark crossroads south of Kimberley, even when he had seen the diamonds gleam in

Hendrick Naaiman's hands, he had not been able to banish Louise's image from his mind: Louise with contempt in her eyes and cold accusation on her lovely lips.

Expert marksman that he was, the shade of Louise had spoiled his aim. He had fired a wink too late, and a touch too wide. He had not killed the Bastaard, but if he had done so, Louise's reaction could have been no more severe.

When he rode back to where she waited, reeling in the saddle, the wounded stallion dragging under him, he had seen her face in the moonlight. Even though she caught him when he might have fallen, and though she had tended his wounds and gone for succour, he had realized that they had crossed a dividing line over which there was no return.

As if to confirm it, he had seen Zouga Ballantyne staring at her in the lantern light with that unmistakable look in his eyes. Many men had looked at her like that over the years, but this time she had returned Zouga's scrutiny openly, making no attempt to hide it from either man.

On the long road northwards, as she walked beside the cart in which he lay wounded, he had challenged her again and she had not denied it.

' – At least Zouga Ballantyne is a man of honour.'

'Then why do you not leave me?'

'You know I cannot leave you now, not as you are—' She left it unfinished, and they had not spoken of it again, though in her icy silences he had sensed the presence in her mind of the other man, and he knew that no matter how desperately unhappy a woman might be she will seldom leave a relationship until she has the prospect of something better to replace it. Louise had that prospect now, and they were both aware of it.

He wondered if he would let Louise go if she finally made the decision. There had been a time not long ago when he would have killed her first; but since they had reached Khami, everything had begun altering even more swiftly. They were rushing towards some climax, and Mungo had sensed that it would be explosive.

For Mungo had forgotten the magnetism that Robyn Ballantyne had once exerted upon him, but now he had been vividly reminded by the mature woman, Robyn Codrington. She was even more attractive to him now than she had been as a girl. He sensed that her strength and assurance would provide a secure port for a man tired to his guts and the marrow of his bones by the storms of life.

He knew that she was the trusted confidante of the Matabele king, and that if his fortune awaited him here in the north, as he had come to suspect, then her intercession with the Matabele would be invaluable.

There was something else, some other darker need within him. Mungo St John never forgave or forgot an injury. Clinton Codrington had commanded the Royal Naval cruiser which had seized *Huron* off the Cape of Good Hope, an action which seemed to Mungo to mark the beginning of his long decline, and herald his dogged misfortune. Codrington was vulnerable. Through this woman Mungo could be avenged, and the prospect was strangely compelling.

He sighed and shook his head, roused himself and used the stick to push himself erect. He found himself confronted by the two small figures. Mungo St John liked all women of whatever age, and though he had not seen his own children in many years, the youngest would be about the same age as these two.

They were pretty little things. Though he had seen them only fleetingly or at a distance, he had felt the stirring of his paternal instincts; and now their presence was a welcome relief from his dark thoughts, and from the loneliness of the past weeks.

'Good afternoon, ladies.' He smiled, and bowed as low as his leg would allow. His smile was irresistible, and some of the rigidity went out of the two small bodies, but their expressions remained pale and fixed; their eyes, huge with trepidation, were fastened upon the fly of his breeches, so that after a few seconds silence even Mungo St John felt disconcerted, and he shifted uncomfortably.

'What service can I be to you?' he asked.

'We would like to see your tail, sir.'

'Ah!' Mungo knew never to show himself at a loss in front of a female, of no matter what age. 'You aren't supposed to know about that,' he said. 'Are you, now?'

They shook their heads in unison, but their eyes remained fixed with fascination below his waist. Vicky was right, there was definitely something there.

'Who told you about it?' Mungo sat down again, bringing his eyes to the level of theirs, and their disappointment was evident.

'Mama said you were the Devil – and we know the Devil has a tail.'

'I see.' Mungo nodded. With a huge effort, he fought back his laughter, and kept his expression serious, his tone conspiratorial.

'You are the only ones that know,' he told them. 'You won't tell anybody, will you?' Quite suddenly Mungo realized the value of having allies at Khami, two pairs of sharp bright eyes that saw everything and long ears that heard all.

'We won't tell anybody,' promised Vicky. 'If you show us.'

'I can't do that.' And there was an immediate wail of disappointment.

'Why not?'

'Didn't your mother teach you that it's a sin to show anybody under your clothes?'

They glanced at each other, and then Vicky admitted reluctantly. 'Yes, we aren't even really allowed to look at ourselves there. Lizzie got whacked for it.'

'There.' Mungo nodded. 'But I'll tell you what I will do – I'll tell you the story of how I got my tail.'

'Story!' Vicky clapped her hands, and they spread their skirts and squatted cross-legged at Mungo's feet. If there was one thing better than a secret, it was a story, and Mungo St John had stories, wonderful scary, bloodthirsty stories – the kind that guaranteed nightmares.

Each afternoon when he reached the lookout under the leadwood tree, they were waiting for him – captives of his charisma, addicted to those amazing stories of ghosts and dragons, of evil witches and beautiful princesses who always had Vicky's hair or Lizzie's eyes when Mungo St John described them.

Then after each of Mungo's stories, he would tactfully initiate a lively discussion of the affairs of Khami Mission. On a typical day he would learn that Cathy had begun painting a portrait of Cousin Ralph from memory, and that it was the considered and unanimous verdict of the twins that Cathy was not only 'soft' but, much worse, 'sloppy' about Cousin Ralph.

He learned that King Ben had commanded the entire family to attend the Chawala ceremony at the new moon, and the twins were ghoulishly anticipating the slaughter of the sacrificial black bull. 'They do it with their bare hands,' Vicky gloated. 'And this year we are going to be allowed to watch, now that we are eleven.'

He was told in detail how Papa had demanded from Mama at the dinner table how much longer 'that infamous pirate' was to remain at Khami, and Mungo had to explain to the twins what 'infamous' meant – 'famous, but only more so'.

Then on one such afternoon, Mungo learned from Lizzie that King Ben had once again '*khombisile*' with his indunas.

Gandang, one of the king's brothers, had told Juba, who was his wife, and Juba had told Mama.

'*Khombisile?*' Mungo asked dutifully. 'What does that mean?'

'It means that he *showed* them.'

'Showed them what?'

'The treasure,' Vicky cut in, and Lizzie rounded on her.

'I'm telling him!'

'All right, Lizzie.' Mungo was leaning forward, interest tempering the indulgent smile. 'You tell me.'

'It's a secret. Mama says that if other people, bad people, heard about it, it would be terrible for King Ben. Robbers might come.'

'It's a secret then,' Mungo agreed.

'Cross your heart.'

And Lizzie was telling it before he had made the sign of good faith. Lizzie was determined that Vicky would not get in ahead of her, this time.

'He shows them the diamonds. His wives rub fat all over him, and then they stick the diamonds onto the fat.'

'Where did King Ben get all these diamonds?' Scepticism warred with the need to believe.

'His people bring them from Kimberley. Juba says it isn't really stealing. King Ben says it is only the tribute that a king should have.'

'Did Juba say how many diamonds?'

'Pots full, pots and pots of them.'

Mungo St John turned his single eye from her flushed and shining face and looked across the grassy golden plains to the Hills of the Indunas, and his eye was flecked golden yellow like one of the big predatory cats of Africa.

Jordan looked forward to this early hour of day. It was one of his duties to check each evening in the nautical almanac the time of sunrise, and to waken Mr Rhodes an hour beforehand.

Rhodes liked to see the sun come up, whether it was from the balcony of his magnificent private railway coach or drinking coffee in the dusty yard of the corrugated iron cottage that he still maintained behind Market Square in Kimberley, from the upper deck of an ocean-going liner or from the back of a horse as they rode the quiet pathways of his estate on the slopes of Table Mountain.

It was the time when Jordan was alone with his master, the time when ideas which Mr Rhodes called his 'thoughts' would come spilling out of him. Incredible ideas, sweeping and grand or wild and fanciful, but all fascinating.

It was the time when Jordan could feel that he was part of the vast genius of the man, as he scribbled down Mr Rhodes' draft speeches in his shorthand pad, speeches that would be made in the lofty halls of the Cape Parliament to which Mr Rhodes had been elected by the constituents of what had once been Griqualand, or at the board table of the governors of De Beers, of which he was chairman. De Beers was the mammoth diamond company which Mr Rhodes had welded together out of all the little diggers' claims and lesser competing companies. Like some mythical boa constrictor, he had swallowed them all – even Barney Barnato, the other giant of the fields. Mr Rhodes owned it all now.

On other mornings they would ride in silence, until Mr Rhodes would lift his chin from his chest and stare at Jordan with those stark blue eyes. Every time he had something startling to say. Once it was, 'You should thank God every day, Jordan, that you were born an Englishman.'

Another time it was, 'There is only one real purpose behind it all, Jordan. It is not the accumulation of wealth. I was fortunate to recognize it so early. The real purpose is to bring the whole civilized world under British rule, to recover North America to the crown, to make all the Anglo-Saxon race into one great empire.'

It was thrilling and intoxicating to be part of all this, especially as so often the big burly figure would rein his horse and turn his head and look to the north, towards a land that neither he nor Jordan had ever seen, but which, during the years that Jordan had been with him, had become a part of both their existences.

'My thought,' he called it. 'My north – my idea.'

'That's where it will really begin, Jordan. And when the time comes, I shall send you. The person I can trust beyond any other.'

It had never seemed strange to Jordan that those blue eyes had looked in that direction, that the open land to the north had come to loom so large in Mr Rhodes' imagination, that it had taken on the aura of a sacred quest.

Jordan could mark the day that it had begun, not only the day but the hour. For weeks after Pickering had been buried in the sprawling cemetery on the Cape Road, Jordan had respected Mr Rhodes' mourning. Then, one afternoon, he had left his office early. He had returned to the camp.

He retrieved the bird image from where it had been abandoned in the yard, and with the help of three black workmen, he moved it into the cottage. The living-room had been too small to hold it; it hindered access to both the dining-table and the front door.

In the small cottage, there was only one free wall, and that was in Mr Rhodes' bedroom, at the head of his narrow cot. The statue fitted perfectly into the space beyond the window. The next morning, when Jordan went to call him, Mr Rhodes had already left his cot and, wearing a dressing-gown, was standing before the statue.

In the fresh pink light of sunrise, as they rode down to the De Beers offices, Mr Rhodes had said, suddenly: 'I have had a thought, Jordan, one which I'd like to share with you. While I was studying that statue, it came to me that the north is the gateway, the north is the hinterland of this continent of ours.' That is how it had begun, in the shadow of the bird.

When the architect, Herbert Baker, had consulted Mr Rhodes on the decoration and furnishings of the mansion that they were building on his Cape Estate, 'Groote Schuur' – 'The Great Barn', Jordan had sat aside from the two men. As always in the presence of others he was unobtrusive and self-effacing, taking the notes that Mr Rhodes dictated, supplying a figure or a fact only when it was demanded, and then with his voice kept low, the natural lilt and music of his rich tenor subdued.

Mr Rhodes had jumped up from his seat on the box against the wall of the cottage and begun to pace, with that sudden excitable and voluble mood upon him.

'I have had a thought, Baker. I want there to be a theme for the place, something which is essentially me, which will be my motif long after I am gone, something that when men look at it, even in a thousand years' time, they will immediately recall the name Cecil John Rhodes.'

'A diamond, perhaps?' Baker had hazarded, sketching a stylized stone on his pad.

'No, no, Baker. Do be original, man! First I have to scold you for being stingy, for trying to build me a mean little hovel and now that I have prevailed on you for magnificently barbaric size and space, you want to spoil it.'

'The bird,' said Jordan. He had spoken despite himself, and both men looked at him with surprise.

'What did you say, Jordan?'

'The bird, Mr Rhodes. The stone bird. I think that should be your motif.'

Rhodes stared at him for a moment, and then punched his big fist into the palm of his left hand.

'That's it, Baker. The bird, sketch it for me. Sketch it now.'

So the bird had become the spirit of Groote Schuur. There was barely one of the huge cavernous rooms without its frieze or carved door jambs depicting it, even the bath, eleven tons of chiselled and polished granite was adorned at its four corners with the image of the falcon.

The original statue had been shipped down from Kimberley, and a special niche prepared for it high above the baronial entrance hall, from where it stared down blindly upon everyone who came through the massive teak front doors of the mansion.

On this morning they had ridden out even earlier than usual, for Mr Rhodes had slept badly and had summoned Jordan from his small bedroom down the corridor.

It was cold. A vindictive wind came down off the mountains of the Hottentots Holland and as they took the path up towards the private zoo, Jordan looked back. Across the wide Cape flats he saw the snow on the distant peaks turning pink and gold in the early light.

Mr Rhodes was in a morose mood, silent and heavy in the saddle, his collar pulled up over his ears, and the broad hat jammed down to meet it. Jordan surreptitiously pushed his own mount level and studied his face.

Rhodes was still in his thirties, and yet this morning he looked fifteen years older. He took no notice of the first unseasonal flush of blue plumbago blooms beside the path, though on another morning he would have exclaimed with delight, for they were his favourite flowers. He did not stop at the zoo to watch the lions fed, but turned up into the forest; and on the prow of land that led to the steeper cliffs of the flat-topped massif they dismounted.

At this distance the thatched roof of Groote Schuur with its twirling barley-corn turrets looked like a fairy castle – but Rhodes looked beyond it.

'I feel like a racehorse,' he said suddenly. 'Like a thoroughbred Arab with the heart and the will and the need to run, but there is a dark horseman upon my back that checks me with a harsh curb of iron or pricks me with a cruel spur.' He rubbed his closed eyes with thumb and forefinger, and then massaged his cheeks as though to set the blood coursing in them again. 'He was with me again last night, Jordan. Long ago I fled from England to this land and I thought I had eluded him, but he is back in the saddle. His name is Death, Jordan, and he will give me so little time.' He pressed his hand to his chest, fingers spread as though to slow the racing of his damaged heart. 'There is so little time, Jordan. I must hurry.' He turned and took the hand from his heart and placed it on Jordan's shoulder. His expression became tender, a small sad smile touched his white lips. 'How I envy you, my boy – for you will see it all and I shall not.'

At that moment Jordan thought his own heart might break and, seeing his expression, Rhodes lifted his hand and touched his cheek.

'It's all too short, Jordan, life and glory – even love – it's all too short.' He turned back to his horse. 'Come, there is work to do.'

As they rode out of the forest, the course of that mercurial mind had changed again. Death had been pushed aside and he said suddenly:

'We shall have to square him, Jordan. I know he is your father – but we shall have to square him. Think about it and let me have your thoughts, but remember time is running short and we cannot move without him.'

The road over the neck between the main massif of Table Mountain and Signal Hill was well travelled and Jordan passed twenty coaches or more before he reached the top, but it was another two hours' ride beyond that and the road became steadily less populous, until at last it was a lonely deserted track which led into one of the ravines in the mountainside.

In this winter season the protea bushes on the slopes beyond the sprawling thatched building were drab and their blooms had withered and browned on the branches. The waterfall that smoked down off the mountain polished the rocks black and cold, and the spray dripped from the clustering trees about the pool.

However, the cottage had a neat cared-for look. The thatch had recently been renewed. It was still bright gold, and the thick walls had been whitewashed. With relief Jordan saw smoke curling from the chimney stack. His father was at home.

He knew that the property had once belonged to the old hunter and explorer Tom Harkness, and that his father had purchased it with £150 of his royalties from *A Hunter's Odyssey*. A sentimental gesture perhaps – for old Tom had been the one who had encouraged and counselled Zouga Ballantyne on his first expedition to Zambezia.

Jordan dismounted and hitched the big glossy hunter from the stables of Groote Schuur to the rail below the verandah, and he walked to the front steps.

He glanced at the pillar of blue marbled stone that stood at the head of the steps like a sentinel, and a little shadow flitted over his face as he remembered the fateful day that Ralph had hacked it out of the Devil's Own claims and brought it to the surface.

It was the only thing that remained to any of them from all those years of labour and travail. He wondered not only that his father had transported it so far with so much effort, but that he had placed it so prominently to rebuke him.

For a moment he laid his hand upon the stone, and he felt the faint satiny bloom that other hands had made on the same spot on the surface, like the marks of worshippers' hands on a holy relic. Perhaps Zouga also touched it every time he passed. Jordan dropped his hand and called towards the shuttered cottage.

'Is anybody there?'

There was a commotion in the front room, and the front door burst open.

'Jordan, my Jordie!' howled Jan Cheroot, and came bounding down the steps. His cap of peppercorn hair was pure white at last, but his eyes were bright and the web of wrinkles around them had not deepened.

He embraced Jordan with the wiry strength of brown arms; but even from the advantage of the verandah step he did not reach to Jordan's chin.

'So tall, Jordie,' he chuckled. 'Whoever thought you'd grow so tall, my little Jordie.'

He hopped back and stared up into Jordan's face. 'Look at you, I bet a guinea to a baboon turd that you've broken a few hearts already.'

'Not as many as you have.' Jordan pulled him close again, and hugged him.

'I had a start,' Jan Cheroot admitted, and then grinned wickedly. 'And I've still got the wind left for a sprint or two.'

'I was afraid that you and Papa might still be away.'

'We got home three days ago.'

'Where is Papa?'

'Jordan!'

The familiar, beloved voice made him start and he broke from Jan Cheroot's embrace and looked beyond him to Zouga Ballantyne standing in the doorway of the cottage.

He had never seen his father looking so well. It was not merely that he was lean and hard and sun-browned. He seemed to stand taller and straighter with an easy set to his shoulders, so different from the defeated slump with which he had left the diamond fields.

'Jordan!' he said again, and they came together and shook hands, and Jordan studied his father's face at closer range.

The pride and the purpose that had been burnt away in the diamond pit had returned, but with their quality subtly changed. Now he had the look of a man who had worked out the terms on which he was prepared to live. There were the shadows of a new thoughtfulness in his green eyes, the weight of understanding and compassion in his gaze. Here was a man who had tested himself almost to the point of destruction, had explored the frontiers of his soul and found them secure.

'Jordan,' he said again quietly for the third time, and then he did something that demonstrated the profound change he had undergone. He leaned forward and briefly he pressed the soft golden curls of his beard to Jordan's cheek.

'I have thought of you often,' he said without embarrassment. 'Thank you for coming.' Then with his arm about his shoulders he ushered Jordan into the front room.

This room always pleased Jordan, and he moved across to the log fire in the walk-in hearth and held out his hands to the blaze while he looked about him. It was a man's room – shelves filled with men's books, encyclopaedias and almanacs and thick leatherbound volumes of travel and exploration.

Weapons hung upon the walls, bows and quivers of poisoned Bushman arrows, shields and assegais of Matabele and Zulu, and, of course, the tools of the trade to which Zouga had reverted, firearms, heavy calibre sporting rifles by famous gunsmiths, Gibbs, Holland and Holland, Westley Richards. They were racked on the wall facing the fireplace, blued steel and lovingly carved wood.

With them were the souvenirs and trophies of Zouga's

work, horns of antelope and buffalo, twisting or curved or straight as a lance, the zig-zag stripes of a zebra hide, the tawny gold bushed mane of the Kalahari lion, and ivory, great yellow arcs reaching higher than a man's head, yellow as fresh butter and translucent as candlewax in the cold winter light from the doorway.

'You had a good trip?' Jordan asked, and Zouga shrugged.

'It gets more difficult each season to find good specimens for my clients.'

His clients were rich and aristocratic sportsmen, come out to Africa for the chase.

'But at least the Americans seem to have discovered Africa at last. I have a good party booked for next season – young fellow called Roosevelt, Secretary of the Navy.' He broke off. 'Yes, we are managing to keep body and soul together, old Jan Cheroot and I – but I don't have to ask about you.'

He glanced down at the expensive English cloth of Jordan's suit, the soft leather of his riding boots which creased perfectly around his ankles like the bellows of a concertina, the solid silver spurs and the gold watch chain in his fob pocket – and then his eye paused on the white sparkle of the diamond in his cravat.

'You made the right choice when you decided to go with Rhodes. My God, how that man's star rises higher and brighter with each passing day.'

'He is a great man, Papa.'

'Or a great rogue.' Then Zouga smiled apologetically. 'I am sorry, I know how highly you think of him. Let's have a glass of sherry, Jordie, while Jan Cheroot makes lunch for us.' He smiled again. 'We miss your cooking. You will find it poor fare, I'm afraid.'

While he poured sweet Cape sherry into long glasses, he asked over his shoulder:

'And Ralph, what do you hear of Ralph?'

'We meet often in Kimberley or at the railhead. He always asks after you.'

'How is he?'

'He will be a big man, Papa. Already his wagons run to Pilgrims' Rest and those new goldfields on the Witwatersrand. He has just won the fast coach contract from Algoa Bay. He has trading posts at Tati and on the Shashi river.'

They ate in front of the fire, sour bread and cheese, a cold joint of mutton and a black bottle of Constantia wine, and Jan Cheroot hovered over Jordan, scolding him fondly for his appetite and recharging his glass when it was barely a quarter empty.

At last they finished and stretched out their legs towards the fire, while Jan Cheroot brought a burning taper to light the cigars which Jordan produced from a gold pocket case.

Jordan spoke through the perfumed wreaths of smoke.

'Papa, the concession—' And for the first time an angry arrowhead creased the skin between Zouga's eyes.

'I had hoped that you came to see us,' he said coldly. 'I keep forgetting that you are Rhodes' man, ahead of being my son.'

'I am both,' Jordan contradicted him evenly. 'That's why I can talk to you like this.'

'What message has the famous Mr Rhodes for me this time?' Zouga demanded.

'Maund and Selous have both accepted his offers. They have sold their concessions to Mr Rhodes, and both are ten thousand pounds richer.'

Maund was a soldier and an adventurer. Fred Selous, like Zouga, a hunter and explorer. Also, like Zouga, Selous had written a well-received book on the African chase, *A Hunter's Wanderings in Africa*. Both of these men had at different times prevailed on Lobengula to grant them concessions to ivory and minerals in his eastern dominions.

'Mr Rhodes wants me to point out to you that both the

Maund and Selous concessions are over the same territory as the concession that Mzilikazi granted to you. He owns both of them now – the validity of all the treaties is hopelessly confused and hazy.'

'The Ballantyne concession was granted first – by Mzilikazi; the ones that followed have no force,' snapped Zouga.

'Mr Rhodes' lawyers have advised—'

'Damn Mr Rhodes and his lawyers. Damn them all to hell.'

Jordan dropped his eyes and was silent, and after a long pause Zouga sighed and stood up. He went to the yellow-wood cupboard and took out a stained and dog-eared document, so ragged that it had been pasted onto a backing to prevent it falling to pieces.

The ink had faded to brown, but the script was bold and spiky, the hand of an arrogant and cocksure young man.

The document was headed:

EXCLUSIVE CONCESSION TO MINE GOLD
AND HUNT IVORY
IN THE
SOVEREIGN TERRITORY OF MATABELELAND

And at its foot was a crude wax seal with the image of a bull elephant, and the words:

NKOSI NKHULU – GREAT KING

Below it a shaky cross in the same faded ink:

MZILIKAZI – *his mark*

Zouga laid the document on the table between them, and they both stared at it.

'All right,' Zouga capitulated. 'What do Mr Rhodes' lawyers advise?'

'That this concession could be set aside on five separate points of law.'

'I would fight him.'

'Papa. He is a determined man. His influence is enormous. He will be Prime Minister of the Cape Parliament at the next session, there is little doubt of that.' Jordan touched the red wax seal. 'His fortune is vast, perhaps ten million pounds—'

'Still I will fight him,' Zouga said, and then stopped Jordan speaking with a hand on his arm. 'Jordan, don't you understand. A man must have something, a dream, a light to follow in the darkness. I can never sell this, it has been all of my life for too long. Without it I shall have nothing.'

'Papa—'

'I know what you will say, that I can never make this into reality. I do not have the money it would need. You might even say that I no longer even have the strength of purpose. But, Jordan, while I have this piece of paper I can still hope, I still have my dream to follow. I can never sell it.'

'I told him that, and he understood immediately. He wants you to be a part of it.'

Zouga lifted his head and stared at his son.

'A seat on the Board of Governors of the company for which Mr Rhodes will petition a Royal Charter from Her Majesty. Then you will have grants of farm land, gold claims, and an active command in the field. Don't you see, Papa, he is not taking your dream away from you, he is making it come true at last.'

The silence drew out, a log crumbled and crashed softly in the hearth; sparks shot up and the flare lit Zouga's face.

'When will he see me?' he asked.

'We can be at Groote Schuur in four hours' ride.'

'It will be dark by then.'

'There are fifteen bedrooms for you to choose from,'

Jordan smiled, and Zouga laughed like a man who has been given back all the excitement and eagerness of youth.

'Then why are we sitting here?' he asked. 'Jan Cheroot, bring my heavy coat.'

Z ouga strode out onto the verandah of the cottage, and on the top step he checked and reached out with his right hand to the pillar of blue stone. He touched it with a strangely formal caress, and with the same hand touched his own lips and forehead, the gesture with which an Arab greets an old friend.

Then Zouga glanced at Jordan, and smiled.

'Superstition,' he explained. 'Good luck.'

'Good luck?' Jan Cheroot snorted from below the steps where he held Zouga's horse. 'Damn stone – all the way from Kimberley, trip over the thundering rubbish.' He went on muttering to himself as Zouga mounted.

'Jan Cheroot would pine away if he didn't have something to complain about.' Zouga winked at Jordan, and they trotted out from under the milkwood trees onto the track.

'I often think back to that day when we hit the blue,' Jordan said. 'If we had only known!'

'How could we know?'

'It was I – I feel sure of that. It was I who convinced you that the blue ground was barren.'

'Jordan, you were only a boy.'

'But I was supposed to be the diviner of diamonds. If I had not been so certain that it was dead ground, you would never have sold the Devil's Own.'

'I never sold it. I gambled it away.'

'Only because you thought it was worthless. You would never have accepted Mr Rhodes' bet if you had known that the blue was not the end – but only the beginning.'

'Nobody knew that, not then.'

'Mr Rhodes sensed it. He never lost faith. He knew what the blue was. He knew it with a certain instinct that nobody else had.'

'I have never been back to Kimberley, Jordie.' Zouga settled down in the saddle, riding with long stirrups like a Boer hunter. 'I never wanted to go back, but of course the news filters down the line of rail. I heard that when Rhodes and Barnato made their deal, they valued the Devil's Own claims at half a million pounds.'

'They were the keys to the field,' Jordie explained. 'It just happened that they were the central claims in the main enrichment. But you could never have guessed that, Papa.'

'Strange how right one man's instincts can be,' Zouga brooded. 'And how wrong another man's. I always *knew*, or thought I knew, that my road to the north began in that hole, that terrible hole.'

'Perhaps it still does. The money to take us all to the north will still come from it. Mr Rhodes' millions.'

'Tell me about the blue. You have been with Rhodes through it all. Tell me about it.'

'It changes,' Jordan said. 'It's as simple as that, it alters.'

Zouga shook his head. 'It's like some sort of miracle.'

'Yes,' Jordan nodded. 'Diamonds are nature's beautiful miracles. I'll never forget my own astonishment when Mr Rhodes showed it to me. That hard blue rock is unyielding as any granite when it comes out of the earth, and yet after it has been laid out in the stacking fields for a year or two it starts to crumble. It's the sunlight, we think, that does it. It crumbles up like a loaf of stale bread – and the diamonds, oh Papa, the diamonds. Incredible stones, eleven thousand carats of diamonds each day. The blue is the mother lode, the blue is the heart.' He broke off in embarrassment. 'Sometimes I run away with myself,' he confessed, and Zouga smiled with him. Who could resist this beautiful young man, that was the word to describe him – not handsome, not good-looking, but beautiful, with a quality of gentleness and goodness that seemed to form an aura about him.

'Papa.' Jordan sobered. 'Oh Papa, you will never know how happy I am that you are to be part of it, after all. You and Mr Rhodes.'

'Mr Rhodes,' Zouga thought indulgently. 'Always Mr Rhodes. And yet it's a good thing for a young man to have a hero. Pity this poor world of ours when the last hero passes.'

C an you judge a man by his books? Zouga wondered. The library was choked with them. One complete wall packed to the ceiling with the sources and references which Gibbon had consulted for his *Decline and Fall*. So impressed had Rhodes been with this work that he had ordered Hatchards of London to collect and, if necessary, translate and bind the complete authorities. Jordan said it had cost him £8,000 thus far, and was not yet complete.

Ranked beside this formidable array were all the published lives of Alexander, of Julius Caesar and of Napoleon. What dreams of empire they must sustain. Zouga smiled inwardly as he listened to the high hypnotic voice of the burly figure with the flushed swollen face as he sat behind the vast desk into whose panels were chiselled the stylized figures of the bird, the falcon of Zimbabwe.

'You are an Englishman, Ballantyne, a man of honour and dedication; these things have always attracted me to you.' He was irresistible, able to conjure up a gamut of emotions with a few words, and Zouga smiled at himself again. He was in danger of the same hero worship as his own son.

'I want you even more than this concession of yours. You understand, you know what it is we seek, not merely wealth and personal aggrandizement. No, no, it is something beyond that, something sacred.'

Then he came to it abruptly, without flourish.

'There,' Rhodes said. 'You know what I need – you and your concession. What do you want from me in return?'

'What task will I perform?' Zouga asked.

'Good.' Rhodes nodded the untidy leonine head. 'Glory before gold. You please me, Ballantyne – but to business. I had thought to ask you to lead the occupying expedition, to guide it over the ground you know so well – but other men can do something as simple as that. I shall let Selous do it. I have something more important for you. You will be my alter-ego at the kraal of the Matabele king. The savages know and respect you, you speak their language, know their customs, you are a soldier, I have read your military paper on the tribe – and we must not deceive ourselves, Ballantyne, it may come to a military option. Few other men can do all these things, have all these qualities.'

They stared at each other across the desk, both men leaning forward, and then Rhodes spoke again.

'I am not a mean man, Ballantyne. Do the job for me and you can name your rewards. Money, ten thousand pounds – land, each land grant will be four thousand acres – gold claims, each will be five hundred yards square. How many shall we say – five of each – ten thousand pounds in cash, twenty thousand acres of prime land of your choice, five claims on the rich gold reef over which you shot the great elephant that you described in *Hunter's Odyssey*. What do you say, Ballantyne?'

'Ten of each,' said Zouga. 'Ten thousand pounds, ten land grants, ten gold claims.'

'Done!' Rhodes slapped the desk. 'Write it down, Jordan, write it down. But what of your salary while you are agent at Lobengula's kraal? Two thousand, four thousand per annum? I am not a mean man, Ballantyne.'

'And I am not a greedy one.'

'Four thousand, then – and we are all agreed, so we can go to lunch.'

Zouga stayed five days at Groote Schuur, days of talking and planning and listening.

It amused him to see the legend dispelled. The idea of Rhodes as a solitary and brooding man – withdrawn to some high Olympus where other men could not follow – was proved to be a myth.

For Rhodes surrounded himself with men; there was not a meal at which less than fifteen sat to his generous board. What men they were, clever or rich or both, belted earls or farm-born Boers, politicians and financiers, judges and soldiers. And if they were not wealthy, they were powerful or useful or merely amusing. At one dinner there was even a poet, a bespectacled little shrimp of a man on passage from Indian Service back to England. Jordan had read his *Plain Tales from the Hills* and secured an invitation for him, and despite his appearance, the company was quite taken with him. Rhodes invited him to return and write about Africa: 'The future is here, young Kipling, and we shall need a poet to sing it for us.'

Men by the dozen, and never a woman. Rhodes refused to have a woman servant in the house. There was not even a painting of a woman on the walls.

And the taciturn, brooding figure of legend never stopped talking. From the back of a horse as they rode through the estate, striding over the lawns with his clumsy uncoordinated gait, seated behind the teak desk or at the head of the long, laden dining-table, he talked. Figures and facts and estimates poured from him without reference to notes, other than an occasional glance at Jordan for confirmation. Then came the ideas, fateful, ludicrous, prophetic, fascinating or fantastic – but never-ending.

To a visiting member of the British Parliament: 'We have to make a practical tie with the old country, for future generations will be born beyond its shores; it must be useful, physical and rewarding for both, or we shall drift apart.'

To an American senator: 'We could hold Parliament for five years in Westminster and for the next five in Washington.'

To a rival financier who enviously sniped at his monopoly of the diamond industry: 'Without me, the price of diamonds would not make it worthwhile turning over a stone to pick one up. Kimberley would revert to desert and thirty thousand would starve.'

When they began to plan the grand expedition to the north, Zouga had imagined that Rhodes would concern himself with each detail. He was wrong.

He defined the objective: 'We need a document from Lobengula, ratifying and consolidating all these grants into a single concession, that I can take to London.' Then he picked the man. 'Rudd, you have the legal mind.' And gave him carte blanche. 'Go and do it. Take Jordan with you. He speaks the language. Take anyone else you need.'

Then to Zouga: 'We need an occupying force, small enough to move fast, large enough to protect itself against Matabele treachery. Ballantyne, that will be your first concern. Let me know what you decide, but remember there is little time.'

What might have taken another man six months, was accomplished in five days, and when Zouga left Groote Schuur, Jordan rode with him as far as the neck of the mountain. The wind had gone up into the north-west, and then came down like a ravenous beast, roaring dully against the crags of the mountain and bringing in cold, steely-grey rain squalls off the Atlantic.

It could not blunt their spirits, and although their wind-driven oilskins flogged their bodies and the horses shivered and drooped their ears, they shouted above the wind.

'Isn't he a great man? Every minute spent in his company is like a draught of fine wine, intoxicating with excitement. He is so generous.'

'Though he is the one who profits most from his generosity,' Zouga laughed.

'That's mean, Papa.'

'A saint does not make such a fortune in so short a time. But if anybody can do this thing, then it is Rhodes, and for that I will follow him into hell itself.'

'Let's pray that won't be necessary.'

At the top of the pass the wind was stronger still, and Jordan had to turn his horse in until their knees touched.

'Papa, the column – the occupying column. There is one person who has the wagons, who knows the route, can requisition the supplies and recruit the men.'

'Who is that, Jordie?'

'Ralph.'

Zouga watched Jordan ride back down the pass, towards the wind-darkened waters of Table Bay and the sprawling white buildings that clung to the lower slopes of the mountain under the dingy scudding sky. Then he turned his own mount into the wind and went down the other side.

The excitement stayed with him. He realized that it was Rhodes' particular genius to awaken this feeling in men around him. Even though there were quicksands ahead in which he knew he might soon be engulfed, the enthusiasm and quickness of spirit persisted.

Ten land grants meant forty thousand acres of land, but it would take more than £10,000 to hold it. Homestead and wells and fences to build, cattle to stock it, men to work it – all that would cost money, a great deal of money.

The gold claims – he could not even begin to imagine how much it might cost to transport stamp mills and sluice boxes from the railhead. Of course, for lack of money to exploit them, he would have to pass by a hundred opportunities that the new land would offer. In the beginning the land grants of other men would be for sale at bargain prices, hundreds of thousands of acres of the land that he had always thought of as his own, and because he did not have the money, it would go to others.

None of this could break the mood, not the cold rain in his face that numbed his cheeks, not the realization that his dream was still merely a dream. For now at last they were on the move at the breakneck pace set by an impatient man – towards the realization of that dream. So Zouga could lift his chin and sit up straight in the saddle, ignoring the icy snakes of rainwater that wriggled down inside his collar, buoyed high above mundane doubts by the gambler's certainty that at last his luck had changed, the dice were hot for him and every time he rolled the aces would flash like spearheads.

The sheets of rain hid the cottage from Zouga until he turned in under the milkwood grove; then a fluke of the wind opened the slanting silver sheets of water, and his mood popped like a bubble.

He had been mistaken, his luck had not changed, it had all been words and illusion, the caravan of his misfortunes rolled on unchecked – for before him his home was partially destroyed.

One of the ancient milkwoods, weary of resisting the gales of a hundred winters, had succumbed at last; it had come crashing down across the front of the cottage. The roof had given under the blow, and sagged in. The supports of the verandah had shattered and a tangle of fallen roof beams and milkwood branches blocked the front entrance.

The living-room would be swamped with rain – his books, his papers.

Appalled at the havoc, he dismounted and stood before it, and his spirits slid further. He felt his ribs constricting his breathing and dread uncoiled in his guts like an awakening serpent. It was the superstitious terror of one who has offended the gods.

The pillar of blue marbled rock that he had set to guard his threshold had been thrown down. It lay half under the tumbled thatch with the shattered verandah support beside it. Once it had been hard and smooth as granite, but the sunlight and the air had rotted it and the fall had shattered it like chalk.

Zouga went down on one knee and touched a rough, irregular lump of the smashed blue ground. The destruction of his home was as nothing. This was the only one of his possessions that was irreplaceable, and the omen of its destruction struck frost into the secret places of his soul.

Almost as a chorus to his dread, a fresh rain squall came booming down the valley, thrashing the trees and ripping at the scattered thatch. Rain beat down onto the broken surface of the rock he was touching, and at Zouga's fingertips there was a tiny burst of white lightning, so dazzling, so searing, that it seemed it could flay the skin from his finger as he touched it. But it was cold, cold as a crystal of Arctic ice.

It had never been exposed to the light of day, not once in the two hundred million years since it had assumed its present form, and yet it seemed in itself to be a drop of distilled sunlight.

Zouga had never seen anything so beautiful, nor touched anything so sensual – for it was the beacon and the lodestone of his life. It made all the striving and the heartbreak seem worthwhile, it was justification for the years he had believed squandered, it exonerated his once firmly held belief that his road to the north began in the gaping chasm of De Beers New Rush.

With hands that shook like those of a very old man, he fumbled open the blade of his clasp knife and gently prised that rainbow of light from its niche in the shattered blue rock, and held it up before his own eyes.

'The Ballantyne diamond,' he whispered, and staring into its limpid liquid depths like a sorcerer into his divining ball of crystal, he saw light and shadow ripple and change and in his imagination become vistas of enchanted pastures rich with sweet grass; he saw slow herds of cattle and the headgear of winding wheels of fabulous gold mines spinning against a high blue sky.

They didn't expect him. He came so swiftly that no runner brought word ahead of him. He had left Rudd and the rest of the party to follow from the Shashi and ridden on ahead, leading two spare horses and changing as soon as the mount beneath him tired. The horses were the pick of De Beers' stables, and it took him five days from the frontier of Matabeleland to Khami Mission.

'I'm Jordan Ballantyne,' he said, and looked down on the family that had hastily assembled on the front verandah of the Mission. The siege was over without a shot fired; he walked in with his curls shining and that warm, almost shy, smile on his lips, and took their hearts, every one of them, by storm.

The gifts he brought had been chosen with obvious care, and spoke of a knowledge of each of them and their individual needs.

There were two dozen packets of seeds for Clinton – unusual vegetables and rare herbs – comfrey and okra, horseradish and turmeric, shallot and sou-sou. For Robyn a box of medicines, which included a bottle of chloroform, and a folding wallet of shiny, sharp surgical instruments.

The latest volume of Tennyson's poetry for Salina, a pair of marvellous lifelike china dogs with moving eyes for the twins, and for Cathy the best of all, a box of oil paints, a bundle of brushes, and a letter from Ralph.

In the first week, while he waited for Rudd and the rest of the party to come up from the Shashi, Jordan used a green twig to divine water, an art that Clinton had never acquired, and helped him dig the new well. They hit clear, sweet water ten feet down. He recited to Cathy a biography of Ralph from the day and hour of his birth, which was so minutely detailed that it took instalments over the entire week to complete, while she listened with a fixed avidity.

He rolled up his sleeves and from the black wood-burning stove produced a flow of culinary phenomena – quenelles and soufflés, croques-en-bouche and meringues, sauces both Hollandaise and Béarnaise – and while Salina hovered near him, eager to learn and help, he quoted to her the entire 'In Memoriam' of Alfred, Lord Tennyson, from memory:

> 'So fret not, like an idle girl,
> That life is dash'd with flecks of sin.
> Abide: thy wealth is gathered in,
> When Time hath sunder'd shell from pearl.'

And she was utterly enchanted by his golden spell.

He showed the twins how to cut and fold from a piece of newspaper all manner of fantastic bird and animal shapes, and he told stories that were the best they had heard since Mungo St John had left Khami.

For Robyn he had the latest news from the Cape. He was able to describe for her the rising stars on the political horizon, and categorize their strengths and weaknesses. He had the latest assessments of the political scene at home. Members of both Houses of Parliament, Cape and home, were constant guests at Groote Schuur, so he could repeat the gossip of that 'wild and incomprehensible old man', as the Queen had called Gladstone. He could explain the Home Rule issue and tell her what the odds were for a Liberal victory at the next election, even after Gladstone's failure to rescue Gordon from Khartoum and his consequential loss of popularity.

'At the Queen's Jubilee the common people on the pavements cheered him, but the aristocracy hissed him from the balconies,' he told her.

For Robyn, this was nectar to a woman lost over twenty years in the wilderness.

Dinners at Khami usually finished by the fall of dark, and the family was abed an hour later, but after Jordan's arrival, the talk and laughter sometimes lasted until midnight.

'Jordan, there is no doubt that if we want Mashonaland, we shall have to square your aunt. I hear that Lobengula will not make a major decision without Dr Codrington. I want you to go on ahead of Rudd and the others. Go to Khami and talk to your aunt.' That had been Mr Rhodes' parting injunction to him, and Jordan's conscience found no conflict between this duty and his family loyalties.

Again and again in that week Jordan returned to extol Mr Rhodes to Robyn, his integrity and sincerity, his vision of a world at peace and united under one sovereign power.

Instinctively he knew which areas of Rhodes' character to emphasize to Robyn, patriotism, charity, his sympathetic treatment of his black workers, his opposition to the Stropping Act in the Cape Parliament which, if passed, would have given employers the right to lash their black servants, and only when he judged that she was swayed to his views, did Jordan mention the concession to her. Yet, despite his preparations, her opposition was immediate and ferocious.

'Not another tribe robbed of its lands,' she cried.

'We do not want Matabeleland, Aunty. Mr Rhodes would guarantee Lobengula's sovereignty and protect him—'

'I read the letter you wrote to the *Cape Times*, Aunty, expressing your concern over the Matabele raids into Mashonaland. With the British flag flying over the Shona tribes, they would be protected by British justice.'

'The Germans and Portuguese and Belgians are gathering like vultures – you know, Aunty, that there is only one nation fit to take on the sacred trust.'

Jordan's arguments were calculated and persuasive, his manner without guile and his trust in Cecil John Rhodes touching and infectious, and he kept returning to his most poignant argument.

'Aunty, you have seen the Matabele bucks returning from Mashonaland with the blood caked on their blades and the captured Shona girls roped together. Think of the havoc that they have left behind them, the burned villages, the murdered infants and grey heads, the slaughtered Shona warriors. You cannot deny the Shona people the protection that we will offer.'

That night she spoke to Clinton, lying beside him in the darkness in the narrow cot on the hard straw-filled mattress; and his reply was immediate and simple:

'My dear, it has always been clear to me as the African sun that God has prepared this continent for the protection of the only nation on earth that has the public virtue sufficient to govern it for the benefit of its native peoples.'

'Clinton, Mr Rhodes is not the British nation.'

'He is an Englishman.'

'So was Edward Teach, *alias* Blackbeard the pirate.'

They were silent for many minutes and then Robyn said suddenly:

'Clinton, have you noticed anything wrong with Salina?'

His concern was immediate. 'Is she sickening?'

'I'm afraid so, incurably. I think she is in love.'

'Good gracious.' He sat abruptly upright in the bed. 'Who on earth is she in love with?'

'How many young men are there at Khami at the present time?'

In the morning, on the way to her clinic in the church, she stopped at the kitchen. The previous evening Clinton had slaughtered a pig, and now Salina and Jordan were making sausages. He was turning the handle of the mincing machine while she forced lumps of pork into the funnel. They were so absorbed, chatting so gaily together, that while Robyn stood in the doorway watching them they were unaware of her presence.

They made a beautiful couple, so beautiful indeed, that Robyn felt a sense of unreality as she watched them, and it was followed immediately by uneasiness, nothing in life was that perfect.

Salina saw her, and started – and then unaccountably blushed so that her pixie pointed ears glowed.

'Oh Mama, you startled me.'

Robyn felt a rush of empathy, and, strangely, of envy for her eldest daughter. She wished that she were still capable of that pure and innocent emotion, and suddenly she had the contrasting image of Mungo St John, lean and scarred and unscrupulous, and what she felt shocked her so her voice was brusque.

'Jordan, I have made up my mind. When Mr Rudd arrives, I will go with you to Lobengula's kraal, and I will speak for your case.'

After a prolonged and unprofitable trading expedition as far as the Zambezi, Mungo had returned with Louise to the kraal at GuBulawayo, where they were kept almost seven months. But Lobengula's procrastinations worked in Mungo St John's favour.

Robyn Codrington had refused to speak to the king on Mungo's behalf, and consequently he was only one among dozens of white concession-seekers camped around Lobengula's royal kraal.

The king would not have let Mungo leave, even if he had wanted to. He seemed to enjoy talking to him, and listened eagerly to Mungo's accounts of the American War and of Mungo's sea voyages. Every week or so he would summon Mungo to an audience and question him through his interpreter, for hours at a time.

The destructive power of cannon fascinated him, and he demanded detailed descriptions of sundered walls and human bodies blown to nothingness. The sea was another source of intense interest, and he tried to grasp the immensity of waters and the blast of storm and gale across it. However, when Mungo delicately hinted at a land grant and trading concession, Lobengula smiled and sent him away.

'I will call for you again, One Bright Eye, when I have thought on it more heavily. Now is there aught you lack in food or drink? I will send my women to your camp with it.'

Once he gave Mungo permission to go out into the hunting veld so long as he stayed south of the Shangani river and killed neither elephant nor hippopotamus. On this expedition Mungo shot a huge cock ostrich and salted and dried the skin with its magnificent plumage intact.

On three other occasions the king allowed him to return to Khami Mission Station when Mungo complained that his leg was paining him. Mungo's predatory instinct was that Robyn Codrington was disturbed and excited by these returns, and each time he was able to draw out the visit for days, gradually consolidating his position with her so that when he again asked her to intercede with Lobengula on his behalf, she actually thought about it for a full day before refusing once more.

'I cannot set a cat upon a mouse, General St John.'

'Madam, I freed my own slaves many years ago.'

'When you were forced to,' she agreed. 'But who will control you here in Matabeleland?'

'You, Robyn, and gladly would I submit to that.'

She had flushed and turned her face away from him to hide the colour.

'Your familiarity is presumptuous, sir.' And she had left him so that he could keep his revived assignations under the leadwood tree with the twins. His absence since those first encounters in his convalescence had not dimmed their fascination for him. They had become invaluable allies. Nobody else could have extracted from Juba the vital information he needed for his planning. Mungo had expressed doubts as to the existence of the diamonds, and declared that he would only be convinced if the twins could tell him where Lobengula kept the treasure.

Juba never suspected danger from such an innocent pair, and in the late afternoon, when she had drunk a gallon pot of her own famous brew, she was always genial and garrulous.

'Ningi keeps the diamonds under her sleeping place,' Vicky informed Mungo.

'Who is Ningi?'

'The king's sister, and she is almost as fat as King Ben is.'

Ningi would be the most trusted of all Lobengula's people – and her hut in the sanctuary of the forbidden women's quarters was the most secure in all Matabeleland.

'I believe you now. You are clever girls, both of you,' Mungo told them, and they glowed with pleasure. There was nothing he could not ask of them.

'Vicky, I need some paint. It's for a secret thing, I will tell you about it later, if you can get the paint for me.'

'What colour?' Lizzie cut in. 'I'll get it for you.'

'Red, white and yellow.'

In the end Lizzie stood guard while Vicky raided Cathy's paintbox, and they delivered their offering to Mungo and basked in his extravagant praise.

In his planning, it was not enough merely to get the diamonds into his hands; even more vital was to escape the consequences. No man or woman could hope to reach the frontier without the king's permission; it was hundreds of miles of wild country patrolled by the border impis. He could not grab and run. He had to use guile and perhaps turn the Matabele dread of darkness and witchcraft to his own advantage.

So he planned with meticulous concentration, and waited for the right moment with the patience of the stalking leopard, for he knew that this was his last attempt. If he failed this time, then not even his white skin nor his status as a guest of the king could save him.

If he failed, the Black Ones would wield their knobkerries, crushing in his skull – and his corpse would be flung from the cliffs to the waiting vultures or into the flooded river pools where the crocodiles would rip it into chunks with their spiky yellow saurian teeth. Louise would suffer the same fate, he knew, but it was a chance he was prepared to take.

He was careful to conceal his preparations from her – and this was made easier by the distance that she had for long now been maintaining between them. Though they shared the thatched hut that Lobengula's men had built for them in the grove beyond the royal kraal, and though they ate the same meals of beef and sour milk and stone-ground maize cakes that the king sent down to them each evening, Louise spent her days alone, riding out on one of the mules in the early morning and not returning until dusk. Her mattress of straw in the farthest recesses of the hut she had screened with the tattered canvas sunshade from the cart, and he only once tried to pass the screen.

'Not again,' she hissed at him. 'Never again!' And she showed him the knife that she kept under her skirts.

So he was able to work uninterrupted, during the day, and to hide his equipment under his own mattress each evening. He carved the mask from the naturally curved portion of a hollow tree trunk, a hideous grimacing ape-like visage with staring eyes and a gaping mouth full of white fangs – and he painted it with the colours from Cathy's paintbox.

From the plumed ostrich skin he tailored a cloak that reached from neck to ankles, and for his feet and hands he made grotesque mittens of black goatskin. In full costume he was enough to paralyse even the bravest warrior with supernatural terror. He was the very embodiment of the *Tokoloshe* of Matabele mythology.

Robyn Codrington had given him repeated doses of laudanum for the persisting pain in his leg, but he had saved these for the occasion. He had decided on one of the Matabele festivals, and he waited until the third night when every man and woman of the entire nation, surfeited with beer and three days and nights of wild dancing, had fallen asleep where they fell.

At nightfall he gave the laudanum to Louise in a cup of soured milk, and the tart flavour concealed the musky taste of the drug. An hour after dark he crept across the hut, drew aside the screen and listened to her even breathing for a minute before leaning over her and slapping her cheeks lightly. She did not move nor murmur, and the rhythm of her breathing did not alter.

He dressed swiftly in the feather cloak, not yet donning the mask and mittens – but blackening his face and limbs

485

with a mixture of crushed charcoal and fat. Then with the mask and a length of rope under one arm and a heavy assegai in the other hand, he crept out of the hut.

The grove was deserted, no Matabele would venture here when the spirits were abroad, so he hurried through it – and from the treeline surveyed the stockade of the royal kraal.

There was a sliver of the old moon rising, and it gave just enough light for him to pick his way, but not enough to betray him to watchful eyes. There would be few eyes open on this night. Even so he crouched low as he crossed the open ground; the cloak made a shaggy hyena shape that would excite no real interest.

At the outer stockade he paused to look and listen, then flicked the length of manila rope over the barrier of sharpened poles.

He climbed up carefully, favouring his bad leg, and peered into the kraal.

It was deserted, but a low watch-fire burned in front of the barred gateway.

Mungo slid down the rope and he crossed quickly to the shadows of the nearest hut, and there paused to pull on his mittens and settle the cumbersome mask over his head before creeping on again towards the inner stockade that guarded the women's quarters.

In the preceding weeks, using his brass telescope from the vantage point of the nearest hilltop, he had been able to see over the walls and to study the layout of the wives' quarters.

There was a double circle of huts, like the concentric rings of a target, but at the centre, the bull's-eye, was a larger hut with intricate patterns of thatch and lacing proclaiming its greater importance. His guess that this was the king's sister's residence had been confirmed when he had seen, through the telescope, Ningi's elephantine gleaming naked body, escorted by a dozen hand-maidens, emerging into the early sunlight from the low doorway.

Now he reached the gateway in the inner stockade, and studied it from around the sheltering wall of the nearest hut. Again his luck held. He had been prepared to use the assegai here, but both the guards were stretched out, wrapped in their furs, and neither of them moved as Mungo stepped over their prostrate bodies.

From inside one hut he heard the low regular snores of one fat wife, and in another a woman coughed and muttered in her sleep, but though his nerves jumped, he went on swiftly.

The door to Ningi's hut was closed. Mungo had honed the edge of the assegai to a razor edge, and with it he sawed through the fastenings of bark rope that secured the opening. The rasp and rustle of the blade sounded thunderous in his ears, and his skin prickled as he waited for a shouted challenge from within. It did not come, but he found that he was sweating as he stepped back and brought out the bladders of goats' blood from under the cloak.

He slit the bladders and splashed the stinking, congealing blood over the portals of the doorway. He had learned from the twins, who were authorities on the supernatural, that a *Tokoloshe* always spurted blood on any doorway through which it passed. It was one of the creature's more endearing characteristics.

Now with the assegai gripped in his right hand, Mungo stooped into the hut and, crouched in the doorway, he waited for his eyes to adjust to the gloom.

The fire in the centre of the large hut had burned low. There was just enough light to make out two figures curled like dogs on the sleeping-mats on each side of it – and beyond it the ponderous bulk of the princess under her furs.

Her snores started as a low grumbling like a volcano,

and rose to a whistling crescendo that covered any sound Mungo might make as he slipped across to the first of the sleeping hand-maids.

Before she could stir he had slipped a gag of goat's skin into her mouth and trussed her at the ankles and wrists with a leather thong. She did not struggle, but stared up at his horrific mask with huge white eyes in the firelight. He tied and gagged the second woman before crossing to Ningi's sleeping platform.

That afternoon, as one of the king's guests, Mungo had watched Ningi sitting beside her brother and swilling pot after pot of French champagne. She went on snoring and grunting as he bound her arms and legs. Only when he thrust the gag into her gaping mouth did she snuffle and moan and come out of her alcoholic slumbers.

He rolled her off the platform and she fell with a thump to the clay floor. He dragged her across to where her bound servants lay. It was heavy work, for she weighed 300 pounds or more.

He threw a log on the fire, and when it flared he pranced and capered around his captives, thrusting his hideous mask into their faces and gibbering at them in fiendish menace. In the firelight their sweat of fear burst out and ran in little rivulets down their bodies as they writhed and wriggled against their bonds.

Suddenly there was a spluttering explosive rush as Ningi voided her bowels with sheer terror, and the hot stink of faeces filled the hut. Mungo threw a fur kaross over them and immediately they were still, their grunts and muffled groans ceased.

He moved quickly then. Returning to the sleeping platform he threw the furs aside, and found a pallet of woven bamboo. It lifted like a trap door, and in the low recess below it were a dozen small clay pots.

His hands began to shake as he reached for one and lifted it out of the recess. His own sweat half blinded him

– but through his blurred vision he saw the soapy gleam of reflected firelight in the mouth of the pot.

He could not take it all, there was too much for him to carry and too much for him later to conceal. Moreover, his survivor's instinct warned him that the more he took the more remorseless would be the search and pursuit.

He spilled the contents of all twelve pots into a glittering heap beside the fire, and in its uncertain light made his choice of the biggest and brightest stones from the hundreds that teased him with their twinkling smiles. Thirty of them filled the leather drawstring bag he had brought with him. He tied it back at his waist, snatched up the assegai and slipped out of the hut.

The guards at the inner stockade still slept, and he passed them silently. Below the wall of the outer stockade he stripped off his cloak, mittens and mask and dropped them on the untended watch-fire. Then he heaped branches over them – there would be only ash by morning.

He went up the rope swiftly, hand over hand, and pulled it up after him. The royal kraal behind him was silent in heavy midnight stupor, and he climbed lightly down the outer wall of the stockade.

He bathed in the pool below the camp, washing off the charcoal and fat, and then found his shirt and breeches where he had left them in the hollow of a tree trunk beside the pool.

In the hut he knelt beside Louise and placed one hand, still icy cold from the pool, upon her cheek. She sighed and rolled over onto her side. He felt like laughing and shouting his triumph out loud. Instead, he hid the bag of precious stones under his mattress and rolled into his blanket. He did not sleep for the rest of the night, and in the dawn he heard the hubbub of superstitious fear from the king's kraal, the screams of women and the shouts of men, loudly bolstering their courage against the spirits and the demons.

'This is a cruel thing for a good king to do,' Robyn told Lobengula bitterly.

'Nomusa, you are a wise woman, the wisest that I have ever known – but you do not understand the spirits and demons of Matabeleland.'

'I understand that the world is full of evil men, but that there are very few evil spirits.'

'The thing that entered my sister's hut came from the air. All the gates to the kraal were guarded by men unsleeping; they have sworn to me that they stood at their posts from dusk to dawn, with eyes wide and spears in their hands. Nothing passed them.'

'Even your best men can doze, and then lie to protect themselves.'

'Nobody dare lie to the king. It came from air, and it sprayed rotten stinking blood upon the portals of Ningi's hut.' Lobengula shuddered despite himself. 'On Chaka's scrawny buttocks, that is a *Tokoloshe* trick. No man can do that.'

'Except if he carry blood in a pot to hurl on the doorway.'

'Nomusa—' Lobengula shook his head sorrowfully. 'My sister and her servants saw this great hairy thing, black as midnight and stinking of the grave, with blood and not sweat oozing from its skin. Its eyes were like the full moon, and its voice that of lion and eagle; it had no hands and no feet, just hairy pads.' Lobengula shuddered again.

'And it stole diamonds,' Robyn told him. 'What does a demon want with diamonds?'

'Who knows what a demon needs for his spells or his magic, or to please his dark master?'

'Men lust after diamonds.'

'Nomusa, to black men diamonds have no value, so it could not have been a black man. On the other hand, if a white man had entered my sister's hut he would not have been satisfied with a few stones. A white man would have taken them all, for that is their way. So it could not have been either a white man or a black man – what is left but a demon?'

'Lobengula, Great King, you cannot allow this thing to happen.'

'Nomusa, there has been a terrible witchcraft perpetrated within the royal kraal. An evil person or many evil persons have conjured up a black demon, and I would be no king at all if I allowed them to live. The evil ones must be smelled out, and my birds must feast before we are cleansed of this filthy thing.'

'Lobengula—'

'Say no more, Girlchild of Mercy, words cannot divert my purpose, for you and your family and all the guests at my kraal are summoned to see justice done.'

It took ten days for the Matabele people to come in to GuBulawayo; they came in their regiments, warriors and maidens, ringed indunas and fruitful matrons – the toddlers and the greyheaded toothless old droolers – in their thousands and tens of thousands; and on the morning that Lobengula had appointed, the nation assembled, rank upon rank, regiment upon regiment, a black ocean of humanity that overflowed the great cattle stockade.

There was a peculiar stillness over such an immense gathering, only the plumed headdresses moved softly in the small restless breeze, and a pall of fear hung over them, so palpable that it seemed to take the heat from the sun and dim its very rays.

The silence was oppressive; it seemed to crush the breath from their lungs. Only once when a black crow flew low over the serried ranks and screeched its raucous cry into the silence, all their heads lifted and a soft sigh shook them, like the wind through the top branches of the forest.

Before the gates of the royal kraal, facing this huge concourse, were drawn up the senior indunas of the Matabele, Somabula and Babiaan and Gandang and the lesser princes of Kumalo, while behind them again, their backs to the poles of the stockade, were Lobengula's white guests, almost one hundred of them, Germans and Frenchmen, Dutchmen and Englishmen, hunters and scholars and businessmen and adventurers, petitioners and missionaries and traders. Soberly clad in broadcloth, wearing hunting leathers and bandoliers or dressed in spangled and gaudy uniform, they waited in the sweltering silence.

There were only two white women present, for Robyn had flatly refused to bring her daughters from Khami for the smelling-out ceremony, and Lobengula had relented and made an exception for them.

The king had given permission for the two women to be seated. Robyn sat beside the entrance to the stockade, and Clinton stood over her protectively while the members of Mr Rhodes' deputation flanked her. Mr Rudd, red-faced and whiskered, with his Derby hat set four square on his head, and Jordan Ballantyne, bare-headed and golden-haired at Robyn's other hand.

Further down the line of guests, Louise St John sat on a stool of leather thongs. Her thick sable plaits hung to the waist of her simple white dress, and the eyes of the men around her kept returning surreptitiously to her exotic high-cheeked beauty. Behind her stood Mungo St John, one eye hidden by the black patch, leaning easily on his cane and smiling to himself as he saw the direction of the eyes of the men about him.

The nation surged like a slumbering black sea struck by a sudden gale of wind, and the plumes tossed like spume. There was a single clap of sound like the volley of massed cannon as every right leg was lifted shoulder high and brought down to stamp the hard earth, and every throat corded and strained to the royal salute.

'Bayete!'

The Great Black Elephant of Matabele came through the gateway, and behind him his wives led by Ningi swayed and shuffled and sang his praises.

With the toy spear of kingship in his hand, Lobengula paced towards the mound of packed clay on which the bath chair, which had been his father's throne, was set, and Gandang and Babiaan, his brothers, came forward to help him ascend the steps.

From his platform, Lobengula looked upon his people, and those closest to him saw the terrible sorrow in his eyes.

'Let it begin,' he said, and slumped into his chair.

There was a ragged chorus of shrieks and whines and maniacal laughter from beyond the stockade walls, and through the gateway came a horrid procession of beldams and crones, of prancing hell-hags and gibbering necromancers.

At their throats and waists were hung the trappings of their wizardry, skull of baboon and infant, skin of reptile, of python and iguana, carapace of tortoise, and stoppered horns, rattles of lucky bean pods and bones, and other grisly relics of man and animal and bird.

Wailing and hooting they assembled before Lobengula's throne.

'Dark sisters, can you smell the evil ones?'

'We smell their breaths – they are here! They are here!'

One of the witches collapsed in the dust, with froth bubbling over her toothless gums; her eyes rolled back into her skull and her limbs twitched spasmodically. One of her sisters dashed the red powder from a snuff-horn in her face, and she shrieked and leaped into the air.

'Dark sisters, will you bring forth the evil-doers?' Lobengula asked.

'We will bring them to you, Great Bull of Kumalo. We will deliver them up, son of Mzilikazi.'

'Go!' ordered Lobengula. 'Do what must be done!'

Some of them went whirling and cavorting, brandishing their divining rods, one the tail of a giraffe, another the inflated bladder of a jackal on a staff of red tambooti wood, still another the stretched and sun-dried penis of a black-maned lion, the rods with which they would point out the evil ones.

Others crept away, slinking and sly as the night-prowling hyena. Others again crawled on all fours, snuffling the earth like hunting hounds quartering for the scent as they spread out amongst the rows of waiting people.

One of the witches came down the line of white guests, hopping like an ancient baboon, her empty teats flapping against her withered belly, her skin crusty grey with filth and her charms clattering and jangling; and she stopped in front of Mungo St John and lifted her nose to sniff the air, then she howled like a bitch in season.

Mungo St John took the long black hand-rolled cheroot of native tobacco from between his lips and inspected the ash on its tip. The crone hopped closer and looked up into his face, and he returned the cheroot to his lips and returned her stare without interest.

She leapt up to thrust her face inches from his and noisily sniff the breath of his nostrils, and then she danced away – until she faced him again, lifted the long giraffe tail above her head, shrieked like a stooping owl and rushed at Mungo, the tail raised to strike into his face.

In front of him she froze in the act of striking, and Mungo St John took the cheroot from his mouth and he blew a perfect smoke ring, that spun upon itself until it broke in the witch's face and blew away in soft wisps.

She cackled, wildly, madly, and passed on down the line to pause in front of Robyn Codrington.

'You stink like the hyena that spawned you,' Robyn told her evenly in perfect Matabele, and the witch whirled and raced away to where Juba stood in the front line of noble matrons; she raised the switch to strike and looked back at Robyn, gloating loathsomely.

Robyn had gone white as bone, and came to her feet clutching her own bosom.

'No,' she whispered. 'Please, fair sister, let her be.'

The witch dropped her arm and came back to strut and preen in front of Robyn; then again she shrieked, whirled and rushed at Juba, this time she struck, and the tail hissed and snapped on black flesh – but at the very last second the witch had diverted her aim, and the blow flew into the startled face of the young woman who stood beside Juba.

'I smell evil,' shrieked the witch, and the woman fell to her knees. 'I smell blood.'

The witch struck again and again, the tail cutting stingingly into the woman's unprotected face until the tears started and ran down her cheeks.

The executioners came forward and pulled her to her feet. The woman's legs were paralysed, so they dragged her unprotesting before Lobengula, and he looked down on her, saddened and helplessly compassionate, before he lifted the forefinger of his right hand.

One of the executioners swung his war club, a full blow that stove in the back of the woman's skull. The bone crunched like a footstep in loose gravel, and the woman's eyes were driven from their sockets like overripe grapes by the force of it. When she fell face forward in the dust there was a bloodless depression in the back of her head into which a man could have placed his fist. The witch scurried away to continue the hunt, and Juba looked across at Robyn. Robyn had fallen back on her chair, trembling and pale, while Clinton put an arm around her shoulders to steady her.

In the packed ranks there was another triumphant shriek, and the executioners dragged a fine-looking young warrior from his place. He threw off their hands and strode to drop on one knee before Lobengula's throne.

'Father of the nation, hear my praises. Great Thunderer, Black Bull, let me die with your name on my lips. Oh Lobengula who drives like the wind—'

The king lifted his finger and the club fell with the flute of a goose's wing.

The chorus of howls and shrieks was unending now as the sisters warmed to their work, and the victims were dragged out and slaughtered – until their corpses were a high mound before the king's throne, a tangle of black limbs and shattered heads, that grew and grew.

A hundred, two hundred, were added to the pile, while the sun reached its zenith and the dust and heat and terror formed a suffocating miasma, and the blue metallic flies swarmed in the staring eyes and open mouths of the dead, and the witches cavorted and giggled and struck with their rods.

Here and there a maiden, overcome with the fear and the blazing heat, fell swooning from her place and the witches pounced upon this irrefutable evidence of guilt and rained blows upon her bare back or glossy breasts, and the executioners hurried to keep pace with their dreadful task.

The sun began its slow descent towards the western horizon, and at last one at a time the witches crept back to the mountain of death they had created. They staggered with exhaustion – the dust had caked on their running sweat, but they bayed and whined like dogs as they pored over the corpses, selecting those they would take with them – back to their caves and secret places – a sliver of the womb of a virgin was a powerful fertility charm, a slice of the heart of a blooded warrior was a wonderful talisman in battle.

'Is the work done?' Lobengula asked.

'It is done, oh king.'

'Are all the evil ones dead?'

'They are all dead, son of Mzilikazi.'

'Go then – and go in peace,' Lobengula said wearily.

'Stay in peace, Great King.' They chuckled and hooted and, bearing their gruesome plunder with them, they shuffled away through the gateway of the stockade.

Three times in as many weeks Mungo St John petitioned the king – asking him to 'give the road' to the south – but each time the king chatted affably for an hour and then waved him away. 'I will think on it, One Bright Eye, but are you unhappy here? Does the beef and beer I send you not fill your belly? Perhaps you would like to go once again on the hunt?'

'I want to go south, oh King.'

'Perhaps in the next full moon, One Bright Eye, and then again perhaps after the rain has passed, or after the Chawala Ceremony, who knows? We will see in good season.'

Then one morning Louise rode out early, as had become her custom – but after she had been gone some hours Mungo realized that this time she had the rifle and bandolier of ammunition, her blanket roll and the gallon water-bottle with her.

He puzzled over her behaviour for the rest of that day, but he was not alarmed until night fell and she had not returned. He sat up beside the fire all that night, and at first light he took the second mule and crossed the river to where Rudd's party was camped in grand style in a pleasant glade of the forest. They had six wagons and as many tents made of best quality waterproof canvas, each with sun flysheets.

The horses on the picket line were all blood Arabs, one of which would carry Mungo and his small bag of precious stones to the Shashi river in six days or less. He was eyeing them hungrily, when Robyn Codrington stooped out of one of the tents. She saw him and would have gone in again, but he called to her and jumped down from the mule.

'Dr Codrington, please, it is a matter of extreme urgency.'

Reluctantly she turned back.

'My wife is missing, she did not come in last night.'

Immediately her distant expression changed to one of concern.

'Did she say where she was going?'

He shook his head. 'I can only think that she might have ridden back to Khami – you know she was becoming friendly with your elder daughter—'

'I shall send a servant to the mission.'

'Can you not ask the king to let me go?'

'The king has gone in to his wives – nobody, not even I, dare disturb him until he comes out from the women's quarters.'

'How long will that be?'

'A day, a week – there is no way of telling. I shall send word to you as soon as I have news.'

That night Mungo waited again, and then in the dawn as he crouched, haggard and bleary-eyed, over the smoky fire, listening for the hoof beats of the mule or the sound of Louise's voice out of the darkness – he was struck instead by a thought that chilled his blood and made his guts slide with dread.

He leapt up from the fire, ran into the hut and scrabbled frantically under the mattress. With a blessed soaring relief his fingers closed on the bag, and he pulled it out and fumbled the drawstring open. He poured the bright stones into the palm of his hand. They were all there, but with them was something that had not been there before. It was a folded sheet of paper – and he took it to the fire and held it to catch the light.

When you find this you will know why I have gone. Even as I write this the memory of those poor wretches who died in their hundreds to pay for your greed rises before me to torment me. With them died the last of my love for you.

I leave you those blood-spattered stones in the certain knowledge that they are accursed.

Do not follow me. Do not send after me. Do not think of me again.

She had not signed it.

Rudd's party was at breakfast under the open-sided dining-tent.

It was a fresh and cool morning. The conversation around the table was intelligent, informed and yet quick and witty, Robyn revelled in it.

She sat at the head of the trestle table and the gentlemen deferred to her. Mr Rudd had been very obviously taken with her from their first meeting, and addressed all his remarks to her directly.

Jordan had supervised the preparation of a gargantuan English breakfast, fresh eggs and grilled gammon, salted kippers and tinned pork sausage, potted shrimps and bloater paste, with freshly-churned yellow butter and hot scones.

Mr Rudd, quite carried away with the spontaneous festive mood, called for a bottle of champagne that had been hung overnight in a wet sack to cool.

'Well,' he lifted his glass to Robyn, 'I am sure we shall be able to survive this rough life and rude fare until the good king makes up his mind.'

Despite Robyn's intercession, Lobengula had not yet ratified the concession that they sought. His senior indunas had been in secret conclave for weeks, but could not reach a consensus of agreement – while Lobengula vacillated and reacted to Mr Rudd's insistence by retiring to his women's quarters where nobody could reach him.

'It may take months yet.' Robyn lifted her own glass and returned Rudd's salute. 'I would not expect Lobengula to make a decision on such an important matter without going into the Matopos Hills to consult the oracle, the Umlimo.'

Suddenly Clinton looked down towards the river, frowned and whispered to Robyn. 'It's that scoundrel St John, what does he want coming here?'

Mungo St John had dismounted at the periphery of the camp, but he did not approach the company under the open-sided marquee.

Robyn stood up quickly. 'Please excuse me, gentlemen. General St John's wife is missing, and he is naturally worried.'

'Thank you for coming,' Mungo said, as she hurried to him. 'I have nobody else to turn to, Robyn.'

She tried to ignore the intimacy of his appeal, and the little jolt that his use of her given name always gave her.

'Do you have news?' she asked.

'I have discovered a note that Louise left for me.'

'Let me see it.' Robyn held out her hand.

'I am sorry. It contains most personal and, I fear, embarrassing, references,' Mungo told her. 'But what is important is that Louise is trying to leave Matabeleland by the southern road.'

'That is madness,' Robyn whispered. 'Without the king's permission, without an escort. The road is obscure, the country wild and infested with lions, she cannot hope to pass the border impis – and they have orders to kill all who do not have the road from Lobengula.'

'She knows all this,' Mungo said.

'Then what possessed her to make the attempt?'

'We argued. She resented the feeling which she knows that I still have – for you.'

Robyn fell back a pace, her cheeks paling and her breath catching in her throat.

'General St John, I forbid you to talk in that fashion.'

'You asked me, Robyn, and once, long ago, I told you that I would never forget that night aboard *Huron*—'

'Stop it! Stop it, this instant! How can you speak like this when your wife is in dire danger?'

'Louise was never my wife,' he said quietly, staring into her green eyes with that single penetrating gaze. 'She was my travelling companion, never my wife.'

Robyn faltered, colour rushed back into her cheeks, and with it came a strange unaccountable pagan joy.

'You told me – once – that you were married.'

'I was, Robyn. Not to Louise. That other lady died many years ago in Navarre in France.'

Robyn confounded herself. She was married to a brave, kind man – in his own way a saintly man – while before her stood the embodiment of evil, the veritable serpent of Eden; and yet she could not suppress this wicked unconscionable elation at the knowledge that he was free – free for she knew not what, or could not bring herself to think on it.

'I shall go to the king,' she said, painfully aware of the quaver in her voice. 'I shall ask him to send men after your – after the lady. I shall ask him also to give you the road, General, and I would consider it full repayment if you would take it immediately, and never return to Matabeleland.'

'What is between us can never be denied, Robyn, as long as we both live.'

'I do not wish to see you again.' With an effort of all her will she steadied her voice and met his eye.

'Robyn—'

'I shall send a messenger to you with the king's reply.'

'Robyn—'

'Please.' Her voice cracked again. 'In God's holy name, please leave me alone.'

H owever, it was two more days before Robyn sent Jordan Ballantyne to Mungo's camp.

'Dr Codrington bids me tell you, sir, that the king has already sent one of his trusted indunas with a picked body of warriors after your wife. They have orders to protect her from the border guards and to escort her to the Shashi river.'

'Thank you, young man.'

'Furthermore, she asked me to tell you that the king has given you the road. You may follow your wife immediately.'

'Again my thanks to Dr Codrington.'

'General St John, you do not remember me—'

'I am afraid—' Mungo frowned up at Jordan on the back of the dancing Arab mare.

'Jordan – Zouga Ballantyne's son. We met in Kimberley some years ago.'

'Ah! Of course, forgive me. You have changed.'

'General, I know that it is none of my business, but as you are a trusted friend of my father's, it is my duty to warn you that there were unpleasant rumours after your departure from Kimberley.'

'I did not know,' Mungo told him indifferently. 'Still, it is one of life's unpleasant truths that the more prominent a man becomes, the more determined are the mean little men to tear him down.'

'I know that, General. I am associated with a great man—' Jordan checked himself. 'However, a police agent, a Griqua named Hendrick Naaiman claimed that you attended an I.D.B. rendezvous and that when you realized it was a trap you attempted to kill him.'

Mungo made an impatient gesture. 'Why should somebody of my standing, my estate, take such a ridiculous risk as to indulge in I.D.B.?'

'That was what Mr Rhodes said, sir. He has repeatedly expressed certainty of your innocence.'

'After I have found my wife I shall return immediately to Kimberley to confront this Naaiman person.'

'General St John, that will be neither necessary nor possible. Naaiman was killed some months ago in a knife fight in one of the drinking canteens. He cannot give evidence for or against you. Without either witness or accuser, your innocence is presumed.'

'Damn it—' Mungo frowned to cover his immense relief. 'I should have welcomed the chance to force his words down his lying throat, now there will always be doubts in some men's minds.'

'Only in the minds of the mean little men.' Jordan touched the brim of his cap. 'I shall not detain you further; you must be anxious to follow and find your wife. Good luck and God speed. I am sure we shall meet again, General.'

Mungo St John stared after Jordan as he rode away. It was hard to grasp the extent of his good fortune – the spectre of unrelenting justice that had pursued him from the south had vanished; he had the road to leave Matabeleland, and an immense fortune in diamonds to carry with him.

An hour later he had visited one of the traders and exchanged the cart and the other meagre possessions he no longer needed for a good rifle and one hundred rounds of ammunition, and he sat the broad comfortable back of the mule, its head pointed southwards, as it skirted the granite hills of the indunas.

Mungo looked neither left nor right: his eye was fixed ahead, towards the south, so that he did not see the slim almost boyish figure on the slopes high above him. Robyn shaded her eyes with the brim of her bonnet and peered after him until the little feather of dust raised by the mule's big heavy hooves subsided into the mimosa forests.

L ouise St John was driven on by her need to keep ahead of any pursuit, obsessed with the knowledge that she must avoid the kraals along the road, ridden by the guilt she knew she must share with Mungo, her senses and emotions in terrible turmoil – so that she did not have a chance to regret her hasty action, taken in the shock of discovering the diamonds, nor did she realize the depths of her loneliness – until she had successfully skirted the last of the great kraals and left the pleasant grasslands of the plateau.

Now ahead of her the escarpment fell into the wild land, hot and heavily forested, which she knew was teeming with wild animals and guarded by the merciless border impis.

It was a measure of her desperate need to be free of Mungo St John and all he stood for that she never once considered turning back – though she knew there was sanctuary for her at Khami Mission, though she knew that Robyn Codrington would go to the king on her behalf and he would give her an escort of warriors to the border.

She could not go back, she could not bear the prospect of being close to Mungo St John ever again. The love she had once borne him had sickened into a total revulsion. No risk was too high to escape him and she had to do it now. There was no going back.

She lay the last night beside the wagon ruts that were her tenuous link with civilization and life itself, her own thread through the maze of the Matabele Minotaur, and she listened to the mule cropping grass close at hand and, far away down the escarpment, the faint roar of a hunting lion, while she tried to reconstruct in her mind the map that had formed the frontispiece to Zouga Ballantyne's book *A Hunter's Odyssey*. The account of Zouga's journeys had fascinated her, even before she had met him, and she had studied the map with minute attention.

She judged that from where she now lay the Tati river was not more than one hundred miles due west. No pursuer would expect her to take that direction. No impi would guard that desolate untravelled quarter, and the Tati river was the border between Matabeleland and Khama's country. By all accounts King Khama was a gentle and honourable man; his country was under suzerainty of the British crown, and British justice was ensured by the presence of Sir Sidney Shippard at Khama's kraal.

If she could reach the Tati river and follow it south until she met some of Khama's people who could take her to Sir Sidney – then he would see to it that she was sent on southwards to Kimberley.

The thought of that town made her realize the true reason for her desperate haste. For the first time she became aware of the terrible hunger within her to be with a man whom she could trust, whose strength would shield her and make her strong again. The man to whom she could at last acknowledge she had transferred the love which Mungo St John had long ago forfeited. She must reach Zouga, and reach him soon – that was the only thing certain in her confusion, and her despair, but first there were a hundred miles of wilderness to cross.

She rose in the first pale light of day, kicked sand over the fire, saddled the mule, and slid the rifle into its scabbard, she buckled the water-bottle and blanket to the pommel and swung up onto his back. With the unearthly red glow of the sunrise at her back, she urged the mule forward, and after fifty paces, when she glanced back, the faint double track of wagon wheels was no longer discernible.

The land through which she rode had a harsh and forbidding grandeur; the horizons were infinite and the sky was tall and milky blue. It was empty of all life, she saw no bird nor animal, and the sunlight was white and fierce. In the nights the stars filled the heavens with whorls and eddies of cold bright light and she felt herself shrinking under the immensity and loneliness of it all.

On the third evening, she knew that she was lost, hopelessly and irretrievably lost. She was barely certain of the direction of the sunset, but she had no idea of distances and her memories of the sketch map which she had thought vivid and clear, had become fuddled and confused.

The gallon water-bottle was empty. She had drunk the last bloodwarm mouthful a little before noon. She had seen no game to provide meat, and she had eaten the last stale maize cake the previous evening. The mule was too exhausted and thirsty to graze. He stood miserably under the wild sycamore tree that she had chosen for her night's camp; but though she put the knee halter on him, she knew that he would not wander. His head hung to his knees. An arrowhead of flint had lacerated the frog of his left fore. He was dead lame, and she had no idea how much farther it was to the Tati, nor in which direction the river lay.

She put a little round white pebble under her tongue to draw her saliva and lay down next to the fire. Exhausted, sleep came like sudden black death – and she woke as though she were struggling up from the depths of hell itself.

The moon was up, full and yellow, but it was the mule's fearful snorts and the stamp of his hooves on the stony earth that had roused her. She dragged herself up with the help of the sycamore trunk and peered about her. Something moved at the edge of her vision, something big and ghostly pale, and as she stared at it she caught the acrid ammoniacal whiff of cat. The mule whinnied with terror and broke into a maimed lunging gallop, the halters holding his forelegs so that he was awkward and slow, and the big pale thing came flashing lightly upon him, rising like a huge white bat against the moonlit sky, and settled upon the mule's back.

The mule screamed once and clearly Louise heard his spinal column break as the lioness on his back bit into his neck and in the same movement reached forward to sink her claws into his cheek and twist his head backwards against the hold of her jaws.

The mule went down with a thumping impact on the hard earth, and the lioness immediately flattened herself behind the shuddering and spasmodically kicking carcass and began ripping into the soft skin around the anus – making an opening into the belly cavity through which to reach the titbits of kidney and spleen and liver and guts.

Behind her Louise saw other pale cat shapes coming out of the shadows, and she had just presence of mind enough to snatch up the rifle before she scrambled up into the fork of the sycamore and climbed upwards, driven by a suffocating terror.

She clung to an upper branch and listened to the grisly feast below her, the growling and squabbling of a dozen lions over the carcass, the lapping sounds as they licked the meat off the bones with tongues like wood rasps, and the awful guttural purring and slurping.

As the light of day slowly strengthened, so the noises subsided. The big cats had eaten their fill and slunk away into the bush. Then Louise looked down the trunk of the sycamore into two implacable yellow orbs that seemed to search out new depths in her terror.

A full-maned lion stood at the base of the tree. He seemed as broad across the back as a carthorse, and his colour was a dark bluish-grey in the bad light. He was looking up at her, and as she stared in horror, the great black ruff of his mane came erect in excitement, so that he seemed to swell in size to fill the whole field of vision.

Suddenly he reared up on his hindlegs and reached up towards her, the long, curved, yellow claws unsheathing from their massive pads, and he ripped long parallel wounds down the bark of the sycamore from which the sap swelled in white milky beads.

Then the lion opened his jaws, and she stared into the deep pink cave of his throat. The long velvety tongue curled like the fleshy petal of some weird orchid, and each gleaming ivory fang was long as a man's forefinger and sharp as the point of a guardsman's pike.

The lion roared up at her. It was a gale of sound that struck her like a blow from a mailed fist. It drove in her eardrums and it jellied every muscle in her body. Then the huge beast came up the tree. It climbed in a series of lunges, the yellow claws raking slabs of wet bark off the trunk as it bunched its quarters and drove upwards, those painful gusts of sound still bursting from its throat, the enormous yellow eyes fastened upon her coldly and remorselessly.

Louise began to scream and the tree rocked, the branches tossed and crackled as the great tawny body forced its way through them with a speed and power she would never have believed possible. Still screaming, she pushed the long barrel of the rifle downwards, without aiming she jerked at the trigger and nothing happened except that the lion was closer still.

In her panic she had forgotten the safety catch of the rifle. It was almost too late; the lion reached up and struck the barrel with one enormous paw. The blow jarred her wrists and numbed her arms, but she kept her grip and slid the catch forward with her thumb and thrust the muzzle into the animal's jaws as she pulled the trigger again. The shot was almost drowned in the lion's roars.

The recoil broke her grip on the weapon and it went spinning away, clattered against the branches, leaving her utterly defenceless. Just below her perch the lion still clung to the tree trunk, but the huge shaggy head was thrown back on the arch of the thick neck, and a bright fountain of blood spurted up out of the open jaws, and the gleaming fangs turned rosy red as it washed over them.

Slowly the hooked claws released their deep grip on the bark of the tree trunk, and the cat fell, twisting and convulsing in mid-air until it struck the ground at the foot of the tree. Lying on its side, it stretched out its limbs and arched its back, one last breath choked with blood rattled up its throat – and then it slumped and softened into the total relaxation of death.

Timidly Louise clambered down from the sycamore and, keeping well clear of the carcass, she retrieved the rifle. The butt was cracked through and the breech block jammed solid. She struggled with it futilely for a few minutes, and then dropped it.

Terror still stifled her breathing, and congested her bladder – but she did not pause to relieve it. Frantically she snatched up the small canvas bag that contained her tinder-box and steel, a clasp knife and a few items of jewellery and other personal oddments. She left the bandolier and blanket and the empty water-bottle, for she was desperately driven by the need to leave this place, and she stumbled away from the sycamore.

Once only she looked back. A pair of jackals were already at the lion's carcass, and out of the lemon-pale morning sky the first vulture came planing down on wide elegant wings to roost, hump-backed, in the top branches of the sycamore. It bobbed its foul boiled-looking naked head in gluttonous anticipation.

Louise began to run. She ran with a panicky desperation, looking over her shoulder, so that the thorn bushes ripped at her and her high-heeled riding boots tottered over the broken ground. She almost exhausted herself in that wild run, and when she fell at last she lay face down, racked by the sob of each breath, and with the tears of fear and despair mingling with the sweat of her cheeks.

It took her until almost noon to recover her strength, and gather her determination and get her racing terror under control.

Then she went on.

In the mid-afternoon one heel broke off her boot, and she twisted her ankle painfully. She hobbled on until darkness gathered around her and with it all her fears returned.

She climbed to the high fork of a mopani tree. The cramped position on the hard trunk, the cold and her own fears prevented her from sleeping. In the dawn she climbed down. Her ankle had swollen and turned a deep purple-rose colour. She knew that if she removed her boot once more she would never get it on again. She pulled up the straps as hard as she could and cut a branch of mopani to use as a crutch.

The noon was windless and fiercely hot. The mucous membrane of her nostrils had dried out and swollen so that she was forced to breath through her mouth. Her lips cracked and began to bleed. The metallic salt of her own blood seemed to scald her tongue. The crutch of raw rough mopani rubbed the skin from her armpit and flank, and by mid-afternoon her tongue had swollen into a choking gag like a ball of oakum jammed into her mouth.

That night she did not have the strength to climb to a tree fork. She crouched at its base, and when at last exhausted sleep assailed her, she was tormented by dreams of running mountain streams – from which she woke mumbling and coughing to the worse torment of reality.

Somehow she dragged herself up again when the light woke her. Each step now was an effort to which she had to steel herself. She leaned on the staff, staring through bloodshot eyes and swollen lids at the spot where she would place her foot, then she lunged forward and swayed to catch her balance before she drew her injured foot up beside the other.

'Five hundred and four—' She counted each step, and then steeled herself for the next pace. At every count of 'one thousand' she rested and peered around her at the wavering heat mirage.

In mid-afternoon she lifted her head during one of the rest pauses and saw ahead of her a file of human figures. Her joy was so intense that for a moment her vision darkened, then she roused herself and tried to shout. No sound came out of her dry, cracked, swollen mouth.

She lifted the crutch and waved it at the oncoming figures – and realized at that moment that the mirage and her own hallucinations had tricked her. In her wavering, uncertain vision the line of human figures resolved into a troop of wild ostrich, and they scattered away across the plain.

There were no tears to tell the depths of her disappointment. Her tears had dried long ago. At dusk she fell face down, and her last conscious thought was, 'It's over. I cannot go on.'

But the dawn chill roused her and she lifted her head painfully and in front of her face she saw a stalk of grass curved under the weight of the drops of dew that hung from it, trembling precariously and sparkling like precious jewels. She reached out her hand and touched it, and instantly the lovely drops fell into the dry baked earth and left no trace of their going.

She crawled to the next stalk and this time let the liquid diamonds fall into her black swollen mouth. The pleasure was so intense as to change its shape to pain. The sun came up swiftly to dry the dew, but she had taken enough strength at least to push herself upright and go on.

The following night there was a small warm breeze that nagged at her while she slept, and because of it there was no dew, and she knew that this was the day she would die. It would be easier to do it here where she lay, and she closed her eyes – then opened them again and struggled into a sitting position.

Each thousand paces seemed to take an infinity, and she was hallucinating again. Once her grandfather walked beside her for a while. He wore his war bonnet of eagle feathers, and his beaded and tasselled buckskins. When she tried to talk to him he smiled sadly at her and his face folded into ancient leathery brown seams, and he disappeared.

At another time Mungo St John galloped past on Shooting Star. He did not look in her direction and the great golden stallion's hooves made no sound. They whirled away into the dusty distances. Then suddenly the earth opened under her and she fell, lightly as a feather from the breast of a goose, lightly as a snowflake, twisting and turning, down and down, then a jarring impact shocked her back to reality.

She lay face down in a bed of sugary white sand. For a moment she thought it was water, and she scooped a double handful and lifted it to her lips, but the dry sharp grains were like salt on her tongue. She looked about her and realized with a sort of bitter triumph that she had at last reached the Tati river and that she lay now in the parched river bed. The fine sand, white as salt, reached from bank to bank – she was about to die of thirst in a river.

'A pool—' she thought. 'There must be a pool.' She began to crawl through the sand, down towards the first bend in the course.

It opened to another long vista of tall banks, and overhanging trees – but the white glittering unbroken sand taunted her. She knew she did not have the strength to crawl as far as the next bend. Her vision was starring and breaking up again; but she frowned with concentration at the piles of brown ball-shaped lumps in the centre of the river bed, and vaguely realized that they were heaps of elephant dung, and that near them were mounds of sand, like children's sandcastles on the beach.

She remembered suddenly a description of the elephant digs from Zouga Ballantyne's book – and it gave her the final burst of strength to pull herself onto her feet and stagger to the nearest sandcastle. The elephants had kicked aside the sand, and made an excavation in the bottom of the river bed as deep as a man's waist. She slid down into it and began frantically to dig with her bare hands. Within minutes her nails were broken and her fingertips bleeding, and the sand kept collapsing back into her hole, but she dug on doggedly.

Then the white sand changed colour, became damp and firm, and at last there was a glint in the very bottom. She tore a strip of cloth from the hem of her ragged skirt and pressed it down into the hole, then after a moment lifted it to her mouth, and with bleeding fingers squeezed out a drop of water onto her cracked and blackened tongue.

I t was as Zouga had always imagined that it would be.

He crossed the Shashi river an hour before high noon on a hot windless day, with the silver and blue thunder-heads piled on the far horizons and the teeming forests and hunting veld of Matabeleland ahead.

He sat astride a fine salted horse, and at his right hand rode his eldest son, a man full grown, straight and strong, a man to delight his father's heart.

'There she is, Papa.' Ralph swept his hat from his head

and gestured with it to include the horizon of smoky-blue hills and green forests. 'There is your north at last. We are coming to take her now.'

Zouga laughed with him, his golden beard glowing in the sunlight and his teeth as white and even as his son's.

'Not quite yet, my boy. This time we have come to woo her – and the next time to take her as a bride.'

Zouga had broken his journey three months at Kimberley, and with the full resources of De Beers Diamond Mines at his disposal had done the planning that Rhodes had ordered.

He had decided on a band of two hundred men to take and hold Mashonaland, to ride the boundaries of the farms and peg the gold reefs. They were to be supported by a detachment of Sir Sidney Shippard's Bechuanaland Police from Khama's kraal – and another detachment of Rhodes' own police which he would raise. Zouga detailed the arms and equipment that they would need – one hundred and sixteen pages of schedules and lists – and Rhodes approved it with that bold sweeping signature and a curt injunction. 'Do it!'

Four days later Ralph had come into Kimberley with two dozen wagons from the Witwatersrand goldfields, and Zouga sat with him all night in his suite in Lil's new hotel.

In the morning Ralph had whistled with excitement.

'It's so big, so many men, so much equipment—'

'Can you do it, Ralph?'

'You want me to tender for a price to recruit the men, buy the equipment and assemble it here at Kimberley, provide the wagons and oxen to carry it all, horses for the men, rifles and ammunition, machine-guns, a steam engine to power a searchlight; then you want me to tender to build a road to get it all to a map reference, a place which you call Mount Hampden, somewhere in the wilderness, and you want it all to be ready to leave in nine months?'

'You have grasped it fairly,' Zouga smiled. 'Can you do it?'

'Give me a week,' Ralph said, and five days later he was back.

'It's too big for me, I'm afraid, Papa,' he said, and then grinned mischievously at Zouga's expression of disappointment. 'I had to take in a partner – Frank Johnson.'

Johnson was another young man in a hurry, and, like Ralph, had already acquired a reputation for being able to get things done.

'Have you and young Johnson worked out a price?'

'We'll do it for eighty-eight thousand two hundred and eighty-five pounds and ten shillings.' Ralph handed him the signed tender and Zouga studied it in silence. When at last he looked up he asked:

'Tell me, Ralph, what is that ten shillings on the end for?'

'Why, Papa—' Ralph widened his eyes disarmingly. 'That is our profit on the deal.'

Zouga had cabled the tender price to Rhodes at Claridge's Hotel in London, and the following day Rhodes had cabled back his acceptance in principle.

All that was still needed was Lobengula's ratification of the consolidated concessions – and Zouga was under Rhodes' orders to go immediately to GuBulawayo and find out from Rudd the reasons for the delay.

Ralph had immediately elected to ride with Zouga.

'Once Mr Rhodes gives us the word to go – there will be no time for anything else. I have some unfinished business in Matabeleland, at Khami Mission and beyond—' And an uncharacteristic dreamy look had come into Ralph's eyes. 'This is the time to do it. While I still have the chance.'

So now, side by side, Zouga and Ralph spurred their mounts up the bank of the Shashi river and rode into Matabeleland.

'We will outspan here for a few days, Papa,' Ralph said; it was still strange for Zouga to have his son make decisions without deferring to him. 'The grazing is good and sweet, and we will rest the oxen and do a little hunting; there is still plenty of game up near the confluence of the Tati river.'

At the beginning of this long journey together, Zouga had been disconcerted by his son's competitive spirit that turned even the most mundane task into a contest. He had forgotten this trait of Ralph's in the time they had been separated but found now that it had grown stronger and fiercer during that period.

His energy daunted Zouga, who found that on this journey – for lack of other opposition – he was a foil for his son's need to compete.

They shot bird, on foot in heavy cover – guinea-fowl and francolin, Ralph counted the bag and scowled when Zouga outgunned him. They sat late at each outspan over the ivory dice, or the greasy dog-eared pack of cards, and Ralph glowed when he won a shilling, and growled when he lost one.

So now, when he said, 'We'll hunt together tomorrow, Papa,' Zouga knew he was in for an early start, and a long hard day.

They rode out from the wagons an hour before the first glimmer of dawn.

'Old Tom is getting *madala* – he's getting old – but I have a sovereign that says he'll run rings around that fancy beast of yours,' Ralph offered.

'I cannot afford that sort of money,' Zouga told him. He was hard and fit, his long professional hunting expeditions had kept him that way but the pace that Ralph set once he was aroused would be punishing. There was something else that troubled Zouga. When Ralph hunted competitively, he could be murderous. If he were challenged, there was only one consideration for him, the size of the bag.

Zouga had been a hunter for the greater part of his life. He had hunted for ivory, and for the peculiar fascination of the beautiful and noble animals he pursued. It was almost a form of love, that made a man want to study and understand and finally take the quarry irrevocably for his own.

These last seasons he had hunted, of necessity, with many men, but he had never yet met a man who hunted like his own son when his blood was up. It seemed as if the game were merely counters in another of Ralph's contests, the score all that counted. 'I don't want to be a sportsman, Papa. I leave that to you. I just want to be a winner.'

'I cannot afford that sort of money,' Zouga repeated, trying lightly to defuse Ralph's escalating tension.

'You can't afford a sovereign?' Ralph threw back his darkly handsome head, and his green eyes flashed as he laughed delighted. 'Papa, you have just sold that fat diamond of yours for thirty thousand pounds.'

'Ralph, let's make an easy day of it. If we get one giraffe, or a buffalo, that's all we need.'

'Papa, you are getting old. A sovereign. If you can't pay immediately, why then, your credit is always good!'

In mid-morning they cut the spoor of a troop of giraffe, feeding slowly eastward along the river bank.

'I make out sixteen of them.' Ralph leaned from the saddle to examine the huge double bean-shaped spoor in the sandy earth. 'They'll not be an hour ahead of us.' And he put his heels into old Tom's flanks.

The forest alternated with open glades through which meandered little streams, draining the escarpment down to the Shashi river. They were dry at this season of the year, but that did not account for the paucity of game.

When Zouga had first travelled this road, going south

from old King Mzilikazi's kraal, the herds had darkened every one of these open glades. In one day's ride he had counted over a hundred monstrous grey rhinoceros, but there had been no counting the silvery herds of fat zebra and clowning purple wildebeest.

In those days, after a man had fired a shot, the dust rising from the galloping herds had looked like the smoke from a bush fire – and yet this day they had ridden since dawn without seeing a single wild animal.

Zouga brooded on it as he rode stirrup for stirrup with his son. Of course, this area was on the direct road to Lobengula's kraal, over which steadily more and more wagons and travellers passed. There were still vast areas beyond where the herds were thick as the grass on which they grazed. But after the road they would cut into Mashonaland – and the railway line that would follow – he wondered what would remain.

Perhaps one day his grandchildren would live in a land of which every corner was as barren as this. He did not envy them the prospect; and even as he thought that, his trained hunter's eye picked up the tiny speck just above the forest line, far ahead.

For a moment he was reluctant to call Ralph's attention to it. It was the head of a giraffe, raised inquisitively high above the mimosa tree on which it was feeding.

For the first time in the hunting veld Zouga felt sick to the gut at the slaughter he knew was about to follow – and he thought to distract Ralph's attention from the herd of huge spotted animals in the mimosa forest ahead. But at that moment Ralph shouted gaily:

'There they are, I'll be damned! They are shy as blushing virgins, they are off already.'

There had been a time when Zouga had been able to ride up to within two hundred yards of a herd before they took alarm. These were still a mile away and already galloping from the two horsemen.

'Come on, Papa. We'll catch them when they try to cross the Shashi,' and they tore into the stand of flowering mimosa.

'Tally-ho!' yelled Ralph. His hat came off and, hanging on its thong, it slapped against his back; while his long dark hair fluttered in the wind of their gallop. 'By God, Papa – you'll have to work to win your sovereign today,' he warned laughingly.

They crashed out of the forest onto another level open plain. The entire herd of huge vulnerable animals were spread before them: bulls and cows and calves, but that was not what caught Zouga's attention.

He pulled his horse down out of its gallop and swung his head away to the west.

'Ralph,' he shouted, 'let them go!'

Ralph looked back at him through the flying dust. His face was flushed with the hunter's fever.

'Warriors,' Zouga shouted. 'War party, Ralph. Close up!'

For a moment it seemed that Ralph would not obey, but then his good sense prevailed. It would be reckless to separate when there was a war party out, and he broke back to Zouga's side and let the panic-driven giraffe tear away towards the river.

He reined Tom to a halt. 'What do you make of them?' he asked, shading his eyes and peering through the heat-distorted air at the squiggly black line, like a shoal of tadpoles in the bottom of a rippling pool, which moved across the far side of the open plain. 'Khama's men? Bamangweto raiders? We are only a few miles from the frontier.'

'We won't take any chances until we know,' Zouga told him grimly. 'Let the horses blow. We may have to make a run—'

But Ralph interrupted him. 'Long shields! And they are red, those are the Moles, Bazo's fellows,' Ralph urged Tom towards the approaching impi. 'And I'll be damned if that isn't Bazo himself out front.'

By the time Zouga came up, Ralph had dismounted and, leaving Tom to stand, had run to embrace his old comrade – and he was already joshing Bazo cruelly.

'Lo, the Moles-that-burrow-under-a-mountain are returning from a raid without women or cattle. Did Khama's people give you the steel farewell?'

Bazo's delighted smile slid off his face at such levity, and he shook his plumes sternly.

'Not even in jest, Henshaw – do not talk like a giggling girl. If the king had sent us to Khama,' and he stabbed the air with his assegai, 'there would have been a beautiful killing.' He broke off as he recognized Zouga.

'Baba!' he said. 'Bakela – I see you, and my eyes are white with joy.'

'It has been too long, Bazo – but now you have the headring on your brow and an impi at your back – we shall shoot a beast and feast together this night.'

'Ah Bakela, it grieves me – but I am on the king's business. I return to GuBulawayo in haste to report the woman's death to the king.'

'Woman?' Zouga asked without real interest.

'A white woman. She ran from GuBulawayo without the king's word, and the king sent me after her—' Bazo broke off with an exclamation. 'Hau! But you know this woman, Bakela.'

'It is not Nomusa, my sister?' Zouga asked with quick concern. 'Not one of her daughters?'

'No, not them.'

'There are no other white women in Matabeleland.'

'She is the woman of One Bright Eye. The same woman who raced her horse against yours at Kimberley – and won. But now she is dead.'

'Dead?' All the blood had drained from Zouga's face, leaving his tan muddy and yellow. 'Dead?' he whispered, and swayed in the saddle so that, had he not grabbed at the pommel, he would have fallen.

'Louise – dead.'

Zouga found the sycamore that Bazo described to him, merely by back-tracking the impi.

They had left a good wide spoor, and Zouga reached the tree in the middle of the afternoon.

He did not know why he tortured himself so. There could be no reasonable doubt that she was dead. Bazo had showed him the pathetic relics he had retrieved. The damaged rifle and bandolier, the empty water-bottle, and the tatters of cloth and saddlery ripped and chewed by the omnivorous jaws of the hyena.

The ground under the sycamore was beaten and swept of all traces of Louise by the pads of jackal and hyena, by the fluttering wings and the talons of hundreds of feeding, squabbling vultures. It smelled like a chicken coop, smeared with vulture dung, and loose feathers blew aimlessly hither and thither on the soft dry breeze.

Except for a few splinters of bone and tufts of hair, every trace of animal carcasses and the human body had been devoured. The hyena would have gobbled up even the leather of Louise's boots and belt, and the few remaining shreds of blanket and cloth were bloodstained.

It was quite easy to reconstruct what had happened. Louise had been set upon by a pride of lion. She had managed a single shot, there was an empty shell in the breech of the damaged rifle, and had killed one of the cats before being pulled off the mule.

Zouga could imagine every moment of her agony, almost hear her screams as the great jaws crunched through her bone and the yellow claws hooked into her flesh. It left him physically nauseated and weakened. He wanted to pray on the spot where she had died, but he did not seem to have the energy for even such small effort. It was as though the very force of life had gone out of him. Until that moment he had not realized what Louise's memory had meant to him, how the certainty that their lives were intertwined had sustained him while they were apart, how his belief in their eventual reunion had given his life purpose and direction. She had become part of his dream, and now it had been snuffed out on this wild and bloody patch of earth.

Twice he turned back to his horse to mount and leave, but each time he hesitated and then wandered back to sift through the reeking dust with his fingers for some last trace of her.

At last he looked at the sun. He could not reach the wagons before nightfall. He had told Ralph to leave Jan Cheroot and the spare horses at the drift of the Shashi when he went on with the wagons, so there was no urgency. There was no hurry. Without Louise there was no flavour in his life. Nothing really mattered any more, but he crossed to his horse, clinched the girth and mounted. He took one more lingering look at the trampled earth and then turned his horse's head back towards the Shashi and the wagons. He had not gone fifty yards when he found himself circling. It was not a conscious decision to begin casting for outgoing spoor. He knew it was futile, but his reluctance to leave the place dictated his actions.

Once he circled the sycamore, leaning out of the saddle and examining the broken and stony earth, then he moved farther out and circled again, then again, each time opening the radius of the circle. Suddenly his heart leaped against his ribs, and new hope flooded his devastated soul, but he had to steel himself to lean from the saddle and examine the thorn twig, in case he was to be disappointed once again.

The white tear had caught his eye, the twig had been

broken half-through and now hung from the main branch at the level of a man's waist. The soft green leaves had wilted, the break was two or three days' old, but that was not what made Zouga's fingers shake.

From one of the curved red-tipped thorns hung a fine red thread of spun cotton. Zouga lifted it reverently and then touched it to his lips as though it were a sacred relic.

He was to the west of the sycamore; he could just make out the top branches above the surrounding bush, which meant that Louise had left that thread on the grasping thorn after she had run from the tree. The height above ground showed she had been on foot, and the broken twig and shredded cloth were evidence of her haste.

She had run from the sycamore and kept going in the direction which she had been stubbornly following, westwards, towards the Tati and Khama's country.

Zouga thumped his heels into the horse's flanks and galloped in the same direction. It was useless to look for spoor three days' old on this rocky ground. The wind had blown steadily for most of that time, and it would have scoured the last traces.

He must rely on luck and speed. He had seen the empty water-bottle and he knew what were the chances of survival on foot, without water, in this country between the rivers. He galloped on the line of her flight, quartering from side to side, searching grimly – not allowing himself to doubt again, concentrating all his mind on the search for another tiny sign. In the last minutes of dusk he found it. It was the heel of a brown riding boot torn from the sole. The gleam of the steel nails had caught his eye. He drew the rifle from its holder and fired three spaced shots into the darkening sky.

He knew she had no rifle to reply – but if somewhere out ahead she heard his signal, it might give her hope and strength. He waited beside a small fire until the moon came up – and then by its light he went on, and every hour he stopped and fired signal shots into the great starry silence, and afterwards he listened intently, but there was only the shriek of a hunting owl overhead and the yipping of a jackal far out across the silvery plain.

In the dawn he reached the wide white course of the Tati river. It was dry as the dunes of the Kalahari Desert, and the hopes which he had kept alive all night began to wane.

He searched the morning sky for the high spiral of turning vultures which would show a kill, but all he saw was a brace of sand grouse slanting down on quick stabbing wings. Their presence proved that there was surface water – somewhere. She might have found it – that was the only chance. Unless she had found water she would be dead by now. He took a cautious mouthful from his own bottle, and his horse whickered when he smelt the precious liquid. Soon the thirst would begin wearing him down as well.

He had to believe that if Louise had reached the river, she would follow it downstream. She was part Indian, and she would surely be able to get her direction from the sun and to know that her only chance was southwards towards the confluence with the Shashi. He turned in that direction, staying up on the bank, watching the river bed and the far bank and the sky.

Elephant had been digging in the bed, but their holes were dry now. He trotted on along the edge of the high bank. Ahead of him there was a rush of big purple-beige bodies as a herd of gemsbuck burst through the rank undergrowth on the far bank. Their long straight horns were like lances against the pale horizon sky, and the diamond-patterned face masks that gave their name seemed theatrical and frivolous. They galloped away into the deserts of Khama's country.

They could live without water for months at a time, and their presence gave Zouga no hope, but as he watched them go, his attention shifted to another distant movement much farther out on the flat open ground beyond the river.

There was a chacma baboon foraging there – the humanoid shape was quite distinctive. He looked for the rest of the troop – perhaps they were in the treeline beyond the plain. Chacma baboon would drink daily, and he shaded his eyes against the glare to watch the distant moving dark blob. It seemed to be feeding on the green fruit of the vine of the wild desert melons, but at this range it was difficult to be certain.

Then abruptly he realized that he had never before encountered baboon this far to the west, and at the same moment he was convinced that there was no troop. It was a solitary animal, unheard of with such a gregarious species, and immediately after that he saw that this animal was too big to be a baboon, and that its movements were uncharacteristic of an ape.

With a singing, soaring joy he launched into a full gallop, and the hooves beat an urgent staccato rhythm on the iron-hard earth, but as he dragged his horse down to a plunging halt and swung down out of the saddle, his joy shrivelled.

She was on her knees, and they were scratched bloody by the stony ground. Her clothing was mostly gone, and her tender flesh was exposed in the rents. The sun had burned her arms and legs into red raw blisters. Her feet were bound up in the remains of her skirt, but blood had soaked through the rags.

Her hair was a dry tangled bush about her head, powdered with dust and with the ends split and bleached. Her lips were black scabs, burned and cracked down into the living meat. Her eyelids were swollen as though stung by bees and she peered up at him like a blind old crone through slits that were caked with dried yellow mucus. The flesh had fallen off her body and her face. Her arms were skeletal and her cheekbones seemed to push through the skin. Her hands were blackened claws – the nails torn down into the quick.

She crouched like an animal over the flat leaves of the vine, and she had broken open one of the wild green melons with her fingers and stuffed pulp into her ruined mouth. The juice ran down her chin, cutting a runnel through the dirt that plastered her skin.

'Louise.' He went down on one knee, facing her. 'Louise—' His voice choked.

She made a little mewling sound in her throat and then touched her hair in a heart-breakingly feminine gesture, trying to smooth the stiff dust-caked tresses.

'Is it?' she croaked, peering at him with bloodshot eyes from slits of sun-swollen red lids. 'It isn't—'

Fumbling, she tried to cover one soft white breast with the rags of her blouse. She started to shake, wildly and uncontrollably, and then she closed her eyes tightly.

He reached out gently and at his touch she collapsed against his chest, still shaking, and he held her. She felt light and frail as a child.

'I knew—' she mumbled. 'It didn't make sense, but I knew somehow that you would come.'

'Will you not dowse the lantern, Ralph?' Cathy whispered, and her eyes were huge and dark and piteous as she crept in under the canvas of his wagon.

'Why?' he asked, smiling, propping himself on one elbow on the wagon cot.

'Somebody may come.'

'Your father and mother are still at Lobengula's kraal. There is nobody—'

'My sister – Salina—'

'Salina is long ago asleep, dreaming of brother Jordan, no doubt. We are alone, Cathy, all alone. So why should we put out the lantern?'

'Because I am shy, then,' she said, and blushed a new shade of scarlet. 'All you ever do is tease me. I wish I had never come.'

'Oh Cathy.' His chuckle was fond and indulgent, and he sat up on his cot, and the blanket slid to his waist. Quickly she averted her eyes from his naked chest and muscled upper arms. The skin was so white and marble-smooth in comparison to his brown forearms and face. It set strange unfamiliar emotions loose within her.

'Come!' He caught her wrist and drew her towards the cot, but she hung back until he jerked her forward and, taken off balance, she fell across his legs.

Before she could break free, he had taken a handful of the thick dark hair at the back of her head and turned her pale face up to his mouth. For a while she continued to struggle unconvincingly, and then her whole body softened, like wax in the candle flame, and seemed to melt over him.

'Do you still wish you had not come, Cathy?' he asked, but she could not reply; instead she tightened her arms around his neck convulsively. Once more she searched for his mouth with hers, and made a little moaning sound.

He goaded her with his mouth and tongue, the way Lil had first taught him so long ago, and she was defenceless as a beautiful soft-bodied insect in the spider's gossamer toils. It excited him as none of the practised and calculating women on whom he had spent his gold sovereigns ever had.

His own breathing started to hunt roughly, and his fingers shook at the lacings of her bodice. The skin of her shoulder was without blemish, silky and warm. He touched it with the tip of his tongue, and she shuddered and gasped, but when he pulled down the light cotton, she shrugged her shoulders to let the cloth come free. It caught for a moment and then slid to the level of her lowest rib.

He was unprepared for those tender and terribly vulnerable young breasts, so pale and rosy-tipped and yet at the same time hard and jubilant in their marvellous symmetry.

He stared at her body, and she watched him through half-closed lids, but made no effort to cover herself, though her cheeks were wildly flushed and her lips trembled as she whispered.

'No, Ralph, I don't want to go – not now, or ever.'

'The lantern—' He reached for it, but now she caught his hand.

'No, Ralph, I'm not ashamed of you and me. I don't want darkness, I want to see your dear face.'

She jerked the ribbon loose from her waist and then lifted her dress over her head and let it flutter to the wagon floor. Her limbs were long and coltish, her hips still bony as a boy's, and her belly concave as a greyhound's above the dark triangular bush of her womanhood. Her skin shone in the lantern light with that peculiar lustre of healthy, vibrant youth. He stared at it for only an instant and then she had lifted the corner of the rough woollen blanket and slid in under it. The long slim arms and legs wrapped around him.

'There is nothing I would not do for you. I would steal and lie and cheat – and even kill for you, my wonderful, beautiful Ralph,' she whispered. 'I'm not sure what a man and woman do, but if you show me I will be the happiest girl on this earth to do it with you.'

'Cathy, I didn't mean this to happen—' He tried with a last sudden lash of his conscience to push her away.

'I did,' she said, clinging stubbornly to him. 'Why else do you think I came here?'

'Cathy—'

'I love you, Ralph, I loved you from the very first moment I ever saw you.'

'I love you, Cathy.' And he was amazed to find that what be said was the truth. 'I really and truly love you,' he said again, and then later, much later: 'I didn't realize how much until now.'

'I didn't know that it would be like this,' she whispered. 'I have thought about if often, every day since you first came to Khami. I even read about it in the Bible – it says that David *knew* her. Do we know each other now, Ralph?'

'I want to know you better – and more often,' he grinned at her, his tousled hair still damp with sweat.

'I felt as though I had fallen through a dark hole in my soul into another beautiful world, and I didn't want to come back again.' Cathy's voice was awed and marvelling, as though she were the first in all the infinite lists of creation to experience it. 'Didn't you feel that, Ralph?'

They held each other close under the blanket, and they talked softly, examining each other's faces in the yellow lantern light, breaking off every few minutes to kiss the other's throat and eyelids and lips.

It was Cathy who pulled away at last. 'I don't want to know the time, but listen to the birds, it will be light too soon.' Then, with a rush of words, 'Oh Ralph, I don't want you to go.'

'It will not be for long, I promise you. Then I will be back.'

'Take me with you.'

'You know I can't.'

'Why not – because it's dangerous, isn't it?'

But he avoided the question by trying to kiss her again. She put her hand over his mouth.

'I'll die a little every moment of the time you are gone, but I'll pray for you. I'll pray that Lobengula's warriors do not find you.'

'Don't worry about me,' he chuckled fondly. 'We'll fall through that dark hole in your soul again soon.'

'Promise,' she whispered, and brushed the damp curls off

his forehead with her lips. 'Promise me you will come back, my beautiful, darling Ralph.'

Ralph started his wagon train south again on the road to the Shashi, and for the first morning he rode at the head of the unusually lightly loaded vehicles. At noon he gave the order to outspan. He and Isazi slept away the hot afternoon, while the bullocks and horses grazed and rested.

Then at dusk they cut the five chosen bullocks out of the herd and tied them to the wagon wheels by leather reins around the boss of their horns while they fitted the back packs. Ralph and Isazi had selected these beasts for their strength and willingness, and during the long trek up from Kimberley he had trained them to accept these unusual burdens with resigned docility.

Jordan had provided Ralph with the precise measurements and weight of the bird statue that now graced the entrance to Mr Rhodes' new mansion, Groote Schuur, and Ralph had used these figures to design the back packs and constructed them with his own hands, not trusting anyone else with his secret intentions.

Each pack could carry two statues like the one at Groote Schuur. They would be slung in woven nets of good mania rope on each side of the bullock, and Ralph had worked meticulously to ensure a perfect fit of the saddle to protect the beasts' back from galling, and prevent the load from shifting even over the roughest ground or on the steepest inclines.

Now, when Isazi, the little Zulu driver, led the file of three bullocks quietly out of the camp and disappeared into the darkening forest, they followed meekly. Ralph stayed behind just long enough to repeat his orders to the other drivers.

'You will double-march to the Shashi river. If the border impis question where I am, you will tell them I am hunting to the east with the king's permission, and that you expect me to rejoin the wagons at any time. Do you understand?'

'I understand, Nkosi,' said Umfaan, who, although now promoted from *voorlooper* to driver, still answered to the name of 'Boy'.

'Once you cross the Shashi, you will trek on as far as the Bushman wells, five days' march beyond the frontier. Lobengula's impis will not follow you that far. Wait there until I come, do you understand, Umfaan?'

'I understand, Nkosi.'

'Then repeat it to me.'

Satisfied at last, Ralph stepped up into Tom's stirrup and looked down at them from his back.

'Go swiftly,' he said.

'Go in peace, Nkosi.'

He trotted out of camp, following Isazi's bullock train and dragging behind him a bulky branch of thorn mimosa to sweep their spoor clean. By mid-morning the following day they were well clear of the wagon road and had entered the mystical Matopos Hills. While the oxen grazed and rested, Ralph rode ahead to mark a trail between the soaring granite kopjes, and through the deep and sullen gorges. At dark they resaddled the bullocks with their packs and went on.

The next day Ralph made a noon observation of the sun with the old brass sextant. From experience he made allowance for the cumulative error in his boxed chronometer, and worked out a position which he knew was accurate to within ten miles. Also from experience, he knew that his father's observations, made before he was born, were usually as accurate. Without them he would never have found the caches of ivory which had been the start of his growing fortune.

His calculations compared to his father's showed that

he was one hundred and sixty miles west of the ancient ruined city that the Matabele called Zimbabwe, the burial place of the old kings.

Then, while he waited for darkness to resume the march, he took from his saddle-bags the sheaf of notes which Zouga had given him as a parting gift when he first left Kimberley. He read the description of the route to Zimbabwe, and of the city itself, for possibly the hundredth time.

'How much longer must we march through these hills?' Isazi broke his concentration. He was cooking maize cakes on a small smokeless fire of dry wood. 'My beasts suffer on these rocks and steep places,' he grumbled. 'We should have gone farther south and passed below the hills on the open ground.'

'Where Lobengula's bucks wait and pray every day for the chance to stick an assegai through a skinny little Zulu,' Ralph smiled.

'There is the same danger here.'

'No,' Ralph shook his head. 'No Matabele comes into these sacred hills without good reason. We will find no impi here, and once we come out on the far side, we will be beyond the farthest regimental kraals.'

'And this place of stone to which we go? There will be no impi waiting for us there?'

'Lobengula forbids any man even to look into the valley in which the stones stand. It is a death-marked place, cursed by Lobengula and his priests.'

Isazi shifted uncomfortably. 'Who sets store by the curse of a fat Matabele dog?' he demanded, and touched the charm on his belt which warded off devils and hobgoblins and other dark secret things.

Despite his assurances to Isazi, Ralph moved with utmost caution in threading the maze of the Matopos. During daylight he hid the bullocks in some thick patch of bush in a rock gorge, and he went ahead to reconnoitre every yard of the way and to mark it for Isazi to follow with a discreetly blazed tree trunk or a broken twig of green leaves at every turning or difficult place.

These precautions saved him from disaster. On the third day he had tied Tom in good cover and gone forward on foot to the ridge from where he could look into the next valley.

Just below the brow he was alerted by the raucous alarm call of a grey lourie, the 'Go-Away' bird of the African bush. The cry came from just beyond the ridge, and as he froze to listen he heard a gentle susurration like the wind in tall grass; he ducked and jumped off the path, sprawling on his belly with his rifle tucked into the crook of his elbows, and rolled under the spreading branches of a low red berry bush – just as the first rank of Matabele warriors came sweeping over the rise ahead of him, with their cloaks and kilts and headdresses rustling – the sound which had warned him.

From where he lay under the bush beside the path, Ralph could see only as high as their knees as they passed, but their gait was that determined businesslike trot which the Matabele call '*minza hlabathi*', to eat the earth greedily.

He counted them. Two hundred warriors in all went past, and the soft rustle of their feet dwindled – but Ralph lay frozen beneath his bush, not daring even to creep deeper into the undergrowth. Minutes later, he heard the soft chant of bearers coming up from the next valley, and then they were trotting past his hiding-place, singing the praise song to the king in their deep melodious voices.

Ralph could tell by the spacing and weight of their gait that they were carrying a heavy litter.

He had guessed that the leading band was merely a vanguard. This was the main party, while the person on the litter was without any doubt Lobengula himself, and following him were his attendants, his high indunas and other important personages. After them again, more bearers carrying sleeping-mats and karosses of fur, beer pots and leather sacks of maize meal and other burdens. They filed past and disappeared, but still Ralph did not rise from hiding.

Another long silence, and then, with only a soft warning rustle, came the rear guard, two hundred more picked warriors trotting past. After five minutes Ralph felt it was safe to crawl out onto the path and dust the damp leaf mould from his knees and elbows.

From the top of the ridge he stared back in the direction which Lobengula's party had taken, puzzled as to where they were all headed and why. He knew from Cathy that Rudd and his party were still at GuBulawayo and that Clinton Codrington and Robyn were with them, negotiating the concession that Mr Rhodes so desperately needed.

Why would Lobengula leave such important guests at his kraal and come up here into these sacred and deserted hills?

There was no answer, and Ralph had to be content with having so narrowly escaped discovery, and to be now alerted to the presence of large parties of warriors in the area.

He moved forward with even more caution than before so that it took three more nights of travel at the pace of the bullocks before they came out of another pass between bald granite cliffs and saw the open forests of tall and lovely trees rolling away below them, silver and charcoal in the moonlight.

In the dawn Ralph climbed the cliff to the peak of the last of the Matopos Hills, and on the eastern horizon – almost exactly where he had hoped to find it – he picked out the far blue silhouette of a solitary kopje standing above the forested plain. It was still thirty miles distant, but the shape of a crouching lion was unmistakable, and it fitted exactly the description in Zouga Ballantyne's notes:

The hill which I have named 'Lion's Head' stands high above the surrounding terrain, and points the traveller unerringly towards great Zimbabwe—

A man might have walked in the shadow of the massive stone walls and never known they were there, so dense was the growth that covered them. It was a jungle of liana and flowering creepers, while from the very walls themselves grew the twisting serpentine roots of the strangler figs, wedging open the mortarless joints of the stonework and bringing it down in screes of fallen blocks.

Above the level of the high walls soared the heads of other tall trees, grown to giants in the time since the last inhabitant had fled this place or died within its labyrinth of passages and courtyards. When Zouga Ballantyne had discovered this massive keep before Ralph's birth, it had taken him almost two days to find the narrow gateway under this mass of tangled vegetation, but now his directions and descriptions led Ralph immediately to it.

Ralph stood before the ancient portals and looked up at the pattern of chevron stone blocks which decorated the top of the wall thirty feet above his head, and was seized with a primeval superstitious awe.

Though he could see the marks of his father's axe, and the old stumps cut away on each side of the opening, a veil of trailing plants had regrown to screen the gateway – proof that no human being had entered it since Zouga's visit more than twenty-five years before.

The steps that led up to the gateway had been dished by the passage of the feet of the ancient inhabitants over the centuries. Ralph drew a deep breath, and silently reminded himself that he was a civilized Christian; but his superstitious fears lingered as he climbed the stairs, ducked under the trailing creepers and stepped through the gateway.

He found himself in a narrow twisted stone gut between high walls open to the sky. He followed the passage, clambering over fallen stonework blocks and forcing his way through brush and undergrowth that choked it, until abruptly he came out into a wide courtyard, dominated by an immense cylindrical tower of lichen-coated grey granite.

It was exactly as his father had described it, even to the damaged parapet of the tower where Zouga had broken in to discover whether the interior of the towering structure contained a secret treasure chamber. He knew that his father had ransacked the ruins for treasure, he had even torn up and sieved the earth of this temple enclosure for gold. He had retrieved almost a thousand ounces of the yellow metal, small beads and flakes of foil, finely woven gold wire and tiny ingots the size of an infant's finger, and Ralph knew that the only treasure left for him were the idols of green soapstone.

With a stoop of his spirits, Ralph thought for a moment that someone else had forestalled him. According to Zouga, the stone falcons should have been here in this courtyard, and he started forward, his superstitious chills forgotten in the bleaker fear of having been deprived of his booty.

He plunged into the waist-high undergrowth and waded through it towards the tower – and he tripped over the first of the statues, and almost fell. He crouched over it and with his hands tore away the tangle that covered it, and then he looked into the blank cruel eyes above the curved beak that he remembered so well from his childhood. It was the identical twin of the statue that had stood on the verandah of Zouga's cottage at Kimberley, but this falcon had been cast down and lay half buried by roots and brush.

He ran his hands over the satiny green soapstone, then with one finger traced the well-remembered shark's-tooth pattern around the plinth.

'I've come for you at last,' he whispered aloud, and then looked around him quickly. His voice had echoed eerily against the surrounding walls, and he shivered though the sun was still high. Then he stood up and went on searching.

There were six statues, as Zouga had counted them. One was shattered as though by the blows from a sledgehammer, the battered head lay beside it. Three others were damaged to a lesser extent, but the remaining two statues were perfect.

'This is an evil place,' a sepulchral voice intoned unexpectedly, and Ralph started and spun to face it.

Isazi had followed and stood close behind him, preferring the terrors of the narrow passages and ominous walls to the greater terror of remaining alone at the gateway to the city.

'When can we leave here, Nkosi?' Isazi shot restless little glances into the dismal corners of tumbled passageways. 'It is not a place where a man should stay overlong.'

'How soon can we load these onto the oxen?' Ralph squatted and patted one of the fallen images. 'Can we do it before nightfall?'

'*Yebho*, Nkosi.' Isazi promised fervently. 'By nightfall we will be a good march away from here. You have my word upon it.'

The king had once again chosen Bazo for a special task – and Bazo's heart was big with pride as he led the vanguard of his impi along the secret road that took them deeper and deeper into the dreaming Hills of the Matopos.

The road was well beaten, wide enough for two warriors to run abreast with their shields just touching, for it had been used since the time when Mzilikazi, the old king, had first brought the nation up from the south.

Mzilikazi himself had blazed the trail to the secret cavern

of the Umlimo. At every crisis in the nation's history, the old king had followed this road – in drought or pestilence or plague, he had come to hear the words of the chosen one. Every season he had come for advice on the herds and the crops, or to help him decide in which direction to send his raiding impis.

Lobengula, himself an initiate of the lesser mysteries, had first entered the cavern of the Umlimo as a youth – led by the crazed old magician who had been his mentor and his tutor. It had been the Umlimo's word which had placed the toy spear of kingship in Lobengula's hand when Mzilikazi had let it fall from his grasp. It was the Umlimo who had chosen Lobengula in preference to Nkulumane or the other older brothers of nobler birth – and it was the Umlimo who had made him the favourite of the ancestral spirits and had sustained him in the darkest hours of his reign.

Thus it was that Lobengula, plagued by the importunate demands of the emissaries of a white man whom he had never seen, confused by scraps of paper whose signs he could not read, troubled by doubts and tormented by fears, badgered and pulled by the conflicting advice of his senior indunas – was at last returning to the secret cavern.

He lay on his litter, on a mattress of the soft yellow and black spotted furs of the leopard, rocked by the motion of the trotting bearers, so that the naked folds and bulges of his gross black body shook and rippled, and he looked ahead with dark and haunted eyes.

Lodzi – that was the name on every white man's lips. Everywhere he turned, Lobengula heard the name Lodzi.

'Is this Lodzi a king, as I am a king?' he had asked the white man with the red face; for Lobengula, as a Matabele, could not pronounce the 'R' of the name.

'Mr Rhodes is not a king, yet he is greater than a king,' Rudd had replied.

'Why does not Lodzi come to me himself?'

'Mr Rhodes has gone across the sea, he sends us lesser men to do this business.'

'If I could look upon the face of Lodzi, then I would know if his heart was great.'

But Rhodes would not come, and day after day Lobengula had listened to the insistence of Lodzi's minions, and in the nights his indunas cautioned and questioned him, and argued amongst themselves.

'If you give the white men a finger, they want the hand,' Gandang told him, 'and having the hand, they desire the arm and then the chest and the heart and the head.'

'Oh King, Lodzi is a man of pride and honour. His word is like Lobengula's own. He is a good man,' said Nomusa, whom he trusted as he trusted few others.

'Give each of the white men a little – and give the same thing to each of them,' counselled Kamuza, one of his youngest but most cunning indunas, a man who had lived with the white men and knew their ways. 'Thus every white man becomes the enemy of the other. Set one dog on the other, lest the pack set upon you.'

'Choose the strongest of the white men and make him our ally,' said Somabula. 'This Lodzi is the herd bull. Choose him.'

And Lobengula had cocked his ear to each of them in turn, and become more desperate and more confused with every conflicting view, until now there was only one path open to him, the path into the Matopos.

Behind his litter came the bearers with the gifts for the oracle, rolls of copper wire, leather bags of coarse salt, pots of trade beads, six great tusks of yellow ivory, bolts of bright cloth, knives made by his master smith with handles of rhinoceros horn, a considerable treasure to pay for the words which he hoped would give him solace.

The path twisted down like a maimed serpent into the gut of the hills, so that the sun was lost and there was only a narrow strip of blue sky showing between the tops of the granite cliffs.

The rank and thorny vegetation crowded the pathway and at last met overhead, forming a dreary tunnel, and the silence was a heavy oppressive presence, for no bird sang and no animal squeaked or scurried in the undergrowth.

But Bazo led on at the same pace, his head swinging from side to side, scanning for danger or menace, and his grip on the shaft of his stabbing spear was firm, his sweat-oiled muscles tense as the springs of a mantrap, ready to hurl his body forward to meet an enemy at any twist in the path.

There was a stream of slow green water and algae-slick boulders across the track, and Bazo leapt it easily with barely a break in his stride; and fifty paces farther on the bush thinned and the cliffs pinched in to form a natural gateway of stone that led into the looming precipice.

Here a determined spearman could hold a thousand and Bazo surveyed it with the swift appraisal of a soldier; and then he raised his gaze to the ledge high above on which was perched a small thatched watch-hut.

Bazo grounded the butt of his long red shield – and called up the cliff. 'I, Bazo, induna of one thousand, demand passage.' His voice boomed and broke into a myriad echoes against the stone walls.

'In whose name do you come to trouble the spirits of the air and earth?' a querulous old man's voice replied, and a sticklike figure, foreshortened by the height of the cliff, appeared upon the lip.

'I come in the king's name, Lobengula the Black Bull of Matabele.' Bazo scorned to wait on permission or favour and, sweeping his shield up onto his shoulder, he sprang forward through the ominous portals.

The passageway beyond was so narrow that his warriors

could follow only in single file, and the grey sand that covered the floor sparkled with starry chips of mica and crunched under their bare feet. The passageway curved upon itself and then opened again without warning over a hidden valley.

The valley was completely enclosed by sheer cliffs, and this narrow passage was its only entrance. The bowl of the floor was lush with green grass, and watered by a clear fountain that sprang from the cliff face beside the gateway and meandered down into the valley bottom.

In the centre of the valley, a thousand paces ahead, was a tiny village, twenty or so thatched huts laid out in a neat circle. Bazo led his warriors down and, with a gesture of his assegai, formed them into a double rank on each side of the pathway that led to the huts.

They waited in stillness and silence until the distant chant of the litter-bearers grew louder, and at last the king's party emerged into the hidden valley – and Bazo led his men in a deep chorus of praise and salutation.

T he royal party camped two days beside the tiny stream, waiting on the Umlimo's pleasure.

Each day her attendants came to Lobengula to receive gifts and tribute on the oracle's behalf. They were a strange and macabre motley of lesser wizards and witches; some of them, touched by the spirits they served, were crazed and wild-eyed, others were young nubile girls, their bodies painted and their eyes blank and empty like the smokers of the hemp pipe. There were children with wise old eyes who did not laugh or play like other children, and ancients with withered bodies and sly eyes who spoke with the king in low, wheedling tones and took his gifts and promised: 'Perhaps tomorrow; who knows when the power of divination will descend upon the Umlimo.'

Then on the dawn of the third day Lobengula sent for Bazo, and when he came to the king's camp fire, his father Gandang was already with the king, dressed in full regimentals, plume and fur and tassels of valour at elbow and knee, and with him were six of the other senior indunas.

'Bazo, my fine axe with a sharp edge, I have chosen you to stand by my shoulder when I face the Umlimo – to guard my back against treachery,' ordered Lobengula, and Bazo felt his chest swell with pride at such a mark of the king's trust.

A witch led them, prancing and mumbling and mouthing, through the village and up the far side of the valley. Burdened by his great bulk, Lobengula paused often on the climb, his breathing sobbing in his throat, and he rested on Gandang's arm before going on again, until at last they reached the foot of the sheer high cliff. Here there was a cave in the rock. Its entrance was a hundred paces wide, but its roof low enough for a man to reach up and touch. Some time long ago the entrance had been walled up with square blocks of dressed stone, but the wall had tumbled down, leaving dark gaps like the missing teeth in an old man's mouth.

At a nod from his father, Bazo placed the king's carved stool facing the cave and Lobengula lowered his great black haunches upon it gratefully. Bazo stood at the king's back, his assegai gripped underhand, and pointed forward towards the dark entrance in the rock.

Suddenly there came the terrible spitting, tearing snarl of an angry leopard from the cave mouth, so loud and close and real that the band of hardened old warriors started and swayed, and stood their ground only with an obvious effort of will. The old witch giggled and spittle ran down her chin.

The silence fell again, but charged with promise and the threat of an unseen presence watching them from the utter darkness of the cave's recesses.

Then there was a voice, the voice of a child, sweet and piping clear. It issued not from the cave but from the air above the king's head, so that all of them raised their eyes. There was nothing there except the voice.

'The stars will shine upon the hills, and the Black Bull will not quench them.'

The little group of indunas drew closer together as though to take comfort from one another, and the silence fell again. Bazo felt himself shivering, although his sweat tickled like an insect as it ran down between his shoulder blades. Then he jerked his head as another voice spoke. It came from the ground at the king's feet, and it used the liquid purring tones of a beautiful and seductive woman.

'The sun will shine at midnight, and the Great Elephant will not dim it.'

Again that fraught and frightening silence, before something croaked from the cliff high above them, a hoarse inhuman sound, like the croak of a carrion crow.

'Heed the wisdom of the vixen before that of the dogfox, Lobengula, King of—' The voice broke off abruptly, and there was a scuffling sound deep in the black maw of the cave, and the old crone who had been nodding and grinning at Lobengula's feet scrambled up and shouted an order in an unknown tongue.

Now there was a flash of movement within the cave, and it caused consternation to Lobengula and his indunas, for they had visited the cave a hundred times and more but they had never seen the Umlimo nor had any glimpse of her presence in the depths of the cave.

This was something beyond ritual and custom, and the crone hopped forward, shouting angrily; and now they could make out what was happening in the gloom. It seemed that two of the macabre attendants of the Umlimo were trying to restrain a smaller and more agile figure. They were unsuccessful, for the person threw off their clutching, claw-like hands and ran forward to the threshold of the cave, where the early sunlight revealed the Umlimo at last.

She was so beautiful that all of them, even the king, gasped and stared. Her skin was oiled and polished to the colour of dark amber.

Her limbs were long and supple as a heron's neck, her feet and hands finely shaped. She was in the prime of her womanhood, her body not yet distorted by childbearing; although her belly was luscious as a ripening fruit her waist was narrow as a lad's. All she wore was a single string of crimson beads about her waist, knotted at the level of the deeply sculptured pit of her navel. Her hips flared with a delicate line, forming a broad basin to contain the spade-shaped wedge of her sex. It nestled there like a dark furry little animal possessed of separate life and existence.

Her head was perfectly balanced on the long stem of her neck; the neat cap of her hair set off the marvellous domed contours of her skull and exposed the small neat shape of her ears. Her features were oriental, the huge eyes slanted, her cheekbones high and her nose delicate and straight – but her mouth was twisted with anguish and her eyes blinded with tears as she stared at the young induna who stood at the king's back.

Slowly she lifted one hand and reached out towards him; the long, delicate palm was pink and soft, the gesture infinitely sad.

'Tanase!' whispered Bazo, staring at her, and his hands shook so that the blade of his assegai clattered against the rim of his shield.

This was the woman he had chosen and who had been so cruelly taken from him. Since her going Bazo had sought no other to wife, though the king had chided him, and others whispered that it was unnatural, yet Bazo had held to the memory of this bright, sweet maid. He wanted to rush to her and seize her, to swing her high upon his shoulder and bear her away, but he stood rooted, her anguish reflected in his own eyes.

For though she stood before him, she was as remote as the full moon. She was a child of the spirits and protected by their horrid servants, far beyond the reach of his loving hands and constant heart.

Her attendants came now from the cave behind her, to scold and whine. Slowly Tanase lowered her arm, though for a moment longer her whole body yearned towards Bazo, and then her lovely head wilted like a flower upon the long, graceful stalk of her neck and she allowed them to take her arms.

'Tanase!' Bazo said her name for the last time, and her shoulders jerked at the sound of his voice.

Then a terrible thing happened. A shuddering convulsion ran up Tanase's back, from the perfect globes of her tight, hard buttocks to the nape of her neck, so that the nerves and muscles twitched and contracted on each side of her spine. Then her spine began to bend backwards like a hunter's bow.

'The spirit is upon her,' shrieked the old witch. 'Let the spirit take her!'

They let her be, drawing back from her wracked body.

Every muscle in her body was under such strain that it stood out in clear and separate definition under her glossy skin – and her spine arched to an impossible angle, the base of her skull almost touching the soft flesh at the back of her knees.

Her face was contorted with the unbearable agony of divination; her eyes rolled back into her head so that only the whites showed. Her lips were drawn back so that the small perfect white teeth were exposed in a frozen rictus and creamy froth bubbled from the corners of her mouth.

Though her lips did not move, a voice boomed from her tortured throat. It was the deep bass of a man, the stentorian voice of a warrior, and it bore no trace of the terrible travail of the young woman from whom it issued.

'The falcons! The white hawk has torn open the nest of stone. The falcons are flying. Save the falcons! The falcons!'

The voice rose abruptly into a wild shriek, and Tanase collapsed and writhed like a squashed insect upon the earth.

'No black man, neither Matabele nor Rozwi nor Karanga, none of them would dare desecrate the nest of the falcons,' said Lobengula, and the circle of indunas nodded. 'Only a white man would have the effrontery to defy the word of the king and chance the wrath of the spirits.'

He paused and took snuff, drawing out the little ritual to put off the moment of decision.

'If I send an impi to Zimbabwe and we take a white man in the red act of plundering the ancient place, dare I send steel through his heart?' Lobengula turned to Somabula, and the old man lifted his grey head and looked sadly at his king.

'Kill one of them, and the others will come swarming like ants,' he said. 'Set not a feast for the birds, when it will bring a pride of lions instead.'

Lobengula sighed and looked to Gandang:

'Speak, my father's son.'

'Oh King, Somabula is wise and his words have the same weight as boulders of black ironstone. Yet the king's words are heavier still, and the king's words have been given – *the despoilers of the ancient places must die*. Those are the words of Lobengula.'

The king nodded slowly.

'Bazo!' he said softly, and the young induna dropped on one knee before the king's stool.

'Take one of the wizards to guide your impi to the nest of the falcons. If the stone birds are gone, follow them. Find the despoiler. If it is a white man, take him where no other eyes can see you, not even those of your most trusted warriors. Kill the man and bury him in a secret place, and speak of it to no man but your king. Do you hear the words of Lobengula?'

'I hear, oh Great King, and to hear is to obey.'

Dutchman, the bullock with the narrowest spread of horns, was the only one which Isazi could coax down the narrow passageways and over the tumbled stonework into the temple enclosure of the ruins. In the baskets on his sturdy, dappled back, they ferried out the bird images, even the damaged ones, and repacked them onto the backs of the other oxen which waited outside the massive walls.

With Isazi's skilful handling of the bullocks and their burdens, the work was finished by mid-afternoon, and they roped the oxen in single file. With patent relief, Isazi led them away through the forest towards the south.

Ralph's relief was every bit as intense. He had been uneasy ever since that chance encounter with the Matabele impi in the hills. Now he let Isazi go on with the oxen, while he circled back across their incoming tracks to the north-west of the ruined city, examining the ground with the hunter's eye for any sign that they had been followed, or that there were any other human beings in the area. It need not be a war party – even a band of honey-gatherers or a hunter could carry word back to Lobengula's kraal or alert the border impis.

He knew what he would have to do if he found a wanderer or solitary hunter, and he eased the rifle in the leather boot at his knee. These forests were populous. He saw troops of big-eared striped kudu, sable antelope with snowy bellies and sweeping scimitar horns, big black bovine buffalo and spreading herds of plump zebra with alert pricked ears and stiff, black manes, but there was no sign of human presence.

He was only slightly mollified when he turned back and picked up the spoor of the bullock file five miles on the other side of the ruins. He trotted along the widely beaten sign, and his misgivings returned at full strength. This was too easy to follow.

He caught up with Isazi and his bullock train as the dusk was falling, and he helped him lift the heavy packs down from the backs of the oxen and examine them for galling or saddle sores, before hobbling them and letting them graze. More than once during the night he started awake, and listened for the sound of men's voices – but heard only the yipping of jackal.

In the early light they entered a wide grassy plain; the trees on the far side were a dark line on the horizon, and there were huge troops of zebra grazing out in the open. They lifted their heads to watch the strange little caravan go past, and sounded their curiosity and concern with their sharp, almost dog-like, barks.

Halfway across the plain Ralph turned the bullock train at a right angle to their track, and they marched due east until noon, when they re-entered the forest. Still Ralph headed on east until darkness fell and they camped.

Isazi muttered and complained about the wasted day, and the detour of so many miles out of their direct route towards the Limpopo river and the Bushman wells beyond, where Umfaan waited for them with the wagons.

'Why do we do this?'

'For the benefit of anyone who follows us.'

'They will still be able to follow the spoor we have laid,' Isazi protested.

'I will change that, in the morning,' Ralph assured him, and in the dawn he allowed Isazi to resume the southerly direction again.

'If I do not rejoin you, do not wait for me. Keep on until you reach the wagons, well beyond the frontier of the Matabele. Wait for me there,' he ordered, and he left Isazi and rode back on their spoor of the previous day.

He reached the open grassland where they had made such a dramatic change of direction the preceding morning, and the zebra barked at him. Their stripes were indistinguishable at this distance, and the herds were moving silver-grey masses on the yellow grassland.

'You are going to enjoy this, old Tom.' Ralph patted the horse's neck and then trotted out onto the plain towards the nearest herd of zebra. There were more than a hundred animals in the group, and they let horse and rider approach to within a few hundred paces before bunching up and galloping away.

'After them, Tom!' Ralph whooped, and they tore into the bellowing dust cloud, gaining swiftly on the chubby, striped ranks of bobbing hindquarters. Ralph quartered and turned them, and they gathered up another herd, and then another, until there were two or three thousand zebra in stampede ahead of them.

He rode out onto one flank and pushed the herd over the ground which his bullock train had crossed the previous day. Thousands of broad hooves churned the earth into soft explosions of dust. When they reached the far side of the plain, Ralph forced Tom ahead of the leading zebras and rode across their front, yelling and waving his hat about his head. The dense mass of animals turned like a living whirlpool, and the dust boiled up into the sky.

Back they went across the open ground with Tom delighting in the chase, and Ralph worked them northward until the zebra herds reached the forest line and swung parallel with the trees, and they scoured the earth with driving hooves in a swathe five hundred yards wide.

Back and forth again Ralph drove them, sheep-dogging them deliberately over the bullock tracks on each pass, until at last even Tom's pace was short and knocked up, and he was sweating in black streaks down his shoulders and flanks and blowing like a south-easterly gale over False Bay.

Ralph off-saddled in the shade of the treeline, while out on the plain the zebra herds, skittish and nervous at the harassment – still galloped in aimless circles, or snorted and pawed the torn earth.

'Nobody, not even a Bushman, will be able to pick the spoor through that,' Ralph told Tom, and stooped to lift each of his hooves in turn.

With his clasp knife Ralph prised off Tom's iron horse-shoes and bundled them into the saddle-bag.

Without shoes, Tom's tracks were almost identical to those of a zebra stallion. He might go lame before they reached the wagons at Bushman wells, but they could limp in at their own speed, sure at last that there would be no pursuit. Once they reached the wagon, there was forge and anvil to re-shoe him, and Tom would suffer no lasting injury.

Ralph wiped Tom down with the saddle blanket and let him rest for another hour before re-saddling. Then he rode back amongst the scattered zebra herds to mingle and lose Tom's hoof prints amongst theirs before deliberately turning westwards, the opposite direction to Isazi's bullocks. He settled down in the saddle to lay a false trail into the forest before circling back southwards to find Isazi.

R alph slept until sunrise the following morning, secure at last, and the temptation to drink coffee was too much for him. He chanced a small fire and delighted in the strong hot brew.

When they rode on, the sun was well up, and clear of the forest tops. Ralph let old Tom amble along at his own pace to save his unshod hooves, and he pushed his hat onto the back of his head and repeated the opening bars of Yankee Doodle over and over in a flat tuneless whistle.

The morning was cool and fresh. He felt elated at the success of his coup; already he was planning the sale of the statues. He would send letters to the British Museum and the Smithsonian Institution in Washington, D.C.

Out on his right a red-breasted cuckoo uttered its staccato call that sounded like a greeting 'Pete-my-friend!'.

Tom flicked his ears but Ralph went on whistling happily, slouched down in the saddle.

Old J. B. Robinson, one of the Kimberley millionaires who had made millions more on the new Witwatersrand goldfield, would buy at least one of the birds simply because Rhodes had one. He could not bear—

In the grassy glade ahead of Ralph a francolin called harshly, 'Kwali! Kwali!' only twice, and it rang falsely to Ralph's ear. These brown partridges usually called five or six times, not twice.

Ralph checked Tom and stood up in the stirrups. Carefully he surveyed the narrow open strip of head-high elephant grass. Suddenly a covey of brown partridge burst out of the grass and whirled away on noisy wings.

Ralph grinned and slouched down again in the saddle, and Tom trotted into the waving stand of coarse grass – and instantly it was full of dark figures of dancing plumes and red shields. They swarmed around Tom and the sunlight sparkled on the long silver blades.

'Go, Tom!' Ralph urged, and kicked his heels into his

flank, while he jerked the rifle from its bucket and held it against his hip.

As Tom lunged forward, one of the plumed warriors leapt to catch his bridle, and Ralph fired. The heavy lead bullet hit the Matabele in the jaw and blew half of it away; for a moment teeth and white bone flashed in the shattered face, and then were smothered in an eruption of bright blood.

Tom bounded into the gap in their line that the man had left, but as he went through, one of them darted in from the side and grunted with the strength of his stroke.

With a thrill of horror Ralph saw the long steel blade go into Tom's ribs, an inch in front of his toe cap. He swung the empty rifle at the warrior's head, but the man ducked under it, and while Ralph twisted in the saddle, a second Matabele darted in, and Tom's whole body shuddered and convulsed between Ralph's knees as the man stabbed deep and hard into Tom's neck, an inch in front of his plunging shoulder.

Then they were through the line of Matabele, but the assegai had been plucked from the warrior's hand and the shaft stuck out of Tom's neck at a brutal angle that showed the point must be buried in his lungs. Still the gallant old pony carried his master on across the glade and into the first trees of the forest.

Then abruptly a double stream of frothy bright lung-blood burst from Tom's nostrils, and splattered back against Ralph's boots. Tom died in full run. His nose dropped to the earth and he went over in a somersault that pitched Ralph high over his head.

Ralph smashed into the earth, and he felt as though his ribs were stoved in and his teeth cracked from his jaws, but he crawled desperately to his fallen rifle and jammed a fresh cartridge into the breech.

When he looked up, they were almost upon him, a line of racing red shields and pounding bare feet below; the war rattles on their ankles clashed and the hunting chorus was like the deep baying of hounds.

One tall *indoda* lifted his shield high to clear his spear arm for the killing stroke, and the blade flashed as it started down, and then the movement froze.

'Henshaw!' The name exploded out of the warrior's straining throat, and then Bazo continued the stroke, but at the last instant rolled his wrist and the flat of the heavy blade smashed against Ralph's skull above his temple; and he pitched forwards, face down against the sandy earth, and lay still as death.

'Y ou took the irons from the horse's hooves.' Bazo nodded approval. 'That was a good trick. If you had not slept so long this morning, we might never have caught up with you.'

'Tom is dead now,' replied Ralph.

He was propped against the trunk of a mopani tree. There was a bright scarlet smear of gravel rash on one cheek where he had hit the ground when he was thrown from the saddle. The hair above his temple was caked with black dried blood where the flat of Bazo's blade had knocked him senseless, and he was bound at ankles and wrists with thongs of rawhide. Already his hands were puffy and blue from the constriction of his bonds.

'Yes!' Bazo nodded again gravely, and looked at the carcass of the horse where it lay fifty paces away. 'He was a good horse, and now he is dead.' He looked back at Ralph. 'The *indoda* whom we will bury today was a good man – and now he is dead also.'

All about them squatted ranks of Matabele warriors, all Bazo's men drawn up in a dense black circle, sitting on their shields and listening intently to every word spoken.

'Your men fell upon me without warning, as though I

were a thief or a murderer. I defended myself as any man would do.'

'And are you not a thief then, Henshaw?' Bazo interrupted.

'What question is that?' Ralph demanded.

'The birds, Henshaw. The stone birds.'

'I do not know what you speak of,' Ralph challenged angrily, pushing himself away from the tree trunk and staring arrogantly at Bazo.

'You know, Henshaw. You know about the birds, for we have spoken about them many times. You know also the king's warning that to despoil the ancient places is death to any man, for I myself have told you of it.'

Still Ralph glared his defiance.

'Your spoor led straight to the burial place of the kings and straight away from it – and the birds are gone. Where are they, Henshaw?'

A moment longer Ralph continued his show, and then he shrugged and smiled and sank back against the tree.

'They are gone, Bazo, flown afar where you cannot follow them. It was the prophecy of the Umlimo, beyond the powers of mortal men to prevent.'

At the mention of the prophetess, a shadow of sorrow passed over Bazo's face.

'Yes, it was part of the prophecy,' he agreed. 'And now it is time to carry out the orders of the king.' He stood up and addressed the squatting ranks of Matabele.

'All of you heard the king's word,' he said. 'What must be done, must be done in secret; it must be done by me alone, and no other may witness it, nor speak of it after, even in a whisper, on pain of slow and lingering death. You have heard the king's word.'

'We have heard the king's word,' they agreed in deep sonorous chorus.

'Go!' Bazo commanded. 'Wait for me at great Zimbabwe, and wipe from your eyes the things you have seen this day.'

His warriors sprang up and saluted him. They shouldered the body of the man that Ralph had slain, using their shields as a litter, and they bore him away. The double column of running warriors snaked away across the glade and into the forest.

Bazo watched them go, leaning on his own shield, and then he turned back to Ralph, heavily and unwillingly.

'I am the king's man,' he said softly. 'Strictly charged with your death. What I have to do today will leave a deep scar in my heart for all my life, though I live to be an old greyhead. The memory of this thing will keep me from sleep, and turn the food sour and heavy in my belly.' Slowly he paced to where Ralph lay and stood over him. 'I will never forget this deed, Henshaw, though I will never be able to speak of it, not to my father or my favourite wife. I must lock it in the darkness of my soul.'

'If you must do it, then do it swiftly,' Ralph challenged him, trying to show no fear, trying to keep his gaze steady.

'Yes,' Bazo nodded, and shifted his grip on the haft of the spear. 'Intercede for me with your God, Henshaw,' he said, and struck.

Ralph cried out at the stinging burn of razor steel, and his blood burst from the wound and spilled into the dry earth.

Bazo dropped to his knee beside him and scooped up the blood in his cupped hands. He splashed it on his arms and chest. He smeared it on the haft and blade of his spear, until the bright steel was dulled.

Then Bazo leapt up and ripped a strip of bark from the mopani tree. He plucked a bunch of green leaves and came back to Ralph's side. He held together the lips of the deep wound in Ralph's forearm, then he placed the bunch of leaves over it and bound it up with the strip of bark.

The bleeding slowed and stopped, and Bazo hacked the rawhide bonds from Ralph's ankles and wrists and stood back.

He gestured at his own blood-sullied arms and weapon.

'Who, seeing me thus, would believe that I am a traitor to my king?' he asked softly. 'Yet the love of a brother is stronger than the duty to a king.'

Ralph dragged himself upright against the mopani trunk, holding his wounded arm against his chest and staring at the young induna.

'Go in peace, Henshaw,' whispered Bazo. 'But pray to your God for me, for I have betrayed my king and forfeited my honour.'

Then Bazo whirled and ran back across the glade of yellow grass. When he reached the trees on the far side he neither paused nor looked back, but plunged into them with a kind of reckless despair.

Ten days later, with his boots scuffed through the uppers and the legs of his breeches ripped to tatters by arrow grass and thorn, with his inflamed and infected left arm strapped to his chest by a sling of bark, his face gaunt with starvation and his body bony and wasted, Ralph staggered into the circle of wagons that were outspanned beside the Bushman wells – and Isazi shouted for Umfaan and ran to catch Ralph before he fell.

'Isazi,' Ralph croaked, 'the birds, the stone birds?'

'I have them safe, Nkosi.'

Ralph grinned wickedly, so that his dried lips cracked and his bloodshot eyes slitted.

'By your own boast, Isazi, you are a wise man. Now I tell you also, that you are beautiful to behold, as beautiful as a falcon in flight,' Ralph told him, and then reeled so that he had to catch his balance with an arm around the little Zulu's shoulders.

Lobengula sat cross-legged on his sleeping-mat, alone in his great hut. Before him was a gourd of clear spring water. He stared into it fixedly.

Long ago, when he had lived in the cave of the Matopos with Saala, the white girl, the mad old witchdoctor had instructed him in the art of the gourd. Very occasionally, after many hours' staring into the limpid water, and after the utmost exercise of his concentration and will, he had been able to see snatches of the future, faces and events, but even then they had been murky and unclear, and soon after he left the Matopos this small gift had gone from him. Sometimes still, in desperation, he resorted to the gourd – although, as it was this night, nothing moved or roiled darkly beneath the still surface of the spring water, and his concentration kept slipping away. Tonight he kept toying with the words of the Umlimo.

Always the oracle spoke obliquely, always her counsel was shrouded in imagery and riddles. Often it was repetitive, on at least five previous visits to the cavern the witch had spoken of 'the stars shining on the hills' and 'the sun that burns at midnight'. No matter how doggedly Lobengula and his senior indunas had picked at the words, and tried to unravel the meaning that was tied up in them, they had found no answer.

Now Lobengula set aside the fruitless gourd, and lay back upon his kaross to consider the third prophecy, made in the croaking raven's voice from the cliff above the cavern.

'Heed the wisdom of the vixen before that of the dogfox.'

He took each word and weighed it separately, then he considered the whole, and twisted it and studied it from every angle.

In the dawn there remained only one possible solution that had survived the night. For once the oracle seemed to have given advice that was unequivocal. It was only for him to decide which female was the 'vixen' of the oracle.

He considered each of his senior wives – and there was not one of them that had any interest in anything beyond the begetting and suckling of infants, or the baubles and ribbons that the traders brought to GuBulawayo.

Ningi, his full-blooded sister, he loved still as his one link with the mother he barely remembered. Yet now when Ningi was sober she was elephantine and slow-witted, bad-tempered and cruel. When she was filled with the traders' champagne and cognac, she was giggling and silly to begin with, and then incontinent and comatose at the end. He had spoken with her for an hour and more the previous day. Little that she had said was sensible, and nothing she had said could possibly bear on the terrible pressures of Lodzi and his emissaries.

So at last Lobengula returned to what he had known all along must be the key to the riddle of the Umlimo.

'Guards!' he shouted suddenly, and there were quick and urgent footfalls, and one of his cloaked executioners stooped through the doorway and prostrated himself on the threshold.

'Go to Nomusa, the Girlchild of Mercy, bid her come to me with all speed,' said Lobengula.

W hereas I have been much molested of late by divers persons seeking and desiring to obtain grants and concessions of land and mining rights in my territories –

Now, therefore, for the following considerations:

Item One, payment by the grantee to the grantor of £100 per month in perpetuity.

Item Two, the provision by the grantee to the grantor of One Thousand Martini-Henry rifles, together with

One Hundred Thousand rounds of ammunition for the same.

Item Three, the provision by the grantee to the grantor of an armed steamboat to patrol the navigable reaches of the Zambezi river.

Now, therefore, I, Lobengula – King of the Matabele people, and Paramount Chief of Mashonaland, Monarch of all territories South of the Zambezi River and Northwards of the Shashi and Limpopo Rivers, do hereby grant –

Complete and exclusive charge over all metals and minerals in my Kingdom, Principalities and Dominions, together with full power to do all things that they may deem necessary to win and procure the same and to enjoy the profits and revenues, if any, derivable from the said metals and minerals.

In his fair hand, Jordan Ballantyne wrote out the document from Mr Rudd's dictation.

Robyn Codrington read the text to Lobengula, and explained it to him, then she helped him attach the Great Elephant seal. Finally, she witnessed the mark that Lobengula made beside it.

'Damn me, Jordan, there's none of us here that can ride the way you can.' Rudd made no effort to conceal his jubilation when they were alone. 'It's speed now that counts. If you leave immediately, you can reach Khami Mission by nightfall. Pick the three best horses from those that we left there, and go like the wind, my boy. Take the concession to Mr Rhodes – and tell him I will follow directly.'

The twins ran down the front steps of Khami Mission and surrounded Jordan as he stepped down from the stirrup.

At the head of the steps, Cathy held a lantern high, and Salina stood beside her with her hands clasped demurely in front of her, and her eyes shining with joy in the lantern light.

'Welcome, Jordan,' she called. 'We have all missed you so.'

Jordan came up the steps. 'I can rest one night only,' he told her, and a little of her delight died and her smile with it. 'I ride south tomorrow at first light.'

He was so beautiful, tall and straight, and fair, and though his shoulders were wide and his limbs finely muscled, yet he was lithe and light as a dancer and his expression gentle as a poet's as he looked down into Salina's face.

'Only one night,' she murmured. 'Then we must make the most of it.'

They ate a dinner of smoked ham and roasted sweet yams, and afterwards they sat on the verandah and Salina sang for them while Jordan smoked a cigar and listened with obvious pleasure, tapping the time on his knee and joining with the others in the chorus.

The moment Salina had finished, Vicky leapt to her feet.

'My turn,' she announced. 'Lizzie and I have written a poem.'

'Not tonight,' said Cathy.

'Why?' demanded Vicky.

'Cathy,' wailed the twins in unison. 'It's Jordan's last night.'

'That is precisely why.' Cathy stood up. 'Come on, both of you.'

Still they cajoled and procrastinated, until suddenly

Cathy's eyes slitted viciously, and she hissed at them with a vehemence that startled them to their feet, to bestow hasty pecks on Jordan's face and then hurry off down the verandah, with Cathy close behind.

Jordan chuckled fondly and flicked the cigar over the verandah rail. 'Cathy is right, of course,' he said. 'I'll be in the saddle for twelve hours tomorrow – it's time we were all abed.'

Salina did not reply but moved to the end of the verandah farthest from the bedrooms and leaned on the rail, staring down across the starlit valley.

After a moment, Jordan followed her, and asked softly:

'Have I offended you?'

'No,' she answered quickly. 'It's just that I am a little sad. We all have such fun when you are here.'

Jordan did not reply, and after a minute she asked:

'What will you do now, Jordan?'

'I shall not know until I reach Kimberley. If Mr Rhodes is at Groote Schuur already, then I shall go there – but if he is still in London, then he will want me to join him.'

'How long will it take?'

'From Kimberley to London and back? Four months, if the sailings coincide.'

'Tell me about London, Jordan. I have read about it and dreamed about it.'

He talked quietly, but lucidly and fluently, so that she laughed and exclaimed at his descriptions and anecdotes, and the minutes turned to hours, until suddenly Jordan interrupted himself.

'What am I thinking of; it's almost midnight.'

She grasped at anything to keep him from going.

'You promised to tell me about Mr Rhodes' house at Groote Schuur.'

'It will have to wait for another time, Salina.'

'Will there be another time?' she asked.

'Oh, I am sure there will,' he answered lightly.

'You will go to England, and Cape Town, it could be years before you come back to Khami.'

'Even years will not dim our friendship, Salina.' And she stared at him as though he had struck her.

'Is that it – Jordan – are we friends, just friends?'

He took both her hands in his. 'The dearest, most precious friends,' he confirmed.

She was pale as ivory in the dim light, and her grip on his hands was like that of a drowning woman as she steeled herself to speak – but her voice, when at last she summoned it, was so strained that she was not sure he had understood her.

'Take me with you, Jordan.'

'Salina, I don't know what you mean.'

'I cannot bear to lose you – take me. Please take me.'

'But—' he was confused and shaken, 'but what would you do?'

'Whatever you tell me. I should be your slave, your loving slave, Jordan – for ever.'

He tried to free his hands from hers, but he did it gently.

'You cannot just go away and leave me, Jordan. When you came to Khami, it was like the sun rising into my life; and if you go you will take the light with you. I love you, Jordan, oh sweet Jesus, forgive me, but I love you more than life itself.'

'Salina, stop! Please stop now.' He pleaded with her, but she clung to his hands.

'I cannot let you go without telling you – I love you, Jordan, I shall always love you.'

'Salina.' His voice was stricken. 'Oh Salina, I love somebody else,' he said.

'It's not true,' she whispered. 'Oh, please say it's not true.'

'I am sorry, Salina. Terribly sorry.'

'Nobody else can love you as much as I do, nobody would sacrifice what I would.'

'Please stop, Salina. I don't want you to humiliate yourself.'

'Humiliate myself?' she asked. 'Oh, Jordan, that would be so small a price – you don't understand.'

'Salina, please.'

'Let me prove to you, Jordan, let me prove how joyfully I will make any sacrifice.' And when he tried to speak, she put her hand lightly over his mouth. 'We need not even have to wait for marriage. I will give myself to you this very night.'

When he shook his head, she tightened her grip to gag his words of denial.

> 'So fret not, like an idle girl,
> That life is dash'd with flecks of sin.'

She whispered the quotation, with quivering voice. 'Give me the chance, dear Jordan, please give me the chance to prove that I can love and cherish you more than any other woman in all the world. You will see how this other woman's love pales to nothing beside the flame of mine.'

He took her wrist and lifted her hand from his mouth, and his head bowed over hers with a terrible regret.

'Salina,' he said, 'it is not another woman.'

She stared up at him, both of them rooted and stricken, while the enormity of his words slowly spread across her soul like hoar frost.

'Not another woman?' she asked at last, and when he shook his head, 'Then I can never even hope – never?'

He did not reply, and at last she shook herself like a sleeper wakening from a dream to deathly reality.

'Will you kiss me goodbye, Jordan, just one last time?'

'It need not be the last—' But she reached up and

crushed the words on his lips so fiercely that her teeth left a taste of blood on his tongue.

'Goodbye, Jordan,' she said, and turning from him she walked down the length of the verandah as infirmly as an invalid arising from a long sick-bed. At the door of her bedroom, she staggered and put out a hand to save herself, and then looked back at him.

Her lips moved, but no sound came from them. 'Goodbye, Jordan. Goodbye, my love.'

R alph Ballantyne carried up the rifles, one thousand of them, brand new and still in their yellow grease, five in a wooden case, and twenty cases to a wagonload. There were another ten wagonloads of ammunition – all for the account of De Beers diamond mines – another three wagonloads of liquor for his own account, and a single wagon of furniture and household effects for the bungalow that Zouga was building for himself at GuBulawayo.

Ralph crossed the Shashi river with a certain thousand-pound profit from the convoy already safely deposited in the Standard Bank at Kimberley, but with a nagging hollow feeling in the pit of his stomach.

He had no way of knowing whether Bazo had reported him to Lobengula as the abductor of the stone falcons, or whether one of Bazo's warriors had recognized him and, despite the king's warning, had told a wife, who had told her mother, who had told her husband. 'Nothing moves in Matabeleland but the whole nation knows of it,' Clinton Codrington had warned him once. However, the profits on this run, and the prospect of visiting Khami Mission again, were worth the risk.

On the first day's march beyond the Shashi, that risk was vindicated, for it was Bazo himself at the head of his red shields who intercepted the convoy, and greeted Ralph inscrutably.

'Who dares the road? Who risks the wrath of Lobengula?' And after he had inspected the loaded wagons, as he and Ralph sat alone by the camp fire, Ralph asked him quietly:

'I heard that a white man died in the bush between great Zimbabwe and the Limpopo. What was that man's name?'

'Nobody knows of this matter, except Lobengula and one of his indunas,' Bazo replied, without lifting his gaze from the flames. 'And even the king does not know who the stranger was or where he came from, nor does he know the site of the grave of the nameless stranger.' Bazo took a little snuff and went on. 'Nor will we ever speak of this matter again, you and me.'

And now he lifted his eyes at last, and there was something in their dark depths that had never been there before, and Ralph thought that it was the look of a man destroyed, a man who would never trust a brother again.

In the morning, Bazo was gone, and Ralph faced northwards, with the doubts dispelled and his spirits soaring like the silver and mauve thunderheads that piled the horizon ahead of him. Zouga was waiting for him at the drift of the Khami river.

'You've made good time, my boy.'

'Nobody ever made better,' Ralph agreed, and twirled his thick dark moustache, 'and nobody is likely to, not until Mr Rhodes builds his railroad.'

'Did Mr Rhodes send the money?'

'In good gold sovereigns,' Ralph told him. 'I have carried them in my own saddle-bags.'

'All we have to do is get Lobengula to accept them.'

'That, Papa, is your job. You are Mr Rhodes' agent.'

Yet three weeks later the wagons still stood outside Lobengula's kraal, their loads roped down under the tarpaulins while Zouga waited each day from early morning until dusk in front of the king's great hut.

'The king is sick,' they said.

'The king is with his wives.'

'Perhaps the king will come tomorrow.'

'Who knows when the king will tire of his wives,' they said, and at last even Zouga, who knew and understood the ways of Africa, became angry.

'Tell the king that Bakela, the Fist, rides now to Lodzi to tell him that the king spurns his gifts,' he ordered Gandang, who had come to make the day's excuses, and Zouga called to Jan Cheroot to saddle the horses.

'The king has not given you the road.' Gandang was shocked and perturbed.

'Then tell Lobengula that his impis can kill the emissary of Lodzi on the road, but it will not take long for the word to be carried to Lodzi. Lodzi sits even now at the great kraal of the queen across the water, basking in her favour.'

The king's messengers caught up with Zouga before he reached Khami Mission, for his pace was deliberately leisurely.

'The king bids Bakela return at once, he will speak with him at the moment of his return.'

'Tell Lobengula that Bakela sleeps tonight at Khami Mission and perhaps the night after – for who knows when he will see fit to talk with the king again.'

Somebody at Khami must have put a spy-glass on the dust raised by Zouga's horses, for when they were still a mile from the hills, a rider came out to meet them at full gallop, a slim figure with long dark plaits streaming behind her lovely head.

When they met, Zouga jumped down from his saddle and lifted her from hers.

'Louise,' he whispered into her smiling mouth. 'You will never know how slowly the days pass when I am away from you.'

'It's a cross you make us both carry,' she told him. 'I am fully recovered now – thanks to Robyn – and still you make me loiter and pine at Khami. Oh, Zouga, will you not let me join you at GuBulawayo?'

'That I will, my dear, just as soon as we have a roof on the cottage, and a ring on your finger.'

'You are always so proper.' She pulled a face at him. 'Who would ever know?'

'I would,' he said, and kissed her again, before he lifted her back into the saddle of the bay Arab mare which had been his betrothal gift to her.

They rode with their knees touching and their fingers linked, while Jan Cheroot trailed them discreetly out of earshot.

'We shall have only days longer to wait,' Zouga assured her. 'I have forced Lobengula's hand. This matter of the rifles will be settled soon and then you can choose where you will make me the happiest man on earth, the cathedral at Cape Town perhaps?'

'Darling Zouga, your family at Khami has been so kind to me. The girls have become like my own sisters, and Robyn lavished care upon me when I was so ill, so burned and desiccated by the sun.'

'Why not?' Zouga agreed. 'I'm sure that Clinton will agree to say the words.'

'He has already, but there is more to it. The wedding is all planned, and it is to be a double wedding.'

'A double wedding – who are the others?'

'You would never guess, not in a thousand years.'

They looked more like brothers than father and son, as they stood before the carved altar in the little whitewashed church at Khami.

Zouga wore his full dress uniform, and the scarlet jacket, tailored twenty years before, still fitted him to perfection. The gold lace had been renewed to impress Lobengula and his indunas, and now it sparkled bright and untarnished, even in the cool gloom of the church.

Ralph was dressed in expensive broadcloth with a high stock and cravat of watered grey silk that on this hot June day brought beads of sweat to his forehead. His thick dark hair was dressed with pomade to a glossy shine, and his magnificent moustache, twirled with beeswax, pricked out in two stiff points.

Both of them were rigid with expectation, staring fixedly at the altar candles which Clinton had hoarded for such an occasion, and lit only minutes before.

Behind them one of the twins fidgeted with excited anticipation, and Salina pumped up the little organ and launched into 'Here comes the Bride', while Ralph grinned with bravado and, out of the side of his mouth, muttered to his father, 'Well, here we go then, Papa. Fix bayonets and prepare to receive cavalry!'

They turned with parade ground precision to face the church door, just as the brides stepped through it.

Cathy wore the mail-order dress which Ralph had brought up from Kimberley, while Robyn had lifted her own wedding dress from its resting place in the leather-bound trunk and they had taken in the waist and let down the hem to fit Louise. The delicate lace had turned to the colour of old ivory, and she carried a bouquet of Clinton's yellow roses.

Afterwards they all straggled across the yard. The brides tottered on their high heels and tripped on their trains, clinging to the arms of their new husbands; and the twins pelted them with handfuls of rice, before running ahead to the verandah where the wedding board was piled with mountains of food and lined with regiments of bottles, the finest champagne from Ralph's wagons.

At one end of the table Ralph loosened his stock and held Cathy in the circle of his arm and a glass in his other hand as he made his speech:

'My wife—' he referred to her, and the company hooted with laughter and clapped with delight, while Cathy clung to him and looked up at his face in transparent adoration.

Then when the speeches were ended, Clinton looked across the table at his eldest daughter. His bald head shone with the heat and excitement and the good champagne.

'Will you not sing to us, my darling Salina?' he asked. 'Something happy and joyous?'

Salina nodded and smiled, and lifted her chin to sing in her gentle voice:

> 'However far you go, my love,
> I will follow too.
> The highest mountain top, my love,
> Across deepest ocean blue.'

Louise turned her face towards Zouga, and when she smiled the corners of her dark blue eyes slanted upwards and her lips parted and glistened. Below the tabletop Clinton reached for Robyn's hand, but his gaze stayed upon his daughter's face.

Even Ralph sobered, and sat attentively while Cathy laid her cheek upon his shoulder.

> 'No arctic night too cold, my love,
> No tropic noon too fierce.
> For I will cleave to you, my love,
> 'Til death my heart do pierce.'

Salina sat very straight on the wooden bench with her hands in her lap. She was smiling as she sang, a sweet serene smile, but a single tear broke from her lower lid and descended, with tortuous slowness, the velvet curve of her cheek, until it reached the corner of her mouth.

The song ended, and they were silent for a long moment, and then Ralph pounded on the table with the flat of his hand.

'Oh bravo, Salina, that was superb.'

Then they were all applauding, and Salina smiled at them and the single tear broke and fell to her breast, to leave a dark star upon the satin of her bodice.

'Excuse me,' she said. 'Please excuse me.'

And she stood up and, still smiling, glided down the verandah. Cathy sprang to her feet, her face twisted with concern, but Robyn caught her wrist before she could follow.

'Leave her be,' she whispered. 'The child needs to be alone a while. You will only upset her further.' And Cathy sank back beside Ralph.

'Shame on you, Louise,' with forced jocularity, Clinton called down the table. 'Your husband's glass is empty, are you neglecting him so soon?'

An hour later Salina had not returned, and Ralph's voice had become louder and even more assertive. 'Now that Mr Rhodes has got his charter, we can begin to assemble the column. Cathy and I will start back tomorrow with the empty wagons. Heaven knows we will need every pair of wheels, and I thought old King Ben would never take those rifles off my hands.'

But Cathy was for once not drinking in every one of his words; she kept looking down the verandah, and again she whispered to Robyn, who frowned and shook her head.

'You talk as though the whole affair was arranged for your personal profit, Ralph.' Robyn turned from Cathy to challenge her new son-in-law.

'Perish the thought, Aunty.' Ralph laughed, and winked at his father down the length of the table. 'It's all for the good of Empire and the glory of God.'

Cathy waited until they were once more embroiled in amiable argument, and then she slipped away so quietly that Robyn did not notice until Cathy reached the end of the verandah. For a moment she looked set to call her back, but instead she made a move of annoyance and addressed herself to Zouga.

'How long will you and Louise remain at GuBulawayo?'

'Until the column reaches Mount Hampden. Mr Rhodes doesn't want any misunderstanding between the volunteers and Lobengula's young bucks.'

'I will be able to send up fresh vegetables and even a few flowers while you are at the king's kraal, Louise,' Clinton offered.

'You've been too kind already,' Louise thanked him, and then broke off, and an expression of deep concern crossed her face.

They all turned hurriedly in the direction she was staring.

Cathy had returned and climbed the verandah steps. She leaned against one of the whitewashed columns. Her face was the muddy yellow of a malaria sufferer, and her brow and chin were blistered with droplets of sweat. Her eyes were tortured, and her mouth twisted with horror.

'In the church,' she said. 'She's in the church.' And then she doubled over, and retched with a terrible tearing sound, and it came up her throat in a solid yellow eruption that soaked the virginal white skirts of her wedding gown.

Robyn was the first to reach the church door. She stared for only a moment and then she whirled and hid her face against Clinton's chest.

'Take her away,' Zouga ordered Clinton brusquely, and then to Ralph. 'Help me!'

The garland of pink roses had fallen from Salina's head,

and lay below her on the floor of the nave. She had thrown a halter rope over one of the roof beams, and she must have climbed up on the table that Robyn used for her surgery.

Her hands hung open at her sides. The toes of her slippers were turned in towards each other in a touchingly innocent stance, like those of a little girl standing on tiptoe; but they were suspended at the height of a man's waist above the flagged floor.

Zouga had to look up at her face. The rope had caught her under one ear and her head was twisted at an impossible angle to one side. To Zouga her face seemed swollen to twice its normal size, and it was mottled a dark mulberry hue.

At that moment a merciful little breeze came in through the doorway and turned her slowly on the rope to face the altar, so that Zouga could see only her lustrous golden hair which had come down and now hung to her waist. That was still beautiful.

Cathy Ballantyne had never known such happiness as the months spent in the British South Africa Company camp on the Macloutsi river.

She was the only woman among nearly seven hundred men, and a favourite of all of them. They called her 'Missus', and her presence was eagerly sought at every social activity with which officers and men diverted themselves during the long term of waiting.

The harsh conditions of camp life might have daunted another newly married girl of her age, but Cathy had known no others, and she turned the hut of daub and thatch that Ralph built for her into a cosy retreat with calico curtains in the glassless windows and woven grass native mats on the earth floor. She planted petunias on each side of the doorway, and the troopers of the column vied for the honour of watering them. She cooked over an open fire in the lean-to kitchen, and her invitations to dine were eagerly sought after by men who subsisted on canned bully beef and stamped maize meal.

She glowed with all the attention and excitement, so that from being merely pretty, she seemed to become beautiful – which made the men cherish her the more. Then, of course, she had Ralph, and she wondered some nights as she lay awake and listened to his breathing, how she had ever lived without him.

Ralph had the rank of major now, and he told her with a wink and an irreverent chuckle, 'We are all colonels and majors, my girl. I'm even thinking of making old Isazi a captain.' But he looked so handsome in his uniform with frogged coat and slouch hat and Sam Browne belt, that she wished he would wear it more often.

With each day Ralph seemed to her to become taller, his body more powerful and his energy more abundant. Even when he was away down the line hustling up the wagons, setting up the heliograph stations, or meeting with the other directors of the British South Africa Company in Kimberley, she was not lonely. Somehow his presence seemed always with her, and his absence made anticipation of his return a sort of secret joy.

Then suddenly he would be back, galloping into camp to sweep her up and toss her as high as if she were a child, before kissing her on the mouth.

'Not in public,' she would gasp and blush. 'People are watching, Ralph.'

'And turning green with envy,' he agreed, and carried her into the hut.

When he was there, everything was a breathless whirl. He was everywhere with his long assured stride and merry infectious laugh, driving his men along with a word of encouragement or of banter, and occasionally with sudden murderous black rages.

His rages terrified her, although they were never directed at her; and yet at the same time they excited her strangely. She would watch him with fearful fascination as his face swelled and darkened with passion, and his voice rose into a roar like a wounded bull. Then his fists and boots would fly and somebody would roll in the dust.

Afterwards she felt weak and trembly, and she would hurry away to the hut and draw the curtains and wait. When he came in, he would have that savage look on his face that made something flutter in the pit of her stomach, and it took all her will not to run to him – but to wait for him to come to her.

'By God, Katie my girl,' he said to her once as he leaned on his elbow over her, the sweat still glistening on his naked chest, and his breathing as rough as though he had run a race, 'you may look like an angel, but you could teach the devil himself a trick or two.'

Though she prayed afterwards for strength to control the wanton sensations and cravings of her body, the prayers were perfunctory and lacked real conviction, and that lovely smug and contented feeling just would not go away.

With Ralph it was excitement all the time, day and night, when they were alone and when they were in company. She loved to watch the deference with which other men treated him, rich and famous men older than he was like Colonel Pennefather and Dr Leander Starr Jameson, who were the leaders of the column. But then, she told herself, so they should. Ralph was already a director of the Chartered Company, Mr Rhodes' British South Africa Company, and when he sat down at the boardroom table in the De Beers building, it was in the company of lords and generals and of Mr Rhodes himself, though Ralph grinned and told her wickedly, 'Great men, Katie, but not one of them whose feet don't stink in hot weather – same as mine.'

'You are awful, Ralph Ballantyne,' she scolded, but she felt all puffed up with pride when she overhead two troopers talking of him and one said: 'Ralph Ballantyne, there's a man for you, and no mistake.'

Then at night, after they had made boisterous un-ashamed love, they would talk in the darkness, sometimes through most of the night, and his dreams and plans were the more enchanting for she knew that he would make them come true.

Her personal rapture was heightened by the mood of the seven hundred men around her, and each day's restraint as they waited for the word to move off increased the tension which gripped them all. Ralph's oxen brought up the guns, two seven-pounders, and the artillery fired shrapnel over the deserted veld beyond the camp, while the watchers cheered them as the fleecy cotton pods of smoking death opened prettily in the clear dry air.

The four Maxim machine-guns were unpacked from their cases and de-greased – and then, on a memorable day, the monstrous steam engine came chugging into the encampment, dragging behind it the electric generator and the naval searchlight which would be just another precaution against night attack by the Matabele hordes.

That night as she lay in his arms, Cathy asked Ralph the question they were all asking one another.

'What will Lobengula do?'

'What can he do?' Ralph stroked her hair, the way he might caress a favourite puppy. 'He has signed the concession, taken his gold and guns, and promised Papa the road to Mashonaland.'

'They say he has eighteen thousand men waiting across the Shashi.'

'Then let them come, Katie, my lass. There are not a few amongst us who would welcome the chance to teach King Ben's buckeroos a sharp lesson.'

'That's a terrible thing to say,' she said without conviction.

'But it's the truth, by God.'

She no longer chided him when he blasphemed so lightly, for the days and ways of Khami Mission seemed to be part of a fading dream.

Then one day, early in July of 1890, the mirror of a heliograph winked its eye across the dusty, sunwashed distances. It was the word for which they had waited all these months. The British Foreign Secretary had at last approved the occupation of Mashonaland by the representatives of the British South Africa Company.

The long ponderous column uncoiled like a serpent. At its head rode Colonel Pennefather in company uniform, and at his right hand the guide Frederick Selous, whose duty it would be to take the column wide of any Matabele settlements, to cross the low malarial lands before the rains broke and to lead them up the escarpment to the sweet and healthy airs of the high plateau.

The Union Jack unfurled above their heads and a bugler sounded the advance.

'Heroes every one of them,' Ralph grinned at Cathy. 'But it's up to the likes of me to see our heroes through.'

His shirtsleeves were rolled high on his muscled arms and a disgracefully stained hat was cocked over one eye.

'When I come back, we'll be richer by eighty thousand pounds,' he told her, and lifted her off the ground with his embrace.

'Oh Ralph, how I wish I were coming with you.'

'You know Mr Rhodes has forbidden any women to cross the frontier – and you'll be a damned sight safer and more comfortable at Lily's Hotel in Kimberley with Jordan to keep an eye on you.'

'Then be careful, my darling,' she cautioned him, breathless from his hug.

'No need for that, Katie, my sweet. The devil looks after his own.'

'These are not men coming to dig holes.' Gandang stood forth from the circle of indunas. 'They are dressed as soldiers; they bring guns that can break down the granite hills with their smoke.'

'What did the king promise Lodzi?' demanded Babiaan. 'That he may come in peace to look for gold. Why does he march against us like an army?'

Bazo spoke for the young men. 'Oh great King, the spears are bright and our eyes are red. We are fifteen thousand men; can the king's enemies stand against us?'

Lobengula looked at his handsome eager young face. 'Sometimes the most dangerous enemy is a hasty heart,' he said, softly.

'And at other times, Bull Elephant of Kumalo, it might be a tardy spear arm.'

A shadow of irritation at importunate youth passed behind the king's eyes; then he sighed. 'Who knows?' he agreed. 'Who knows where the enemy lies?'

'The enemy lies before you, great King; he has crossed the Shashi river and he has come to take your land from you,' Somabula told him. And then Gandang stood again:

'Let the spears go, Lobengula, Son of Mzilikazi, let your young men run – or as the sun will rise tomorrow, that surely will you live to regret it.'

'That I cannot do,' Lobengula said softly. 'Not yet. I cannot use the assegai when words may still suffice.' He roused himself and his voice firmed.

'Go, Gandang, my brother, take your hot-hearted son with you. Go to the leader of these soldiers and ask him why he comes into my lands in battle array, and bring his answer to me here.'

Frederick Selous rode ahead, a trooper with an axe following him, and he pointed out the trees to be cut.

The trooper blazed them with a slash of the axe, and followed Selous on. The axemen came up behind them, fifty of them, riding in pairs. One man dismounted, handed his reins to his partner, spat on his already callused hands and, hefting the axe, addressed himself to the trunk of the doomed tree.

While his axe thudded and the wood chips flew white as bone in the sunlight, the second man sat in the saddle, his rifle in his hands, and he watched the forest around him for the first plumed head and long tasselled shield to appear. When the tree crackled and toppled, the axeman mounted and they rode on to the next, where he took his turn on guard while his mate swung the axe. Behind them the bullock spans came plodding to chain the fallen trunks and drag them out of the road, and then the whole ponderous caravan rumbled forward.

It was slow work, and on the third day Ralph rode to the head of the column to discuss with Selous the possibility of using the steam engine to haul the smaller trees, roots and all, from the sandy earth. They had left their horses with a trooper and walked forward for a better view of the way ahead when Ralph said quietly: 'Stand your ground, Mr Selous. Do not draw your pistol, and, in God's name, do not show any agitation.'

There were dark and moving shadows in the forest all around them, and then suddenly the dreaded long shields were there, forming a wall across their front.

'Has the king killed any white men?' a deep voice challenged. 'If he has not, then why has this impi of warriors crossed his border?'

'Lobengula has killed nobody,' Ralph called back.

'Then have the white men mislaid something of value – that they come to seek it here?'

Ralph said quietly to Selous. 'I know this man. He is one of the king's senior indunas. The one with the red shield behind him is his son; between them they disposed of eight thousand men. It would be as well to tread warily, Mr Selous. We are surrounded by an army.'

Then he addressed himself to the watching and waiting warriors: 'The king has given us the road.'

'The king denies that he called an army to enter his domain.'

'We are not an army,' Ralph denied, and Gandang threw back his head and laughed briefly and bitterly. Then he spoke again:

'Hear me, Henshaw, no white man steps beyond this place without the word of Lobengula. Tell that to your masters.'

Ralph whispered briefly with Selous, and then faced Gandang again.

'We will wait,' he agreed, 'for the king's word.'

'And we will watch while you wait,' Gandang promised ominously, and at a gesture the warriors melted away into the forest again and it seemed they had never been.

'Pull in the pickets,' Colonel Pennefather ordered. 'Put the wagons into laager. Ballantyne, can you get a message back to Tuli on the heliograph and have someone post up to GuBulawayo to find what are Lobengula's real intentions.' And, as Ralph turned to hurry away, 'Oh, one other thing, Ballantyne, can you start the generator and have the searchlight ready to sweep the area around the camp tonight. We don't want those fellows creeping up on us in the dark.'

Gandang and his son stood together on the crest of one of the little rocky kopjes that dotted the wide hot plain between the rivers.

They were alone, although when Bazo turned his head and looked down the steep back-slope of the hill, he could see the bivouac of their combined impis. There were no cooking fires to disclose their presence to the white men; they would eat cold rations and sleep in darkness this night. The long, black ranks squatted with enforced patience, dense as hiving bees beneath the shading branches of the mopani.

Bazo knew that he had only to lift his right arm above his shield to bring them to their feet and send them racing away, silent and ferocious as hunting leopards, and the thought gave him a savage joy. Reluctantly he turned back, and stood quietly with his shield not quite touching his father's.

The little afternoon breeze coming up from the river stirred their war plumes, and they gazed down upon the laager of the white men.

The bullocks had been penned within the circle of the wagons, and they could see the field guns and the Maxim machine-guns posted at the points of the barricade, their positions fortified with biscuit boxes and ammunition cases from the wagonloads. The gun crews lounged near their weapons, yet somehow the whole scene appeared tranquil and unwarlike.

'In the dark hour before the dawn, we could take them before they could stand to their guns,' murmured Bazo. 'It would be so quick, so easy.'

'We will wait on the king's word,' his father replied, and then started and exclaimed.

'What is it, my father?'

Gandang lifted his assegai and pointed with it southwards, to the pale blue horizon, far beyond the Shashi river, to the faint line of hills, shaped as fantastically as the turreted towers of a fairy castle.

On those far pale hills, something flickered and sparkled, a tiny speck of brightest white light, like a fire-fly in flight, or like the twinkle of the morning star.

'The stars,' Gandang whispered with superstitious awe, 'the stars are shining on the hills.'

The little group of officers stood behind the tripod of the instrument and focused their telescopes on the distant twinkle of light.

The heliograph operator called the message aloud, at the same time scribbling it on his signal pad. 'Jove advises hold your position pending clarification Lobengula's intention.' Jove was the code for Mr Rhodes.

'Very well.' Pennefather closed his telescope with a snap. 'Acknowledge message received and understood.'

The operator bent to the prism of the instrument and made a minute adjustment in its focus, turning one mirror to catch the sunlight and the second to reflect it directly towards the line of distant hills; then he seized the handle and the shutter clattered as it blinked the beam of sunlight, speeding the dots and dashes of the Morse code instantaneously across fifty miles of wilderness.

Pennefather turned away and crossed briskly to the

massive steam engine on its tall steel wheels. He looked up at Ralph on the footplate.

'Are you ready to light up, Ballantyne?'

Ralph removed the long black cheroot from between his teeth, and gave a parody of a military salute.

'We've got sixty pounds of pressure on the boiler. Another half hour and she'll be whistling out of the valve.'

'Very well.' Pennefather hid his mystification. He neither understood nor admired these demoniacal contraptions. 'Just as long as we have light by nightfall.'

Gandang sat on his shield with his fur kaross of monkey skins over his shoulders. The winter evenings were cold, even here in the lowlands. There were no fires in the bivouac – and he could barely make out the faces of his junior commanders who sat opposite him, for the last flush of the sunset was fading from the western sky.

'It was something that all of us saw, and something that we have never seen before.'

They murmured agreement.

'It was a star, fallen from the heavens, and it lay upon the hills. We all saw it.'

'In the morning I will send two of our swiftest runners to the king. He must know of this terrible witchcraft.' He stood up and let his kaross fall. 'Now I am going—' He did not finish the sentence.

Instead he dropped into a defensive crouch and flung up his shield to cover his head, and around him his warriors wailed like frightened children, their eyes wide and white, glinting in the flood of light that burst down upon them from the sky.

The evening stars were washed out by the brilliance of

the great white beam that reached from earth to heaven, and threw the hills into crisp black silhouette.

'The sun has returned,' Gandang croaked in religious terror. 'It is the prophecy, the whole prophecy. The stone falcons have flown, the stars shine on the hills, and now the sun burns at midnight.'

Fort Salisbury
20th Sept. 1890

My darling Kate,
  Over two months since last I kissed you – and I am missing your cooking, amongst other things!

You will see by the address that we have reached our destination – although we lost a man drowned, another to drink, a third bitten by a mamba and a fourth eaten by a lion – the Matabele touched not one of us.

So Lobengula kept his word – to the surprise of all, and the disappointment of not a few. After one exchange of insults with old Gandang at the head of 8,000 of his bully boys, they let us pass – and the rest of it was rather tedious – just sweat and blisters!

The great Selous almost lost us once – but then I showed him the pass through the hills which Isazi and I found when we made our little foray to Great Zimbabwe. Selous called it Providential Pass (providential that I was with him, I'd say), and he took the kudos (to which he is welcome). He will probably write another book about his feat!

We reached Mount Hampden on the 6th instant, and it gave me a turn to think that Papa had been the first man here all those years ago.

However, Pennefather, in his great wisdom, decided

there was insufficient water there and moved us all twelve miles across here. Of course the man is a new chum, fresh out from home, so how is he to know that this place will turn into a swamp with the first rains. (I intend to be well away by then!)

I have visited some God-forsaken places on my travels – but this one gets the coconut! It's infested with lions – and I've lost 15 oxen to them already. The grazing is sour veld – the remaining beasts are losing condition – oh, how I long for the sweet-veld of Matabeleland. Trust the Matabele to pick the best stock country, so I'll not be too surprised when others start thinking about Lobengula's herds and pastures. If only the cunning old blighter had thrown his war spear and given us the excuse, we might be hoisting the flag over GuBulawayo now – rather than over this dreary spot.

Oh well! At least I am the only one here with whisky – two wagonloads of it – and doing a roaring trade at £10 the bottle. You shall have the prettiest bonnet in Kimberley when I return, Katie my heart.

The day Pennefather hoisted the flag the boys were free to go their own way – and what a stampede there was! Everyone intent to be the first to peg the gold reef we've heard so much about. Some of them are crawling back already, tail between their legs. This is no Eldorado – if there is gold, they'll have to work for it – and then, of course, Mr Rhodes and his British South Africa Company will take half of it. Of course, they all were happy enough about the Company's cut when they signed on – but they are starting to bellyache about it now.

We had a message on the 'Helio' this morning that the British South Africa Company shares are selling for £3–15s-0d. each in London, and 5,000 new shareholders on the books in the first week. Well, all I can say is that whoever is paying that price has never seen Fort Salisbury!

'Young Ballantyne,' says Leander Starr Jameson to me, 'you were damnably lucky to take half your fees payable in B.S.A. shares valued at £1 each.'

'Jameson,' says I, 'it's strange how the harder I work and the harder I think, the luckier I get.'

So I have 40,000 B.S.A. shares, Katie my love, and you will find here attached a letter addressed to Aaron Fagan, my solicitor in Kimberley, instructing him to sell every last one of them. Take it around to him post-haste, that's a good girl. We'll be well rid of them at a profit of £2–15s-0d. each, and that's God's truth! Perhaps I'll buy you two bonnets when I come back!

Oh, if only we had Matabeleland – no wonder Lobengula left Mashonaland to the Mashonas! Though they don't call it that any more. The new name that is all the rage is Rhodesia – no less!

What an ungainly name it is, but no doubt Mr Rhodes will be flattered and my brother Jordan will be delighted. They are welcome to my share of Rhodesia – Don't forget to take the letter to Fagan, mind!

Nonetheless, there is still a penny to be made here. I have taken a partner, and we are building a General Store and Bar-room. He will run both businesses, as well as the Salisbury Depot for my wagons. He seems an honest lad, our Tom Meikle, and hard-working, so I have given him a wage of £5 a month and ten per cent of the profits – no point in spoiling him! Just as soon as we get the building up and the stocks on the shelves, I will leave him to it and be on my way back to you.

Mr Rhodes wants me to contract to erect the telegraph line from Kimberley to Fort Salisbury for him at a price of £25,000. I reckon there will be £10,000 profit in it. You shall have three bonnets, Katie, I swear it to you!

I must leave here by the 10th of next month if I am to beat the rains. Once they start the mosquitoes are going to take over Fort Salisbury, and every river between here and the Shashi will be a flood that would break even Noah's heart.

Thus I expect to reach Kimberley by the end of October, so take a good look at the floor, Katie my sweet, for when I get there you will be looking at nought but the ceiling for a week – and my word on it!

Your loving husband,
Ralph Ballantyne
(Ex Major B.S.A. Police Retired!)

'We must have Matabeleland. It is as simple as that,' said Zouga Ballantyne, and Jordan looked up sharply from his pad of Pitman's shorthand.

His father sat in one of the deep buttoned leather chairs facing Mr Rhodes' desk. Beyond him the green velvet curtains were open and held with yellow tasselled ropes of silk. The view from this top floor of the De Beers Company buildings took in a wide sweep of the dry Griqualand plain dotted with camel-thorn trees, and closer to hand the stacking ground where the blue earth from the Kimberley mine was left to deteriorate in the brilliant sunshine before being made to yield up its precious diamonds.

Jordan had no eyes for the view now; his father's words had shocked him. But Mr Rhodes merely hooded his eyes and slumped massively at his desk, gesturing for Zouga to continue.

'The Company shares are six shillings in London, against three pounds fifteen on the day we raised the flag at Fort Salisbury three years ago—'

'I know, I know,' Rhodes nodded.

'I have spoken with the men that remain; I have spent the last three months travelling from Fort Victoria to

Salisbury as you bid me. They won't stay, Mr Rhodes. They won't stay unless you let them go in and finish it.'

'Matabeleland.' Rhodes lifted his great shaggy head, and Jordan thought how terribly he had aged in these last three years. 'Matabeleland,' he repeated softly.

'They are sick of the constant menace of Lobengula's hordes upon their borders; they have convinced themselves that the gold they did not find in Mashonaland lies under Lobengula's earth; they have seen Lobengula's fat herds of choice cattle and compared them to their own lean beasts that starve on the thin sour veld to which they are restricted—'

'Go on,' Rhodes nodded.

'They know that to reach them the telegraph and the railroad must come through Matabeleland. They are sick to the guts with malaria and the constant fear of the Matabele. If you want to keep Rhodesia, you must give them Matabeleland.'

'I have known this all along. I think we all have. Yet we must move carefully. We must be careful of the Imperial Factor, of Gladstone and of Whitehall.' Rhodes stood up and began to pace back and forth before the shelves laden with leather-bound books titled in gold leaf.

'We need to prepare ourselves. You must remember, Ballantyne, that we have technically only the right to dig for gold. As long as Lobengula does not molest us, we cannot declare war upon him.'

'But if Lobengula were to interfere in any way with our people and their rights?'

'That would be another matter.' Rhodes stopped in front of Zouga's chair. 'Then I should certainly end his game for him.'

'In the meantime the company's shares are six shillings each,' Zouga reminded him.

'We need an incident,' said Rhodes. 'But in the meantime we have to prepare and I dare not put it on the wires.

I want you to leave immediately for Fort Victoria to speak to Jameson.' Rhodes swung his big head towards Jordan. 'Do not make notes of this, Jordan,' he ordered, and Jordan dutifully lifted his pencil from the pad. 'Instruct Jameson to send me a series of telegrams on the new wires. Telegrams advising against war, that we can show the British Government and people when it is all over – but in the meantime tell him to prepare for war.'

Rhodes turned back to Jordan. 'Take an instruction, Jordan. Sell fifty thousand B.S.A. Company shares for what they will fetch. Jameson must have what he needs to do the business. Tell him that, Ballantyne. I shall be behind him all the way – but we need an incident.'

Ralph Ballantyne sat his horse on the heights of the escarpment which fell away before him, in a tumbled splendour of rocky hills and forests. The spring foliage turned the groves of msasa trees into clouds of pink and swelling scarlets, and the air was so clear and bright that he could pick out the telegraph line all the way to the horizon.

The wires were a gossamer thread that glistened red gold in the sunlight, so fragile, so insubstantial, that it seemed impossible that they ran, arrow straight, six hundred miles and more to meet the railhead at Kimberley.

Ralph's men had laid this line. The surveyors riding ahead to set up the beacons, the axemen following to clear the line, then the wagons bringing up the poles and finally the enormous spools of gleaming copper wire uncoiling endlessly.

Ralph had hired good men, paid them well, and visited them less than once a month. Yet he was proud as he saw the wires sparkle and thought of the importance and significance of this achievement.

Beside him his foreman cursed suddenly. 'There it is! The thieving bastards!' And he pointed to where the line of telegraph poles marched up the side of one forested hill. Ralph had thought that cloud shadow had dimmed the sparkle of the copper wire up this slope, but now when he focused his binoculars upon them he saw that the poles had been stripped bare.

'Come on,' he said grimly, and rode forward. When they reached the bottom of the slope they found that one of the telegraph poles had been chopped through at the base, and felled like timber. The wires had been hacked through, and the scuff marks in the earth where it had been rolled into bundles had not yet been erased by the wind.

Slowly they rode on up the slope, and Ralph did not have to dismount to read the sign of bare feet.

'There were at least twenty of them,' he said. 'Women and children with them – a family outing, damn them to hell.'

'It's the women that put them up to it,' the foreman agreed. 'That wire makes beautiful bracelets and bangles. The black girls just love it.'

At the top of the slope another telegraph pole had been felled and the wire snipped through.

'They have got away with five hundred yards of wire,' Ralph scowled. 'But next time it could be five thousand. Do you know who they are?'

The foreman shrugged. 'The local Mashona chief is Matanka. His village is just the other side of the valley. You can see the smoke from here.'

Ralph slipped his rifle out of its boot under his knee. It was a magnificent new Winchester Repeater Model 1890 with his name engraved and chased with gold into the metal of the block. He levered a round into the breech.

'Let's go to see brother Matanka.'

He was an old man, with legs like a stork and a cap of pure white wool covering his head. He trembled with fear and fell on his knees before this furious young white man with a rifle in his hand.

'Fifty head,' Ralph told him. 'And next time your people touch the wires it will be a hundred.'

Ralph and his foreman cut the fattest cattle out of Matanka's herds and drove them ahead of them, up the escarpment and into the little white settlement of Fort Victoria which had grown up mid-way between the Shashi river and Fort Salisbury.

'All right,' Ralph told his foreman. 'You can take them from here. Turn them over to the auctioneer, we should get ten pounds a head for them.'

'That will cover the cost of replacing the wires fifty times over,' the foreman grinned.

'I don't believe in taking a loss when I don't have to,' Ralph laughed. 'Get on with you, I'll have to go down and square it with the good doctor.'

Doctor Jameson's office, as administrator of the Charterlands of the British South Africa Company, was a wood and iron building with an untidily thatched roof directly opposite the only canteen in Fort Victoria.

'Ah, young Ballantyne,' Jameson greeted Ralph, and secretly enjoyed Ralph's frown of annoyance. He did not share the general high opinion of this youngster. He was too bumptious and too successful by a half, while physically he was all that Jameson was not; tall and broad-shouldered, with a striking appearance and forceful presence.

The wags were saying that one day Ralph Ballantyne would own the half of the Charterland that Rhodes did not already have his brand on. However, even Jameson had to grant that if you wanted something done, no matter how difficult, and if you wanted it done swiftly and thoroughly, and if you were prepared to pay top dollar, then Ralph Ballantyne was your man.

'Ah, Jameson.' Ralph retaliated by dropping the mousy

little doctor's title from the greeting, and by turning immediately to the other man in the room.

'General St John.' Ralph flashed that compelling smile. 'How good to see you, sir! When did you get into Fort Victoria?'

Mungo St John limped across the room to take Ralph's hand, and his single eye gleamed.

'Got in this very morning.'

'Congratulations on your appointment, sir. We need a good soldier up here, the way things are going.' Ralph's compliment was an oblique jibe at Dr Jameson's own military aspirations. Rhodes had very recently appointed Mungo St John as the Company's Chief of Staff. He would be under Jameson's administration, naturally, but would be directly responsible for police and military affairs in the Charterlands of Rhodesia.

'Did your men find the break in the wires?' Jameson interrupted them.

'Bangles and bracelets,' Ralph nodded. 'That's what happened to the wires. I have given the local chief a lesson that I hope will teach him to behave himself. I fined him fifty head of cattle.'

Jameson frowned quickly.

'Lobengula considers Matanka to be his vassal. He owns those cattle, the Mashona merely tend the herds on the king's behalf.'

Ralph shrugged. 'Then Matanka will have some explaining to do, and rather him than me, and that's the truth.'

'Lobengula won't let this pass—' Jameson broke off, and the frown cleared. He began to pace up and down behind his desk with excited, hopping, bird-like steps. 'Perhaps,' he twitched at his scraggly little moustache, 'perhaps this is what we have been waiting for. Lobengula will not let it pass – nor, by God, will we.' He paused and looked at Ralph. 'How soon will you have the wires restored?'

'By noon tomorrow,' Ralph told him promptly.

'Good! Good! We must get a message through to your father at GuBulawayo. If he protests to Lobengula that his vassals are stealing Company property, and informs him that we have fined him in cattle, what will Lobengula do?'

'He will send an impi to punish Matanka.'

'Punish him?'

'Cut his head off, kill his men, rape his women and burn his village.'

'Exactly.' Jameson punched his fist into his palm. 'And Matanka is on Company ground and under protection of the British flag. It will be our duty, our bounden duty, to drive off Lobengula's men.'

'War!' said Ralph.

'War,' agreed St John softly. 'Well done, young fellow. This is what we have been waiting for.'

'Ballantyne, can you give me a tender to provide wagons and supplies for an expeditionary force, say five hundred men; we'll need twenty-five wagons, six hundred horses, when we drive for GuBulawayo.'

'When do you expect to march?'

'Before the rains.' Jameson was decisive. 'If we go, then we'll have to finish it before the rains break.'

'I will have a tender for you by the time the telegraph is reopened tomorrow.'

Ralph jumped down from the saddle and tossed his reins to the groom who came running.

Although it was only a temporary lodging which Ralph used on his infrequent visits to check the progress of his construction gangs, his transport stages and his trading posts – yet it was the grandest house in Fort Victoria, with glass in the windows and insect mesh screening the doors.

His spurs clattered on the steps as he stormed up onto the verandah, and Cathy heard him and came running with the baby on her hip.

'You are home so soon,' she cried delightedly, rebuttoning her bodice from the feeding.

'Couldn't stay away from you two.' He laughed and smacked a kiss on her mouth, then snatched the baby from her and tossed him high.

'Do be careful.' Cathy hopped anxiously to try and take him back, but Jonathan gurgled joyously and kicked with excitement, and a trickle of milk reappeared and ran down his chin.

'Mucky little devil.' Ralph held him high and sniffed at his son. 'Both ends at once, by God. Here, Katie.' He handed the infant to her and held her around the waist.

'We are going to GuBulawayo,' he said.

'Who?' She looked up at him in confusion.

'St John and the good doctor and I, and when we get there B.S.A. shares will go to five pounds. Last price I heard before the wires were cut was five shillings. The first message that goes out tomorrow is my buying order to Aaron Fagan – for fifty thousand British South Africans!'

Bazo's impi came sweeping down out of the western forests, silent as shadows and murderous as wild hunting dogs.

'Kill that dog Matanka,' the king had ordered. 'Kill him and all his men.' And Bazo caught them in the dawn, as the first of them came out of their huts yawning and rubbing the sleep from their eyes, and then they chased the young girls cackling and shrieking like hens amongst the huts, and roped them in bunches.

'And all his men,' had been the king's order, and some of Matanka's men were working for the white men, at the

Prince Mine, one of the very few paying gold reefs in Mashonaland. They were breaking and carrying the rock.

'Do not interfere,' Bazo told the mine overseer. 'This is the king's business. No white man will be hurt, that is the king's order.' And they chased the Mashona labourers into the crushing plant and stabbed them as they hid under the sorting-tables.

They came racing down the telegraph line, five hundred red shields. The Mashona wiremen were unwinding the huge drums and stringing the shining strands.

'No white men will be hurt,' Bazo shouted as he let his young men run. 'Stand aside, white men.' But now Bazo was mad with blood and boastful with the killing fever. 'This is not for you, white men. Not yet, white men, but your day will come.'

They dragged the Mashona down from the telegraph poles, and bayed about them like hounds tearing a fox to pieces, while the Mashona screamed to their white masters for protection.

'Bring in the cattle, all Matanka's cattle,' the king had ordered, and Bazo's men swept the Mashona pastures, and drove the sprawling multi-coloured herds back into the west in the clouds of their own dust; and with the herds were mingled some of the white men's cattle – for one beast looks like another, and the marks burned by hot iron into the hide meant nothing to the Matabele warriors.

It was all done so swiftly that Jameson had to ride hard with his band of hastily assembled volunteers to catch them before they reached the frontier of the Charterland.

He had thirty-eight men with him, and when he saw the horsemen, Bazo turned back and with the massed warriors at his back he greeted Jameson.

'*Sakubona, Daketela!* I see you, Doctor! Fear not, by the king's orders no white man will be molested.'

But the volunteers bunched their horses, and there was the snick of breech blocks and the rattle of bolts as they loaded. Thirty-eight against five hundred, and they were jumpy and white-faced.

The little doctor spurred forward, and Ralph murmured to St John: 'By God, the man is a bantam cock, and he'll get us all into it yet.'

But Jameson showed no agitation as he stood in the stirrups and called: 'Men of Matabele, why have you crossed the border?'

'*Hau, Daketela!*' Bazo answered him with mock astonishment. 'What border is this you speak of? Surely this land, all of it, belongs to Lobengula. There are no borders.'

'The men you have slaughtered are under my protection.'

'The men we killed were Mashona,' Bazo replied scornfully. 'And the Mashona are Lobengula's dogs – to kill or keep as he wishes.'

'The cattle you have stolen belong to my people.'

'All the Mashona cattle belong to the king.'

Then St John shouted over him, 'Careful, Jameson, there is treachery here, watch those men on your left.'

Some of Bazo's men had pressed forward, the better to see and to hear. A few of them were armed with ancient Martini-Henry rifles, probably those with which Rhodes had paid the king for his concession.

Jameson swung his horse to face them.

'Back!' he shouted. 'Back, I say.' He lifted his rifle to enforce his order, and one of the Matabele instinctively copied the gesture, half threatening the little group of mounted white men with his rifle.

Mungo St John flung up his rifle, and as it touched his shoulder he fired. The shot was a thunderous burst of sound in the heated dusty air, and the heavy bullet smashed into the Matabele's naked chest. His rifle clattered on the ground, and a little feather of bright crimson sprayed from his chest. The warrior pirouetted slowly, almost gracefully, until they looked into the shocking gape of the exit wound between his shoulder blades. Then the warrior collapsed, and his legs kicked convulsively.

'Do not touch a white man!' Bazo bellowed into the terrible silence, but not more than half a dozen of the horsemen understood the language. To the others it sounded like a killing order. The crash of volleyed rifle fire mingled with the trample of hooves and whinny of panicky horses. The banks of blue gunsmoke blended with the billowing pale dust and the rippling plumes of running warriors.

Bazo's impi was streaming away into the forest, carrying their wounded with them, and slowly the rifle fire stuttered and faded, and the horses quietened. The little group sat, silent and appalled, and stared at the Matabele dead strewn across the open ground ahead of them. They looked like the abandoned toys of a petulant child.

Ralph Ballantyne had not drawn the gold-engraved Winchester from its boot, and there was a long unlit cheroot between his white teeth. He spoke around it, smiling ironically, but his eyes were cold and green and hard.

'I count thirty-three of 'em down, Doctor Jim,' he said loudly. 'Not a bad bag really, even though they were sitting birds.' And he struck a Vesta against the thigh of his riding breeches and lit the cheroot; then he gathered the reins and turned his horses's head back towards the fort.

L obengula turned the small canvas bag of sovereigns in his narrow graceful hands. He stood in the centre of the goat kraal, and there were only three Matabele with him, Gandang and Somabula and Babiaan. The others he had sent away.

Before him stood a little white group. Zouga had brought

Louise with him to the meeting. He had not dared leave her alone in the cottage beyond the stockade of the royal kraal, not with the mood of the Matabele as it had been ever since Jameson's massacre at Fort Victoria.

Facing the king also, but a little separated from the other couple, stood Robyn and Clinton Codrington.

Still fingering the bag of gold, Lobengula turned his face to Robyn.

'See, Nomusa, these are the gold queens that you advised me to accept from Lodzi.'

'I am deeply ashamed, oh King,' Robyn whispered.

'Tell me faithfully, did I give away my land when I signed the paper?'

'No, King, you gave away only the gold beneath it.'

'But how can men dig for gold without the land over it?' Lobengula asked, and Robyn was silent and miserable.

'Nomusa, you said that Lodzi was a man of honour. So why does he do these things to me? His young men swagger across my land and call it their own. They shoot down my warriors, and now they gather a great army against me, with wagons and guns and thousands of soldiers. How can Lodzi do this to me, Nomusa?'

'I cannot answer you, oh King. I deceived you as I was myself deceived.'

Lobengula sighed. 'I believe you, Nomusa. There is still no quarrel between us. Bring your family, all your people here to my kraal that I may protect you through the dark times that lie ahead.'

'I do not deserve the king's consideration.' She choked on the words.

'No harm will come to you, Nomusa. You have Lobengula's word upon it.' He turned slowly back to Zouga.

'This gold, Bakela. Does it pay me for the blood of my young men?' And he threw the bag at Zouga's feet. 'Pick up your gold, Bakela, and take it back to Lodzi.'

'Lobengula, I am your friend – and I tell you this as a friend. If you refuse the monthly payment, then Lodzi will look upon it as a breaking of faith.'

'Was not the killing of my young men a breaking of faith, Bakela?' Lobengula asked sadly. 'If it was not, then my people believe it to be so. The regiments are gathered, so that they darken the Hills of the Indunas; they wear their plumes and carry their assegais and their guns, and their eyes are red. The blood of Matabele has been spilled, Bakela, and the enemies of the king gather against him.'

'Hear me, oh King, think a while before you let your young men run. What do they know of fighting Englishmen?' Zouga was angry now, and the scar on his cheek burned red as a welt raised by the lash of a whip.

'My young men will eat them up,' said Lobengula simply. 'As did the Zulu at the Hill of the Little Hand.'

'After the Little Hand came Ulundi,' Zouga reminded him. 'The earth was black with the Zulu dead, and they put chains on the legs of the Zulu King and sent him to an island far across the sea.'

'Bakela, it is too late. I cannot hold my young men, I have held them too long. They must run now.'

'Your young men are brave when there are old Mashona women to stab, and young babies to disembowel, but they have never met real men.'

Gandang hissed with anger behind the king's shoulder, but Zouga went on firmly.

'Send them home to dally with their women and preen their feathers, for if you let them run, then you will be lucky if you live to see your kraal burning and your herds being driven off.'

This time all three of the senior indunas hissed, and Gandang started forward impulsively, but Lobengula spread his hand to restrain him.

'Bakela is a guest of the king,' Lobengula said. 'While he stands in my kraal, every hair of his head is sacred.' But the king's eyes had never left Zouga's face. 'Go, Bakela, leave this day and take your woman with you. Go to Daketela and tell him that my impis are ready. If he crosses the Gwelo river, I will let my young men go.'

'Lobengula, if I leave then the last link between black men and white men is broken. There will be no more talking. It will be war.'

'Then let it be so, Bakela.'

I t was hard riding. They took the road that Ralph Ballantyne's wagons had recently pioneered from Fort Salisbury to GuBulawayo. They left all their furniture and possessions in the cottage outside the stockade of the king's kraal – and they rode light, with a blanket roll on the pommel of the saddle and a food bag on one of the spare horses that Jan Cheroot brought up behind on a lead rein.

Louise rode like a man, astride and uncomplaining, and on the fifth day, unexpectedly, they came up with Jameson's column in camp around the skeletal headgear of Iron Mine Hill, where the volunteers from Salisbury and Fort Victoria had joined up.

'Zouga, is that how Jameson is going to challenge Lobengula's impi?'

The little encampment looked pathetically inadequate. There were two dozen wagons, and on the canvas tents of most of them Zouga could make out the insignia of Ralph's transport company. But he pointed to the corners of the laager.

'Machine-guns,' he said. 'Six of them, and they are worth five hundred men each. They have field guns also, look at their emplacements.'

'Oh Zouga, do you have to go with them?'

'You know that I do.'

They rode down into the camp, and as they passed the

pickets there was a hail that startled the sentries and made Louise's horse shy and skitter.

'Papa!' Ralph came hurrying from the nearest wagon.

'My boy.' Zouga jumped down from the saddle, and they embraced happily. 'I should have known you would be wherever there was something doing.'

Louise bent from the saddle and Ralph brushed her cheek with his fine moustache.

'I still find it difficult to believe that I have a stepmother so young and beautiful.'

'You are my favourite son,' she laughed. 'But I'd love you more if you could arrange a hot bath—'

From behind the canvas screen Louise kept calling for more buckets of hot water, and Zouga had to carry them from the fire and top-up the galvanized hip-bath in which she sat with her thick, dark braids piled on top of her head, glowing pinkly from the almost boiling water and taking full part in the conversation beyond the screen.

Ralph and Zouga sat at a camp table with a blue enamel pot of coffee and a bottle of whisky between them.

'We have six hundred and eighty-five men all in.'

'I warned Rhodes that he would need fifteen hundred,' Zouga frowned.

'Well, there are another five hundred volunteers under Major Goold-Adams ready to move off from Macloutsi.'

'They would never get here in time to take a part in the fighting.' Zouga shook his head. 'What about lines of supply and reinforcements? What happens if we get into trouble with the Matabele? What chance of a relieving force?'

Ralph grinned devilishly. 'I am the whole commissariat – you don't think I would split the profits with anyone else, do you?'

'Re-supply? Relieving force?'

Ralph spread his hands in negation. 'The doctor informs me that we don't need them. God and Mr Rhodes are on our side.'

'If it goes against us, it will be death and mutilation for every man, woman and child this side of the Shashi river. Lobengula's impis are mad for war now. Neither the king nor his indunas will be able to control them once they begin.'

'That thought had occurred to me,' Ralph admitted. 'I have Cathy and Jonathan at Fort Victoria, packed and ready, old Isazi is with them and one of my best young men. I have fresh relays of mules posted all the way from Fort Vicky to the Shashi. The hour Jameson gives the word for the column to march, my family will be on their way south.'

'Ralph, I am taking Louise to Fort Victoria. Can she stay with Cathy and leave with her?'

'Nobody asked me,' Louise called from behind the screen, and there was an angry splash of water. 'I took a vow, until death us do part – Zouga Ballantyne.'

'You also vowed to love, honour and obey,' Zouga reminded her, and winked at Ralph. 'I hope you don't suffer the same insubordination from your wife.'

'Beat them regularly and give them plenty of babies,' Ralph advised. 'Of course, Louise must go with Katie, but you had better leave for Fort Vicky right away – the Doctor is champing at the bit to settle Lobengula's hash.' He broke off, and gestured at a trooper who was hurrying towards their wagon across the laager. 'And it looks as though he has heard of your arrival at last.'

The trooper saluted Zouga breathlessly. 'Are you Major Zouga Ballantyne, sir? Dr Jameson asks you please to come to his tent at your earliest convenience.'

D r Jameson jumped up from the travelling-desk and bustled across the tent to meet Zouga.

'Ballantyne, I was worried about you. Have you come directly from Lobengula? What are the chances? What force do you reckon he disposes?' He broke off and scolded himself with a deprecatory chuckle. 'What am I thinking of. Let me get you a drink, man!'

He led Zouga into the tent. 'You know General St John, of course—' And Zouga stiffened, his face expressionless.

'Zouga.' Mungo St John lounged in a canvas camp chair – but he made no effort to rise or offer his hand. 'How long it is. But you are looking well. Marriage agrees with you – I have not had the opportunity to congratulate you.'

'Thank you.' Zouga nodded. Naturally he had known that Mungo was the Doctor's Chief of Staff – but still he was not ready for his anger and bitterness at the confrontation. This was the man who had kept Louise as a mistress, had held her tender precious body. He found that he was trembling, and he thrust the picture from his mind, but it was replaced instantly by the image of Louise as he had found her in the desert, her skin burned off her in slabs by the sun – and it was Mungo St John who had let her go and made no effort to follow her.

'I have heard that your wife is in camp with you—' St John's single eye glowed maliciously. 'You must dine with me tonight; it will be gratifying to discuss old times.'

'My wife has had a long, hard journey.' Zouga kept his voice level; he did not want to give Mungo the satisfaction of knowing how angry he was. 'And in the morning I am taking her into Fort Victoria.'

'Good!' Jameson cut in briskly. 'That suits my own plans – I need a trustworthy man to put a message on the telegraph line for Mr Rhodes. But now, Ballantyne, what is the news from GuBulawayo, and how do you rate our chances?'

'Well, Doctor Jim, Lobengula's ready for you – his young men are spoiling for a fight – and you have a scanty enough force here. In the ordinary way I would say that to take it into Matabeleland without reinforcements or a relieving force in the offing would be suicide. However—'

'However?' Jameson demanded eagerly.

'Four of Lobengula's regiments, those he sent against Lewanika, the king of the Barotse, are still on the Zambezi, and Lobengula will not be able to use them.'

'Why not?'

'Smallpox,' Zouga said. 'It's broken out in those regiments, and he dare not recall them to the south. They can take no part in the fighting.'

'Half the Matabele army out of it,' Jameson exulted. 'That's a nudge from on high, St John – what do you think?'

'I would say it's still a risk, a damnable risk. But think of the stake. A whole country to be won with all its lands and herds and gold. I'd say if we are ever to march, we must march now.'

'Ballantyne, your sister – the missionary woman, what's her name – Codrington, is she still at Khami? Is her family there with her?'

Zouga nodded, mystified, and Jameson snatched up a pencil and scribbled a message on his pad. Then he tore off the sheet and handed it to Mungo St John. Mungo read it and smiled. He looked like a bird of prey, beak-nosed and fierce.

'Yes,' he said. 'Perfect.' He passed the sheet to Zouga. Jameson had written in block capitals.

URGENT FOR JOVE MATABELE REGIMENTS MASSED TO ATTACK STOP ENGLISH WOMEN AND CHILDREN IN THE POWER OF THE MATABELE TYRANT STOP IMPERATIVE WE MARCH AT ONCE TO SAVE THEM REPLY SOONEST

'Even Labouchère couldn't quibble with that,' Zouga remarked wryly. Labouchère was the London editor of *Truth* magazine, a champion of the oppressed and one of Rhodes' most eloquent and persistent adversaries. Zouga proffered the sheet, but Jameson waved it back.

'Keep it. Send it. I don't suppose you could leave this evening?' Jameson asked wistfully.

'It will be dark in an hour, and my wife is exhausted.'

'Very well,' Jameson agreed. 'But you will return here as soon as you can with Mr Rhodes' reply?'

'Of course.'

'And there will be something else I want you to do on your return, a most important assignment.'

'What is it?'

'General St John will explain.' And Zouga turned suspiciously to Mungo.

Mungo's manner was suddenly placatory. 'Zouga, there's not one of us who hasn't read your book *Hunter's Odyssey*. I would say that it's the bible of anybody wanting to know about this country and its people.'

'Thank you.' Zouga was unbending still.

'And one of the most interesting sections is the description of your visit to the oracle of the Umlimo in the hills south of GuBulawayo.'

'The Matopos,' Zouga told him.

'Yes, of course, the Matopos. Could you find your way back to the witch's cavern? After all, it has been over twenty-five years?'

'Yes, I could find it again.' Zouga did not hesitate.

'Excellent,' Jameson interrupted. 'Come along, St John, do tell him why.' But Mungo seemed to digress.

'You know the old Zulu who works for your son—'

'Isazi, Ralph's head driver?' Zouga asked.

'That's the one. Well, we captured four Matabele scouts and we put Isazi in the stockade with them. He can pass for a Matabele, so the prisoners spoke freely in front of him. One of the things we learnt is that the Umlimo has called all the witchdoctors of the nation to a ritual in the hills.'

'Yes,' Zouga agreed. 'I heard of it before I left GuBulawayo. The Umlimo is preaching war, and promises a charm to the impis that will turn our bullets to water.'

'Ah, so it's true then.' Mungo nodded – and then, thoughtfully: 'Just what influence does this prophetess have?'

'The Umlimo is a hereditary figure, a sort of virgin demi-deity that has her origins long before the arrival of the Matabele in this land, perhaps a thousand years or more ago. First Mzilikazi and then Lobengula have fallen under her spell. I have even heard it whispered that Lobengula served an apprenticeship in sorcery under the Umlimo's guidance, in the Matopos.'

'Then she does wield power over the Matabele?'

'Immense power. Lobengula makes no important decision without her oracle. No impi would march without her charms to protect them.'

'If she were to die on the day we march into Matabele-land?'

'It would throw the king and his warriors into consterna-tion. They would probably act recklessly. The Umlimo's charms would perish with her; her advice might turn like a serpent and strike the receiver. They would be demoralized – and it would take at least three months to choose a prophetess to replace her. During that time the nation would be vulnerable.'

'Zouga, I want you to take a party of mounted men – the toughest and the best we have. I want you to ride to the witch's cave and destroy her and all her witchdoctors.'

Will Daniel was Zouga's sergeant. He was a Canadian who had been twenty years in Africa without losing his accent. He had fought the tribes on the Fish river and in Zululand. He boasted that he had killed three of Cetewayo's men with a single shot at Ulundi and made his tobacco pouch from the scalp of one of them. He had been in the Gazaland rebellion and fought at the Hill of the Doves against the free burghers of the Transvaal Republic. Wherever there had been trouble and shooting, Will Daniel had forged his bloody reputation. He was a big man, heavy in the gut, prematurely bald with large round ears that stood out from his polished scalp like those of a wild dog. His fists were gnarled, his legs bowed from the saddle, and he wore a perpetual wide white grin which never touched his cold little eyes.

'You don't have to like or trust him,' Mungo St John had advised Zouga. 'But he is the man for the job.'

With Will Daniel went his henchman, Jim Thorn, half Will's size but every bit as vicious. A skinny little cockney with the grey tones of the slum-dweller so deeply etched into his gaunt melancholy face that five thousand African suns had been unable to erase them. Dr Jameson had released him from the Fort Victoria gaol, where the was waiting trial for beating a Mashona servant to death with a rhinoceros-hide *sjambok*. His pardon dependent on his conduct during the campaign. 'So you can rely on him to do whatever needs doing,' Mungo had pointed out to Zouga.

The other thirteen troopers were men of a similar type. They had all volunteered under Doctor Jim's Victoria Agreement and signed the enlistment document, a document which Jameson made sure remained secret. No copy of it went to the High Commissioner in Cape Town nor to Gladstone's Government in Whitehall, for it promised the volunteers a share of Lobengula's land and cattle and treasures; the word 'loot' was specifically mentioned in the text.

On the first night out Will Daniel had come silently to where Zouga slept a little apart and, as he stooped over Zouga's recumbent form, a wiry arm had whipped suddenly around his neck and the muzzle of a Webley revolver was thrust under his ribs with sufficient force to drive the air from his lungs.

'Next time you creep up on me, I'll kill you,' Zouga hissed into his face; and Will's teeth flashed in the moonlight as he grinned appreciatively.

'They told me you were a sharp one.'

'What do you want?'

'Me and the boys want to sell our land rights – three thousand *morgen* each, that's ninety thousand acres. You can have them for a hundred each.'

'You haven't earned them yet.'

'That's a chance you gotta take, skipper.'

'I thought you were on guard duty, sergeant.'

'Well, it was just for a moment, sir.'

'Next time you leave your post, I'll shoot you myself, without bothering about a court martial.'

Daniel stared into his face for a moment.

'Yep, I reckon you would too,' Will grinned mirthlessly.

Zouga led the patrol south and westwards through the forests where once long ago he had hunted the wandering herds of elephant. Now the tuskers were all gone, and even the herds of lesser game were wild from the unrestrained hunting of the new settlers and they scattered at the first approach of the small party of horsemen.

Zouga avoided the established roads between the

Matabele regimental towns, and when they had to pass close to a settlement or the cultivated lands surrounding it, they did so at night. Though he knew that the impis had all answered Lobengula's call and were already assembled at Thabas Indunas, still he felt a vast relief when the granite domes of the Matopos rose above the treetops ahead of them and in single file his horsemen followed him into one of the steep-sided valleys.

That night there was a deputation of four troopers led by Will Daniel and Jim Thorn.

'The boys have all voted, skipper. We will take a hundred for the lot.' Will grinned ingratiatingly. 'There's not one of us have the price of a drink to celebrate when we get home – and you have that money belt around your belly. It must be damned heavy by now, and no good it will do you if a Matabele sniper puts a bullet in your back.'

The smile was still on Will's face, but the threat was naked in his eyes. If Zouga did not buy their land grants, it might be a bullet in the back. They would divide up the contents of his money belt anyway.

Zouga considered defying the big ugly sergeant, but there were fifteen of them. The gold in his belt could be his death warrant. He was in enough danger from the Matabele.

'I have seventy-five sovereigns in my belt,' he said grimly.

'Fine,' Will agreed. 'You've got yourself a bargain, Major.'

Zouga wrote out a contract of land grant sale on the back page of his message pad, and twelve of them signed it. Will Daniel and two other illiterates made their marks, and then they squabbled over the division of the gold sovereigns from Zouga's belt. Zouga was relieved to be rid of them, and as he returned the pad to his saddle-bag, he realized abruptly that, if those grants were valid, then Will

Daniel was right. He had got a bargain. He decided that when he rejoined Jameson's column, he would buy up all the other grants that were on offer from any of the rootless drifters who wanted to sell for the price of a bottle of whisky.

Zouga had forgotten just how intense were the peculiar brooding silences of the magical Matopos hills. The silence was a thing of weight and substance that made their spirits quail. No bird twittered or danced upon a twig in the dense undergrowth that pressed in upon the narrow path, and no breeze reached into the depths of the granite-sided valleys.

The silence and the heat weighed even upon the hard and unsusceptible men who followed Zouga in single file. They rode with their rifles held across their laps, their eyes narrowed against the glare from the sparkling chips of mica in the granite walls, watchful and anxious, the dense dark green bush about them charged with a nameless menace.

At times the narrow game trails they were following pinched out or ended abruptly in the gut of a valley, and they were forced to retrace their route and try another; but always Zouga kept working south and west. Then, on the third day, he was rewarded.

He cut the broad beaten road that led from GuBulawayo to the hidden valley of the Umlimo. It was wide and smooth enough for Zouga to spur his horse into a canter. At Zouga's orders, his troopers had muffled their equipment, and put leathers over the hooves of their mounts, so the only sound was the creak of saddlery and the occasional brush and whip of an overhanging branch.

The earlier uneasiness was gone now, and they leaned forward in their saddles, eager as hunting dogs on the leash with a hot scent in their nostrils. Jameson had promised them a bonus of twenty guineas each and all the loot that they could carry away from the valley of the Umlimo.

Zouga began to recognize landmarks that he passed. There was a pile of rocks, the largest of them the size of St Paul's dome, and three others, graded down in size, all of them weathered to almost perfect spheres and balanced one upon the other, and he knew they would reach the entrance to the valley before noon. He halted the patrol and let them snatch a quick meal standing at their horses' heads as he went down the line checking their equipment and assigning each of them a separate task.

'Sergeant, you and Trooper Thorn are to stay close behind me. We will be the first through the pass and into the valley. There is a small village in the centre of it, and there may be Matabele amongst the huts. Don't stop for them – even if there are warriors with them, leave them for the others. Ride straight on to the cave at the end of the valley; we must find the witch before she can escape.'

'This witch, what does she look like, skipper?'

'I am not sure, she may be quite young, probably naked.'

'You leave 'er to me, mate.' Jim Thorn grinned lasciviously and nudged Will, but Zouga ignored him.

'Any woman you find in the cave will be the witch. Now don't be put off by the sound of wild animals, or strange voices – she is a skilled ventriloquist.' He went on, giving precise details, and ended grimly: 'Our orders are harsh, but they may eventually save the lives of many of our comrades by breaking the morale of the Matabele fighting impis.'

They mounted again, and almost immediately the road began to narrow so that the branches brushed their stirrups as they passed, and Zouga's horse stumbled in a narrow stream, clumsy with the leathers over its hooves. Then he was through and he looked up the sheer granite cliff that blocked their way. The entrance to the passage through the rock was a dark vertical cleft and high above it a thatched watch-hut was perched in a niche of the granite.

As he stared up at it, Zouga saw an indistinct movement on the ledge.

'Look out above!' Even as he yelled, a dozen black men appeared on the lip of the cliff, and each of them hurled a bundle of what looked like staves out over the edge. They scattered as they fell, and the steel sparkled as the weighted heads dropped, points first, towards them. There was a fluting sound in the air all around them, soft as swallows' wings, then the rattle of steel against rock and the thud of the points into the earth beneath the hooves of the horses.

One of the steel-headed javelins caught a trooper in the side of his neck, driving down behind the collar bone, deep into one lung so that when he tried to scream the blood gagged him and bubbled out over his chin. His horse reared and whinnied wildly, and he fell backwards out of the saddle; and then all was milling, shouting confusion on the narrow track.

Through it Zouga craned to watch the ledge, and saw the defenders lining the lip again, each with another bundle of javelins on his shoulder. Zouga dropped his reins and used both hands to aim his rifle vertically upwards.

He emptied the magazine, firing as rapidly as he could pump cartridges into the breech, and though his aim was spoiled by the dancing horse under him, one of the men on the ledge arched over backwards with his arms wind-milling wildly and then fell free, writhing and twisting and shrieking in the air until he hit the rock in front of Zouga's horse, and his screams and struggles ceased abruptly.

The rest of the men on the ledge scattered away, and Zouga waved the empty rifle over his head.

'Forward!' he yelled. 'Follow me!' And he plunged into the forbidding crevice that split the cliff vertically from base to crest.

The passage was so narrow that his stirrup irons struck

sparks from the rock walls on each side of him, but he looked back and saw Will Daniel pounding along behind. He had lost his slouch hat. His bald head was washed with sweat, and he was grinning like a hungry hyena as he reloaded his rifle from the bandolier across his chest.

The passage turned sharply, and the white sand that floored it splashed up under the hooves, and the mica chips sparkled even in the gloom. Ahead of Zouga a tiny freshet of clear water fountained from the rock, and his horse gathered its front feet under its chest and jumped the stream easily; then suddenly they burst out from the narrow passage, back into the sunlight again.

The hidden valley of the Umlimo lay in a green basin below them, the little village of huts as its centre; and in the base of the cliff beyond it, a mile or so away, Zouga could make out the low entrance of the cavern, dark as the eye cavity in a bleached skull. It was all exactly as he remembered it.

'Troop, into line wheel!' he shouted as his horsemen galloped out into the open behind him; and they swung into extended formation, facing the valley, the rifles unsheathed and cocked, impatient and fierce as they saw before them the prize they had come so far to find.

'*Amadoda!*' shouted Will Daniel, pointing at the band of warriors that were trotting out of the village to face the line of horsemen.

'Twenty of them,' Zouga counted swiftly. 'They'll give us no trouble.' And then he stood in his stirrups. 'Walk march, forward!'

The horsemen moved down the slope, keeping their line – while the warriors lifted their shields high and raced to meet them.

'Troop, halt.' Zouga ordered when the nearest Matabele was a hundred paces ahead. 'Pick your targets.'

The first volley, carefully aimed by hard and experienced soldiers, scythed the line of charging warriors like the reaper's steel; and they went down, falling over their shields, plumes tumbling from their heads, assegais pinning harmlessly into the earth, and yet a handful of them came on without checking.

'Fire at will!' Zouga called, and looked over the sights of his rifle at a bounding Matabele, watching him grow in size with every pace, seized by a strange reluctance to kill a brave man such as this one.

'Jee! Jee!' the Matabele yelled defiantly, and raised his shield to clear his spear arm. Zouga shot him in the notch of bone at the base of his throat and the Matabele spun sharply round, hit the ground with one shoulder and rolled against the legs of Zouga's horse.

Half a dozen of the Matabele had broken in the face of those deadly volleys, and were running back towards the village. The others were strewn about in front of the line of horsemen.

'After them.' Zouga hardly raised his voice above a conversational tone. 'Forward! Charge!'

'Sergeant Daniel, Trooper Thorn, to the cave.' He swung his horse's head to gallop clear of the cluster of huts, and there was the body of one of the fallen Matabele directly in his path. He altered course again to miss it, and both Thorn and Daniel pulled a length ahead of him.

Then the Matabele rolled lithely to his feet, and dodged in front of Zouga. Playing dead was an old Zulu trick, and Zouga should have been ready for it. But his rifle was in his left hand, and he tried to get it across, at the same time trying to turn his horse and shouting an impotent challenge at the warrior.

The Matabele extended his spear arm stiffly and let the running horse impale itself upon the broad silver blade. It went deeply into the heaving chest between the front legs, and the horse reeled from the blow and then went over on its side.

Zouga barely had time to kick his feet out of the irons

and jump clear before the carcass hit the earth with all four legs kicking briefly at the sky.

Zouga landed badly, but gathered himself and whirled to face the warrior. He was only just in time to deflect the blood-smeared assegai as the Matabele struck at his belly. The steel rang against the barrel of his rifle and then they were straining chest to chest.

The man smelled of woodsmoke and ochre and fat, and his body was hard as carved ebony and slippery as a freshly caught catfish. Zouga knew he could not hold him for more than a few seconds, and with one hand on the muzzle and the other on the breech, Zouga rammed the barrel of the rifle up under the man's chin into his bulging corded throat, and hooked desperately with the rowel of his spur for the ankle.

They went over backwards, Zouga on top, and he threw all his weight onto the rifle at the moment they hit the hard earth, savagely driving it into the Matabele's throat, and the neck broke with a crunch like a walnut in a silver nutcracker. The warrior's lids fluttered down over the smoky bloodshot eyes and the body went limp under Zouga's chest.

Zouga pushed himself to his feet and looked around him quickly. His troopers were amongst the huts, and there was the thudding of scattered rifle fire as they finished off the survivors of that gallant but futile charge. He saw one of his men chase a scampering old naked crone, her empty dugs swinging and her thin legs almost giving under her with terror. He rode her down, and then backed his horse up to trample her – shouting and swearing with excitement and firing down into the frail, withered body that lay crushed against the earth.

Beyond the village, Zouga saw two horses going up the slope towards the base of the cliff at full gallop, and even as he started forward, they reached it and Daniel and

Thorn jumped from the saddles and disappeared into the mouth of the cavern.

It was half a mile from where Zouga had fallen to the base of the cliff. He reloaded his rifle as he ran. The fight with the Matabele had shaken him, and his riding boots hampered each step. It took him many long minutes to toil up the slope to where Daniel and Thorn had left their horses, and by then he was badly winded.

He leaned against the stone portal of the cavern, peering into the black and threatening depths, while each breath he drew jarred his whole body. Tumultuous echoes boomed out of the blackness of the cavern, the shouts of men and the bellowing and snarling of wild animals, the screams of a woman in terrible anguish and the crash of rifle fire.

Zouga pushed himself away from the cliff and stooped through the entrance. Almost immediately he stumbled over a body. It was that of an old man, his hair pure white and his skin wrinkled like a dried prune. Zouga stepped over him, into a puddle of his dark, sticky blood.

As he moved forward, Zouga's eyes accustomed to the gloom, and he peered about him at the mummified bodies of ancient dead piled haphazard against the walls of the cavern. Here and there white bone gleamed through the parchment of leathery dried flesh, and an arm was raised in a macabre salutation or a gesture of supplication.

Zouga moved on through this grisly catacomb, and ahead of him there was a diffused source of light. He quickened his pace as another gale of wild screams was this time mingled with booming inhuman laughter that bounced from the rocky walls and roof.

He turned a corner of jagged rock and looked down into a natural amphitheatre in the floor of the cavern. It was lit by the flames of a flickering orange fire, and from above by a single beam of sunlight that came in through a narrow crack in the high arched roof. The sunbeam was dimmed to an unearthly blue by the tendrils of curling smoke from the fire, and like the limelights of a theatre stage it dramatized the group of struggling figures on the floor of the amphitheatre beyond the fire.

Zouga ran down the natural steps, and had almost reached them before he realized what they were doing.

Between them Daniel and Thorn had the body of a young black girl stretched out on the rocky floor, the girl was naked, on her back with her limbs spreadeagled. Her oiled body was as glossy as the pelt of a panther, her limbs were long and shapely. She was struggling with the desperation of a wild animal in a trap. But her screams were muted by the fur kaross wrapped about her head, and Jim Thorn knelt upon her shoulders, pinning her helplessly while he twisted her arms back against the joint of the elbows and roared with cruel laughter that was too loud for his skinny body.

Will Daniel was over the girl, his face swollen and dark with congested blood. His belt and breeches were down across the back of his knees. He was grunting and snuffling like a boar at the trough. His pale buttocks were covered with a fuzz of sparse curly black hair. He drove against the girl with a wet slapping sound like a washerwoman pounding laundry on a slab.

Before Zouga could reach him, Will Daniel's whole body stiffened and jerked spasmodically and then he rolled off the tender young body, and he was bloodied from the knees to the navel of his sagging, hairy paunch.

'By God, Jim my lad,' he panted at the little trooper, 'that was better than a belly ache. Get up on the bitch for your turn—' Then he saw Zouga out of the shadows, and he grinned at him. 'First come, first served, Major—'

Zouga took two strides to reach him, and then he kicked him in his smiling mouth with the heel of his riding boot. Will Daniel's bottom lip split open like the petals of a rose, and he scrambled to his feet, spitting out white chips of tooth, and hauling up his breeches over his monstrous nakedness.

'I'll kill you for that.' He tugged at the knife on his dangling unclinched belt, but Zouga thrust the muzzle of his rifle into his belly, doubling him over at the waist, and then whirled to slam the butt against Jim Thorn's temple, as Thorn was reaching for his abandoned rifle.

'Get on your feet,' Zouga told him coldly, and, swaying and clutching the swelling above his ear, Jim Thorn backed off against the wall of the cave.

'I'll get you for this,' Will Daniel wheezed painfully, still holding his belly, and Zouga turned the rifle back onto him.

'Get out,' he said softly. 'Get out of here you filthy bloody animals.'

They shuffled up the steps of the amphitheatre; and from the shadows of the cavern entrance, Will Daniel yelled again, his voice blustering and angry.

'I'll not forget this, Major bloody Ballantyne. I'll get you yet!'

Zouga turned back to the girl. She had pulled the kaross off her head, and she crouched on the stone floor with her legs curled up under her. She was trying to staunch the flow of her virgin blood with her hands, but she stared at Zouga with the tortured ferocity of a leopard held by the serrated jaws of a spring trap.

Zouga felt an overwhelming compassion sweep over him – yet he knew there was no succour he could give her.

'You, who were Umlimo, are Umlimo no longer,' he said at last, and she drew back her head and spat at him. The frothy spittle splattered against his boots, but the effort made her whimper with pain and press her hands against her lower belly. A fresh trickle of bright arterial blood snaked down her thigh.

'I came to destroy the Umlimo,' he said. 'But she is destroyed not by a bullet from a gun. Go, child. The gift of

617

the spirits has been taken from you. Go swiftly, but go in peace.'

Like a wounded animal she crept on her hands and knees into the dark maze of tunnels beyond the amphitheatre, leaving a speckle of bloody drops upon the stone floor.

She looked back at him once. 'Peace, you say, white man. There will be no peace, ever!'

And then she was gone into the shadows.

The rains had not yet come – but their heralds soared up to the heavens, great ranges of cumulus cloud, their heads shaped like mushrooms. Silver and blue and imperial purple, they stood above the Hills of the Indunas.

The heat seemed trapped beneath them. It clanged down upon the iron hills like a blacksmith's hammer on the anvil. The impis were thick as safari ants upon the slopes; they squatted in dense ranks their shields under them, their assegais and guns laid on the rocky earth before them – thousands upon thousands they waited, every plumed head craning down towards the royal kraal at the foot of the hills.

There was the beat of a single drum. Tap – tap! Tap – tap! And the great black mass of warriors stirred like an amorphous sea monster rising from the depths.

'The Elephant comes! He comes! He comes!' It was a soft growl in all their throats.

Through the gates of the stockade filed a small procession, twenty men wearing the tassels of valour, twenty men walking proud, the blood royal of Kumalo, and at their head the huge heavy figure of the king.

Lobengula had thrown off all the European gee-gaws,

the brass buttons and mirrors, the gold brocaded coat – and he was dressed in the regalia of a Matabele king.

The headring was on his brow, and heron feathers in his hair. His cloak was royal leopard skin, spotted gold, and his kilt was of leopard tails. His swollen ankles, crippled with gout, were covered by the war rattles, but he mastered the agony of the disease, striding out with ponderous dignity, so the waiting impis gasped with the splendour of his presence.

'See the Great Bull whose tread shakes the earth.'

In his right hand he carried the toy spear of polished redwood, the spear of kingship. Now he raised the puny weapon high, and the nation came bounding upright; and the shields, the long shields that gave them their name, bloomed upon the slope of the hill, covering it like a garden of exotic deadly flowers.

'*Bayete!*' The royal salute roared like the surf of a winter sea breaking on a rocky headland.

'*Bayete!* Lobengula, son of Mzilikazi.'

After that great burst of sound, the silence was daunting, but Lobengula paced slowly along the ranks, and in his eyes was the terrible sorrow of a father for the sons who must die. This was the hour which he had dreaded from the first day he took the little redwood spear in his right hand. This was the destiny which he had tried to avoid – and now it had overtaken him.

His voice boomed, and he lifted the spear and pointed to the east. 'The enemy that comes upon us now is like—' the spear shook in his hand, 'like the leopard in the goat kraal, like the white termites in the kingpost of a hut. They will not stop until all is destroyed.'

The massed regiments of Matabele growled, straining like hunting dogs against the leash, and Lobengula stopped in the centre of their lines and threw the leopard skin cloak back from his right arm.

He turned slowly until he faced into the east, where Jameson's columns were massing far over the horizon, and his spear arm went back to its full stretch. He stood poised in the classic stance of the javelin-thrower, and there was a soft susurration in the air as ten thousand lungs filled with breath and held it.

Then, with a heart-stopping shout, the cry of a man crushed under the iron wheel of his own destiny, Lobengula hurled the war spear into the east, and his shout was echoed by ten thousand throats.

'Jee! Jee!' They roared, and stabbed at the air with the broad silver blades, stabbing at the still invisible enemy.

Then the impis formed, one behind the other. Led by their indunas, their matched shields overlapping, they swept past the king, fierce in their pride, leaping high and flashing their assegais, and Lobengula saluted them: the Imbezu and the Inyati, the Ingubu and the Izimvukuzane, the 'Moles-that-burrow-under-a-mountain,' with their matt red shields held high and Bazo, the Axe, prancing at their head. They wound away into the eastern grasslands, and Lobengula could still hear their singing, faintly on the heated air, long after the last of them had disappeared from view.

A little group of indunas and guards still attended the king, but they waited below at the gate of the stockade.

Lobengula was alone upon the deserted hillside; all the dignity and regal pride had gone out of his bearing. His grossly swollen body slumped like that of a very old and sick man. His eyes were rheumy with unshed tears, and he stared out into the east without moving, listening to the fading war chants.

At last he sighed, shook himself, and hobbled forward on his crippled distorted feet.

Painfully he stooped to retrieve the little redwood spear, but he paused before his fingers touched it.

The blade of the spear of kingship had snapped through.

He picked up the broken pieces and held them in his hands, and then he turned and shuffled slowly down from the Hills of the Indunas.

The Company flag stood high above the laager on a slightly crooked pole of mopani.

It had hung limply in the stupefying heat all that morning, but now as the patrol rode in across the open ground above the river bank, it unfurled briefly on a random current of air, snapped as though to draw attention to itself, and then extended its full glory for a moment, before sagging wearily once again.

At the head of the patrol, Ralph Ballantyne turned to his father who rode at his side. 'That flag makes no bones about it, Papa.'

The pretty crosses of St George, St Andrew and St Patrick that made up the Union Jack, had the Company insignia superimposed upon them, the lion gardant with a tusk of ivory held in its claw and the letters under it 'B.S.A.C.' – British South Africa Company.

'Servants of the Company first, and of the Queen a good deal later.'

'You're a cynical rascal, Ralph.' Zouga could hardly suppress his smile. 'Are you suggesting that there is a man in all our Company here for personal gain rather than glory of Empire?'

'Perish the thought.' This time Ralph chuckled. 'By the way, Papa, how many land grants have you bought up so far? I am losing count – is it thirty or thirty-five?'

'This is a dream I worked for all my life, Ralph. It's coming true before our eyes – and when it does, I'll have my fair reward, and nothing more.'

The laager was drawn up in its rigid square three hundred yards from the steep banks of the Shangani river, in the centre of a dried-out clay pan. The surface was as flat and bare as a tennis court. The clay had cracked into irregular briquettes that curled up at the edges. They crunched under the horses' hooves as Zouga led the patrol in.

They had been out for two days, scouting the road beyond the river, and Zouga was pleased to see that during his absence St John had taken Zouga's advice and had his axemen hack down the brush around the edges of the pan to open the field of fire. Now any attacker would have to cross three hundred yards of bare clay to reach the square of wagons, all of it under the evil little Cyclopean scrutiny of the Maxims.

As they cantered up, a party unchained the wheels of one of the wagons and dragged it aside to allow them to enter, and a sergeant in Company uniform saluted Zouga as he passed and called after him.

'General St John's compliments, sir, and will you report to him directly.'

'My bet is that you need a drink.' Mungo St John took one look at the dust that clung like flour in Zouga's beard and the dark patches of sweat that had soaked through his shirt. Coldly Zouga nodded his thanks and poured from the bottle that held down one corner of the map.

'The impis are out in full array,' he said, and let the whisky soak the cloying dust from the back of his throat before going on. 'I have identified most of them. There's Gandang's Inyati, and Manonda's Insukamini—' He reeled off the names of the indunas and their impis, glancing at the notes he had made on his pad. 'We had a brush with the "Moles" and had to shoot our way out and ride for it, but still we reached the Bembesi river before turning back.'

'Where are the impis, Ballantyne? Damn it, man, we have advanced seventy miles from Iron Mine Hill and seen neither hide nor hair of them,' Jameson demanded almost petulantly.

'They are all around us, Doctor. A thousand or more in the trees just across the river, and I cut tracks that showed that two more impis have circled out behind us. They are probably lying across the Longiwe Hills watching every move we make.'

'We must bring them to battle,' Jameson fretted. 'Every day the campaign lasts is costing the shareholders money.'

'They won't attack us here, not while we are in laager, not across open ground.'

'Where then?'

'They will attack in the Zulu way, in broken ground, or thick bush. I have marked four likely defiles ahead of us, places where they will be able to creep up close on either side or lay to ambush the wagons as we pass.'

'You want us to walk into their trap – rather than draw them out?' Mungo asked.

'You'll not draw them out. I think their commander here is Gandang, the king's half-brother. He is far too cunning to come at us in the open. If you want to fight them, it must be in the bad ground.'

'W'hen the serpent is coiled, with his head drawn back and his mouth agape to show the venom hanging like drops of dew upon his fangs – then the wise man does not stretch out his hands towards him.' Gandang spoke softly, and the other indunas cocked their heads to listen to his words. 'The wise man waits until the serpent uncoils and begins to creep away, then he steps upon the head and crushes it. We must wait. We must wait to take them in the forests, when the wagons are strung out, and the outriders cannot see one another. Then we cut the column into pieces and swallow each one, a mouthful at a time.'

'Yet my young men are tired of waiting,' said Manonda,

facing Gandang across the fire. Manonda was the commander of the elite Insukamini impi, and though there was silver on his head, there was still fire in his heart. They all knew him to be brave to the edge of folly, quick to take an insult, and quicker still to revenge it. 'These white barbarians have marched unopposed across our lands, while we trail around them like timid girls guarding our maidenheads and giggling behind our hands. My young men grow weary of waiting, Gandang, and I with them.'

'There is a time for timidity, Manonda, my cousin, and there is a time to be brave.'

'The time to be brave is when your enemy stands brazenly before you. They are six hundred, you have counted them yourself, Gandang, and we are six thousand.' Manonda grinned mockingly around the circle of listening men. On the brow of each was the headring of high office, and on their arms and legs the tassels of courage. 'Shame on those that hesitate,' said Manonda, the Bold. 'Shame on you, Bazo. Shame on you, Ntabene. Shame on you, Gambo.' His voice was filled with scorn, and as he said each of their names they hissed with angry denial.

Then suddenly there was a sound from beyond the circle of squatting indunas, a sound in the night that chilled and silenced them all. It was the eerie wail of mourning for the dead, and as they listened it came closer, and with it were many other voices.

Gandang sprang to his feet and challenged loudly. 'Who comes?'

And out of the darkness a dozen guards, half dragged and half carried an old woman. She wore only a skirt of untanned hyena skin, and around her neck the grisly accoutrements and trappings of the witch's trade. Her eyes were rolled up into her head so that the whites flashed in the firelight, and her spittle foamed on her slack lips. From her throat issued the wails of mourning for the dead.

'What is it, witch?' Gandang demanded, his superstitious fears twisting his mouth and darkening his eyes. 'What tidings do you bring?'

'The white men have desecrated the holy places. They have destroyed the chosen one of the spirits. They have slaughtered the priests of the nation. They have entered the cave of the Umlimo in the sacred hills – and her blood is splashed upon the ancient rocks. Woe unto all of us. Woe unto those who do not seek revenge. Kill the white men. Kill them all!'

The witch threw off the restraining hands of the guard and, with a wild shriek, hurled herself into the midst of the leaping flames of the watch-fire.

Her skirt burst into flames. Her wild bush of hair burned like a torch. They drew back in horror.

'Kill the white men,' screamed the witch from out of the flames, and they stared as her skin blackened and her flesh peeled from off her bones. She collapsed and a torrent of sparks flew up into the overhanging branches of the forest, and then there was only the crackle and drum of the fire.

Bazo stood in the stunned silence, and he felt the rage rising from deep within his soul. Staring into the flames at the black and twisted remains of the witch, he felt the same need of sacrifice – an atonement and a surcease from the rage and the grief.

He saw in the yellow flames an image of Tanase's beloved face, and something seemed to tear in his chest.

'Jee!' he said, drawing out the war cry, giving expression to his rage. 'Jee!' He lifted the assegai and pointed the blade in the direction of the river and the white men's laager which lay not more than a mile beyond the dark silhouette of the hills. 'Jee!' and the night breeze turned the tears cold as the snow-melt from the Drakensberg mountains upon his cheeks.

'Jee.' Manonda took up the chant, and stabbed towards

the enemy, and the divine madness descended upon them. Gandang was the only one who had reason and fear of consequence left to him.

'Wait!' he cried. 'Wait, my children and my brothers.' But they were gone already, racing away into the darkness to rouse their sleeping impis.

Zouga Ballantyne could not sleep, though his back and thighs still ached for rest from hard riding, and the earth under his blanket was no harder than that on which he had passed a thousand other nights. He lay and listened to the snores and occasional dreamers' gabble from the men around him, while vague forebodings and dark thoughts kept him from joining them in slumber.

Once again vivid memories of the little tragedy in the cave of the Umlimo returned to plague him – and he wondered how long it would be before the news of the atrocity reached the king and his indunas. It might take weeks for a witness to come down from the cave of the Matopos, but when that happened, he would know it by the actions of the Matabele indunas.

From the opposite side of the laager a sky-rocket went hissing up into the night sky, and popped into little red stars high in the heavens. The pickets had been firing a rocket every hour, to guide a missing patrol into the laager.

Now Zouga reached under the saddle that was his pillow and brought out the gold hunter watch. In the light of the sky-rocket he checked the time. It was three o'clock in the morning. He threw off his blanket, and groped for his boots. While he pulled them on, his premonition of lurking evil grew stronger.

He strapped on his bandolier and checked the Webley service revolver hanging on the webbing. Then he stepped over the sleeping blanket-wrapped forms around him and went down to the horse lines. The bay gelding whickered as it recognized him, and Jan Cheroot woke.

'It is all right,' Zouga told him quietly, but the little Hottentot yawned and, with the blanket over his shoulders like a shawl, hobbled across to stir the ashes of his cooking-fire. He set the blue enamel coffee pot on the coals and, while it was heating, they sat side by side and talked quietly like the old friends that they were.

'Less than sixty miles to GuBulawayo,' Jan Cheroot murmured. 'It's taken us more than thirty years – but now at last I feel we are coming home.'

'I have bought up almost forty land grants,' Zouga agreed. 'That is nearly a quarter of a million acres. Yes, Jan Cheroot, we are coming home at last. By God, it's been a long, hard road, though, from the pit of Kimberley mine to the Zambezi—' Zouga broke off and listened. There had been a faint cry, almost like a night bird, from beyond the laager.

'The Mashona,' Jan Cheroot grunted. 'The general should have let them stay in the laager.'

During the slow trek up from Iron Mine Hill, many small groups of Mashona had come to the wagons, begging protection from the assembling Matabele. They knew from bitter experience what to expect when the impis swept across the land in battle array.

'The general could not take that chance.' Zouga shook his head. 'There may be Matabele spies amongst them, he has to guard against treachery.'

Mungo St John had ordered the refugees to keep clear of the laager, and now there were three of four hundred, mostly black women and children, camped amongst the thorn trees on the river bank, five hundred yards from the nearest wagon.

Zouga lifted the coffee pot from the coals and poured the steaming black brew into his mug, then he cocked his head again to listen. There was a faint hubbub, a distant chorus of shrieks and shouts from the direction of the river. With the mug in his hand Zouga strolled across to the nearest wagon in the square, and climbed up onto the disselboom. He peered out of the laager, towards the river.

The open expanse of flat clay was ghostly pale in the starlight, and the treeline beyond it was solid blackness. There was nothing to be seen – except – he blinked his eyes rapidly, for they were playing him false. Nothing, except the blackness of the treeline seemed to be closer, the blackness was spreading towards the laager across the pale clay, like spilled oil or a pool of blood.

Now there was a sound, a rustle like locust wings when the swarms pass overhead, and the engulfing blackness was coming closer, with eerie swiftness.

At that moment another sky-rocket went swooshing up into the night sky, and when it burst, it flooded the pan with a soft, pink light and Zouga dropped the mug of steaming coffee.

The earth was black with the Matabele horde. It swept like a black tide towards the wagons, rank upon rank of great oval shields, and the assegais twinkled in the reflection of the rocket flare.

Zouga pulled the pistol from its holster, and fired towards the racing black wall of shields.

'Stand to your guns,' he bellowed, the heavy revolver bouncing and crashing in his fist. 'The Matabele are coming! Stand to your guns.' And from the black tide swelled a sound like a swarm of bees when the hive is overturned.

The hammer of Zouga's revolver clicked on a spent cartridge, and he jumped down from the disselboom and raced down the line of wagons to where the nearest Maxim was emplaced.

Throughout the laager there was a rush of bodies and the shouts of frightened men running to their posts, and as Zouga reached the corner of the square, the machine-gunner came stumbling out from his bed under a wagon body. His face was a pale blob, and his hair was hanging into his eyes. He was in stockinged feet and his braces dangled down his legs as he hitched his breeches and plumped himself down on the little seat that was built onto the rear leg of the Maxim tripod.

His number two loader was nowhere to be seen, perhaps lost in the milling confusion of newly-awakened bodies, so Zouga stuffed the revolver into his belt and dropped upon his knees beside the ungainly weapon. He yanked the top off the ammunition box and lifted out the first length of the canvas belt.

'Good-oh, mate!' muttered the gunner, as Zouga lifted the shutter in the side of the breech and passed the brass tag loader of the belt through the block.

'Ready! Load one!' he snapped, and the gunner jerked back the crank handle on the opposite side of the block and let it fly home, and the gib at the top of the extractor gripped the first round.

The spears were drumming on the rawhide shields now, and the deep humming chorus of the running warriors was almost deafening. They could only be yards from the barricade of wagons, but Zouga did not look up. He concentrated all his attention on the intricate task of loading the Maxim.

'Load two!' The gunner cranked again, and the feed block clattered. Zouga jerked the brass tag leader and the gunner let the handle fly back the second time. The first round shot smoothly into the breech.

'Loaded and cocked!' Zouga said, and tapped the gunner on the shoulder. Now they both looked up. The front rank of shields and war plumes seemed to curl over where they squatted beside the weapon, like a wave breaking on a beach.

It was the moment of the 'closing in' that the *amadoda* loved and lived for, already the shields were going up on

629

high to free the spear arms and the steel rasped as the blades were cleared for the stabbing.

The joyous roar of the killing chant sundered the night; they were at the wagons, breaking into the laager, and the gunner sat stiffly upright with the gun between his knees and both hands on the traversing handles. He hooked his fingers through the rings of the safety guard, and as it lifted, he pressed his thumbs down on the chequered firing button.

The muzzle was almost touching the belly of a tall plumed warrior coming in between the wagons when the thick barrel shuddered, and a bright bar of flickering light sprang from the muzzle and the hammering clatter dinned upon Zouga's eardrums. It sounded as though a giant was drawing a steel bar horizontally across a sheet of corrugated iron, and miraculously the warrior was blown away.

The gunner traversed the Maxim back and forth, like a meticulous housewife sweeping a dusty floor, and the continuous muzzle flashes lit the open clay pan with a dancing unearthly light.

The black tide of Matabele was no longer advancing; it stood static in front of the wagons; and though its crest foamed with dancing plumes and the shields that formed the body of the wave heaved and clattered and tumbled, they came no closer. They were dammed by the stroking, flickering bar of light that sprang from the Maxim gun. The solid stream of bullets played like a jet of water from a firehose upon them, and as each of the chanting warriors came racing up, he died on the same spot as the man in front of him had died, and he fell upon his corpse, while another warrior appeared in the space he had left, and the gun swung back, hammering and jerking, and that man went down, his shield clattering on the baked clay of the pan and the flash of the gun reflected from the burnished steel of his assegai as it went spinning from his nerveless hand.

All around the square the Maxims ripped and roared,

and six hundred repeating rifles underscored that hellish chorus. The air was blue with gunsmoke, and the reek of cordite burned the throats of the troopers and made their eyes run, so that they seemed to be weeping for the terrible butchery in which they were engaged.

Still the Matabele came on, though now they had to clamber over a shapeless barricade of their own dead, and the gunner beside Zouga lifted his thumbs from the button trigger and twirled the elevation wheel of the Maxim, lifting the muzzle an inch so as to keep the fire on the belly line of the warriors as they climbed over the mounds of corpses.

Then once again the gun fluttered and roared, the glossy black bodies jerked and twitched and bucked as the stream of bullets tore into them.

Still the Matabele came on.

'By God, will they never stop!' yelled the gunner. The muzzle of the gun glowed cherry red, like a horseshoe fresh from the forge, and the steam from the water jacket whistled shrilly as the coolant boiled. The bright brass cases spewed from the extractor; they pinged and pattered against the iron-shod wheel of the wagon and formed a glittering mound beneath it.

'Empty gun!' Zouga yelled, as the end of the belt whipped into the clattering breech. They had been firing for less than sixty seconds, and the case of five hundred belted cartridges was empty.

Zouga kicked it aside and dragged up a fresh case, and the Matabele surged towards the silent gun.

'Ready, load one!' Zouga yelled.

'Load two!' They were swarming into the gap between the wagons.

'Loaded and cocked!' And once again that fluttering beat like the wings of a dark angel dulled their senses, and the barrel swung back and forth, back and forth, washing them away into the darkness.

'They're running,' shouted the gunner. 'Look at them run!'

In front of the wagons lay nothing but the piles of bodies. Here and there a dying man made feeble little movements, groping for a lost assegai or trying to staunch one of the awful holes in his flesh with fumbling fingers.

Beyond the massed corpses, the wounded and maimed were dragging themselves back towards the treeline, leaving dark wet smears on the clay. One of them was on his feet, staggering in aimless circles, using both hands to hold his bulging entrails from falling out of the open pouch of his belly. The Maxim had gutted him like a fish.

Beyond the trees the sky was a marvellous shade of ashes of roses, and the clouds were picked out in smoking scarlets and pipings of pale gold as the dawn came up in silent fury over the reeking field.

'Them black bastards have had enough.' The Maxim gunner giggled with mirthless, nervous reaction to that glimpse that he had just had into hell itself.

'They'll be back,' said Zouga quietly, as he dragged up another case of belted ammunition and knocked off the lid.

'You did all right, mate,' the gunner giggled again, staring with wide horrified eyes at the piles of dead.

'Refill the water in your condenser, soldier,' Zouga ordered him. 'The gun's over-heating, you'll have a jam when the next wave hits.'

'Sir!' The gunner realized suddenly who Zouga was. 'Sorry, sir.'

'Here is your loader.' The number two came up breathlessly. He was a fresh-faced lad, curly-headed and pink-cheeked. He looked more like a choirboy than a machine-gunner.

'Where were you, trooper?' Zouga demanded.

'Checking the horses, sir. It was all over so quickly.'

'Listen!' Zouga ordered, as the boy took his place at the gun.

From the treeline, across the bloodied clay pan, came the sound of singing – deep and sonorous in the dawn. It was the praise song of the 'Moles-who-burrow-under-a-mountain'.

'Stand to your gun, trooper,' Zouga ordered. 'It's not over yet.' And he turned on his heel and went striding down the line of wagons, reloading the revolver from his belt as he went.

Singing, Bazo strode down the squatting lines of his impi, and they sang with him.

He had held their shattered ranks just beyond the edge of the treeline as they came streaming back from the square of wagons. They were re-grouped now, singing as they screwed their courage for the next assault. What remained of Manonda's impi was mingled with his. They had been in the first wave of the attack, and very few of them were left.

Suddenly there was a great rushing sound in the air above the tree tops, like the onrush of the first wild storm of summer. Then in the midst of the squatting ranks a tall column of smoke and dust and flame sprang into the air, and the bodies of men were flung high with it.

'Kill the smoke devil,' somebody screamed, and another shell burst amongst them, and another, leaping fountains of smoke and flame; and the maddened warriors fired their ancient Martini-Henry rifles at these smoke devils, killing and wounding their comrades on the far side.

'They are not devils,' shouted Bazo, but his voice was lost in the barrage of artillery fire, and the pandemonium of warriors trying to defend themselves against something they did not understand.

'Come!' Bazo bellowed. There was only one way to bring them under control again.

'To the wagons. Forward to the wagons.' And those close enough to hear him followed, and the others, seeing them go, went bounding after them. They came out of the treeline in a swarm, and the other shattered impis heard the war chant go up, and turned again back onto the open pan of pale grey clay – and immediately that terrible clattering din, like the laughter of maniacs, began again and the air was filled with the flute and crack of a thousand whiplashes.

'They are coming again,' Zouga said quietly, almost to himself. 'This is the fifth time.'

'It's madness.' Mungo St John murmured, as the racing ranks came out of the trees and over the lip of the river bank, their plumes seething like the surface of boiling milk as they came onto the guns.

The field guns were depressed to the limit of their travel, the fuses screwed down to their shortest range, and the shrapnel bursts were strangely beautiful in the morning sky, popping open like pods of new cotton, shot through with pretty red fire.

The storm of small-arms fire was like the monsoon rains beating on an iron roof, and as the impis came into the drifting banks of gunsmoke, the dense ranks thinned out, and lost momentum, like a wave sliding up a steep beach.

Once again the wave faltered, and just short of the wagons it stopped, hesitated and then was going back, and the storm of gunfire continued long after the last of them had disappeared amongst the trees. In a kind of insensate fury the Maxim bullets tore wet white slabs of bark off the tree trunks, and then one after the other fell silent.

Standing beside Zouga, Dr Jameson scrubbed his hands

together gleefully. 'It's all over. Their impis are destroyed, shattered, blown away. It's better than we could ever have hoped for. Tell me, St John, as a military man, what do you estimate their losses to be so far?'

Mungo St John considered the question seriously, climbing up onto one of the wagons the better to survey the field, ignoring the spattering of Martini-Henry rifle fire from the edge of the treeline where a few Matabele snipers were making very poor practice; convinced that raising their sights to the maximum made the bullets more powerful, most of their fire crackled high over the heads of the men manning the wagons.

Standing on the wagon Mungo St John lit a cheroot without transferring his attention from the carnage which surrounded them. At last he said gravely, 'Not less than two thousand casualties – perhaps as many as three.'

'Why don't you send a party out to count the bag, Doctor?' Zouga suggested, and Jameson did not recognize the sarcasm.

'We cannot spare the delay – more is the pity. We can still get in a full day's trek. That will look good in the Company report.' He pulled the gold chain from his fob pocket and sprang the lid of his watch with his thumbnail 'Eight o'clock,' he marvelled. 'It's only eight o'clock in the morning. Do you realize that we have won a decisive battle before breakfast, gentlemen, and that by ten o'clock we can be on our way to Lobengula's royal kraal? I think we have done our shareholders rather proud.'

'I think,' Zouga cut in gently. 'That we still have a little more work to do. They are coming again.'

'I don't believe this,' Mungo St John marvelled.

Bazo paced slowly down the sparse ranks. This was no longer an impi. It was a pathetic little band of desperate survivors. Most of them had bound up their wounds with bloody bunches of green leaves, and their eyes had that strange fixed stare of men who had just looked into eternity. They were no longer singing, they squatted in silence – but they were still facing towards the white men's laager.

Bazo passed beyond the shortened line and paused under the spreading branches of a wild teak tree. He looked up.

Manonda, the commander of what had once been the glorious Insukamini impi, hung by his neck from one of the main branches. There was a thong of rawhide around his throat, and his eyes were still open, bulging in a defiant glare towards his enemies. His right leg, shattered above the knee by machine-gun fire, was twisted at an ugly angle and hung lower than his other leg.

Bazo lifted his assegai in a salute to the dead induna.

'I greet you, Manonda, who chose death rather than to drink the bitter draught of defeat,' he shouted.

The Insukamini impi was no more. Its warriors lay in deep windrows in front of the wagons.

'I praise you, Manonda, who chose death rather than to live a cripple and a slave. Go in peace, Manonda – and speak sweetly to the spirits on our behalf.'

Bazo turned back and stood before the waiting, silent ranks. The early morning sun, just clearing the tree tops, threw long black shadows in front of them.

'Are the eyes still red, my children?' Bazo sang out in a high clear voice.

'They are still red, Baba!' they answered him in a bass chorus.

'Then let us go to do the work which still waits to be done.'

Where ten *amadoda* had raced in that first wave, now two made the last charge across the blood-soaked clay. Only one of that pitiful band went more than halfway between the tree lines and the wagons. The rest of them turned back and left Bazo to run on alone. He was sobbing with each stride, his mouth open, the sweat running in oily snakes down his naked chest. He did not feel the first bullet that struck him. It was just a sudden numbness as though part of his body was missing, and he ran on, jumping over a pile of twisted corpses, and now the sound of the guns seemed muted and far-off, and there was another greater dinning in his ears that boomed and echoed strangely like the thunder of a mighty waterfall.

He felt another sharp tug, like the curved red-tipped thorn of the 'wait-a-bit' tree hooking into his flesh, but there was no pain. The roaring in his head was louder, and his vision narrowed so that he seemed to be looking down a long tunnel in the darkness.

Again he felt that irritating but painless jerk and tug in his flesh, and he was suddenly weary. He just wanted to lie down and rest, but he kept on towards the flashing white canvas of the wagon tents. Yet again that sharp insistent pull as though he was held on a leash, and his legs buckled under him. Quite gently he toppled forward and lay with his face against the hard sun-baked clay.

The sound of the guns had ceased, but in its place was another sound, it was the sound of cheering; behind the wall of wagons the white men were cheering themselves.

Bazo was tired, so utterly deathly tired. He closed his eyes and let the darkness come.

The wind had swung suddenly and unseasonably into the east, and there was a cold dank mist lying on the hills, the fine *guti* which made the trees drip dismally and chilled every bone in Tanase's body as she trudged up a narrow path that led to a saddle between two pearly grey granite peaks. Over her shoulders was a leather cloak and on her head she balanced a bundle of possessions which she had salvaged from the cave of the Umlimo.

She reached the saddle and looked down into yet another valley choked with dense, dark green undergrowth. She searched it eagerly, but then her spirits slowly fell again. Like all the others, it was devoid of any human presence.

Since she had left the secret valley, the moon had reached its full, and waned to nothingness, and was once again a curved yellow sliver in the night sky. All that time she had searched for the women and children of the Matabele nation. She knew they were here, hiding somewhere in the Matopos, for it was always the way. When a powerful enemy threatened the nation, the women and children were sent into the hills – but it was such a vast area, so many valleys and deep labyrinthine caves that she might search a lifetime without finding them.

Tanase started slowly down into the deserted valley. Her legs felt leaden, and another spasm of nausea brought saliva flooding from under her tongue. She swallowed it down, but when she reached the floor of the valley, she sank down onto a moss-covered rock beside the little stream.

She knew what was the cause of her malady; though she had missed her courses by only a few days, she knew that the loathsome seed that her pale, hairy, balloon-bellied ravisher had pumped into her had struck and taken hold, and she knew what she must do.

She laid aside her load and searched for dry kindling under the trees where the *guti* had not yet dampened it. She piled it in the protected lee of a sheltering rock, and crouched over it.

For many long minutes she concentrated all her will upon it. Then at last she sighed, and her shoulders slumped. Even this minor power, this small magic of fire making, had gone from her. As the white man with the golden beard had warned her, she was Umlimo no longer. She was just a young woman, without strange gifts or terrible duties, and she was free. The spirits could make no demands upon her, she was free at last to seek out the man she loved.

As she prepared to make fire in the conventional manner, with the tiny bow for twirling the dry twig, two passions gave her strength to face the ordeal ahead of her – her love and her equally fierce hatred.

When the contents of the little clay pot boiled, she added the shreds of dried bark of the tambooti to it, and immediately the sweet odour of the poisonous steam cloyed upon the back of her throat.

The straight sharp black horn of the gemsbuck had been clipped off at the tip so that it could be used for cupping blood, or as a funnel for introducing fluids into the body.

Tanase spread the leather cloak below the rock shelter and lay on it, flat upon her back, with her feet braced high against rough granite. She had lubricated the horn with fat, and she took a deep breath, clenched her jaw upon it, and then slid the horn into herself. When it met resistance, she manipulated it carefully, but firmly, and then her breath burst from her in a gasp of agony as the point found the opening and forced its way still farther into her secret depths.

The pain gave her a strange unholy joy, as though she were inflicting it upon the hated thing that had taken root within her. She lifted herself on one elbow, and tested the contents of the little clay pot. It was just cool enough for her to be able to bear the heat when she plunged her forefinger into it.

She took up the pot and poured it into the mouth of the long black funnel, and this time she moaned, and her back arched involuntarily, but she poured until the pot was empty. There was the coppery salt taste of blood in her mouth, and she realized that she had bitten through her own lip. She seized the horn and plucked it out of herself, and then she curled up on the leather cloak and hugged her knees to her bosom, shuddering and moaning at the fire in her womb.

In the night the first terrible cramps seized her, and she felt her belly muscles spasm up hard as a cannon ball under her clutching hands.

She wished there had been something formed, a tiny replica of that white animal that had rutted upon her, so that she could have wreaked a form of vengeance upon it. She would have delighted in mutilating and burning it, but there was nothing substantial on which to expend her hatred. So despite the purging of her body, she carried her hatred with her still, fierce and unabated, as she toiled on deeper and deeper into the Matopos.

The joyful cries and sweet laughter of children at play guided her, and Tanase crept along the river verge, using the tall cotton-tipped reeds as a screen until she over looked the green pool between its sugary sandbanks. They were girls sent to fetch water. The big, black clay pots stood in a row on the white sand with green leaves stuffed in the mouths to stop them slopping over when carried balanced on the girls' heads.

However, once the pots were filled, they had not been able to resist the temptation of the cool, green waters, and they had thrown off their skirts and were shrieking and sporting in the pool. The eldest girls were pubescent with swelling breast buds, and one of them spotted Tanase in the reeds and screamed a warning.

Tanase was just able to catch the youngest and slowest child as she was disappearing over the far bank, and she held the wriggling little body, glossy black and wet from the river, against her bosom while the child wailed and struggled with terror.

Tanase cooed reassurances and stroked the little girl with gentling hands until she quietened.

'I am of the people,' she whispered. 'Don't be afraid, little one.'

Half an hour later the child was chattering gaily and leading Tanase by the hand.

The mothers came swarming out of the caves at the head of the valley to greet Tanase, and they crowded about her.

'Is it true that there have been two great battles?' they begged her.

'We have heard that the impis were broken at Shangani and again those that remained were butchered like cattle on the banks of the Bembesi.'

'Our husbands and our sons are dead – please tell us it is not so,' they pleaded.

'They say the king has fled from his royal kraal, and that we are children without a father. Is it true, can you tell us if it is true?'

'I know nothing,' Tanase told them. 'I come to hear news, not to bear it. Is there not one amongst you who can tell me where I may find Juba, senior wife of Gandang, brother of the king?'

They pointed over the hills, and Tanase went on, and found another group of women hiding in the thick bush. These children did not laugh and play, their limbs were thin as sticks, but their bellies were swollen little pots.

'There is no food,' the women told Tanase. 'Soon we will starve.' And they sent her stumbling back northwards, seeking and questioning, trying to blind herself to the agonies of a defeated nation, until one day she stooped in through the entrance of a dim and smoky cave, and a vaguely familiar figure rose to greet her.

'Tanase, my child, my daughter.'

Only then did Tanase recognize her, for the abundant flesh had melted off the woman's frame and her once bounteous breasts hung slack as empty pouches against her belly.

'Juba, my mother,' Tanase cried, and ran into her embrace. It was a long time after that before she could speak through her sobs.

'Oh my mother, do you know what has become of Bazo?'

Juba pushed her gently to arm's length and looked into her face. When Tanase saw the devastating sorrow in Juba's eyes, she cried out with dread.

'He is not dead!'

'Come, my daughter,' Juba whispered, and led her deeper into the cave, along a natural passageway through the living rock – and there was a graveyard smell on the cool dark air, the odour of corruption and rotting flesh.

The second cavern was lit only by a burning wick floating in a bowl of oil. There was a litter against the far wall. On it lay a wasted skeletal body, and the smell of death was overpowering.

Fearfully Tanase knelt beside the litter and lifted a bunch of leaves off one of the stinking wounds.

'He is not dead,' Tanase repeated. 'Bazo is not dead.'

'Not yet,' agreed Juba. 'His father and those of his men who survived the white men's bullets, carried my son to me on his shield. They bid me save him – but nobody can save him.'

'He will not die,' said Tanase fiercely. 'I will not let him die.' And she leaned over his wasted body and pressed her

642

lips to the fever-hot flesh. 'I will not let you die,' she whispered.

The Hills of the Indunas were deserted; no beast grazed upon them for the herds had long ago been driven afar to try to save them from the invaders. There were no vultures or crows sailing high above the hills, for the Maxim guns had laid a richer feast for them barely twenty-five miles eastwards at the Bembesi crossing.

The royal kraal of GuBulawayo was almost deserted. The women's quarters were silent. No child cried, no young girl sang, no crone scolded. They were all hiding in the magical Matopos hills.

The barracks of the fighting regiments were deserted. Two thousand dead on the Shangani, three thousand more at Bembesi – and nobody would ever count those who had crawled away to die like animals in the caves and thickets.

The survivors had scattered, some to join the women in the hills, the others to cower, bewildered and demoralized, wherever they could find shelter.

Of all the fighting impis of Matabele, only one remained intact, the Inyati regiment of Induna Gandang, the king's half-brother. Gandang alone had been able to resist the madness of hurling his men over open ground at the waiting Maxim guns, and now he waited for his king's orders in the hills just north of the royal kraal with his impi gathered about him.

In all of GuBulawayo, there was one small group remaining. Twenty-six of these were white men and women. They were the traders and concession-hunters who had been at the kraal when Jameson had marched from Iron Mine Hill. With them, were the Codrington family, Clinton and Robyn and the twins. Lobengula had ordered them all to remain under his protection, while the impis were out in battle array, and now he had called them to the goat kraal for his last audience.

Drawn up before the two new brick-built houses which had replaced the great thatched hut, were Lobengula's four Cape wagons with the teams already in the traces.

About the wagons were a small party of the royal retainers: two of the king's senior wives, four elderly indunas, and a dozen or so slaves and servants.

The king himself sat on the box of the leading wagon. In that wagon were all Lobengula's treasures, a hundred big tusks of ivory, the little sealed pots of uncut diamonds, and the canvas bags stencilled with the name 'The Standard Bank Ltd' containing the sovereigns paid to him during the four years since he had granted the concession to the British South Africa Company, four thousand sovereigns, less than a sovereign for every one of his dead warriors.

Around the wagon were gathered the white men, and Lobengula looked down upon them. The king had become an old man in the few short weeks since he had thrown the war spear on the Hills of the Indunas. There were deep lines of sorrow and despair carved around his mouth and eyes. His eyes were rheumy and shortsighted, his hair bleached silver-grey, his body bloated and misshapen, and his breathing was racked and irregular like that of a dying animal.

'Tell your queen, white men, that Lobengula kept his word. Not one of you has been harmed,' he wheezed. 'Daketela and his soldiers will be here tomorrow. If you go out upon the eastern road, you will even meet them before nightfall.' Lobengula paused to catch his breath, and then went on. 'Go now. There is nothing more I have to say to you.'

They were silent, subdued, and strangely chastened, as they trooped out of the goat kraal. Only Robyn and her family remained.

The twins stood on each side of Robyn. At twenty-one years of age, they were as tall as she. It seemed that the three of them were sisters – for they all had the clear eyes and glossy hair of healthy young women.

Clinton Codrington, standing behind them, stooped and bald, dressed in sober broadcloth that was mossy green with age and shiny at the cuffs and elbows, seemed father to Robyn as well as to the twins.

The king looked down upon them with a terrible regret.

'It is the last time that you will make my eyes glad, Nomusa,' he said.

'Oh King, my heart is on fire for you. I think of what has happened and how I advised you.'

Lobengula held up his hand to silence her. 'Do not torture yourself, Nomusa. You have been a true friend of many years, and what you did was done in friendship. Nothing you or I could have done would have changed the manner of it. It was the prophecy; it was as certain as the fall of the leaves from the msasa trees when the frosts are on the hills.'

Robyn ran forward to the wagon, and Lobengula stooped to take her hand.

'Pray to your three gods that are one god for me, Nomusa.'

'He will hear you, Lobengula, you are a good man.'

'No man is all goodness or all evil,' the king sighed. 'Now, Nomusa, soon Daketela and his soldiers will be here. Tell him that Lobengula says thus. "I am beaten, white men, my impis are eaten up. Let me go now, do not hunt me further, for I am an old sick man. I wish only to find a place where I may mourn my people – and at last die in peace."'

'I will tell them, Lobengula.'

'And will they listen, Nomusa?'

She could not face him, and she dropped her eyes. 'You know they will not listen.'

'My poor people,' whispered Lobengula. 'Will you look after my poor people when I am gone, Nomusa?'

'I swear it to you, oh King,' Robyn said fiercely. 'I will stay at Khami Mission until the day that I die, and I will devote my life to your people.'

Then Lobengula smiled, and once again there was a flash of the old mischievous twinkle in his eye.

'I give you the royal permission which I denied you all these years, Nomusa. From this day forward any of my people – man or woman or child of Matabele who wish it of you – you may pour water on their heads and make the cross of your three gods over them.'

Robyn could not reply.

'Stay in peace, Nomusa,' said Lobengula, and his wagon rumbled slowly out through the gates of the stockade.

Clinton Codrington reined in the mule on the crest of the rise above the royal kraal, and he groped for Robyn's hand. They sat silently on the seat of the little Scotch cart, watching the last pale shreds of dust thrown up by the king's wagons disappearing away in the north across the grassy plain.

'They will never leave him in peace,' Robyn said softly.

'Lobengula is the prize,' Clinton agreed. 'Without him, Jameson and Rhodes will have no victory.'

'What will they do with him?' she asked sadly. 'If they catch him.'

'Exile, certainly,' Clinton said. 'St Helena Island, probably. It's where they sent Cetewayo.'

'Poor tragic man,' Robyn whispered. 'Caught between two ages, half savage and half civilized man, half cruel despot and half a shy and sensitive dreamer. Poor Lobengula.'

'Do look, Papa!' Vicky called suddenly, pointing down

the rude track towards the east. There was a thick column of dust rising above the tops of the thorn trees, and even as they watched, a distant troop of mounted men rode out onto the grassy plain with badges and weapons twinkling in the sunlight.

'Soldiers,' whispered Lizzie.

'Soldiers,' repeated Vicky gleefully. 'Hundreds of them.' And the twins exchanged a bright ecstatic glance of complete understanding and accord.

Clinton picked up the reins – but Robyn tightened her grip on his hand to restrain him.

'Wait,' she said. 'I want to watch it happen. Somehow it will be the end of an age, the end of a cruel but innocent age.'

Lobengula had left one of his trusted indunas in the royal kraal, with instructions to lay fire to the train as soon as the last wagons were clear. In the mud-brick building behind the king's new residence were the remains of the hundred thousand rounds of Martini-Henry ammunition for which he had sold his land and his people. There were also twenty barrels of black powder.

'There!' said Robyn, as the pillar of black smoke and flame shot hundreds of feet straight up into the still air.

Only many seconds later did the shock wave and the great clap of sound pass over where they watched from the ridge, and the smoke, still spinning upon itself, blossomed into an anvil head high above the shattered kraal.

Lobengula's house that had given him such pleasure and pride was only a shell, the roof blown away and the walls fallen in.

The beehive huts of the women's quarters were ablaze, and even as they watched, the flames jumped the stockade and caught in the roofs beyond. Within minutes the whole of GuBulawayo was in leaping, swirling flames.

'Now we can go on,' Robyn said quietly, and Clinton shook up the mule.

There were thirty horsemen in the advance scouting party – and as they galloped up, the tall straight figure leading them was unmistakable.

'Thank God that you are safe!' Zouga called to them. He was handsome and heroic in the frogged uniform with his brass badges of rank ablaze in the sunlight, and the slouch hat cocked forward over his handsome, gravely concerned features.

'We were never in any danger,' Robyn told him. 'And well you knew that.'

'Where is Lobengula?' Zouga sought to divert her scorn, but she shook her head.

'I am guilty of one act of treachery against Lobengula—'

'You are an Englishwoman,' Zouga reminded her. 'You should know where your loyalties lie.'

'Yes, I am an Englishwoman,' she agreed icily, 'but I am ashamed of that today. I will not tell you where the king is.'

'As you wish.' Zouga looked at Clinton. 'You know that it is for the good of everyone in this land. Until we have Lobengula, there will be no peace.'

Clinton bowed his bald head. 'The king has gone to the north with his wagons and wives and the Inyati regiment.'

'Thank you,' Zouga nodded. 'I will send an escort with you to the main column. They are not far behind us. Sergeant!'

A young trooper with triple chevrons on his sleeve spurred forward. He was a fine-looking lad, with high English colour in his cheeks and broad shoulders.

'Sergeant Acutt. Take the six men from the rear three files and see this party to safety.'

Zouga saluted his sister and brother-in-law curtly and then ordered, 'Troop, at the gallop. Forward!'

The first two dozen troopers went clattering away towards GuBulawayo, while the sergeant and his six men wheeled in alongside the cart.

Vicky turned her head and looked directly into the young sergeant's eyes. She took a long slow breath that pushed her bosom out under the faded cotton of her blouse. The sergeant stared, and the flush of dark blood rose from the high stock of his tunic and suffused his cheeks.

Vicky wetted her pouting lips with the tip of a pink tongue, and slanted her eyes at him – and Sergeant Acutt seemed about to fall out of the saddle, for Vicky's gaze had struck him from a range of less than six feet.

'Victoria!' Robyn snapped sharply, without looking back over her shoulder.

'Yes, Mama.' Hurriedly, Vicky slumped her shoulders forward to alter the cheeky thrust of her bosom to a more demure angle, and composed her expression into dutiful gravity.

TELEGRAM MESSAGE RECEIVED FORT VICTORIA 10TH NOVEMBER 1893 RELAYED BY HELIOGRAPH TO GUBULAWAYO:

FOR JAMESON STOP HER MAJESTY'S GOVERNMENT DECLINES TO DECLARE MATABELE A CROWN COLONY OR PLACE IT UNDER THE JURISDICTION OF THE HIGH COMMISSIONER STOP HER MAJESTY'S FOREIGN SECRETARY AGREES THAT THE CHARTER COMPANY IS TO PROVIDE THE MACHINERY OF GOVERNMENT FOR THE NEW TERRITORY STOP BOTH MASHONALAND AND MATABELELAND NOW FALL WITHIN THE ADMINISTRATIVE AREA OF THE COMPANY STOP COMPANY SHARES QUOTED AT £8 LONDON CLOSE STOP HEARTIEST CONGRATULATIONS TO YOU YOUR OFFICERS AND MEN FROM JOVE

FOR JAMESON URGENT AND CONFIDENTIAL
DESTROY ALL COPIES STOP WE MUST HAVE LOBEN-
GULA STOP NO RISK TOO GREAT TO PRICE TOO HIGH
FROM JOVE

'Reverend Codrington, I am sending out a considerable force to escort Lobengula in.' Jameson stood
at the fly of his tent, looking out beyond the
laager to the blackened ruins of the royal kraal. 'I have
already sent this message after the king.' Jameson came
back to his desk and read from his pad:

'Now, to stop this useless killing, you must at once come
back to me at GuBulawayo. I guarantee that your life
will be safe and that you will be kindly treated.'

'Has the king sent you a reply?' Clinton asked. He had
declined a seat and stood stiffly in front of the camp table
that served Jameson as a desk.

'Here.' The doctor handed Clinton a grubby, folded
scrap of paper. Clinton scanned it swiftly:

I have the honour to inform you that I have received
your letter and have heard all what you have said, so I
will come . . .

'This is written by a half-caste rogue, named Jacobs,
who has joined up with Lobengula,' Clinton muttered, as
he glanced through the rest of the wandering, misspelt and
barely literate note. 'I know his handwriting.'

'Do you think the king means it?' Mungo St John asked.
'Do you think he means to come in?'

Clinton did not turn his head towards where Mungo
lolled in a canvas camp chair across the tent.

'Dr Jameson, I do not condone your actions or those of your infamous Chartered Company, but I came here at your bidding in order to do what little I can to redress the terrible wrongs that have been perpetrated on the Matabele people. However, I draw the line at having to speak or in any way communicate with this henchman of yours.'

Jameson frowned irritably. 'Reverend, I would like you to bear in mind that I have appointed General St John as Administrator and Chief Magistrate of Matabeleland—'

Clinton cut in brusquely. 'You are, of course, aware that your Chief Magistrate was once a notorious slave trader, buying and selling the black people over whom you now give him supreme powers?'

'Yes, thank you, Reverend, I am aware that General St John was once a legitimate trader, and I am also fully aware that while a serving officer of Her Majesty's navy, you led an attack on his ship – an action which led to your being court martialled, imprisoned and cashiered from the service. Now let us continue, Reverend. If you do not wish to talk directly to General St John, you may address me instead.'

In the camp chair Mungo St John crossed his beautifully polished riding boots and smiled lazily, but his eye was bright and sharp as a bared blade. 'Doctor Jameson, would you ask the good priest if he is of the opinion that Lobengula will give himself up?'

'Would you?' Clinton asked, still without a glance in St John's direction.

'No,' Mungo replied, and nodded his head significantly at Jameson.

'Reverend, General St John is taking out a flying column to bring Lobengula in. I want you to go with him, please,' Jameson said.

'Why me, Doctor?'

'You speak the language fluently.'

'So do many others – Zouga Ballantyne is one of them. He is also a soldier.'

'Your brother-in-law has other important work to do—'

'Stealing the king's cattle,' Clinton cut in acidly.

It was already common knowledge that Zouga Ballantyne had been given the task of rounding up the vast Matabele herds and bringing them in to GuBulawayo for distribution.

However, Jameson might not have heard the remark, and he went on smoothly. 'Besides, Reverend, you and your wife have been close friends of Lobengula for many years, he trusts and likes you. But, since it was Major Ballantyne who delivered our ultimatum, Lobengula looks upon him as an enemy.'

'Not without reason,' Clinton murmured dryly. 'However, Doctor, I refuse to be your Judas goat.'

'Your presence with the column may help to avert another bloody conflict, with the inevitable result of hundreds if not thousands more Matabele slaughtered. I would think it your Christian duty to try to prevent that.'

Clinton hesitated, and Mungo murmured. 'Do point out, Doctor Jim, that after Lobengula surrenders, Reverend Codrington will be in a position to comfort and protect him, to ensure that the king is kindly treated and that no harm befalls him. I give him my word on that.'

'Very well,' Clinton capitulated sadly. 'On the understanding that I am to be the king's protector and advisor, I will go with your column.'

'They follow,' Gandang said softly. 'They still follow.' And Lobengula lifted his face and looked at the sky. The rain drops, heavy and hard as newly minted silver shillings, struck his cheeks and forehead.

'The rain,' said Lobengula. 'Who said they could not follow us in the rain?'

'It was me, my King, but I was wrong,' Gandang admitted. 'When he marched from GuBulawayo, One-Bright-Eye had three hundred men and four of the little guns with three legs which chatter like old women. He also had wagons and one big cannon.'

'I know this,' said the king.

'When the rains came, I thought that they had turned back, but now my scouts have come in with heavy news to tell. One-Bright-Eye has sent back half of his men and the wagons, the cannon and two of the little three-legged guns. They could not ride over the mud – but—' Gandang paused.

'Do not try to spare me, my brother, tell me it all.'

'He comes on with half his men, and two little machine-guns drawn by horses. They are travelling fast, even in the mud.'

'How fast?' the king asked quietly.

'They are a day's march behind us, tomorrow evening they will camp here on this very river.'

The king pulled the tattered old coat around his shoulders. It was cold in the rain, but he did not have the energy to crawl under the canvas of his wagon tent. He looked out across the watercourse. They were camped on the Shangani river, but almost a hundred and fifty miles higher than where the first battle of the war had been fought upon the headwaters of this same river.

They were in thick mopani forest, so thick that a road had to be chopped through it to allow the king's wagons to pass. The terrain was flat and relieved only by the clay hills of the termite nests that dotted the forest, some of them as large as houses, others the size of a beer keg, just big enough to smash the axle of a wagon.

The sky, grey and heavy as the belly of a pregnant sow, pressed down upon the tops of the mopani. Soon it would rain heavily again, these fat drops were merely a warning of the next deluge to come, and that trickle of muddy water, the colour of a drunkard's bile, down the middle of the watercourse would be a roaring torrent again within minutes of the onslaught.

'One hundred and fifty men, Gandang,' the king sighed. 'How many have we?'

'Two thousand,' said Gandang. 'And perhaps tomorrow or the next day Gambo may come to join us with a thousand more.'

'Yet we cannot stand against them?'

'The men we would eat. It is those little guns with three legs, oh King, not even ten thousand warriors, each with the liver of a lion, could prevail when they begin to laugh. But if the king commands, we will run—'

'No! it is the gold,' Lobengula said suddenly. 'The white men will never let me be until they have the gold. I will send it to them. Perhaps then they will leave me in peace. Where is Kamuza, my young induna? He speaks the language of the white men. I will send him to them.'

Kamuza came swiftly to the king's bidding. He stood attentively in the spattering rain beside the front wheel of the wagon.

'Place the little bags of gold in the hands of the white men, Kamuza, my trusted induna, and say to them thus, "You have eaten up my regiments and killed my young men, you have burned my kraals and scattered the women and children of Matabeleland into the hills where they burrow for roots like wild animals, you have seized my royal herds, and now you have my gold. White men, you have it all, will you now leave me in peace to mourn my lost people?"'

There were ten bags of white canvas, stamped with black lettering. They made a heavy burden for one man to carry. Kamuza knelt and tied them together in bunches, and then packed each bunch into a leather grain bag.

'To hear is to obey, Great Elephant,' Kamuza saluted his king.

'Go swiftly, Kamuza,' Lobengula ordered softly. 'For they are close upon us.'

W ill Daniel sat his own horse, with the brim of his hat pulled down to protect the bowl of his clay pipe from the drizzling rain, and over his shoulders he wore a rubber groundsheet which glistened with moisture and gave him a pregnant, clumsy look as he slumped barrel-bellied in the saddle.

On lead reins he held two other horses, one was a pack animal whose burden was covered by a white canvas sheet. Daniel no longer bore the lofty rank of sergeant. After his conduct at the secret valley of the Umlimo, Zouga Ballantyne had seen him reduced to trooper, and as an additional mortification, he was now acting as batman to one of the officers of the flying column. The packhorse carried Captain Coventry's traps.

The other horse belonged to Will's old comrade in arms, Jim Thorn. That worthy was crouched behind a thorny shrub a short way off, with his belt hanging around his neck and cursing bitterly in a low monotone.

'Filthy bleeding water, stinking bloody rain – God-forsaken country—'

'Hey, Jimmo, your backside must be on fire by now. That's the twelfth time today.'

'Shut your ugly face, Will Daniel,' Jim shouted back, and then dropped back into his dismal monotone. 'Bloody gut-breaking trots—'

'Come on, Jim my lad.' Will lifted the brim of his hat to peer about him. 'We can't fall too far behind the rest, not with the bush crawling with bloody black savages.'

Jim Thorn came out from behind the bush re-buckling his belt, but wincing with another bout of stomach cramps. He climbed gingerly up into the saddle, and the three horses plodded along in the deep yellow muddy ruts of the horse-drawn carts which carried the two Maxim machine-guns.

The rear of the column was out of sight ahead of them amongst the dripping mopani trees. The two of them had soon learned to loiter at the back away from the scrutiny of the officers, so that they would not be ordered into the thigh-deep mud when the Maxim carts bogged down and had to be man-handled through one of the glutinous 'mopani holes.'

'Look out, Will!' Jim Thorn yelled suddenly, and his oilskins flapped like the wings of a startled rooster as he tried to draw his rifle from its scabbard. 'Look out, bloody savages!'

A Matabele had stepped silently out of the thick bush alongside the cart tracks, and now he stood directly in front of the horses and held up his empty hands to show the white men that he was unarmed.

'Wait, Jimmo!' Will Daniel called. 'Let's see what the bastard wants.'

'I don't like it, man. It's a trap.' Jim searched the bush around them nervously. 'Let's shoot the black bugger and get out of it.'

'I come in peace!' the Matabele called in English. He wore only a fur kilt, without armlets and leg tassels, and the rain shone on his smoothly muscled torso. On his head was the headring of an induna.

The two mounted men both had their rifles out now, and were aiming from the hip, covering Kamuza at point-blank range.

'I have a message from the king.'

'Well, spit it out then,' Will snapped.

'Lobengula says take my gold, and go back to GuBula-wayo.'

'Gold?' demanded Jim Thorn. 'What gold?'

Kamuza stepped back into the scrub, picked up the leather grain bag, and carried it to them.

Will Daniel was laughing excitedly as he pulled out the little canvas bags. They jingled softly in his hands.

'By God, that's the sweetest music I ever heard!'

'What will you do, white men?' Kamuza demanded. 'Will you take the gold to your chief?'

'Don't fret yourself, my friend.' Will Daniel clapped him delightedly on the shoulder. 'It will go to the right person, you have the word of William Daniel hisself on it.'

Jim Thorn was unbuckling his saddle-bags and stuffing the canvas sacks into it.

'Christmas and my birthday all in one,' he winked at Will.

'White men, will you turn and go back to GuBulawayo now?' Kamuza called anxiously.

'Don't worry about it another minute,' Will assured him, and ferreted a loaf of hard bread out of his own saddle-bag. 'Here's a present for you, *bonsela*, present, you understand?' Then to Jim. 'Come on, Mr Thorn, it's Mister I'll be calling you now that you are rich.'

'Lead on, Mr Daniel,' Jim grinned at him, and they spurred past Kamuza, leaving him standing in the muddy pathway with the mouldy loaf of bread in his hands.

Clinton Codrington came slipping and sloshing along the bank of the Shangani river. The lowering clouds were bringing on the night prematurely, and the forests on the far bank were dank and gloomy.

The thunder rumbled sullenly, as though boulders were being rolled across the roof of the sky, and for a few seconds the rain spurted down thickly and then sank once more to a fine drizzle. Clinton shivered and pulled up the collar of his sheepskin coat as he hurried on to where the Maxim carts stood at the head of the column.

There was a tarpaulin draped between the two carts and beneath it squatted a small group of officers. Mungo St John looked up as Clinton approached.

'Ah, Parson!' he greeted him. Mungo had learned that this address irritated Clinton inordinately. 'You took your time.' Clinton did not reply; he stood hunched in the rain and none of the officers made room for him beneath the canvas.

'Major Wilson is going to make a reconnaissance across the river with a dozen men. I want you to go with him to translate, if he meets any of the enemy.'

'It will be dark in less than two hours,' Clinton pointed out stolidly.

'Then you had best hurry.'

'The rains will break at any minute,' Clinton persisted. 'Your forces could be split—'

'Parson, you bother about brimstone and salvation – let us do the soldiering.' Mungo turned back to his officers. 'Are you ready to go Wilson?'

Allan Wilson was a bluff Scot, with long, dark moustaches and an accent that burred with the tang of heather and highlands.

'You'll be giving me detailed orders then, sir?' he demanded stiffly. There had been ill-feeling between him and St John ever since they had left GuBulawayo.

'I want you to use your common sense, man,' St John snapped. 'If you can catch Lobengula, then grab him, put him on a horse, and get back here. If you are attacked, fall back immediately. If you let yourself be cut off, I will not be able to cross the river to support you with the Maxims until first light, do you understand that?'

'I do, General.' Wilson touched the brim of his slouch hat. 'Come on, Reverend,' he said to Clinton. 'We do not have much time.'

Burnham and Ingram, the two American scouts, led the patrol down the steep bank of the Shangani; Wilson and Clinton followed immediately behind.

Clinton's lanky, stooped frame, in the scuffed sheepskin jacket and with a shapeless stained hat pulled down over his ears, looked oddly out of place in the middle of the uniformed patrol of armed men. As he came level with Mungo St John, standing on the top of the bank with his hands clasped behind his back, Clinton bent low from the saddle of his borrowed horse and said, so quietly that only Mungo heard him, 'Read II Samuel, chapter eleven, verse fifteen.' Then Clinton straightened, gathered the old grey gelding with which he had been provided by the Company, and the two of them went sliding untidily down the cutting in the steep bank which the Matabele had dug to take Lobengula's wagons across.

At this point, the Shangani river was two hundred yards across, and as the little patrol waded the deepest part of the channel, the muddy waters reached to their stirrup irons. They climbed the far bank and almost immediately were lost from view in the dripping woods and poor light.

Mungo St John stood for many minutes, staring across the river, ignoring the fine, drizzling rain. He was wondering at himself, wondering why he had sent such a puny force across the river, with only hours of daylight left. The priest was right, of course, it would rain again soon. The heavens were leaden and charged with it. The Matabele were in force. The priest had seen the Inyati impi under its old and crafty commander, Gandang, escorting the wagons away from GuBulawayo.

If he were going to reconnoitre the lie of the land beyond the river, then he knew that he should have used the last of the daylight to ford his entire force. It was the correct tactical disposition. That way the patrol could fall back under the protection of the Maxims at any time during the night, or he could go forward to relieve them if they ran into trouble.

Some demon had possessed him when he gave the orders. Perhaps Wilson had finally irritated him beyond all restraint. The man had argued with him at every opportunity, and had done his best to subvert Mungo's authority amongst the other officers, who resented the fact that he was an American over British officers. It was mostly Wilson's fault that this was such an unhappy and divided little expedition. He was well rid of the overbearing and blunt Scotsman, he decided. Perhaps a night spent in company with the Inyati regiment would take some of the pepper out of him; and he would be a little more tractable in the future – if there was a future for him. Mungo turned back to the sheltering tarpaulin strung between the gun carriages.

Suddenly a thought struck him, and he called down the line. 'Captain Borrow.'

'Sir?'

'You have a Bible, don't you? Let me have it, will you?'

Mungo's batman had a fire going, and coffee brewing in the shelter, and he took Mungo's coat to dry and spread a grey woollen blanket over his shoulders as Mungo squatted beside the fire and paged slowly through the little leather-bound, travel-battered Bible.

He found the reference and stared at it thoughtfully:

And he wrote in the letter, saying, Set ye Uriah in the forefront of the hottest battle, and retire ye from him, that he may be smitten, and die.

Mungo wondered that he was still capable of surprising himself. There were still strange places in his soul that he had never explored.

He took a burning stick from the fire and lit his cigar,

then plunged the glowing red of the brand into the black coffee to enhance the taste of the brew.

'Well, well, Parson!' he murmured aloud. 'You have a sharper instinct than I ever gave you credit for.'

Then he thought of Robyn Codrington, trying to consider his feelings objectively, and without passion.

'Do I love her?' he asked, and the answer was immediate.

'I have never loved a woman, and by God's grace, I never will.'

'Do I want her, then?' And again there was no hesitation. 'Yes, I want her. I want her badly enough to send anybody who stands in my way to his death.'

'Why do I want her?' he pondered. 'When I have never loved a woman – why do I want this one? She is no longer young, and God knows, I have had my pick of a hundred more beautiful. Why do I want her?' and he grinned at his own perception. 'I want her because she is the only one whom I have never had, and whom I will never have completely.'

He closed the Bible with a snap, and grinned wickedly across the wide river at the dark and silent mopani forest.

'Well done, Parson. You saw it long before I did.'

The tracks of Lobengula's wagons were clear to follow, even in the worsening light, and Wilson pushed the pace to a canter.

Clinton's aged grey was exhausted by two weeks of hard trekking. He fell back little by little, until after five miles they were loping along with Captain Napier's rear file. The mud thrown up by the hooves ahead speckled Clinton's face as though he was suffering from some strange disease.

The mopani thinned out dramatically ahead of the tiny patrol, and there were low bare hills on either hand.

'Look at them, Padre,' Wilson called to Clinton, and gestured at the hills. 'There must be hundreds of them.'

'Women and old men,' Clinton grunted. The slopes were scattered with silent watching figures. 'The fighting men will be with the king.'

The twelve riders cantered on without a check, and the thunder muttered and shook the sky above the low, swirling clouds.

Suddenly Wilson raised his right hand high.

'Troop, halt!'

Clinton's grey stood, head hanging and chest heaving between his knees – and Clinton was as grateful. At his best he was no horseman, and he was unaccustomed to such hard riding.

'Reverend Codrington to the front!' The order was passed back, and Clinton kicked the grey into a plodding walk.

At that moment a squall of rain stung his face like a handful of thrown rock-salt, and he wiped it off with the palm of his right hand.

'There they are!' said Wilson tersely, and through the drizzle Clinton could make out the stained and ragged canvas tent of a wagon rising above the scrub, not more than two hundred paces ahead.

'You know what to say, Padre.' Wilson's Scots accent seemed even stronger and was incongruous at this place and in these circumstances.

Clinton walked the grey forward another few paces, and then drew a deep breath.

'Lobengula, King of the Matabele, it is me – Hlopi. These men wish you to come to GuBulawayo to parley with Daketela and Lodzi. Do you hear me, oh King?'

The silence was broken only by the scraping of a wind-blown branch and the rustle of the rain on the brim of Clinton's old hat.

Then quite clearly, he heard the snick of a Martini-Henry rifle being loaded; and a young voice asked in whispered Matabele from the scrub near the wagon:

'Must we shoot, Baba?'

A deeper, firmer voice replied in the same language. 'Not yet. Let them come closer so there can be no mistake.'

And then the voices were blotted out by a grumbling roll of thunder overhead, and Clinton backed the grey up.

'It is a trap, Major. There are armed Matabele in ambush about the wagons. I heard them talking.'

'Do you think the king is there?'

'I would not think so, but what I am sure of is that even now the main impi is circling back between us and the river.'

'What makes you think that?'

'It is always the Zulu way, the encirclement and then the closing in.'

'What do you advise, Padre?'

Clinton shrugged and smiled. 'I gave my advice on the bank of the river—' He was interrupted by a shouted warning from the rear of the column. It was one of the Americans, his accent unmistakable.

'There is a force moving in behind us.'

'How many?' Wilson shouted back.

'Plenty, I can see their plumes.'

'Troop, about wheel!' Wilson ordered. 'At the gallop, forward!'

As the horses plunged back down the rough trail, the rain that had been threatening so long burst upon them in an icy silver cascade. It slashed at their faces, and stung their eyes, and drummed on their oilskins.

'This will cover our retreat,' Wilson grunted, and Clinton flogged the grey's neck with the loose end of the reins, for the old horse was falling back again.

Through the thick silver lances of falling rain, he caught

a glimpse of waving war-plumes above the scrub; they were racing in to head off the patrol. At that moment the grey stumbled and Clinton was thrown onto his neck.

'Jee!' He heard the war chant go up, and he clung desperately to the grey's neck as it plunged to regain its balance.

'Come on, Padre!' somebody yelled, as the other troopers went pounding past him in the mud and the rain.

Then his horse was running again. Clinton had lost a stirrup, and he bumped painfully on the wet saddle, clinging to the pommel for a grip, but they were through. There were no shields or plumes in the bush around them, only the twisting streamers of rain and the gloom of gathering night.

'Are you telling me, Napier, that Major Wilson has deliberately chosen to spend the night on the far bank, despite my direct orders to return before nightfall?' Mungo St John asked. The only light was that of a storm lantern. The rain had washed out the fires.

The tarpaulin over the heads of the two officers flogged in the wind, spilling gouts of rainwater over them, and the lantern flame fluttered uncertainly in its glass chimney, lighting Captain Napier's face from below so that he looked like a skull.

'We got so close to Lobengula, General, within hail of the wagons. Major Wilson considered a retreat would not be justified. In any event, sir, the bush is swarming with the enemy. The patrol has a better chance of surviving the night by stopping in thick bush and waiting for daylight.'

'That is Wilson's estimate, is it?' Mungo demanded, putting on a grim expression. Yet inwardly, he congratulated himself on such an accurate assessment of the Scotsman's impetuous character.

'You must reinforce the patrol, sir. You must send at least one of the Maxims across – now, this very hour.'

'Listen carefully, Captain,' Mungo ordered him. 'What do you hear?'

Even over the rain and the wind there was an echo like the sound in a seashell held to the ear.

'The river, Captain,' Mungo told him. 'The river is spating!'

'I have just forded it. You can still get across, sir. If you give the order now! If you wait until dawn, it may well be in full flood.'

'Thank you for your advice, Napier. I will not risk the Maxims.'

'Sir, sir – you can take at least one Maxim off its carriage. We can carry it in a blanket and swim across.'

'Thank you, Captain. I will send Borrow across with twenty men to reinforce Wilson until morning – and this force will follow, with both Maxims, only when it is light enough to see the ford and make the crossing in safety.'

'General St John, you are signing the death warrant of those men.'

'Captain Napier, you are overwrought. I shall expect an apology from you when you have recovered yourself.'

Clinton sat with his back against the bole of a mopani tree. He had one hand thrust into the front of his sheepskin jacket, to hold his travelling Bible out of the rain. He wished above any other creature needs that he had light enough to read it.

All around him the rest of the tiny patrol lay stretched out on the muddy earth, bundled up in their rubber groundsheets and oilskins, though Clinton was certain that, like himself, none of them was asleep – nor would any of them sleep that night.

Clutching the Bible above his heart, he had the certain prescience of his own death, and he made the astonishing discovery that it had no terrors for him. Once, long ago, before he had discovered how close at hand was God's comfort, he had been afraid, and now the release from fear was a blessed gift.

Sitting in darkness, he thought of love, the love of his God and his woman and his daughters – and that was all that he would regret leaving behind him.

He thought of Robyn as he had first seen her, standing on the deck of the American slaver *Huron* with her dark hair aflutter on the wind and her green eyes flashing.

He remembered her upon the rumpled sweat-soaked childbed as she struggled to give birth, and he remembered the hot slippery and totally enchanting feeling of his first infant daughter's body as it slithered from Robyn's body into his waiting hands.

He remembered the first petulant birth wail, and how beautiful Robyn had been as she smiled at him, exhausted and racked and proud.

There were other small regrets – one that he would never dandle a grandchild, another that Robyn had never come to love him the same way he loved her. Suddenly Clinton sat up straighter against the mopani, and inclined his head to listen, peering out into the utter blackness from whence the sound had come.

No, it was not really a sound – the only true sound was the rain. It was more like a vibration in the air. Carefully, he returned the precious book to his inside pocket, then he made a trumpet of his bare hands and pressed them to the wet earth, listening intently with his ear to the funnel.

The vibration coming up from the ground was that of running feet, horny bare feet, thousands of feet, trotting to the rhythm of an impi on the march. It sounded like the very pulse of the earth.

Clinton crawled and groped his way across to where he

had last seen Major Wilson lie down under his plaid. There was no glimmering of light under the midnight clouds, and when his fingers touched coarse woven cloth, Clinton asked softly:

'Is that you, Major?'

'What is it, Padre?'

'They are here, all around us, moving back to get between us and the river.'

They stood-to while the dawn tried vainly to penetrate the low roof of cloud above them. The saddled horses were merely humped shapes just a little darker than the night around them. They were drawn up in a circle, with the men standing on the inside, rifles resting on the saddles as they peered out into the thick bush that surrounded them, straining for the first glimpse as the grey light settled gently, like a sprinkling of pearl dust upon their dark, wet world.

In the centre of the circle of horses, Clinton knelt in the mud. With one hand he held the reins of the grey horse, and with the other he held the Bible to his chest. His calm voice carried clearly to every man in the dark waiting circle.

'Our Father which art in heaven,
Hallowed be Thy name—'

The light grew stronger; they could make out the shape of the nearest bushes. One of the horses, perhaps infected by the tension of the waiting men, whickered and scissored its ears.

'Thy will be done
in earth, as it is in heaven—'

Now they all heard what had alarmed the horse. The faint drumming approached from the direction of the river, growing stronger with the dawn light.

> ' – for Thine is the Kingdom,
> the Power and the glory—'

There was the metallic clash of a rifle breech from the silent waiting circle of dismounted men, and half a dozen gruff voices echoed Clinton's quiet 'Amen!'

Then suddenly someone shouted. 'Horses! Those are horses out there!'

And a ragged little cheer went up as they recognized the shape of slouch hats bobbing against the sullen grey sky.

'Who is it?' Wilson challenged.

'Borrow, Sir, Captain Borrow!'

'By God, you're welcome.' Wilson laughed as the column of horsemen rode out of the forest into their defensive circle. 'Where is General St John; where are the Maxims?'

The two officers shook hands as Borrow dismounted, but he did not return Wilson's smile.

'The general is still on the south bank.'

Wilson stared at him incredulous, the smile sliding off his face.

'I have twenty men, rifles only, no Maxims,' Borrow went on.

'When will the column cross?'

'We had to swim our horses across. By now the river is ten feet deep.' Borrow lowered his voice so as not to alarm the men. 'They won't be coming.'

'Did you make contact with the enemy?' Wilson demanded.

'We heard them all around us. They called to each other as we passed, and we heard them keeping pace with us in the forest on either hand.'

'So they are massed between us and the river, and even if we cut our way through to the river, the ford is impassable. Is that it?'

'I am afraid so, sir.'

Wilson took his hat from his head and against his thigh he beat the raindrops from its brim. Then he settled it again carefully on his head at a jaunty angle.

'Then it seems there is only one direction that we can take, one direction in which the Matabele will not expect us to move.' He turned back to Borrow. 'Our orders were to seize the king, and now our very lives depend on it. We must have Lobengula as a hostage. We have to go forward – and that right smartly.' He raised his voice. 'Troop, mount! Walk march, trot!'

They rode closed up, tense and silent. Clinton's old grey had benefited from the night's rest, and kept his place in the third file.

A young trooper rode at Clinton's right hand.

'What is your name, son?' he asked quietly.

'Dillon, sir – I mean, Reverend.' He was smooth-cheeked, and fresh-faced.

'How old are you, Dillon?'

'Eighteen, Reverend.'

They are all so young, Clinton thought. Even Major Allan Wilson himself is barely thirty years of age. If only, he thought, if only—

'Padre!'

Clinton looked up sharply, his attention had been wandering. They had long ago emerged from the thick bush, and were now coming up to the same spot from which they had retreated the previous evening.

The wagons were still standing abandoned beside the rude track; the tents made pale geometrical oblongs of solid canvas against the dark wet scrub.

Once again, Wilson halted the patrol, and Clinton walked the grey forward.

'Tell them we do not wish to fight,' Wilson ordered.

'There is nobody here.'

'Try anyway,' Wilson urged. 'If the wagons are deserted, then we will ride on until we catch up with the king.'

Clinton rode forward, shouting as he went:

'Lobengula, do not be afraid. It is me. Hlopi.'

There was no reply, only the flutter of the wind in the torn wagon canvas.

'Warriors of Matabele – children of Mashobane, we do not wish to fight—' Clinton called again; and this time he was answered by a bellowing bull voice, haughty and angry and proud. It came out of the gloom and rain, seeming to emanate from the very air, for there was no man to be seen.

'Hau, white men! You do not wish to fight – but we do, for our eyes are red and our steel is thirsty.'

The last word was blown away on a great gust of sound, and the shrub about them misted over with blue gunsmoke and the air about their heads was torn by a gale of shot.

It was twenty-five years and more since Clinton had stood to receive volleyed gunfire; yet he could still clearly differentiate between the crack of high-powered rifles and the whistle of ball thrown from ancient muzzle loaders, and in the storm the 'whirr-whirr' of beaten pot-legs tumbling as they flew; so that, glancing up, Clinton expected to actually see one come over like a rising pheasant.

'Back! Fall back!' Wilson was shouting, and the horses were all rearing and plunging. The fire was, most of it, flying overhead. As always, the Matabele had raised their sights to the maximum; but there must have been a hundred or more of them hidden in the shrub and random bullets were scoring.

One of the troopers was hit in both eyes, the bridge of his nose shot away. He was reeling in the saddle, clutching his face with blood spurting out between his fingers. His number two spurred in to catch him before he fell, and with an arm around his shoulder led him at a gallop back along the trail.

Young Dillon's horse was hit in the neck, and he was thrown in the mud, but he came up with his rifle in his hands, and Clinton yelled at him as he galloped back.

'Cut off your saddle-bags. You'll need every round in them, lad.'

Clinton came in for the pick-up, but Wilson rode him off like a polo player.

'Your moke's half done, Padre. He'll not carry two. Get on with you!'

They tried to make a stand in the thicket where they had spent the night, but the hidden Matabele riflemen crept in so close that four of the horses went down, kicking and struggling, exposing the men who had been standing behind them, firing over their backs, and three of the men were hit. One of them, a young Afrikander from the Cape, had a pot-leg slug shatter the bone above his right elbow. The arm was hanging on a tattered ribbon of flesh, and Clinton used the sleeves of his shirt to make a sling for it.

'Well, Padre, we are for it now – and that's no mistake.' The trooper grinned at him, white face speckled with his own blood, like a thrush's egg.

'We can't stand here,' Wilson called. 'Two wounded to a horse and a man to lead them. They'll go in the centre with those who have lost their own horses. The rest of us will ride in a box around them.'

Clinton helped the young Afrikander up onto the grey's back, and one of the lads from Borrow's volunteers up behind him. The sharp slivers of his shin bone were sticking out of the meat of his leg.

They started back slowly, at the pace of the walkers, and from the thickets beside the track the muskets banged and smoked; but the Matabele were all of them well hidden. Clearly, they were taking no chances, even with this tiny band of thirty-odd men.

Clinton walked beside the grey, holding the good leg of the wounded man to prevent him slipping from the saddle. He carried the two rifles belonging to the wounded men slung over his shoulder.

'Padre!' Clinton looked up to find Wilson above him. 'We have three horses that are fresh enough to try a run for the river. I have ordered Burnham and Ingram to try and get back to the main camp and warn St John of our predicament. There is one horse for you. They will take you with them.'

'Thank you, Major,' Clinton answered without a moment's hesitation. 'I am a sailor and a priest, not a horseman; besides, I rather think I have work to do here. Let somebody else go.'

Wilson nodded. 'I expected you to say that.' He pushed his horse to a trot and went up to the head of the dismal little column. Minutes later, Clinton heard the quick beat of flying hooves and he looked up to see three horsemen wheel out of the straggling line and plunge into the brush that surrounded them.

There was a chorus of angry yells and the low humming 'Jee!' as the Matabele tried to head them off, but Clinton saw their hats bobbing away above the low bush, and he called after them.

'God speed you, boys!'

Then, as he trudged on in the mud that was balling to the soles of his riding boots – he began silently to pray.

On the outside of the column, another horse fell, throwing its rider over its head, and then lunged up again to stand on three legs, shivering miserably in the rain, its off-fore hanging limply as a sock on a laundry line. The trooper limped back, drawing his revolver from its webbing holster, and shot the animal between the eyes.

'That's a wasted bullet,' Wilson called clearly. 'Don't waste any more.'

They went on slowly, and after a while Clinton became aware that they were no longer following the wagon tracks. Wilson seemed to be leading them gradually more towards the east, but it was hard to tell, for the sun was still hidden by low, grey cloud.

Then abruptly the column stopped again, and now for the first time the insistent banging of muskets from hidden skirmishers in the mopani scrub was silenced.

Wilson had led them into a lovely parklike forest, with short, green grass below the stately mopani trees. Some of these trees stood sixty feet high and their trunks were fluted and twisted as though moulded from potter's clay.

They could see deep into the forest, between the widely spaced trunks. There, directly ahead of the patrol, stretched across their front, waited the army of Lobengula. How many thousands, it was impossible to tell, for their rearguard was hidden in the forest; and even as the little band of white men stared at their host, the *Jikela* began, the 'surrounding' which had been the Zulu way ever since great Chaka's time.

The 'horns' were being spread, the youngest and swiftest warriors running out on the flanks, their naked skins burning like black fire through the forest. A net around a shoal of sardines, they were thrown out until the tips of the horns met to the rear of the band of white men – and again all movement ceased.

Facing the patrol was the 'chest of the bull', the hard and seasoned veterans; when the 'horns' tightened, it was the 'chest' that would close and crush, but now they waited, massed rank upon rank, silent and watchful. Their shields were of dappled black and white, their plumes were of the ostrich, jet black and frothing white, and their kilts of spotted civet tails. In their silence and stillness, it was not necessary for Wilson to raise his voice above conversational tones.

673

'Well, gentlemen. We will not be going any farther – not for a while anyway. Kindly dismount and form the circle.'

Quietly the horses were led into a ring, so that they stood with their noses touching the rump of the one ahead. Behind each horse, his rider crouched with the stock of his rifle resting on the saddle, aiming across at the surrounding wall of silent, waiting black and white dappled shields.

'Padre!' Wilson called softly, and Clinton left the wounded whom he was tending in the centre and crossed quickly to his side.

'I want you here to translate, if they want to parley.'

'There will be no more talking,' Clinton assured him, and as he said it the massed ranks of the 'chest' parted and a tall induna came through. Even at a distance of two hundred paces, he was an imposing figure in his plumes and tassels of valour.

'Gandang,' said Clinton quietly. 'The king's half-brother.'

For long seconds Gandang stared across at the circle of rain-streaked horses and the grim, white faces that peered over them, and then he lifted his broad assegai above his head. It was almost a gladiatorial salute, and he held it for a dozen beats of Clinton's heart. Then his voice carried clearly to where they waited.

'Let it begin!' he called, and his spear arm dropped.

Instantly, the horns came racing in, tightening like a strangler's grip on the throat.

'Steady!' Wilson called. 'Hold your fire! No bullets to waste, lads! Hold your fire, wait to make sure.'

The blades came out of the thongs that held them to the grip of the shields with a rasping growl, and the war chant rose, deep and resonant:

'Jee! Jee!' And now the silver blades drummed on the dappled rawhide, so that the horses stamped and threw their heads.

'Wait lads.' The front rank was fifty yards away, sweeping in out of the gentle silky grey rain mist.

'Pick your man! Pick your man!' Twenty yards, chanting and drumming to the rhythm of their pounding bare feet.

'Fire!' Gunfire rippled around the tight little circle, not a single blast but with the spacing that told that every shot had been aimed, and the front rank of attackers melted into the soggy earth.

The breech blocks clashed, and the gunfire was continuous, like strings of Chinese crackers, and an echo came back, the slapping sound of lead bullets striking naked black flesh.

At two places the warriors burst into the ring, and for desperate seconds there were knots of milling men, and the banging of revolvers held point blank to chest and belly. Then the black wave lost its impetus, hesitated and finally drew back, the surviving warriors slipping back into the forest, leaving their dead scattered in the wet grass.

'We did it, we sent them off!' someone yelled, and then they were all cheering.

'A little early to celebrate,' Clinton murmured drily.

'Let them shout,' Wilson was reloading his pistol. 'Let them keep their courage up.' He looked up from the weapon at Clinton. 'You'll not be joining us then?' he asked. 'You were a fighting man once.'

Clinton shook his head. 'I killed my last man over twenty-five years ago, but I will look to the wounded and do anything else you want of me.'

'Go around to each man. Collect all the spare ammunition. Fill the bandoliers and dole 'em out as they are needed.'

Clinton turned back to the centre of the circle, and there were three new men there – one was dead, shot in the head – another with a broken hip – and the third with the shaft of an assegai protruding from his chest.

'Take it out!' his voice rose as he tugged ineffectually at the handle. 'Take it out! I can't stand it.'

Clinton knelt in front of him and judged the angle of the blade. The point must lie near the heart. 'It's better to leave it,' he advised gently.

'No! No!' The man's voice rose, and the men in the outer circle looked back, their faces stricken by that hysterical shriek. 'Take it out!'

Perhaps it was best after all – better than lingering, shrieking death to unnerve the men around him.

'Hold his shoulders,' Clinton ordered quietly, and a trooper knelt behind the dying man. Clinton gripped the shaft. It was a beautiful weapon, bound in decorative patterns with hair from an elephant's tail and bright copper wire.

He pulled and the wide blade sucked with the sound of a boot in thick mud, and it came free. The trooper shrieked only once more, as his heart's blood followed the steel out in a bright torrent.

The waves of warriors came again four times before noon. Each time it seemed impossible that they could fail to overwhelm the waiting circle, but each time they swirled and broke upon it like a tide upon a rock, and then were sucked back into the forest.

After each assault the circle had to be drawn a little smaller, to take up the gaps left by fallen horses and dead and wounded men, and then the Matabele musketeers would creep in again, moving like quick and silent shadows from mopani to mopani, offering meagre targets, the bulge of a shoulder around the stem of a mopani trunk, little cotton pods of gunsmoke in the patches of green grass, the black bead of a head bobbing above the summit of one of the scattered termite nests as a warrior rose to fire.

Wilson walked quietly around the circle, talking calmly to each man in turn, stroking the muzzle of a restless horse, and then coming back into the centre.

'Are you coping, Padre?'

'We are doing fine, Major.'

The dead were laid out with what little dignity was left to them, and Clinton had covered their faces with saddle blankets. There were twelve of them now – and it was only a little past noon, another seven hours of daylight.

The lad who had lost his eyes in the first volley was talking to somebody from long ago in his delirium, but the words were jumbled and made little sense. Clinton had bound his head in a clean white bandage from the saddle-bag of the grey – but the bandage was now muddied, and the blood had seeped through.

Two others lay still, one breathing noisily through the hole in his throat from which the air bubbled and whistled, the other silent and pale, except for a little dry cough at intervals. He had been hit low in the back, and there was no use nor feeling in his lower body. The others, too gravely wounded to stand in the circle, were breaking open the waxed paper packages of cartridges and refilling the bandoliers.

Wilson squatted on his haunches beside Clinton. 'Ammunition?' he asked softly.

'Four hundred rounds,' Clinton replied as softly.

'Less than thirty rounds a man,' Wilson calculated swiftly. 'Not counting the wounded, of course.'

'Well, look at it this way, Major, at least it is no longer raining.'

'Do you know, Padre, I hadn't even noticed.' Wilson smiled faintly, and looked up at the sky. The cloud belly had risen and at that moment a pale ghostly silhouette of the sun appeared through it; but it was without warmth and so mild that they stared at it without paining their eyes.

'You are hit, Major,' Clinton exclaimed suddenly. He had not realized it until that moment. 'Let me look at it.'

'It's almost stopped bleeding. Let it be.' Wilson shook his head. 'Keep your bandages for those others.'

He was interrupted by a shout from one of the troopers in the outer circle.

'There he is again!' And immediately firing rifles whip-cracked, and the same voice swore angrily.

'The bastard, the bloody bastard—'

'What is it, soldier?'

'That big induna – he's moving about again out there; but he's got the devil's luck, sir. We just wasted a packet of bullets on him.'

As he spoke, Clinton's old grey horse threw up his head and fell on his knees, hit in the neck. He struggled to rise again, then rolled over on his side.

'Poor old fellow!' Clinton murmured, and immediately another horse reared up, thrashed frantically at the air with his fore hooves and then crashed over on his back.

'They're shooting better now,' Wilson said quietly.

'I would guess that is Gandang's work,' Clinton agreed. 'He's moving from sniper to sniper, setting their sights for them and coaching their fire.'

'Well, it's time to close the circle again.'

There were only ten horses still standing; the others lay where they had fallen, and their troopers lay belly down behind them, waiting patiently for a certain shot at one of the hundreds of elusive figures amongst the trees.

'Close up.' Wilson stood and gestured to the ring of troopers. 'Come in on the centre—'

He broke off abruptly, spun in a half circle and clutched his shoulder, but still he kept his feet.

'You're hit again!' Clinton jumped up to help him and immediately both his legs were struck out from under him, and he dropped back onto the muddy earth and stared at his smashed knee caps.

It must have been one of the ancient elephant guns, the four-to-the-pounders that some of the Matabele were using. It was a weapon that threw a ball of soft lead weighing a quarter of a pound. It had hit him in one knee and torn through into the other.

Both his legs were gone; one was twisted up under his buttocks, and he was sitting on his own muddy riding boot. The other leg was reversed, the toe-cap of his boot was dug into the mud and the silver spur stuck up towards the swirling cloud belly of the sky.

G andang knelt behind the trunk of the mopani tree and snatched the Martini-Henry rifle out of the hands of a young brave.

'Even a baboon remembers a lesson he is taught,' Gandang fumed. 'How often have you been told not to do this.'

The long leaf sight on top of the blued barrel was at maximum extension, set for one thousand yards.

Under Gandang's quiet instructions, the young Matabele rested the rifle in a crotch of the mopani, and fired.

The rifle kicked back viciously, and he shouted joyously. In the little circle a big sway-backed grey horse dropped to its knees, fought briefly to rise and then flopped over on its side.

'Did you see me, my brothers?' howled the warrior. 'Did you see me kill the grey horse?'

Vamba's hands were shaking with excitement as he reloaded and rested the rifle again.

He fired, and this time a bay gelding reared up and then crashed over on its back.

'Jee!' sang Vamba, and brandished the smoking rifle over his head, and the war chant was taken up by a hundred other hidden riflemen, and the volley of their fire flared up.

'They are almost ready,' Gandang thought, as he glimpsed another of the defenders struck down in the renewed gale of gunfire. 'There can be few of them who still can shoot. Soon now it will be time to send the spears for the closing-in, and tonight I will have a victory to take to my brother the king. One little victory in all the terrible defeats – and so hard bought.'

He slipped away from the shelter of the mopani trunk, and loped swiftly across towards where another of his riflemen was firing away as fast as he could reload. Half-way there Gandang felt the jarring impact in his upper arm, but he covered the open ground to shelter without a check in his stride, and then leaned against the bole of the mopani, and examined the wound. The bullet had gone in the side of his biceps and out the back of his arm. The blood was dripping from his elbow, like thick black treacle. Gandang scooped a handful of mud and slapped it over the wounds, plugging and masking them.

Then he said scornfully to the kneeling warrior at his side. 'You shoot like an old woman husking maize.' And he took the rifle out of his hands.

Clinton dragged himself backwards on his elbows, and his legs slithered loosely after him through the mud. He had used the webbing belt from one of the dead men as a tourniquet, and there was very little bleeding. The numbness of the shock still persisted, so the pain was just bearable, though the sound of the shattered ends of bone grating together as he moved brought up the nausea in a bitter-acid flood in the back of his throat.

He reached the blind boy, and paused for his breathing to settle before he spoke. 'The others are writing letters, afterwards somebody may find them. Is there anybody at home? I'll write for you.'

The boy was silent, did not seem to have heard. An hour earlier Clinton had given him one of the precious laudanum pills from the kit which Robyn had prepared for him before he left GuBulawayo.

'Did you hear, lad?'

'I heard, Padre. I was thinking. Yes, there is a girl.'

Clinton turned a fresh page of his notebook and licked the point of his pencil, and the boy thought again and mumbled shyly:

'Well then, Mary. You'll have read in the papers, we had quite a scrap here today. It's nearly over now, and I was thinking about that day on the river—'

Clinton wrote quickly, to keep up.

'I'll be saying cheerio, then Mary. Isn't one of us afraid. I reckon as how we just want to do it right – when the time comes—'

Quite suddenly, Clinton found his vision blurring as he wrote the final salutation, and he glanced up at the pale beardless face. The eyes were swathed in bloody bandages, but his lips were quivering and the boy gulped hard as he finished.

'What is her name, lad? I have to address it.'

'Mary Swayne. The Red Boar at Falmouth.'

She was a barmaid then, Clinton thought, as he buttoned the folded page into the boy's breast pocket. She would probably laugh at the note if she ever got it, and pass it around the regulars in the saloon bar.

'Padre, I was lying,' the boy whispered. 'I am afraid.'

'We all are.' Clinton squeezed his hand. 'I tell you what, lad. If you like, you can load for Dillon here. He's got eyes to shoot, but only one arm – you've got two good arms.'

'Bully on you, Padre,' Dillon grinned. 'Why didn't we think of that.'

Clinton draped a bandolier across the blind boy's legs. There were only fifteen cartridges in the loops – and at that moment, out in the mopani, the singing started.

It was slow and deep and very beautiful, echoing and ringing through the forest. The praise song of the Inyati. And Clinton turned his head and looked slowly around the circle.

All the horses were dead; they lay in a litter of saddlery and broken equipment, of crumpled yellow scraps of waxed paper from the ammunition packets, of empty brass cartridge cases and discarded rifles. In the confusion, only the row of dead men was orderly. How long was that row, Clinton thought, oh God, what a waste this is, what a cruel waste.

He raised his eyes, and the clouds were at last breaking up. There were valleys of sweet blue sky between the soaring ranges of cumulus. Already the sunset was licking the cloud mountains with soft, fleshy tones of pink and rose, while the depths of the billowing masses were the colour of burnt antimony and tarnished silver.

They had fought all day on this bloody patch of mud. In another hour it would be dark, but even now there were dark specks moving like dust motes against the high singing blue of the evening sky. The tiny specks turned in slow eddies, like a lazy whirlpool, for the vultures were still very high, waiting and watching with the infinite patience of Africa.

Clinton lowered his eyes, and across the circle Wilson was watching him.

He sat with his back against the belly of one of the dead horses. His right arm hung uselessly at his side, and the wadding over the wound in his stomach was crimson with seeping blood, but he held his revolver in his lap.

The two men held each other's gaze while the singing soared and fell and soared again.

'They'll be coming now – for the last time,' Wilson said.

Clinton nodded, and then he lifted his chin, and he, too, began to sing:

'Nearer my God to Thee,
Nearer to Thee—'

His voice was surprisingly clear and true, and Wilson was singing with him, holding the wadding to his stomach wound.

'– Darkness comes over me,
My rest a stone—'

The blind boy's voice cracked and quavered. Dillon was beside him; though his ankle and elbow were shot through, he lay upon his back with a rifle propped on his crossed knees, ready to fire one-handed when they came. His voice was flat and tuneless, but he winked cheekily at Clinton and grinned:

'– Angels to beckon me—'

Eight of them, all that were left, every one of them wounded more than once, but all of them singing in the wilderness of the mopani forests – their voices tinny and thin, almost lost in the great crashing chords of the praise song of the Inyati regiment.

Then there was thunder in the air, the drumming of two

683

thousand assegais on black and white dappled shields, and the thunder came rolling down upon their little circle.

Allan Wilson dragged himself to his feet to face them. Because of his stomach wound, he could not stand erect, and the one arm dangled at his side. His service revolver made a strangely unwarlike popping sound in the roar of the war chant and the drumming blades.

Dillon was still singing, snatching the loaded rifles and firing, and singing, and grabbing the next rifle. The blind boy fed the last cartridge into a rifle breech, and passed the hot rifle back to Dillon, and then he groped for another round, his fingers becoming frantic as he realized the bandolier was empty.

'They're finished,' he cried. 'They are all finished!'

Dillon pushed himself erect on his one good leg, and hopped forward, holding the empty rifle by the muzzle, and he swung the butt at the wave of shields and plumes that reared over him, but the blow lacked power and was deflected harmlessly aside by one of the tall oval shields; and then quite miraculously a long, broad blade sprang from between his shoulder blades, driven through from breast bone to spine, and the silver steel was misted pink.

'I don't want to die,' screamed the blind boy. 'Please hold me, Padre.'

And Clinton put his arm around his shoulders and squeezed with all his strength.

'It's all right, lad,' he said. 'It's going to be all right.'

The bodies were stripped naked. Their skin, never touched by the sun, was snowy white and strangely delicate-looking, like the smooth petals of the arum lily. Upon this whiteness, the wounds were the shocking colour of crushed mulberries.

Around the killing ground was gathered a vast concourse of warriors, some of them already wearing items of the looted uniforms, all of them still panting with the exhilaration of that last wild charge and the stabbing with which it had ended.

From the dense ranks, an old grizzle-headed warrior stepped forward with his assegai held under-handed, like a butcher's knife. He stooped over the naked corpse of Clinton Codrington. It was the time to let the spirits of the white men free, to let them escape from their bodies and fly, lest they remain on earth to trouble the living. It was time for the ritual disembowelment. The old warrior placed the point of his blade on the skin of Clinton's stomach, just above the pathetic shrivelled cluster of his genitals, and gathered himself to make the deep upward stroke.

'Hold!' A clear voice stopped him, and the warrior stood back and saluted respectfully as Gandang came striding through the parting ranks of his warriors.

In the centre of that awful field, Gandang stopped, and looked down at the naked bodies of his enemies. His face was impassive, but his eyes were terrible, as though he mourned for all the earth.

'Let them lie,' he said quietly. 'These were men of men, for their fathers were men before them.'

Then he turned and strode back the way he had come, and his men formed up behind him and trotted away into the north.

Lobengula had come to the end of his domains. Below him the earth opened into the steep escarpment of the Zambezi valley, a wild infernal place of broken rocky gorges and impenetrable thickets, of savage animals and a smouldering crushing heat.

At the limit of the eye the dark serpentine growth of

riverine bush outlined the course of the father of all waters, and in the west a tall silver cloud of spray stood against the sky: it marked the place where the Zambezi river went crashing over a sheer ledge of rock in an awesome, creaming torrent, falling over three hundred feet into the narrow gorge below.

Lobengula sat upon the box of the leading wagon and looked upon all this savage grandeur with listless eyes. The wagon was drawn by two hundred of his warriors. The oxen were all dead, the ground had been too rugged and rocky for most of them and they had broken down and died in the traces.

Then the migration had run into the first belt of the tsetse fly, and the dreaded little insects had come to swarm on the dappled hides of the remaining bullocks and plague the men and women in Lobengula's sprawling caravan. Within weeks, the last of the fly-struck beasts was dead, and men, more resistant to the sting of the tsetse, had taken their places in the span and drawn their king onwards in his hopeless, aimless flight.

Now even they were daunted by what lay ahead, and they rested on the yokes and looked back at Lobengula.

'We will sleep here this night,' said the king, and immediately the weary, starving host that followed the wagons spread out to begin the chores of making camp, the young girls to carry water in the clay pots, the men to build the temporary lean-to shelters and cut the wood for the fires, and the women to eke out the contents of the almost empty grain bags and the few shreds of dried meat that remained. The fly had killed the last of the slaughter beasts with the draught bullocks, and game was scarce and shy.

Gandang went forward to the lead wagon and saluted his half-brother.

'Your bed will be ready soon, Nkosi Nkulu.'

But Lobengula was staring dreamily up at the steep

rocky kopje that towered above their bivouac. The great bloated trunks of the cream-of-tartar trees had forced the black boulders apart. The little twisted branches, loaded with smooth furry pods, reached towards the uncaring sky like the maimed arms of a cripple.

'Is that a cave up there, my brother?' Lobengula asked softly. A dark cleft was riven into the rock face that girdled the crest of the hill. 'I wish to go up to that cave.'

Twenty men carried Lobengula on a litter of poles and furs, and he winced at each jolt, his great swollen body riddled with gout and arthritis, but his eyes were fastened on the crest high above him.

Just below the rock face Gandang made a sign to the bearers and they lay the litter gently upon the rocky slope while Gandang shifted his shield onto his shoulder and freed his broad blade from its thong as he went ahead.

The cave was narrow but deep and dark. The small ledge at its mouth was littered with the furry remains and chewed bones of small animals, the hydrax and baboon, gazelle and klipspringer. The cave itself gave out the fetid odour of the cage of a carnivorous animal, and when Gandang squatted at the entrance and peered into the sombre depths, there was the sudden vicious spitting snarl of a leopard, and dimly he saw the beast move in the shadows and caught the glint of its fierce golden eyes.

Gandang moved slowly out of the sunlight, and paused to let his eyes adjust to the gloom. The leopard warned him again with a terrifying crackle of anger in the confined spaces of the cavern. It had crept closer and was lying flat upon a narrow ledge above the level of Gandang's head. He could just make out the shape of its broad adder-like brow; the ears were laid back flat and the eyes slitted with rage.

Carefully, Gandang moved into position below the ledge, for he did not want to trigger the charge until he was ready to receive it. Balanced lightly in a half crouch, with the assegai's point lifted and lined up on the enraged animal's throat, Gandang flirted his shield and called to it.

'Come, evil one! Come, devil spawn.' And with another stunning burst of rage, the leopard launched itself, a blurr of gold, upon the tall dappled shield. But as it dropped, so Gandang lifted the point and took the leopard upon it, letting its own weight drive the steel through its heart; and then he rolled backwards under the shield and the cruel hooked talons raked the cured iron-hard hide unavailingly.

The blade was still buried in the leopard's chest. It coughed once, choking on its own blood, and then it wrenched itself free of the steel and bounded out through the mouth of the cavern. When Gandang followed it cautiously into the sunlight, the beautiful beast was stretched out on the rocky ledge in a spreading puddle of its own blood. It was a magnificent old male, the pelt unscarred. The sable rosettes upon its back were not much darker than the dark amber ground, that shaded down to a pure buttery cream on the underbelly. A noble animal, and only a king might wear its fur.

'The way is safe, oh King,' Gandang called down the slope, and the litter-bearers carried Lobengula up and set him gently upon the ledge.

The king dismissed the bearers, and he and his half-brother were alone on the hillside, high above this harsh and barbaric land. Lobengula looked at the dead leopard and then at the dark mouth of the cavern.

'This would be a fitting tomb for a king,' said Lobengula reflectively, and Gandang could not answer him. They were silent for a long while.

'I am a dead man,' said Lobengula at last, and raised a graceful hand to still Gandang's protest. 'I walk, I speak still, but my heart is dead within me.'

Gandang was silent, and he could not look upon the king's face.

'Gandang, my brother. I want only peace. Will you grant me that? When I order it, will you bring your spear to me and by piercing my dead heart let my spirit free to find that peace?'

'My King, my brother, never once have I disobeyed your order. Ever your word was the centre of my existence. Ask anything of me, my brother, anything but this. Never can I lift my hand towards you, son of Mzilikazi, my father, grandson of Mashobane, my grandfather.'

Lobengula sighed. 'Oh Gandang, I am so weary and sick with grief. If you will not give me surcease, then will you send for my senior witchdoctor?'

The witchdoctor came and listened gravely to the king's command; then he rose and went to the carcass of the leopard.

He clipped off the long, stiff, white whiskers and burned them to powder in a tiny clay pot over a small fire. To make the potion stronger still, he pounded a dozen seeds of the poison rope shrub to a paste and mixed it with the lethal ashes. Then from a stoppered buck-horn on his belt, he poured and stirred an acrid green liquid.

On his knees, with face to the ground, he wriggled towards the king like an obsequious cur-dog and placed the pot on the rocky ledge before him. As his withered claw-like fingers released the deadly vessel, Gandang rose silently behind him and drove his assegai between the witchdoctor's bony shoulder blades and out of his pigeon chest.

Then he picked up the wizened skeletal body and carried it into the recesses of the cavern. When he came back he knelt again before Lobengula.

'You are right,' Lobengula nodded. 'No man but you should know the manner of the king's going.'

He picked up the pot and held it between his cupped pink palms.

'Now you will be the father of my poor people. Stay in

peace, my brother,' said Lobengula, and lifted the pot to his lips and drained it at a single draught.

Then he lay back on the litter and pulled a fur kaross over his head.

'Go sweetly, my beloved brother,' said Gandang. His noble features were set like weathered granite, but as he sat beside the king's bier the tears coursed down his cheeks and wet the great battle-scarred muscles of his chest.

They buried Lobengula in the cavern, sitting upright on the stone floor and wrapped in the wet green skin of the leopard. They dismantled his wagons and carried them up the hill and stacked the parts at the back of the cave.

They piled Lobengula's tusks of yellow ivory at each hand, and at his feet Gandang placed his toy spear of kingship and his beer pots and eating plates, his knives and mirrors and snuff-horn, his beads and ornaments, a bag of salt and another of grain for the journey – and finally the little sealed clay pots of uncut diamonds to pay his way into the spirit world of his forefathers.

Under Gandang's supervision, they sealed the mouth of the cavern with heavy slabs of black ironstone, then, dolefully singing the king's praises, they went back down the hill.

There were no cattle to slaughter for the funeral feast, nor grain for the beer pots. Gandang called the leaders of the mourning people to him.

'A mountain has fallen,' he said simply. 'And an age is past. I have left behind me my wife and my son and the land that I loved. Without those things a man is nothing. I am going back. No man need follow me. Each must choose his own path, but mine is south again to

690

GuBulawayo and the magical hills of the Matopos – to meet and talk with this man Lodzi.'

In the morning, when Gandang started southwards again, he looked back and saw what was left of the Matabele nation straggling along behind him, no longer a great and warlike people, but a bewildered and broken rabble.

Robyn Codrington stood on the cool shaded verandah of Khami Mission. It had rained that morning, and the air was washed sparkling clean and the wet earth smelled like newly baked bread as the bright sunshine warmed it.

Robyn wore the black ribbons of mourning sewn on her sleeves.

'Why do you come here?' she demanded quietly, but unsmilingly, of the man who mounted the front steps of the verandah.

'I had no choice,' Mungo St John answered her. He stopped on the top step, and studied her for a moment without any trace of mockery on his face.

Her skin was scrubbed and fresh, devoid of either rouge or powder. It was smooth and fine-textured. There was no pouching below her clear green eyes, no blurring of her jawline, and her hair drawn back from her temples and forehead was innocent of silver lacing. Her body was small-breasted and narrow-hipped, tall and supple, but when she saw the direction of his gaze, the line of Robyn's lips hardened and set.

'I should be grateful, sir, if you would state your business and leave.'

'Robyn, I am sorry, but perhaps it is best that the uncertainty is over.'

In the four months since the return of the flying column from the Shangani, a dozen rumours had come out of the bush.

That fateful morning, Mungo St John's column, cut off by the flooded river, had heard heavy firing on the opposite bank. Then almost immediately they had themselves come under fierce attack by elements of the Matabele army. They had been forced to retire, a long weary fighting retreat in the rain that had taken weeks of starvation and privation, until at last the harrying impis had let them go, but not before the gun carriages had been abandoned and half the horses lost.

Nobody had known what had happened to Allan Wilson's patrol on the north bank of the Shangani, but then the word had reached GuBulawayo that the little band had cut their way through the impis, gained the Zambezi, and rafted down it to the Portuguese settlement of Tete, three hundred miles downstream. Later that was denied by the Portuguese and hopes plunged, to be revived again when a Matabele induna coming in to surrender suggested that the white men had been taken prisoner by the Inyati regiment – rumour, denial and counter-rumour for four harrowing months, and now Mungo St John was standing before Robyn.

'It's certain,' he said. 'I did not want a stranger to bring the news to you.'

'They are dead,' she said flatly.

'All of them. Dawson reached the battlefield and found them.'

'He would not have been able to recognize them or be certain of how many bodies. Not after all these months, not after the hyena and vultures—'

'Robyn, please.' Mungo held out a hand to her, but she recoiled from him.

'I won't believe it, Clinton could have escaped.'

'In the bush Dawson met the senior induna of the

692

Matabele. He was coming in with all his people to surrender. He described to Dawson the patrol's last stand, and how in the end they all died.'

'Clinton could have—' She was very pale, shaking her head firmly.

'Robyn, it was Gandang. He knew your husband well. "Hlopi" he called him, the man with white hair. He saw him lying with the other dead. It is certain. There can be no more hope.'

'You can go now,' she said, and then quite suddenly she was weeping. Standing very erect and chewing her lower lip to try and stop herself, but her face had crumpled and the rims of her eyelids turned rosy-pink with grief.

'I cannot leave you like this,' he said and limped down the stoep towards her.

'Don't come near me,' she husked through her tears, and she retreated before him. 'Please don't touch me.'

He came on, lean and rangy as an old tom-leopard; but the cruel and swarthy planes of his face had softened with an expression she had never seen upon them before, and his one good eye held her swimming green ones with a deep and tender concern.

'Don't, oh please don't—' Now she held up both hands as if to ward him off, and she turned her face away. She had reached the end of the verandah; her back was pressed to the door of the bedroom which Cathy and Salina had once shared, and she began to pray, her voice muffled by her own tears.

'Oh Gentle Jesus, help me to be strong—' His hands fell upon her shoulders; they were hard as bone and cool through the thin cotton of her blouse. She shuddered, and gasped.

' – Have pity. I beg you. Let me be.'

He took her chin in the cup of his hand and forced her face up to his.

'Will you give me no peace, ever?' she mumbled

brokenly, and then his mouth covered hers and she could not speak again. Slowly the rigidity went out of her body, and she swayed against him. She sobbed once, and began to slump into the embrace of his hard muscled arms. He caught her behind the knees, and around the shoulders, and lifted her like a sleeping child against his chest.

He kicked open the door to the bedroom, stepped through and pushed it closed with his heel.

There was a dustsheet on the bed, but no pillow or eiderdown. He laid her upon it, and knelt beside her, still holding her to his chest.

'He was a saint,' she choked. 'And you sent him to his death. You are the very devil.'

Then with the shaking, frantic fingers of a drowning woman, she unfastened the mother-of-pearl buttons down the front of his linen shirt.

His chest was hard and smooth, the olive skin covered with crisp, dark curls. She pressed her open lips to it, breathing deeply the man-smell of him.

'Forgive me,' she sobbed. 'Oh God, forgive me.'

From his cubbyhole beside the pantries, Jordan Ballantyne could overlook the cavernous kitchens of Groote Schuur.

There were three chefs at work over the gleaming, anthracite-burning Aga ranges, and one of them hurried across to Jordan with the enamelled double-boiler and a silver spoon. With it Jordan tasted the Béarnaise sauce that would go with the galjoen. The galjoen was a fish of the stormy Cape waters; fancifully its shape could be likened to that of a Spanish galleon, and its delicate greenish flesh was one of the great African delicacies.

'Perfect,' Jordan nodded. '*Parfait, Monsieur Galliard, comme toujours.*' The little Frenchman scurried away beaming, and Jordan turned to the heavy teak door leading to the wine cellars below the kitchens.

Jordan had personally decanted the port that afternoon, ten bottles of the forty-year-old Vilanova de Gaia of the 1853 vintage; it had faded to the beautiful tawny colour of wild honey. Now a Malay waiter in long white Kanzu robes, with crimson sash and pillbox fez, came up the stone steps, reverently carrying the first Waterford glass decanter on a Georgian silver tray.

Jordan poured a thimbleful into the chased silver *tastevin* which he wore on the chain about his neck. He sipped, rolled it on his tongue and then drew breath sharply through pursed lips to let the wine declare itself.

'I was right,' he murmured. 'What a fortunate purchase.'

Jordan opened the heavy leatherbound wine register, and noted with pleasure that they still had twelve dozen bottles of the Vilanova, after he had deducted today's decanting. In the 'remarks' column he wrote, 'Extraordinary. Keep for best,' and then turned back to the Malay steward.

'So then, Ramallah, we will offer a choice of Sherry Finos Palma or Madeira with the soup, with the fish the Chablis or the 1889 Krug—' Quickly Jordan ran down the menu, and then dismissed him. 'The company will be coming through presently, kindly see that everyone takes their places now.'

The twelve waiters stood with their backs to the oak panelling of the dining-hall, their white-gloved hands clasped in front of them, expressionless as guardsmen, and Jordan gave each one a quick appraisal as he passed, looking for a stain on the brilliant white robes or a sloppily knotted sash.

At the head of the long table, he paused. The service was the silver gilt queen's pattern presented to Mr Rhodes by the directors of the Chartered Company, the glass was long, finely stemmed Venetian, lipped with twenty-two carat gold to complement the gilt. There were twenty-two settings this evening, and Jordan had agonized over the seating arrangements. Finally he had decided to place Dr Jameson at the bottom of the table and put Sir Henry Loch, the High Commissioner, on Mr Rhodes' right. He nodded his satisfaction at that arrangement, and took one of the Alphonso Havanas from the silver humidor and sniffed it before crackling it against his ear – that too was perfect; he replaced it and took one last lingering look around the hall.

The flowers had been arranged by Jordan's own hands, great banks of protea blooms from the slopes of Table Mountain. In the centrepiece, yellow English roses from the gardens of Groote Schuur, and of course Mr Rhodes' favourite flowers, the lovely blue plumbago blossom.

From beyond the double doors came the clatter of many feet on the marble floor of the hall and the high, almost querulous voice which Jordan knew and loved so well carried to him.

'And we shall just have to square the old man.' Jordan smiled fondly at the words, the old man was certainly Kruger, the President of the Boer Republic, and 'square' was still one of the central words in Mr Rhodes' vocabulary. Just before the doors swung open to admit the company of brilliant and famous men clad in sombre dinner jackets, Jordan slipped out of the hall, back to his little cubbyhole – but he raised the hatch beside his desk an inch, so that he could hear the conversation at the long, glittering table in the hall beyond.

It gave him a glorious feeling of power, to be sitting so close to the centre of all this and to listen to the pulse of history beating, to know that it was within him subtly to alter and direct, and to do so in secrecy. A word here, a hint there, even something so trivial as the placing of two powerful men side by side at the long dinner table. On occasions, in privacy, Mr Rhodes would actually ask, 'What do you think, Jordan?' and would listen attentively to his reply.

The tumultuous excitement of this life had become a drug to Jordan, and barely a day passed that he did not drink the heady draught to the fill. There were special moments that he treasured and whose memory he stored. When the meal ended, and the company settled down to the port and cigars, Jordan could sit alone and gloat over these special memories of his.

He remembered that it had been he who had written out that legendary cheque in his own fair hand for Mr Rhodes to sign the day that they had bought out the Kimberley Central Company. The amount had been £5,338,650, the largest cheque ever drawn anywhere in the world.

He remembered sitting in the visitor's gallery of Parliament as Mr Rhodes rose to make his acceptance speech as Prime Minister of Cape Colony, how Mr Rhodes had looked up and caught his eye and smiled before he began speaking.

He remembered after that wild ride down from Matabeleland when he had handed the Rudd Concession with Lobengula's seal upon it to Mr Rhodes, how he had clasped Jordan's shoulder and with those pale blue eyes conveyed in an instant more than a thousand carefully chosen words ever could.

He remembered riding beside Mr Rhodes' carriage down the Mall to Buckingham Palace and dinner with the queen, while the Union Castle mailship delayed its sacred sailing by twenty-four hours to wait for them.

This very morning had added another memory to Jordan's store, for he had read aloud the cable from Queen Victoria to 'Our well-beloved Cecil John Rhodes', appointing him one of Her Majesty's Privy Councillors.

Jordan started back to the present.

It was after midnight, and in the dining-hall Mr Rhodes

was abruptly breaking up the dinner in his characteristic fashion.

'Well, gentlemen, I'll bid you all a good night's rest.'

Quickly Jordan rose from his desk and slipped down the servants' passageway.

At the end he opened the door a crack and anxiously watched the burly, appealingly awkward figure mount the stairs. The company had done justice to Jordan's choice of wine, but still Mr Rhodes' tread was steady enough. Though he stumbled once at the top of the sweeping marble staircase, he caught his balance, and Jordan shook his head with relief.

When the last servant left, Jordan locked the wine cellar and the pantry. There was a silver tray left upon his desk, and on it a glass of the Vilanova and two water biscuits spread thickly with salted Beluga caviar. Jordan carried the tray through the silent mansion. A single candle burned in the lofty entrance hall. It stood upon the massive carved teak table in the centre of the floor.

Jordan paced slowly across the chequer board of black and white marble paving, like a priest approaching the altar, and reverently he laid the silver tray upon the table. Then he looked up at the carved image high in its shadowy niche, and his lips moved as he silently began the invocation to the bird goddess, Panes.

When he had finished, he stood silent and expectant in the fluttering light of the candle, and the great house slept around him. The falcon-headed goddess stared with cruel blind eyes into the north, a thousand miles and more towards an ancient land, now blessed, or cursed, with a new name, Rhodesia.

Jordan waited quietly, staring up at the bird like a worshipper before a statue of the Virgin, and then suddenly in the silence, from the bottom of the gardens, where grew the tall dark oak trees that Governor van der Stel had planted almost two hundred years before, came the sad and eerie cry of an eagle owl. Jordan relaxed and backed away from the offering that he left upon the table. Then he turned and went bounding up the marble staircase.

In his own small room he quickly stripped off his clothing that was impregnated with the odours of the kitchen. Naked, he sponged down his body with cold water, admiring his own lithe form in the full-length mirror on the far wall. He scrubbed himself dry with a rough towel, and then rinsed his hands in eau-de-Cologne.

With a pair of silver-backed brushes he burnished his hair until his curls shone like whorls of pure gold wire in the lamplight; then he slipped his arms into the brocaded gown of midnight blue satin, belted it around his waist, picked up the lamp to light his way and stepped out into the passage.

He closed the door to his bedroom quietly and listened for a few seconds. The house was still silent, their guests slept. On silent, bare feet, Jordan glided down the thick carpet to the double doors at the end of the passage to tap lightly on one of the panels, twice then twice again, and a voice called to him softly,

'Enter!'

'These are a pastoral people. You cannot take their herds away from them.' Robyn Ballantyne spoke with a low controlled intensity, but her face was pale and her eyes sparkled with furious green lights.

'Please, won't you be seated, Robyn.'

Mungo St John indicated the chair of rough raw lumber, one of the few furnishings in this adobe mud hut that was the office of the Administrator of Matabeleland. 'You will be more comfortable, and I will feel more at ease.'

Nothing could make him appear more at ease, she thought wryly. He lolled back in his swivel chair, and his booted ankles were crossed on the desk in front of him. He was in shirtsleeves, without a tie or cravat, and his waistcoat was unbuttoned.

'Thank you, General. I shall continue to stand until I receive your answer.'

'The costs of the relief of Matabeleland and the conduct of the war were borne entirely by the Chartered Company. Even you must see that there must be reparation.'

'You have taken everything. My brother, Zouga Ballantyne, has rounded up over a hundred and twenty-five thousand head of Matabele cattle—'

'The war cost us a hundred thousand pounds.'

'All right.' Robyn nodded. 'If you will not listen to the voice of humanity, then perhaps hard cash will convince you. The Matabele people are scattered and bewildered; their tribal organizations have broken down; the smallpox is rife amongst them—'

'A conquered nation always suffers privation, Robyn. Oh, do sit down, you are giving me a crick in the neck.'

'Unless you return part of their herds to them, at least enough for milk and slaughter, you are going to be faced with a famine that will cost you more than your neat little war ever did.'

The smile slipped from Mungo St John's face, and he inclined his head slightly and studied the ash of his cigar.

'Think about this, General. When the Imperial Government realizes the extent of the famine, it will force your famous Chartered Company to feed the Matabele. What is the cost of transporting grain from the Cape? A hundred pounds a load. Or is it more now? If the famine approaches the proportions of genocide, then I will see to it that Her Majesty's Government is faced with such a public outcry, led by humanitarians like Labouchère and Blunt, that they may be obliged to revoke the charter and make Matabeleland a crown colony after all.'

Mungo St John took his bottle off the desk and sat upright in his chair.

'Who appointed you champion of these savages, anyway?' he asked. But she ignored his question.

'I suggest, General, that you relay these thoughts to Mr Rhodes before the famine takes a hold.'

She gloried in the visible effort it took him to regain his equanimity.

'You may well be right, Robyn.' His smile was light and mocking again. 'I will point this out to the directors of the Company.'

'Immediately,' she insisted.

'Immediately,' he capitulated, and spread his hands in a parody of helplessness. 'Now is there anything else you want of me?'

'Yes,' she said. 'I want you to marry me.'

He stood up slowly and stared at her.

'You may not believe this, my dear, but nothing would give me greater pleasure. Yet, I am confused. I asked you that day at Khami Mission. Why now have you changed your mind?'

'I need a father for the bastard you have got on me. It was conceived four months after Clinton's death.'

'A son,' he said. 'It will be a son.' He came around the desk towards her.

'You must know that I hate you,' she said.

His single eye crinkled as he smiled at her.

'Yes, and that is probably the reason that I love you.'

'Never say that again,' she hissed at him.

'Oh, but I must. You see I did not even realize it myself. I always believed that I was proof from such a mundane emotion as love. I was deceiving myself. You and I must now bravely face up to that fact. I love you.'

'I want nothing from you but your name, and you shall have nothing from me but hatred and contempt.'

'Marry me first, my love, and later we will decide who gets what from whom.'

'Do not touch me,' she said, and Mungo St John kissed her full on the mouth.

It had taken almost ten full days of leisurely riding to make a circuit of the boundaries of the ranch lands that Zouga had claimed with his land grants.

It stretched eastwards from the Khami river, almost as far as the Bembesi crossing and southwards to the outskirts of GuBulawayo, an area the size of the county of Surrey, rich grasslands with stretches of parklike forests and low golden hills. Through it meandered a dozen lesser rivers and streams, which watered the herds that Zouga was already grazing.

Mr Rhodes had appointed Zouga the custodian of enemy property – with powers to take possession of the royal herds of Lobengula. The hundred troopers who volunteered for the duty rounded up almost 130,000 head of prime cattle.

Half of these belonged to the Chartered Company, but that left 65,000 to be distributed as loot to the men who had ridden in to GuBulawayo with Jameson and St John. However, at the very last minute, Mr Rhodes had changed his mind, and telegraphed St John with instructions to redistribute 40,000 head to the Matabele tribe.

The volunteers were incensed at having lost more than a third of their rightful loot, and word was soon spreading through the improvised bars and canteens of GuBulawayo that the cattle had been given back to the tribe after threats and representations by the woman doctor of Khami Mission. Credence was given to the rumour by the fact that the same telegraph message authorized the grant of six thousand acres of land to Khami Mission. Mr Rhodes was squaring the God-botherers, and the volunteers were not going to stand for it.

Fifty troopers, all full of whisky, rode out to burn down the mission and string up the hag responsible for their loss. Zouga Ballantyne and Mungo St John met them at the foot of the hills. With a few salty sallies, they had them laughing; then they took it in turn to curse them fluently and roundly, and finally they drove them back to town, where they stood them a dozen rounds of drinks.

Despite the redistribution to the tribe, still the flood of cattle upon the market brought the price down to two pounds a head, and Zouga used half the proceeds of the Ballantyne diamond to buy up ten thousand of them to stock his new estates.

Now as Zouga and Louise rode together, with Jan Cheroot following them in the Scotch cart with the tent and camping equipment, they passed small herds of the cattle tended by Matabele herders that Zouga had hired.

Zouga had been able to select only the best animals, and he had graded them by colour, so that one herd might consist of all red beasts while the next of only black ones.

Ralph had contracted to bring up all the materials for the new homestead from the railhead at Kimberley – and with the same convoy would be twenty thoroughbred bulls of Hereford stock that Zouga intended running with his cows.

'This is the place,' Louise exclaimed with delight.

'How can you be so certain – so soon?' Zouga laughed.

'Oh, darling, it's perfect. I can spend the rest of my life looking at that view.'

Below them the land fell away steeply to deep green pools of the river.

'At least there will be good water – and that bottom land will grow excellent vegetables—'

'Don't be so unromantic,' she chided him. 'Look at the trees.'

They soared above their heads like the arched and vaulted spans of a great cathedral, and the autumn foliage was a thousand shades of reds and golds, murmurous with bees and merry with bird song.

'They will give good shade in the hot season,' Zouga agreed.

'Shame on you,' she laughed. 'If you cannot see their beauty, then look at the Thabas Indunas.'

The Hills of the Indunas were whalebacked and dreaming blue beneath the tall silver clouds. The grassy plains between were scattered with small groups of Zouga's cattle, and of wild game – zebra and blue wildebeest.

'They are close enough,' Zouga nodded. 'When Ralph's construction company finally reaches GuBulawayo with the railway line, then we shall be a few hours' ride from the railhead and all the amenities of civilization.'

'So you will build me a home here – on this very spot?'

'Not until you give it a name.'

'What would you like to call it, my darling husband?'

'I'd like to have a touch of the old country – King's Lynn was where I spent my childhood.'

'That's it then.'

'King's Lynn.' Zouga tested the name. 'Yes, that will do very nicely. Now you shall have the home you want.'

Louise took his hand, and they walked down under the trees towards the river.

A man and a woman came down the narrow winding pathway through the thick riverine bush.

The man carried his shield on his left shoulder, with the broad-bladed assegai secured to it by the rawhide thongs; but his right arm was shortened and deformed, twisted out from his shoulder as though the bone had been broken and badly set.

There was no superfluous flesh upon his powerfully boned frame; the rack of his ribs showed through, and his skin lacked the lustre of health. It was the dull lifeless colour of lamp-black – as though he had just risen from a long sickbed. On his trunk and back gleamed the satiny rosettes of freshly healed gunshot wounds, like newly-minted coins of pure blue cobalt.

The woman who followed him was young and straight. Her eyes were slanted and her features those of an Egyptian princess. Her breasts were fat and full with milk, and her infant son was strapped tightly to her back so that his head would not jerk or wobble to her long, swinging gait.

Bazo reached the bank of the river and turned to his wife.

'We will rest here, Tanase.'

She loosened the knot and swung the child onto her hip. She took one of her swollen nipples between thumb and forefinger until milk spurted from it, and then she touched it to the boy's lips. Immediately he began to feed with little pig-like snuffles and grunts.

'When will we reach the next village?' she asked.

'When the sun is there.' Bazo pointed halfway down the sky. 'Are you not weary of the road we have travelled so far, so long!'

'I will never weary, not until we have delivered the word to every man and woman and child in Matabeleland,' she replied, and she began to joggle the baby and croon to it:

'Tungata is your name, for you will be a seeker.

'Zebiwe is your name, for what you will seek is that which has been stolen from you and your people.

'Drink my words Tungata Zebiwe, even as you drink my milk. Remember them all your days, Tungata, and teach them to your own children. Remember the wounds on your father's breast, and the wounds in your mother's heart – and teach your children to hate.'

She changed the infant to her other hip, and her other breast, and she went on crooning until he had drunk his fill and his little head drooped sleepily. Then she slung him upon her back once more, and they crossed the river and went on.

They reached the village an hour before the setting of the sun. There were less than a hundred people living in the scattered huts. They saw the young couple from afar and a dozen of the men came out to greet them with respect and lead them in.

The women brought them grilled maize cakes and thick soured milk in calabash gourds, and the children came to stare at the strangers and to whisper to one another. 'These are the wanderers – these are the people from the Hills of the Matopos.'

When they had eaten, and the sun had set, the villagers built up the fire. Tanase stood in the firelight, and they squatted in a circle about her, silent and intent.

'I am called Tanase,' she said. 'And once I was the Umlimo.'

There was a low gasp of shock at her mention of that name.

'I was the Umlimo,' Tanase repeated. 'But then the powers of the spirits were taken from me.'

They sighed softly and stirred like dead leaves when a random breeze passes.

'There is another who is now the Umlimo and lives in the secret place in the hills, for the Umlimo never dies.'

There was a little hum of assent.

'Now I am the voice of the Umlimo only. I am the messenger who brings you the word of the Umlimo. Listen well, my children, for the Umlimo prophesies thus.' She paused and now the silence was charged with religious terror.

'When the noon sun goes dark with wings, and the trees are bare of leaves in the springtime – then warriors of Matabele put an edge to your steel.'

Tanase paused and the firelight gleamed on the hundreds of eyes that watched her.

'When the cattle lie with their heads twisted to touch their flank and cannot rise – then will be the time to rise up and to strike with the steel.'

She spread her arms like a crucifix and cried out:
'That is the prophecy. Harken to it, children of Mashobane; Harken to the voice of the Umlimo. For the Matabele will be great once again.'

In the dawn the two wanderers, carrying the infant who was named the 'Seeker after what has been stolen', went on towards the next village, where the elders came out to greet them.

In the southern springtime of 1896 on the shores of a lake near the southern extremity of the Rift Valley, that mighty geological fault which splits the African Continental Shield like an axe stroke, a bizarre hatching occurred.

The huge egg masses of *schistocerca gregaria*, the desert locust, that were buried in the loose earth along the border of the lake, released countless multitudes of flightless nymphs. The eggs had been laid by females in the solitary phase of the locust's life cycle; but so vast was the hatching of their progeny that the earth could not contain them, and though they spread out over an area of almost fifty square miles, they were forced to crawl upon one another's backs.

The constant agitation and stimulation of contact with other nymphs wrought a miraculous change in this teeming tide of insects. Their colour turned to a vivid orange and midnight black, unlike their parents' drab brown. Their metabolic rate surged and they became hyperactive and nervous. Their legs grew longer and stronger, their gregarious instincts more powerful, so that they flowed in a compact body that seemed to be a single monstrous organism. They had entered the gregarious phase of the life cycle, and when at last they moulted for the last time and their newly-fledged wings had dried, the entire swarm took spontaneously to the air.

In that first baptism of flight, they were spurred by their high body temperature, which was raised further by their muscular activity. They could not stop until the cool of evening, and then they settled in such dense swarms that the branches of the forest snapped under their weight. They fed voraciously all night, and in the morning the rising heat spurred them into flight once more.

They rose in a cloud so dense that the sound of their wings was the drumming roar of hurricane winds. The trees they left behind were stripped completely of their tender springtime foliage. As they passed overhead, their wings eclipsed the noonday sun, and a deep shadow fell over the land.

They were headed south towards the Zambezi river.

From the Great Sud where the infant Nile river weaves its way through fathomless swamps of floating papyrus, southwards over the wide savannahs of eastern and central Africa, down to the Zambezi and beyond, roamed vast herds of buffalo.

They had never been hunted by the primitive tribes,

who preferred easier game; only a few Europeans with sophisticated weapons had ventured into these remote lands, and even the lions which followed the herds could not check their natural multiplication.

The grasslands were black with the huge bovine black beasts. Twenty or thirty thousand strong, the herds were so dense that the animals in the rear literally starved, for the pasture was destroyed before they could reach it. Weakened by their own vast multitudes, they were ripe for the pestilence that came out of the north.

It was the same plague that Moses' God had inflicted on the Pharaoh of Egypt, the rinderpest, the *peste bovine*, a virus disease which attacks cattle and all other ruminants. The stricken animals were blinded by the discharge of thick mucus from their eyes. It poured in ropes from their gaping jaws and nostrils to contaminate the pastures and infect any other animal that passed over them.

Their emaciated bodies were wracked by spasms of profuse diarrhoea and dysentery. When at last they dropped, the convulsions twisted their heads back upon their tortured necks, so that their noses touched one of their flanks – and they could never rise again.

So swift was the passage of the disease that a herd of ten thousand great horned black beasts was wiped out between dawn and sunset. Their carcasses lay so thickly that they touched each other, and the characteristic fetid odour of the disease mingled with the stench of rotting flesh; for although the vultures gorged, they could not devour one thousandth part of this dreadful harvest of death.

Swiftly, carried by the vultures and the blundering, bellowing herds, the plague swept southwards towards the Zambezi river.

On the banks of that mighty river Tanase stood beside another watch-fire and repeated the prophecy of the Umlimo:

'When the noon sun goes dark with wings,
and the trees are bare of leaves in the
springtime –
        'When the cattle lie with their heads
twisted to touch their flank, and cannot
rise—'

Thus she cried, and the people of the Matabele listened
and took new heart and looked to their steel.